SHIRA

❧ ❧ ❧ ❧ ❧ ❧ ❧ ❧ ❧

S. Y. AGNON

SHIRA

Translated from the Hebrew by Zeva Shapiro

With an Afterword by Robert Alter

❧

SCHOCKEN BOOKS · NEW YORK

S

English translation copyright © 1989 by Schocken Books Inc.

Afterword © 1989 by Robert Alter

All rights reserved under International and Pan-American Copyright Conventions. Published in the United States by Schocken Books Inc., New York, and simultaneously in Canada by Random House of Canada Limited, Toronto. Distributed by Pantheon Books, a division of Random House Inc., New York. Originally published in Isreal by Schocken Publishing House Ltd., Tel Aviv, in 1979. Copyright © 1979 by Schocken Publishing House Ltd., Tel Aviv.

Library of Congress Cataloging-in-Publication Data

Agnon, Shmuel Yosef, 1888–1970.
[Shirah. English]
Shira / by S.Y. Agnon ; translated from the Hebrew
by Zeva Shapiro ; with an afterword by Robert Alter.
p.   cm.
Translation of: Shirah.
ISBN 0-8052-4043-8
I. Title.
PJ5053.A4S51913   1989   88-43129
892.4′35—dc20

Manufactured in the United States of America

First American Edition

*This translation has been made possible in part
by a grant from the Wheatland Foundation.*

CONTENTS

BOOK ONE

1

It was almost twilight when Manfred Herbst brought his wife to the hospital. After a few minutes, footsteps were heard, and Axelrod, the clerk, arrived, talking over his shoulder to an aide, to the aide's wife, to both of them at once. As he walked and talked, he shifted his glasses from his eyes to his forehead and looked around in alarm, as if he had come into his house and found a stranger there. He asked what he asked, said what he said, took out a notebook, put his glasses back in place, and wrote what he wrote. Finally, he brought Mrs. Herbst to the room where women in labor wait to be assigned their beds. Manfred dragged along behind his wife, then came and sat with her.

Manfred sat at Henrietta's side with the other women about to give birth, thinking about her and her pregnancy, which had come upon them not by design for, being past midlife, she was, presumably, beyond such concerns. How would she withstand the anguish of birth and how would she endure what follows? But what is done is done. Now, we have no choice but to accept whatever windfall comes our way as a gift from heaven. He reached over to stroke her tired arms, her withered cheek. When she dozed off, a sad smile playing on her swollen lips, he dozed off too, becoming his wife's partner in anguish and in joy.

The hospital nurse arrived—tall, mannish, with glasses that towered over her eyes arrogantly and lit the freckles in her ashen cheeks so that they shone like nailheads in an old wall. Manfred had seen her for the first time some three or four years earlier. On that day, Jerusalem was in deep mourning. A young man from a leading family had been killed by a Gentile, and the entire city was gathered for the procession to the graveyard. Just then, with everyone grieving, that very woman saun- tered out of the hospital in her uniform, head held high, a lit cigarette protruding from her mouth, her entire person arrogant and defiant. From that day on, whenever they crossed paths, Manfred Herbst would turn away rather than see her. Now that she had appeared, he was angry at the hospital administration for putting her in charge. A vulgar-spirited person, who behaved arrogantly and defiantly while a city mourned, could hardly be expected to have compassion for those who need compassion. She had come to extend her harsh hand over these tender women, and Henrietta too was in her power for life and death. His thoughts returned to his wife, who was about to give birth, and once again he began to reflect on the things that confront a woman in labor and thereafter. Imperceptibly, his eyelids began to contract with sympathy.

How did I happen to think of Lisbet Neu, Herbst asked himself. I wasn't really thinking of her, but I'll think of her now. And, remembering her, a breath of innocence swept over him, as it did whenever she came to mind. The radiant darkness of her eyes, without a hint of anger, the cast of her delicate face, her grace, her beauty, her fetching stance, her fine limbs—all were evidence that the Creator had not lost the power to fashion splendid creatures. Add to this her family connections, her manner, her burdened life, her Ashkenazic piety, all of which were barriers, so that, even as his thoughts were becoming schemes, they were pushed beyond her domain. That nurse, the one he called Nadia, was back again. Her name was actually Shira. Her father, a Hebrew teacher and an early Zionist, had called her Shira after his mother, Sarah.

Shira did not show the women to their rooms. She came and sat with them, as if she were sick or about to give birth herself. As Herbst closed his eyes to avoid looking at her, a beggar appeared, blind in both eyes, and began to mill about among the women. Herbst was surprised at the hospital staff for allowing this fat beggar to roam through the building, among weary women about to deliver, dragging his feet, touching each one of them while humming a mo-notonous tune with neither beginning nor end, his red headdress ablaze with derisive laughter. Nadia, *i.e.*, Shira, *i.e.*, Nadia, opened a pack of cigarettes and said to him in Russian, "My dove, would you like a cigarette?" He spoke no Russian and answered in Turkish, a language Shira, *i.e.*, Nadia, didn't know, touching her shoulder as he spoke. Herbst thought of telling her: The blind man is a Turk and doesn't know your language. But he kept his mouth shut, saying nothing, as he did not wish to speak with her.

Shira sat confined to her body, which began to expand and grow so that her ample limbs enveloped the fat beggar. Herbst shifted his eyes and mused: The nerve of that woman. She is shameless and of such poor taste as to reach out and embrace a blind beggar with a foul stench coming from his eyes. The women were now astir, watching Shira and the beggar. They watched, less baffled than curious. Then suddenly something baffling occurred. The two of them were so close together that they began to dwindle and dissolve, until nothing was left of Shira except her left sandal, which was baffling, for a sandal is only one of the body's trappings, and how could two persons—one fat, the other somewhat fat—be enclosed in it? And what if they were not enclosed in the sandal? Where were they then? Our eyes have been fixed on them constantly, but we didn't see them go. We insist they are in the sandal. Nevertheless, it makes sense to ask Henrietta what is fact and what is fancy. Before he had a chance to ask, he felt her long, warm fingers stroking his forehead and heard her saying, "My love, they're coming to take me to my bed. I'm going now."

Manfred opened his eyes and saw his wife standing up, a small hospital nurse holding both her hand and her small suitcase. He took leave of his wife, who clung to him, as she always did when she was about to give birth, as she had done when she was about to give birth to Zahara and when she was about to give birth to Tamara. Manfred gave her a parting kiss, the same sort of kiss he he had given her half a generation ago, when she was about to give birth to his eldest daughter, Zahara, and when she was about to give birth to her sister, Tamara. After kissing her, he kissed her again and went on his way.

He thought to himself as he walked: I know the entire episode was a dream. In which case, why agonize over it, why not dismiss it from my mind, why not accept it as a dream? I will now abandon all those fruitless struggles and see just what I need to do. He searched his mind and found nothing that needed to be done, surely nothing that needed to be done immediately and couldn't just as well be put off until after Henrietta gave birth, even until she was back home. He turned toward home and began to consider the dinner he would prepare as well as the book he would read.

Engrossed in thought, he walked on, looking in his notebook to see if there was anything he had to do on the way home. There was nothing he had to do, but there were addresses, among them the phone number of Lisbet Neu, a relative of his celebrated mentor, Professor Neu. He remembered telling her that he would almost certainly call one day soon. In truth, this was neither the day nor the hour to telephone a young woman. Moreover, he had nothing to say to her. But, Herbst thought, since I promised to call, I will keep my promise. As he was near a phone booth, he went in to call her.

— 2 —

How did Herbst know Lisbet Neu? It happened that one Saturday, before noon, in a lull between rains, Herbst went to congratulate Dr. Ernst Weltfremdt, who had been promoted that same week from associate to full professor. While Herbst was at Weltfremdt's, two women, one old and one young, came to congratulate the new professor. Weltfremdt introduced Dr. Herbst to them. The older woman, tilting her head slightly, offered the tips of her right fingers. The younger one offered her hand and said to him, "I was once in your house." Herbst replied, "Odd that I didn't see you." She smiled and said, "I didn't see you either. You were out." Herbst said, "Much to my regret. When was this?" She said, "When my uncle, Professor Neu, was in Jerusalem, he went to call on you, and I went with him." Herbst said, "What a misfortune, my dear lady; to think that Professor Neu came to my house, and I wasn't there to welcome him. But I hope to see him soon, and perhaps I will have the good fortune to see you with him." The older woman said, "Our uncle is old, and the discomforts of travel are a strain on him. I doubt if he will come again." Herbst said, "In any case . . ." and didn't elaborate. But he thought to himself: Though he won't come because of his age and the strain of travel, you, my dear lady, are young, and the roads leap out toward you. Perhaps you will come again.

He left Weltfremdt's house and had not gone far when he began to picture Lisbet Neu's face, realizing how rare it was to see such a woman. He was sorry he hadn't said something to her that could be pursued. But, even if he had said something that could be pursued, he could not have pursued it, for he was married, the father of two grown daughters; even if he were to speak with her again, what did it matter? Still, Lisbet Neu was certainly worth seeing.

Like people who choose a vocation in their youth, Manfred Herbst put Lisbet Neu out of mind. When he did remember her, he remembered only so he could tell himself that even if he were to find her, he wouldn't recognize her, because he didn't have an eye for faces and wouldn't recognize anyone after a single meeting, even a woman as lovely as Lisbet Neu. Perhaps he should have asked her to be sure to say hello, should she happen to see him first, because of his age, because of his vision, or because of both of these infirmities. Having neglected to ask, there was no hope of seeing her.

What hope did not accomplish was accomplished through luck. Not many days later, he met her, recognized her, and, what is more, it was he who recognized her instantly, whereas she didn't know him until he told her his name, for, when she had come with her mother to congratulate Professor Weltfremdt on becoming a full professor, she hadn't had a chance to engrave Herbst's image in her heart. For one thing, all of Professor Weltfremdt's furnishings were black, a setting in which it is hard to discern a person's face, and, for another, immediately after conveying their good wishes, they left to give the two scholars a chance to talk about their own affairs.

She was plainly dressed and wore a straw hat, which was out of season, for summer was over and the days were rainy. It was clear from her appearance that she was poor. Those immigrants from Germany, who had lived in an abundance of wealth and honor until they were exiled from their splendid houses by Gentiles and who finally went up to the Land of Israel, were penniless and financially pressed by the time they found jobs. But her poverty was masked by charm, charm that was enhanced by reticence. At first glance, she seemed to have no self-confidence, like someone who has landed in a place where she is totally unknown. But, in this case, her reticence was in her character. She felt that she didn't deserve to enjoy the bounty of a land others had toiled over—for her father's and mother's families had lived complacently, fulfilling their commitment to the Land of Israel through donations to the poor of Jerusalem and to charitable organizations, while the Jews of Russia, Poland, Galicia, and Rumania came and built houses, planted vineyards, made citrus groves, established settlements, and prepared the country for their brothers-in-exile. Much as Herbst scorned both racist theory and the would-be scholars of this would-be theory, when he discovered Lisbet Neu, in whom youthful grace was joined with ancient splendor, he was glad, despite himself, to be of her people.

Since Lisbet Neu is destined to occupy several sections of the book *Shira*, I will include some of the conversation between Dr. Herbst and

Lisbet Neu. But, rather than present it in dialogue form, I will relate
the general content of their conversation.

Herbst began by telling Lisbet Neu about the recent book by her aged
uncle, Professor Alfred Neu, which even his adversaries conceded was
a scholarly breakthrough that would soon be considered a classic in the
field. Lisbet was very surprised. In all the years she had known her
uncle, it had never occurred to her that his distinction derived from
books. She regarded him as an uncle, one of her closest relations. He
was actually a distant relative, but, since we have no special word for
this relationship, and since it is customary to use the term *uncle* broadly,
she called him Uncle, though he was not her uncle but her grandfather's uncle, having been born to an elderly father at an advanced age,
so that, as it turned out, he was younger than her own grandfather, who
was the grandson of Professor Neu's grandfather. "But," Lisbet Neu
said, "my mother and I are now worried, for it is more than a year and
a half since our uncle wrote to us, and he used to write three or four
times a year, apart from sending New Year greetings." "He wrote to
you four or five times a year?" Herbst cried in amazement. "Four or
five times a year. . . . He must be very fond of you. Scholars from all
over the world send him letters that remain unanswered. If he does
answer, he answers one out of many, so he takes time from them for
you and writes to you four or five times a year!" Herbst did not take
leave of Lisbet Neu without promising to inquire about Professor
Neu's health and report back to her.

As it happened, Herbst happened to stop in to see his friend Professor Lemner and found him in a state of elation, having just received a
letter from Professor Neu. And, as it happened, he happened to run
into Lisbet Neu that very day. He said to her, "I have something good
to tell you, my dear lady. I just saw a letter from Professor Neu that
was received today, written in a hand that proves he has the strength
of seven youths." Lisbet Neu laughed and said, "We had a letter too.
He must have written both letters on the same day. Uncle Alfred sets
aside special days for letter writing." From then on, whenever Manfred
Herbst met Lisbet Neu, he would discuss Professor Neu with her.
So-and-so had a letter from Professor Neu; in such-and-such a journal,
there was an article about her uncle or about his theory. Since she knew
so little about Professor Neu's field, Herbst could not engage her with
words. Since he could not engage her with words, the conversation
ended where it began. He was aware that he was not one to win a
maiden's heart through fine conversation, so he was brief rather than
risk inflicting boredom. To her, this was a virtue, for she understood,

in her own way, that Dr. Herbst was a distinguished scholar, and it was not the way of scholars to converse with simple girls endowed with neither Torah, wisdom, nor anything else.

A month passed, then another month. The world was occupied with its affairs, as was Dr. Herbst. Who can relate the affairs of the world? The affairs of Dr. Herbst I can relate.

I'll begin with essentials and relate one thing at a time. He prepared lectures and delivered them to his students. He read many books and journals in his field, as well as related fields. When he found something worthwhile, he copied it by hand and put it in a box. If it was not worth copying, but nonetheless of interest, he would mark it in pencil, sometimes even in ink. In addition to all this, he talked with his colleagues at the university, with his students, and at times with ordinary people, such as the bus driver, the shopkeeper who sold him stationery, or the neighbors, and, needless to say, with his wife and daughters when they were at home. Zahara, his eldest daughter, lived on a *kvutza*, and Tamara lived at home and didn't burden her father with conversation. I will not dwell on the daughters now, though I mean to tell about them in time.

And so several months passed, during which he didn't see Lisbet Neu. He was too busy to notice. When he did notice, he thought to himself: How is it that one doesn't see Neu's relative? Finding no one to answer his question, he answered it himself: She must have gone to Tel Aviv or to some other place. Finding no one to ask, he observed to himself: Actually, what's it to me if she's in Jerusalem or not? Even if she is in Jerusalem, and if I do see her, I have nothing to say to her. Still, what a joy it is for a tent dweller to venture into town and see a fine young woman there.

— 3 —

I will add several words on this subject. Manfred Herbst didn't tell his wife about the young woman he met at Ernst Weltfremdt's when she and her mother came to congratulate Weltfremdt on becoming a professor. Though it was Manfred's custom to tell Henrietta everything, he didn't breathe a word about Lisbet Neu, though he knew that if he were to say anything to her, she would make nothing of it. Henrietta doesn't follow every turn of Manfred's eye, especially when the young woman in question is the relative of an eminent professor, and Henrietta had surely noted, when she came with her uncle, that she wasn't one of those meddling spinsters who pursue other women's husbands.

I will clarify something that needs to be clarified. When Lisbet Neu told Dr. Herbst that she and her uncle had been in his house but hadn't found him in, he expressed regret at having been denied the privilege of receiving his eminent professor in his home. Though Herbst didn't see him, Henrietta did, and she surely told him so. Still, his words suggested that he hadn't heard about the visit at all. In fact, Henrietta did tell him, and Professor Neu told him too, before leaving the country, so that what Herbst told Lisbet Neu was mere rhetoric.

Let us linger awhile with Henrietta. At about this time, she had begun to age rapidly. Wrinkles appeared on her face, and, though it is common for blondes to age before their time in this country, in her case it was due less to climate than to stress. Her relatives in Germany were in great distress, so her mind was totally fixed on getting them out of there and into the Land of Israel. Her concerns were imprinted on her face in the form of wrinkles, which, unlike others her age, she did nothing to conceal, making no attempt to improve herself for her husband. At night, when a woman is unencumbered by household tasks and can give her mind free rein, she would be scheming: what to do next, and how. And what she decided by night she acted on by day, running to the Jewish Agency, to lawyers, to the immigration office, from there to brokers, agents, advisers who, though they were not evil, behaved unscrupulously. When evil pervades the world, even those who are not evil behave in an evil fashion. Henrietta took all this on, sparing her husband the runaround and abuse so many of our people were subjected to in those days by English officials, Arabs, and those Jewish officials who allied themselves with all the others and were more cruel than the Gentiles. Since Manfred was spared these troubles, the One who was created only to make trouble came and troubled him, saying: Take a look at yourself and you'll see—if you're not young, you're not old either. Though you and Henrietta are equal in years, there is a difference between man and woman. She is already aging, but you still have your youthful vigor. In such matters, one tends to accept idle talk as ultimate truth. This was true even for Manfred Herbst, the renowned scholar, the author of a six-hundred-page tome on the artifacts in the Byzantine church of Santa Sophia at the time of Leo III, a work praised by most scholars, who found nothing to delete or add, beyond two or three questions which, according to other scholars, had to be studied further in order to determine whether the small beakers actually existed in Leo's time or were introduced later. This same Manfred Herbst began to say: I'd better take over before old age overtakes me. How? Through the company of attractive young women. As long as Henrietta was young, while the girls were small and the house was in good order, he sat with his books, collecting material for an essay on burial customs of the poor in Byzantium, without giving a thought to finding companionship away from home. Now that Henrietta was aging, the girls were grown, and he was less confident about finishing his paper, he was drawn to follow his roving eye. But his eyes were slow to find what his heart was after. Then he made the acquaintance of Lisbet Neu. Though he realized she was not the girl he was seeking, his loftiest thoughts were of her. Were it my tendency to analyze, I would suggest that deep in his heart he was displeased with the winds that disperse illicit fantasies.

One day Manfred Herbst came out of the French Library on Ben Yehuda Street, carrying new novels from Paris. Some scholars boast of not having read a poem, story, novel, or anything else outside of their field since their schooldays. Others, when they wish to read for pleasure, choose a detective story and read it discreetly, so as not to be seen. Herbst read a great deal of poetry, as well as short stories and novels, and he was open about this. As he walked down the street, he treated himself to a taste of what he would soon be reading. Suddenly he felt a rush of warmth, a flash of radiance. Even before he could identify the source of the warmth and radiance, Lisbet Neu came toward him. She looked up, her black eyes flashing. Herbst forgot that he had told himself he had nothing to say to her and forgot that he had told himself that, should he talk to her, he had best be brief, as they were barely acquainted. By some miracle, it was she who began speaking. She said, "Please, Dr. Herbst, could you possibly give me a bit of your time? It won't take long. I need some advice." His heart was stirred by her voice, even more so by her eyes: the look of concern—had she overstepped? Perhaps she had asked too much. . . . Herbst hugged the novels he was holding and said, "Wherever you choose, I'll be there. Anytime." Lisbet was bewildered. This was beyond what she had in mind, though the consultation did, in fact, require a time and place. She braced herself and said, "If it's all right with you, I'll be at the Café Zichel tomorrow at six." When Herbst repeated her words so he wouldn't forget them, a note of furtive joy rang in every syllable he

uttered. He was breathless, like someone anticipating joy but unable to
wait for it. She soon took leave of him and was on her way.

Herbst didn't watch her go, but in his mind he followed her footsteps
as she made her way among passersby, unaware of the company they
were in and that her every step was putting distance between them. All
of a sudden he remembered something he did not want to miss. He
turned to look after her. She was already far away, so that he could
barely make out the fringe of her hat, blown by the evening breeze like
a curtain designed to shut out the street.

I am skipping an entire day, which was in no hurry to pass—the day
between meeting and meeting—but let's see what followed. This sort
of thing, O ye who seek novelty, is already common and recurs every
day, at any time, at any hour: a married man, father of two daughters,
lecturer at a university, arranges to meet a twenty-four-year-old woman
of good family in a café. I will nonetheless recount it as if it were news,
from beginning to end: how he waited for her, how he went into the
café with her, sat with her, what he said to her, and all that ensued.

About an hour before the appointed time, Herbst stole away from
home, since he had no way of knowing what his wife might ask of him,
nor could anyone know who might suddenly appear at his door and
how long it would be necessary to tarry, since a friend could drop in
without calling ahead, and Herbst would not be free until the friend
was ready to go. For these reasons, Herbst left home an hour before the
appointed time.

When he got to Ben Yehuda Street, Herbst crossed from sidewalk
to sidewalk, from the side the Café Zichel was on to the opposite side,
then the reverse, afraid someone would engage him, for it is the custom
in this land that, if you run into a friend and you are not busy, you
attach yourself to him, whether or not you have something to say. One
can imagine Herbst's concern. Still, except for the cigarettes he took
out and lit, one after the other, nothing engaged him. Between cigarettes, he consulted his watch, which did not alter its time, like an
hourglass in which the grains of sand will not move until it is time,
however much one taps it. When the appointed hour arrived and Lisbet
Neu was not there, Herbst began to review every word he had said the
previous day. He had, perhaps, said something inappropriate that
turned her against him. Reviewing the entire conversation and weighing each word, he found no flaw, so his mind was at rest, but not his
feet. He went into the café to see if she was there. Pressed between the
crowded tables, he searched every corner without finding Lisbet Neu.
As he didn't find her, he left.

Again he crossed from sidewalk to sidewalk in despair, then anticipation; in anticipation, then despair. When these two emotions faded and were replaced by a vague sense of weariness, he spotted Lisbet Neu. There she stood: face to face with him, eye to eye.

There was Lisbet Neu. She came and said, "I've wasted your time, Dr. Herbst. I kept you waiting." Hearing this, Herbst would have liked to say: I would wait for you until tomorrow or the day after. But, saying nothing, he bowed, shook her hand, and went into the café with her.

Again Herbst was pressed between crowded tables and chairs with back legs that were straight and indifferent to the fact that everyone knocked into them. The whole point of a chair is that one sits on it however he likes, with no concern for passersby who knock into it. Herbst was in the café again. The first time he had felt sad and abandoned, but now Lisbet Neu was at his side. He was surprised that everyone in the café did not get up to offer her a chair. Since no one offered her a chair, he began looking for one. He couldn't find an empty chair. Then someone did get up to go—to a meeting, a conference, home—and there was an empty chair. Herbst brought it to Lisbet Neu. He stood beside her and would have stood there until the end of time. Another chair was vacated. he grabbed it but remained standing. He suddenly realized he could place it near Lisbet Neu's chair and actually sit down. He took the chair, put it near Lisbet's, and sat down.

Lisbet Neu sat there, as did Dr. Herbst. They seemed to be sitting for the sake of sitting. The waitress came and asked in a coarse voice, "What will you have?" Herbst answered harshly, "What will we have? Everything. And if there is not enough here, run and bring us Jerusalem's best." Lisbet laughed and said to the waitress, "Bring me cocoa made with water rather than milk. And you, doctor, what will you drink?" Herbst asked, "Cake, how about cake?" Lisbet Neu said, "I can't have cake." Herbst said, "Why?" She said, "They're made with butter." Herbst said, "So much the better. They're better with butter." Lisbet Neu said, "It has not been six hours since I ate meat." Herbst was astonished to discover that there were people who still waited six hours between eating meat and milk. She was astonished by his surprise. She told him, among other things, that when she, her mother, and little sister came to the country, they had no means of support. She was hired to cook in a restaurant that was certified to be strictly kosher, and observant Jews did not hesitate to eat there. One day she saw meat dishes and dairy dishes being washed together in the same basin. She would never again taste anything that was cooked there. From then on,

she did not eat hot food until she got home after midnight and cooked
for her mother and sister. Her mother was too sick to stand on her feet
long enough to cook more than a simple porridge, her sister was still
young, and she, Lisbet Neu, loathed porridge. So she cooked for herself
and her little sister, who lived with them while she was still in school.
The girl was now living in Amsterdam with her mother's aunt.

Manfred Herbst learned from Lisbet Neu that her mother was sickly
and, for the most part, bedridden. He learned that Lisbet's sister was
too young to support herself, and he learned that the entire burden of
the household was on Lisbet's shoulders, that there were many days
when she went hungry, that as a result she had come down with
jaundice but was now fully recovered. Neither the rigors of life nor an
excess of piety were congenial to Manfred Herbst, an enlightened man
who lived an orderly life. But the religious feelings Lisbet Neu conveyed when she spoke of the practical commandments were unlike
those of other observant Jews Herbst had occasion to know, for whom
he had little regard.

"What am I doing now?" Lisbet Neu continued, not wanting him
to think she was still employed in the restaurant. "I am a clerk in a
furniture store." Herbst didn't ask if she was being paid enough or what
the job entailed. The word *clerk* has many connotations. The woman
who cleans and takes customers up in the elevator could call herself a
clerk. It could even be that Lisbet Neu is merely a caretaker.

The waitress brought the cocoa and coffee. Herbst said to Lisbet
Neu, "It took so long to bring the cocoa, it must be six hours by now.
You could have it with milk and eat the cookies, which probably don't
have a trace of butter." Lisbet Neu smiled politely, but it was evident
that she did not approve of his joke, that even a mild joke about religion
disturbed her.

Herbst remembered that Lisbet Neu needed advice. He couldn't
decide whether or not to remind her. If he reminded her, the entire
matter might be concluded in three or four minutes, and their meeting
would be over, which would not be the case if he failed to remind
her—then their meeting would be prolonged. He weighed the two
options and admonished himself: Unless you give her an opening, she
won't begin; but, since you enjoy the company of this lovely young
thing, you allow her to flounder while you subject her to bad jokes.
Lisbet Neu got up and said, "It's time for me to go. Forgive me, Dr.
Herbst, for troubling you to come here." When she got up to put on
her coat and he got up to help her, she added, "I don't deserve it."
When she realized he meant to see her home, she was surprised, for not

only had she taken his time, but he was going to take more time and see her home.

As they walked, she said, "The matter I wanted to consult you about has worked itself out, and I am glad not to have to bother you. I'm really surprised at myself. I can't believe that I was going to bother anyone with it." As she spoke, her face seemed to cloud over, and Herbst concluded that, though the matter was settled, it was not settled in her favor and, furthermore, that he had no right to ask about it. They walked on in silence, in close physical proximity but at a distance in their thoughts. Lisbet Neu was considering: I went to a café with a stranger. I let him pay for my cocoa, and now I am walking with him, while Mother is at home alone, worrying about me. Herbst was considering: The conversation I had with Miss Neu has no future. With this sort of young woman, you imagine you've come close when in fact you've created a barrier. Wish her well and don't try to court her.

He did not act on this intelligence. The next day he ran into her in the post office, at the next window. Having met her, he spoke to her, and when their business was concluded he joined her. While they walked, he talked on and on. He suddenly had so much to say. With no preparation, the words came. Not of themselves, but by way of a story about a postal worker who collected stamps. He used to remove valuable stamps from international letters and keep them. Nothing was said about this, for what would be the point of speaking out when your letters could be confiscated? Then, suddenly, someone saw the matter differently. He went and told a supervisor, who would have dismissed the matter in deference to British honor, for no servant of the British Empire would violate its laws, but he was not content until the fellow was reprimanded. In addition to the reprimand, he was ordered to return the stamps. He denied taking them. His house was searched, and many undelivered letters were found.

A story that doesn't really pertain to either Dr. Herbst or Lisbet Neu gave them something to talk about. If we were to monitor their conversation, we would find nothing that hasn't been said by others. Still, it wasn't wasted. For, having begun a conversation, they continued to walk and talk, like people who know each other well and enjoy talking to each other. As things happen, it happened that, before taking leave of each other, she gave him the telephone number of the store she worked in and, as it was closed at night, added the number of the grocery she shopped in; the grocer and his wife were there until 10:00 and would call her to the phone at any time. The night Dr. Herbst took leave of his wife when she was about to give birth, it was hard for him to go back to his empty house. He thought of various people but was

not drawn to any of them. He was reminded of Professor Neu's relative. He thought of calling her. One doesn't really call a young woman
at such an hour, but Lisbet Neu was different,

This is the beginning of the story of Manfred Herbst and Lisbet Neu,
a relative of Professor Alfred Neu, Dr. Herbst's distinguished teacher.
I think I have made things as clear as they can be. But this is not the
essence of the story. The essence of the story involves Manfred Herbst
and the nurse Shira, the Shira I began with, whose conduct I will
continue to recount insofar as it touches on the story of Herbst.

— 4 —

Now, after taking leave of his wife, he went to telephone Lisbet Neu.
He found a phone booth, but it was at an intersection, and he was
worried that he wouldn't be able to hear Lisbet Neu's lovely voice over
the traffic. So he passed it up and went on to another phone, only to
realize that the numbers were jumbled in his mind. He wasn't sure
which was her work number and which was the grocery number. He
opened the telephone book to verify the numbers. They were spotted
with dirt and illegible. He put down the book with the illegible numbers and went on. He found another booth.

When he opened the door, he found a woman inside. He retreated
and was about to turn away. The woman said, "I finished my conversation. If I'm not mistaken, it's Dr. Herbst, Mrs. Herbst's husband."
Herbst stared at her and at the red turban on her head, his face turning
red, like the turban. She said, "I am sure that Mrs. Herbst is well. She
is comfortable with us and has whatever she needs."

Herbst asked himself: Who is this woman in whose hands Henrietta
is so comfortable? One thing is clear: the red turban on her head is
becoming. And it is equally clear that she is the nurse I call Nadia,
though her name is not Nadia but Shira. He was gracious to her, so that
she would be gracious to his wife.

Shira said, "Did Dr. Herbst want to use the phone?" He blushed and
muttered, "Yes." Shira said, "Is there trouble with the phone? Here, I'll
make the call." She lifted the receiver, placed a coin in the slot, and said,
"This is the nurse Shira. S-h-i-r-a. How is Mrs. Herbst? H-e-r-b-s-t. I

said Mrs. Herbst, the wife of Dr. Herbst. Dr. Herbst from the university. Mrs. Herbst who checked into the hospital this afternoon. She's doing well? If so, Mr. Axelrod, her husband sends regards. Her husband, Dr. Herbst, who is right here having trouble with the phone. Can you hear me? *Heeeeaaar meee?* Or do I have to repeat everything? You heard me. Good."

Herbst thought to himself: That nurse took on a hard job. I must thank her and pay her for the call. But will that make us even? He looked her in the eye and said, "If Miss Shira is free, I would be glad to take her for coffee." Shira answered, "I am free, and I would be delighted to go." Herbst realized his timing was right, that he had done the correct thing, and that to have done otherwise would have been rude.

Shira adjusted her turban, took a mirror from her purse, powdered the tip of her nose, and said, "Let's find a café with a phone so we can inquire about Mrs. Herbst." Herbst opened the door of the phone booth for her, thinking: This woman is tough on the outside, but inside she is soft. As for me, what am I like? I'd rather not inquire or analyze. He looked at Shira again. Her freckles were no longer visible, because of the darkness or the powder. Either way, she was tall and well dressed, so one would not be embarrassed to be seen with her in public. She opened her purse but, instead of a cigarette, took out a mirror and peered into it, as young women do.

They went into the café and sat down—Herbst like a man unaccustomed to the company of a woman, and Shira like a woman intending to relax rather than talk. When Herbst realized she wasn't eager for conversation, he was relieved and took the opportunity to observe her. He noted that she was sitting distractedly, sitting without crossing her legs, sitting and drinking tea with milk, sitting without smoking, sitting contentedly without looking this way or that, simply gazing at the small space in front of her, which was being filled with her tranquil presence. Though one cannot quite say this, for space is space and she is no more than herself—how could her mere gaze fill it up?

When she had finished about half of the tea, she took her purse, got up, went to the phone, picked up the receiver, and asked how Mrs. Herbst was doing. She came back, smiling, and said, "This time I was lucky and more successful. I spoke with the night nurse, not with Axelrod, who never hears you, who just keeps talking to everyone and his wife, as they say. As for Mrs. Herbst, she is doing well and is in good hands. The nurse I spoke to is the one in charge."

Herbst said to Shira, "Really, that Axelrod is an odd fellow. He talks over his shoulder to everyone at once." But what I am saying is irrele-

vant too. I should thank her for taking the trouble to inquire about my
wife for me, and I end up talking, in Shira's words, about "everyone
and his wife."

Shira didn't answer. She sat with her legs crossed. When she crossed
her legs, it seemed to Herbst that she began to dwindle. Not as she had
dwindled there in the hospital, when he and Henrietta sat as one, and
Shira and that beggar merged and were enclosed in whatever place that
was. Though it was clear to him that it had all been a dream, he looked
around and was surprised that the same beggar, blindman, Turk, wasn't
there now. As soon as he saw that he wasn't there, he smiled and
murmured to himself: In any case, it's clear that he didn't disappear in
that sandal.

While Herbst was struggling to extricate himself from matters that
are inherently impossible to extricate oneself from, a man appeared,
dressed in black, elegant, and so closely shaved that there was a blue
cast to his cheeks. He bowed and asked if they were pleased to be in
his café, if they had received what they ordered, if what was served to
them was satisfactory. When they answered that they were pleased
with the service, that whatever they were served was good, he went on
to say, "I hope that from now on you won't pass me by." He then took
the opportunity to introduce himself. Actually, he had already introduced himself and told them his name. He had introduced himself
earlier so he would be able to talk to them. He was introducing himself
now to assert his position.

Now that he had joined them, he thought it would not be inappropriate to say a few words. He began telling about himself: that he was
new here in Palestine and in Jerusalem, that it had never occurred to
him that he would come here, certainly not to live. "But," he continued, "having come here, I wanted to set up a café like the one I had
in Berlin. At first, I thought I would open a café in Tel Aviv, a dynamic
city, teeming with action. But when I saw the cafés there, which are
half out-of-doors, I decided against Tel Aviv. For I, dear sir and dear
madam, see the café as an enterprise that should offer refuge from the
street rather than drag the street along with it. In Tel Aviv, coffee
drinkers sit outside, as if they're drinking soda, not coffee. With your
permission, madam, and yours, sir, let me say a few words on the
subject of drinks. Every drink has its place. Wine loves a fine room,
furnished like a parlor with chandeliers that light the room as well as
the wine in the goblet. Your eyes are fixed on the goblet, and its eyes
are fixed on you. Being gay and jubilant, you bring the goblets together
and sing out, '*L'hayim.*' Tea loves grayish yellow walls and a low
ceiling. It inhabits its cup like a mandarin ruling his domain. Cocoa

loves a cloth embroidered with roses and butterflies, with cake along-side the cocoa and cream topping them both. Beer loves an old, dusky cellar with oak tables, heavy and bare. A cocktail is at home anywhere, asking nothing of those who drink it. It sits watching with sadistic pleasure as people clamor for an illicit drop whose mother doesn't know who its forebears were and is even unsure of her own daughter's genealogy. And so on, with every sort of drink. Each one has its place. Coffee is foremost, with a special place named for it. Whoever comes for a cup of coffee comes to relax, to be refreshed. There, in Tel Aviv, you sit on the street, drinking, without knowing what you are drinking, engaging every passerby, arguing, shouting, contending, though no one can be heard, while a small, dark Yemenite crawls about applying the tools of his trade to the assorted footwear. He alone, I would say, is of any consequence. While he shines a man's shoes, the fellow's head could be switched with someone else's, and neither of them would notice, in the general commotion, that head and shoulders are mis-matched. Even here in Jerusalem, all is not well. It's hard to find a good spot and hard to find waiters. You're forced to hire waitresses. I don't deny that waitresses have something waiters lack, but they're impatient. They don't have the patience guests deserve. There are guests who don't know what they want, and a waiter must know what to suggest and how to use hypnosis sometimes to make them think it was their own idea to order as they did. Not only do waitresses fail to help a guest, but their brash manner confuses him. I stand by in silence. If I speak up, the union will be after me. If you will permit me, sir and madam, I would like to tell you what happened to me here in Jerusalem. I once threw a waitress out of my café. I won't claim I was one hundred percent right, but surely ninety-nine. Picture this: I am standing and talking to her, and she yawns in my face. I yelled at her and said, 'Take your rag and get out.' As soon as she left, her friends stopped working and followed her, declaring that they were on strike. I laughed and said, 'Strike, my girls, strike. Such meager chicks . . . you're not even worth the price of slaughtering.' I tried to find other waitresses, but they all belonged to the union and would have nothing to do with an employer involved in a strike. A gentleman came from the Histadrut, carrying a briefcase, like a lawyer, and began talking to me as if he owned my café. In short, he talks and I answer, I talk and he answers. Meanwhile, the customers rush in, and there is no one to serve them. Having no choice, I decide to negotiate with the waitresses, all except for that brazen one, so they'll go back to work. Do you know what that man from the Histadrut said? He said to me, 'If you don't want her, we don't want you.' Ha, ha, ha, ha—I'm the boss, and she's merely my servant.

Yet he has the nerve to say to me, to the one who set up this place, 'We don't want you.' If things hadn't happened as they did, who knows how it would have ended? Exactly what happened? The sort of thing that happens only in Palestine. That gentleman had his eye on the waitress, and she had her eye on him. They were married, and, believe it or not, I sent them an enormous tart with 'Mazel Tov' written on it in chocolate. Which is not to say that we made up. But I did win their hearts, and they are now regular customers. He comes for coffee and she comes for ice cream. It's the sort of thing that occurs only in Palestine. There are many basics missing here. I won't mention the ones a cultured person misses all the time. But even some of the things a modern man needs only two or three times a year can't be found here. There is not a single synagogue with an organ or a choir. I have dealt with one such need by setting up this café. I hope it suits you and that I will have the pleasure of seeing you here again. Good night, dear lady. And a restful night to you, sir. I am at your service. *Au revoir.*"

The conversation with the café owner rescued Herbst from a whirlpool of imagination. When he left the café with Shira, his mood was light. When he went to the hospital with Henrietta, his mood had not been so light. To add to the lightness, he took off his cap, turned to Shira, and said, "What a splendidly grotesque performance." Shira said, "It's hard for those *yekkes* to adjust." Herbst smiled and said, "I'm a *yekke* too." Shira said, "A *yekke*, but one who came willingly, unlike that lout who never considered leaving Germany and coming here. Such a person could not possibly be comfortable here, apart from the absence of an organ or the presence of the Histadrut. There are other forces undermining him." Herbst said, "If I had permission, I would ask: What about Miss Shira? Is she comfortable here?" Shira said, "Comfortable or not, wherever I am there are sick people, and what difference does it make if I am with them here or somewhere else? I wear the same white *kittel* here as there." "And apart from the white *kittel*, is there nothing else?" "Apart from the *kittel*, there are the sick, who are sick whether they speak Russian, Yiddish, or Hebrew." Herbst said, "In that case, I'll ask no more questions." Shira said, "I have nothing more to add. Jerusalem is already asleep. There's not a soul on the streets. Anyone who happens to be out has one thing in mind: to find refuge in his doorway and then inside his home." Herbst said, "A perfect definition of night in Jerusalem. . . . Night in Jerusalem, just as it is." Now what? Herbst pondered. I'll see Shira to her door, go to my empty house, get into bed, wake up early, and in the morning I'll go to see Henrietta. When I knock at the hospital gate, they'll open it and call a clerk, who will talk to me over his shoulder and ask in alarm,

"What do you want?" To which I will say, "My name is Herbst—
Herbbbst—husband of Mrs. Herbst." To which the clerk will answer,
"You mean Mrs. Herbst who came with you for, for——" I will grab
his notebook and show him what she came for. What if I had called
Lisbet? Before Herbst could pursue this train of thought, Shira stopped
and said, "This is my house." "This one here?" Herbst asked, somewhat dismayed. When he saw that she was dismayed by his dismay, he
added, "Since the walk was short and the company pleasant, I am sorry
to be here already." Shira said simply, "Would Dr. Herbst like to come
in?" Herbst looked at his wrist, as if he were consulting the time, and
said, "I'll come in, but I won't stay long." He stared at the house in
wonder, amazed that such a structure existed. It had been there for
several generations. One could tell from the style of the structure. But
Shira's words gave it new vitality, deriving not from the stone, wood,
mortar, plaster of which it was constructed, but from its own power,
imbued with life and will which, at will, gives life. Vivid thoughts took
over, though not yet in full color, showing Herbst more than his eyes
could see. In just a few minutes, he might enter that house, for Shira
had explicitly said, "Come in, sir," and he had answered, "With your
permission, madam, I will come in." His legs were suddenly heavy, his
knees began to quiver, his entire body was inert, and he was afraid he
would be too weak to move. Still, with heavy heart and in high anticipation, he stood peering in and looking to see whether the house had a
door and whether it was a door one could enter.

Shira took a bunch of keys from her purse. In the light from the
window of the house across the way, she chose a key and opened the
door for Herbst. Standing at the entry, she said, "Wait a minute. I'll
go in and turn on a light. Or would it be better to go in while it's dark
and close the door before turning on the light, to keep out mosquitoes
and sand flies?" Herbst nodded and said, "Let's close the door first and
then turn on the light."

They entered the room in darkness. Shira dropped her purse on the
bed, along with the keys, and said, "I opened the door with the wrong
key." She groped for a match, then turned on the lamp. "Success!
Three cheers for success!" Herbst said—as if it were remarkable to
succeed with the first match.

Herbst was now in Shira's room. There was a bed, a table, a chair,
a closet, a chest with five or six books on it, and above it the Böcklin
painting with the skull. Two windows overlooked the street and the
neighboring houses. There was also a door, covered with a curtain, that
led to the kitchen. The scent of coffee mixed with burnt alcohol wafted
through the room. Everything was in perfect order, though it didn't

seem as if a guest was expected. Nor did Shira seem to be paying attention to the guest she had brought.

Shira lowered the blinds on both windows, taking her time, as if no one else were there. Finally, she turned toward Herbst and said, "My room is small, but it's mine." She sat on the edge of her bed, still wearing the turban, and said to herself: What was I going to do? Try the key and see if it fits the lock. . . . I'll leave that for tomorrow. She suddenly looked up at Herbst, gave him a long, searching look, reached out wearily, and pointed to the chair without telling him to sit down. Though she sat down and took off her turban, Herbst remained standing. She waved the turban at him and said, "Why not sit down. Here's a chair." Herbst said, "Should the lady wish to change her clothes, I can turn the other way." Shira said, "That's a fine idea. If the professor doesn't mind, I will go and change my clothes."

She got up from the bed, went to the closet, and stood behind the open door, lingering as long as she lingered, then appeared in dark blue slacks and a thin shirt. Herbst looked at her and was astonished: now that she was wearing men's clothes, her masculine quality seemed to fade. She sat down on the bed again, and he sat on the chair between the table and the bed. His mind remained fixed on this miracle, this miraculous reversal: when she took off her dress, which was womanly attire, her masculinity was dispelled. As that thought became more and more dim and as his mind became vacant, once again everything was concrete and once again he saw Shira as she was, namely, in those particular dark blue slacks and in that particular thin shirt. He saw her, not face to face, but in a vision. He remained in this state of mind but started when he heard Shira say, "One can assume the professor would not like tea, having just had some in the café. If so, I'll pour us some cognac." She got up and bent down to get the cognac from the chest. Then, straightening up, she said, "Dr. Herbst is a smoker, right? Here are cigarettes, matches, an ashtray." She took a box from the table, opened it, and said: "I haven't tried these yet, but the company that makes them wouldn't turn out inferior cigarettes. Most important, I trust the source."

Herbst asked himself: Who is it that gives this woman cigarettes she is so confident about? The question exploded in his mind. He, no doubt, brought the cigarettes to her room. Yes, to her room. And when he brought them to her room, he was obviously in the room, as I am now. And when he was in her room, she sat on the bed as she did a few minutes ago. And he too may have suggested that she change her clothes. And when she changed, she changed into those slacks and that shirt, those blue slacks and that thin shirt. His heart was suddenly heavy, his shoulders drooped, his eyes began to sweat, and he felt as if his head had been hit with a metal pole. He was caught in a muddle of hate and envy, hating the shade of dark blue that enclosed her hips and belly, the shirt that pressed against her heart, and envying the cigarette giver, who had been here in this room in this place with this woman while she changed into those slacks and that shirt. But his envy and hatred were short-lived. They had appeared suddenly and vanished just as suddenly, leaving panic in his heart.

Those familiar with Dr. Manfred Herbst's character might wonder at this degree of emotion, and even he wondered about himself—how he had suddenly become excited to the point of altered sensibilities. Nonetheless, as if to protest against those cigarettes, he took out a battered pack and lit one of his own.

Meanwhile, Shira had made herself at home on her bed. Realizing she was tired and in need of rest, she reached for a pillow, which she propped up between her head and the wall, taking no notice of what had happened. When Herbst lit his cigarette, which was not one of hers, she let the pillow slip, looked at him, bewildered, and said, "What is it, doctor? Is there something wrong with my cigarettes?" Herbst shook his head and said, "No, no, no." He grasped her hand reassuringly, as if it were the way of the world, when one turns down a woman's cigarette, to comfort her by taking her hand. Now that her hand was in his, he took the other one too. Her hands were cold and his were warm.

Herbst knew he was behaving childishly, that this was, no doubt, apparent on his face, that he was surely ridiculous, that Shira knew he was ridiculous and was laughing to herself at his expense. Herbst, like those who always behave properly but suddenly do something improper, was afraid of appearing ridiculous. He let go of her hands and relit his cigarette, for it had gone out. When it was lit, he set it down, turned back toward Shira, moistened his lips with his tongue, and stared at her. He saw not a trace of ridicule. On the contrary, her face was opaque. Or, as they say in modern Hebrew, her face was "serious." In any case, Shira's mind was elsewhere. Herbst stretched out his arm, his fingers open, like someone on the edge of despair who doesn't know what to do. Shira was still in the same position, her head against the wall, her eyes closed. Whether or not you knew Shira, you could recognize that Shira was tired, that she was waiting for you to get up and go so she could entrust her weary limbs to sleep.

Herbst looked at her and said in a whisper, "Miss Shira is tired. I will go now so she can sleep." Shira said, "I'm not tired. I don't want to sleep, and there's no reason to go." Herbst said, "Then I have some advice to offer." Shira covered her eyes and, peering through the cracks, said, "We'll hear, then we'll see." Herbst said, "Miss Shira should stretch out and close her eyes." Shira opened her eyes wide, stared at him with the aforementioned curiosity, and asked, "What will Dr. Herbst do meanwhile? Will he sit with me and sing me a lullaby? But I'm worried you'll be bored. Besides, I'm not a baby, and you, who are the father of two grown girls, may not remember any lullabies. It's too bad that I don't have a phone. We can't call the maternity ward and check on Mrs. Herbst, who may have just now presented her lord and master with a glorious songbird. You see that I am treating you as an adult. I haven't mentioned the stork that brings babies from heaven." Herbst was startled and began praying he would forget all that had transpired here. He looked at Shira, wishing that she too would erase from her heart all that had happened. Knowing this was a futile wish, a deep sigh erupted from his heart.

Shira smoothed her shirt, touched her thumb to one of her freckles, and sat watching Dr. Herbst. She watched him for a long time, her eyes growing bigger and bigger. Herbst sat with Shira like a man who sees that his downfall is imminent and there is no way to avert it. He shifted from one foot to the other, let his shoulders droop, and stood ready to submit. After a while, since Shira hadn't said a word, he thought to himself: What will be will be, but I ask only one thing—that she not mention my wife. As Shira sat in silence, not saying a word, he repeated to himself: Why is she so silent, why doesn't she speak, why doesn't she say something to me? Shira remained silent, giving no sign that she intended to speak.

All of a sudden, she stirred and said in a singsong, like a woman telling some old tale, "Now let's go back to the beginning. You said I should close my eyes and try to sleep, that you would sit beside me. I said I was afraid it would take too long and be boring. If I hadn't interrupted you, you might have added, 'How can anyone be bored in Shira's presence?' So much for that. Let's deal with another matter. I didn't serve you cholent, and the cognac I offered never appeared. Now, doctor, all the evil spirits in the world will not keep me from pouring you a drink."

She straightened up and, moving gracefully, with a youthful stride, went to the chest. She took out a bottle and a glass, poured a drink, and said, "Have some. As a licensed nurse, I can assure you that this drink is harmless." "And what about you?" Herbst asked in a whisper. "If you insist, I'll drink with you." She went to get another glass, poured herself a few drops, lifted her glass, and said, "*L'hayim*, doctor, *l'hayim.*" She drank up and was about to refill his glass when Herbst cried in alarm, "No, no, no!" She glanced at him, and in a flash she understood: He is afraid I will drink to his wife.

She stood over him, her arm on his shoulder, and declared, "Dr. Herbst, you *are* a baby." Earlier, when he had held her hand, it was cold. Now it was warm, so much so that he felt it through his clothes. He grabbed her hand and held it in his. Shira withdrew it and, stroking his head, remarked, "What a full head of hair, like a young man's." Herbst said, "I meant to get a haircut." She said, "It's good you didn't. I prefer a full head of hair." Herbst brushed his hand over her head and said, "Then why do you cut your hair?" She said, "Did I say I like my own hair? That's not what I said." While she was talking, he brushed her cheek with his hand. As his hand brushed her cheek, fingering its freckled surface, the blood rushed to his hand, emitting flashes of violent fire that stemmed from his blazing blood. Shira closed her eyes, opened them again, and stared at him. A bond seemed to stretch between her eyes, not a bond of curiosity, as before, but more like the bond that marks a woman whose heart has turned to love, who would give her life for love. She tilted her head to the left, and her eyes turned toward him, studying him obliquely, fixing themselves there, unswerving.

I will stop in the middle, leaping over those things that transpired between him and her, and continue to relate what followed, that is to say, after Manfred Herbst took leave of Shira.

— 5 —

What happened then? Manfred Herbst left Shira and went on his way, not knowing if he was happy or sad. But he was perplexed. How could he not be perplexed? He, the father of two daughters, the husband of a fine woman with whom he lives amicably, is on his way back from a woman he met in a telephone booth and was drawn to follow home, staying from early evening until past midnight. Despite all this, he sees no change in himself. Nor has there been any change in the world.

The small filigreed streetlamps, designed to bestow romantic sleep on the city—by a shortsighted mayor who regarded himself as the last scion of the Crusaders and prided himself on doing as they did—these

small beacons gave off light that was scarcely visible. Though Jerusalem
already had electricity, it was expensive, and most people used kerosene. The city was quiet; there was not a person in sight. Earlier, when
we were seeing Shira home, there was not the image of a person in
sight; now there was not even the image of an image. Who is it who
said, "In Jerusalem, if you see anyone stirring about at night, he is
heading for the safety of home"? Now I am the one seeking the safety
of home.

Herbst has already left Shira's street. He is winding his way through
the alleys that serve as shortcuts. Alley bites alley, lane is joined to lane,
yard to yard. And from alley to alley, from lane to yard, you imagine
you are back where you started, that you will have to retrace your steps
and find another way out. But we are fortunate, for, along with the
earth under us, we have sky, moon, stars above, so that, when we look
up, we are never lost. Herbst looked up at the sky, oriented himself,
and found the intersection from which a broad street led to the upper
valley and to his house.

By now, other winds were blowing, cool winds from Talpiot, where
the good winds gather to give life to the entire region. On such a night,
at such an hour, when Herbst happened to come home and find restful
quiet pervading every rock, every mound, every hill, breezes blowing
and bringing with them the fragrance of cypresses, pine, garden flowers, wild grasses, desert plants, cool earth, his heart was tranquil and his
soul soared. Now his mind was distracted, his heart impassive, his soul
in turmoil. When Herbst happened to be coming home from an academic meeting or lecture on such a night and at such an hour, he would
take short steps, enjoying every breath. Now he was running, though
there was no one waiting for him at home, no one to ask where he had
been and why he was late. Earlier would have been better. Why, he
didn't know.

His thoughts suddenly shifting to his wife, he speculated: While I
was with Shira, my wife could have given me a son or a daughter.
"No!" Herbst shouted. "The good Lord wouldn't do such a thing!"
Herbst lifted his head toward the sky, as if to probe God's mysterious
ways. The skies were pure; the stars were in place, showing no trace
of evil design. But Herbst's mood was foul, more so than at first, for
it occurred to him that, while he was with Shira, his wife could have
had a difficult delivery and died. He pulled off his hat and crumpled
it angrily. Among his numerous thoughts, not one was of sorrow, grief,
sympathy for his wife. His were thoughts of revenge, retribution,
recompense for his malice and villainy. All of a sudden he laughed
derisively and said to himself, still laughing: Now, Manfredchen, all

you need is for that freckled one to come and say, "Now that your wife is dead and you are without a wife, take me as your wife." Where is my hat? My God, I left it at Shira's. He didn't realize he was holding it. When he realized his hat was in his hand, he recovered, and his thoughts were once more with Henrietta. You are a good woman, Henriett, you're a good woman, Henriett, he singsonged sadly. You were with me, and you are with me now. You raised the girls, you made me a home, looked after my interests, seeing that I did my work, not letting me be distracted by these troubled times. And when we began to be discouraged about my academic prospects, you never came to me with recriminations or complaints. You gave me support and kept me from joining that thwarted lot that degrades itself through gossip and slander. After all this, that woman could come and say, "Take me as your wife." But the choice is mine, and what Miss Shira wants is not what I want. An evil spirit responded, saying: If so, if the choice is yours. Where were you an hour ago, when Henrietta was in the throes of labor? And what will you do when Shira informs you that she is carrying your child? No need to worry about that. Women like Shira protect themselves. If she was careless, there are ways to terminate a pregnancy. And if she wants to have the child, there are places in the world where no one asks the mother if she is properly married. In any case, Shira is not one of those who attach themselves to a man against his will. And, in any case, from now on I will never again darken her doorstep.

Herbst was already at his house. When he saw he was there, he lunged toward the gate to the garden that surrounded the house and found it was locked, just as he had left it when he took Henrietta to the hospital. But there was a break in the fence. When Arab shepherds notice there is no one home, they poke a stick through the wiring and make a hole, a bit yesterday, a bit today, until the fence is destroyed and their sheep have the run of the garden. I see, Herbst said, that, first thing in the morning, I must fix the fence, or not a single bush or flower will survive. Now I'll go and see if there are any letters.

There were no letters in the box. Only notices, announcements, invitations, and other printed matter that comes our way, to which we pay no attention, except for a reprint that would have interested him at any other time, as there were arguments in it challenging Alfred Neu's theories. His eyes skimmed the article, but his mind was elsewhere. He was in a hurry to get to bed, for he had to be at the hospital early to see Henrietta. By and by, his mind lighted on Lisbet Neu.

If I were to speak to you today, Lisbet Neu, I would not choose my words so carefully, and you, my dear, would not be such a sheltered rose. When he left Shira, he was not aware of any change in himself, but he now had the air of a youth, confident of success.

Enough about Lisbet Neu, who is only an accessory to the story, and enough about Shira, who is not yet at its core. I will merely take what comes, event by event, and set it in its place.

— 6 —

The next morning, he was up early, shaved with a new blade, changed his clothes, and put on the tie Henrietta had bought him for his birthday. It was the color of dark Bordeaux, woven of silk thread that popped up in balls between the rows like berries between the furrows of a garden. Then he rinsed the kettle to make coffee. While waiting for the water to boil, he picked up that fool's article and, with a single glance, skimmed his misguided version of Professor Neu's theories. Herbst laughed, ranted, laughed again, threw it on the floor, flung it in the air, drew donkey's ears on it. Then he made his snack, which he ate and drank. He looked in the mirror, adjusted his tie, locked the door, and jumped down the three steps in front of the house.

He noticed that the hole in the garden fence was higher than it had been the previous night. A large creature could shove its way in. As he was in a hurry to get to Henrietta, time was precious. He looked around for a neighbor he could ask to keep the Arabs from sending their animals into his garden. There was no one in sight. Just as well, he thought. Since there's no one around, I don't have to account for myself.

"A most felicitous morning, sir!" A voice was heard, hoarse as an old parakeet, and an odd creature appeared, perhaps male, perhaps female, perhaps priest, perhaps actor. Herbst pretended not to hear. The greeting was repeated: "Good morning, professor! Good morning, professor! I see you are already up tending your garden. *Morgen shtunde, hat gold in munde*—he who makes the early rounds will reap success beyond all bounds." Herbst answered curtly, "Good morning." And that creature Sacharson, that convert, that priest of Jewish Christians, ignoring his neighbor's grudging tone, leaped over to join him, walking and talking like those agitators who speak when no one listens and are nevertheless paid for their words. Herbst pointed to an approaching bus, jumped on, pushed his way in, and adjusted his tie. A child on her way to school got up to give him a seat. Someone else grabbed the seat, so Herbst and the child both had to stand. Like a man whose senses are impaired, he took no notice. She was offended and enraged—enraged at the Arab policeman who took the seat she had given up for Dr. Herbst and offended that Herbst did not acknowledge the seat. Herbst suddenly recognized her, asked about her parents, how she was doing, all the other questions one asks a friend's daughter. The child was appeased and answered all his questions. When they arrived in town, she took another bus to the high school, and he went on to the hospital.

The hospital gates were open, but no one was allowed in, as a truck was delivering ice and the help was working frantically to finish before the heat set in. Herbst moved aside to make way for the ice carriers, whose hands were red and chilled. One of them looked up from the ice and informed him that his wife had borne him a daughter. "A daughter?" Herbst starnmered. "A daughter is not a son," the informant added. "But, in these times, with wars raging everywhere, it's a blessing to have female children rather than males, who are likely to be sent off to war." Herbst nodded and moved out of the way. Someone shouted, "Make way for the doctor!" Herbst tried to make himself inconspicuous, so he wouldn't be mistaken for a doctor of medicine, and went in. When he arrived at the maternity section, he asked, "Which room?" Realizing the question was vague, he added, "Mrs. Herbst's room, please." They opened a door and led him to Henrietta's room. He scanned it quickly and went to her bed. She was lying there, radiant. She offered him her hand, gazing up at him like a woman gazing at the beloved husband whose child she has just borne as if to proclaim, "Look, my darling, look—I have overcome all obstacles and fulfilled all your hopes."

He didn't say a word. Henrietta took no notice. She was peering at him, watching him lovingly, without a word, without speech, without end. Roses sent forth their scent from the small table beside her bed, and their fresh redness sparkled. Who had already brought Henrietta flowers, and why hadn't it occurred to him to bring some? He blushed and began to stammer, "I'm embarrassed, Henrietta, I'm embarrassed." Henrietta looked at him fondly and asked, "Why are you embarrassed, my dearest?" Again he stammered. "Because, because I should have brought you flowers." Henrietta pressed his hand in hers and caressed it, saying, "Never mind, my love. At a time like this, how could you have thought of bringing flowers? Tell me, my dearest, tell me truly: Did you sleep? Did you sleep enough? Now, my love, let's call the nurse, and she'll show you your little daughter. There's the bell, my love. Put your finger on the button and push three times. Like that, my darling."

He barely touched the button. He touched it again and pressed it with trepidation—once, then once, then once again, without turning this way or that—for it might be Shira who responded. A groundless fear. Another nurse, an old woman, was on duty in that room at that hour. The old woman came and glanced fondly at the new mother and her husband. She offered her small, sturdy hand to Herbst, smiled, and said pleasantly, "Mazel tov, doctor. I must say one thing: Your wife is brave. The courage she showed last night should be engraved in gold on a marble plaque. Look and see if there are signs of fatigue on her face. Because of the evil eye, we are keeping her in bed. Otherwise, you could order a horse and she could ride to Motza or Kiryat Anavim. If you don't believe me, ask the other nurses. They all agree."

Henrietta's eyes pointed toward a wicker basket. The old woman smiled and said sweetly, "In your place, Mrs. Herbst, I wouldn't be in such a hurry. I would let him ask again and again, and each time I would demand a gold dinar or, in the currency of our land, a shiny new lira. But since the baby is eager to see her father, I will bring her." The old woman brought out a tidbit of flesh, swathed in linen, and began to mumble and coo, "My sweet honeycomb, my luscious nectar, look and see who is here. It's your father, your sire, who has come to consider your dowry. But I can tell, you won't need a dowry. The boys are all after you already. They'll have you as you are, my pet."

She took out the baby and presented her to her father, watching to see if he could tell how fetching she was. Manfred stared at the rosy tidbit, its two spots of twinkling blue fixed on him, not knowing what to say. Henrietta turned her eyes toward her husband and toward the infant, not knowing what to say either. She fixed her eyes on his. Manfred knew he was expected to say something. He arched his lower lip and said, "So this little worm is our daughter." The nurse put the infant back in the basket and left silently. Manfred went to sit beside his wife.

Once more, Henrietta took his hand in hers and spoke. "Now, my love, you must relay our news to the girls, so they know they have a little sister. And now, my love, let's get down to essentials. What name will we give our daughter? I should confess I have already given her a name, not one of those new names that are chirped over every cradle, but a name from the Bible."

"What do you call her?" Manfred asked. Henrietta answered, "What do I call her? If I tell you, you'll agree." "So?" Herbst asked impa-

tiently. "So," Henrietta answered, "so I call her Sarah." Manfred heard
and was silent. After a while he asked, "Why did you choose that
name?" Henrietta looked up at her husband with special affection and
answered with a question. "Wasn't your mother called Sarah?" Manfred nodded and said, "Yes. Yes, my mother's name was Sarah, but she
was called Serafina." Henrietta said, "Tell me this, my love. Can a child
be called Serafina in this country?" Manfred said, "It's truly impossible." Henrietta said, "So let's name her for your mother's grandmother,
who was probably called Sarah." Manfred said, "Yes, yes." Henrietta
said, "I assumed my lord and master would be thrilled to name his
daughter after his mother," Manfred said, "Yes, yes. Of course, Henriett. Of course." Henrietta said, "Unless you prefer one of those new
names, such as Aviva or Zeva." At this point Henrietta puckered her
lips and chirped like one of those women, the mothers of Aviva and
Zeva, "Avivale, Zevale. Remember Elizabeth Modrao, the daughter of
Professor Modrao? Do you remember telling us that her grandfather
was called Samuel, a rare name for a Christian in Germany? Do you
remember why he was called Samuel? You don't remember? She told
you, and you told me. It was because he was born in Jerusalem, on
Shavuot, and his father saw fit, in honor of the land and the festival,
to give his son a name from the Hebrew Bible. After what the Germans
did to us," Henrietta added, "why say anything good about them. Still,
it must be admitted, they did pay homage to Palestine."

Another nurse came in and whispered something in the new
mother's ear. Henrietta glanced at her husband and said, "You must
leave now, Fred. It's really too bad. I want so much to talk to you, but
I can't delay the nurse, who is here to take care of me. So, for now, Fred,
let's say goodbye. Come back this afternoon, if you can. In about four
hours, or four and a half. Did you have breakfast? Did you eat any of
the eggs Zahara sent us from her *kvutza?* Please, be sure to have an egg
in the morning and another in the evening. If you have two at a time,
all the better. The natives say seven olives are the equivalent of one egg.
If you ask me, an egg is an egg. As for olives, if you happen to like them,
they spice up a meal. But not for a main dish—even eggs themselves
don't have such pretensions. According to Dr. Taglicht, the Talmud
states that whatever is like an egg—that's right, whatever is *like* it—
doesn't match it in quality. Now, my dearest, tell me where you plan
to have lunch. I insist, my dearest, that you go to a good restaurant and
have a solid meal. Meat, not vegetables. When you eat out, be sure to
avoid salads, since you can't be sure the greens were properly washed.
I'm told restaurants buy their greens from Arab women, and you know
they water their gardens with sewage, which is the source of most of

the disease in Jerusalem. Now then, my love, are you listening? Say goodbye to Sarah." "Sarah? Who's Sarah?" Henrietta smiled and said, "My little Sarah, you chose a forgetful father. He hears your name is Sarah and forgets." "Ah," said Manfred, rummaging in his pockets. It seemed to him that it was the anniversary of his mother's death, and he wanted to consult the calendar. "Now you know who Sarah is," Henrietta continued. "Sarah, your daddy is saying goodbye to you, and I'm saying goodbye to your daddy in your name. I'll say bye to you too. Goodbye, Fred. Don't forget to write the girls. I would ask you to phone them if I didn't know how hard that is to do." "I'll phone." "You will? Bless you, my love. When they let me out of bed, I'll go to the phone and call each of them. See you at four. If you promise to rest after lunch, I won't expect you until five. Right away, nurse. Bye, Fred. At five."

—— 7 ——

Herbst left the hospital and stood near the fence, trying to recall the precise date of his mother's death. By his calculation, it was not the previous evening, but he wanted to consult the calendar to be certain. He looked in his pocket, but the calendar wasn't there. He had changed his clothes in the morning, and the calendar was still in yesterday's jacket.

He had left the calendar in his old jacket. He was haunted by the thought that what had happened to him the night before could have occurred on the eve of the anniversary of his mother's death. It was good that it did not occur on the actual anniversary. Still, the event was bad in itself. Even if I was after something of that sort, now that it has come to pass, I see it wasn't what I was after. In seven days, Henrietta will be home again. May the intervening days be straightforward and uncompromised. If a man sins once, only once, the sin is not erased; still, one offense is less than two. What did Henrietta ask of me? Henrietta asked me to inform the girls that they have a sister. And something further. When he remembered what else she had asked, he looked at his watch to see how many hours remained until lunch. He noticed that his watch strap was worn. He took off the watch, put it in his jacket, and straightened his tie.

Julian Weltfremdt, a relative of Ernst Weltfremdt's, appeared. They were related in family but not in fortune, for one was a full professor and the other was not even a lecturer. He deserved to be a lecturer, even in one of the great European universities, and if Professor Weltfremdt had supported him, he would have secured an appointment. But Ernst Weltfremdt was afraid he might be charged with nepotism, that is to say, with bestowing favors on relatives. Ernst used to say to Julian, "Would you have me behave like that administrator who made his brother secretary, found jobs for his mother and father, and then changed their names, so no one would know they were related?" Since Julian Weltfremdt considered himself a victim, he allied himself with other would-be victims and, like them, engaged in challenging the establishment. Unlike most of them, a thwarted lot that indulged in gossip and slander, Julian Weltfremdt was devoted to truth. Since scholarship has many branches and truth has many violators, he became more and more outspoken against those who mock the truth.

At that time, the entire country was astir with Professor Wechsler's discovery. He had found a manuscript attributed to Saint Justin the Martyr on the subject of the profane aspects of life and the love of purity. I am not an expert on the writings of the Church Fathers, nor do I know whether he uncovered an ancient source or was misled by one of the counterfeits common in Jerusalem for three generations now. Between eagerness to innovate and the proliferation of counterfeiters, the world has been inundated with parchments, jugs, burial chests, figurines, idols, and gods from Enoch's time and earlier. Moreover, most of the scholars from Germany came to this country intent on discovering antiquities, and they found what they were after. Actually, Professor Wechsler was legitimate, as was his enterprise. But he was also extremely eager to publicize his discoveries. To this end, he invited a host of journalists, as administrators often do in the interests of their institution, attracting attention to themselves as if they were the institution. Wechsler presented his discoveries to the journalists, glorifying himself at every opportunity. The journalists listened, sent telegrams to their newspapers, and provided Wechsler with a public. Scholars of other nations began to view this country's scholars and academics with suspicion, which gave Julian Weltfremdt an opportunity to deplore the university's scholars, especially Wechsler, whose behavior he considered scandalous. However Herbst viewed Wechsler's activities, he dismissed them with a casual gesture and proceeded to enumerate some of Wechsler's accomplishments. Weltfremdt was enraged and shrieked, "What I am telling you is deplorable, and that's how you respond! Go and tell your father you need to be born again. Maybe this time you'll turn out to be a man. By the way, did your wife give birth yet? Boy or girl?" "What if it was a girl?" Weltfremdt said, "Don't tease me, Herbstlein. I believe you have two girls already." Herbst said, "Now I have three." "Three daughters? So now you have one more daughter. Don't be disheartened. The world needs girls too. I see you've bought a new tie. Come, let's wet our palates in honor of both these events. There's a new café nearby. They try to serve real coffee. Let's go there." Herbst said, "You sound as if you're their agent." Weltfremdt said, "Not yet. If you prefer, we'll go to another café."

They tried one place, but it was crowded. Here, there were young men with pipes in their mouths; there, old men with canes in their hands. Here, there were young women waiting for young men; there, young men waited for young women. Here and there, young men and women sat together, engulfing each other in clouds of smoke. "Look," Weltfremdt said to Herbst. "Look—every face is clean-shaven, every mouth holds a pipe. They all talk out of the corner of their mouth, like native Englishmen. If France had the mandate, our boys would grow beards and start whistling like birds. Get moving, man. Let's go to the place I mentioned before."

The café owner recognized Herbst, brought their order, bowed, and then retreated, so as not to give the gentleman who had been there the previous evening the idea that he intended to bother him. The two friends sat. They sat, and Weltfremdt talked about the university, about its professors, about other matters, talking, as the saying goes, about everyone and his wife, while Herbst stared straight ahead, wondering: Where was that space, the space he had seen here the night before? Weltfremdt sensed that Herbst was preoccupied. He assumed that he was worried. He certainly had cause for worry, with another daughter in addition to the first two. Feeling sorry for his friend, he insisted on paying the check.

After they took leave of each other, Herbst went to the jeweler to buy a new strap for his watch. While the worn strap was being removed, he looked at the watches, designed for a single purpose yet made in many forms. Time is constant, yet manifest in varied forms. All things are like time, even rumors, even words. A single lesson can be learned from many texts. Herbst had once said to Lisbet Neu, "I'm old enough to be your father." She had said, "I don't know your age, but I see your face and you look young." At the time, he had thought she was being generous. Now he viewed her words differently.

So much for the parable of the clocks. After fastening the new strap around his wrist, he stuck in his finger to stretch it. All of a sudden he felt bewildered. Where was the pure spirit that used to be invoked by the mere mention of Lisbet? One thought led to another, as thoughts do, and he had another thought: What if I had a son and this son was drawn to Lisbet? One thought led to still another: Henrietta will, undoubtedly, be unable to nurse the baby, so we'll have to hire a wetnurse, which will mean extra expense and put us even more in debt. Moreover, while the baby is young, wherever we put her to sleep, I will hear her and be distracted from my work, which requires concentration. My paper will remain a mess of notes, and I will remain a lecturer, with a lecturer's salary, rather than that of a professor or even an associate professor.

I will now convey some of what was implicit in Herbst's thoughts. The author of a thorough and comprehensive work on Leo III, the Byzantine ruler, a work that established his academic reputation, so that, when our university was opened in Jerusalem, he was recommended by Professor Neu and appointed lecturer—such a man should have produced another book. But days and years had passed, and he had produced nothing. When he was a student, still single, and the university was full of German women, Russian women, Jewish women— among them, some who sought his company—he turned away, out of devotion to his studies. Now that he was married, all the more reason to avoid distractions. Yet, in the end, it was he who pursued them. Who was to blame? Certainly not Henrietta. I doubt there are many like her. In terms of intelligence, beauty, and competence, Henrietta has no peer. Without regular help, without her husband's assistance, she did all the household chores. She cooked, baked, sewed, ironed, even made her own clothes. And when the girls were young, she chose to take care of them herself, without a nursemaid. As for their house—when the Herbsts came up to Jerusalem, they couldn't find a place to live. Talpiot and Beit Hakerem were new neighborhoods, and there were no apartments to be had there. Rehavia was in the planning stages. This left the Bukharan Quarter, which in those days was as important and as lovely as Rehavia is now. And there were areas that were free of flies and mosquitoes, but every space was occupied, taken over by intellectuals from abroad. In Baka, however, Henrietta found a hovel filled with garbage, considered unfit to live in. She rented this hovel, got rid of the garbage, and fixed it up. We were astonished; the hovel was transformed into a delightful, even glorious house. Henrietta made herself a garden, too. She made it with her own hands. Without the help of a gardener, without the help of her daughters. Tamara, as you know, loves flowers that come from the store rather than from trash and dung.

Her sister Zahara has many tasks to perform for her teachers—she collects money for Keren Kayemet's land-reclamation projects, sells ribbons for charitable causes, et cetera—and, because of all these tasks, she has no time for homework and never eats at mealtimes. Henrietta's only helper is Manfred, who waters the garden. Not that Henrietta needs him to do this, but it gets him out of his room and gives him a chance to exercise, rather than acquire a belly, like Professor Welt-fremdt and Professor Lemner, who are all belly, below their middle and above it—a mound of neck topped by a tiny head.

Having referred to Herbst's study, let me say a word about the room. It was the largest and most spacious room in the house, but its dimensions were not apparent because of the books lining its four walls. The wall opposite the door had a square window in it that looked onto the street, bringing the outdoors in. There was no end to what went on outside or to the shifts of scene from day to day, from hour to hour. There was another window in the south wall, and, if not for the tall piles of books on the floor, it would be possible to get to the window and see the earth's marvels: rocks rising from the ground, looking like shepherds with their flocks. Or are those shepherds with their flocks that look so like rock? Either way, there are rocks in Jerusalem that look like sheep, as well as sheep that look like rocks, and the shepherds look equally ambiguous.

The desk, the chair next to Herbst's chair, the guest chair opposite the desk—all these, like the walls, were filled with books. When a guest came, he would clear a place for him, either with a single gesture or book by book, lingering over each one. In some fields, new replaces old. Not so with Herbst. He was fond of every book that passed through his hands, even if it was outdated, even if its conclusions were outdated when it first appeared. A scholar ought to consult those naive works, Herbst would say, for we learn from them that knowledge has arrived at its current positions by way of false hypotheses, invalid conclusions, groundless evidence. In truth, it was not for this reason alone that Herbst filled his room with books. He began collecting books as a child, and what he was accustomed to do as a boy he continued to do as he grew older. In the past, before his house was filled with books, the walls of the room were decorated with antique maps of Byzantium, shaped like ships in the heart of the sea, like mountains floating in pale blue air, like many-colored towers. But, in time, these maps gave way to bookshelves.

Many other things could be found in Herbst's room, on his desk, on the windowsills. Such as pipes and ashtrays, some of which he bought in Jerusalem's markets and some of which were gifts, like the pebbles he had collected in Ashkelon, on which one can discern symbols of a language not yet decoded. Next to the pebbles were thorns, the ones that seem to have a human face. Since they are not relevant to Dr. Herbst's field of study, I will not deal with them, though I will mention the polished brass inkstand he bought from the crippled scribe who sits at the entrance to the courthouse, who was rescued by Herbst from under the hooves of a wild horse on Ramadan—its drunken rider was a judge in that very courthouse at the time.

Herbst's study is his domain, and he works with few distractions. Henrietta has a discerning eye, and whoever calls on her husband is closely scrutinized to determine whether or not he is one of those who lead to idleness. There are many idlers in Jerusalem, those employed by national institutions as well as people who know the value of work but, not having found anything to do themselves, keep others from their work.

Just as Henrietta protects her husband from idlers, she protects him from excessive burdens. She even spares him the burden of the girls' education. You, of course, know how hard it is to raise a daughter in this country. Not only a daughter like Tamara, who is as full of thorns as a cactus, but even one like Zahara, who is softer than butter. What's more, she—that is, Henrietta—manages her household without complaints or bitterness on thirty-five lirot a month, her husband's salary from the university. Were the entire sum available for household expenses, it would be simple. But it isn't simple, as some of it is earmarked for the National Fund, some for the Foundation Fund and various other funds not yet founded, which, when they are founded, will be superfluous. But who can withstand such an appeal, the word-filled drone that drowns everyone and everything? Despite all this, Henrietta carries on and maintains her home with dignity. Everyone who sees Henrietta Herbst is moved to remark, "That woman has sprung out of a painting. She's a Rubens in the flesh."

But Henrietta is flawed in one respect: she began to age prematurely. Though Manfred is still in his prime, she is aging rapidly. Another flaw: she works too hard and doesn't look after herself—all so Manfred can devote himself to his work, prepare lectures that will not bore his audience, produce a new book on a par with the first, which made his reputation. After giving him a second child, Henrietta began to behave as if she were not wife to her husband. If not for his birthday nine months ago, Sarah would not have come into being.

Manfred was faithful to his wife, even if his fantasies were sometimes illicit. From several of Henrietta's remarks, one learns about Manfred's fantasies. She has said to him many times, "Are there no attractive girls

in this country? Is that why you're always after me? Go find yourself
a young girl. If you look, you'll find one." I don't know how long a
man's wife would tolerate another woman. Even if she did put up with
it, in the name of domestic peace, one would do well to beware. Manfred Herbst neither looked nor found, either out of respect for Henrietta or because it was not his style. A man who marries his wife out
of love at first sight isn't likely to have eyes for other women. He was
once on an ocean voyage, and, finding himself on the high seas for
several days with nothing to do, he considered: If an attractive woman
were to appear, would you keep your distance? But nothing came of
this. Herbst assumed he was the cause. He was in the habit of telling
his wife everything; should he take up with another woman, he would
tell his wife and cause her sorrow. Which is not to say that, in the time
he was abroad, no woman was warm to him, but only a fool would
assume that every attractive woman who behaves warmly is open to
love. The episode ended as it began. Dr. Manfred Herbst came home
bringing new books, nothing more. When would he read them? As
book collectors know, not every book has to be read. All a book needs
is a buyer, and all a buyer needs is a bookcase that can take one book
more. It is to their credit that books contract to make room for others.

Suddenly, all of a sudden, there were newcomers in the land. They
were unexpected, and if anyone had said to them two or three years
earlier that they would emigrate, they would have protested. Suddenly,
all of a sudden, they were here. These people whose fathers and forefathers preferred the soil of Germany to that of the Land of Israel, loving
Germany perhaps even more than the Germans did, felt the ground
crumbling under them and could find no foothold anywhere in Germany. Some of them went from nation to nation, from exile to exile.
Others sought refuge in the Land of Israel, waiting there for Germany's
rage to be spent, assuming Germany would soon recover. They came
to the Land of Israel, continuing to refer to it as Palestine, as its
detractors always do.

Among the recent newcomers from Germany were various scholars
and their wives, their sons and daughters. Herbst had studied with some
of them and had known their daughters when they were in high school,
at the university, hiking together in the woods of Berlin. One elderly
professor with a sharp tongue, who was hostile to women, hearing that
the students were planning a hike, had offered this advice: "My dear
colleagues, be sure to invite some women. If there are mosquitoes, they
will attack the women, and you will be spared." Many years had passed.
Young women Herbst had known in Germany were now married, and
he had a wife too. Hearing that some of them were in Jerusalem, he

was stirred and began to recall each one, what she was like, or rather, what she had been like in those days. These thoughts led him to imagine ties of affection. He forgot that there had been nothing between them beyond prosaic words. Time plays odd tricks: what never was, pretends to have been. Some of these girls, who were once extremely beautiful, had lost their beauty and radiance. There were others whose beauty endured, but it was not the sort of beauty that revives the soul. Living in Germany, we regarded blonde hair, blue eyes, and the like as the ultimate in beauty. Having settled in the Land of Israel, another beauty arrests our eye, another sort of beauty is appealing. If he happened on one or another of these friends from the past and gathered from the conversation that she was unable to pay for lodging, he would tell Henrietta, and she would put her up. Even after the friend was settled in an apartment, Henrietta would invite her, as is the custom in this country, for lunch, dinner, sometimes for the weekend. If Manfred became deeply involved in conversation with the woman, Henrietta was never jealous. It happened that they invited one of these women for Shabbat. On the following day, Sunday, Henrietta had to go to Tel Aviv. She went to Tel Aviv, leaving her husband alone with the woman. Manfred thought to himself: I see that Henrietta trusts me. In the evening, she came home and put on the kettle. Then they had coffee with the cakes she had brought from Tel Aviv. Henrietta was not in the habit of buying baked goods. She and her family were accustomed to home baking, but, when she had occasion to be in Tel Aviv, she would bring all sorts of treats, for the confections one finds in Tel Aviv are unlike anything in Jerusalem, where pastries all taste alike. Though they come in many shapes, they have one taste.

Among the learned men who came from Germany, there were several distinguished scholars. Some were experienced medical doctors; some occupied academic chairs and were renowned throughout Germany and beyond. There were those who had been a thorn in the flesh of their Christian colleagues and those whose learning served them well, so that their Christian peers took note of their learning but not of their Jewishness. They now roamed the streets of Jerusalem, destitute, with no prospect of a livelihood. This country has only one university, and all its academic positions were occupied. Not many people would act as the scholars of Bathyra did, yielding to the authority of Rabbi Hillel. What an opportunity to make Jerusalem a metropolis of medicine and scholarship! But, because of financial calculations and narrow vision, these great men did not find a footing here. They left the country, and their wisdom was dispersed in other lands.

When these exiled scholars arrived from Germany, Manfred Herbst was like a man who wakes up and is unable to find his clothes.

Since the meaning is simple, I will not pursue the metaphor.

As we know, Herbst was one of the first lecturers at the first Hebrew university in the world, and, as such, he was honored, along with others who, being the first to be appointed lecturers and professors at the Hebrew University, were important in other people's eyes as well as their own. They lived serenely, relishing this honor, delivering lectures, reading books, each man in his own field. They wrote books too. Those who produced many books rejoiced in them and displayed them prominently; those who produced only one or two maintained that more books do not equal more wisdom; and those who didn't produce any books at all turned out the sort of dutiful papers that are referred to in the footnotes of scholarly journals and, after a certain number of years, become a monograph.

What about Herbst? After his book on the life of Leo III, the Byzantine emperor, he published nothing except for several papers that appeared in various collections. But he continued to read widely, even outside of his field, to take notes, compare texts, and collect material for a new book he intended to write on burial customs of the poor in Byzantium. With the arrival of the great academics in exile from Germany, he emerged from the complacency enjoyed by his colleagues, the professors of the Hebrew University.

Herbst began to examine his behavior and was forced to attribute his position to the fact that he had come to the country early, when the university was being established and there were many openings. He recognized that he had been recommended by his renowned professor, Alfred Neu, and made a lecturer on the basis of a book that he had by now fully exploited. Now he had only those tedious notes and references, which became more tedious as their number increased.

Out of habit, and because he had no proper plan, Herbst pored over his books, read prodigiously, took notes, and added more and more references, assuming that in time he would make them into a book—like those instructors who assume that in time they will be granted tenured positions. As the old saying goes: What reason doesn't do is often done by time.

Herbst sits in his study, reading, writing, making note after note. His note box is filling up. The connection between the notes becomes less and less apparent, every additional part seeming to diminish the whole. Learning can become impotent; fed on its regular diet, in the end it loses its potency.

His reward came from an unexpected source. Herbst, as we know, in addition to reading everything in his field, also read books that were totally unrelated—even books one would be shocked to know he was reading.

Through one such book, Herbst made a discovery envied by more than one scholar of Italian church history. Even Professor Ernst Weltfremdt, who was not known to lavish praise on a friend, was moved to exclaim, "Bravo, dear colleague, you have made an important discovery!"

Since everyone conceded that Dr. Manfred Herbst had made an important discovery, we will go into some detail about it.

Scholars of Italian church history were struggling to determine when churches were first built to honor Prieguna the Meek, the duck-eyed saint. As the earliest existing church in her name was known to have been built at the time of Pope Clement IV, it was assumed that churches were first built for her in his time. Dr. Herbst discovered that, in the very heart of Venice, there was a church named for her that predated Clement IV. How did he know this? From a collection of letters written by courtesans. He found one such document in which a courtesan reports to a friend that she has left her lover, the cardinal, because he scolded her for being late, although it was his fault that she was late rather than her own: she always took the shortcut through the courtyard of the Church of Prieguna the Meek, but on that day there was a detour, because of a woman in labor who was taken into the church and on whose account passersby were denied access to the courtyard. As His Eminence the Cardinal knew, it was he who made the unfortunate woman pregnant and caused the event that forced the courtesan to take the longer route.

Although the Holy See removed Prieguna the Meek from the Catholic calendar after the pope's committee on Catholic saints concluded that the Meek One herself as well as her story was a legend, and she was divested of her holiness, still and all, Herbst's discovery remains important. For, even if Prieguna the Meek never existed, the churches built in her name surely do.

A greenish light shines on Herbst from the south window. Herbst looks away from the light, concentrating on the books at his side and the pencil in his hand. He sits copying out material that will pull his book together. His book is still but an embryo in the womb of scholarship; at full term, a book will emerge. Meanwhile, Henrietta was at full term and bore him a daughter.

You may remember that when Professor Ernst Weltfremdt was promoted to the rank of full professor, Herbst went to congratulate him and met a relative of Professor Alfred Neu's, and a furtive love developed between the two of them, so that, whenever he saw her, it seemed to Herbst that he was suffused with a breath of innocence and in the end it turned out that when he meant to call her he found Shira. How do we relate to this incident, wherein innocence led to its opposite?

Herbst was already engaged in the struggle to eradicate the Shira episode from his heart. If he did remember it, he assured himself: It was an accident, involving no sequel; tomorrow I'll be back at work, with no time for frivolous thoughts. Still, Herbst was curious about one thing. Did Shira plan to invite him to her room; did she do what she did deliberately and with forethought? In other words, Herbst wanted to analyze his acts, to know who had initiated them, he or Shira. Much as he thought about them, only one thing was clear: Shira was adept at lovemaking, and he was not the first of her lovers. Still, he had no wish to know who her lovers were and if she was still involved with them.

Thoughts are devious. Before his thought was complete, it turned to the dream he had had in the hospital, when Shira was with the women, and the blind Turk with the red turban on his head was with Shira, who offered him a pack of cigarettes. Thus far, everything is clear. From here on, one must look beyond the obvious—at Shira's turban (when Herbst found her in the telephone booth, she was wearing a red turban), as well as the pack of cigarettes she handed him when they sat together in her room, the very pack she had handed to that blind Turk. Remembering the time he spent with Shira in her room, Herbst's heart began to flutter longingly.

— 8 —

Wishing to please his wife, Herbst stepped into a restaurant known for its fine food and ordered a meat meal. He hadn't enjoyed a meal as much since Henrietta checked into the hospital. A wife knows more about her husband than he does. He imagined he would be revolted by meat, and here he was, enjoying it thoroughly. When he finished his coffee, he leaned his head against the back of the chair and began composing letters to his daughters.

As he sat there, his mind wandering from Zahara to Tamara and from Tamara to Zahara, he lifted his eyes and looked around. The waitress noticed and came over, assuming he wanted something. Since she was there, he asked for paper and envelopes, which she brought him. They sent off a pleasing fragrance. He sniffed them and said, "If I could find this fragrance, I would take some to my wife in the hospital." The waitress asked in a hush, "Is your wife sick?" He ran his hand through his hair, laughing heartily, and said, "She's not sick, she wasn't sick, and she won't be sick. She has given birth to a daughter. She has given me a sweet new baby, whom all the boys are already after." The waitress said, "When you came in, I said to myself: This man is celebrating. Mazel tov, sir. Mazel tov." To which Herbst said, "And what sort of good wishes may I offer in return? I could wish for a husband for you, but such a fine young woman has probably been spoken for already."

The restaurant owner strutted over, bowed perfunctorily, glanced harshly at the waitress, and was off. Herbst asked the waitress, "Who is that absurd-looking man?" "He owns the restaurant," she replied. "And it annoys him to see us talking," Herbst said. "Even nurses in a hospital are allowed to talk to visitors, and this *yekke* doesn't want you to talk to me. In fact, your words have more of an effect than any of this *yekke*'s delicacies." The waitress smiled and said, "But, sir, aren't you from Germany too?" Herbst said, "True, I was born in Germany, but I left before you were born." "An exaggeration, sir! What an exaggeration!" Herbst said, "Then let's say I left Germany while lullabies were still being sung to you."

The proprietor was back, glaring darkly at the waitress. Herbst gathered up the paper and envelopes, and said, "Rather than arouse that fool's envy, I will just sit here and write to my daughters. Many thanks for the paper, the envelopes, for everything."

The waitress left, and Herbst began to write. The scented paper reminded him of its owner. He thought to himself: Too bad about that man and all that befell him. He had a further thought: A man becomes intimate with a woman, and, in a flash, all her sisters begin to notice him. He found some newspapers to lean on and composed this letter to Zahara or Tamara: "Our mother fair / To whom poems are dear / Wishing to spare poets the effort / Has added to Zahara and Tamara / A new rhyme, namely, Sarah."

After writing this, he glanced at the newspapers that were under the letters. He saw a puzzle, which he tried solving. While working on it, he noticed a poem. He put down the puzzle and looked at the poem. He read: "Flesh such as yours / Will not soon be forgotten. . . ." He folded his letters and left.

Every day after lunch, Herbst used to lie down on his bed, read, and doze. On this day, having eaten in town, he was far from home, and there wasn't time to go back and forth. He was planning to go back to the hospital to see his wife. But the hospital would not be open for two more hours. What was he to do in the meanwhile?

He saw a pharmacy sign and remembered that he meant to take his wife some perfume, the scent that had been on the envelopes given to him by the charming waitress. He went into the drugstore and handed the druggist the envelope, so he could smell it and give him the same perfume. The druggist thought he wanted envelopes. He glared at him pompously and said, "This is a pharmacy, not a stationery store." Herbst explained and said, "I will surely find what I want here." The druggist clapped his hands to call his wife to come and sniff, since he himself had no sense of smell. She came, sniffed, and handed Herbst a bottle of perfume. He said, "I trust you to give me the right thing." Hearing this, the pharmacist began to celebrate her sensibilities. "She is so sensitive, especially about smells. Once our daughter came from the kibbutz, stopped in to use the phone, and left immediately. A little later, her mother came back from marketing and had to phone one of the stores she had been in to see if her keys, which she had left some-where—she didn't know where—had been found. As soon as she picked up the receiver, she asked me, 'Was our daughter here.' I said, 'Did you see her?' She said to me, 'No, I didn't see her.' I said to her, 'Then how do you know?' She said, 'From the smell on the receiver.'" Herbst said, "You mentioned the telephone and I remembered that I must make a call. May I use your phone?" He picked up the receiver and said what he said. Believe it or not, before long, the telephone was answered in the *kvutza*.

And, believe it or not, Herbst was not satisfied. He still had almost two hours and didn't know how to spend them. He went to a florist and bought a bouquet of red roses. From there, he went and bought some chocolate. If Henrietta didn't eat it, the nurses would. He bought another box for the old nurse who had first showed him Sarah.

He left the store, holding two boxes under his arm and a bottle of perfume in his hand. He looked at his watch. It still wasn't time to go to the hospital. When one's patience is short and the time is long, the clock seems to slow down. He took a short walk, then a long walk, and turned into another street. He noticed a locked store with a sign on the door explaining that the family was in mourning. He recognized from the sign that this was where Lisbet Neu was employed, and he knew she would not be working for seven days. If she wasn't at work, she was sitting at home with her mother and had most likely been home the previous night as well, perhaps even expecting his call. For his own sake, he was sorry he hadn't called her. And he was sorry that when he went to call her events unfolded as they did. He rolled his lips and slipped his finger between the watch strap and his wrist. He looked and saw it was time to go to his wife. He stopped at the locked door and put down the flowers and perfume, so he could adjust his tie. Then he picked up his packages and was on his way.

9

While he was sitting with his wife, hand in hand, the door opened and the nurse Shira came in. Henrietta looked at her warmly and said, "If my husband hasn't already done so, let me thank you doubly for taking the trouble to ask about me on the telephone last night." Shira answered, "It was no trouble at all, but Dr. Herbst has already thanked me beyond what I deserve." Henrietta said, "Men do tend to be ungrateful, and I wouldn't pretend that my husband is any different in this regard. Isn't that so, Fred? Now, let me ask you this, Fred. Did you do as I ordered?" "What did you order?" Fred asked in alarm. "What did I order? Nothing. I asked you to eat a decent meal." Manfred replied, "I did as I was told. I filled up on meat, left nothing on my plate, and I don't know when I'll ever have room for food again." Henrietta said, "Don't talk like that. When it's time for supper, you should have supper and eat solid food, not nonsense such as salads. Now, listen to me, my sweet. I hear that the nurse Shira doesn't work nights, and, if she has no plans, I will give her some good advice: I suggest that she have dinner with my husband tonight. Look at him, Miss Shira, the father of three daughters blushing like a schoolboy. So, Miss Shira, what do you say? But you must take him to a big restaurant and see that he has a solid meal, since he has learned to make do with fruits and vegetables. It's a miracle that he hasn't become a vegetarian. I have nothing against vegetable dishes if they come with meat, but as for grazing in a meadow, I leave that to the goats. By the way, how is our garden doing? Did you water the plants? Is the mallow growing? You look as if you're sitting on hot coals. I know, my sweet, that you're longing for your desk, but our little Sarah deserves another evening of your time. Isn't that so, Nurse Shira? Where is that nurse? She's disappeared." When Henrietta realized she was alone with her husband, she took his hand and said, "Don't be annoyed that I'm troubling you to take Shira to dinner. You don't know what a wonderful woman she is, how she puts herself out on my behalf, beyond the call of duty. The mysterious hand that brought these flowers was hers. If you take her to a restaurant, it won't pay even half the debt. . . . You're embarrassed to be seen with her? Don't be embarrassed. When she takes off her uniform and puts on her own clothes, she's like any other woman. . . . You're afraid you'll have to go out with her again? Don't worry. She's the sort of woman who doesn't ask for more than she's offered. And if you're afraid you'll be bored, don't worry, my sweet. Light conversation will help you sleep." "Good, good," Manfred said. "You have a new habit," Henrietta observed. "You say, 'Good, good,' all the time." Manfred said, "Good, good." Henrietta said, "There you go again, it must mean you're feeling good." Manfred said, "I feel good. Yes, I feel good." Henrietta said, "If you feel good, then I feel good." Manfred answered, "Good, good." Henrietta smiled and said, "You said it again: 'Good, good.'" There was a smile on her lips, but inwardly she wasn't smiling.

She withdrew her hand from his and groped for something on the bedside table. She brushed aside the roses sent by the mysterious hand, as well as the presents brought by her husband. Manfred said, "What are you looking for?" Henrietta said, "I'm not looking for anything. Did you write to the girls?" Manfred said, "I wrote, and I also phoned Zahara." Henrietta said, "You phoned Zahara? What did she say?" "She didn't say anything." Henrietta said, "Please, Fred, what do you mean, 'she didn't say anything'? You just told me that you phoned her." "I did, but the fellow who answered the phone wouldn't stop talking, and by the time they called Zahara, my time was up and we were disconnected." Henrietta sighed and said, "Too bad. But will they tell her you called?" "They'll tell her." "You didn't call Tamara? Why didn't you call Tamara?" "Why? Because she has no telephone." Henrietta said, "She has no telephone? She always had a phone." Manfred said, "She used to have one, but she doesn't now." Henrietta said, "Just for spite—when we didn't need to call her, she had a phone. Now that we need to call her, she has no phone." Manfred said, "It's not a matter of spite. Like most things that happen, it's chance." Henrietta said, "So we're into philosophy." Manfred said, "That's not philosophy. When she lived in a house with a phone, she had a phone. Since she moved to a house without a phone, she has no phone." Henrietta said, "Good, good." Manfred said, "Who's saying 'good, good'?" Henrietta said, "By chance, I am." Manfred said, "Then you admit, Henriett, that there is such a thing as chance." Henrietta said, "Did I claim there was no such thing as chance? Of course there is." Manfred said, "When I said it was chance, you laughed at me and cried, 'Philosophy!' " Henrietta laughed and said, "Dear Fred, I have no answer, only 'good, good.' Now, my darling, get ready for the nurse. Don't you want to see Sarah?" "Sarah? Who's Sarah?" Henrietta said, "Didn't we agree to call our new daughter Sarah?" "We agreed? Good, good." Henrietta said, "A good heart says, 'Good.' The nurse will soon come and show you Sarah. Actually, I could show her to you myself, but as long as the baby is here, the nurses are in charge."

The nurse Shira was back. We barely recognized her. She wore a midlength gray dress and a silver filigree necklace, which set off her face to advantage, like that of a chaste woman whose beauty is emphasized by some trinket. One more striking thing: on her lovely, small feet she wore shoes made by a skilled craftsman, which lent special elegance to her bearing, and, as the day was beginning to darken, her elegant bearing was evident, but not its source. She held her hat in her hand, as a girl does, and it hid her purse, so one couldn't tell she was ready to go. Henrietta glanced at her and said, "Shira the nurse looks charming. If I had known she would change so much, I would not have been so eager to put my husband in her hands. He might decide to leave me for her." Shira said, "Do I give Mrs. Herbst a little pleasure?" Mrs. Herbst said, "That's a big question. Not just a little. More than a little. Now, Fred, my dear, have a pleasant evening." "We'll try, Mrs. Herbst, we'll try," Shira said. Mrs. Herbst offered Shira her hand and said, "Yes, yes, nurse. Now let's show the father his daughter. . . . Now that you've seen her, give me your hand, and I'll say goodbye. If you want a kiss, no need to be shy. These are ordinary events. Good night, Fred. Good night, nurse." Shira answered, "A fine and blessed night."

— 10 —

When they were outside, Shira said, "Actually, I would rather not go to a restaurant." "Then where would you like to go?" Herbst whispered, his heart beginning to flutter. Shira said, "Let's walk a little, so I can clear my head." Herbst said, "I don't know where one can walk in Jerusalem without being stopped at every step." Shira said, "We don't have to go to Rehavia." Herbst said, "Beit Hakerem or Talpiot wouldn't be any better. In Beit Hakerem, you run into teachers; in Talpiot, you meet professors. Wherever you turn, there are people you know. They choose to live out of the city in order to escape its tumult, and they drag the tumult with them. By now, the only difference between a suburb and the city proper is the distance and the bus fumes. This nation does everything in public. Because religion is public, it has become the custom to do everything in public."

Shira looked at him searchingly and asked, "Are you Orthodox, Dr. Herbst?" "Why?" "Because you referred to religion. I don't care for the Orthodox, nor do I care for religion." Herbst said, "In your childhood, you were probably Orthodox too." Shira said, "Even my father wasn't Orthodox. He enjoyed tradition, and for that reason alone he fulfilled some of the commandments, but only those that didn't require much effort. And, even then, he was rather casual, which is surely the case with me. I hardly know what tradition is or what it is for." Herbst said, "I have very little information about the nurse Shira." Shira said, "And my knowledge about the professor is limited as well." Herbst said, "Actually, I know nothing about you." Shira said, "When I get to know someone, I never concern myself with his beginnings." She reached into her purse and rummaged around without taking anything out. Herbst said, "I think the lady was going to say something." Shira said, "No, I wasn't going to say anything." Herbst said, "Then I was wrong." Shira said, "Yes, Dr. Herbst was wrong." She took a step and stopped. Herbst stopped and circled her with his eyes. Shira said, "I wasn't going to say anything, but now I will. The only person about whom I knew everything was someone I loathed more than anyone." Herbst said, "Am I allowed to ask who he was?" Shira said, "You are allowed to ask, and I am allowed not to answer." Herbst said, "Pardon me, madam. In that case, I won't ask." Shira said, "Pardon me, sir, for not giving a proper answer." They took a few steps. She stopped, groped in her purse, and said, "You asked who it was that I loathed more than anyone, and I didn't answer. It's not really a secret, only a memory, a piece of the past that is no longer painful. If you want to know about it, I'll tell you." Herbst said, "When I get to know a person, I want to learn all about him, and the more I learn about him, the closer he is to me." Shira said, "Someone removed from life would say that, but those who know the world and are involved in it pay no attention to the past." "Really!" Herbst declared, astonished. Shira laughed and said, "Yes, really." Again she reached into her purse. She took out a cotton ball, rubbed the tip of her nose, threw the cotton away, and said, "Let's take this turn. There's a new road that connects this neighborhood with Sanhedria. No one comes this way. What is it, professor? You're pouting like a child whose nanny has promised to tell him a lovely story but doesn't keep her word. Dear professor, my story is not at all lovely. The man I loathed more than anyone was my husband." Herbst asked in a whisper, "You were married?" Shira said, "I was married." Herbst said, "I assumed that——" Shira interrupted him, laughing, "What did you assume? That . . . that I was a virgin?" Herbst stammered, "No, but I . . . In fact, I don't know what I assumed." Shira said, "Don't torture yourself over it. It's not worth the trouble. Let's stand here awhile and watch the sun."

Shira continued, "The sun is setting, painting the empty new houses red, painting the bare windows no one looks out of yet with its golden flush. I'm a city girl, born in an old house. Here in Jerusalem, I live in an old house too, built several generations before I was born. But when the sun begins to set and I walk through the new neighborhoods and see all the new houses being built, my heart is filled with yearning and desire. Why is my heart so full of yearning and desire? Perhaps because I yearn to live in houses no one has lived in yet. But why, when in a day the novelty will be gone and they'll be like other houses? Nonetheless, that desire becomes more and more intense. The sun has already set. Its golden flush has vanished. Everything sinks and disappears, even the sun, with all its dazzle, leaving nothing behind, no further dramas to unfold."

Herbst rolled his lip into his mouth, pressing one lip over the other. He walked quickly, but his heart was in a state of suspense. What was Shira saying, and what did he want to hear? Shira was totally distracted. She walked in silence. The houses were all dim by now. Mounds of lime and piles of cement peeked out from among the unfinished buildings, and the road in between glittered like a silver chain. Shira lifted the hem of her dress, took a few steps, smoothed her eyelashes with her hands, and spoke. "What was I going to say?" Herbst lowered his eyes, so she wouldn't see how eager he was to hear. Renewed passion stuck in his eyes like thorns. His heart was stiff, and his teeth began to chatter. He lowered his eyes further, to avoid looking at her, now that they were alone. He saw her small feet in the slippers she had waved at him the night before. He remembered the night's events, how he had slipped them off and exposed her feet, how she had put the slippers back on and he had slipped them off again, how her feet had wriggled, stockingless, bare, lovelier than any feet in the world. Now those same feet walked a few steps, then stopped, then walked on along the dim road, and she seemed unaware of him. It may be that not even twenty-four hours have elapsed since those events occurred. In terms of time, it can't be determined; in terms of truth, what is true cannot be denied. He came to a standstill, like someone confronting a riddle for which he finds no solution. She stopped too and said, "What was I going to tell you?" And then she began to talk.

—— 11 ——

"I should begin when I was a baby, but the impact of the war that engulfed us in the interim minimized the importance of early events. I will, therefore, begin after the war, when I was on my own and began observing my actions—becoming so much the observer that they unfold before me and I can recount them as if reading from a book.

"My father taught Hebrew and was highly involved in culture and Zionism. After the war, Father wanted to take me to the Land of Israel. But we were not allowed to leave Russia. Father was able to prove that he was born in Poland, and the emigration laws did not apply to natives of Poland. After considerable efforts, we left for Poland, intending to go to Israel from there. We were joined by others, who made Father into a sort of patron of emigration, then appointed him to administer a savings fund called the Emigrants' Bank. We remained in Poland. I enrolled in the Hebrew high school and joined the Hehalutz movement.

"Once you're involved in community work, you don't get out so fast. At first, Father was upset when his departure was delayed. By and by, he began to take comfort in the fact that I belonged to Hehalutz and would leave with my pioneering friends, leading the way for him. Father had picked out a companion for me. He was the son of a widow—a pampered young man, active, ambitious, well spoken. His promise was already being fulfilled, for he held an important post in the Zionist movement, and a prominent position awaited him in the Land of Israel. He was especially appealing to Father, who had been a tutor in the home of this young man's mother in his youth. Father took pride in the fact that the young man was now a regular caller at our house and had his eye on me. I didn't like him, nor did I hate him. How is it possible to hate or like anyone? When he started treating me possessively, I began to put him off. I don't think this was the only reason. There were surely others. He once asked, 'What do you have against me?' I answered, 'I don't know.' He said, 'Please think about it.' I said, 'There's nothing to think about.' I assumed he would leave me alone. But he seemed to cherish me all the more.

"At about this time, a group of our friends went to the country for agricultural training. He didn't go, because he said he had work to do in town. I didn't go, because my father wanted me to stay in school another year and make up what I had missed during the war.

"The village they went to was ruled by an old duchess. Before the war, she had several Russian villages under her jurisdiction. But, after the Revolution, she was left with only one, which was annexed to Poland. The village had a Jewish overseer, who had stood by her during the Revolution and managed to save some of her property. It was rumored that there was something more to their relationship. Was this true or half-true? She was jealous of his relationships with women. They say that, when she discovered that one of the servants was pregnant by him, she stripped the girl naked and beat her to death. This took place much earlier, long before the war, when nobles could do as they pleased. After the war, their power diminished, especially in the case of this duchess, who was half-paralyzed and depended on the overseer to conduct the affairs of the village, which was part of her estate and was where the *halutzim* were lodged. Father boasted that it was through the efforts of our Sokolow that this duchess was granted authority over the village. When lands were being distributed and boundaries set, Sokolow convinced the League of Nations that this was Polish territory, citing evidence from an old book that referred to it as Poland. And so it became Poland.

"One day, I went to see my friends in the village, and my protector was there to deliver a lecture. He saw me and was pleased, assuming I would hear his lecture and then return to town with him. I had no desire to hear his lecture or to be with him. When he was on the platform, about to begin his speech, I got up and left.

"The road was in disrepair, full of obstructions. It was piled high with dirt. Leaves, both green and wilted, covered the dirt and were covered by it. I left the road and entered the forest. I didn't know the way. One didn't normally venture into the forest, certainly not alone, because of the deserters who roamed there. I followed the sound of the church bells and was beginning to enjoy being among trees and bushes that smelled of the wild berries we often ate without knowing where they grew. As long as it was light, I relished every single step and every single breath. When dusk began to fall and the trees took on another aspect, my joy was mixed, and I began to be afraid of army deserters who might be hiding in the woods. I heard hoofbeats and thought: This is the end.

"A tall man dressed in leather appeared on horseback. My terror dissolved instantly, and I asked, 'Which is the way to town?' He said, 'Do you ride?' 'No.' 'Then we'll walk.' He got off the horse and walked to town with me. In bed that night, I reviewed what had happened and was astonished. Had I not seen him later on, I would have believed he was from a fairy tale. But fairy-tale characters were dead before we were born, and if they still exist, they exist to deny their reality. Dr. Herbst has something to say? No? Then I'll get back to my story.

"A few days later, he rode past our house. He tied up his horse and came in. He gave me his hand and said, 'I was passing your house, and I stopped in to ask where it is nicer, in the woods or at home.' At this point, I saw no trace of what I had seen in him before, yet there was a special quality I could not define, and his image was not diminished. Meanwhile, the horse was neighing. He said to me, 'If you could ride, I would put you on my horse and race to the end of the world with you.' I said to him, 'Since I don't ride, you will have to race alone.' He pursed his lips and said, 'Touché. You win.' A few days later, he returned. Father took out the Carmel wine. I spread out a cloth and brought cakes. I noticed that he looked at me with pleasure, that Father was pleased too. We sat together. Father spoke about the Balfour Declaration, rebuilding the land, and the like. When our conversation turned to the *halutzim*, Father told about Sokolow's influence, as a result of which the duchess had been granted jurisdiction over the village. When he left, Father said, 'He is a real man. Too bad we can't interest him in Zionism.' I laughed inwardly. A real man, romantic whims and all.

"One night, when I came back from a drama workshop, Father came out of his room and said, 'The forest prince was here.' I said to him, 'I'm sorry I didn't see him.' Father said, 'I guarantee that he'll be back.' He paused, then added, 'You don't wonder why?' I said to Father,

'Why are you smiling?' Father said, 'If I tell you, you'll smile too. That man, who is as old as I am, asked what I would say if he wished to marry my daughter.' I said to Father, 'What was your answer?' Father said, 'What should I have answered?' I said, 'You gave him an answer. Tell me what you said.' Father said, 'I told him that my daughter's heart already belongs to another.' I began to wonder whom he had in mind. Then, suddenly, I became enraged and shrieked, 'If you mean that climber, that Pickwick, let me tell you—you're making a big mistake!' Father said, 'I thought you would smile, and instead you're angry.' I said to Father, 'I'm not angry at him, I'm angry at you! You think I have no taste, that I would give my heart to someone I can't stand.' Father said, 'Tell me, please, what do you have against him?' I said, 'You want to know, then I'll tell you. He calls Herzl, Gerzl.' Father said, 'That's the only reason?' I said to Father, 'There's more.' 'What else?' 'He calls Heine, Geinrich Geine.' Father said, 'His Russian diction is impeccable, yet you hold that against him?' I said to Father, 'I agree that those reasons are inadequate. I regret that I am not intelligent and knowledgeable and that I don't know the true answer, but hopefully he will leave me in my ignorance.'

"The next day, I didn't stir from the house. I knew I would turn down the man Father had told me about. Still, I waited for him. Why? Just to say: 'I don't want you'! The day passed, and he didn't come. When, after several more days, he still didn't appear, I stopped thinking about him, and Father didn't mention him either. One day, at sunset, I heard a knock at the door. I thought to myself: He has finally come. The door opened, and Pickwick came in. He flung his hat angrily and said, 'I'm here to congratulate you.' 'What for?' He sneered and said, 'On your betrothal.' 'My betrothal?' I cried in surprise. He repeated, 'Your betrothal to that old lecher, the gigolo who carries on with the old duchess.' I was silent. He changed his tone and began to address me tenderly. 'Really, Shira, really, its unbecoming for a young Hebrew woman, the daughter of a distinguished Zionist, to marry someone like that, who has lived with gentile women. Listen, Shira, let's go to the Land of Israel, let's join a kibbutz, let's live a pure life.' I answered him, 'As for your speech about a Hebrew woman and all the rest, the fact is that I now have the opportunity to rescue a Jew from Gentiles. As for its being unbecoming, there are many unbecoming things in the world, and I don't believe the world will be any uglier if I add one more. As for the Land of Israel, it seems to me that the first two answers include an answer to that idyll.' After he left, the one who wanted me to be his wife arrived. I answered him, saying yes. So I was married, then divorced. I was divorced from him because I married him. I'm not joking. I'm simply reporting what happened. Dr. Herbst has a question? No? Then I'll get back to the subject. I must say, I don't really like talking about myself, least of all about that chapter. If I were to be interrupted, I would not return to my story."

— 12 —

"Where was I? I was telling that story. Although I was mature beyond my years, I had no concrete picture of married life. As long as we were engaged, he behaved like a rich uncle. He used to bring me presents and speak to me affectionately. I can't deny that those days were pleasant, but they didn't last. I was not quite seventeen when we were married.

"The wedding was large and elegant. Zionist lumber merchants and householders came to share in our joy, and the flow of gifts and telegrams was a burden to me. Father had one drink too many and made a long speech about the apple of his eye and her chosen one. Other speeches followed in endless succession, after every speech a drink, and after every drink—joy. Everyone was happy, except for me. I was irritated and bored, the sort of boredom you feel at a gala concert. You sit there, stuck to your seat, not daring to stir. Meanwhile, something is bothering you, perhaps your skin, perhaps your clothes. Your eyelids droop. You strain to keep your eyes open. You watch the violin bow, make an effort to focus on it, but it looks menacing, and your mind is blank. I forgot I was at my own wedding, and all sorts of places where I had once been came together, lining up side by side, one after the other. Finally, all those places vanished, and I was in a forest with no way out. I was expecting a man in leather to come and lead me out, and I was surprised that he didn't come. I heard the sound of a horse and looked up. I saw that very man seated beside me in fancy clothes, with another man standing over him, dressed like the one who had led me out of the forest. He pointed at the guests, most of whom were intoxicated. He pointed at them again, saying, 'They need something, but who knows what? Get up, Shira. Put on some warm clothes, and let's go out into the world.' When I was outside, he covered me with fur and lifted me into a sleigh, which glided off into the forest."

Shira paused and said, "I'll leave the rest for another night. Now, Dr.

Herbst, let's go back to town and find a restaurant, as Mrs. Herbst instructed." Shira suddenly laughed and said, "Don't be afraid I'll be another Scheherazade. Even if I recount every detail, I won't take a thousand and one nights."

Manfred Herbst was a curious person, like all those who deal with books and are so unfamiliar with the world that their ears perk up at any news of it. But now that he was out with Shira, he regretted every word she spoke, for she was involved with her story rather than with him. By and by, he relaxed and began to be intrigued by her words. When she paused, he started, expecting events to unfold as they had the previous night, when they were alone in her room. But, no. Shira returned to her story.

"The sleigh stopped in a field in the forest, surrounded by snowy hills and snow-covered trees. That man leaped out of the sleigh, wrapped me in his arms, and said, 'Here is our house.' I saw no sign of a house, only smoke rising from the snow, sending forth the fragrance of burnt pine. He brought me to a heated room. My limbs were heavy with fatigue, and my eyes sought sleep. He looked at me strangely, pointed to the wide bed, and said, 'You're tired. Take off your clothes and get into bed.' He saw I was ashamed to undress with him there, and he left. An old woman came to help me. I said, 'Don't bother, I'll undress myself.' She wished me well and left. I threw off my clothes and my shoes, everything but my stockings, which I didn't have the strength to remove. I stood there, wondering what was going on, just what I was doing there. Exhausted, I flung myself on the bed, curled up in the feather quilt, and gave myself to sleep.

"Hearing footsteps, I started. I assumed the old woman was coming to see if I needed anything. I closed my eyes, so she would think I was asleep. The quilt lifted itself, and a cold wind engulfed me. I opened my eyes and saw a naked man, totally undressed. I screamed in terror, 'Get out!' He whispered, 'Don't be afraid, I'm your husband.' I screamed as loud as I could, 'I'll scream if you don't get out!' He said, 'What's the point, when you're screaming already?' And he began to caress me, to embrace me, his mouth dripping kisses. I freed myself from his embrace, leaped from the bed to the door and from the door to the hall. By the time he recovered from the shock, I was outside.

"The woods were covered with snow, and the trees were totally still. The snow vibrated underfoot in the stillness. I ran through the snow, not knowing whether I was cold or warm. A hand gripped me, and in an instant I was in that man's arms. He ran with me, yelling, 'If I hadn't found you immediately, you would have frozen to death. A babe in the woods on a freezing night, without clothes, without shoes.' He brought

me to the room I had escaped from and stood me on my feet, sighing
and whispering, 'Oh, my darling, my darling, I didn't know how much
I love you. Kill me, but let me have one hour with you.'

The old woman came with a hot drink, put me to bed, covered me
with several blankets, and brought a hot brick wrapped in towels,
which she placed at my feet. She sat beside me, singing sad and lovely
songs about water creatures, wood sprites, and other sprites that assume
human form and cohabit with the sprites, all of whom give birth to male
children they hide in trees, where they grow up, unbeknownst to
anyone. In springtime, when young girls go to the woods, these boys
pop out, snatch the ones who are virgins, whisk them away, and marry
them. When their babies are born, they deposit them in trees, unbeknownst to anyone. And when they grow up, the cycle is repeated.
That's how it is, that's how it was, and that's how it will be until the
end of time.

"Night passed and day came. That man appeared and began to coax
me, to promise me everything if only I would relent. I sobbed, I cried,
I begged. 'Take me back to my father. I don't want to stay here even
a minute.' He no longer kissed and hugged me. He spoke to me gently,
then harshly. When he spoke gently, I asked myself why he was not
harsh; when he spoke harshly, I asked myself why he was not gentle.
In either case, my heart was bitter and hard. While he was trying to
win me with words, he was told guests had come to congratulate him.
His manner changed, and he went to greet his guests. When he left,
the old woman he had provided to serve me appeared. This happened
several times in the course of the day.

"The old woman was the mother of the girl he had made pregnant,
who was beaten to death by the duchess. The old woman used to sit
and talk with me. 'He's a real man,' she would say. 'A real man. No
girl can resist him. And you, my dove, are trying to run away. How
will you do it? None of the farmers will give you a ride, for fear of your
husband. If you walk, your little feet will sink into the snow. These
darling feet were out on a snowy night; it's a miracle the skin didn't
peel right off. Your dead mother probably came and put her good hands
under the soles of your feet. The dead know the sorrows of the living
and share them, though we are sometimes too stingy to light a candle
in their memory. Give me one of your feet, my dove, and I'll kiss it.
My daughter didn't have feet like yours, though she was lovely and
good. Alas, she wasn't favored by the Mother of God, who could have
saved her from our mistress, the duchess. Probably because my daughter was born Christian and our lord, your husband, is a Jewish man.
You, my dove, are Jewish too, so why resist your husband? You won't

find another man as powerful as he is. Be still, my dove, be still. Don't look so enraged. The rage of the Lord God is enough, why add to it? You are, after all, a woman, and a woman's heart is soft and good. Why be defiant? You are an orphan with no mother, and I am a mother with no daughter. Let's live in peace, rather than upset each other. The Lord God and all those with him make enough trouble. Wouldn't it be better if my daughter had lived and I had died, like your good mother who died, leaving you alive? She left you a kind father, too. Listen, my dove, listen: I hear the sound of a sleigh. Your kind father is coming. He will make peace between you and your husband.'

"The door opened, and Father came in. I fell on his neck and sobbed, 'Father, Father.' He pushed me away and said, 'You've brought us shame, you've brought us shame.' I was stunned. My tears dried up. I stopped crying and didn't say a word. Father began to praise the man he called my husband, to describe all the good things he would be able to give me. I didn't answer. I was as mute as a tree in the snow, but for the fact that a tree is alive on the inside though covered with snow, whereas I was like snow through and through. At night, that man gave a big party for Father, who had one drink too many and began muttering, 'It will work out, it will work out.' He kissed me and kissed the one they called my groom.

"It didn't work out. On the contrary, it became more complex. At first, I had nothing against the man, but, in the end, my heart was filled with seething hatred. When he came near me, I shouted, 'Get away from me, you wretch!' I called him every vile name, and he loved me all the more. I was a captive in his house, seeking escape. Because of the snow, it was impossible to escape. Once, while he was drinking with friends who came to congratulate him on his marriage, I sneaked out of the house, hid in a sleigh belonging to a gentleman from my town, and rode off. Father was not happy to see me. Having married off his only daughter, he had his eye on a wife. Whom did he have in mind? The mother of the young man I had rejected. Knowing this, she hated me doubly—once for her son, once for herself—for I was interfering with the pleasure she sought from my father. Fate is a clown, and when he clowns, he doubles the laughs.

"Father hardly spoke to me. By day he was busy at the bank, and in the evening he was with the widow. I was on my own. I invited friends. They didn't come. When I went to meetings, they avoided me, and those who didn't avoid me spoke with feigned respect and addressed me as Madame So-and-so, wife of that man. When I was first betrothed, my friends began to keep some distance. Now they treated me as a stranger. I went home humiliated and swore I would never go back, nor would I forgive them. I stayed at home, without father or friends, without joy, without anything.

"One day the old woman appeared. She came in and said, 'You don't come to us, so I am coming to you.' She sat with me, singing the praises of her master, my husband, who had always been a good man but, since I ran away, had become evil. 'You must, therefore, go back to him, if not for my sake, then for the sake of others. Considering how little goodness there is, every good soul should promote goodness with his own body, all the more so women, who were created solely for the pleasure and benefit of men.' This is how the old woman spoke. She mentioned the Son of God, who died for mankind and doesn't harm even those who sin against him. He is generous even with the sinful duchess, so much so that her children, who were assumed to have been killed by the Bolsheviks, were, in fact, alive. Then the old woman praised my husband again and said, 'What a pity to see this powerful man declining, all because my mistress, his wife, has left him.'

"A little later, that man came himself and talked to me like a merchant discussing business. He said roughly this: 'Come back to me and stay; I won't ask anything of you. I want only to be able to see you.' He sent relatives, men and women, to urge me to go back to him. All this occurred again and again. Sometimes the old woman came, sometimes he came, sometimes all sorts of relatives came. In all this time, Father showed no sympathy. I'm not angry, I'm not complaining. He, of course, had my good in mind, as would any father with an only daughter. Scorning his efforts, I not only caused him pain and torment but prevented him from pursuing his own interests, for, as long as I was at home, the woman was unwilling to move in. And living with her would have been difficult for both of them, because of her son.

"Once Father brought a man home, took him into his room, and closed the door. When they emerged, Father's face was dark. Father turned to me and said, 'A splendid turn of events. If he runs off to America, you'll be lost forever. Do you know what it is to be an abandoned wife? You don't know, so I'll tell you. If your husband goes to America, you will never be free as long as you live.' I wasn't very familiar with religious law, so I answered Father calmly, 'What do I care? Let him go wherever he likes, as long as I don't have to see him.' Father began pulling at his beard and shouting, 'God in heaven, isn't it enough that You plagued me with such a daughter, did You have to impair her intelligence too?'

"The guest calmed Father down and said, 'Why all the excitement? He's not running off empty-handed, and if his wife goes with him, she won't lack for anything either.' Father repeated this to me: 'Listen, he's not empty-handed. Come to terms with him and go along.'

"After the guest left, Father sat for about an hour, in a state of shock. Then he said, 'Come, let me tell you what made your husband decide to go to America. He was managing the property of the duchess as if it were his own, assuming that her sons were killed by the Bolsheviks. They are actually alive and are on their way here. When they come, they will demand an accounting, which he cannot and does not wish to provide. For him, escape is the best solution. If you don't go with him, you will be an abandoned wife.' As I said, I was not familiar with religious law, and I didn't know that, until my husband handed me a piece of paper called a *get,* I was, by religious law, his wife. When Father realized I was firm in my decision and determined not to go with that man, he didn't rest until he had prevailed upon him to give me a *get.* I was finally rid of him by Jewish law, having already rid myself of him on my own.

"What happened next? Did the professor want to ask me something? No? I'm surprised. I thought I was about to be interrupted. About six months after the *get,* I decided to come to this country. I didn't come with my father, who was too deeply involved in his work and various other activities. I didn't come with my friends from the youth movement, as we were no longer in touch with each other. But my mother's mother lived in Jerusalem, so I went to stay with her.

"I'll make a brief digression to explain some things that had happened several years earlier. A Russian boy was arrested for revolutionary activities and escaped to Galicia. He came to a town where he began teaching Hebrew. He set his heart on a student of his, who was the only daughter of a well-to-do family, and married her despite her parents' objections. That man was my father and the woman was my mother. After a while, Father heard that conditions had improved in Russia. He took me and my mother back to Russia. Mother was homesick. She missed her parents, as well as her town. They sent her money for the fare. She went to visit them. One day, Mother was sitting in the park. A cavalry officer saw her, and, in the course of events, she went off with him. Not long afterward, she died. Her father and mother, wishing to atone for her sin, went up to Jerusalem.

"When I came to Jerusalem, my grandfather was already dead and my grandmother was living in an old-age home. I couldn't stay with her, since she was in the home, nor could I find myself a room, as I had very little money. I decided to go to a kibbutz. My grandmother began to weep and begged me not to do anything so shameful.

"A rich woman from Hamburg lived next door. She took sick and was planning to leave the country. I looked after her in exchange for room and board. When she left, she took me along as a companion. I went with her to Hamburg. In Hamburg, once again I didn't know what to do. The woman's daughters-in-law advised me to study nursing. They helped me out while I was in school. When I completed the course, I was sent to Jerusalem to work in the hospital where Dr. Herbst made my acquaintance."

— 13 —

While she was telling her story, Herbst was haunted by this question: What sort of people did Shira know between the time she ran away from her husband and the present? Since she was silent, Herbst asked in a whisper, "After you were rid of your husband, you must have known other men?" Shira bit her lip and said, "I'm not someone who answers unwelcome questions. Not that I mean to cover up my past, but an unwelcome question makes me tight-lipped. Will the eminent professor please say if he grasps my meaning." Herbst was silent, and Shira too was silent.

Finally she laughed and said, "I've upset you, now I'm ready to make up. What were you asking? If I knew other men. Is that it? You should say so without embarrassment." Herbst nodded and said, "That's roughly what I asked." Shira said, "Yes, I did know some men." Herbst asked in a whisper, "And you didn't run away from them?" She laughed and said, "A big question. In the interim, Shira grew up. I beg of you, dear professor, a mature woman of ample years—and you ask such a question? Now, on a more appropriate subject: Wasn't it a good idea to walk here? It's restful, quiet, with a fresh breeze. The moon has even come up. Too bad we didn't see it rise. How delightful it is here. The moon and stars are in the sky, and we're alone on the earth." Herbst peered at her and saw her face inundated with moonlight and smiling, like someone who smiles at himself for wanting what he can never have. He took her hand and was about to kiss her on the mouth. Shira said, "When I said we're alone here, I didn't mean to suggest that sort of nonsense." Herbst was offended and responded with a growl,

"Good, good." Shira said, "What's good?" Herbst said, "Shira's mouth, for example." Shira said, "If so, you should be good too and not do anything that displeases Shira. If there is no man here, then you should try to act like a man, not a boy. If it weren't so far away, I would find myself a room in this neighborhood."

"So she wants to move?" Herbst asked. Shira said, "Whether I want to or not, I won't change my place. And any night, whenever I'm not working, you can find me in my room." "And tonight?" "Tonight, as you can see, I am walking with Dr. Herbst in this new neighborhood." "And then?" "Then we'll go to a restaurant, where you will eat your fill, as Mrs. Herbst requested." "And after we eat, what then?" "After we eat, the eminent professor will return home, climb into bed, and have good dreams about his good wife." Herbst asked Shira, "Why did you mention my wife?" Shira said, "Why shouldn't I? I might as well tell you that I am fond of Mrs. Herbst, and I don't intend to cause her grief. Now let's get back to town, go to a restaurant, and eat." "Good, good," Herbst answered, irritated. Shira said, "After a good meal, you'll cheer up, and when you say, 'Good, good,' it will be from the goodness of your heart. Why so silent?" Herbst said, "Not at all." Shira said, "But, you're not talking." Herbst said, "You talk like a logic teacher." Shira asked, "What is logic?" Herbst said, "You did go to school, and you studied logic." Shira said, "Since the day I left school, I've managed to forget everything they taught me. You want to know how many years I've been out of school. That I won't tell. If I did, you'd know my age." Herbst said, "Even if you don't tell me, I can figure it out." "How?" "You were about seventeen when you married, after which, you didn't return to school. But I don't know how long it was between the divorce and your second arrival in this country." Shira laughed and said, "So—despite all your calculations, you aren't sure." Herbst said, "You are dear to me even if you're forty." Shira said, "I'm not yet forty." Herbst said, "I didn't mean to provoke you." Shira said, "What do you gain by provoking me?" Herbst said, "Forgive me, Shira, far be it from me to provoke you."

From here on, whenever the two of them were alone, Herbst and Shira addressed each other in the familiar second person.

Shira said, "We're already at Jaffa Road. Where would you like to eat?" Herbst said, "As long as it's not where I ate this afternoon." "Why? Didn't you like the food?" Herbst said, "Not only did I find good food, but I also found a lovely waitress." Shira said, "Then let's go there." Herbst said, "Aren't you jealous?" Shira said, "It's not time for jealousy yet." Herbst took her hand in his and said, "Forgive me,

Shira. Forgive me." Shira slipped her hand away and took out some powder, which she sprinkled on the tip of her nose. When she returned the powder to her purse, she straightened her eyeglasses and held on to her necklace with her left hand. The moon was bright, and Shira's face was melancholy.

— 14 —

Henrietta came home from the hospital, bringing an additional daughter. The little one occupied minimal space, but her presence filled the house. Herbst tried to get back to work and to prepare lectures for the winter term.

He was busy preparing his lectures, and his wife was busy with her child and with the wetnurse. The Fashioner of All Things creates many needy souls with a symmetry that maintains life, giving this one a daughter and that one a daughter. One has no milk for her child; the other has no way to support her family. He brings them together. One nurses the other's child and is paid for the service, so that each one lives off the other's flaw. One is from Kurdistan, the other from Germany. Kurdistan and Germany being far from each other, what does He do? He brings them both to Jerusalem, for a Jew's eyes look to Jerusalem.

Sarini, the Kurdish wetnurse, is a handsome, healthy woman. Her face is dark brown, her hair dark gray. Her shiny eyes are green, her teeth like peeled garlic cloves and harder than rock. She is always laughing, and every year she gives birth. She has already produced eight male children, apart from the daughter we mentioned, all of them alive and healthy. They are no trouble during pregnancy or birth, being aware that none of them is an only child, that, should she wish to, she can produce many more. They don't trouble her for another reason: it is she who supports them. Their father—which is to say, their mother's husband—has many trades, none of which provides much income. There are times when he is a scholar in the yeshiva, times when he ties a rope around his waist to be a porter, times when he sells books, times when he does magic. He can look into a glass of clear water and tell if a particular woman was a virgin when she married. And, whispering gently over a pinch of salt and a sugar cube, he can cause you to forget to say the prayer for the new moon. He has many other accomplishments, foremost among them the fact that he is the husband of this prolific, powerful, shrewd woman who supports a houseful of children, besides two sets of parents, and is at war with the Mandate government for obstructing immigration. And, of course, she does her bit at home, so that the seed of our father Abraham will not vanish from the earth. Although Sarini has intelligence and good deeds to her credit, Henrietta has to exert considerable effort to get her to bathe and wear clean clothes, and to provide her with a wholesome diet, since she comes from a neighborhood of tin huts and lives in a dingy room with straw mats for bedding, coarse food, and foul water.

Henrietta is busy with other matters, apart from the wetnurse and the kitchen, such as driving away the goats the Arab shepherds send into the garden. While in the garden, she picks three or four flowers to put in a vase. If they are especially nice, she brings them to Manfred and sets them on his desk. She tiptoes in and tiptoes out again, going back to her pots and her stove until lunch is ready. After lunch, she has a short nap and tends to the remaining tasks, such as mending, ironing, and collecting milk so the baby won't be hungry when the wetnurse is gone. Since Sarini can't support her family on what Herbst can pay she has to supplement her income elsewhere. When Henrietta has an extra bit of energy, she goes into town on other business, such as obtaining certificates for her relatives in Germany, and making bank payments. On the way, she stops at the doctor to consult about the baby, at the dentist to have her teeth checked, at the tinsmith to have the kettle repaired, and at Krautmeir, the gynecologist. With all this business to attend to, Henrietta has no time for her husband. Similarly, he, with all his business, has no time for Henrietta. New students from Germany cannot be offered the usual fare; you have to be well prepared, for they come from German schools, where scholarship is serious. They each go their own way: Manfred doesn't intrude on Henrietta's domain, and Henrietta doesn't intrude on Manfred's.

Herbst is at his desk, which is filled with open books, reading a page here and a page there, writing, copying, adding to the pile of notes and comments, to the series of lectures on such-and-such an emperor—a Byzantine whose name I forget, a very short fellow who required that all his ministers stoop to a level below his shoulders. Herbst takes no shortcuts. He consults every book in Jerusalem pertaining to his field and orders books and photographs from abroad. Though the books are numerous and there is no shortage of scholars, there is room for innovation. If he had more books, he would make more discoveries, for it is in the nature of books that each one offers a different theory, and a reader with the capacity to innovate adds his own opinion. If his wisdom is significant, what he adds is significant. Whether you know it or not, Dr. Manfred Herbst is an expert on the Byzantine period, and, when Byzantine scholars are mentioned, his name is always included. So he has reason to be pleased with himself.

But this is not the case. Often Herbst shoves away his books, photographs, index cards, and notes, rests his left arm on the desk, and leans his head on his arm. This pose, if I am not mistaken, is hardly the one in which painters portray learned men. When he sits in this position, he resembles a man trying to dismiss his worries. Which of them did he succeed in dismissing, and which did he fail to dismiss? He succeeded in dismissing Lisbet Neu from his mind, but he failed to dismiss Shira.

Shira displays herself in an array of guises, and every one of her guises compels his eyes and heart. But he does not move from his spot or run to her, and he is surprised at himself for not running to her. A single verse he read by chance remains fixed in his mouth, and he mumbles, "Flesh such as yours / Will not soon be forgotten." He determines to go to her. When night comes, he finds an excuse and doesn't go. He looks for Henrietta and insists on helping her in the kitchen, even though she has told him he doesn't belong among the pots. This sometimes becomes a quarrel. And when she hears his footsteps, she locks the door. What does he do? He takes Sarah out of her crib, carries her in his arms, knocks on the door, and says, "I think the baby needs you." Henrietta comes out, takes the baby, and walks Manfred to his room and to his desk, saying, "This is where you belong, Fred. Sit down and do your work." What does he do? He remembers there is no butter in the house. Since there is no dairy in Baka, he goes to Talpiot to buy butter. In Talpiot, he meets up with some of his students, who are protecting the neighborhood from Arab snipers. Herbst does another thing: he writes letters to friends abroad, as well as to his two daughters who are in the same country, for a father is required to educate his daughters. If he didn't educate them when they were at home, he is educating them now, from a distance. He also occupies himself with a matter that occupies few of his Jerusalem colleagues: he is engaged in clarifying and establishing just who deserves to be considered a Church Father. As Vincent of

Lerins has already noted, not all the early Church writers should be considered Church Fathers, since God was testing the Christians through these great teachers, et cetera.

This is how Herbst spent those of his nights that seemed to be seeking Shira. When a night passed and he hadn't gone to Shira, he felt he was in control.

A contradiction: If it was Shira he was seeking, why didn't he go to her? But Herbst had a wife; he was the husband of an intelligent, attractive woman. He was the father of three daughters and a lecturer at the Hebrew University in Jerusalem. Whether or not the Hebrew University is required to uphold the teachings of the prophets and the Jewish moral code, whether or not it is a university like all others, university faculty should not behave frivolously. And, needless to say, they should not waste time indulging the body at the expense of the soul. There was a further reason: Herbst was a reticent man, attached to his wife. She was his first love, and it was with her that his love matured, which is to say that, until he knew Henrietta, he didn't know a woman's love.

So, if the night passed and he hadn't gone to Shira, he considered himself in control. Even more so on a night when he knew she was at home. There were nights when he knew she wasn't working and would be at home; when she told him this, it was quite deliberate, so he would know when he could find her in.

Herbst stayed away from Shira's house. Shira didn't stay away from Herbst's house. She showed herself in seventy forms: her little feet escaping to the forest on a snowy night, the wolf pelt her husband flung over her on their wedding night when he took her to the house in the woods, the blanket wrapped around her in her husband's room, the feet the old servant woman wanted to kiss, the slippers he slid off her feet and she replaced. When she appeared to him, her voice sounded as it did that night when they walked as one in the new neighborhood. And he was engulfed in the same stillness, not finding the courage to reach out and caress her. When, after a few weeks, the same face continued to impel him to run to her, he began summoning up her other face, the one he had seen the day the entire city was mourning a young Jerusalem boy who was killed and Shira appeared with that defiant cigarette in her mouth. When that face began to blur, he pictured her sitting with the women in the waiting room of the maternity section, her limbs expanding, encircling the blind Turk and reaching to embrace him. These things are certainly ugly, so reason would cause him to pluck her from his heart and avert his eyes from her. He did just this, pressing his eyes into their sockets so he wouldn't see her. What did that Turk do? Believe it or not, he sneered from his blind eyes into Herbst's tightly clenched eyes, chirping, "Flesh such as yours / Will not soon be forgotten."

—— 15 ——

Manfred was having a hard morning. His head was heavy, and his shoulders were as inert as rocks. He was utterly debilitated. His bed annoyed him so, he couldn't lie in it. He got up, settled his feet in his slippers, and began shuffling back and forth from one end of the room to the other.

Henrietta bathed and oiled Sarah, and put her on the scale to check her weight. The baby wriggled her round feet and raised them high, upsetting the scale, so no one could tell how much she had gained. Henrietta laughed and spoke as if to an adult, "I don't have time for your mischief, Sarah. Father is awake, and I haven't made his coffee yet." Even if the child had understood Henrietta, it would have been impossible to find out her weight, as the scale wasn't working because of a missing screw. When Henrietta realized this, she began searching the house. She remembered that a neighbor had come to weigh her son, and all his brothers had come along; they had played with the scale and, undoubtedly, broken it. Henrietta was irritated with herself. Why did I have to teach the Arab women what they and all their sisters never knew? Now that I need to weigh my daughter, the scale is broken.

Henrietta heard Manfred's footsteps. They didn't sound right to her. She handed the baby to Sarini and went to Manfred. His face looked strange. She assumed he had been awake all night with his books. She looked at the lamp and noted that it was still full of kerosene. It occurred to her that his stomach might be upset. Since she knew there were no spoiled ingredients in her cooking, she attributed this to some vegetarian dish, such as a radish he might have pulled up and eaten. Manfred tended to fill up on fruits and vegetables, on the misguided premise that live vegetation gives life. She looked at him again and saw that his eyes were red, his face somber. His shoulders drooped, and his entire body was dejected. Feeling sorry for him, she said, "Fred, I'm taking a chair out to the garden for you. I'll bring out your coffee. Waste one day in the garden rather than several days in bed. If we were in Germany, wouldn't we spend two or three months in a summer house? It's about four years since you took a vacation. You surely deserve a day off." Henrietta had forgotten that he once went abroad to a conference of Byzantine scholars and spent a few days at the seashore.

Manfred went out to the garden, and Henrietta brought him a lounge chair. She went to bring him coffee and milk, toast, butter, and honey, and to tell Sarini she could go home early, since it was a holiday for her—her brother Ovadiah was being released from jail for the fifth time. Not because of any crime, God forbid, but because he had no luck with women. When Sarini's father and mother and their entire clan came to the holy city of Jerusalem, they brought Ovadiah along. He was like a brother, having nursed at her mother's breast. On the way, Ovadiah went to the well for a drink. There was a large rock there in the shape of a wicked woman. She stared at him, and he forgot to come back. They went on to Jerusalem without him. There was a man in Jerusalem, strong as an ox, who said, "I'll bring him back." He went and brought him back. Seeing that he was a good boy, he gave him his daughter as a wife. Ovadiah was fifteen years old, and the girl they gave him for a wife was thirty-five. Ovadiah stayed with her a year and half and gave her two children. He lost interest in her and left. Some women's organization came and said, "You are required to give her ten lirot a month." Ovadiah went to a rabbinical court and proved to the wise men that the woman couldn't become pregnant again, while he wanted more children. The wise men said, "Give her a *get,* and take another wife." He threw a *get* at her and took a young wife. The first woman came to grief and died. Ovadiah had no life with the child-wife because he had no luck with women. So he left her. There was an outcry from the women's organization: "If you don't want her, you don't want her, but you must give her ten lirot a month." Ovadiah said, "Ten lashes, yes, but not ten lirot. In the name of Moses, I myself never had ten lirot." The women's organization maligned and slandered him. They sent a policeman to arrest him. This happened once, twice, three times—again and again, making five. His prison term was now up. Sarini was eager to see him, so Mrs. Herbst gave her permission to leave early.

As soon as Sarini left, Mrs. Herbst took a chair out to join Manfred. She brought Sarah out in her cradle and sat down, although there was much work and little time. Manfred looked at Henrietta, and he saw how concerned she was. He wept inwardly for her and for himself, that they had arrived at such a pass.

Manfred sat, Henrietta sat, and Sarah lay in her cradle, a rubber doll

with a black face at her side, brought to her by Dr. Taglicht. Amid sun
and shade, the garden shrubs sent forth their fragrance. Not a sound
was heard from the neighbors. Even Sacharson, who could usually be
found where he wasn't wanted, was not in sight. The day was neither
hot nor cold. The sun had lost its intensity, as the month of Av was
over and it was now Elul, which often shows an autumnal aspect. Such
a day and such an hour are a delight to anyone, all the more to a man
and woman touched by the hand of God, which the faithless call the
hand of destiny. Henrietta was not yet aware of that hand upon her,
but Manfred was aware of it, and he was aware more of sin than of
punishment.

Henrietta got up and stood next to her husband, smoothing his brow
to erase the wrinkles. She said to him, squinting a bit, "I wish I knew
the thoughts that make those wrinkles. I know your work involves
heavy thought, but this is too much." Manfred answered, "Henriett,
you ask about the thoughts that are wrinkling my brow; actually it's
the lack of thought that makes wrinkles. You see, Henriett, when a
waterskin is empty, when it has no water, it begins to wrinkle. Me,
too—I'm an empty vessel. If I give a hundred lectures, if I copy a
thousand quotations, nothing will change. When I was a boy, I wanted
to read many books. When I grew up, I wanted to write books. Now,
my dear, now I don't want to read books, and I don't want to write
them either. When I visited you in the hospital the day Sarah was born,
you mentioned Lisbet Modrao, the daughter of Professor Modrao. You
mentioned her because of her grandfather's name, and I am reminded
of her for another reason. Lisbet told me—but why did I call her Lisbet,
when her name is Elizabeth?—anyway, Elizabeth told me about her
eldest brother, who was a minister, a Protestant minister in a small town
in Thuringia. He wasn't especially bright or learned, just an honest
man, one who never had a chance to misbehave. During the war, some
heretical texts fell into his hands. He read them, and his faith was
undermined. He began to loathe his job, as it involved teaching what
he no longer believed. One Sunday, after his sermon, he threw off his
robes and decided to give up the ministry. At dinner he said to his wife,
'Thus far and no farther.' Those were the war years, when food was
scarce. But, being a minister, he lacked nothing, as the peasant women
used to bring him eggs, chickens, vegetables, butter, cheese, and meat
in such quantity that his household was provided for and there was a
surplus to send to other relatives. His wife listened and wrote to his
father, the professor. The professor came, hoping to restore his faith.
When he realized his words were having no impact, he said to him,
'Truth and justice are fine and praiseworthy, but a man must be con-

cerned with his livelihood. If you abandon the ministry, how will you sustain yourself?' Economic pressure, Henriett, is not unique to Jews. With the power of German philosophy, which can be used to prove anything, the distinguished professor proved to the honest minister that it was essential that he keep his job and that, in order to do his job justice, he must become more devout. It ended well. A minister is a minister. His sermons were so fervent that he was promoted and his salary was increased, so much so that two of his daughters could study at the university, and the other five found husbands privileged to be in Hitler's retinue. Why did I tell that story? It's about me, Henriett. Yes, me. This instructor at the university in Jerusalem is where that minister was at the beginning. Don't worry, Henriett. I won't leave my job, and I don't need a dose of German philosophy. I've had a bellyful of it already and wouldn't mind vomiting some of it up."

Henrietta asked Manfred, "If you had a choice, what field would you choose?" Manfred answered, "Do you remember Axelrod, who looks in his notebooks and sees prophecies about everyone and his wife? What do you think? If I wanted a job like Axelrod's, would they give it to me?" Henrietta said, "You have so little respect for your work that you would rather be a hospital clerk?" Manfred said, "It's not that I underestimate my work, but I'm no longer happy with it. Others are happy with their work; I'm not. I'm not happy. I'm not happy, Henriett, my dear."

Henrietta said, "Is there some other sort of work that would please you?" Manfred said, "Whether there is or not, isn't there a song that goes 'Forest, forest, how far away you are'? Who sang that song to us?" Henrietta said, "Taglicht sang it." Manfred said, "You remember everything, Henriett. You hear something once, and you never forget it. Since you mention Taglicht, I'll tell you something I heard from him.

"Taglicht was at a conference of scholars in Jerusalem, seated next to a certain Hebrew poet. This country is so full of poets that I don't remember his name. Taglicht said to the poet, 'See what respect the world showers on learned men, but you poets never achieve it.' The poet remained silent. Taglicht added, 'Apart from the high regard in which they are held, they also make a living.' The poet said to Taglicht, 'You runt, I'll tell you a splendid story that's told about your great-great-grandfather, renowned for his righteousness.' You've surely heard, Henriett, that our Taglicht's forebears were noted for piety and virtue; they were distinguished rabbis, whom you probably read about in Buber's books. How hard it is for people like us to talk about Jewish subjects. Everything needs an introduction, and every introduction needs to be explicated." Henrietta said, "What did he tell you?" Man-

fred said, "He told me a splendid story. But if I tell it to you, I doubt
you'll enjoy it. It would be better to hear it directly from him than from
me."

Much as he resisted, she persisted. He began the story.

"There was once a crippled beggar who sat on a heap of rags at a
crossroads, tending his deformity. Passersby took note of him and
threw him coins—one, two, three, depending on their resources and
compassion. The beggar made a fortune. A son was born to him. He
whispered to the midwife, 'Cripple him, and when the boy grows up,
God willing, people will see his handicap and give him money. He
won't have to work for a living.' The midwife did as she was told.
Another son was born to him. He told her what he told her, and she
did what she did. So it was with each of his sons; they were provided
with a livelihood at birth and spared the need to exert any effort. When
his sixth son, or perhaps the seventh or eighth, was born, he went to
the midwife again and whispered, 'Cripple him.' She saw that the child
was good. She felt sorry for him and didn't cripple him. The father saw
this son and preferred him to all the others, because of his charm, and
beauty, and because he was not impaired. He held him in his arms, lifted
him high, played with him, bounced him on his knee, and taught him
all sorts of tricks, when he was small as well as when he grew up, in
accord with the boy's intelligence and the wisdom of the father, who,
having sat in the marketplace observing all sorts of people and their
behavior as they passed through, was full of wisdom. The boy surpassed
all the brothers who preceded him and everyone in the city as well.
While the brothers were occupied with their handicaps, tending them
and grooming them to arouse sympathy and bring in wealth, while
most people were snatching half-swallowed food from one another as
others snatched what they could from both parties—which is typical
of this generation, as it probably was in earlier times too—that son
devoted himself to his father's teachings. To these, he added his own
ideas. And, being occupied with wisdom, he had no interest in anything
unrelated to wisdom, which certainly included money, a commodity
he didn't value at all, having watched people throw it around. He
himself, being occupied with ideas, didn't notice that people gave his
father money, sometimes out of sympathy, sometimes to delude themselves, thinking they enjoyed every advantage while that poor man sat
on a heap of rags in the heat, cold, rain, and snow.

"One day, the man collected his sons and said to them, 'You're all
crippled. You carry your livelihood with you. All you have to do is
display your handicap, and everyone throws you money. All but your

little brother, who is healthy and whole, charming and pleasant, with no handicap other than poetry, which most people consider a handicap. How will the boy make his way? How is he to earn his bread? I am, therefore, leaving him my entire fortune. The rest of you can go out and sit on your rags, displaying your handicaps. You will lack for nothing.' "

Henrietta said, "If there's a moral in that tale, what is it?" Manfred said, "I enjoyed the tale so much that I forgot most of the moral. I'll try to tell some of what I remember.

"The man sitting on a heap of rags is the Creator. He tends His handicap, a reference to the world He has created. The passersby are human beings, passing through, only to return to dust. They throw a penny or two—people's good deeds, which are worth but a penny. The favored son is the poet, engaged in poetry, and his brothers are scholars who derive honor from their livelihood. What did that father do? He rejected them all and gave everything to the son who was most precious to him, who had devoted himself to poetry and was unsuited to the pursuit of honor and a livelihood."

Henrietta laughed and laughed. While she was laughing, the sun reached the middle of the sky and it was noon, time for a meal, although Henrietta had not so much as put a pot on the fire or made any other move toward lunch. Henrietta left Manfred, went to the kitchen, and turned to her pots. She checked the vegetables and the fruit basket, and actually made a meal of what she found there. Believe it or not, this meal, which she hardly fussed over, was more satisfying than most others involving far more fuss. Not only to Dr. Herbst, but to Mrs. Herbst as well, and you know Mrs. Herbst usually says how much she likes fruit and vegetables along with meat, but not when they pretend to be a main course.

The Herbsts sat in the garden, eating, drinking, discussing what we eat, what we drink, the sort of people that cross our paths. It happened that their conversation touched on Taglicht, who is endowed with two talents, one for scholarship and one for poetry. Neither leads him to action as poetry alienates scholarship, and he doesn't value scholarship enough to engage in it. But he has another talent, the most supreme of all: he has a soul. Henrietta said, "The fact that he's still a bachelor doesn't speak well for the daughters of Jerusalem." Manfred said, "You may remember that young woman—the relative of Professor Neu's, who came to our house with him. I told you I met her at Ernst Weltfremdt's when I went to congratulate him on his professorship and was introduced to two ladies, a mother and daughter. If Taglicht were to meet the daughter, the outcome might be good for both of them. What do you think, Henriett, should we invite the two of them together? I know you have a lot on your mind, and I don't want to add to your burdens. But Taglicht is worth the effort. In any case, I'll talk to Weltfremdt first, since he knows both the girl and Taglicht."

—— 16 ——

Manfred Herbst and Taglicht both went up to Jerusalem when the university was first established, Herbst, because he was a bit of a Zionist; and Weltfremdt, because his luck was turning where he was. Weltfremdt was a lecturer in patristics at some German university. This subject is normally in the domain of the Department of Religion, but, since Weltfremdt was a Jew, not a Christian, he was made an adjunct to the Department of Philosophy. With the publication of his major work, *Can We Assume Origen Was Familiar with "Hermes the Shepherd" as We Know It?* he gained renown and his audience grew. Because he had such a following, it was often necessary to assign him the large hall in the university, which had not been done for any other professor in several years. All in all, things were going well with him, but not with the world. In those years, after Germany's downfall, the bewildered Germans were asking who had caused their decline. Inasmuch as no nation is likely to take the blame on itself, least of all the Germans, who pride themselves on their exemplary behavior, they began searching for someone to whom to attribute their stench, and found the Jews. They failed to remember that twelve thousand Jews had fallen in Germany's war, which was two percent of the Jewish population of Germany. Weltfremdt began to feel the fist of malice. Students began to challenge him; colleagues he had supported began to make themselves scarce and avoided being seen with him in public. The newspapers began to berate him and to call him a parasite of German scholarship. He assumed his fellow professors would deplore these affronts. Not only did they fail to rally to his defense, but, when he asked them to respond to these charges, they begged him not to press them, explaining that, for various reasons that could not be enumerated, they could not get involved in the controversy, although they naturally did not agree with the anti-Semitic propaganda. As for the substance of the matter, in their scholarly journals they had already expressed the opinion that his papers were among the best research produced in German in this generation. At first, Weltfremdt saw himself as an academic martyr, which enabled him to accept the pain with love. They continued to torment him, and the university authorities refrained from protecting him, so he soon realized there was no future for him in a German university. He heard they were starting a university in Jerusalem. Weltfremdt imagined that, if Jews were creating a university, its language would be German. He intimated to the head of the Zionists in his city that he would not rule out the possibility of becoming a professor in Jerusalem. When he learned that lectures at the Jerusalem university were to be conducted in Hebrew, he withdrew and looked elsewhere for a position. He got no response, so he began to negotiate with the trustees of the Hebrew University. Before long, he went up to Jerusalem and was appointed to the Faculty of Philosophy, where he specialized in Jewish Hellenistic writings, first as an associate professor and then as a full professor.

Ernst Weltfremdt and Manfred Herbst were on the same ship when they went up to the Land of Israel. Inasmuch as they were shipmates who came from the same country, spoke the same language, and had the same purpose, a friendship developed, which endured so long as the university remained small, the *yishuv* population sparse, and Jerusalem's neighborhoods few. When the trouble in Germany and other Nazi-controlled countries began to escalate, many Jews arrived. The *yishuv* grew, the university expanded, new teachers came. Everyone found new friends, and Weltfremdt and Herbst rarely met up with each other. Herbst didn't notice that he no longer visited Weltfremdt, nor did Weltfremdt notice that Herbst seldom appeared at his door. When they noticed, they saw no reason for a change. When they did meet, they met as friends with an ongoing friendship. Occasionally Weltfremdt dragged Herbst home with him, and occasionally Herbst came on his own to borrow a book, more frequently as Herbst grew interested in patristics. Weltfremdt had brought his books on the subject with him, this being the field he had studied and in which he had earned renown. He was still hoping to return to it, at first in England or the United States, and later on in Germany itself. What was it that attracted Herbst to patristics? He apparently wanted to find out whether he could still deal with unfamiliar material, for he often wondered if what he did in his own field was largely habit.

A few days after Manfred and Henrietta's conversation about Taglicht and Lisbet Neu, it happened that Manfred went into town. When he was in town, it happened that he was in Rehavia. Once he was in Rehavia, he stopped at Weltfremdt's.

Weltfremdt was busy preparing lectures for the spring term. He used to write them in German, and Taglicht would translate them into Hebrew, adding comments he considered appropriate from the Gemara and the Midrash, but no one was aware that Weltfremdt was plowing with Taglicht's horse. Were you to mention this, Weltfremdt himself probably wouldn't know what you were referring to. How could this be? He paid Taglicht generously, giving good money for what he got. Furthermore, although Taglicht was praised by everyone and considered highly accomplished in every field and discipline, his learning was a mass of disjointed fragments. If not for Professor Weltfremdt, who used this expertise as a resource for lectures, articles, and books, that expert would be lost in his own wisdom.

As soon as Herbst mentioned Taglicht, Weltfremdt was alarmed. When he told him why he had come, he was relieved. He got up and hid his lecture notes, placed his hand on Herbst's shoulder, and said, "Neu, Neu. Yes, yes. . . . I know a woman called Neu. Yes, yes. If I'm not mistaken, she's considerably older than Taglicht." Herbst said, "If you're referring to the mother, she's older than Taglicht. As for the daughter, she's younger." Weltfremdt said, "Yes, yes, Dr. Herbst, the old are old, and the young are young. Incidentally, just yesterday I read your paper comparing the Code of Leo the Isaurian to the Hammurabi Code. Not bad, not bad at all. But, judging by the date under the paper, you wrote it two years ago. Two years ago, and you haven't published anything since. Not a thing. This is contrary to university policy. We don't require that each faculty member produce a weighty tome annually, but it would be appropriate to publish an article or a monograph every year or so. And you, doctor, turn out one article in two years. As for the piece itself, others have in fact dealt with the same subject, though yours is not without new insights. I pointed it out to our colleagues, especially to Professor Bachlam, who resents other people's insights and always uses them to support what he has written or what he means to write, even in fields whose terminology he doesn't understand. What were we talking about? Yes, yes, about Professor Neu's relative. If I'm not mistaken, you—that is, you and Mrs. Herbst—are interested in making a match between Taglicht and Miss Neu, mainly because he and she are available. In that case, one should speak to them first, to both Dr. Taglicht and Miss Neu. Though you and Mrs. Herbst both agree that they—I mean, Taglicht and Neu—are suited to each other, that's not good enough. You—I mean, you and Mrs. Herbst—have taken on a big job. I myself can't imagine how these things happen—how you come to a fellow and say, 'I've found a girl for you,' not to mention coming to a girl and delivering the same message with the appropriate changes. Yes, indeed. Incidentally, doctor, have you noticed that Leo's Code, though he is considered an outright atheist, is derived from the Torah and from the Evangelists, which is not the case with Justinian? Incidentally, doctor, if you see my cousin Julian, tell him that, though he maligns me in every café in Jerusalem, he is welcome for coffee at my house anytime. I see you're hurrying. If you wait a bit, we can have coffee together. Not the kind you usually drink, which keeps you awake, but a harmless brew. Incidentally, tell me, how did you arrive at the comparison between the Code of Leo the Isaurian and the Hammurabi Code? If I were allowed to allow myself the liberty, I could, perhaps, give myself some of the credit, as I was the one who lent you David Heinrich Miller's edition of the Hammurabi Code. Yes, yes. Incidentally, what do you think about Bachlam? Taglicht says that Bachlam writes 'flaxen Hebrew.' I can't imagine what 'flaxen Hebrew' is. Welcome, Mrs. Weltfremdt. Did you manage to rest a bit? Now, Herbst, you can't escape without drinking coffee with us first. What do you think, Dikchen, will Professor Herbst find some coffee in our house?"

Herbst stayed at Weltfremdt's, where he drank coffee that doesn't keep one from sleeping and ate cake that doesn't keep one's middle from expanding. They talked about the university, its faculty, and many other matters. When Dr. Ernst Weltfremdt publishes his autobiography, we'll have more details.

To please his wife, Weltfremdt suggested that she show their guest the rhymes she had composed on the marriage of their eldest daughter. Professor Weltfremdt's wife, Rikchen, poetized every family event. Her relatives in Germany were fond of her rhymes, but here in Jerusalem, where public events tended to overshadow personal ones and the Hebrew language was beginning to take over from German, she had no audience. If not for her husband, who sometimes told his guests about her rhymes, we would be unaware of Mrs. Weltfremdt's talent.

While she went to get her rhymes, Weltfremdt gave Herbst the galleys of his article for Bachlam's jubilee volume. As Herbst leafed through the galleys, Weltfremdt began discussing other individuals who had been similarly honored. Typically, as they approached the age of fifty or sixty, these men would go from professor to professor, asking how to avoid the notoriety to which they were about to be subjected. They would confide that the most erudite scholars had already met and formed a jubilee committee—a committee of unprecedented distinction—which they nevertheless considered flawed, "because Ernst Weltfremdt's name is not included." "Whether I want to or not, I add my name. They press me to contribute an article to the jubilee volume to be published in honor of that academic pest. They press me to hand it in immediately and then delay my article, along with the entire book, so that, when it finally appears, my insights are outdated. A learned man once said wisely, 'All those jubilee volumes are burial grounds for the written word.' I would amend this—they're burial grounds for mummies. Yes, for mummies!"

Mrs. Weltfremdt returned, carrying a bunch of notebooks tied together with colorful string. She looked warmly at Professor Herbst, who had agreed to hear her verses, and imploringly at her husband, wishing he would stop talking and let her read. Her husband took no notice but went on talking to Herbst, explicating every new point in his article, for he gravely doubted that his colleagues would grasp it. "I'm not saying that all of our eminent colleagues are imbeciles. There are surely one or two—perhaps even three—who are capable of grasping my insights, but since they measure with their own yardsticks, they have the impression that my insights are no better than theirs. In any case, there's nothing to stop them from claiming my insights as their own, with a change of language or an additional phrase, to the point where the sheer verbiage disguises the source." If not for Lemner, who loved to disclose the sources authors use, none of them would realize that many of Weltfremdt's insights were incorporated in their books. Mrs. Weltfremdt saw there was no end in sight and went off. In the interim, the sun set, the day darkened, and Herbst got up to go.

Weltfremdt remembered his wife and her verses. He opened the door and called, "Dikchen, Dikchen, what's going on? We have here one-third of one-half of one dozen distinguished gentlemen eager to bask in your delightful verse, and you withhold its light."

Mrs. Weltfremdt heard him and appeared. Professor Weltfremdt said, "It's good you came, Dikchen. I was talking to our friend, Doctor Herbst, about our revered cousin, who never deigns to come to us, and I asked Doctor Herbst, if he should see our cousin, to tell him to be so kind as to come. What's your opinion, Dikchen? Will he find a place to sit in our house? As for your verses, it's good you brought them. Let me see if you brought the notebook with the humorous ones. Yes, yes. Here's the notebook, and here are the verses. Bravo. What was I going to ask? Yes, yes. . . . Who's that knocking? Isn't there a bell in the house? Problems with the electricity again. Storrs may be right to keep everything modern out of Jerusalem. Even the electric lights go out most nights, leaving us in darkness. Dikchen, I see we won't get to your verses tonight. I certainly won't agree to let you ruin your eyes in the light of the kerosene lamp. I don't know how anyone reads in that light. When I touch a kerosene lamp, I can't get rid of the smell.

Now, Doctor Herbst, it isn't right to keep you here in this dark dungeon. Dikchen, allow me to go two or three steps with Doctor Herbst, and don't be upset if I make it four or five. You know I'm no mathematician."

When they were outside, Weltfremdt said to Herbst, "Dear doctor, why is it that Julian finds it necessary to malign me everywhere? In any case, I can say, like King David in his time, my throne and I are pure. I don't know if I've quoted the phrase correctly, but I've made my point. Incidentally, your article was very successful. I said this in so many words at the senate meeting. You ought to publish more articles like that one, doctor. Just like it. Yes, indeed. I have an important subject for you to investigate: when Athanasius went to Rome to seek support, why did the journey take a whole year? As for my cousin Julian, when he discredits Wechsler and Bachlam, we can say that, if he isn't one hundred percent justified, he is surely fifty or sixty percent right. I'm not a mathematician, and I can't formulate the precise percentage. But when he maligns me, he does himself harm, because everyone knows he's not familiar with my field. All of Jerusalem has light, except for my house. My best to Mrs. Herbst and to you, too, doctor. Above all, let's get together again. Really. Yes, yes. Back to the subject of Julian. When his little girl got sick and was taken to Hadassah Hospital, where she stayed many days, who was it who tried to get the bill canceled, if not me? And when the child died, who paid for her burial? I was the one who paid to have her buried. In Jerusalem, nothing is free. Now I have to go home too. I assume it was the printer's messenger knocking at the door, coming for the galleys of my article for Bachlam's jubilee volume. See you soon, doctor. I really mean it. I hope to see you soon."

— 17 —

How long did he keep himself at home, occupied with things he hadn't done in years, for one purpose—so he wouldn't go into town? If he were to go to town, his feet would run to Shira. How he agonized the night he visited Weltfremdt! And he triumphed. In the end, he didn't go to Shira, though he knew she was at home, perhaps even expecting him. That witch, she never said, "I expect you to come." Still, even someone inept in the realm of women's wiles could sense it. So he kept himself at home, hanging around his wife while she worked. At this point, Henrietta even allowed him to do household chores without protesting. Sometimes she even asked him to relieve her, teasing, "If you had teats, we wouldn't need a wetnurse."

Manfred is with Henrietta, arranging Sarah's crib, spreading her rubber sheet, smoothing the wrinkles, while Henrietta plays with the baby, cooing at her like any mother with an infant daughter. Manfred watches them, thinking: If I didn't know otherwise, I would think the baby was with her grandmother. Manfred looks furtively for some trace of youthful charm, but he sees an old woman. He starts to pity her and is overcome with renewed affection. He engraves its new form in his heart. He is warmed by this affection. The One who was created only to cause trouble asks: Isn't she an obstacle in your path, the one that keeps you from living your life? Manfred sighs and reflects: Life . . . the life that seduces us is, perhaps, not really life. It may be the mission of our life to live with the wife we were given. If not for a man's wife, he would sink from bad to worse.

Those were good days. His evil thoughts lost their sting, and he began to cherish his wife, for it was through her that he avoided a reckless course. At first he kept himself at home, helping his wife just to prevent his feet from heading toward town; now he was helping her in order to ease her burdens. Henrietta would take note and say, "Thank you, thank you, my dear. You did such a good job. Now, dear, you can go back to your own work." Manfred would take her advice, go to his room, and sit at his desk, editing lectures he had prepared for the winter term. Should you stop in he doesn't behave as if you've kept him from discovering the symbol for zero, for example, or impeded him in his conquest of Mesopotamia. Should a student stop in, Herbst receives him warmly, gives him a chair, hears his questions, provides advice as well as research data from the box of notes, gratis, without suggesting he has offered all the Indies as a gift. A student who arrives at teatime is served tea with a slice of cake, along with cordial conversation unrelated to scholarly work. Dr. Herbst doesn't have many students, but if you combine all of them over his entire career, there are more than a few.

We could dwell a bit on Dr. Herbst's students without arresting the pace of our story. They came from various countries, where they roamed the roads for many years, sustaining themselves as porters. Even here, their sustenance doesn't simply land in their mouths. Some of them deliver newspapers; others are teachers and accountants. Those privileged to deliver papers are up before dawn. After distributing the papers, they race up to class on Mount Scopus, on foot, since even those who do well can't afford the busfare. Sometimes they are up early, but to no avail, because of a hand that tampers with the papers: censors appointed by the Mandate government often allow things to be printed, only to ban them suddenly. The Hebrew newspapers remain in their place and never reach their readers. Those who deliver them are demoralized by the wasted time and loss of income. The others—those who are accountants or teachers—are no better off. But those with a talent for writing fare worst. They hire themselves out to all sorts of operators, do-gooders, and ordinary people who wish to perpetuate themselves through memoirs, although they haven't the ability to write two or three lines properly. They write what they write and hire a poor student to translate their words into civilized language. They pay by the hour and include proofreading in the price. Not only do the students invest their strength in others, whose business is of no interest to them, but they don't get to do what is suited to their talents. There is even a young woman, the mother of a baby, among those who listen to Herbst's lectures. She is in Jerusalem five days a week, cleaning office floors for a living. On Friday nights, she goes down to Tel Aviv to enjoy her husband and the small daughter she leaves with her mother-in-law. On Sunday mornings, she returns to Jerusalem, to her studies and her job. What moves them to learn about subjects such as the history of Byzantium? Perhaps they are eager for knowledge, and it is not the subject that is crucial, but the learning process. Herbst is a splendid teacher, the sort one can learn from. Even if you wanted to, how could you pursue the subject of your choice, when the university is small and in many areas there are no teachers, so that what you want to study may be taught by some imbecile who distorts the material?

We have mentioned the students' occupations; let us now mention their housing. They live in tin huts in Nahlat Achim, two or three to a room. Their beds are flimsy, their tables unsteady, their chairs lame. At night, they go out and learn to handle rifles. You, sir, lie in bed secure, get up the next morning, and sit at your lavish table reading the paper, assuming that mighty Britain is spreading a tabernacle of peace. Actually, it is a small band of fellows with empty tables and flimsy beds—they and other Haganah members—who protect you. Herbst isn't one of them. He belongs to Brit Shalom, and he used to sit at Brit Shalom meetings devising plans to prevent Jews from victimizing the Arabs. Herbst once went to a friend's home for a housewarming; he had built a new house in Rehavia. There was food, drink, conversation. Herbst noticed that his friend was sad and asked, "Did something happen to you?" He answered, "The same thing that happened to you,

to me, to every Jew who lives in this country. Every Jew that lives here
is driving out an Arab, since the land is his."

As soon as Herbst started to get close to his students, listening to
their talk and watching their actions, he began observing the land and
those living in it. His eyes were opened, and he saw what most of his
friends did not see, for they had found there a place to rest their weary
feet, a comfortable and painless livelihood, a place where their sons and
daughters would be safe from those evil doctrines that lead to extinc-
tion. It was not because of the Arabs that they found what they found,
but because of those who formed the *yishuv*, transforming desolate
wilderness into habitable land. They built cities and established settlements, which they defend with body and soul against a desert sword
that threatens annihilation. And even these predators exist because of
those who built the land. Both sides are governed from above, so no one
knows whether to build or destroy.

For some time now, Herbst had in mind to put his views on paper.
But he was concerned that his knowledge of the history of the land and
its settlement would not provide an adequate base, and Herbst was a
professional and a scholar, subject to a thousand research criteria, who
would not make any work of his public until it was validated. Besides,
this wasn't the time for research and validation, since Ernst Weltfremdt
had asked him to collaborate on a book about those terms in the writings of the contested Church Fathers that are not found in the writings
of the true Church Fathers. Nonetheless, Herbst's views were not
wasted. He conveyed some of them in a letter to his elder daughter,
Zahara, who belonged to a *kvutza*. Realizing that he was in accord with
those engaged in building up the land, he began to be proud of his
daughter, and she became an extension of his ideas about the land and
its settlement.

While Manfred arrived at this truth through conversation with his
students, Henrietta arrived at it on her own. All those years, living in
the Land of Israel, she watched the land being built and saw who its
builders were; and that there were others who would destroy it, and
who they were. This being the case, to whom does the land belong?
To the builders, of course. She objected to those who were cloistered
in their homes, buried in their own affairs as if eternal peace had been
achieved, who in the event of trouble would be unable to defend
themselves and would surely be slaughtered, as was the fate of Jews in
Hebron and Safed during the massive slaughter of 1929. She even used
to argue with Manfred: any man who volunteered to fight in Germany's war, who can handle weapons, who wrote an article about the
strategy of Emperor Valens—how could he not enlist in defense of his

people and his land? This woman, who always fought to protect her husband from any task that might distract him from his work, was demanding this of him. But she didn't press him. I will now add a small detail, from which one can learn about everything else. When Henrietta rented a house in Baka, it was a ruin filled with garbage rather than a house, and no one would have considered it suitable to live in. Henrietta cleared out the garbage, repaired the house, and made herself a garden with fruit trees, vegetables, and flowers. When the land began to be productive, Arab shepherds appeared with their sheep and cattle, and what she had been tending all year was consumed in two or three days. She hired workers to fence in the garden. What did the shepherds do? They poked a stick in the fence, made openings, and sent their flocks into the garden. Henrietta found an olive tree that wasn't bearing fruit; she dug up the soil and fertilized it, and it flourished. What did the shepherds do? They sneaked into the garden and pulled off leaves, which they fed to their sheep, or brought in goats to demolish the olives.

During one of those days when Manfred was keeping himself at home, sitting there for hours on end, this is what happened. That day he went out into the garden. The heat was past its peak, and the soil was fragrant. Above the earth, trees and bushes and grasses made a wreath of varied hues—some derived from innate power granted by God, others from His power being renewed all the time, at every moment. Just then, in fact, the skies were testing all the hues to determine which was most suited to the moment, shifting from hue to hue and back again.

Manfred looked around and saw Henrietta getting up from the ground, a bunch of flowers in her hand. His senses drifted back to a time when they were both young. He, a student at the university, and she, a clerk in a music store, used to meet in the evening, among rows of flowers in a park in Berlin. Not that evenings there were like this one; nor were there flowers such as these. Still, the scents and after-scents of those flowers wafted from the shadows of those vanished evenings. Manfred's heart began to throb, as it had in those days of his youth when he used to run to those parks and see Henrietta walking through rows of flowers, waiting for him with a bouquet in hand. God-who-is-good-and-renders-good, man's spirit lives not only in the present but in every good memory of days long past. His eyes were moved to tears, and he whispered, "Let's sit a minute." Henrietta heard him and said, "We can sit, if you like." She repeated, "Yes, let's sit."

They sat together and exchanged pleasantries. Manfred was afraid he might say something inappropriate, for in such a setting and at such a time one might very well say words it would be embarrassing to recall, because of their banality. Manfred took the flowers from Henrietta and put her hand in his rather gruffly. He placed the flowers on a rock and closed his eyes. He saw Henrietta's affection rising up before him, completely engulfing him. Now her hand was in his, lifeless. Only the afterscent of the flowers he took from her hand and placed on the rock was still alive. Manfred knew that the stress of caring for the household and the children had consumed the years of love. Add to this the anxiety about her relatives in Germany, where God's wrath was loose. To remain alive, her relatives and acquaintances needed certificates. Henrietta used to spend half her day dealing with the household and the other half in pursuit of certificates. The household had its routines. As for the immigration officials, if no tears can move their ruthless hearts, from whence will our help come? While Manfred held Henrietta's hand, the day darkened, the garden grew dusky, the array of colors vanished from the sky, and an evening chill set in. Henrietta went to get her shawl. Manfred followed her. As she wrapped herself in the shawl, Manfred reached out his arms and embraced her. She teased him and said, "What do you want with this withered stick of wood?" And she slipped out of his arms.

—— 18 ——

Zahara and Tamara, Manfred and Henrietta's daughters, came to welcome their little sister. Zahara is about nineteen, and Tamara is a year and a half younger as well as half a head taller, for she was only a baby when her parents brought her to this country, whose special milk makes people tall. Their faces are tanned, their hands steady—Zahara's as a result of work, and Tamara's from bathing in the sea and rowing on the Yarkon. Zahara belongs to a *kvutza* called Kfar Ahinoam, and Tamara is a student at a teachers' seminary in Tel Aviv. They were both slow to arrive. One, because of a group of youngsters from abroad she was asked to take charge of; the other, because she went hiking with some friends.

Before dealing with the daughters, let us deal with the parents. Henrietta is blonde; her limbs are full and relaxed, responding to her at work as well as at rest. Her eyes are a medium blue that can turn fierce. Her hair is pulled across the middle of her ears and folded up in back, framing her face and leaving her neck exposed. Manfred is dark. His hair is thick, so that, seeing him in the street, you assume he is on the way to get a haircut. His eyes, either laughing or bemused, suggest a pleasant temperament. His mouth is small. A narrow mustache separates his nose from his mouth, and a wrinkle begins between his eyes, curving up to his broad forehead, where it joins with the other three and a half wrinkles that are there. This is approximately how Manfred and Henrietta look.

Now I will give about a pen's worth of ink to a description of their daughters. But I will precede this with a few remarks about our other sisters in this land, as well as about ourselves.

When we came to the Land of Israel, we were shy young men with no interest in women, our every thought being centered on the land and on work. Finding work, we found a slice of bread, a plate of greens, and a cup of tea, and we were grateful for the land and its bounty. If we didn't find work, we were hungry. In a hungry period, we sometimes danced to take our minds off our hunger. Whether or not the Lord of Hunger saw our situation, we paid no attention to Him. Either way, we were devoured by malaria and the other scourges of the land. If a young woman fell in with our group, we paid no attention to her looks, since it was not for the sake of beauty that she came to this country, but to work the land. When we sat discussing land, labor, farmers, and workers, it didn't occur to us that the One who made farmers different from laborers made young men and women different too. If a fellow had his eye on a girl, it was her virtues that interested him, not her anatomy; if he had romantic tendencies, he would be interested in her doleful eyes, her plaintive voice. If she brought us songs of her homeland, in Yiddish, Polish, Russian, Ruthenian—which is now called Ukrainian—and sang them to us, we enjoyed these times on the beach at Jaffa far more than any concert we later attended in Europe's great cities.

There were other young women, whose families were Sephardic exiles descended from the ruling class of Judea, from the tribe of Judah, like David our king and like our righteous Messiah, who will come to deliver us from exile in the lands of Edom and Ishmael. They would sit at a window and never come out of the house, for their dignity enclosed them. Unlike their Ashkenazic sisters, their dignity was interior. Their eyes were black; their black hair was parted in the middle and flowed to the edge of the forehead. A blue-black or black-blue spark flashed from their eyes, settling on their eyebrows with a fiery glow. A baffled smile fluttered over their mouth. Between eyes and mouth, the nose loomed, angry and menacing.

There were others, also descendants of exiles from Spain. They took on any job that came their way to earn their bread. Both their hair and their eyes were black. Their eyebrows glistened with warm compassion. Their mouth seemed about to cry, and, when they opened their lips to sing, their voice would embrace you and you would want to cry for no reason. If you took notice of such a one, she would turn away from the window and withdraw into the house. Why? Because you could have asked her father for her hand, but you did no such thing; you merely peered and gazed at her.

There were other young women, Moroccans, with full faces, oval heads, eyes almost as large as their face. I mean not to disparage but to praise these eyes, for they animated the entire face. They spoke a brand of Arabic not many people in this country would recognize. We include ourselves, realizing that, if we were to speak Arabic, the Arabs would assume it was Russian.

There were still others, descendants of the exile into Yemen, the cruelest of all exiles. They came to this country with a purpose—to welcome the Messiah, for our righteous Messiah will reveal himself here first, before other countries. They left homes filled with every comfort and came empty-handed, with only the clothes on their back, carrying their books, which were written with ink on parchment and on parchmentlike paper. Some were copied from the manuscripts of our great Maimonides; others, we had heard of but never seen until these immigrants from Yemen came to the country. They wandered from desert to desert, hungry and thirsty. Their days were consumed by drought, their nights by frost, and they couldn't sleep for fear of snakes, scorpions, or bandits. Still, they never said, "Why did we forsake a settled place to wander in this wasteland?" When they reached this country, they were not welcomed with bread; no door was opened to shelter them from the night, for their brothers regarded them as strangers. They slept in the woods, foraged for food, accepted their fate without rebelling. God opened the eyes of a few unique individuals, who saw the plight of their brothers from Yemen, bought Kfar Hashiloah, and built them houses there, so they could live off the yield of their labor. This, in summary, is the tale of our brothers, the early settlers from Yemen who have been a boon to the country.

So much for the fathers, for I mean to deal only with the daughters.
They were like children, though already mothers. Only yesterday

they were nurslings; today it is they who offer the breast. We noticed their work but not their charm. The good Lord, cherishing their reserve, spread a film over our eyes, so we would not be led astray.

There were others, from the land of Queen Esther. Their eyes were as sweet as the raisins from which wine is made for Pesah, and their hair soft as the neck of a songbird. They wore so many layers that their limbs didn't show. Their ragged clothes concealed their beauty, like the wretched exile they had come from.

We will also mention those distant sisters we saw in Jerusalem when we made a pilgrimage there. On special occasions and holidays, we used to stroll through the Bukharan Quarter. It was the largest and most sweeping of Jerusalem's neighborhoods. All its houses were grand and elegant. Grandest of all was the splendid house built for the Messiah, our king, who, when he comes, will come to Jerusalem first. Our forefathers, elders, prophets, kings, generals, and scribes will come to receive him, along with many righteous men and dignitaries. To house them all, our brothers from Bukhara have prepared grand and elegant quarters.

So much for the houses; I will now deal only with the daughters. Their faces were full. Their colorfully embroidered garments adorned the streets. They were round, absolutely round, the embodiment of good fortune. We walked the streets of the neighborhood, our eyes on the locked doors, the closed houses—the lovely girls will appear now, they'll come out for us to see. When they came out, it didn't occur to us that young men such as we were could approach them. The reserve was so intense in that generation that a young man—even one who devoured romantic novels and perhaps composed his own—would never presume to approach a girl not destined by God to be his wife.

There were other young women from the cities of Lebanon, from Damascus, Aleppo, Izmir, Babylonia, all the cities of Ishmael—each with unique charm and beauty. The Creator made pots of goodness and offered them to us, but their loads are so heavy that, before we get a good look at them, their beauty fades. This is how it was when we were young.

Between yesterday and today, our generation has changed its aspect. Its young women have done likewise. The world was stripped of its original beauty; primeval beauty was eclipsed, and other concepts of beauty began to dominate our minds, then our hearts. Neither lovely eyes nor a warm face make a woman attractive now. Shapely limbs, a proud bearing, and light-footedness are the qualities that count. A body like an aspen, quaking with every breeze, is considered beautiful.

Now, to get back to the two Herbst daughters. I will begin with

Tamara. True, Zahara is the older one, but when they appear together, one sees Tamara first.

Tamara, as I have noted, is tall, and her cheeks are full—you might say plump. Her forehead is narrow. Her eyes are small, suggesting two bronze specks in which the artist has engraved the trace of a smile. Her hair, like her eyes, has a bronze cast to it, and she wears it loose and disheveled. As I already suggested, her eyes have a mysterious smile, but her mouth laughs openly, and it's hard to find anything that doesn't elicit laughter from this mouth. I have listed all her obvious qualities. As for the less obvious ones, who can say? So much for Tamara. Now I will turn to Zahara.

Zahara is blonde, like her mother. But she is shorter than her mother, father, or sister, as she was born in Germany during the lean years, when a pregnant or nursing woman had to struggle to find food to sustain her child. Henrietta used to tell that, when she was pregnant with Zahara, a bottle of oil fell into her hands, and she exulted over it all day. Because of this meager prenatal fare, Zahara arrived in the world serious. Tell her a joke, and you won't get even the ghost of a smile; even when she herself tells an amusing story, such as the tale of the controversy between *kvutza* members and Jewish National Fund officials who called the *kvutza* Tel Vernishevsky, after one of thousands of active Zionists whose names are forgotten once they are dead. The *kvutza* members, however, called it Kfar Ahinoam, after Ahinoam the Holstein, a comely dairy cow, arguing that whereas man eats, drinks, and produces waste, she eats the waste and produces milk, butter, cream, and cheese. Zahara doesn't so much as smile, even when she describes her friend Avraham-and-a-half, who is taller than anyone, as tall as two people, but is called Avraham-and-a-half because of his modesty. Once, when they were on a walk together, Zahara sprained her ankle, and Avraham-and-a-half picked her up and carried her. Anyone who saw them from a distance would have been astonished at such a tall woman. Zahara tells this story, too: There was a Yemenite in another *kvutza*, near Ahinoam, who was installed there by the religious party to slaughter poultry in the ritual manner and perform marriages throughout the area. He used to sit in his hut composing poems, which he sold to collectors. He tucked his legs under him and leaned to the left or on his knees as he wrote, adding poems to the cycle he was composing. Being preoccupied with his poetry, he often appeared at a wedding after the event. But everyone was so eager to please him, they set up the canopy and had him perform the ceremony anyway.

The father of these daughters sat in his study, with the mounds of printed matter this country provides in profusion laid out before him. He didn't discard it, out of respect for the written word. He didn't look it over, because he knew there was nothing of substance there. Being an orderly man, Herbst took the trouble to put these papers in order: announcements with announcements, reminders with reminders, letters with letters; another pile for memos, appeals, political flyers, and the like, put out by national and charitable institutions, scholarly and political groups, children's schools and academies, jubilee committees and plain committees—the assorted material one receives daily. An entire lifetime is not long enough to look it over.

Tamara came in and stood behind him. She leaned over him and said, "So, Manfred, you've made us a sister." At that moment, the father was not comfortable with his daughter's impudence, and he asked, "How are your classes?" Tamara answered, "Don't worry, I'll get my diploma." Her father said, "When I was your age, my studies were more important to me than the diploma." Tamara responded coyly, "When you were my age, you weren't expected to know when Issachar Ber Schlesinger was born, and you weren't expected to know that poem about the statue of Apollo wrapped in phylacteries." Herbst regarded her harshly and said, "That's absurd." Tamara said, "You see, Father, we're expected to learn those absurdities, and they determine whether we advance to the next class or fail. That's how it is, Manfred." Herbst placed both his hands on the piles of paper and muttered whatever he muttered. Tamara stared at his papers out of the corner of her tiny eyes and said, "Wow! Your desk is popping with wisdom!"

Zahara came in and said, "Hello, Father. The little one is sweet. I've never seen such an adorable baby. She's intelligent, too. When I said, 'You're my sister,' she looked me over to see if I deserve to be her sister. You've acquired some new books, Father. The shelves are full, the desk is full, even the floor is full. I won't be surprised if we have to start coming in through the chimney. What are you up to? Mother says you hardly leave the house. In that case, you'll soon have a book in print."

Herbst took a chair and said, "Sit down, Zahara. Sit down. How are you, my child?" Zahara said, "That's good advice, I'm really tired. It's nice to sit in your room, Father. I can't remember when I last sat on an upholstered chair." Herbst took another chair, moved it, and said to Tamara, "You can have a seat, too. So, Tamara, no marvels to report from school?" Tamara said playfully, "You want marvels? Who expects marvels these days? In my opinion, even small accomplishments are excessive." Herbst said, "I met up with your history teacher, and he said to me——" Tamara said, "Never mind what he said. What did you say? In your place, I would have said to him, 'A deadhead like you ought to cover his tiresome face to keep me from yawning.' " Herbst said, "Don't you think a person should know our nation's history?" Tamara said, "Then the nation should make the kind of history I want to know." Her father said, "Your tongue is quick, my dear." Tamara said, "I can't tie my tongue to a birthing bed." Zahara said, "It's impossible to talk to you, Tamara." Tamara answered, "And you're such a conversationalist? Is it essential to talk? I like people I can sit with in silence. Who's knocking on the door?"

Zahara got up to open the door and returned with a heavy, loose-limbed young man carrying a briefcase, confident he was created for a purpose. He placed his hat on the desk, took a chair, sat down, perspired, opened the briefcase, took out a notebook, leafed through it, and said to Herbst, "You haven't paid your dues; you owe one grush." Herbst paid him, and the young man added, "You probably want to subscribe to the jubilee volume the committee is putting out for Getzkuvitz." Herbst said, "I have never had the privilege of hearing that name." The young man said, "Is it possible you never heard of Getzkuvitz? He's the Getzkuvitz who . . ." and he talked on and on, until Herbst put his hands on his head, wishing for a refuge.

As soon as the visitor left, Zahara asked her father what would be done with the grush he came to collect and why he called it a grush when he meant a shilling. Her father said, "Who knows?" Zahara said, "And you gave it to him without asking what it's for?" Herbst said, "In this country, is it possible to investigate every organization that asks for money? Mother contributes to forty funds whose names she doesn't even know. If you wanted to know the names of all the funds that demand money, you would have to appoint a special secretary, and even that wouldn't do. It's easier to get rid of them with money. Words don't work." Zahara said, "The officials know that, and they set their agents on your trail. Nonetheless, one should ask them what they give you for your money." Herbst laughed and said, "They don't give me anything." Tamara said to her sister, "You're asking such questions—you, a *kvutza* member!" Zahara looked at her disdainfully and offered no response. Tamara realized she had overstepped and said to her sister, "Don't be upset, honey. Let's get back to Sarah. What do you think of her?" Zahara said, "She's a sweetheart." Tamara said, "I can picture you at her age. You were probably a sweetheart too." Herbst looked at Zahara and said fondly, "You really were a sweetheart, Zahara." Tamara stretched to her full height and asked, "What about me, Father?" Her father said, "Your enthusiasm about yourself spares me the trouble of an opinion." Tamara said, "Have I no reason to be enthusiastic about myself?" Her father smiled and said, "If I say otherwise, you won't believe me anyway. Now, what are your plans for today?" Tamara answered, "Whatever comes my way is already in my plans." Zahara answered, "I came to attend to some business for the *kvutza.*" Tamara said, "And if a sister hadn't suddenly been born to you, the business would remain undone." Zahara said, "They would have sent someone else to attend to it." Tamara asked, "Tell me, sister, did they at least pay part of your expenses?" Zahara said, "Whether they did or not makes no difference." Tamara said, with a wink, "Father, explain to her that her *kvutza* costs you more than my tuition."

Henrietta came in, carrying the baby. Zahara was quick to take the baby and give her mother her chair. Henrietta asked, "What were you talking about? I seem to be interrupting." Tamara said, "On the contrary, it's we who are interrupting your lunch preparations. What, for instance, is Mrs. Herbst preparing for her daughters' lunch? Sarahke, hush yourself and stop shrieking. Can't you see there are serious people here dealing with a weighty question?" Henrietta got out of the chair, took the baby from Zahara, and began cooing to her. Tamara said, "Bravo, Mother. You sound as if she were your first child. Sarahke, tell us, whom do you look like?" Zahara said, "I'm going out, Mother. Do you need anything from the market?" Henrietta said, "Don't be long, and bring back a good appetite." Zahara said, "I'll try, Mother. Goodbye, all you good people." Tamara said, two and a half times, "Goodbye, goodbye, and bring me back some ice cream."

— 19 —

The girls had gone, each to her place, and the household resumed its routine. Henrietta deals with the baby, the wetnurse, all the household affairs. Still, she manages to run around for certificates. Oh, those certificates! It seems that if you reach out, they'll give you one. But when you get to the office, there are none, and the official you saw yesterday, who promised to give you one today, isn't there either. There—in Berlin, Frankfurt, Leipzig, all the cities of Germany— brothers, sisters, in-laws, uncles, and aunts are rotting away, and, if you postpone bringing them here, they will be erased from the earth. Every report from there is worse than the preceding one. Sad letters, imploring letters, reproachful letters arrive daily. They reproach us for being complacent, for not lifting a finger to rescue them. Henrietta is miserable. She cries and is full of reproach—not for the English who have closed the country, nor for the malevolent officials who do their bidding and withhold certificates. She reproaches her relatives who reproach her, as if their immigration were in her control and she were obstructing it. Unaware of the runaround and abuse she endures, they repeat what they already wrote yesterday. Once again, Henrietta dresses up, runs to the Jewish Agency, to the immigration offices, to those who rule the country and, in a most cordial manner, pleads gently, ever so gently, on behalf of her sisters and brothers. She no longer distinguishes between herself and her family; she has taken in their sorrow and is one of them. Henrietta is advised to bring in her relatives on the sort of certificate that is backed up by a bank account of one thousand lirot to guarantee each immigrant's support. The Herbsts have no such resources, even if they were to sell the clothes off their backs. And besides, there are so many relatives that they would need countless thousands. Nonetheless, Henrietta does not relent. Julian Weltfremdt and Taglicht, Herbst's two friends, agree to be cosigners. Henrietta runs to a savings and loan bank to borrow money for deposit in Barclay's Bank. The manager looks at the signatures and rejects Taglicht's for, being a man of meager means, his signature is worthless. As for Weltfremdt's signature, the bank manager clucks his tongue and says, "Weltfremdt, Weltfremdt. . . . Which Weltfremdt?" "Dr. Julian Weltfremdt." If she could get Professor Ernst Weltfremdt to sign, they would accept the document and lend the money. Of course, you know Professor Ernst Weltfremdt all too well. He would give you an offprint and sign it, but a financial note—never. Still, rather than trouble her husband, Henrietta deals with most of their business, leaving him free to work. Manfred sits in his study, working.

Herbst has already prepared his lectures for the fall term. When he finished this task, it seemed to him that he had done everything. Herbst did not remember Professor Weltfremdt's suggestion that it was desirable for a faculty member to publish an occasional book or, if not a book, at least an article. Some things are desirable and some are not. Manfred Herbst's desires are in abeyance. He produces neither books nor articles, yet he assists others who produce books and articles. They all accept his help, assimilate his comments, acknowledge his editorial skills. Since they are the authors, the books are theirs. And if not for them, Herbst would have nothing to comment on. Still and all, to be correct, they thank him. Herbst doesn't mind if comments offered generously to friends are not acknowledged, nor does he blush with pleasure when they thank him. If you like, this is apathy. Or, if you prefer, it's because his mind is elsewhere. And where is it? Believe it or not, it's with Shira.

It is Manfred's way to help Henrietta with the daily chores. So much so that when she goes into town, he does the dishes, keeps an eye on the kerosene lamp, takes the laundry off the line, and, needless to say, watches the baby and chases the cattle sent into the garden by Arab shepherds, which exposes him to Sacharson's monologues, designed to prove that Arab hostility is not directed against Jews in particular, for his garden is invaded too, although everyone knows he is thoroughly Christian. Whatever Herbst does is done, not out of actual will, but in an attempt to keep himself at home. Were he to go into town, he would stop at Shira's, and he doesn't want to stop at Shira's. What does this mean, he doesn't want to? Not an hour passes without his thinking of her. Still, although he can't control his thoughts, he can control his feet. And, as long as he can control them, he keeps them at home, despite the fact that, were he to go to Shira, he and his conscience would be clear: if a man's wife doesn't offer him comfort, he has the right to do as he likes.

Henrietta doesn't offer Manfred comfort or intimacy, and Manfred no longer attempts to be intimate with her; she, because of her concerns, and he, because she has trained him not to bother her. Twice a day they eat together, discussing their relatives in Germany, the university, the students and teachers. At the core of the conversation are their daughters, who no longer need them. Zahara lives in Ahinoam. She is accepted by everyone and seems to feel she belongs there. When Zahara first said, "I'm going to a *kvutza*," her parents laughed and said, "When you see the privation and hard work, you'll come running home to Mama." But she didn't come home to Mama. She works hard—in the fields, in the garden, anywhere—enjoying her work and eating what she produces, and even her parents benefit from her labor. She sends eggs from the *kvutza*, each one the size of an ostrich egg. She sends tomatoes whose equal cannot be found in any Jerusalem market and flowers that charm the eye, give off a lovely scent, and have such sweet names. In our textbooks, flower names are translated from Latin, French, and a variety of other languages. Children in the *kvutza* give them Hebrew names, which I'm inclined to believe go back to the third day of Creation. Zahara has even found herself a young man in Ahinoam. We don't know who he is—either that tall Avraham whom they call Avraham-and-a-half, who carried her in his arms when she sprained her ankle, or Heinz the Berliner, who manages the *kvutza*'s business, or yet another one of the young men who live there. When Henrietta met Manfred, she linked her soul to him for the rest of her life. In this time and place, a young girl doesn't know to whom to cling. So much for Zahara.

Tamara still hasn't finished her studies. She plans to live in Tel Aviv until she gets her certificate and a teaching job. When does she study? We wonder about that; one more wonder to add to the seven wonders of the world. In the summer? She spends all day at the beach, swimming, sunbathing, exercising, sailing, doing all sorts of delightful things on land and sea. In the winter? She goes hiking, to get to know the length and breadth of the land. When she's in Tel Aviv, she sleeps all day. As for the night, she spends most of it in one of the cafés. Tamara and Zahara are sisters, with the same father and mother, yet they are not related in looks, height, or dress. But they do resemble each other. I will tell you something that happened to me in this connection. Once, in the winter, I was in Kfar Ahinoam, where I met Zahara. That summer I went down to Tel Aviv to bathe in the sea, where I happened to meet Tamara. I said to her, "I saw you in Kfar Ahinoam." She stretched to her full height, laughed her bronze laugh, and said, "I grew two heads taller in the interim." I looked at her, saw my error, and laughed with her. I have related all this to demonstrate that, though they seem dissimilar, they are actually alike. Not only these two, but all of the country's youth: our young men and women are all alike. When you and I were young, we studied in one room, in one school, from one Gemara text, hoping to resemble our fathers and teachers. But, in the end, we were different from them and different from each other. Here, the schools are all different, the texts are different, and the students end up resembling one another.

I will get back to the heart of my story. Actually, I have nothing new to add. Everything is in order in the Herbst household. Henrietta deals with her concerns, and Manfred deals with his. They eat together and converse with each other. When she is free from her chores for a while, he reads the news to her and adds details excluded from the paper. Many things are happening. Every day Jews are killed in secret as well as in public, and every day there are black borders in the newspaper. At first, when we saw a black band in the paper and read that a Jew had been murdered, we left our meal unfinished. Now that there is so much misfortune, one sits at the table eating bread with butter and honey, reading, and remarking, "A Jew was killed again, another man, woman, child." We sit with folded hands, yielding to murder, proclaiming, "Restraint, restraint!" They murder, kill, incinerate, while we exercise restraint. As for the authorities, how do they react? They enact a curfew. Our people are contained in their houses. They don't go out lest they be struck by an arrow, for those who shoot the arrows roam freely, unleashing their weapons anywhere. You can't say the authorities aren't doing their job, nor can you say we're not doing ours. We exercise restraint and show the world how beautiful we are, how beautiful the Jewish ethic is: even when they come to kill us, we are silent.

Manfred sits with Henrietta, reading her the news of the day, explaining England's strategy, along with the importance of the Arab factor, listing all our disappointments from the Balfour Declaration to the present. Manfred and Henrietta are not politically knowledgeable, and I doubt if Herbst has read a single book about English policy, not to mention Henrietta, who doesn't even read the newspaper. But since the riots of 1929, even they pay attention to what is going on in the country. With Jews being murdered every day, anyone who lives in the Land of Israel hears his brother's blood crying out to him from the earth, and he too cries out. The Herbsts, who were remote from politics, began to dabble in them, like every other Jew, when the trouble became more constant.

Manfred and Henrietta are sitting together. He reads and she listens; she questions and he responds, stimulating her with his responses, so that she asks further questions. Manfred says to Henrietta, "You think those who hate Jews love Arabs and those who love Arabs hate Jews. But, in fact, when they denounce Zionism, they denounce us, hoping to win the Arabs." Manfred, whose ideas lead to memories and whose memories lead to ideas, recounts earlier history, written and unwritten, provocative newspaper articles and virulent sermons delivered in mosques, inciting Arabs against Jews. Henrietta marvels at Manfred's ability to fathom politics and to put things together. Henrietta accommodates her opinions to his and makes his thoughts hers. If Henrietta understood Manfred in other areas as well as she understands his remarks on the delusions of politics, they would both be better off.

The Herbsts' position among their Arab neighbors in the Baka area began to deteriorate. Before 1929, Baka was settled by Jews who lived with Arab neighbors in peace and harmony. They rode in the same buses, the same pharmacists filled their prescriptions, and good wishes winged their way from a Jew's mouth to an Arab's ear and from an Arab's mouth to a Jew's ear. When a Jew greeted an Arab, he greeted him in Arabic, and when an Arab greeted a Jew, he greeted him in Hebrew. It was not mere lip service but a sincere, loving exchange, so that there were those who prophesied that Arabs and Jews would become one nation in the land. How? This could not be spelled out, but what reason doesn't accomplish is often accomplished by time. The power of time exceeds the power of reason, even of imagination. Suddenly, all at once, came the riots of 1929. Jewish blood was spilled by Arab neighbors who had lived alongside them like beloved brothers. Fear of the Arabs fell upon the Jews, and anyone living in their midst ran for his life. All the Jews who lived in Lower Baka or Upper Baka fled and never returned to their homes in Arab neighborhoods.

When calm was restored, several families picked up and went back to Baka. Those who found that their homes had been plundered retrieved their remaining property and settled somewhere else. Those who found their homes intact went back to live in them while they looked for housing in a Jewish neighborhood.

Herbst was the first one to go back. On Sunday, after calm was restored, Herbst emerged from the hiding place in which he, his wife, and several neighbors had taken refuge that entire previous day and night. He met Julian Weltfremdt, who asked, "What happened to your books?" He said, "They were either flung into the street or burned." Weltfremdt said, "I see a police officer. Come, I'll tell him you left a roomful of books and you want to see if they survived." They went and told the officer. He invited them into his car, and they drove to Baka.

They arrived in Baka and found that the house and study were both intact. The officer saw the books and was astonished that one man could own so many volumes. He was charmed by Dr. Herbst and said to him, "You and your family can go back to your house today, and I will guarantee your safety." Three or four days later, the Herbsts were back in their house. Manfred returned because of his books, and Henrietta returned because she was attached to the home she had put together with her own hands. Mrs. Herbst had found a mound of trash and transformed it into a delightful home.

The Herbst family lived in an Arab neighborhood in a lovely house in the midst of a lovely garden, as if the riots had never occurred. *Kaddish* was still being said for those murdered in the Land of Israel, and the land was still in mourning for these victims, yet the Herbsts' neighbors were already coming to "Madame Brovessor Herberist," one to borrow a utensil, another to bare a troubled soul: her husband was threatening divorce because of her repeated miscarriages. She asked Madam Brovessor to take her to a Jewish doctor, as she had done for other neighbors whose homes were now teeming with children, for

Jewish doctors deliver live babies. Once again Herbst's neighbors anticipated his greeting, as in the old days; in those days, however, they greeted him in Hebrew, whereas they now greeted him in Arabic or English. In the interim, England had sent many troops to the Land of Israel, and the English language was becoming widespread. Before the riots, there were four hundred English soldiers in the land; since the riots began, you couldn't make a move without running into an Englishman.

I will skip the years between the disturbances and the unrest (1929 to 1936), recounting events that occurred from 1936 on and relating them to Manfred's story. Suddenly, without the leaders of the community and its great men being aware that a catastrophe was imminent, there was a new round of violence known as the riots, in which Jewish blood flowed unrestrained, and there were so many murders and massacres that no self-preserving Jew would venture out at night, certainly not a Jew living among Arabs, for his life would be at risk.

In the Mishnah, in *Nezikin,* we are told that Tur Malka was destroyed because of a rooster and a hen, that Betar was destroyed because of a chariot peg. What was it that brought on these riots? A straw mat. They tell a story about a Polish rabbi who went up to Jerusalem and prayed at the Western Wall on Yom Kippur. He gave an order, and a straw mat was hung up to separate the men from the women. Arab leaders complained to the English governor. The governor sent soldiers to demolish the divider. Jewish leaders called a protest meeting. Arab leaders incited their people against the Jews. The Arabs came out to demolish, eliminate, annihilate all the Jews. Blessed is the Lord, who didn't abandon us.

Manfred Herbst sits at home nights and doesn't go into town. Which is a good thing, for, if he were to go there, he would stop at Shira's, and he doesn't want to stop at Shira's. In other words, he does and he doesn't want to, and, since he is ambivalent, he assumes he really doesn't want to.

A person can't give up going into town night after night—because of a friend he needs to talk to there, or for some other reason. There are countless reasons. Most important: anyone who turns away from society will find society turning away from him. As for the dangerous roads, it is dangerous to go on foot but safe in a car, even in a bus, since the buses have been equipped with iron window bars that keep out the rocks Arabs fling at passengers. The way it works is this: one puts off compulsory trips and undertakes the optional ones. Since an optional trip is optional, it ends up becoming compulsory. One night Herbst happened to be in town, which did not gratify him. So he decided to go to Shira.

He didn't really want to see her. On the way there, he began to wish that she wouldn't be in, that her house would be locked, that some passerby would detain him. As he approached her house, his legs began to tremble with desire.

He arrived at her house, saw a light, and remarked in despair, "She does seem to be at home." He began to mutter, "Let her be sick, let her not be able to get out of bed to open the door for me."

He stood at the entrance to Shira's house like a man whose mind is on a woman, who is wondering just what he sees in her, why she is in his mind, and what moved him to go to her, who concludes that, since he's there, he might as well go in and stay just long enough to say hello, then take leave of her and go home.

He came to Shira's and found she was in good health. Her face showed annoyance at having an uninvited guest. But in her heart she was glad to see him. He didn't see what was in her heart, only what was in her face. She was sitting near the light, reading a German magazine. When he came in, she took off her glasses, held the magazine in her right hand, and greeted him with the left. Her fingers were cool, and Shira herself was like her fingers. There was something about her that puzzled Herbst.

A man has his eye on a woman and is eager to see her. After a while, he goes to her. He wonders what he saw in her, what it was that attracted him to her. She is not his type, and he is not hers.

He peered at the magazine in her hand, his mouth twisted with contempt, and said, "Put down that rag." Shira answered, "It's not a rag, and I have no reason to put it down." Herbst said, "Why so angry?" Shira answered him, "It's not anger, and there's no reason for you to ask me questions." Herbst shrugged his shoulders and said, "All right, all right." Shira said, "Could it be that Dr. Herbst has nothing to say?" Herbst said, "What, for example, should I say?" Shira said, "After not showing yourself to me for weeks—a number that adds up to months, in fact—you come and start a fight. But I won't fight with you. On the contrary, I'll prove how eager I am to know how you're doing. So, how is Dr. Herbst doing? And how is Mrs. Herbst? And the baby? I think she's called Sarah. If you change the vowels, her name is like mine. So you are all well? A man whose wife and children are well is truly fortunate. Please take a chair, Dr. Herbst, and sit down, rather than wear out your legs pacing. You might like to try a new kind of cigarette; they say it's easy on the nerves."

Herbst was pacing around the room in an agitated state. He didn't look at Shira, but her evil presence was palpable wherever he turned. He encircled his left thumb with his right hand and pressed it hard. After a while, he went over to Shira, looked down at the magazine she was holding, and took her glasses. Shira said, "What are you doing? Give me my glasses and I'll read you something nice." Herbst said, "If that's the verdict, I'll sit and listen." After she had read awhile, he got up and said, "There are people who write such nonsense, and there are people who read such nonsense. For the life of me, I can't understand it." Shira said, "Tell me, please, what's so bad about this article?" Herbst said, "Tell me, please, what's so good about it?" He recognized from these words that such an argument would not lead to a meeting of hearts. He shut his mouth and thought to himself: If I hadn't lingered this long, we wouldn't be arguing.

Shira saw that his face was becoming more and more gloomy. She looked up at him and asked, "What's wrong, dear? Did something happen?" There was a trace of pity in her voice. Herbst answered, "It's nothing." Shira said, "Then why so sad?" Running her hand through his hair, she said, "A fine head of hair, no doubt about it. And a fine forehead, the forehead of a scholar. I suppose there are fine thoughts rumbling around in your head when you are at work. Manfred, will I ever see you at work?" Herbst stretched out his arms to embrace her. Shira said, "I'm making meaningful conversation, and you want to be silly." He caught her and sat her on his lap. But he wasn't happy. Although she seemed to be in his hands, she could slip away. And what was in his mind she acted upon. She slipped off his lap, stood up, arranged her blouse, and said, "I'll go and make you tea. I could even make you supper. When did you leave home? Aren't you hungry? You could sit and read the magazine while I go to the kitchen."

Shira went off to the kitchen, while Herbst sat browsing through the magazine. What he read didn't add up to anything of interest, nor did his thoughts add up to anything. Only one thing interested him: when would Shira be back, and how would she behave with him?

Shira has already been gone longer than it takes to put a kettle on the fire, boil water, and brew tea. What is taking so long? She must be preparing supper. Yes, Shira is preparing supper. She invited him to eat with her. All day she works with patients; when she gets home, she has household chores to do. In this respect, she is no different from most single people in Jerusalem and throughout the land. Some of these

women are her betters, yet their fate is in no way better than Shira's.
Before looking to them, let's look to Lisbet Neu. But Herbst was not
faring so well either: when he took the time to come to Shira, she went
off to the kitchen, leaving him all alone.

— 20 —

Shira returned and set the dishes on the table, along with butter, cheese,
tomatoes, cocoa, grapes, and berries. She moved slowly, singing some
inane song. Her voice was not pleasant, and the words were banal.
Herbst was irritated by the voice, the words, and most of all her pace.
Such a leisurely pace would provoke even the most easygoing person,
such as myself, to murder. In the interests of peace, he shut his mouth,
rather than risk saying a harsh word.

When the dishes and food were arranged, Shira went to bring a jar
of pickled olives. She sniffed them and said, "You don't have to worry
about garlic. I'll bring us some cognac. I'll have mine with the meal,
and you can drink yours before, during, after—however you like, my
dear. There's no rule." Then, with a start, she tapped her forehead and
said, "What a fool I am. I have gin, and I didn't bring it. Do you like
gin?"

Herbst sat silently, thinking to himself: The devil take you, gin and
all. He remembered that night when he was in her room for the first
time; he remembered suggesting that she change her clothes, and he
remembered everything that followed. He wouldn't offer such a suggestion now—if she went to change her clothes, she would be sure to
linger, and his chief desire was to be with her.

By now, the many kinds of food and drink that Shira had were
arranged on the table. Nothing was missing, not a fork, a knife, a bowl,
a glass. By all reason, it was time for her to sit down. What did Nadia
do? She went behind the curtain to the sink and washed her hands,
singing that same song. Her voice, like the song, was not pleasant, not
lovely. When she had dried her hands, she came to Herbst and said,
"There's water, soap, a towel. Wash your hands and we'll eat." Herbst
answered, "I don't want to wash my hands." Shira said, "You don't
want to wash your hands? One should wash before eating." Herbst said,
"I don't want to eat." Shira said, "As a nurse, an expert in health, I tell

you that a person must eat. If he doesn't eat, he'll be hungry; if he's hungry, he'll have no strength; and if he has no strength, he'll end up sick. Hurry up, sweetheart, and wash your hands. I'm hungry, and I want to eat." As she spoke, she sliced some bread, buttered it, and began to eat. Then she put down her bread and asked, "Why aren't you eating?" He said, "Because I don't want to." She said, "You're acting like a baby—not a good baby, but an obstinate one. Do you know how we handle obstinate children? We make them eat." She took the bread, stuffed it into his mouth, and said in a singsong, in baby talk, "A bite for Mommy, a bite for Daddy, and a bite for little Fredchen. Chew it well, my little one, or an ogre will come to put you in his sack and carry you off to a place where they make you eat porridge every day. Be good, my sweet. Eat up, and don't make Mommy sad. You're angry, my child. A good boy shouldn't be angry. Now you're smiling. Smile, my boy, smile. A smile is good for the heart. Tomorrow, my boy, we'll take you to the barber and ask him to make a part in your hair. But first, eat well." She brushed his head with her hand, took a pinch of hair, leaned over his head, and sniffed. As she stood there, he encircled her hips with his arms. She didn't make a move, nor did she seem to object to his gesture. Suddenly she slipped away and fled. He muttered under his breath, "Damn!" Shira put her hand to her nose and said, "Didn't they teach you not to swear, my child?" She moved close to him again, brushed her hand over his head, and said, "Eat, my friend. The cocoa will get cold." Herbst said, "The light is blinding." Shira said, "Which light?" He pointed to the lamp. "What do you mean, doctor? Should we sit in the dark?" Herbst said, "I didn't mean the lamp. I meant the light from the neighbors' houses. Please, Shira, lower the blinds." Shira said, "The more light, the more joy." Herbst made a wry face and said, "The light of your eyes is enough for me." Shira said, "I beg you, don't talk nonsense. I know my own eyes, and I know they don't glow. Unless you're referring to my glasses." Herbst went to the window and rattled the blind. Shira said, "Easy, easy, you're breaking it." Herbst said, "Then you lower it." She went to the window, singing that same song, stood looking outside, and said, "Enlightened professor, all the houses are dark. You've wrecked the pulley, and I can't lower the blind. What a schlemiel! Everything he touches breaks." She tugged at it, this way and that, over and over again. Then, turning her head, she said, "It's hopeless." Just then, the blind lowered itself. She went to the other window and lowered the blind in one move, turned her head again, and said, "Are you satisfied, my friend?" He nodded and closed his eyes. She said, "Do you have a headache?" He looked at her and said, "Why do you ask?" Shira said, "I saw you squinting, as if you were in pain."

He said, "No, it's nothing." She said, "Good." He said: "Not good." She said, "Not good?" He said, "Good, good." She said, "When someone feels good, he doesn't yell, 'Good, good.' " He said, "Good, good." Shira laughed and said, "There you go again. Please tell me, just who is feeling good?"

Herbst opened his arms and said, "Come, Shira, come." Shira said, "But I'm here." He said, "Come, sit on my lap." She said, "He can barely hold himself up, and he wants to hold this heavy load—freckles, eyeglasses, and all. Eat first. It might make you stronger." Herbst said, "I don't need food." "You don't need food, but you do need this dismal load on your lap. You're swaying like a windmill. I wonder if you have a fever. Give me your hand; I'll check your pulse. The pulse is all right, but Fredchen isn't. Let me listen to your heart." After she listened to his heart, he said, "Now let me listen to yours." Shira said, "I, my friend, am normal. I don't need to be examined." Meanwhile, he reached out and put his hand on her heart. She shouted at him, "You're out of your mind! Anyone could peek in and see." Alarmed, he looked around and then began to shout, "That's a lie, Shira! A lie! No one is looking." Shira said, "But someone could look." Herbst said, "You pulled down the blinds, so no one can see." Shira said, "But they can guess what you're doing." Herbst said, "If they can guess, let them guess." Shira said, "It doesn't matter at all to you, my friend, but it matters to me." Herbst said, "Don't be——" Shira said, "What is my Manfredchen asking me not to be?" Herbst said, "I'm not asking anything." Shira laughed and said, "If you were asking nothing, you'd be doing nothing." Herbst said, "So what am I doing?" As he spoke, he put his arm around her hips. She loosened his grip. His head drooped, and he was silent.

Shira said, "You're tired. Lie down for a while, then you can get up and go home." Herbst stretched out on her bed, closed his eyes, and waited, expecting Shira to come and sit near him. When she didn't come, he opened his eyes and discovered she was nowhere in sight. He muttered, "The hell with her, where did she go?" He looked around and saw that the table was bare: Damn; she went to do the dishes. She has to do them now, when I feel as if I was flung into a blazing furnace.

And, in truth, the fire had already taken hold. He was like fire within fire, flaming and enflaming; he was overwhelmed by a sweetness that melts the whole body. He no longer existed; nor did any part of him exist, other than that mounting sweetness. When he stirred and realized he was alone, he pricked up his ears but heard nothing. He began to wonder. When some time had passed and she wasn't back, he began to worry: What if she doesn't come back? If she didn't come back and he were found stretched out on her bed, he'd be in trouble. Anyway, she certainly hadn't gone far. If she had, she wouldn't have left her purse and her powder. Then he saw his shadow on the wall, and his blood froze. Shira returned.

Shira came back, dressed in light clothes, giving off the good scent of lavender. Herbst reached out to her and whispered, "Come, Shira. come." She sat beside him, her body quivering. He thought to himself: If I had any sense, I would lie here and let her quiver, let her know what it's like. But he had no sense, and he didn't lie calmly. Shira said gently, "You're in such a frenzy, so stormy and wild. Take off your jacket and cool off." She got off the bed to make room. As he struggled to get his jacket off, with her standing by, there was an uproar outside and the sound of running. Shira opened a window, stuck her head out, then turned back toward Herbst, saying, "It's the curfew. They've announced another curfew until six in the morning." Herbst was in a panic. He didn't know what he would do, but he knew he had to get back immediately, that he couldn't not go home.

"When does it start?" he asked in alarm. Shira said, "It starts now and is in effect until morning. You want to go? Do you have a pass?" Herbst said, "I don't have any such thing." Shira said, "Then how will you go? The police will stop you." Herbst said, "But I must get home." Shira said, "You must get home, but how? If you go out, a policeman will stop you immediately and take you to the station. You'll have to spend the night there." Herbst said, "I'm sure you understand, Shira, that I have to go. Think of something, Shira. I'm dying, I'm going crazy." Shira looked at him irately and said, "No need to go crazy. I'll talk to Axelrod, my neighbor. He may agree to take you home." Herbst said, "Go on, Shira. Ask Axelrod to take me home. Who's Axelrod?" Shira said, "Axelrod is Axelrod's son." Herbst said, "You're teasing me." Shira said, "It's as I said. This Axelrod is the son of the Axelrod you met at the hospital when you brought Mrs. Herbst to the maternity section. Papa Axelrod is a pest of the first water, but the son is a daring young man who drives a bus for Hamekasher. I'll see if he's in." Herbst looked at her imploringly and said, "Go on, Shira, go. But can you allow yourself to be seen in those clothes?" A few minutes later, he heard the sound of a car. A broad-shouldered young man came in and said, "Hop in, professor. Don't worry, I'll take you home."

Herbst parted from Shira on the run. He got into the car and sat on the edge of the seat, compressing himself into his body, his mouth agape with wonder that, at an hour when no one was allowed to be out, a driver had agreed to take him home. He watched the driver, who held the steering wheel in his hand and made the car move. Herbst realized what a great favor the driver was doing for him and wanted to thank him, but he couldn't find the words. He sat gaping, his lips on fire, dismayed to find himself in a car in the heart of the dark night. He sank into the cushions, listening to the wheels of the car turning and rolling onward. He began to reflect: It's good that I'm going home, but the essence of the matter isn't good. He covered his eyes with both hands and reviewed what had happened to him with Shira. Actually, nothing at all had happened, so why the embarrassment and regret? After a while, he uncovered his eyes. He looked at his hands and was surprised to find that the darkness had not clung to them.

Again he buried himself in the cushions, alerting his ears to the sound of the car wheels clattering through the silent city, the silence receding before them as he approached his home.

Near the Allenby Barracks, two armed Syrian policemen popped out and stopped the car. They were so short that their rifles overshadowed them. They rattled their weapons to intimidate the passengers, made menacing faces, and spoke menacingly—like warriors seizing captives. Axelrod eyed them calmly, like a customer examining toy soldiers to see whether they are made of lead or tin. He said to them, "The man I am driving is a great professor, one of our great university professors, and he can't be detained." Whether or not the policemen knew what a professor was, they understood from the driver's tone that his passenger was important and to be treated with respect. They signaled with their rifles and cleared the road for him. Shortly thereafter, Herbst found himself at home.

— 21 —

On the twenty-first of Heshvan, Herbst went up to Mount Scopus for the opening ceremonies of the academic year. It was his habit to go to these ceremonies without his wife, as Henrietta had trained him to go alone whenever he could manage without her.

The main hall of the Rosenblum Building was full. In addition to professors, lecturers, advisers, students, and university officials, there were guests from Jerusalem, Tel Aviv, Haifa, and the rest of the country's towns and settlements—invited guests who were guaranteed a seat, as well as uninvited guests, the sort who push their way into every public place and grab the reserved seats.

It was past three in the afternoon. Early autumn permeated the spacious, high-ceilinged room with air for which any attire was suitable. One would not feel chilly in summer clothes, nor would winter clothes be too heavy. Similarly with the doors: when they were open, they didn't let in a chill and when they were closed, it wasn't too warm. The guests chatted with one another about the university, its buildings, the courses for which there were still no teachers, and Mount Scopus and its environs. They didn't raise their voices as they talked; even those who were in the habit of making themselves heard, at any time and in any place, behaved respectfully. The windows drew light directly from the sky itself, with nothing intervening. There were many people present who felt, at that moment, that this structure was unique among structures and this setting unique among settings. Individuals who tended to respond only to what was created to be useful to man were astonished by what they saw from Mount Scopus: the city, the Temple Mount, the wilderness inhabited by infinite colors, the Dead Sea, whose quiet blue flows up from the bottom of the deep, capped by hills and valleys that soar and dip and wrinkle, with every wind etching shapes above like those below, from which a breeze ripples upward and flutters overhead.

On the platform and close by sat the leaders of the *yishuv*, who arrived early, before the proceedings began, unlike those functionaries who make a point of coming late, so they can feast their eyes on the crowd rising to honor them. Suddenly all conversation ceased, the hall was silent. All eyes were on the president of the university, who had begun his speech. He had been a Reform rabbi in his youth and had been forced to leave his post because he was a Zionist. Although he retained some of the mannerisms of the Reform rabbinate, which are considered ridiculous in this country, his height, style, and dignity led even the cynics in the hall to listen to what he had to say.

As he did every year, he expounded on the role of the Hebrew University, which is not merely the university of the Land of Israel, but belongs to Jews everywhere and is destined to break down the boundaries of Jewish learning, fusing Jewish studies with the humanities and natural sciences to form one single discipline—for everything human is Jewish, and everything Jewish is human.

After outlining the future of the university, he enumerated the innovations of the past academic year, as well as those on the agenda for the coming year: who was appointed lecturer and who was promoted to the rank of senior lecturer, associate professor, or tenured professor. Although most of this information was already public knowledge, everyone listened attentively, for it is one thing to hear a rumor in the marketplace and another to hear it from the president of the university at the official opening of the new academic year.

After listing the names of the faculty members and the promotions, he told how many buildings had been built and how many new students enrolled.

After finishing this account, he spoke about the obligations of teachers and students. Their purpose was twofold and manifold, for, apart from coming to this institution for the sake of learning—some to study and some to teach—a further duty was thrust upon them: to fortify the Torah and the Jewish ethic, without which there could be no future for the nation and no basis for society.

After mentioning all the lofty and exalted hopes invested in the university and in rebuilding the land, he lowered his voice and spoke of impending dangers, dangers we did not foresee, with the power to undermine the lofty and sublime hopes that had brought us here.

Everyone sat and listened, not so much to the speech as to a voice from their own hearts that spoke without words and began to take form. Earlier, as long as there was peace in the world, in all the lands of our exile it was possible to dream of the return to Zion, the revival of the people and its language. Some unique individuals added a dream to this dream: the dream of a Hebrew University in Jerusalem. How? The dreamers never explained this dream. When they were awake, they could provide no key to it. Our holy language remained unsuited to scholarship; Hebrew-speaking professors were scarce, and Hebrew was as far from the lips as dreams from reality. The war suddenly erupted, the world was in chaos, and not one of the dreamers dreamed a good dream. The towns Jews lived in were eradicated, and hundreds of thousands of Jews were killed in the war and its aftermath. At last those at war were worn out and no longer able to fight. All weapons were at rest, and there was no more war. Some of those who survived the war thought about returning to their homes. They found no way to travel. There were no vehicles, no horses to ride. Highwaymen prowled the roads, which were in disrepair and difficult to traverse by foot. The survivors were pressed to leave those places in which they had found refuge from the sword of war, because of hardships and a shortage of food. So they plucked up their courage and, without regard for themselves, set off. They returned to their towns and found desolation, their houses burned to the ground. Anyone who found his home intact found it occupied by a vicious Christian, who held on to the house, shouting at him, "Jew, what do you want here? Go to Palestine!" During the war, Britain had issued a declaration and even published a letter saying that she viewed with favor the opening of the gates of the Land of Israel to the people of Israel. This message had not yet reached people's hearts, though the hostile voices of those who stole our houses resounded wherever Jews sought their homes and property.

They swallowed their pride and looked elsewhere. Walking from place to place, they found nothing. They began to despair and asked, "Could it be, God forbid, that Israel's destruction has been decreed and that this is the beginning of the end?" A very few individuals overcame these misfortunes and said, "Salvation will come from these very misfortunes." How? Salvation isn't brought about by reason.

In any case, there were a few individuals who ignored logic and didn't wait for salvation. They banded together and went up to this land. They wandered from nation to nation, from country to country, along with those hordes returning from the war, its disabled victims, wounded human fragments, thieves, and murderers. At last they came to a port and hired leaky vessels that took them up to heaven and down to the abyss. Some reached the gates of death, and some reached the gates of this land. When they arrived, they engaged in hard labor. All day they were consumed by the sun; at night, by insects and other ills with which God blighted the land. Without regard for themselves, they paved roads, made settlements, and cured the ills of the land, preparing it for the next generation and for all our brothers-in-exile. Today they are here in Jerusalem, our glorious city, capital of our land, the Land of Israel, at our sanctuary–university at the opening ceremonies of the academic year. They sit at the Hebrew University, on benches like the ones in a real university. And what is the language of instruction? Hebrew. Disregard the fact that some of the professors are not very learned. You could say that they are like clay shards placed between beams, that great men will come tomorrow and fill the house with scholarship. Do you ask, "Who needs a university in an age such as this, when books are widely available and anyone who wishes can open a book and learn?" As long as other countries support universities, it is fitting for us to have one too.

When the ceremony was over, Herbst left for home. There were many cars at the university gate, waiting to take the guests back to town. But what always happens, on any day, at any hour, happened then. Those who value time, love work, and behave decently are shoved aside by loudmouthed idlers in noisy pursuit of nothing, who push and shove, occupying every space without leaving an inch, preventing you from getting home and back to the work that was interrupted by these

ceremonies. All the cars were occupied and would be filled again when
they returned by those who jump lines and are stronger than you. This
being the case, Herbst chose to go back on foot.

He turned away from the vehicles, toward the edge of the road,
stopping to adjust the elegant tie he had worn for the occasion and to
decide which road to take, for there were many roads branching off this
way and that, each one scenically special, so that it was hard to choose
one over the others. Before Herbst had a chance to decide which he
would take, he heard the sound of a car behind him. He moved aside,
turned toward the car, and saw four or five of his friends in it, among
them Professor Wechsler, who invited him to join them. When Herbst
noticed that Axelrod was driving, he had no wish to get in, for Axelrod
might mention that he had given him a lift the other night, and it would
be best if they knew nothing about it. He thanked them for the invitation and went on.

Twilight. All over the mountain and in the valley, everything was
still. The sky above was overlaid with an array of shifting colors throwing light on each other, blending, modulating, appearing, and disappearing in a flash, only to be succeeded by others, still others. Before
these settle in, another round appears, and they swallow each other up.
Dirt and rock take shape, as do shrubs and grass, fragrant grass which,
along with thorns, briars, and wild brush, fills the arid land with its
good smell as the day dims. Each step bestows peace, each breath cures,
taking in the scent of field grass, a remnant of summer, born of the early
rains. Suddenly, the lights were turned on and the whole city glowed.
Over the city, in the skies above, the moon could be seen beginning its
tour.

The evening was fine and pleasant, the air clear and fresh, like most
autumn evenings in Jerusalem after the first rains. Herbst was in a
similar state. The days spent at home, in his study, in the garden with
Henrietta, peaceful and quiet, had a favorable effect. But for the somber
thoughts that wrinkled his brow, Herbst was like a young man.

Herbst was already at the foot of the mountain, near town. Those
who live in outlying neighborhoods, who come to town and are not
in a hurry to get home, spend an hour or two roaming Jerusalem's
streets or seeing friends. Herbst, who had had his fill of society even
before the ceremonies, wasn't eager for his colleagues or their conversation. But he had an urge to see the whole city, to go beyond the wall,
which he didn't do. If he were to go there, he would become involved,
endlessly so and without limits. Yet much as he resists, he is drawn
there, because of a place he never saw, though he knew he was already
there many times.

He took himself toward the post office, from there to the Jewish Agency, from there to Zion Square, and from there to a small department store. He looked in all the windows and came back to the one with fountain pens that sprang forward as if from inside a mirror. Actually, there was a large mirror beneath the pens, which were suspended over it on invisible string. A tiny light was attached to every pen, shining on it, on its shadow, and on the face of anyone who happened to be studying the display. While Herbst was considering which pen he would like to buy, his reflection peered out at him from the mirror, decked out in the finery he had worn for the opening ceremonies of the new academic year. It was a long time since Herbst had been so elegantly dressed and a long time since he had felt so fresh. He stopped to adjust the tie Henrietta had bought him for his birthday, with money held back from household expenses, and gazed into the mirror.

The tie was in place; it hadn't stirred, not this way, not that. His thoughts, however, were stirring this way and that. He dismissed the pen he had in mind to buy for himself, as well as his thoughts about what he would write with the pen, and began listing the names of the lecturers and professors the president of the university had mentioned in his address. He repeated the names of all those who had been promoted. He considered each one of them—the books they had produced, the articles they had written. He envied neither them nor their works. He would have enjoyed discussing academic politics with his colleagues, but he wasn't drawn to any one of them. This one never makes a clear statement; that one has a wife who doesn't let him get a word in, and, before he has a chance to answer you, the house is brimming with her conversation. This fellow is even worse than the other two. He takes what you say and twists it, so you wear yourself out explaining what you meant, and you can never be sure he won't quote you on something you never said. Still worse is the one who talks only about himself—what Mrs. So-and-so said to him after visiting him with a group of tourists, who felt deeply honored by his hospitality, and what Professor So-and-so wrote to him about his new book. Julian Weltfremdt is the one person worth listening to, but, not being a member of its inner circle, he tends to demolish the university and its professors with every breath. Also, if you come at night, you find him and his wife sitting across from each other at one table with one light. She is reading the novels she reads, while he covers his face with a newspaper or book to avoid seeing them. You begin talking, and, as soon as she says a word, Julian gets up, takes his hat, puts a hand on your shoulder, and says, "How about a walk?"

A man has many friends and no preference about which one to go to, so he doesn't go to any of them. While Herbst was deliberating, he arrived at a point where several roads intersect. One of them leads to Shira. I will waste no words. Of all the roads, Herbst chose the one that leads to Shira.

— 22 —

Shira was dressed in warm, unattractive clothes. Her face was tired, her cheeks smooth. Only her freckles were prominent, so enlarged that it seemed as if a part of her right cheek had been taken away. The room smelled of some liniment, the kind you apply to a bruise. Either she had been tending patients' bruises or she herself was bruised. Herbst stared at her with probing eyes, like a man studying a woman he dislikes in order to identify the power that draws him to her. He saw again what he had already seen: although she wasn't ugly, she certainly wasn't beautiful. He had called her Nadia in the beginning, before he really knew her. Actually, this name suggests no particular image; still, it suits her better than Shira.

Herbst changed his face to register fury and considered: Maybe I won't address her in the familiar second person. He hadn't arrived at a decision when he said, "I've interrupted you." He was prepared to hear her say, "I'm busy," and to answer, "If so, I won't keep you. I'll be on my way." But rather than answer his implied question, she said, "So you got home all right." Herbst said, "That's an old story. It's been almost a month." Shira said, "A month and a half. Still, you haven't forgotten me, and you took the trouble to stop by. One can't say the man has no curiosity." Herbst said, "It's not a question of curiosity. I've been busy. I had to prepare first-rate lectures for the winter semester. Students are beginning to come from all over; many have been at European universities and can't be offered rubbish." Shira said, "And you stopped working to come here." Herbst said, "You want to know how I could stop working to come here? Because, I already prepared some of the lectures, so I'm able to take the time." Shira answered in a relaxed tone, "You prepared your lessons and found yourself with a little time, some of which you've decided to donate to me. Now I need some time to arrange my thoughts and consider what to do with the gift of time you were kind enough to give me. If I were sure I would be able to arrange my thoughts in a single evening, I would tell you to take a chair and sit down. But I'm afraid I, too, might need a month and a half to arrange my thoughts, and that may be too long for you to wait." Herbst said, "If you don't mind, I'll sit down." He thought to himself: I'll stay until she finishes complaining, then I'll be on my way.

Herbst sat and Shira sat, making no move to change her clothes. Didn't she realize such clothes were not likely to win hearts? Not to mention her complaints, or the look on her face. He thought of asking if she was sick but decided not to, for she would surely notice from his tone of voice that he was unsympathetic. He took a cigarette from the pack on the table and began smoking fiercely, to create his own atmosphere. As he smoked, he took out his own cigarettes and offered them to Shira. "I don't want to smoke," she said. Herbst blew smoke rings and said, "You don't want to smoke? Then what do you want?" Shira stared at him and said, "What do I want? I want to know how Mrs. Herbst is doing." Herbst growled a response. "She's fine." Shira said, "She's fine. And how is the baby? Her name is Sarah, isn't it?" Herbst growled at her again, "She's fine." Shira continued to question him. "And Dr. Herbst himself, how is he?" "Me? Yes, I'm fine." Shira stared at him and said, "Then you, the baby, and Mrs. Herbst are all healthy and sound. You are such a successful man, Dr. Herbst. A man whose entire family is in good health, lacks nothing. What else did I want to ask you? What are your views, doctor, about men who beat women?" He looked at her in alarm and said, "What was that?" Shira looked at him with malice and affection, and said, "I asked for Dr. Herbst's views on men who beat women." Herbst answered, "They are depraved, absolutely depraved." Shira looked at him with smiling eyes and said, "I think so too, and I knew that's how you would answer. Tell me, my friend, are you not capable of beating a woman?" Herbst cried out in alarm, "No!" and realized he was on the verge of slapping her face. Shira said, "Well said, my boy. You must never strike a woman. Women are fragile, and one must be gentle with them."

Shira sat on her chair, becoming one with it, her shoulders contracting, while Herbst sat crushing the cigarette with his fingers. The lines on his palms began to jump and were covered by dry, searing heat. His temples throbbed and sweated. Once or twice he was about to speak, but the words remained on the tip of his tongue. He stared with enmity at the remains of the cigarette in his hand, its embers singeing his fingernails. Again he wanted to say something and didn't know how to begin, although he knew that, if only he could begin, words would come. He got up and moved his chair, put the remains of his cigarette in the ashtray, snuffed it out, sat down again, passed his tongue over his lips, and asked in a whisper, "What were you talking about and what did you have in mind, Shira?" Shira looked at him, lowering her head and speaking from deep in her chest. "And if I tell you, will you understand?" Herbst said, "Why wouldn't I understand?" Shira said, "Maybe you will and maybe you won't. Even if you do, I don't know why I asked such an odd question. Tell me, don't you think it's an odd question?" Herbst said, "It is an odd question, but allow me to ask what led to such a question." Shira said, "You think I know?" Herbst said, "Don't you know?" Shira said, "I don't really know, but, because you asked, I will tell you something."

Shira touched the tip of her nose, which was colored by the powder she had sprinkled on it, and asked in a leisurely tone, "What was I going to say?" Herbst said, "You were going to answer my question." Shira said, "You mean about that odd question? I'll tell you, if you like."

Shira said, "The event took place a month and a half ago plus two days. Why did I say 'plus two days,' when actually it was a month and a half ago plus three days, exactly one night after the curfew. Remember, you were here the night they declared the curfew. So, one night later, a certain person happened by, not to my room but to the landlord's apartment. A respectable person, healthy, not young but not old. In any case, his age didn't show. He was an engineer by profession. A marine engineer, or some such thing. What do I know? Until that day, I never knew there were such engineers, though it's logical that, if there are boats, they didn't build themselves, and, just as you need someone to build houses, you need someone to build boats. Anyway, the engineer I'm telling about was related to the landlady, or maybe the landlord. For the life of me, I couldn't say whose relative he was, hers or his. It happened that he came to visit his relatives, but they had gone to some *kvutza* because of a tragedy involving their daughter. The night before, her son, a child of about five and a half, had wandered off and encountered a jackal that devoured him, leaving only a headless skeleton. The architect was alone in his relatives' home. What am I saying? I said 'architect' when, in fact, he was an engineer, a marine engineer. That gentleman, the engineer, was here in the home of his relatives, and I was in my room, paying no attention to him. It's possible that I didn't even know such a person was in the house with me. After dinner I said to myself: Why sit in the room when I could sit on the balcony? Hadn't the landlady given me permission to sit out there whenever she and her husband were out? I put on comfortable clothes and went up to the landlady's apartment and out onto the balcony, where I sat on a chair, allowing the wind to curl my hair and the moon to play hide-and-seek with me. I thought how lucky it was to have such a balcony, and now I was the lucky one. I heard footsteps. I'm not saying the footsteps concerned me. If someone was there, it was his right to move around. After a while, the architect appeared. Manfred, I'm talking, but you're not listening. Are you listening? If so, I'll tell you what followed."

Shira continued. "The engineer came in, straight as a mast. And his shoulders—such shoulders! How can I describe them? Let me just say that, if he were to put me on his shoulders, I wouldn't say, 'There's not room,' although I would hope he wouldn't try to add one more like me. He bowed and said, 'If the lady will allow me, I'll sit for a while.' I answered, 'You have more right to be here than I do.' He bowed again and said, 'With your permission.' And he sat down. I sat as if he weren't there. He began talking and said roughly this: 'You don't seem to be busy, so if I talk, I won't really be interrupting.' I looked at my hands, which were idle, and said, 'I'm not really doing anything.' He sat in silence, and I was silent too. I thought: Why sit idly? I'll go get a sock to darn, or the wool I bought when the curfew began, and I can work on my sweater. I was too lazy to get up. I sat staring straight ahead, making a point of not looking at him, so he wouldn't think I meant to engage him in conversation. I assumed he would take out a thick cigar, which is what that type of powerful man usually smokes. He didn't take out a cigar but began talking again. What did he talk about? If you like, I could repeat every word, but neither you nor I would be enthralled by his words, would we? So I'll summarize the whole conversation in two or three words. What did he say?

"He really didn't say anything. But his voice, Manfred! His voice swept me off to distant places. After sailing with me from sea to sea and from continent to continent, he took me to Paris, which that gentleman was in the habit of visiting every year. To be more concrete let me tell you this: he sat and talked, and I sat and listened. Manfred, anyone who saw us would have said, 'They're like a young man and his maid when their time is ripe.' Manfred, those scowls are uncalled for! What was I saying? He was like a youth courting his girl with engaging words. But I knew that words are one thing, the heart another. After touring those places with me, we were back in Jerusalem. Extending his hand toward Jerusalem, he said, 'This is no city. It's a desert, an eternal desert that sprouts earlocks, old men in frock coats stiff as Jerusalem stone, and even its sun is arid as stone.' After he finished what he had to say about Jerusalem, he started on me. He shook his head at me and said, 'Imagine, a young girl sitting here, lonely and solitary in this arid desert, under this arid sun, not enjoying what's been created for her.' I wanted to say, 'No, sir, I'm neither young nor lonely,' but his voice was so lulling that I didn't say a word. Manfred, I see you are bored. No? Then I'll continue. So I sat in silence while he sat and talked. He said roughly this: 'The lady is alone because she ignores those who seek her company.' All the time he was talking, he held something in his hand—not a cigar, for a cigar is quite thick, but this object was even thicker. All the time, the object kept swinging. Not on its own; the one who held it kept swinging it. I said to myself: I'll look and see what's in his hand. I looked and saw it was a whip—a small whip, but even a small whip is a whip. I began to be afraid he would strike me with the whip. He swings the whip without noticing that I'm afraid. I become more and more terrified that he may strike me—more precisely that he will surely strike me. He has only to extend his hand, swing the whip, and strike. With all my strength, I stare at the whip. He leads the whip this way, then that way and I am in terror. I didn't have the strength to get up. I was too weak to run. What could I do? I could call for help, but even if I was saved from his clutches, I wouldn't be saved from gossip. If he wants to hit me, let him hit me; I'm sure he won't kill me. This gentleman—the one we've been discussing, the one I've been telling you about—is slowly being transformed. His face is malevolent, and there is an evil glare in his eyes. As he gazes at me, malevolently, I see he is reading my mind. I sit there, unable to stir. Every limb contracts. And he—the one I'm telling you about—sits opposite me, staring through those malevolent eyes. And they—those eyes—continue to be transformed, to blaze and glow. I'm not saying his eyes were appealing, but they were powerful. Some serpents immobilize their prey with such eyes. My eyes were drawn to his, so that I forgot the whip and the fear. I knew only that my limbs relaxed. Manfred, are you sleeping? It's not nice to sit with a woman wringing your paws like a bereaved bear." Herbst produced a rasping growl that seemed to mean: Tell me more.

Shira continued. "The fear became more intense, and my teeth began to chatter. I asked myself: Why so frightened? He is a polite, intelligent man with a whip in his hand; so what? If there's a whip in his hand, does that mean I have to be afraid? To convince myself I wasn't afraid, I got up. As I got up, I heard the sound of a whip and felt a burn on my flesh. That man, my dear Manfred, that engineer, swung his whip and hit my arms, which were bare since it was a warm night and I was wearing a sleeveless shirt. After he did what he did, he asked, 'Where to, miss?' He asked in a tender voice, and even his eyes were no longer evil. But, as for me, my dear Manfred, my arms were like torches. Even later, in bed that night, when I looked at them, all the marks of the whip were still coiled around my skin like blue-black snakes. I raised my voice and yelled at him. You'd think he would have panicked and run off. He didn't panic; he didn't run off. On the contrary, he sat down again and looked at me with equanimity. I stood there, immobile. Suddenly, another rattle of the whip, followed by a burning sensation on my knees, which were exposed, since it was a warm night and I was wearing shorts. I was stunned into silence and rubbed my flesh; first my arms, then my knees. A tremor of sweetness filtered through, permeating my entire body. He peered at me and asked, 'Good?' That was his very word, as if someone had asked him for a favor and, after granting it, he were asking if he had performed it well. Manfred, you're wringing your paws like a bear again. What do you want to ask?" Herbst muttered, "And then what?"

Shira said, "That's an odd question. What did you expect? There was nothing further. He threw down the whip and looked at me, his eyes devoid of evil. I asked him, 'Why did you do that to me?' He looked at me in dismay, as though I were ungrateful. I changed my tone and shouted, 'Who gave you permission to do that?' He answered in a whisper, 'But, madam, wasn't it all for you?' I screamed at him, enraged, 'Get out of here! Go!' He got up and said, "With your permission, madam, I am going. Good night, madam.' I pointed to the chair and said, 'Sit down.' He turned and sat down. I said to him, 'You owe me an explanation.' He answered, 'These things are good, and you yourself probably recognize that they're good, so there's no need to explain.' I said to him, 'I have the right to an explanation.' He sat and told me things I don't mean to repeat. What did he tell me?"

Shira told Herbst what the engineer told her, but we will skip the engineer's story and return to our own.

Shira said, "As he talked, he picked the whip up from the floor. I trembled, thinking he was taking the whip in order to strike me again. Believe it or not, I was ready. What did he do? He bowed graciously and left. I expected him to come back, but he didn't. Not that night, nor the next day. Not to the balcony, nor to my room, though I didn't stir from my room. He knew I was there, because I spent the day straightening my room and my things, and when I straighten my room and my things, I always sing. I sometimes sing loudly, though not on purpose, because I know I don't have much of a voice."

Herbst asked Shira, "When did you see him again?" Shira tapped her forehead with her hand and said, "Good morning, sir. His Highness has deigned to wake up? What did you ask? If I saw him again? Why should I see him! I didn't see him; I saw him only three times. Once in the hallway, once on the stairs, and twice in the hall again. When he saw me, he inquired about my health and was supremely polite. I looked at his hands, searching for the whip. His hands were empty. They were firm, smooth, and without hair or wrinkles. When I saw him later on, I asked him where the whip was. He answered in a whisper, 'It's in my briefcase. I'm about to leave.'"

Herbst asked Shira, "And before leaving, he came to say goodbye?" Shira said, "If he had come, I would have thrown him out." "Why?" "You're asking why? After what he did to me, I suppose I was expected to bow my head to my navel and implore him, 'Please come to me; please come, my lord and master'? I'll show you something if you like, Manfred." She bared her arm, and he saw a scar. Herbst asked Shira, "From his whip?" Shira shook her head and said, "I did it myself." Herbst said, "And that was sweet, too?" Shira said, "Please, I'm asking you not to be sarcastic." Herbst said, "But didn't you yourself say . . .——" Shira said, "I said what I said, and you have no right to say things like that to me." Herbst said, "Come, Shira, don't fight with me." He stood up, encircled her hips with his arms, and closed his eyes, leaving a tiny opening. He saw that she was looking at him. He opened his eyes and looked at her. She covered his eyes with her hands and remained in his arms, exhausted.

— 23 —

Late that night, he left her and went on his way. She stood at the window, waving. He waved back and would have run, as it was past the hour when one is normally home in bed. But he couldn't run, lest she see him and say: He's running away from me. Also, what he remembered slowed him down. At the same time, he was pondering:

When Henrietta asks where I've been, what will I say? Actually, she doesn't usually ask questions, but what if she does? He went through all the possible excuses, how plausible they were, and which ones required caution, for the very person you were counting on for an alibi could have been in your house while you were off with that woman. Anyway, whatever he considered either ruled itself out or had a glaring flaw. An honest person finds it hard to tell a lie even when he wants to. Having failed to find an excuse, he felt pathetic. Not because of Shira, not because of the excuse, but because of Henrietta, who made it necessary to seek an excuse. He reached the end of Shira's alley and was somewhat relieved; anyone who saw him now would have no reason to suspect he was coming from Shira's.

There was no one in sight. But the one he had just taken leave of was present, with all her power and intensity. Herbst was not happy. When he was with her, he wasn't happy. Now that he was rushing home, he wasn't happy at all.

It was a fine night, charged with silence; the special silence of Jerusalem, an inner silence that exudes sweetness. Herbst hurried home, indifferent to the antics of the night, which, even for a Jerusalem night may have been unique in its sweet silence, or to the hour, equally unique in its pleasant sweetness.

He was already at King George Road, having come out of the web of narrow alleys near where Shira lived. When Manfred Herbst first came to Jerusalem, one couldn't walk here because of all the stones, rocks, boulders, and gaping potholes. When Rehavia was built, the stones were cleared, the rocks dug up, the boulders uprooted, and the holes filled with dirt. A long, wide road, suitable for pedestrians and vehicles, was built. Traffic was constant, but, as it was past midnight, the Talpiot bus, which stops in Baka and could have brought Herbst home in no time, was no longer running.

The silence had moved on, and wherever it went, it was pursued by cars flying past, one after another. Where were they all coming from? The high commissioner's residence. The high commissioner was having a party attended by many guests—people of wealth and status, diplomats, and even some *yishuv* leaders. They whizzed by in shiny cars with elegant interiors, their rubber wheels drinking up the earth. Manfred Herbst was small and humble. Not only was he on foot, but he had to keep swerving this way and that to avoid being run down. Every day you read in the papers that a man was run over by a car, a car struck a woman and killed her, children were playing in the street when a car came and crushed one of them. Herbst heard about a poor Jew who sold poultry, who happened to live between Mekor Hayim and Talpiot. One day he went out to slaughter a bird. A car ran into him and broke his ribs. He was taken to Hadassah Hospital, where the doctors labored over him until he was out of danger—out of danger, but not out from under the crippling effects of the car. Now he lived with some poor relative, sharing his meager resources. Shattered, broken, disheartened, depleted by the accident, he could no longer use his legs and pursue a livelihood. By rights, the driver should have compensated him for pain and suffering, medical expenses, disability, and embarrassment. But the rich are stingy where they should be extravagant and extravagant where they should be stingy. When the victim's family decided to sue, the driver hired a lawyer who proved, through a little-known clause in the legal code, that his client was not required to pay. The offending party won the case. He paid his lawyer a fee that may have exceeded what the victim would have claimed had he won. That day, the son of the lawyer went with his friends on one of those hikes that have become the vogue. They arrived at some spot where they found a land mine the Mandate soldiers had neglected to clear. They picked it up, played with it, got bored, and threw it down. It hit that boy, the son of the lawyer, leaving him crippled. There are those who see connections, who connect the tale of the son with the tale of the father; may those who are experts in the laws of the Mandate see that there are other laws, higher ones. But what wrong did the child do, and why did he have to answer for his father's sins? Moreover, why wasn't the driver answerable for his car's crime?

Herbst was already at the train station. He turned toward Baka, but he still had no excuse to offer Henrietta. He saw Dr. Taglicht approaching. Where from? Ramat Rachel. Had he been giving a lecture? Not so. Taglicht, that saint and promoter of peace, that mass of spirituality, is training himself to fight. Should the enemy attack, he will stand up with the other Haganah members, so we will not be massacred and plundered, as we were in other years sealed in Jewish blood. Twice a week, Taglicht goes to Ramat Rachel to train with a Haganah group, and now he is on his way home. All this is beside the point. The point is that Herbst now has an excuse. Should Henrietta ask him where he was, he can say he was with Taglicht. Once, Taglicht was on his way to give a lecture. Hemdat met him and went along. After the lecture, several people attached themselves to Hemdat. One of them remarked, "I've read your stories. I won't say they're not good; I could even say

I enjoyed them. But, let me tell you, today's reader is no longer content with reading for pleasure. He expects to find a new message in every creative work. Hemdat said to him, " 'Whither?' is not a question I answer, though I do sometimes respond to 'Whence?' "

Herbst and Taglicht did not have a long conversation; Herbst, because he was hurrying home, and Taglicht, because he had heard good news. On this night, one of many filled with horror and distress, catastrophe, restricted rights, and harsh measures and rulings that limit our every step, a band of youngsters had taken possession of some land, establishing a new settlement there. For this reason, Taglicht was not interested in the sort of conversation academics usually indulge in. They said goodbye to each other and went on their way, Taglicht rejoicing over the birth of a new settlement and Herbst relishing the excuse he had found.

When Herbst reached home, he saw there was a light on. A light at one A.M. meant something had happened. But this was beside the point, the point being that, should Henrietta ask where he was, he now had an adequate and totally reasonable excuse. Herbst put his key in the door, but it didn't open. What's this? Henrietta could have left her key in the lock so she would hear him when he came in.

He stood outside, unable to get into his own house without knocking. But if he knocked, his wife would come to let him in. Even if she didn't ask any questions, shouldn't he offer an explanation? But his face would contradict his answer. He had to get in somehow, and if he didn't knock, no one would open the door. He knocked, and Zahara appeared.

Herbst saw his daughter Zahara and said, "You're here? When did you come?" Zahara embraced her father and kissed him. He wanted to embrace her and kiss her too. But his soul was astir with other embraces, so he restrained himself. He brushed her head with his hand, smoothing her hair, reluctantly, as his hands still blazed with Shira's fire.

Henrietta heard Manfred come in and called out from her bed, "Fred, what do you think about our visitor? Zahara, tell Father why you came." Herbst asked in alarm, "What's happened, what's happened? Something bad again?" Henrietta said in a cheery voice, "What do you mean, 'again,' and why bad when it can be good?"

He hurried to his wife. Zahara followed him. He looked at them with concealed anger and said with open reproach, "Won't you say . . . Won't you tell me what happened." Zahara answered, "Nothing, Father. Honestly. Nothing. I came to Jerusalem and I dropped in to see how you are." Henrietta looked at her with affection and good cheer, and said to her husband, "But wait till you hear what brings her here." Herbst said to Zahara, "Do I have permission to ask what brings you here?" Zahara said, "Honestly, you *are* strange." Herbst said, "I'm strange? In what way?" Zahara said, "Isn't that right, Mother?" Henrietta said, "When a special guest makes a statement, the host must agree." Herbst said, "Nonetheless, I would like to know in what way I'm strange." Zahara said, "You're not strange now, Father." Although at that moment he was actually stranger than ever, she repeated, "Honestly, you're not strange now."

Henrietta asked her husband, "Have you eaten?" Manfred was afraid to say, "I ate but I'm hungry," since that might lead his wife to further questions. He answered, "I had tea with Taglicht." Henrietta said, "Poor thing, you had tea, but nothing to eat." He said, "Tea with some dry cake." Henrietta said, "I'm getting right up to bring you something to eat." Zahara said, "Stay where you are, Mother. I'll fix something for Father." Henrietta said, "Aren't you tired from the trip?" Zahara answered, "Did I walk here? I came in a car, of course. And what a car, a very special one, like a deer with wings. It was quite a trip. Eighty kilometers an hour. If you promise not to report me, I'll confess that we even hit a hundred kilometers an hour. Avraham-and-a-half says such speed causes cars to die an untimely death."

Herbst asked his daughter, "What brings you here?" Zahara said, "Mother, I see Father isn't pleased that I came." Herbst said, "I'm pleased. I'm pleased, and all I'm asking is why." Zahara said, "I came for the workshops. Out of the entire *kvutza,* two of us were chosen." "And who is the other girl?" Zahara said, "Allow me to correct you, Father, dear. You ask about the other girl when you ought to ask about the other person." Herbst smiled and asked, "Then who is the other person?" Zahara said, "If I tell you, will you know? You have a habit of switching people's names, Father." Herbst said, "Yes, honey, I never remember the names of all the boys who surround you." As he spoke, he noticed how ripe she was. He lowered his eyes and thought: She is with young men who have rejected the authority of their fathers. She has come here with one of them, and I'm too preoccupied to look after her. But look at Lisbet Neu—of course, she is older, but she is in constant contact with all kinds of people, clerks as well as customers, and she has an invalid mother and no father. Nevertheless, she behaves impeccably. He stroked his daughter's head and said with concealed emotion, "It's a great privilege to have been chosen to attend these workshops and to have an opportunity to hear things that are probably worth hearing. Did you see your little sister? Isn't she a fine baby? Who will be lecturing?" As he asked this question, he felt a twinge of pain, for he had not been invited to participate. Several years earlier, there was not an intellectual event that didn't include him. Now they were having these workshops, and he wasn't asked to lecture even once. Manfred Herbst was on the way out. He used to be invited to partici-pate in every cultural event, and those who arranged them didn't make a move without consulting him. New people had come, bringing new wisdom. Herbst felt sorry for himself, sad that it had come to this. Yet he justified these omissions, for he had not published anything in sev-eral years, except for two or three trifles in *Kiryat Sefer* and *Tarbitz*. His great book on burial customs of the poor in Byzantium was still a bundle of notes, references, and preliminary drafts.

Whose fault is it that the book lies curled up in a box, like an embryo dead in the womb. This country is at fault; it is not a scholarly environ-ment. Here in the Land of Israel, everyone makes do with the mini-mum. This applies to spiritual needs as well as physical ones. Whatever is not essential to sustain body or soul is a luxury this poor country cannot afford. Our colleagues—those young scholars who came from Germany only yesterday, because they were relieved of their positions there—are amazed that in all these years we have contributed absolutely nothing. They don't realize that this place is unlike any other. In other places, scholarship justifies itself. Not so here, where, unless a scholarly study can be related to Israel's national destiny or to the ethic of the prophets, it is immediately discredited. Those innocents still pretend to be living in a German environment. Give them two or three years and they'll be like the rest of us, making do with articles in jubilee volumes. The ambitious ones will join the bureaucracy, which is the seat of power. In other countries, the bureaucracy serves the needs of the people and the state; here, the bureaucracy itself is primary, and it takes precedence over the needs of the people and the state. Among those who came in the early days of the university, there were some true scholars. Years passed, and they didn't achieve anything important. This being the case, they began to regard their minor achievements as major ones. When Julian Weltfremdt and his cronies remark scorn-fully, "See what those professors are up to," the professors answer, "Their words have the ring of envy; they resent us because they weren't appointed to the faculty." What these malcontents say about the professors, most of the professors say about their own colleagues.

In fact, most of them agree that Bachlam is no scholar, while he says
they have small minds and deal entirely with trivia.

Zahara brought her father his meal. Herbst glanced at his beloved
daughter, who was forfeiting sleep for his sake. He picked up a knife
and fork to eat what she had prepared, but they remained idle. Zahara
peered at him and said, "Father, you're not eating." Herbst answered,
"I'm eating." Zahara laughed gaily and said, "I see you deep in thought,
but I don't see you eating."

Many thoughts troubled Herbst. He dismissed them, one after another, thanks to his beloved daughter. As long as she was in his mind,
he felt relaxed. But he was sorry she hadn't followed his advice. She
hadn't enrolled in the university, and her education was incomplete.
Dr. Herbst had many opinions, among them that one cannot acquire
an education outside of a university. Since settling in the Land of Israel,
some of his opinions had changed, but he remained convinced that one
could not be educated outside of a university, even by reading widely,
listening to lectures, devouring the wisdom of the world. In the end,
such knowledge is incomplete. He applied this rule to everyone, including his daughters.

Father Manfred doesn't really know his daughters. This is surely
true of Tamara, whose character no one really knows. But it is also true
of Zahara, who is attached to her father and whose soul is as transparent
as water from a spring; one can't really say that her father knows her.
Were we to summarize all of Father Manfred's information about
Zahara, it would add up roughly to this: Zahara belongs to a *kvutza*
called Ahinoam, which foreign correspondents with Zionist sympathies mention often and journalists rush in to write about in many
languages, as if it were there that humanity will be renewed—to the
extent that one can barely find a *kvutza* member or even a shrub that
hasn't been photographed for one of these publications. Zahara is a
member of this *kvutza* and is accepted by one and all. Its ways are
congenial to her, and there is no activity in which she doesn't partici-
pate wholeheartedly: the vegetable garden, the kindergarten, the
kitchen, the dining room. Wherever she works, there are people helping her. It is the way of young men to be helpful to young women who
enjoy their work, by lending a hand, giving good advice, or simply
looking on. She occasionally comes to Jerusalem from the *kvutza*,
sometimes with this young man, sometimes with that one. Today, too,
she came with one of them. The early days were good, before Herbst
met Shira. He used to see his daughter and her friends without being
subjected to afterthoughts.

Father Herbst sits eating what his daughter serves him, straining to ward off suspicious thoughts. In these good days, before he knew Shira, he wouldn't have entertained even the trace of a suspicion. Father Herbst raises his head so he can look at his daughter and lowers it without looking at her. He raises it again as if to say, "Go to bed, my child, you must be tired." He also wants to ask for news of Ahinoam. The words are formed and need only to be uttered. A cough disperses them. Father Manfred lowers his head again and eats without tasting the food. Shame and regret are a harsh condiment.

—— 24 ——

In the morning, Herbst made a firm decision to clear his mind of all unessential business and devote himself to his major work, to check his pads, notebooks, and file cards, and determine what was new material—i.e., quotations and summaries distilled from documents unnoticed by other researchers. Caution is crucial to scholarship, and careful verification is crucial to caution. Not once, but constantly, for without frequent verification, material already presented by others could be copied into your book. Many times Wechsler had boasted to him that he had discovered a document no one had seen before; a simple document, one would assume. But not so. Were he to publish it, it would fly in the face of all our historians and reveal that they were, one and all, a band of illiterates. Herbst showed him half a dozen books citing that very document and basing theories on it; finally, he showed him a small volume that dismissed it with a curt phrase from which its fraudulence was obvious.

After eating and drinking, he returned to his study. He took out his pads, his notes, his index cards. Though his notebooks were full, with writing on both sides of the paper, and the box was stuffed with cards, he wasn't arrogant, like those who presume that their book is done if they have enough notes.

Herbst sat at his desk for about two hours, arranging notes by subject, discarding duplicates and triplicates, for sometimes one sees an item and imagines it is new, not remembering he has already copied it two, three, four times. Although he found several new items in his notes, he didn't delude himself into thinking he had achieved his goal.

Nor did he err in the direction of despair, like those who feel helpless when they see they have failed to achieve their goal and say, "Why struggle, when it's clear I'll never finish?" One should know that every beginning has an end. Day after day, one does what he does, until finally the beginnings add up to a conclusion.

There were several articles that were similar in subject and in good shape. If he had retained his youthful vigor, he would not have stirred before finding additional material and combining the fragments into a book. But Herbst's youth was over. This was not the Herbst who used to work so diligently that nothing could distract him. Now some frivolous woman could appear, disrupt him, and turn him on end.

Now that he was thinking of that woman, he began to scrutinize her actions. She sometimes sought distance, sometimes closeness, behaving at times as if there had never been anything between them. If she had allowed him to approach her yesterday, it was only after many rejections. Herbst leaned his head to the left, pondering: Maybe I myself am the guilty one. Had I gone back to her right then, after I was first close to her, she might have offered me her love. Did I think I was so attractive that I could stay away and she would still leap up and shower me with affection whenever I showed my face? She was, no doubt, deeply drawn to me at first, withholding nothing. But I didn't show up again for several months, and when I did, I ran off because of the curfew and didn't come back for a month and a half. Meanwhile, someone else found her. Why did Shira decide to tell me the story of the whip? Did she mean to make me jealous? Does she imagine I'm fool enough to think she keeps herself for me? Anyway, the engineer's behavior was a disgrace. Shira herself is even more of a disgrace, since her behavior provokes insolence, even violence. It's a fact: any woman who invites a man home after one conversation deserves what she gets. She deserves to be beaten, not loved. The man who beat her was wielding his charm, to take revenge, to make her pay for her misbehavior. "What do you want from me?" Herbst cried out, as if Shira were there, torturing him. "My God, my God," he cried out, and as he cried out he was overcome with wonder, like a man in trouble who sees help and salvation.

The night they walked along the road to Beit Yisrael, Shira had asked Herbst, "Are you Orthodox?" She had told him, "I'm not Orthodox, and I don't care for the Orthodox." When she said this, he hadn't given it a second thought. Now that he was alone, thinking of her and her behavior, an undefined question began to form in his mind. It could be articulated in these terms: It's true, isn't it, that, when one rejects religion, spiritual restraints are also suspended, that the soul casts off its restraints, and actions are no longer examined? Herbst was neither a believer nor an atheist. His research never led him to consider questions of faith. Not many of those who studied Byzantium were as familiar as Herbst with the endless strife, disputes, intrigues, conspiracies, murders, and massacres in the name of religion that occupied Christian sects in Byzantium from the time of Christianity's early triumphs to Islam's conquests. Still, his erudition did not compel him to reflect on the nature of his own faith. Now that he was invoking heaven because of his distress, a spark flared up for him and died as soon as it was lit. A spark that goes out immediately gives no light; it doubles the darkness. Out of anger, out of anguish, out of foolish self-pity, out of a need to act, he picked up a book and banged it on the table. With the exception of a cloud of dust, the act achieved nothing.

I don't know how you relate to the contemplative process. When Manfred Herbst has an issue to contemplate, he begins by turning it over, abandoning it midway to consider matters that are tangential but not part of the issue, and ending up where he started. So, at this point, involved as he was with Shira, he moved on to Lisbet Neu. Along with these two, he considered several others—women he had been with at the university, women he had met later at scholarly events. Suddenly, he was overwhelmed with the realization that some of these women were working in the very fields he was working in, although they were very different from him. And it was this difference that unsettled and disturbed his soul. After visualizing their beauty, their coiffures, their fragrance, their manners, he fixed his mind on Lisbet Neu, hoping she would save him from them and from Shira. But the One who was created only to trouble us said derisively: What's it to me if this fool doubles his trouble?

Suddenly, Zahara's cheerful voice was heard calling him to lunch. Herbst answered, "I'll be right there." Zahara called again, "Father, the food is getting cold." Herbst called out, "I'm on my way." He picked up two or three stones from the bunch he had collected on an archeological dig and placed them on his papers, so they wouldn't blow in the wind, arranged his pads and notebooks, and took a quick inventory—not like those scholars who estimate how many pages they can make out of a given amount of material, but like a builder amassing lumber and stone for construction.

Manfred Herbst was sitting there; his wife, Henrietta, was sitting there; Zahara, their daughter, was sitting there. They were eating together. The table was covered with a heavy cloth made of coarse fabric Henrietta had bought from the husband of Sarini the wetnurse. Henrietta was saving the things she had brought from her mother's

house for her daughters, with the idea of dividing them between them
when they had homes of their own. She did this with the silver cutlery,
substituting cheap metal utensils, as well as with the linen tablecloths,
which she replaced with this coarse fabric. Now, the Herbsts were
sitting together. Papa Herbst and Mama Herbst and Zahara, their eldest
daughter, were sitting and eating lunch. Though it was an ordinary day
and the food was ordinary, there was something exceptional about this
lunch. Not only for her father and mother, but even for Zahara. The
vegetables Zahara's mother cooked were not her ordinary fare, though
they came from the *kvutza* and she herself had brought them. The
quality produce grown in the fields of Ahinoam is sent to market, and
the *kvutza* eats only what fails to make the grade. Zahara took a double
helping, feeling love for her mother, for whatever her mother did, and
it seemed to her that she had never loved her mother as she did at that
moment, though she knew, clearly, that she loved her mother then as
always. This was true of the table, the dishes, everything in the house:
in its rooms, which were dearer to her today than ever before; in the
vegetable garden, whose beauty was displayed between every furrow.
Only her mother could dig those little holes so they hugged the seedlings that were at rest there, saturated with rich water, pleased with the
brown earth, content with the fertilizer and with the sun above, welcoming the grasshoppers that leaped over them, circled around,
jumped, flew, and finally landed on their long legs. Not to mention the
wondrous air that stretched between grasshopper and garden row, and
was sometimes endowed with a color known as Berlin blue. Her heart
expanded to include love upon love. This love augmented itself and
engulfed her father. Zahara knew her father well, every line, every
mark on his face. Still, she stared at him as if she had never seen him
before. Zahara studied him, his forehead, his hair, his person—this
precious human being whom she never tired of watching, not realizing
her eyes were closed and what she saw of her father was in her own
mind. This was her father, and she could barely begin to describe to
her friends in Ahinoam even a particle of what she found in him. In
truth, no one in Ahinoam had asked about her father, not even in jest;
for example: What sort of individual is your venerable progenitor? And
no one there seemed interested in such things, not even Avraham-and-
a-half or Heinz the Berliner. They didn't ask about her father either.
Just because no one there asked about her father, she found herself
thinking about him, even now that she was with him and her thoughts
were not colored by the magic of distance. Only good sense kept her
from reaching out and wrapping her arms around his neck, for she
wouldn't have wanted to be considered sentimental.

Zahara served herself and ate slowly, hoping to figure out just what was in the dish. As she ate, she abandoned her research, began eating for pleasure, and took another helping. Again she tried to analyze the dish. She stared at the plate, then at her mother, and stopped trying to guess the ingredients. With her mother's cooking, it wasn't the ingredients that determined the taste. Even when her mother told her how to prepare a particular dish and she passed on the recipe to her friends in Ahinoam, it never turned out like her mother's.

Herbst ate with pleasure too, but he was troubled. He picked up a spoon instead of a fork and assured himself that, if what was on his mind was important, it would make itself known; if not, it would slip away. But it didn't make itself known, nor did it slip away. What could be troubling me so? Manfred wondered. Is it that I didn't praise Henrietta's cooking? If so, I'll say something, and, even if she sees I'm not sincere, I'll be in the clear. He put down the spoon and looked up. His eyes met Zahara's. Affectionate joy flashed from his eyes to hers; identical joy flashed from Zahara's eyes to those of her father. Herbst forgot his troubles and began talking to Zahara.

Manfred said to his daughter, "Now, Zahara, we should ask what's new back in Ahinoam. You ought to tell us without being asked, since we're so citified that we're total boors when it comes to *kvutza* affairs and our questions won't be meaningful. Aren't you pleased, my child, that your father knows himself so well?" Zahara said, "Wrong, Father. You ask and I'll answer, since I don't know what you would like to know." Herbst said, "All your news is important to me." Zahara said, "There are several sorts of news, and I don't know which you have in mind." Henrietta said to Manfred, "You start, Fred."

Father Manfred sat asking questions, and Zahara answered at length, as if it were vital for him to have thorough knowledge of all the things he asked about. She didn't realize that this urban man, this bookworm, probably forgot his question before he finished asking it, that he hadn't noticed she wasn't finished answering and was already asking Henrietta what she had accomplished with regard to the certificates. Before Henrietta could answer, he asked Zahara questions he had already asked and she had already answered. Even things he knew and had no need to ask about, he asked. Zahara and Henrietta didn't notice at first; when they noticed, they laughed about the absentminded professor whose great ideas left no room in his head for their trivial concerns.

Zahara's mind was somewhat like her father's. Her brow was narrow and unwrinkled, but many ideas were spinning around in her brain. Some were the outcome of conversations with Avraham and Heinz; some were inspired by lecturers. She stored some of these ideas in her heart and imparted some of them to her parents. Herbst looked at his daughter fondly and said to his wife, "What do you think of our scholar, Henrietta?" Henrietta answered, "She's your daughter; like father, like child." Herbst was pleased with his wife's words and wanted to say something about his daughter, such as "No need to be sorry that she left school." But his own sorrow suppressed these words, for it was Berl Katznelson, his close friend, who had designed her workshops, bypassing him, neglecting to ask him to give even one lecture. Herbst had one consolation: his great work on burial customs of the poor in Byzantium. It was still a heap of notes, the skeleton of a book, but it would surely become a real book. When it appeared in print, those who ignored him now would be the first to seek him out. Herbst wasn't thinking in terms of revenge: You underestimate me now; tomorrow, when I'm famous, you'll be the first to honor me. But, remembering his book, he was comforted. The book was important, not only because of the sources he uncovered, but because of his ideas, which, at several points, approached the level of a study in religion. The burial customs of the poor in Byzantium, which at first glance, appear entirely opposed to Christian doctrine, were in fact derived from a philosophy that found itself a niche within that very religion. Now that Herbst was thinking about his book, he was determined to do whatever was in his power to complete it. Having reached this decision, his sorrow vanished. Although it vanished, he was not relieved. On the contrary, as he thought about his book he grew more and more angry that, with such a work in progress, he could be treated as if he didn't exist. Actually, it was not because he wasn't invited to the workshops that he was angry, but because of himself, because his mind was not on his work because of Shira.

— 25 —

When they had finished eating, Zahara led her mother to the uphol-stered chair near the window and went to clear the table. As long as Zahara was clearing the dishes, Henrietta sat quietly. When Zahara didn't come back, Henrietta understood that she must be washing them. But she had come for the workshops, not to do dishes, and she ought to rest before going to the lectures. Henrietta pulled herself together, got up, and went to the kitchen to relieve Zahara. Zahara refused to listen to her; she wouldn't let her do household chores after being up most of the night and spending most of the day cooking, with no one to help. When Sarini came to nurse Sarah, she had asked if she could take the day off, as she was being offered the chance to assist at an important ritual—the ransoming of a first-born donkey—to pour drinks for the guests and serve all sorts of sweets, since the wife of the celebrant, a kind and rich Bukharan, was all thumbs and so inept she couldn't even manage the sugar cubes she sucked on, let alone the guests. And it was going to be a great ceremony, like the one with Balfour and Herbert Samuel when the Ashkenazim established a university. Manfred, when he heard Zahara and Henrietta arguing, leaped into the fray and declared, "I'll wash the dishes." Henrietta scolded him, saying, "You, go back to your room. Climb into bed. And after you've slept, you can get back to work."

Neither of them washed the dishes, nor did anyone go back to his room, since Zahara's friend, the lanky young man called Avraham-and-a-half, appeared at that moment. He was as smart as he was tall, having come to the Land of Israel where the sky is tall too, and one's head doesn't scrape the clouds.

Avraham-and-a-half is about twenty-two years old, but he looks younger. He is from a rich family that, generations back, cast off the yoke of the Torah and commandments, renouncing the Hebrew language and the Land of Israel. It was Avraham who rediscovered the Hebrew language and went to the Land of Israel. He is meticulous with language and meticulous in all his actions. His hair is wild, but his thoughts are orderly. His clothes are in tatters, but his soul is intact. Because his hair is golden, as are his eyebrows, and his eyes hide shyly behind long, smiling, golden lashes, bars of gold seem to pour forth from his eyes. He loves everyone, and everyone loves him. Since the time he was hiking with Zahara and she sprained her ankle so he had to carry her in his arms, he loves her twice as much as anyone else. Zahara loves him too, but she still isn't sure whether she loves him or Heinz the Berliner more. It's odd, but, as soon as she decides she loves one, the other appears and makes himself even more lovable; then she decides he is the one she loves more, and the first one appears, and so on, over and over again. Though she is in conflict with herself, Avraham and Heinz are on amicable terms. Affection for Zahara is very special, in that those who love her are not moved to hate one another.

As soon as Avraham-and-a-half appeared, all the arguments about dishwashing came to an end. Zahara made coffee and Henrietta brought cake. They all sat down, drank coffee, and ate cake. Avraham-

and-a-half told about several news items that were reported in the papers with essentials omitted. Then he told about the workshops and the lecturers, most of whom didn't know how to accent words, handle grammar, or construct a proper sentence in Hebrew. They sometimes phrased their sentences in such a way that, if one weren't already familiar with the subject, he would conclude the exact opposite of what was intended. Similarly, there were those renowned orators whose language was meager, whose vocabulary was like a child's but without its charm. As he spoke, Avraham-and-a-half swallowed slice after slice of cake, which Zahara placed on his dish unnoticed, until the ninth or tenth round, when he began wondering how there could still be half a slice in his hand when he had been eating constantly.

Henrietta sat idly, enjoying the boy and his conversation. Even Manfred was aware of his fine qualities. But, if he could have exercised a fatherly prerogative over his daughter, he would have chosen another young man for Zahara, such as Taglicht. Though he already had Taglicht in mind for another young woman, he would have reconsidered on his daughter's behalf.

When there were no more cakes on the table, Zahara tapped Avraham on the shoulder and said, "Let's get going, or we'll be late to Aharaoni's lecture on domestic and nomadic cultures." They got up and left. Henrietta got up and went into the kitchen to wash the lunch dishes, as well as the additional ones from the coffee and cake. Herbst got up and went back to work.

Having had three cups of hot coffee, as well as another half-cup at the end, which was cold by then, he was alert and decided to forgo an afternoon nap and get right to work. He had not slept enough the previous night, and his hands were clumsy and awkward as a result, so that, when he began sorting his notes, not only did he add nothing, but he disturbed the ones that were in good order. It was hard for him to continue working and hard for him to stop, for it was barely two or three hours since he had resolved to keep working until he finished his book. He sat fingering his papers and notecards. He read a bit here, a bit there, and was not pleased with anything. He put down the papers and began looking for something else to occupy himself with.

There are many things asking for attention. One has only to glance at the books piled on the desk, the chairs, and the floor, asking to be put in place. What a waste of time, what a bother to run into them when you don't need them and not be able to find them when you do. This goes for borrowed books as well. They should be returned to their owners, but he hasn't even looked at them yet. And the collections of scholarly papers that, presumably, contain new material, although they must be examined to see if they say anything really new, as well as dissertations that sometimes refer to an unfamiliar book or article. Over and above these are the letters, those written to him that require answers, as well as those he has to write. These are aspects of his work that he deals with regularly, but now his soul seeks replenishment. He glances harshly at the room that has attached itself to him, clinging to him like a skin, unchanged since he first occupied it. Just then, the strip of greenish pink light that shines in from the garden between the rains, just before dark, begins to glow through the window. He goes to the window and gazes out at the garden in amazement, like a man who sees something lovely and is amazed that it still exists. He soon leaves the room and everything in it, and goes out to the garden.

Before he could catch his breath, he saw Sacharson, his neighbor. Last night, when Herbst needed an excuse for Henrietta, he found one. Now that he was looking for a way to escape Sacharson, he couldn't find one. So he prepared himself for the worst. Sacharson glanced at him and, seeing he was upset, slipped away. Herbst forgot about Sacharson, kneeled down to pull up a weed that was growing in Henrietta's flower bed, and cleared some pebbles flung by a shepherd to call back sheep he had sent into the garden. Having begun to tend the garden, Herbst threw himself into the task. He pulled off wilted leaves, evened out a mound of dirt, fixed a furrow, adjusted some stakes that were beginning to slip. Finally he went to get the watering can, happy to have a chance to spare Henrietta the chore. On his way, he stopped in the kitchen to see if there was any dishwater to use for the garden.

He found Sarah lying in her crib, with a fat housefly circling above her nose. He chased the fly and chirped at the baby. She fixed her eyes on him and stared, wondering where the sound was coming from. It seemed she thought the buzz was from his hands and was wondering how hands could have the strength and wisdom to make such a sound.

The fly disappeared somewhere, and still Herbst did not stir from his daughter's crib. He stood chirping through his lips. It occurred to him that he might entertain her by clapping. He began clapping his hands and chirping. It occurred to him that he could dance, and this would surely please her. He began to dance for her while he clapped and chirped. It occurred to him that he could walk on all fours for her. He bent down and began walking on his hands and knees. He jumped around like a rabbit or a hare, only to realize that her crib was too high for her to see what he was doing. He straightened up and stood alongside the crib, clapping and chirping. It occurred to him that all these games were outdated and not very exciting, that, if he wanted to amuse her, he should invent something new. He puffed up his cheeks and tapped them with his fingers so the air would burst out. The baby laughed and reached out to him.

Henrietta came in and saw him playing, the baby laughing. Her throat tightened and she felt like crying with joy at the sight of this child of their old age, lying in the crib, contemplating her father with such perceptive eyes. Henrietta took her husband's hand, pressed it, and said, "Fred, is there anything in the world that we lack?" Suddenly, a sigh was plucked from her heart on behalf of the relatives stranded in that German hell. Her face darkened; she made a fist and said angrily, "What are they up to at the Jewish Agency? They pretend to be working for Zionism, and they're not working at anything. Every day I knock on their doors and list all the calamities, and either their ears are shut tight or their hearts are stone. Fred, my love, I haven't told you even the tiniest fraction of what I go through dealing with those blocks of ice. I know, my love, that I mustn't keep you from your work and I shouldn't distract you from your business. Still, I need advice. Tell me, my love, tell me what to do. I don't expect you to tell me immediately. With your insight, you'll surely find the answer. Don't cry, Sarah. Don't cry, my sweet. I'll feed you in a minute. You're lucky to have been born in this country, so you don't need a certificate."

Remembering the certificates, she pictured all the people she was negotiating with, to no avail. Some of them put her off with "Come back tomorrow"; some didn't even take the trouble to put her off and treated her with total disrespect. Suddenly, they all appeared before her eyes, in a single horde, and, since her heart was bitter, they looked to her like monsters. She was frightened and covered the baby's eyes with her hands, so she wouldn't see them and be afraid.

— 26 —

That night, Taglicht came. He had no particular reason to come, other than to see how the Herbsts were doing, but once he was there, he asked to see Zahara, having heard she was in Jerusalem. To be precise, he had seen her on the street in the company of an extremely tall young man.

As soon as Taglicht appeared, Herbst became uneasy. He was worried that Henrietta might ask what she hadn't asked the night before. He glanced at Henrietta, then at Taglicht, who was unaware of what he could unleash with one wrong word. He envied Taglicht. As a bachelor, he was not accountable to any woman, nor was he afraid she might learn things it would be best to conceal from her. Yet this man, who was free to do as he pleased, was not engaged in any acts that had to be concealed. But what do we know about our friends? Would it have occurred to Wechsler, to Weltfremdt, to Lemner that Herbst was involved with another woman? Even Professor Bachlam, whose nose was everywhere, would never have suspected that a lecturer at the Hebrew University in Jerusalem—someone who ought to be a model of the Jewish ethic proclaimed by prophets of truth and justice—might covet a woman not lawfully his. Who knew about him and Shira? Other than the driver Axelrod, son of Axelrod at the hospital, and the café owner from Berlin, no one has seen him with Shira. How different Herbst had been that night when he spoke with Axelrod the clerk, after bringing Henrietta to the hospital when she was about to give birth. With regard to Henrietta, he had still been free of guilt; with regard to Shira, that evening in the café had been so splendid because he was free of hateful envy.

Taglicht sat at the Herbsts', saying things Herbst would have relished at another time, for Herbst preferred Taglicht's conversation to that of his other friends. Those who go in for paradox say there is one sin even a good man can indulge in: gossip. Not Herbst; he still hadn't acquired a taste for it. Taglicht still hadn't learned the art either. So they discussed those matters that a wise soul can enjoy. Taglicht's words always seem to be transmitted from his heart to his tongue and carefully arranged before they are uttered. Those who are impressed are impressed, and those who are unimpressed say, "If Taglicht had to produce books and write articles, he wouldn't be so free to play with words."

This is true and untrue. It is true that Taglicht does not produce books or write articles, but also untrue, because he did write a dissertation for which he was awarded a doctorate.

We will tell about the dissertation and his years at the university. Taglicht, a perpetual student, spent year after year at the university. There wasn't a subject he failed to explore. After many years, he was still not working on a doctorate. If asked, "When do you expect to complete your studies?" he would answer, "I seem to be just beginning." During those years he made a meager living producing dissertations for doctoral candidates with the ability to pay but without the ability to do the work.

His favorite teacher once asked, "When will you present your own dissertation, so we can grant you a degree?" Taglicht blushed, thinking the professor was suggesting he was engaged in fraud. He stopped working on other people's dissertations and began taking notes and writing for himself. After several months, he produced a fine manuscript on the names of the angels in the poems of Rabbi Amitai, son of Rabbi Shefatyahu, and how these names were interpreted by our sages, as well as in the writings of early German Hasidim.

One night, his professor invited him to his home. They sat for a while and said what they said. As he was leaving, he handed the professor a manuscript. When he was gone, the professor began to read it. He didn't stir until he reached the end of it, at which point he thought: If I knew where Taglicht lived, I would go to him, knock on his door, and say, "You have written a great book."

The next day, the professor told his colleagues about Taglicht's work. They all read it and said approximately, "In all our years at the university, no one has ever submitted such a dissertation." They told Taglicht, "Present your work to the senate, and you'll be awarded a degree." Taglicht didn't submit his dissertation. His devoted teacher saw that all his efforts with Taglicht were futile. He and his colleagues did something that was probably never done in any other university. Let me tell you about it.

One day, his favorite professor invited him to his house for coffee. They sat around talking. Another professor, who was one of Taglicht's teachers, arrived, followed by a second and a third. They sat for a while, talking about this and that, and they did not stir from that spot until Taglicht was granted a doctorate. Taglicht concluded his affairs at the university, went back to his parents' home, from there to Vienna and on to the Land of Israel.

When he came to this country, he looked for work in the fields, the vineyards, the orchards. He didn't find any work on the land. Those jobs were still being done by Arabs. They were everywhere—even in the very settlements that swore not to let in Arab labor after the first round of riots, since the rioters included the very same Arab neighbors who had worked there earlier. The entire country was inundated with Arab labor, so our friend couldn't find work. Taglicht joined the *halutzim* engaged in paving the roads.

Taglicht found work, but the work didn't find him worthy. The youngsters he was with laughed and teased, but they were drawn to him. They instructed him in the ways of work. He took sick and was brought to the hospital. The doctors examined him and discovered all sorts of ailments the patient was unaware of. He stayed for a while, until he was dismissed to make room for others, among them some of the youngsters he had worked with on the roads, who also came down with the local maladies.

From conversation with Taglicht, his doctor recognized that this patient was an intellectual, and not an ordinary intellectual, but one who had both broad knowledge and expertise in several fields. Other doctors who came from abroad and visited the hospital had known Taglicht and were told about his experiences in this country. They said to him, "You see that this country doesn't want your sort of labor, so why not present yourself to the university administrators? Most of the departments still need lecturers." Taglicht answered them, "Could I be so naive as to apply for a position in the university when the world is full of distinguished Jewish scholars seeking appointments and finding none?" This was before the rise of that appalling monster who annihilated one-third of the Jews. Throughout the world, there were still learned men filled with wisdom and knowledge.

The words of Taglicht's champions were not wasted. He didn't listen, but others did. They began seeking him out, courting him, and enjoying his conversation, which became part of them—and, in some cases, of their books.

Some of the departments had already found excellent lecturers, but not everyone was well versed in the Hebrew language. Whoever was somewhat versed in the language, but not fluent, hired an editor to correct errors; those who could barely read Hebrew had their lectures translated. Those who came to Taglicht fared especially well, for, not only did he do his work, but, in the course of translating, he added to the text. And what he added was often more interesting than the rest; this applies to manuscripts he was given to edit as well. He returned translations and edited manuscripts with one condition: that his name not be mentioned. There were those who complied; others, who were of two minds, credited Taglicht with minor contributions, overlooking the significant ones. I have said more than I had to. Still, these details may be of some use.

Little by little, Herbst felt reassured. His worries took flight; his anxiety was dissipated. Henrietta didn't ask, and Taglicht didn't tell. There was really no reason for Herbst to be afraid. It was not Henrietta's way to ask many questions, and it was not Taglicht's way to indulge in many words.

Manfred, Henrietta, and Taglicht sat, as usual, sharing news of the outside world. We used to be baffled by people in the Land of Israel. Every little thing that happened in the country was more important to them than all the monumental things that were happening in the world.

In time, we became like them, ignoring all other countries because of this one. But, in the end, we were back where we started. Once again, because of certain events, our attention was drawn to the lands we left years ago. Foremost among those countries was Germany. The events taking place there were brutal beyond what the most brutal imagination could envision. Anyone who was not affected by the events tried to ignore them. Then, suddenly, everyone was totally obsessed with them. Henrietta's correspondence with relatives and friends in Germany had become limited, and it was sheer habit that kept up the flow of letters; in three or four years, they would, most likely, no longer have been writing to one another. A shift in place leads to a shift in thought; shifts in thought disrupt habit; disrupted habits lead to disrupted action. All of a sudden, there were major actions that affected every other action. There wasn't a postal shipment from Germany that didn't include many bundles of letters. The very people who were appalled at Manfred and Henrietta when they left Germany for this wasteland now urged them to get them out of Germany and into this land, lest they be lost. Some of them meant to settle in the Land of Israel, to live here as Jews. Others hoped to emigrate to America, but, in the meanwhile, they needed certificates for Palestine, as life in the lands of their birth was becoming impossible for Jews. Most difficult of all were the ones who asked nothing. There were rumors that they were already lost; some had taken matters into their own hands, others had fallen into the hands of the Nazis.

Manfred Herbst, Henrietta Herbst, and Taglicht sat together recalling the names of relatives and friends left behind in Germany, some of whom wanted to settle in the Land of Israel, some of whom wanted to use it as a stepping stone. The power of exile is great. Barely out of one exile, a Jew already seeks another. After a while, Henrietta went off to prepare supper.

As soon as Henrietta left, Manfred was relieved. He knew the reason and was ashamed. Anyway, it was good that Henrietta had gone and he didn't have to worry that Taglicht might mention their encounter of the previous night. Herbst thought of referring to it, so the subject would be exhausted by the time Henrietta returned and he wouldn't have to worry that Taglicht might say something about it in her presence. He was about to begin, but it occurred to him that Henrietta might come back while Taglicht was talking. His anxiety began to surface again. He got up and took a cigarette, put it down and took another—one of those black ones with a special tip—lit it, and turned to Taglicht, saying, in a tormented voice, "And you, Taglicht, you still don't smoke? But that's not what I wanted to say. What did I actually want to say?" He put down the cigarette, picked up a book, and waved it in the air, holding it tight, as though afraid it would be taken from him. "What's this?" Herbst said, looking at the cigarette in alarm. "Didn't I put it out?" He turned to Taglicht. "A first edition. I bought it for one shilling. Only one shilling." Taglicht looked at the book Herbst was holding, without saying a word. Herbst glared at Taglicht and said to him, "Wouldn't you like to see it?" Taglicht laughed and said, "But you're holding it so tight that I can't possibly see." Herbst gave him the book. Taglicht opened it, tried to decode the name of the author, and didn't succeed. The letters were stylized, so it wasn't clear whether they were German letters in Greek form or Greek letters in German form. Herbst said, "Did it ever occur to us that, here in Jerusalem, it would be possible to find a first edition of *The Birth of Tragedy?* In Jerusalem's bookstores there are many volumes for which the great collectors would give an eyetooth."

Herbst took back *The Birth of Tragedy* and said, "Since the Nazis came to power, Jerusalem has become a center for German books." He added, changing his tone, "The German immigrants are on a downhill course; every year they move to a smaller apartment. Those who brought crates full of books can't find room for them in a small apartment, so they call in a dealer and sell him a sack of books for a shilling, to make room for themselves. Now every street corner in Jerusalem is overflowing with rare books. One could almost say that you're more likely to find a rare German book in Jerusalem than in Germany. And now," Herbst said, "I'll show you a book that would delight me, were it not for the fact that it came from the estate of a scholarly couple, a man and woman who threw themselves off the roof of their house."

Herbst took out a copy of the Apocrypha and proceeded as with *The Birth of Tragedy.* He waved it at Taglicht and stood watching his face gradually expand and fill with wonder. Herbst said to Taglicht, "Having worked on the Apocrypha, are you familiar with this edition? I wasn't familiar with it myself until it fell into my hands. Incidentally, two rival scholars have already appropriated your insights about the giants in the Book of Enoch, each one proclaiming loudly, 'These are my discoveries,' and I already picture a third one about to claim them as his own. Don't you see, Taglicht, the modesty that keeps you from publishing anything in your own name causes respectable citizens— people one would never suspect of stealing so much as a fingernail—to take credit for stolen wisdom." Taglicht laughed and said, "Still, what they reject survives." Herbst laughed and said, "You are referring to that word in Ecclesiastes that every scholar relates to a different ancient language, but for which you found an explanation in Kohelet Rabba?

I forget the word." He told him. Herbst said, "You told me that the Tanaim and Amoraim went beyond first meanings in their responses to the language of the Torah, yet those who make dictionaries don't always take this into account, a situation that ought to be corrected. If only you would listen to me. . . . I hear Wechsler's voice."

Wechsler barely had time to open the door from outside and already he was closing it from inside. His arms dangled, his face was agitated, his glasses were at an angle—the left lens high and the right one low, or the reverse. He himself was also agitated. He was never a relaxed person, and that night he had a special reason. Bihlul's *Grammar* was the alleged reason, but really it was because of his compassion. Professor Wechsler, as you know, was not excited by books. He was content with the files I have already mentioned. If I haven't already mentioned them, I am ready to do so now. Apart from those files, he had several reference books and several dictionaries, among them Bihlul's *Grammar*. Sitting there for a thousand and one years, Bihlul was never disturbed by Wechsler. Nor was Wechsler disturbed by Bihlul. All of a sudden Hitler appeared, confusing everyone, most of all us. Those who could, escaped from Hitler's land and came to the Land of Israel. Wechsler was occupied with his own affairs, as usual—sorting amulets, seals, and family emblems; making files for each object—leaving Hitler to kill, the Jews to deliver themselves. Now we get to the heart of the matter. Those who maintain that politics is one realm and scholarship another—that a scholar can withdraw from the events of the world and concentrate on his research—don't know how things work. Whether the scholar is willing or not, he becomes involved. If he doesn't involve himself, others involve him. I will offer one example out of many. Many of those exiled because of Hitler came to Jerusalem. Those who brought money were well off, while those who came with a craft were sometimes well off, sometimes not. I can't say that a rich man is well off wherever he goes, because everyone pursues his money. But a craftsman has to pursue potential employers. Just such a craftsman came from Germany or Austria, perhaps Czechoslovakia—can one mention all the countries conquered by Hitler? So, this craftsman came to Wechsler and told him, "I am a bookbinder. Surely the professor has some books that need to be rebound?" Wechsler was filled with compassion for this man, compelled by fate to search for work. There was another reason, which you may already know. In his childhood, Wechsler had been sort of a bookbinder, and he had destroyed more than one pair of shoes to get leather for a binding. If not for his mother's ambitions, he probably would have become a bookbinder rather than a professor, and he probably would be like this man who was searching

for work. So his heart went out to him, and he took about half a meter
of books and handed them over to be rebound without even looking
to see what they were. After the bookbinder left, Wechsler had second
thoughts and realized he had behaved rashly, allowing his emotions to
prevail over his good sense and ordering bindings for books that didn't
need them. He tried to remember which books he had given out. He
thought of one, of another, and finally of Bihlul's *Grammar*. He realized that he needed that particular book. He decided to borrow a Bihlul
from Ernst Weltfremdt. On the way, he thought to himself: When
Weltfremdt lends a book, he expects it back in three weeks. Actually,
he had only one word to look up in Bihlul, but he hated any transaction
that was conditional. So, instead of borrowing Weltfremdt's Bihlul, he
went to borrow a Bihlul from Herbst.

Herbst brought him his Bihlul. Wechsler said to him, "You've
earned my envy. When I need Bihlul, I search through half of Jerusalem without finding it. When you need it, you come up with it instantly. Furthermore, your Bihlul is torn and tattered, and you haven't
sent it to the binder, whereas my Bihlul is good as new, yet I sent it
to be rebound. I'll go now." Wechsler barely had time to open the door
from inside and already he was closing it from outside.

Wechsler never lingered anywhere longer than his business required. Since that amulet fell into his hands, he was even more careful
not to waste time on conversation, though it is more useful than thinking. If so, why did he run off? We know only too well the limits of
scholarship and that new discoveries are not made every day. If Taglicht and Herbst do discover something new, it would be best for the
two of them to clarify it together, and in a day or so we will have word
of it. Then we will copy what we hear from them and file it away.

Having mentioned Wechsler, let me mention a few things about his
history. His father was from Bessarabia. He was employed by the baron
and ought to have educated his son in Paris, as everyone else did, but
Leonid was educated in Germany. His mother came into an inheritance
in Germany and went to collect it, taking her small son along to present
him to her family.

When she came to Germany, she learned that her father's will,
which favored her—a stepdaughter born to his second wife during her
first marriage—was being contested by his sons and daughters. She saw
that the court was not likely to reach a swift verdict and enrolled
Leonid in a German school, so he wouldn't be idle.

The case dragged on. She hired other consultants and lawyers whose
conduct was like that of their predecessors, which is to say that, except
for a slight shift in reasoning and argument, the later round behaved

much like the earlier one. Every month her husband sent money for living expenses, as well as legal fees, and once a year, during vacation, she would visit her husband briefly, taking her son along, so he wouldn't forget his father.

Back to the subject I began in the preceding paragraph. The case dragged on. Leonid did well. He advanced from class to class, from elementary school to secondary school, from secondary school to the university. Too bad about his father, who died in the meantime and didn't live to see his son grow up. And too bad about the mother, whose resources dwindled, for, after her husband's death, she no longer had an income.

As her income declined, so did her appearance. She was no longer the Zenia Wechsler who wore a different outfit every day, with a thin chain of precious jewels adorning her graceful neck, which was without a trace of a wrinkle. Now the wrinkles were everywhere. Her face was prematurely wrinkled, her soul even more so, because of the anguish of the lawsuit. And, if not for her son, who was about to receive his degree, she would have been lost in grief.

Not many relatives remained. Some had left the land of the living; some had left the land of Germany to seek a life in those countries where it was still possible for Jews to live. She had only one relative in Germany, and he, too, was planning to leave.

When he parted from her, he said, "Go back to your home while you can still afford the trip. Your stepfather's children are obstinate. You're worn out and no longer have the strength to fight. It's not only love of money but hostility to the woman who took their mother's place that drives them to prevent you, at all costs, from getting a cent of their father's. The lawyers will extract your last penny, and you'll find yourself in an alien land, alone, without support."

She took these words to heart, having suffered from the case, and settled with her stepfather's legal heirs. She got what she got and didn't listen to the lawyers, who said, "Be patient and see what we do to your adversaries." At this point she went to the Land of Israel, and Leonid stayed in Germany to finish his doctoral work.

When he received his doctorate, he too went to the Land of Israel. The country did well by him, and he was appointed a research member or lecturer at the Hebrew University in Jerusalem. Shortly thereafter, he was promoted to associate professor. When his name became known in the world on account of the amulet he discovered, he was made a full professor. A country whose gifts are carefully calculated can also be generous. So it was in the case of Wechsler and the amulet. Were it not for this amulet, he would still be ordinary professor, with only his name, rank, and salary to speak for him.

I have referred to the amulet. Now let me tell you about it.

Once, at sunset, Wechsler was browsing in some Jerusalem shops that dealt in antiquities. He was both happy and sad. Happy that even skilled counterfeiters didn't try to cheat him, knowing he was an expert; sad that, because of his known expertise, nothing interesting enough to attract the attention of scholars to him was likely to come his way. Confused by this mix of joy and sadness, he noticed another man's shadow extending over his own. He turned around and asked, "What do you want?" The shadowy figure said to him, "In the Monastery of the Outstretched Hand, there is a young monk who has a leather amulet, found in a cave near Ashkelon, with an inscription in ancient Hebrew letters. It is for sale, because the monk would like to help a young woman who is here on pilgrimage and about to give birth." Wechsler did not procrastinate. He undertook the climb to the monastery and looked at the amulet. He did not succeed in buying it, because the seller was asking more than Wechsler could afford. Wechsler left, in a depressed and agitated mood. Several days later, he met someone who said, "So you want to buy the Ashkelon piece, and you can't afford it because the seller is asking such a high price. Then let me whisper that he must sell it now, because it's time for that woman to leave the country and go back to her husband. But she can't go back, because she has given birth in the meanwhile and can't take her child. When she left her husband over a year ago to come to Jerusalem, there was no sign of a pregnancy. Now that she has given birth, she has to hire a wetnurse for the child, and that monk, who offered to help her in her distress, has no choice but to convert the amulet into cash." Once more Wechsler climbed up to see the monk. He met the one who first informed him about the amulet, who now said to him, "So you are going to buy the amulet, and you think you will succeed because the woman has to hire a nurse and can't ask her husband for the money, and the monk wants to help her by selling the amulet. In that case, you might as well know that she no longer has to worry about a nurse. She found a woman doctor, one of your doctors, who took the child and put it in a Jewish foundling home free of charge. So she no longer has to pay a nurse and doesn't need the monk's money. The amulet is, nonetheless, for sale. Now that the monk has sniffed the scent of money, he would like to convert the amulet into cash. An American tourist has turned up and made a good offer, but something he said will work in your favor. The tourist said he would make the monk and his monastery famous, but the monk is concerned about the evil eye. He has no choice but to favor the scholar over the millionaire, since scholars tend to be discreet and to avoid publicity." At night, a Syrian girl came to Professor Wechsler's house, carrying a letter with this message: "The one I spoke of won't sell the amulet to the American, but you must buy it quickly, before someone else does." In less than twenty-four hours, the amulet passed from the monk's hands into the hands of Professor Wechsler.

As soon as the amulet was in Wechsler's hands, he—unlike those who find something rare and disclose it only when it is worth their while, who collect many opinions and finally publish them, prefaced by "in our opinion"—immediately photographed it and circulated the photograph. The amulet acquired renown; Jews and non-Jews were busy decoding it. And, whenever they mentioned the amulet, they mentioned Wechsler. Wechsler's name became known around the world and all the way back to Jerusalem.

Mrs. Herbst returned and was bewildered. When she regained her bearings, she asked, "Wasn't Wechsler here? Did he disappear? I never saw him go. I may have no choice but to believe in magic. I'll bring supper in a minute. Don't go, Taglicht. Stay, your supper is ready. Boiled eggs and a glass of tea."

—— 27 ——

As they ate, the conversation turned to the amulet and from the amulet to Wechsler, who was transformed by the amulet. This lazy fellow, whose laziness exceeded his ambition, was suddenly the darling of the scholarly world because of a snip of an amulet that fell into his hands. Most Orientologists became preoccupied with it and credited it to him.

Let us present their views first, followed by Wechsler's. Some of them wrote, "Traces of three Aramaic letters can be discerned on the amulet. If we identify the middle one as *t* and the final one as *n*, we have two letters of *Satan*, from which we conclude that the amulet was related to Satan and that both the person who made it and the person for whom it was made were Satan worshipers. Inasmuch as there are no other indications of Satan worship in Ashkelon and its environs, it is more likely that it was invoked to counter Satan's power. There are grounds for the assumption that this small object is part of a larger one with a more extended inscription. Which is cause for regret. If the amulet had been preserved in its entirety, we would have the formula for a spell against Satan."

Other scholars maintained that the symbols on the amulet were not letters, and certainly not Aramaic letters; that, if they were letters, they were related to proto-Sinaic script; that the word had to be read from left to right and was one of many words we cannot as yet attach to a particular language group with total certainty. In any case, three letters can now be added to the proto-Sinaic alphabet, whose letters have not as yet all been discovered.

Other scholars regarded it as a transitional sort of script, a bridge between Semitic and ancient Greek, though they weren't sure how it should be read, since it leaned in both directions, toward the Semitic and toward the Greek as well.

What did Professor Wechsler say? Wechsler said, "The inscription is not Aramaic. It is not proto-Sinaic. Nor is it a transition between Semitic and Greek script. Those are Hebrew letters, not three but four of them. They are *t, y, g, y,* which should be read as a segment of *ptygyl,* a word in Isaiah 1. Since the word occurs in Isaiah 1, this bit of leather is obviously from the time of Isaiah 1, one of the earliest and thus most precious disclosures provided by the soil of Palestine. Henceforth, we must dismiss all existing theories about this word. We can no longer say it refers to a silk belt or a fringed buckle—a forced interpretation to begin with—since what we have here is leather, not silk or fringes."

The saga of Wechsler and the amulet adds nothing to our story, but it was useful to Herbst. It distracted him from what had happened with Shira the night before, so that he seemed to himself much as he had been in the old days, before he met Shira.

— 28 —

Although the meal was over, the conversation between Herbst and Taglicht was not. It shifted from the amulet to other objects discovered in the country, from the cave in which it was found to other caves whose mouths remain sealed and, when they are finally dug up, will also yield great rewards. The strip of land known as Palestine, seemingly parched and denuded, is actually a treasure trove with all sort of riches ensconced in it.

Taglicht said, "If you're referring to geology, you're right." Manfred said, "What about archeology?" Taglicht said, "No one can deny that archeology has expanded our horizons. But, when I see how discoveries are interpreted, I'm reminded of biblical criticism. It seems that the people who deal with these subjects don't have enough imagination to write historical novels, so they push themselves to make hypotheses. Scholars from other fields use these as a basis for some system of their own, on which they build vacuous structures—like that famous man who published a book proving whatever it was he proved, using an archeologist's hypothesis that the archeologist had already retracted and declared to be wrong."

Mrs. Herbst shook her finger menacingly and said, "Because a scholar makes a mistake, his entire field isn't invalidated." Herbst laughed and said, "Bravo. But I'm surprised, Henrietta, to hear you champion something you usually scorn." Henrietta said, "Fred, do you want to argue? I don't." Manfred said, "I don't mean to argue, but, tell me, Henrietta, where did you hide the cognac?" Henrietta said, "Now I'll be the one to argue. Tell me, what do you see in that drink that consumes the palate, deadens the mind, and confounds the senses?" Herbst said to Taglicht, "You try. Describe the taste of cognac to her. Come on, Henriett, let's drink to peace." Henrietta said, "If you want to drink, drink. But I'm not drinking." Manfred said, "I am given to understand that I have your permission." Henrietta said, "And without my permission, you won't drink?" Manfred said, "Tell me, Mother, do I ever make a move without your permission?" Mrs. Herbst said to Taglicht, "After such a speech, particularly when you look at his face, would anyone suspect he might make a move without my permission? Sit down, Taglicht. Sit down. There won't be any scenes out of Strindberg. I'm bringing the cognac, and you can drink with Fred." Herbst said, "Taglicht, I renounce all the other women in the world. I love only Henrietta." Henrietta laughed and said, "Listening to you, one would think you're involved with other women." Herbst said, "Taglicht, what's the hurry?"

Taglicht sat down again and stayed another half-hour. At ten o'-clock, he left. Herbst didn't detain him; even though he hadn't mentioned the events of the previous night, there was no way of knowing what might still come up. The fact that it hadn't come up yet didn't mean it couldn't.

After accompanying Taglicht to the bus stop and waiting for the bus with him, Herbst went back to Henrietta. He found her tired from the effort of having company, from the day's work, and from lack of sleep. As usual, just when the lady of the house needed help, there was none at hand. Of all times, on the day when Zahara came with Avraham-and-a-half for the workshops organized by Berl Katznelson, hoping to find some rest at home, just then the Kurdish woman asked for the day off, because she was invited to an important event. What sort of event? It was in this connection, I believe, that Sarini referred to the university, to fingers dipped in fat, to a donkey, to drinks.

Manfred went back to Henrietta. Even before his thoughts were organized, he began talking. About Zahara and Avraham-and-a-half, who were together, alone in the car, with no one else there, such a long distance—all the way from Ahinoam to Jerusalem and from Jerusalem to Ahinoam. Manfred said to Henrietta, "You and I, Henriett, are of the old school, and our road never deviated, so we can't fathom this new generation, whose emotional discipline is lax. Tell me, Henriett, what did Zahara say to you? I myself am out of step with this world, with this generation, with these daughters. But you, Henriett—you as a woman, a mother—are entirely of this world, and you sense what this generation is after." Henrietta looked at him fondly and said, "If I weren't an old woman, I would kiss you for your innocence. What should Zahara have told me? In any case, you can sleep peacefully. It's past eleven, and here we are, chattering away like a pair of youngsters. Go to your room, my dearest. Get into bed and get some sleep. Last night you came in after midnight. Incidentally, where were you last night? What did you do?" "Where was I? What did I do?" Manfred cried in dismay. "Taglicht already told you." "Taglicht told me? Not a word, not even half a word." "What are you talking about? He distinctly said . . ." "What did he say? I didn't hear a thing." Manfred answered her, "You're teasing me, Henriett. He certainly did tell you, and, if you don't remember, I'll remind you. Take a chair and sit down. I don't like to see you standing when you should be lying in your crib. Taglicht came tonight because of last night's events; he was here because of last night, Henriett." "What happened last night?" "Last night? I didn't really want to tell you about last night, but do we keep secrets? Is there anything in the world that I hide from you? You know the meaning of the riots only too well, and all about those young men who refuse . . . refuse to be slaughtered like the Jews of Hebron and Safed. You know all this, and about the Haganah too. But you don't know that even Taglicht, even Taglicht is a member of the Haganah, and, like most Haganah members, he spends most of his evenings training. Tell me, Henriett, would you ever dream that such a fellow holds a rifle? Well, last night he dragged me to their training site. This is a forbidden subject, but we don't have secrets between us. I said 'training,' but actually they were military drills. Real military drills. Please, Henriett, bury this information in your heart and don't mention it to anyone in the world, not so much as a hint, especially not in front of Taglicht. I'm amazed that he revealed all this to me. It's top secret. True, some of the English know what we're up to, but they don't want us to know that they know. Do you see, Henriett? On the one hand, they instigate the Arabs to fight us, and, on the other hand, they're pleased that we create a counterforce. Who can grasp the English mentality? It may all be one scheme: the English want the Arabs to riot against us, and they want us to retaliate. Understand, Henriett?" Henrietta said, "I understand one thing: I understand that what Taglicht is doing is right, and I don't understand why you and your friends stand by with folded arms. If I weren't a woman, I would learn to use all those weapons." "You? You, Henriett?" "Yes, Fred. Or would we do better to wait for the Arabs to come and slaughter us?" Manfred said, "Then I'll confess in a whisper that there are not only young men in the Haganah, but young women as well. In a separate section."

What he had feared the day before had come to pass today. But he emerged unscathed. True, he had given Henrietta an earful of lies. He may or may not have regretted these lies. In any case, he was astonished at his ability to heap lie upon lie without stammering.

He held Henrietta's head in his hands and said, "Now, let's say good night. But first, I want to seal our conversation with a kiss on the forehead—a modest kiss, with no ulterior motives." Henrietta said, "Remember, no ulterior motives. You, my dear, need rest, and I, as you well know, am deadwood. I hope Zahara comes home soon. Liar, I allow one kiss and you pucker your lips for another. Scram. You woke the baby. Let me go to her. Be quiet, little one. Be quiet. Mama's coming."

— 29 —

Herbst lay in bed on the verge of sleep. He put down the book he was meaning to read and turned out the light, in order to yield to sleep. His fatigue should have brought on sleep, but it was dispelled by his thoughts. He got up, turned on the light, and picked up the book. If he had only the book to deal with, he would have either read and enjoyed it or read and fallen asleep. But, apart from the book, he had his thoughts. He stared at the page, only to be diverted by his thoughts; yielded to them, only to have them abandon him and vanish. He turned back to the book, only to have his thoughts return; when he returned to his thoughts, they abandoned him and vanished. After several hours, he put down the book, turned off the light, turned it on again, and picked up the book. Finally, he was overcome by uneasy sleep, the sort of sleep that brings the body little pleasure.

Nevertheless, he was up at the regular time and got right to work. He wrote, erased, rewrote what he had erased. What did he write, what did he erase? What did he add, what did he delete? Between one thing and another, half a day passed, and it was time for lunch. When he heard Zahara calling, he put down his work, got up, and went to the dining room, as Henrietta made a point of promptness, insisting that everything be done on time, and Manfred made a point of not disrupting her routine. In his haste, he forgot to put the stones on his papers, so, when he got back from lunch, he found they had been scattered by the wind. The meal had been prolonged because of Zahara and because it was unusually good. Since he was tired because of his sleepless night, he ignored the scattered papers on the floor and stretched out on his bed. The papers started to fly. He got up and began collecting them. He soon gave up, and went back to bed. All of a sudden, he started, looked at his wristwatch, and saw that he had been sleeping for more than an hour. The house was quiet. Not a sound was heard. Not the baby's voice, not any other voice. The window was open, and the sun shone in. The papers lay scattered but unharmed by the wind. Herbst unbuckled his watch, took it off, and picked up a book, meaning to read for a while. The book slipped out of his hand, and he dozed off again, then fell into a deep sleep.

It was almost twilight when he got out of bed, sat at his desk, and leaned his head on his arms, like someone awake but still in the power of sleep. His vision was blurred, his heart confused, alternately full and empty. He placed his hand on his heart and surveyed the scene. He spotted a slip of paper on the floor under the door and noticed that it was different from the others. He picked it up and read: "Father, I didn't want to wake you All those lectures have turned my stomach so I'm going back to Ahinoam Love and kisses Zahara." He scrutinized her letters. They were large, straight up and down, without connecting strokes, commas, periods, or vowels. He put the note to his mouth, then placed it on the desk. He took a seashell, which was shaped like an eggshell and as sharp, and put the note under it. The room began to darken, and a bird was heard returning to its nest, for it was evening.

The books on the shelves were covered with darkness and gloom. They seemed to merge with the shelves, and the papers seemed to merge with the floor. It was hard to distinguish the shelves from the books or the papers from the floor. But Herbst picked up all the papers and placed them on the desk.

So Zahara, having had her fill of lectures, had left. In fact, she was now with Avraham-and-a-half, and he was driving fast, in order to get to Ahinoam in daylight. With so much unrest in the country, it was unwise to travel after dark. But he was the sort of person one could count on to know that there was a time for everything, and by now he and Zahara were probably back in Ahinoam. So let's return to Herbst now and tell his story.

In the past, after a midday nap, it was Herbst's custom to have some coffee and then sit and work without stopping until supper. If his nap happened to last into the evening, as it did today, he would immediately turn on the lamp and double his efforts, to make up for lost time. Or he would sit and read books related to his work, the sort of texts to which his own book and lectures were indebted, just as these texts were indebted to others, for even a learned man who has read many books and knows their views remains indebted to others. Scholars are not like poets. Poets derive their verse from what they see and feel; if they're not lazy, they write it down. Not so with scholars, whose insights derive from predecessors and from those who preceded them. A scholar who pores over earlier books will not emerge unrewarded and will surely add to the body of literature.

Some scholars, once they have acquired a reputation, pass on to others the drudgery of providing material for their books. They either assign their students to do research or hire a needy scholar. Manfred Herbst is not this sort. Not only are his insights his own, but even the footnotes in his book and articles are derived from his own reading, which is to say, from the books in which they originally appeared— unlike scholars who use secondary or even third-hand sources without having looked at the books they refer to, but, rather than offend anyone, simply add them to their bibliography. Some scholars identify their sources but leave a space between two citations, although both are by one author. One who is not familiar with the material would assume the second entry is original; if, on the other hand, one is familiar with it, the source has been duly acknowledged. Manfred Herbst is not of that ilk. When he cites other people's data, he doesn't manipulate it to get credit for himself. Many researchers are so eager to come up with a theory a day that they publish instantly, only to wake up the next morning and see that the theory is groundless and must be retracted. Then why publish before verifying everything? Because they believe that, even so, they will stimulate study and research from which scholarship will benefit. Not so with Herbst. Nothing issues forth from under his hand until he is convinced of it. You see how Herbst labors over his book and articles. When he feels his work is sloppy, he doesn't force it, unlike those whose work is the product of boredom. What does Herbst do? He puts down his work, picks up a biography or a scholarly monograph, and reads it. Whether we believe all the wonders we read about great men or remain skeptical, a reader loses nothing if the writing is good. The imagination of a competent narrator can affect and arouse the soul, mobilize faltering hands to renewed activity.

At this point, however, Herbst didn't go back to his work, nor did he turn to those biographies and monographs. His depression was so great that it resisted every antidote.

Herbst sat as one whose world has vanished, for whom there is nothing left to do. Even cigarettes, which sometimes pulled him through desolate moments, did not trick him into thinking he was occupied. He sat alone with himself, a cigarette in his mouth, picking at his chin and whispering, "What am I to do?"

He spit out the cigarette, crushed it with his foot, and cried out, "I've got it!" He knew what to do. He went into the bathroom, tossed off his sandals, took off his clothes, got in the tub, and turned on the shower. The water poured over his head, his shoulders, his back, his entire body. The moist chill engulfed him from outside, and some of its sweet freshness seeped in, permeating his body with pleasure. Herbst was renewed from within and without, and was like a new creature. He dried himself, put on his clothes, and went to the kitchen for tea. He found some coffee Zahara had made before she left. He drank it. As soon as it began dripping down his throat, his fatigue was dissipated. After two cups of coffee, he was totally alert. He didn't feel like getting back to work, so he went looking for his wife.

He found her sitting alone in the dusk, her chin on her heart, like someone overwhelmed with worry who obscures it rather than let anyone see her worrying. Henrietta didn't know what she was worrying about, or why. But, since she was alone in the dark, it seemed to her the right time to examine her soul and render an account. Tired from the day's work and from all that had happened to her, she allowed her head to droop and dozed off. Herbst looked at her and whispered, "Henriett, you're sitting in the dark." She was startled and said, by way of an excuse, "Yes, I didn't turn on the light." Herbst said, "Zahara is gone." Henrietta nodded and said, "Yes, Zahara is gone. She went to your room twice, and you were asleep. She didn't have the heart to wake you, so she left a note, but I don't remember where I put it." Manfred said, "You don't remember where you put the note?" Henrietta said, "I'm sorry, but I don't remember." Manfred said, "You have no way of knowing, since Zahara slipped the note under my door. You say Zahara found me asleep. Yes, that's right, Henriett. It's a long time since I've had such a good sleep. Now I'm up, and I don't know what to do. Very simply, I don't know what to do." Henrietta said, "Go for a walk." "A walk?" Manfred asked in dismay. Such a thought hadn't occurred to him. "You suggest I go for a walk? And you, Henriett, will you be stuck here in the house? Will you stay home while I go out?" Henrietta said, "The baby can't be left alone. Besides, my dear, I don't have the strength to pick up my legs. Go ahead, my love. Don't give me a hard time. I know you would rather walk with me than walk alone. Go ahead, and, when you come back, you'll find your supper ready and waiting for you in your room, on your desk. If it's a simple meal, don't be angry. I gave Zahara every last bit of food for the road. Actually, she only took four slices of buttered bread, but Avraham said, 'I'll take the rest and I'll feed her.' " Manfred said, "You ought to turn on the light rather than sit in the dark." Henrietta said, "Of course, of course. Do you think I'll sit here all night in the dark? Don't I have to put Sarah to sleep and make you some supper? I might even eat too." Manfred offered his right hand and said, "Give me your hand, Mother, and I'll say goodbye." Henrietta said, "Here, my love. Goodbye. Don't be late, Fred. Come back before you get tired. I hear Sarah. Go ahead, Fred, don't let me keep you." Fred said, "I'm going, I'm going. Bye, Mother. Bye."

He went out, meaning to walk, but he saw a bus coming from Talpiot and jumped on it. The bus was nearly empty. There were only a few passengers. Because of Arab attacks, people from Talpiot were reluctant to go into town at night. Those who went into town couldn't be sure they would make it back that night, for the authorities could suddenly proclaim a curfew, which would bring transportation to a standstill. Still, the inspector sent out buses rather than disrupt the system. When Herbst arrived in town, he was astonished to see the streetlamps lit as usual, the streets filled with men and women, ambling in a leisurely manner, in no hurry to find refuge at home. Even the shoeshine boys were there, plying their trade. People get their shoes shined, not in order to wear them in bed, but to walk in them, which suggests that the night has not closed in on us and there is no danger of a curfew.

Worried by what he saw and worried by his thoughts, Herbst strolled down Jaffa Road, which was as crowded with people as in peacetime. Soldiers of the Mandate government added to the bustle. Whether they ambled along like everyone else or stood like observers or inspectors, they were different, not only because of their uniforms, or because they were armed, but because of the expression on their faces.

I will dwell on this matter for a moment and explain my remark about the expression on the Englishmen's faces. It seems to me that I speak for Herbst. I may be slightly mistaken in this matter, but surely not by very much.

Before Herbst came to the Land of Israel, he had little contact with other nationalities. Except for Jews and Germans of foreign extraction, he knew no other nation. When he came to this country and saw various peoples, distinct from each other, he became interested in their characters. When he knew a person well, he tried to determine which of his qualities were national traits and which were unique to that individual. I don't know what he achieved or what he failed to achieve. It is clear that, of all the nations and tribes in this country, he was least acquainted with the English. And I would not be straying far from the truth if I were to say he made no effort to know them, although he often had the opportunity for close contact with the English. At public events, such as concerts and exhibits, for example, and even in private homes. I will try to explain why he didn't get to know the English and why he made no attempt to do so.

As soon as Herbst arrived in the Land of Israel, he was imbued with a spirit that was totally new to him. It could be called the spirit of freedom. Herbst suddenly felt that he was in his own land, with his own people, with others like him, who shared many of his qualities and many of whose qualities he shared. He felt that he longer needed to strain to be like others, for he simply *was* like them, which had not been the case before. As long as he was living in Germany, he made an effort to accommodate his ways to those of the Germans and to be like them. Even after becoming a Zionist, he didn't change very much; nor did his Zionist friends.

As for all the other peoples to be found in this country—be they ordinary people or scholars and intellectuals—whether he considered them natives or guests who are here today and gone tomorrow, should this suit them, he saw no reason to change his character on their account. But the Englishman, lording it over a land to which he had no claim, considering himself superior to all its inhabitants, was strange in Herbst's eyes, and he had no wish to make his acquaintance. Since the English were strange to him, the expression on their faces was equally strange.

Herbst was jostled, sometimes by a drunken sailor, sometimes by an ordinary person. Still, Herbst functioned under his own power, dispatching his eyes in whatever direction he chose: at the pedestrians, the houses and stores, the vehicles and their passengers, those little houses in Nahlat Shiva with larger structures and stores built to the right and left of them, about to swallow them up, along with all of Nahlat Shiva. The neighborhood, being modest and discreet, accepted its fate in silence. But, as you and I well remember, it paved the way for the building of modern Jerusalem, providing it with the vigor and courage to expand. When Herbst first arrived in Jerusalem, Nahlat Shiva, with its stone buildings, was still a defined neighborhood. Now it is overshadowed by houses built of concrete and stores with goods Jerusalem had no need of until they appeared, or, let's say, until the shopkeeper explained how necessary they were. Herbst, who generally stayed at home, whose shifts and changes led him from workroom to dining room to bedroom, is suddenly in the midst of a crowd. There are many people on the street, so many that he can't see if there is a friend or acquaintance among them. He doesn't recognize anyone, yet he feels he is a partner, though the nature of the partnership is unclear. He sees himself as part of the crowd. He suddenly finds himself standing in front of a large store. Its windows are brightly lit, and the wares are skillfully arranged to catch the eye of strollers.

What did I want to look at? Herbst asked himself. I didn't want to look at anything. Actually, I did. Before he could decide whether or not he did, he was interrupted by a bell being rung by the shoeshine boy sitting in ambush at the edge of the street. Herbst's thoughts were interrupted. He looked up and saw a small boy sitting at the entrance to an office building, one hand on a bell, the other on a bristled implement. The boy jingled the bell again and said to him, "Here, here, sir. Let me shine your shoes. I'll do it tiptop." The word appealed to Herbst. He laughed and said, "If you can really do it tiptop, I'll let you shine my shoes." The boy said, "If I don't do a good job, you don't have to pay." Herbst said, "That's not the point. Just make it tiptop." The boy said, "All right, sir." Herbst extended his foot. The boy picked up his tools and began to work. Herbst watched him and said, "I see you are really making it tiptop. What do you earn in a day?" Herbst also asked the boy where he lived and if he had a father, a mother, brothers, sisters. I'm not sure just how interested Dr. Herbst really was. But the boy answered, adding even more information than was asked for.

This is roughly his story. His father had left his mother for someone younger, his mother having aged rapidly because she worked so hard, at home and away from home, in the homes of Ashkenazim, who are so rich that they don't have to work and their work is done by others. As for his brothers, one of them, sort of a *halutz*, who studies at night and can even read a newspaper, was in partnership with a Yemenite. The Yemenite would give him a pile of newspapers to distribute and a share of the profits. On Friday nights, he would bring home a newspaper and sit reading it, like a scholar with a sacred text. And what about the sisters? They were up to no good. Victoria went with some Englishman. She was attacked by fanatics, who beat her up and poured acid on her face, which ruined her looks. When the Englishman saw this, he got angry and said he would kill all the Jews. Balfouria heard this and began to cry inconsolably. She said to the Englishman, "Don't kill the Jews." He took her to the movies, and she didn't come back. When she came home in the morning, Victoria jumped on her, bit her, pulled her hair, shouted, and wept. Our brother Musa appeared and beat up Victoria and Balfouria, screaming, "I'll kill all the English! They're making our girls into whores! Even if they kill me, I'll kill them first." Then he joined forces with Fat Musa, who loved Balfouria dearly. They planned to ambush the Englishman, and Mother was terrified that Musa would kill him. Musa has a fierce temper, and, when he is angry, he turns red as a bull's blood; his eyes get twice as red, so he can't see what he is doing. He pounds with his fists, kicks, and thrusts his head into the enemy's belly until the victim collapses in defeat.

After having his shoes shined, Herbst went to a candy shop and bought some bittersweet chocolate. He didn't know what type of chocolate Shira preferred, but the package was attractive and the price was high, so he chose that one.

Herbst left the store pleased with himself, since he knew where he was going and he had succeeded in buying chocolate. Sometimes, when he had in mind to buy something for Shira, he restrained himself, out of fear of being seen. He imagined everyone was watching him and knew just what he was up to. Now, having entered and emerged, unscathed, he directed his feet toward the streets that lead to Shira's.

He met Lisbet Neu. He greeted her, and she returned his greeting, saying, "You still remember me?" He offered her the chocolate. "This is evidence that I was thinking of you. Look and you'll see. I wrote your telephone number on the wrapper. I was about to call you." Lisbet looked at the wrapper and saw no sign of a number. Herbst said, "Oh my goodness, the salesperson switched packages. If you have room in your purse, please take it." Lisbet said, "To waste one's money on such things!" Herbst said, "I bought it for my daughter, but she left." Lisbet said, "Then keep it until she comes back." Herbst said, "When she comes, I'll buy her another. Meanwhile, my dear, eat the chocolate and remember me." Lisbet said, "I remember you even without it." He looked at her fondly, wondering why he didn't feel as he used to feel and respond as he used to respond. Whenever he saw her, he used to be refreshed by a breath of innocence. Now his soul was unmoved and his spirits were low.

Has there been a change in me or in her? Herbst asked himself. It's not that, but . . . I'll watch and see.

The street was buzzing. The pastimes that occupied the passersby were passed back to them by the street. But he withdrew from the tumult into which he had been propelled and eyed Lisbet obliquely to determine if the change was in her. His eyes lighted on the bag slung over her shoulder with the chocolate in it. Your present was taken away, Shira, and given to Lisbet Neu, Herbst remarked to himself.

Lisbet Neu interrupted his conversation with himself and said, "If you would like, Dr. Herbst, you could walk a little way with me. Only a little way. I know you are busy and have no time to waste." Herbst said, "I'd be glad to walk all the way home with you." Lisbet Neu said, "That's more than I asked, and not what I intended." Herbst said, "Intentions don't preclude action." Lisbet Neu looked up at him, struggling to fathom his words.

When they had walked a few paces, his mouth was empty, and he could find nothing to say. He thought: Will we walk in silence, like those couples who are weary of each other? He lit a cigarette and said, "If the lady agrees, we can stop for coffee." Lisbet Neu said, "With your permission, I'd rather walk. I've been sitting in the office all day, and I don't get a chance to stretch my legs. That's why you found me on the street. If it's all right with you, Dr. Herbst, let's walk a bit." Herbst said, "Let's walk."

They left Ben Yehuda and were on a street that had no name yet but is now called Shammai Street. They were suddenly encircled by the quiet that sweetens the summer nights of Jerusalem in those few remaining spots that have not been ruined by this perplexed generation. When they reached such a place, Lisbet Neu began telling about herself, things that astonished Herbst. Lisbet Neu said, "All my energy is wasted selling furniture and dealing with customers." After talking about furniture and customers, she began to discuss how girls were educated, the fact that they were not taught a trade. What were they taught? To hope for husbands. And husbands didn't appear, since most husbands were looking for a dowry and most girls didn't have a dowry. Even back in Germany, where life was orderly and conventional, it was hard to find matches for daughters. Here in the Land of Israel, where there was so little order and few conventions, these young women hoped in vain. From these young women and their plight, she turned to tales of travel in Africa which she had been reading. One can hardly say there is a connection between the education of women and tales of Africa. Still, she saw some connections; but Herbst wasn't listening.

They were already beyond the quiet streets, entering an area filled with houses, stores, pedestrians. When Herbst first came to Jerusalem, this entire territory was desolate. Now it was bustling, mostly with Jews, but with a few Arabs and a few Englishmen as well—Jews because they lived here; Arabs because, if the Jews thought that building houses and opening stores gave them the land, that's not how it was going to be. For the time being, they were simply here; but, in time, they would have a chance to deal with the Jews. And why were the English here? They were here to bestow peace on the land. But, from the day they arrived, they have promoted hatred, envy, and contention, which will end in murder and bloodshed.

Herbst and Lisbet Neu didn't talk about the usual subjects—Lisbet Neu, because she wanted to speak of her own affairs; Herbst, because he wanted to hear what she had to say. But Lisbet didn't get around to her own concerns, because whatever she thought of seemed too trivial to say to this learned man, whose name she first heard from her uncle when he went to visit him. Whether or not her concerns were important, Herbst enjoyed her verbal contortions.

By now they had reached the little neighborhood adjacent to Orhot Hayim, where Lisbet Neu and her mother lived. This neighborhood, too, was sometimes called Orhot Hayim, after its elder sister, which was built first, and sometimes it was called by another name in honor of one of its settlers; there was still no consensus as to its name. How long did Lisbet Neu walk with Herbst? Whether she walked a lot or a little, she was tired, because she had been slaving all day in the store or the office, because she hadn't had a hot meal all day, and because she had walked so far. For all these reasons, she was tired. And, for this reason, she linked arms with Herbst, which she had never done before with a man.

As sometimes happens, a man happened to pass. He stared at her. Perhaps he knew her, perhaps he didn't. But he was surprised, since it was not the custom in Orhot Hayim for a woman to link arms with a man. Because I don't intend to dwell on him—in fact, I doubt that

I will refer to him again—I will ignore him and get back to Herbst and
Lisbet Neu. Herbst was also surprised, not for the same reason, but for
his own reasons, being so aware of her innocence.

Herbst and Lisbet were walking as one in Orhot Hayim, the neighborhood in which Lisbet Neu and her mother found an apartment
when they came to the country. They had gone to Jerusalem the day
they arrived, since, of all the places in the Land of Israel, Jerusalem was
the one place they knew—not only through the prayerbook, but
through fundraising letters sent out by charitable institutions in Jerusalem to everyone everywhere. In those days, when the Jewish community of Germany was tranquil and Lisbet's father, Mr. Neu, was alive,
an emissary arrived from the Land of Israel. He had been sent by an
organization with plans to set up a school near Jerusalem, where Torah
would be taught, as well as trades. The school day would be divided
equally between Torah studies and vocational training, so the boys
would be able to support themselves when they grew up. Mr. Neu was
impressed with this project and made a sizable contribution. When he
heard the school was to be built in Orhot Hayim, adjacent to several
poor neighborhoods with many abandoned children, he began sending
a portion of his annual tithe to the treasurer of this institution. He
enclosed his daughter's tithe as well, having trained her to set aside for
worthy causes a portion of the monthly allowance she received from
him. Mr. Neu used to combine the two sums and send them both
together. I don't know where that school is; even if it no longer exists,
the neighborhood exists, and Mrs. Neu and her daughter, Lisbet, chose
to live there.

That little neighborhood sits in darkness, like a rug on which a
weaver has outlined houses and gardens in blues and grays. The houses
are houses, the gardens are gardens, and their colors are the dusk that
envelops them, for those who live in the neighborhood are mostly
people of limited means. They skimp wherever possible, certainly on
lights on a summer evening, when even the darkness gives off light.
And if it doesn't give light, it's good to sit in the dark. In the darkness
one is unaware of the house's defects—its sinking floor, a crooked wall,
crumbling plaster, a leaky faucet in the kitchen. The sound of a loud
radio blares forth from one of the houses, the occupant having pitched
its volume to let the neighbors hear, since not everyone has a radio. The
tone is political, but the words are from the prophets.

Dr. Herbst and Lisbet Neu traversed the entire neighborhood and
were now at the other end. If this was not the end of the world, it was
surely the end of civilization. There were no houses here, no tents, no

permanent structures, no temporary ones; only rock and bramble. The rock rolls downward, with clefts that form a series of steps. If these clefts were not made by God, they are almost certainly the ones Solomon described in the Song of Songs: "My dove, in the clefts of the rock, hidden in the cliff." Manfred Herbst and Lisbet Neu are already far from the heart of the neighborhood or any part of it, and another scent and another sound take over—the fragrance of grass and the sound of wind stirring the grass; the scent of thorns sun-dried by day and dampened by evening dew. Along with the sound of the wind in the grass, a two-part song is being sung by a girl and boy perched in a cleft of the rock, a song with words that are in the melody, words to suit each listener. The fine scent from the rock and bramble, along with the singing, make this night like those Jerusalem nights long ago when even we were young.

Lisbet Neu withdrew her arm from Herbst's and said, "Let's turn back." Herbst was surprised, though there was no reason for surprise. He had, in fact, meant to see her home, and now that she was there, it was time for her to go in. Herbst asked Lisbet, "What's the hurry?" Lisbet said, "They're playing Mozart tonight, and the man with the radio invited me to listen. I've been wanting to hear Mozart for so long." If Herbst had put his thoughts into words, he would have said to Lisbet, "Forget Mozart, and let's go down to the rocks and sit there like that boy and girl." But not all of a person's thoughts are put into words. Herbst kept thinking: If I run my hand through her lovely hair, she won't object; she might even let her lovely head slip down and rest on my heart. Herbst glanced at her and saw that her ears were tiny, her eyes sparkling. A woman with small ears likes to listen and doesn't turn one away. He continued to look at her. Alarmed by his evil thoughts, he began to scrutinize himself: How depraved this man is, buying a gift for Shira, giving the gift to Lisbet, and telling her, "I bought it for my daughter." He is on his way to Shira, yet he seeks to amuse himself with an innocent young girl.

They were walking away from the steps. Lisbet stopped at one of the houses and said, "This is where I live." "Here?" Herbst asked in despair. Lisbet said, "Most nights I sit inside with Mother. If you ever have some time, Dr. Herbst, you could come over." Herbst said, "I won't come." Lisbet said, "Why won't you come to our house?" Herbst said, "Because of the young lady's mother." "My mother?" Herbst said, "Old women tend to see me as a peer and engage me in conversation, so I don't get to talk to their daughters." Lisbet said, "My mother isn't old." Herbst said, "In any case, my age is closer to hers than to her daughter's. And another thing, my dear Miss Lisbet: I don't want your neighbors to gossip. Now, be well, enjoy the Mozart, and I'll go home." Lisbet said, "I'm sorry I took the professor this far. By now, the last bus has left, and you will have to walk back to town." Herbst said, "Never mind, my feet will find the way. Goodbye."

When Herbst reached the bus station, there was no bus in sight. Had it already left? Was it about to arrive? There was no one to ask. Herbst stood waiting for the bus, as people do in Jerusalem at night, especially then, during the riots, when Jews were being killed and injured every day. Standing there, he heard the sound of violins, harps, drums, and dancing. He looked up and saw that the two Rabinowitz hotels were filled with people in holiday attire. Some were dancing, some clapping, their *shtreimels* bobbing up and down, to and fro. Herbst thought to himself: On the one hand, death and injury, mourning and dirge; on the other, brides and grooms, joy and exultation. He soon grew tired of waiting. He soon grew weary of the instruments and the tunes, which were all one motif repeated over and over. He shifted his mind to Mozart and to Lisbet Neu, who, at that very moment, was sitting near the radio. His mind drifted to his book on burial customs of the poor in Byzantium, which was still a heap of notes and, if he didn't idle away his time, would be a great book. He was sorry to be wasting time waiting for a bus, with no way of knowing when it was due. He decided to walk home. He took a few steps and turned back, took a few more steps and turned back again, thinking the bus might come in the meanwhile, and the driver, seeing no one waiting, would leave. This had happened to him on several occasions, when he was waiting for a bus and stepped back to read the bulletin board, only to be ignored by the driver and forced to wait for the next one or walk.

The driver appeared and saw Herbst waiting. He told him the bus was stuck on the road with holes in its tires, thanks to the nails with which Arabs immobilize our vehicles to disrupt transportation and cut off those living in outlying districts, so they will come to loathe their isolation.

The two of them, Dr. Herbst and the driver, stood discussing the subjects one discussed during the riots, when events were cruel and bitter, when the Arabs conspired to restrict us in every possible way. One of the things they would do was to scatter nails on roads frequented by Jewish vehicles. A bus or car filled with Jews would be traveling along and stop suddenly because a nail in the tire had caused a blowout. The driver would get down to change the tire, and a stone would be thrown at him or at the passengers. Given a miracle, the injuries would be slight. Often, they were serious. The Arabs would stand by laughing while the English policeman meted out justice. How would he do that? He would grab a Jew and order him to get the nails off the road.

Herbst stands listening to the news the driver has to tell. Actually, there is nothing new. Yesterday is the same as today. The only change is in the number of casualties. Still, there is no day without something novel. Since it is novel, I will tell about it.

An old Jewish woman lived at the edge of one of the settlements in the Sharon. Her home was open to passersby, offering shade from the heat of day and shelter from the rain. That day, her house wasn't open, because her years weighed on her, making it hard for her to get out of bed. She had lived almost a hundred years, enduring poverty, grief, and bereavement. She found consolation in the fact that most of the settlement's children, as well as the children of the Arabs in the surrounding villages, were her nurslings, for she had assisted either at their birth or at the birth of their mother and father, perhaps even of their grandmother and grandfather. She had seen them through childhood illnesses and the maladies of the region. From her bed, she heard a knock at the door, followed by a call for water. She managed to get up and open the door. She saw two Arab youths, who asked for a drink. She handed them the water jug. They turned on her and killed her. The driver had other news to tell. What is known is known; what is unknown, who will believe?

By now, the instruments had fallen silent and the wedding guests were beginning to leave the two hotels. Some of them came to the bus stop, intending to ride home. They found a driver, but not a bus. Having celebrated, danced, and feasted, they were tired. They could barely stand on their feet. And the bus was not there. They began quarreling with the driver. He said to them, "What do you want— should I carry you? You heard what happened to the bus. There's a hole in the tire, and it won't budge. If you're not too lazy, you can carry it on your shoulders." They said, "Then what should we do? It's dangerous to walk, and we can't stand outside—if a curfew is announced, the police will arrest us for violating it." After some further argument, the driver went to call the office and ask that another bus be sent. He couldn't find a public telephone that was in working order, so he took the risk of going into one of those dens of iniquity frequented by English soldiers, who would probably be drunk at this hour and up to no good. After a while, the driver returned and informed those waiting for the bus that the office had promised to send a replacement; unless it suffered a fate similar to that of its predecessor, it would almost certainly arrive soon. Had the bus come immediately, Herbst would have taken it and gone home. But, since there was a delay, he grew impatient and went to Shira's.

The blinds were drawn, and a faint light filtered through. Most likely Shira was already in bed, reading a book or, perhaps, that vile magazine. If he didn't hurry, she might turn out the light and close her eyes, in which case he wouldn't have the heart to deprive her of sleep. She had once told him that, when she falls asleep, as soon as her eyes are closed she is asleep for the night. But, if she is awakened, she can't fall back to sleep.

He bent down and picked up a handful of dirt to throw at the window. He decided not to throw it. Were he to throw it, she would open the window and ask who was there. He would have to say his name, which the passersby would hear and note. He discarded the dirt, then brushed his hand, entered the yard, approached her door, and knocked. While he was waiting, he realized she wasn't alone.

Rage, fury, envy burned in his heart like fire. None of the vengeful acts he was considering diminished the intensity of that fire, vengeful acts he had heard of or read about but not believed possible. None of those acts could satisfy his impulses toward that woman who was in bed, the devil knew with whom, while he was on the other side of the door, his heart about to break. He held on to himself by his coat, by his buttons, grinding his teeth. Would she or would she not open the door? His heart was in turmoil. He gasped, "No, she won't."

The door opened and Shira stood before him, surprised that he had come back after having been there the night before. He hadn't shown his face for a month and a half, and now here he was, night after night. Though she wasn't exactly unfriendly, dismay was apparent in every aspect of her being. She offered her hand, greeted him, and said, "You frightened us." As he held on to her hand, she withdrew it, tossed her head back toward the bed, and said, "Let me introduce you."

A woman got up from Shira's bed, greeted him, and said, "Temima Kutchinsky is the name." Shira gestured toward him and said, "This is Professor Herbst." She then gestured toward Temima Kutchinsky and said, "She was my shipmate, and do you know why she is in Jerusalem? She's here for a great event." Herbst said, "I imagine she's here for the workshops." Shira said, "That's right, but how do you know that?" Temima Kutchinsky said, "I, too, am wondering how Professor Herbst knows I've come for the workshops." Herbst said, "It's enough that I know. As for calling me Professor, I must inform you that I am not a professor." Shira said, "If you're not a professor now, you soon will be." Temima asked Herbst, "Are you lecturing at the workshops?" Herbst said, "I wasn't invited, but my daughter is attending them." Temima cried out in amazement, "A grown daughter? I assumed you were a bachelor." Shira laughed and said, "You assume he's a bachelor because he calls on a single woman?" Temima Kutchinsky said, "Is that a sin?" Herbst said, "If you are well received, then it's no sin." Shira said, "Nonsense, didn't we receive you warmly?" Herbst said, "We shall see. Isn't that so, Lady Kutchinsky?" Temima Kutchinsky said, "I'm no lady." Herbst said, "Any woman can be called a lady." Temima Kutchinsky said, "I see you like to be correct." Shira said, "Not merely correct, but most highly correct. A German from the land of the Germans." Herbst said, "I see you are ready for bed, and I am keeping you from your sleep." Temima said, "The night is young. Besides, I don't usually get into bed until past midnight. I was in bed only because Shira insisted. I'm getting right up to help her make tea." Herbst said, "If you're thinking of me, I'm not thirsty." Temima said, "Tea makes people sociable, especially at night. A musician once passed through our town singing, 'Tea is a social brew / And a cure for any bruise.'" Shira said, "You should know, Herbst, that Temima is a nurse, which is why she mentioned that chant. If you want to hear the whole thing, this is how it goes: 'A fish on your line / And tea the social brew / Make every wound fine / And cure every bruise.' Is that right, Temima?" Temima said, "Honestly, I heard him sing it, and you heard it from me. In the end, I only remember half of it, and you remember it all. Now I'll get up and make tea." Shira scolded her, "Stay where you are, Temima. I can boil water without any help." Temima said, "I'm afraid Dr. Herbst won't enjoy sitting with me." Shira said, "Nonsense. What's new in the world?" Herbst said, "I didn't see the evening paper." Shira said, "I wasn't referring to the news in the paper. How is the baby? You should know, Temima, that our friendship is the same age as his little one."

Shira went to boil water, and Herbst was left with Temima Kutchinsky, thinking: If I had asked Lisbet, would she have given up the Mozart, and would she and I now be walking among the rocks? He turned to Temima. "What did Her Ladyship say?" Temima answered, "That Germans remain German. I've already said I'm no lady." Herbst said, "Forgive me." Temima said, "Since there's been no transgression, there's nothing to forgive. So, your daughter has come for the workshops. Then I'll see her tomorrow."

His soul was alarmed, but he recovered quickly. Zahara had already left Jerusalem and was not known by her family name. There were two factors in his favor: first, that they wouldn't run into each other at the lectures, and, second, that he hadn't mentioned Zahara's name. His apprehensions were groundless.

Shira returned with a kettle and glasses. Temina jumped out of bed, fully dressed, leaped toward her bag, and pulled out a yellow tin filled with baked goods, saying, "They're from our village, homemade with our own flour and butter. Dr. Herbst, try some and tell me if they're not better than all the cakes and pastries in town. I know that scholars don't tend to have opinions on food, drink, and the like. Still, you ought to know the difference between our baked goods and what one gets in the city. Here, one dough takes many forms. While we don't bother about the form, we fuss over the contents, and each cake has a different flavor."

Herbst took one of the cakes, thinking: If I hadn't given Lisbet Neu the chocolate, I could have added it to this feast. He reached for a glass of tea. Temima said, "So your daughter came for the workshops." Herbst nodded, thinking to himself: What will Zahara say when she hears where this nurse met her father? Shira peered at him and said, "You look as if you're pondering the seven wonders of the world." Temima said, "We can list more then seven wonders. What does the doctor think about our cakes? They say no one can cook or bake on the *kvutza*, which is outright slander. Try another. No, take this kind. It's even better than the first." Herbst said, "It's time for me to go." Shira said, "Even before you came, it was time for you to go, but since you are here, sit down." Temima said, "So, my friends, you live in Jerusalem. I admit that our Jerusalem is a truly glorious city. The view from Mount Scopus can't be matched anywhere in the Emek. Altogether, I must say that . . . But what can I say, when you already know?"

Herbst lowered his head and lifted a finger toward the left side of his brow while holding on to his cup. After a while, he put down the cup and studied Böcklin's skull. Did Böcklin paint from a model or from his imagination? Why do I ask? Herbst wondered.

Temima continued, "Most of the cultural institutions, headed by the university—which truly belongs here—are in Jerusalem. The National Library and the Bezalel Museum, for example. So naturally there are many cultured people, more than anywhere else in the country, and every new book, as well as every new idea, comes here before it comes to our *kvutza*. Still, I can say that, when I come from my *kvutza* to Jerusalem, I don't feel inadequate. To borrow a term from Freud, I don't have an inferiority complex. After all, we in our villages are also promoting the country's interests. A few days ago, I happened on a book of philosophical essays and I found something on this subject that

I can quote word for word. If the capital is the head of the city, then the villages are its limbs. To which I add: Just as a body can't live without a head, a head can't exist without limbs." Shira said, "I see, Temima, that you're looking for an excuse for living in the country rather than the city." Temima said, "What makes you think I'm looking for excuses? Besides, what difference can one person make in times such as these? I don't mean myself and those like me. What I have in mind is the world at large. You have to consider whatever is going on in the era it is your fate to be living in and account for every single action. We have no right to let actions go by without examining them and concerning ourselves with them." Shira said, "And if you and I don't concern ourselves with whatever is going on in the world, will anything be different?" Temima said, "Really, I don't understand what you mean." Shira said, "I think I'm making myself clear." Temima said, "I'm surprised at you, Shira. After all, a person is a person. Isn't it a primary duty to reflect about and consider whatever is going on in the world, all the more so here in this country, since we came here for a specific purpose?" Shira said, "Well spoken, Temima. We came for a purpose. The question is: For what purpose?" Temima said, "Really, I don't understand what you are saying. What did we come for? For . . . for . . ." Shira laughed and said, "Temima, your name means 'innocence,' and you are as innocent as your name. Don't wear yourself out looking for sublime words. I'm satisfied with what you said. We came for a purpose." Temima said, "Really, I must repeat, I don't understand you." Shira said, "If I were ten years younger, I would envy you. Imagine, you are still looking for reasons to be where you are. We're here because we're here and nowhere else. And, if my view is too simple for you, that doesn't change a thing. I don't presume to phrase my ideas the way you do in the *kvutza,* but they are sincere."

Herbst sat thinking many thoughts, having to do with another place and another time. If we look for a reason, only one comes to mind. Dr. Herbst wished to withdraw from his present company, if not in person, then in thought. Herbst asked himself: This skull of Böcklin's—how was it drawn? From a model or from the imagination? Actually, Böcklin himself has answered my question. Where do we find his answer? He complained that he never had the chance to draw a woman from life, because his wife, who was Italian, was jealous and wouldn't allow him to have a model in his studio. But why am I thinking about Böcklin's skull painting? Is it because that nurse mentioned Bezalel? No, I thought of the question even before she mentioned Bezalel. Yes, Zahara went back and won't be at the workshops. So, obviously, the nurse won't see her and say where she met her father. Herbst looked at his watch and said, "Time to go. What's this? My watch has stopped." He took off his watch and set it, guessing at the time, not bothering to look at the numbers, and thinking to himself: I'm leaving this place, calm and confident, as if there were no reason to worry about the nurse telling Zahara that she met her father. Even if she were to tell her, she wouldn't necessarily say where and when she saw me. Even if she did say when and where she saw me, Zahara, in the innocence of her heart and purity of her mind, would think nothing of it. And, if she were to wonder, her wonder wouldn't last. Many things happen. Before you have a chance to attend to one thing, there is another on the horizon. We, too, rather than dwell on the past, should attend to what's ahead.

Herbst took leave of Shira and Temima. He was on his way, restating to himself what he had said before: I'll put the past behind me and attend to what's ahead.

I'm going home to my wife, who urged me to take a walk before going to bed so my sleep would be sweeter. I went out for a bit, and the time stretched to several hours. What did I find in that time? I found Lisbet Neu. When I left her, I went to the bus stop, meaning to go home. I didn't find the bus. I waited, and it didn't come. Meanwhile, I heard the day's news. If one were to be precise, I doubt it could be called news, since there is nothing new about it. Events that recur every day can hardly be called new. What do we consider new? A story with danger and with Arabs. Two Arabs come to an old woman and ask for water. They shoot her, though she has provided them with water. She falls in a pool of blood and dies. How naive that old woman was. Innocent blood is being spilled in this country, and it didn't occur to her that what happens to others could happen to her. What happened in the end? In the end, they killed her.

So much for the old woman and the villains who killed her. Let's get back to Herbst. Herbst was walking home and thinking as he walked: I left the others waiting for the bus and went to Shira. I arrived at Shira's and found her shipmate there, a good woman, if a somewhat simple one. But what does a man know about a woman? A man doesn't really know a woman except . . . Take Shira. Before I was close to her, didn't I see her the way she makes others see her? Remembering Shira, his voice began to intone, "Flesh such as yours / Will not soon be forgotten."

He grew silent and reviewed the entire Shira episode, since he began to be close to her. He argued with himself: What did I think when I first knew her? Was I so innocent as to think I wouldn't have to put myself out for her, that I could come at any time? What did she do?

When I came, she made it clear that she had a will too, that her will was different from mine. He reviewed all of his struggles with her. There must have been other men, the engineer and his like. Without envy, without hatred, he enumerated all the men Shira had told him about. They had no reality. Shira was the sole reality. Again she was there, before his eyes, revealed in all the forms he had seen her assume, and as each form unfolded, his voice intoned, "Flesh such as yours . . ."

He suddenly waved his hands, as if to repel something unwelcome. But the very knowledge he was trying to repel seemed to become more and more palpable with every thought. He sighed from the heart and mused: As long as she exists, I will not be rid of her, whether or not that's what she wants. As it is in the nature of thoughts to come and go, an evil thought came to him: Should something happen to her, if she were to be hit by a bus and run over, or if she were to come down with one of the dread diseases she treats, he would be rid of her forever.

Shira appeared before him again, as he had seen her that first night in her house, in her room, dressed in dark blue pants and a thin shirt, when, to his astonishment, as soon as she put on male attire, her masculine qualities vanished and she became all the more female. He opened his mouth wide; the edges of his teeth protruded and began to strike each other. He stood, shouting, "If you insist on living, live, as long as you are transformed into a man!"

He gradually calmed down. He wiped his brow and said, "Far be it from me to wish you misfortune, Shira. Live, but let me be, so I can live too. And, if you like, go off with your lovers and marry them. You could marry the one who gave you the cigarettes, or, if you prefer, the one with the whip, or that blind Turk. I won't interfere. I will entertain you with a lovely tune, if you like." He began singing, "Flesh such as yours . . ." Before he got to "Will not soon be forgotten," his limbs became inert, and he was suffused with a pleasant sensation. The entire world became inert and vanished. Even Shira became inert and vanished. Only Herbst continued to exist.

When he got home and climbed into bed, he didn't think about Shira or about anything in the world or about what had happened on the way. He rested his head on the pillow and stared at the ceiling and at his shadow on the wall. While he was watching the shadow, it closed its eyes, exactly as Herbst himself did. The house was quiet. At intervals, a sigh could be heard in Henrietta's room, but it didn't reach Manfred's ears, because of the snore from the wall or from the shadow on the wall.

Now something occurred that was either a dream or I don't know what it was. Manfred Herbst had a childhood friend, a Greek scholar who used to correct Wilamowitz's translations of the Greek tragedies. One day, he abandoned his studies and left for America. The war came, and there was no trace of him until he came back and was exiled to a detention camp. He suddenly appeared in Mea Shearim. Or perhaps in Tel Aviv. No, it was Mea Shearim, because, when he and Manfred went walking, Mount Zion walked with them. During their entire walk, they never asked each other what they had been doing all those years, but they did discuss gender restriction in language, particularly those words that are masculine in one language and feminine in another. Herbst was going to mention Neu's definition of the word *piyyut* (poetry) as an example. Before he could mention it, his friend bent down and said, "I think my shoes are torn." Herbst took him to a shoemaker. When they were at the shoemaker, Herbst noticed that his shoes were also in need of repair. He extended his legs, slipped off his shoes, and handed them to the shoemaker. The shoemaker took them, rounded the toes, and stitched them with white raffia. The American reached into his pocket and paid the shoemaker what he asked, sixty grush. Herbst began arguing with the shoemaker. Not only had he ruined the shoes and changed their shape, but he was asking sixty grush, which was too high a price. Hearing the argument, the neighbors appeared. Everyone at the Bezalel exhibit came too, as well as all those who were praying in the Emet Veemunah Synagogue next to Bezalel. Herbst wanted to tell them what the shoemaker had done. He realized there wasn't time, since he had to rush off to the wedding of Shira and Lisbet Neu. They were marrying each other, and he still hadn't given them a wedding present. He left all the people to wonder about him and ran to a craftsman, from whom he bought a knife of pure silver. He ran and brought it to Lisbet and Shira—a wedding gift to gladden their hearts.

With this I have concluded Book One of the book about the nurse Shira and Dr. Manfred Herbst. I will begin another, in which I will recount what followed.

BOOK TWO

— 1 —

It was two years since Herbst met the nurse Shira. Many things had happened in those years. Not only in the world, but in Herbst's home as well. I will now recount some of what was new with Herbst.

Little Sarah was already walking, like all bipeds, and chattering away like a full-fledged person. Her speech was still a jumble of single words, but her mother knew how to combine them. Apart from this, she was very clever and showed her cleverness in every realm. Henrietta had a chicken coop. Once, when Henrietta was trying to get a chicken out of the coop, it escaped, and another one flew into her hand. Sarah chased it away and caught the fugitive. Another time, two days after her birthday, her mother was baking a cake for Shabbat. Sarah remembered that it was her doll's birthday and she hadn't baked her a cake yet. She went and told her mother, who gave her a pinch of dough, from which Sarah made a cake. These were some of Sarah's tricks, and they provided some solace for Henrietta.

Henrietta managed to get a certificate for her brother. In the interim, he was offered a certificate for South America and went there instead. Henrietta got a certificate for another relative. In the interim, the Nazis harassed him out of existence, and he was dead. Henrietta tried to transfer the certificate to another relative and was told, "Why not?" Again, she ran around in a panic, for what had happened to her dead relative could happen to a live one. It was the anguish over these certificates that aged her prematurely. Since she considered herself old, the whole world seemed old to her, and she made no attempt to improve herself for her husband. Nor did she remark affectionately, as she used to, "Are there no young women in Jerusalem who would be glad to be with you?" Such talk was far from her lips and, needless to say, from her heart. Now all of Henrietta's conversation with Manfred related to their daughters, to Tamara, for instance, who has finished her studies but has no job. All the openings are in depressed villages or in older settlements abandoned by the younger generation. A young teacher ought to be placed in a school in town, so she can learn from experienced teachers and from the principal, which is impossible in a far-flung village where the teachers and principal are second-rate. Meanwhile, she wastes her time on enterprises that please neither her father, her mother, nor even herself. A grown daughter can be an asset to her mother, but Tamara is incompetent in household matters and adds to her mother's work. Henrietta Herbst, who taught Arab women domestic skills, didn't teach them to her own daughter. Tamara spends half the day in bed, the other half in a telephone booth calling half of the directory. She spends evenings in a café, a cigarette in her mouth, a scornful look on her face, young men enveloping her in clouds of pipe smoke while she envelops them in clouds of cigarette smoke. When the band strikes up a tune, she dances, making no attempt to avoid the English officers, whose language she knows if not their intentions. Perhaps she does know their intentions and assumes her scorn will repel them too.

As for Zahara, we had the impression that her heart was drawn to Avraham-and-a-half or Heinz the Berliner. But she suddenly seems attracted to someone else, who doesn't measure up to the former in height or to the latter in intelligence. Who is he? Heinz from Darmstadt. In fact, he is also one of the founders of Ahinoam, a good fellow, too, with some virtues the others lack. But why should a girl wear herself out and be torn between so many? This was not her mother's way. Before Henrietta knew Manfred, she didn't look at another man, and as soon as she got to know him, she clung to him. Before Manfred knew Henrietta, his eyes were buried in his books. Other than Henrietta, no young woman, however scholarly or beautiful, distracted him from his studies, although he lived in Berlin, whose very air loosens the constraints of the heart and the eye. This daughter of theirs lives in a small *kvutza* in the Land of Israel, settled by young men and women who left Germany to live a pure life on the land. But, in the end, she doesn't measure up to her parents. Which is especially perplexing, for she is a girl with a head on her shoulders and eyes in her head. Why should she be groping as if she were blind?

Let me get back to Dr. Herbst. His great work on burial customs of the poor in Byzantium is in progress—a mass of references, notes, index cards, notebooks, quotations, outlines that remain incomplete, material that is still not in order. Herbst sits at his desk, removes a slip of paper, and replaces it with another. He writes, erases, records, copies, pastes in quotation after quotation, and substitutes a more appropriate word wherever possible. A scholar's wisdom is not like dough in a woman's hand, from which a piece can be torn to make a cake for a doll's birthday. It is bothersome, like the chickens in their coop when you reach for one and another comes flying into your hand; not only do you have to pursue the one you want, but you have to struggle to get rid of the one in your hand. This may be a false analogy; still, it applies to the scholar's struggle with his material. However, it must be noted that Herbst's struggles are not in vain. Any author would be proud of the data Herbst has amassed. When he surveys his material, he often thinks: I'll sit down and organize, combine, and copy, and I'll have a book. But wisdom has such scope and is contained in so many volumes that no scholar can know today what tomorrow will bring. He persists, continuing to do today what he did yesterday and every other day, in some cases to support his data and in others to avoid discovering later that he left something out. There are scholars whose expertise is bewildering. Their bibliography alone occupies a third of the book, and when you examine it you realize that most of the books mentioned are irrelevant. Other scholars, after citing many sources, add *see* and *see also*. In fact, they have copied their material from such *see also*s, which is to say that the sources referred to by *see also* are the ones from which they have copied their data, never having seen the original books from which the data are derived. Still, should someone say, "Others have preceded you," they can point out, sanctimoniously, that full credit was given. Other scholars quote extensively from their own books; that is to say, they cite themselves as authorities. If this isn't a matter of extreme innocence, then it's a game, for they play at showing how smart they are, how many books they have already produced. There are scholars who quote the opinions of others, not to support their own, but to dispute them.

Manfred Herbst did not behave in any of the aforementioned ways. One could say that he and his work were clean. So he ought to have been pleased with himself, but he was not. When he confronted his box of notations, his piles of cards, his collection of notebooks, bundles of papers and pads, and heaps of writings, he would sometimes pound the table and cry out, "May flames leap up and consume you." But, as long as they existed, it was his duty to rework, amend, and update them. He went back to his work, continuing to do today what he did yesterday and all the other days. He worked without joy, for there is no joy in amassing papers, even if the papers are full of fine quotations. When Herbst first thought of writing his book, he was inspired by an idea. As he began to support it with facts, the facts took over, and the idea dwindled. Finally, his box was full of facts but short on substance.

Herbst left his desk and notes, lit a cigarette, and went to the west window, which was curtained in a colorful woven fabric. Under it was a bookcase that used to be filled with fine china from the era of Frederick II, made in the royal factory. The pieces were passed on to Henrietta by her parents and grandparents, for the king, known as Frederick the Great, required every Jew in his kingdom who wished to marry to buy dishes produced in his factory. In time, these dishes were broken since the local help in the Land of Israel was unaccustomed to handling such fragile objects. What wasn't broken, Henrietta sold to buy reproductions for Manfred or traded for books, and what they neither sold nor traded, they gave as a gift to the Bezalel Museum. When there was no china left on the shelves, Henrietta began putting volumes of poetry, stories, and novels there. Occasionally, when she was done with her work, she would come in and take a book to read. Manfred, too, when he was despondent and wanted to regain his composure, would reach for a book.

These books lie there, small volumes that don't attract attention or catch the eye because of their form or content. They were written by individuals who, for the most part, never saw the inside of a university and never studied with the scholars of their day. They wrote in the recesses of their rooms, tormented by hunger and other trials. Their wisdom was gleaned in the marketplace and on the streets, from every man, woman, and child; from animals, beasts and birds; from dusty roads and chilly winds; from the sun, the moon, and the stars; from trees in the wood and streaming river waters. These are books about people of no consequence, yet, if one examines the plots, one finds insight as well as basic wisdom of the sort one has to struggle to extract from other sources, heavy tomes written in profound language and complex terminology.

Not all the books the Herbsts brought from Germany were still in the bookcase. Some had been borrowed and never returned. Zahara took some of them with her to the *kvutza*. Though the settlers in Ahinoam have truly turned their backs on Germany, Austria, or Czechoslovakia to make a new life in the Land of Israel, when it comes to books, they behave as they did in their birthplace. What they used to read there, they read here. Even Tamara, who can barely read German, began taking books off these shelves. When she had finished her courses and received a teachers' certificate, she discarded all the books about yeshiva students, old men with earlocks, beggars, and eccentrics of all kinds—all those types celebrated by Hebrew literature—and turned to books in other languages that told about real people, the kind whose thoughts and actions a civilized person is interested in. After reading everything that had been translated into Hebrew, she began reading English and even German. It's an odd thing: visitors who come from Germany say that, since the Nazi rise to power, they have begun to value a single line of Hebrew more than all of Goethe and Kant; yet this girl, conceived, born, and educated in the Land of Israel, whose friends were all born there, who speaks Hebrew fluently—she replaces Hebrew books with gentile books and, what is more, she calls the Hebrew books "drivel." When Herbst's supply of poetry, novels, and stories began to dwindle, he filled the space with biographies. Everyone should study the lives of famous men, as a source of strength and an antidote to despair, evidence that even the finest human beings were human and they too, were subject to the wheel of fortune and often discouraged—although this is not stated explicitly, either because no one reveals everything or because biographers, wishing to glorify the lives of exemplary people, suppress whatever is not praiseworthy about them. Still, whoever can read between the lines is rewarded. Now that Herbst's task seemed lighter to him, he reached into the bookcase and took out a book.

As soon as he began reading, he forgot why he was reading and found himself reading for pleasure. He read on, smiling every so often and shaking his head at the book, as if to say: How innocent this author is! Doesn't he know that even the greatest human being sometimes hits bottom and is flung from soaring heights to earth's deepest abyss? I am not a great man, nor do I have the arrogance of the great; I am, furthermore, grateful to those powers that didn't endow me with a sense of my own greatness. But I would guess that even the great men of the world were not always so wise, that their actions were not always a credit to them, that they were careful to conceal unbecoming actions and not to make them public except, perhaps, when their very faults were praiseworthy.

Very slowly, his rational processes were suspended, and his critical faculties were replaced by a sense of pleasure. He read with utter pleasure and with a yearning that added a physical dimension to his sensual pleasure. His soul was transported from one realm to another, and he began to feel as if he were the character he was reading about. This crossing of souls and spirits was accompanied by envy, the envy scholars indulge in. Tears filled his eyes as he considered his empty, wasted life. But his envy was fruitless, his tears futile, for neither led to action. His notebooks, lists, notations, and manuscript were like an abandoned egg that would never hatch. Herbst put down the biography of some great man and returned to his box of notes, putting one in, taking one out. If Henrietta were watching, she would assume he was busy with his book. Actually, only his hands were busy, like a card player who keeps shuffling the deck even when he is alone, out of sheer habit.

—— 2 ——

As it happened Herbst was at his desk, occupied with his notes, not thinking about anything. He looked at the notes and discovered that the material seemed to fit together to form a discrete chapter. What was not the case with Homer's poems—which, as one scholar has noted, are not mere letters arranged at random—was the case with the book about burial customs of the poor in Byzantium. All of a sudden, at random and inadvertently, an entire chapter had put itself together. Herbst had worked on it for many years; suddenly, it took care of itself. What needs to be done now? It needs to be edited, erasing what should be erased, adding what should be added, correcting the language, explaining abbreviations and the like, until the chapter stands on its own— since, to a great extent, it is a subject in itself.

How is it a subject in itself? In their legal code, a husband cannot divorce his wife, nor can a woman divorce her husband, since the Torah declares, "They became one flesh." Their lawmakers took this to mean that what the Creator has combined into one flesh, no man may put asunder, adding that in some cases a man is allowed to divorce his wife, but a woman may never divorce her husband. The Byzantine emperor, Leo the Isaurian, however, introduced four situations in which a woman could rid herself of her husband; should he get leprosy, for example, the woman could rid herself of him. This ruling, along with related material, formed a chapter in itself for Manfred Herbst. As he looked it over, he decided to copy it out; as he copied it out, he corrected and rewrote. Once it was edited, written, and rewritten, he sent it abroad to the editor of the journal of research in Byzantine antiquities in which all the great Byzantine scholars are published. Believe it or not, although anti-Semitism was intense, and most gentile scholars lent support to our enemies, they welcomed this article by Dr. Herbst of the Hebrew University in Jerusalem. Scholarship has its own dominion, which villainous hands fail to rock.

It was only a few months before the journal arrived in Jerusalem. Believe it or not, even the scholars on Mount Scopus took note of Manfred Herbst's chapter and said, "This makes sense." Sometimes the world tires of its follies and begins to smile on its creatures. Everyone was certainly astonished: this Herbstlein, whom they tolerated because he was such a modest man and because he made no effort to advance himself, took everyone by surprise with this article. Herbst had already published a book of more than six hundred pages, so why the uproar over a single article? If you like, I will tell you. Whatever a scholar wrote in his youth is prehistoric. If you like, I will tell you more. Herbst had already cashed in on his book, having won his appointment because of it. Eminent faculty members now talk about him in favorable terms. Those who seldom speak positively about anyone have nothing negative to say about him. If one of them is forced to mention him, he is sure to add, "Too bad he didn't show me his article before sending it out; I might have made some comments." Saying this, he thinks to himself: If I read it again, I will surely have something to add. In short, suddenly, with very little warning, Herbst's star began to rise.

Let me say a word about envy. A person who develops step by step gives his friends a chance to observe him and become envious, which is not the case when a person's talents emerge suddenly, in full power. Friends, having had no time to observe him, have had no time to become envious. They don't seem to mind that he has achieved a measure of happiness. They even seek his welfare on occasion, and, if he takes the world by surprise with a great book or an important article, they treat him as they always have, for habit goes a long way. As for those who didn't know him before, they are obviously not susceptible to envy or hatred, envy being reserved for intimates or acquaintances.

Since Manfred Herbst didn't arouse the envy of colleagues, what began as a somewhat favorable response to him escalated, becoming intensely favorable. When the board of governors, or the senate, met to consider his promotion, no one objected, except Professor Bachlam, who was always grudging, all the more so toward scholars from Germany, who tended to disparage him and disregard his scholarship, although he had produced books that were on a par with theirs. In brief, it was suddenly the consensus that Manfred Herbst deserved to be promoted—for the moment, to the level of associate professor, not full professor. Though there was no additional salary involved, there was added prestige. Sometimes a lecturer is promoted but makes do with a lecturer's salary, since the university cannot afford to pay a professor's salary to every instructor who is promoted; the university's expenses are soaring rapidly, and its income doesn't grow proportionately. Its employees no longer receive their monthly salary three days early; now they're lucky to be paid three days late.

Back to Herbst. It was about to happen. Manfred Herbst was going to be appointed a professor, like Bachlam and Ernst Weltfremdt and Lemner and Wechsler and all the other professors at the Hebrew University in Jerusalem who achieved this high position because of their books or social connections. Were we to judge by the polished brass nameplates gleaming on their doors, this was a good thing; if we look to the heart, what's so good about it?

There is a simple creature in this world, named Shira. Just when fortune begins to smile on Herbst, this creature, Shira, puts him off. On the face of it, she shows warmth; actually, she shows only the freckles on her face, which is to say that, when he comes to her, she shows only her face, that's all. Unlike that night when he first knew her, when she was so affectionate that there could be no other woman as affectionate; unlike the three or four nights that followed, when she was not as affectionate as on the first night, but she did respond to him, though not as he wished, yet we can say she responded, and he was in another world because of her. Herbst sits wondering why that night was different. When he saw her for the first time, expecting nothing, she was very affectionate, whereas, now that he is obsessed by her, she doesn't notice him. Has she found more adequate companions, lovers? Herbst isn't jealous, nor does he wish to know who they are. Herbst's mind is on Shira, who is above all women, whom none can match. Whether he sees or imagines her, that phrase "Flesh such as yours . . ." is fixed on his lips.

Herbst tries to extricate himself from this chaos of Shira thoughts, which are boundless and infinite, whose sole effect is to suspend all other enterprises. Herbst turns his mind back to his work, to his book, to the material he has compiled, collected, selected, copied, and invented. He begins to relate to his book as if it is already there, as if it exists, as if all the notes were gathered together in a single volume. What does Shira do? Surfacing from the dimness of his thoughts, she appears before him.

When it comes to self-deception, Herbst is cautious, and he examines his actions with total objectivity. He is aware that, even when his book is completed, his ultimate goal will not be realized. He regards the actions of others with the same objectivity. Even those who have published several books will not affect the heavenly bodies, nor will they change the course of our world. Though learning is a dominion in itself, it holds no golden scepter in its hand.

I'll get back to Shira now. Shira is not the same Shira we knew two years ago. Her upper lip is wrinkled, and her hair is beginning to turn gray. She is still in her prime, but she's becoming slovenly. Though her clothes are old, she doesn't replace them. The walls of her room are peeling, but she doesn't arrange to get them repainted. The print of the skull has yellowed frightfully, and it looks as if a real skull is staring at you. What Böcklin's brush didn't accomplish has been accomplished by Shira's slovenliness; she has stopped dusting the picture. Only the bed has changed its place. It used to be in the southeast corner; it is now in the northwest. Was it Shira's idea to move the bed or someone else's? It doesn't really matter, except that all these thoughts of Shira bring on other thoughts that relate to Shira. He tires of them—they never tire. They give him wings, and he takes off and flies to Shira. When he comes, she welcomes him, offers cigarettes, fruit, and tea. Herbst lights a cigarette, takes some fruit, drinks a glass of tea, and thinks to himself: The things she gives me are presents from lovers; just as she gives me the gifts her lovers give her, she gives her lovers the gifts I give her. None of this disturbs him. It does disturb him that, though her hair is graying, she doesn't dye it; though her clothes are worn, she doesn't replace them; though she has lost a tooth, she doesn't get a false one. Is Shira so sure of herself, confident that she is still attractive? Herbst studies Shira and can only wonder: Why am I so drawn to her. If it's habit, Henrietta is more of a habit. Also handsomer, and of superior character. If Henrietta were in trouble, I would be very upset; if this one were in trouble, I would be glad to be rid of her. Herbst studies Shira repeatedly, through investigation and visitation. Before he has a chance to observe very much, his heart begins to flutter longingly.

Shira continues to behave in her usual fashion. On the face of it, she is warm, allowing him not a hairbreadth closer. She is frank with him, concealing none of her activities. That woman's activities are bizarre, and it is hard to come to terms with them. Doesn't she realize how misguided they are? Her talk is not loose, but it is certainly stimulating. Does she even have to stimulate his desire? Is there any reality to her stories? She once told him about an English soldier who came to her

one night. When did he come? He came after midnight. True, she
threw him out. In any case, the question stands: What was an English
soldier doing in the room of a Jewish nurse in the Land of Israel? What
business did Shira have with soldiers anyway? I say "soldiers," in the
plural, because once she went to Netanya, and, since she had to leave
early and didn't know how she would get to the train station with her
heavy luggage, the proprietress told her there was an Englishman there
who would take her luggage to the station. That night, when she was
in bed, the soldier came to her room. She said to him, "I'm old enough
to be your mother; you want to make love to a woman your mother's
age."

What will the future bring? Herbst asks himself. This question pertains not to the events of the world, nor to the murder of six hundred
Jews in a single year by the Arabs and the country's continued policy
of self-restraint, nor to the university or the concerns of his wife and
daughters, but to Shira, whom he has begun to call Nadia again. He
goes to her two or three times a month, and, whenever he happens to
be in town, he tries to make time for Shira. When he comes in, she
welcomes him, says, "Sit down," and offers him cigarettes, fruit, a
sweet, and tea. She discusses the news and whatever is going on at the
hospital. Sometimes, to accommodate him, she tells about herself, about
the past, which she prefers not to recall, on the theory that it no longer
affects her; only for his sake, because he wants to hear, does she talk
about it. When he tries to approach her, she makes a screen with her
hands and says, "Please, don't be childish." Herbst sits there feeling
scolded, praying to himself: If only she would reproach me, if only she
would say, "Don't come here." He himself doesn't want to stop, can't
stop, doesn't stop; he continues to come. And she continues to welcome
him, without allowing him a hairbreadth closer.

Just to please him, Shira returns to a subject she was in the middle
of, something she doesn't like to talk about but he likes to hear. She tells
him about the past, before she was married; about the young man who
saw himself as her protector, whom she rejected because, from early
childhood, she disliked anyone who tried to dominate her. What was
predicted for him in his youth was fulfilled. He had become prominent
as an orator, a politician, first in whatever he undertook. He was fea-
tured in all the newspapers and praised, for, when someone becomes
the head of an institution, many people depend on him, and the writers
hired to provide publicity for the institution weave the name of its head
into their text, sometimes even making him the subject of the entire
article. If some of these writers, seeing their words in print, cursed
whatever had moved them and cursed themselves for being moved, he

was becoming famous anyhow, and already there was a body of literature about him. As soon as the Diaspora began to shrink, so that he
couldn't find anything to do there, he came here. He does the same
things here that he did there. He is involved in everything, everywhere.
He orates, speechifies, takes charge.

Herbst scorned public figures and orators because the country was
so full of them. Still, he was surprised that Shira had plucked the fellow
from her heart. Like all people who tend not to become much involved
with others, Herbst considered everyone who ever crossed his path an
essential part of his world. He was therefore surprised how that was so
easy for her to pluck a childhood friend from her heart. He wondered
about her, but he was even more curious about that man, beyond what
she was willing to tell.

As minds wander, so did his mind wander once again to Lisbet Neu.
There really wasn't anything between them, nor was it possible that
there ever would be anything between them. But thoughts are
thoughts; they take their own course, and you can't tell them, "Please,
don't be childish."

Lisbet Neu is still working in the same place, which she sometimes
calls a store, sometimes an office. In either case, her salary is meager and
hardly adequate to provide for her and her sick mother. How do they
manage? They manage because the Torah instructs them to live. Lisbet
Neu has tried to find a job in a government office, but a young woman's
prospects are limited there. Her monthly salary would be ten lirot, with
no possibility of advancement. One would think that ten lirot a month
is a decent salary for a young woman who now earns only six lirot. But,
as was already noted, government offices offer a young woman no
opportunity for advancement, whereas here, in this store, the owner is
considerate and allows her to earn money on the side. What does this
mean? There are certain products he is not allowed to handle, because
he is the agent for other companies. He is reluctant to forgo the profit,
so he orders these products in Lisbet Neu's name, giving her two
percent of the profit. Two other young women work for him, but he
doesn't treat them as he does Lisbet Neu, who is his right hand. Herbst
doesn't know Lisbet Neu's employer and has no reason to know him.
He is aware of one thing: the man is an elderly bachelor. Why doesn't
he marry Lisbet? She is lovely, of good family, gracious, and skilled in
business. He probably doesn't need a wife. Some women are available
to men without the marriage ceremony.

The gentleman is rich. Surely he has an elegant apartment with fine
furnishings, and, when he invites a girl to his home, it goes to her head.
The first time, she comes feeling honored to have been invited; the

second time, hoping he finds her appealing and may even want to marry her. The third time—the devil knows her thoughts. It goes without saying that none of the above applies to Lisbet Neu. I doubt that she was ever in any man's home without her mother or her elderly uncle, Professor Neu.

Having mentioned young girls here, let me say something further about them. There are young girls in Jerusalem who used to live with their families in other countries, where they wore silk and ate fine food. They lived in splendid houses surrounded by maids who waited on them and gallant young men—intelligent, loving, and eager to please— as well as the finest teachers and educators, whose job it was to develop their sensibilities. Now these girls are up at dawn to earn the price of a crust of bread and a patch of roof. Some of them work in cafés, putting in an eleven-hour day, for which they are paid eight lirot a month. Some work in army canteens, where drink, revelry, and lewdness are the rule. There are other young women who came to Jerusalem to study at the Hebrew University with their parents' support, but, now that their parents are locked in ghettoes, the daughters spend half the day studying and the other half working for meager wages, barely able to support themselves and pay tuition. More than two years ago, the day Sarah was born, Dr. Herbst went to a restaurant for dinner, where he met a lovely and charming waitress, who gave him paper and envelopes so he could write to his daughters and inform them that their sister was born. Some time later he went there again, and, when he asked about her, he was told she had gone elsewhere and was working in a café frequented by Australian soldiers. The Australians are a good lot, easy with money and generous. They're not pompous like the English. They're friendly to us, so it's nice to work in the places they frequent.

As things happen, Herbst happened to see that waitress again. Much later, Herbst went on a trip to the Dead Sea with his wife and Tamara. They stopped at the main hotel for tea. Herbst saw a waitress whom he recognized, though she didn't recognize him. She saw so many people each day that new faces displaced the old ones. She came over and asked, "What would you like?" Her face was burned, her skin parched; her eyes had lost their luster. But she was gracious to the guests, like all waitresses in big hotels. Herbst identified himself to her, and she was pleased, as a lonely child who finds someone she knows in a crowd of strangers. For those who came to the hotel were strangers to her, while she knew him from the good days. What was better about those days? In those days, she was still endowed with the freshness of youth.

Manfred said to Henrietta, "Remember, Henrietta, the day Sarah was born I brought you a bottle of perfume with a scent you admired. I didn't tell you how I found that delicate perfume, but now I'll tell you. This woman gave me paper so I could write letters to our daughters, and the scent of the paper was so pleasant that I went to the pharmacy and asked for a bottle of perfume with that same scent. See, Henriett, I have secrets too. Secrets with young women. But in time every secret is discovered."

Manfred continued, "Would you guess that this girl was actually pretty, in addition to her charming, youthful ways?" Henrietta said, "She's still pretty." Manfred said, "If you hadn't said those words, I would have invited her to join us for a while." Henrietta laughed and said, "You can invite her." Manfred said, "You think it's all right to ask her to sit with us?" Tamara said, "If anyone were listening, he would think you're hammering out a program for the Zionist Congress. Comrade, come join us. This intellectual couple wishes to converse with you." The young woman laughed and came over. Henrietta said, "Won't you join us for a while, if you're free." Herbst was quick to offer her a chair, as if he were the host and she the guest, inviting her to sit down, moving his chair close to hers, asking questions for the sole purpose of making conversation—about the hotel and its guests, the British, the Australians. From there, he turned to questions about fortifications and road work the British were doing. Tamara sat there, inwardly scornful of these Zionists who see without knowing what they see and babble without understanding their own babble. Finally, she got up and left.

As soon as Tamara left, Herbst was relieved. He began asking questions and apologizing for each one. The young woman answered without hesitation and even volunteered information about herself and her family. The essence of her words was that her father had been rich and had provided her with excellent tutors. They taught her whatever one teaches the daughters of the rich, with the exception of Jewish subjects, which she was never taught. When disaster struck, German Jews didn't believe Hitler would remain in power. Her mother and father stayed in Berlin and sent her to the Land of Israel. Though their hearts did not instruct them to save themselves, they did instruct them to save the girl. She knew nothing about this country except what she had heard in speeches. She would have been better off without those speeches, for she would have tried to find out the things one needs to know when going to a new place. She came here and didn't know what to do. She worked as a waitress. When she lived in Berlin, she knew what to do. She wrote poems, some of which were published. In fact, one of her poems appeared in the *Frankfurter Zeitung*. Even here she continued to write, and she sent a story about a little girl in Jerusalem to the *Jüdische Rundschau*. Robert Weltsch sent the payment to her father.

She doesn't write at all now. The heat and work exhaust her; also she's not really inspired to write poems. If she knew Hebrew, the language might inspire her, and she would sing the songs of the land in its own language. It seems to her that a true poet can never make poems in a language alien to the land, But, being burdened with work, she hasn't learned Hebrew. The people she knows don't know Hebrew either. She has learned English, but not Hebrew. One doesn't learn the language unless those who live in the country demand it. One thing sustains her soul: once every two weeks, she has a day off and goes to Jerusalem to be with her friends, young poets from Germany. Their lot is no better than hers, except for the young man who managed to put out a book of poems on a stencil machine. He didn't cover his expenses and had to run around borrowing from one friend to pay the other. How does he live? Off his wife's salary. She makes dolls, but people who value their beauty can't afford to buy them, and those who have money have no taste, so the fate of the dolls is like that of the book. Along with all these misfortunes, there is also some good. She had two good days a couple of weeks back. How? That same couple has an adorable daughter, a child of about seven. They came with her, and the hotel owner allowed her to keep the child in her room, although waitresses are not usually permitted to have guests.

Tamara was back. She came and sat opposite the young woman, crossed her legs, and assumed the scornful manner we know so well. The young woman didn't notice. Or perhaps she noticed, but she paid no attention and kept right on talking, as the daughters of the rich tend to do. Even when overwhelmed by disaster, they talk about themselves without complaining. And yet, from their accounts of their good fortune, one recognizes the sort of trouble they're in.

Henrietta wiped her eyes and recalled various young girls she had known. Some of them, bringing regards from relatives, clung to her, coming again and again, hanging on even after they were settled. Others never returned. She took excessive pains on behalf of some and not enough on behalf of others. However much you delude yourself with the notion that you have done all you could, this is not the point; quite apart from you, a tender soul is involved, which exists and persists just as you do, and this is the point. Henrietta's thoughts were blurred, and even before they had a chance to register, they faded away. Some of these thoughts had to do with a girl Manfred said was related to Neu. But she was displaced by Zahara and Tamara. From the start, she had been thinking about her daughters, but she dismissed these thoughts, rather than connect her daughters' fate with theirs. Suddenly, her daughters came to mind again. Zahara belongs to a *kvutza* and, so far as one can see, she has settled down. But Tamara, Tamara . . .

Tamara sat there, ambivalent. One eye was on the young woman whose woeful tale played on her nerves; the other eye took in every detail and was eager for more. She turned her head to the left and scrutinized her, as if to ask: What do those stories mean? Finally, Tamara pinched her lips together and questioned her. "Tell me, comrade, why didn't you go to a *kvutza?*" The waitress answered, "I don't know why, but, since I didn't go to a *kvutza* when I first came, I didn't go later either. Why don't I go now? Because of a jaw injury. Though it isn't visible, it requires attention, and I may have to go to the hospital. The doctor isn't worried about infection; still, he warned me not to neglect it. Besides, I doubt if I could succeed on a *kvutza*. The only thing I can do is wait on tables, which I can barely do. And I can do that only because I'm used to it. Having worked in several restaurants and hotels, I'm used to the work, so I keep doing it." Henrietta asked, "And what will you do in the summer? The hotel closes in the summer, doesn't it?" The girl said, "I don't know what I'll do yet. I might work in a café in Jerusalem. New ones open every day. Even a waitress like me can find a job. If I don't find one, I won't worry. I'm tired, dead tired. And if you ask what I'll eat, I've saved enough money to support myself for three or four months. I haven't saved a lot, but my needs are few, and I can make do with very little. Food doesn't count as much as sleep. I daydream about sleep. When I get out of the hospital in good health, I'll rent a room and spend my days and nights sleeping. Here in this hotel at the Dead Sea, I don't sleep. True, there are days in the winter when this entire area is like the Garden of Eden—a Garden of Eden for the guests, not for those who serve them. In any case, I'm doing better than most of my girlfriends, not to mention the men, who can barely keep themselves going. Some of them are poets who were widely published and translated in Germany. Here, they make the rounds of editors, and when an article is accepted and they get forty or fifty grush, they are grateful, though they often have to share their pay with a translator."

In the midst of the conversation, the girl got up to wait on a guest. She returned, bringing tea and cakes, sat down again, and talked until it was time for them to go. Herbst took out his wallet to pay. The girl looked at him with imploring eyes and said: "If I may ask a favor, let me ask you to be my guests instead of paying for the drops of tea you drank." Herbst saw the look in her eyes, put back his wallet, and patted her hand in thanks, while Henrietta invited her to visit them at home in Jerusalem.

—— 3 ——

The day was spent in rest and pleasure; then the night began to emerge from various corners, visible and invisible. It was still not fully night-time, yet there were clear signs of night. The world was ringed by hushed dimness and filled with it. Within the hushed dimness, a light twinkled, darkened, glowed, and darkened again, so that the whole world was darkness within darkness. The sort of warmth that causes no discomfort wrapped itself around the small band of travelers waiting for the Jerusalem bus. Suddenly a clear speck split the sky, followed by a second speck and a third, from which stars were created. Some remained stuck in the sky; others ignited higher stars; still others ignited low stars in the Dead Sea. The travelers waited silently. Soon the bus came. They boarded, took seats, and looked back at the salty still-ness, watching it revert to solitude. As the driver put his hand on the steering wheel, the bus began to roll across the silent roads, where there was no sound, no aftersound.

Manfred and Henrietta sat together, with Tamara across from them. Their minds were at rest, filled with joy and tranquility, which occurs when a day is spent peacefully and appropriately. Two or three times, Herbst reached into his pocket for a cigarette but didn't take one. He suddenly seized Henrietta's hand, pressed it fondly, and said in a whis-per, "Weren't we smart to come here?" Henrietta nodded and said, "You were smart, Fred." Tamara heard and remarked to herself: I've been here many times, but I never enjoyed the trip as much as I did today with these two old folks.

The road provided Herbst with a respite from memories of Shira. When he became aware of this fact, he thought to himself: Then there are ways to put her out of my mind. He clutched his wife's hand again and said, "We should go on a trip such as this every month." Henrietta nodded and said, "Yes, dear, every month." Manfred added, "Then you agree, Henriett?" Henrietta answered, "By all means." Manfred knew these were empty words, that once he was back in Jerusalem he would sink into his space, go back to his desk—to his note box, pads, notebooks, and outlines—and who knows when he would travel again; in a few months, or a few years. But he recognized that one should get out of the house at regular intervals, that getting out of the house fortifies one's body, settles one's mind, relieves all sorts of stress. Once again he looked at his wife: Henrietta, mate and companion, who shared his fate, sustained him, was concerned with his welfare since long ago, before he was in the army, throughout the war, and in the days that followed, in Berlin as in Jerusalem.

Henrietta carried herself like a woman who has thrived and been successful most of her life, who knows through whom she has achieved this success and that she deserves whatever she has achieved. For she has labored over him, looked after him, made it possible for him to concentrate on his work, and protected him from other business. Even when she was involved with matters it was hard for her to handle alone, she didn't intrude on his work.

Considering his age, he was healthy and sound, young and vigorous. She gazed at him with pride and pleasure. Compared to his friends, he was a youth. True, she had lost her own spark along the way, but Manfred made it worthwhile. Besides, all she required or wanted was some peace of mind, her daughters' happiness, and Fred's success.

Henrietta sat curled up, as she used to sit sometimes when she was young, in the old days. When something pleasurable came her way, her shoulders contracted with pleasure and contentment. In those days, she would stretch out gracefully, whereas now she didn't have the strength to straighten up, so her shoulders simply sagged. Her mind began to wander and rove in many directions—what was, as well as what she had hoped for that never came to be. How wonderful everything was, even now, after so many years, undisturbed by time. Henrietta extricated herself from a tangled thicket, like the night's brightness shining through its murky darkness. She saw herself and Manfred as they were in Berlin.

Manfred is standing at the clock in front of the train station at the zoo. Countless men and women come and go, but he doesn't notice, as if none of them exist. Henrietta is the one he wants to see, and he doesn't see her. But he yearns to see her. His patience gives out, and his eyes, eager for her, begin to speak, to shout: Come, Henrietta, come. She is there, but he doesn't see her. There are so many people separating them. He closes his eyes for an instant, so that when he opens them he'll see her standing before him or at his side. Henrietta observes all his moves and knows how to interpret them. Henrietta smiles. And she's right to smile, for, just when she is close enough so he could see her, he turns away to look at his watch. What does she do? She puts her hand on the watch. He looks up and sees her. He grabs her hand and wants to say something to her but can't find the words. He leads the way, walking with her in silence. They find their train and go together to one of those lovely spots outside of Berlin where woods, streams, lakes, and rivers exist side by side, and, in these streams, rivers and lakes, boats of all sizes skim the water, carrying men and women, boys and girls, the sun shining down on them from above and love shining from their hearts. The two of them, Henriett and Fred, are doubly warmed—by sunshine and by love. At last, they get out of the boat and hike through the woods. They come to a river, and, since there is no one else there, they take off their clothes and jump in, floating and frolicking like fish. Later on, later on they rent a boat and row down the river. They are alone on the water, far from anyone else and closer to each other than ever before.

These events were at the edge of Henrietta's memory. God in heaven, when did such things happen? Unless we say that we had an existence before this one, it's not possible to imagine that such things happened to us. A salty tear fell from her weary eyes onto her wrinkled face. She brushed it away with her little finger, gazing out at the ravines gleaming in the darkness of the salty desert. Manfred's heart was stirred, and he directed his eyes to the landscape Henrietta was gazing at. He took her hand again and clasped the finger with which she had brushed away her tear.

They sat without saying a word; they sat in silence. After a while he lifted her hand, put it down, lifted it again, and put it down with a smile, saying, "So, Henrietta, we saw the Dead Sea today, and now we are traveling though the Jericho Valley." Henrietta nodded. Her shoulders contracted as she whispered, "Yes, Fred. Yes, Fred." He began explaining how the Dead Sea was created, how the Jericho Valley was formed, where the palm trees come from. Henrietta sat listening as Manfred continued his discourse. "And now," Manfred said, "now, Henriett, I'll tell you something worth knowing. I was hiking in the Dead Sea Valley with a group that included heads of institutions and various scholars, among them Warburg. When we approached Masada, I wanted to climb up, but Warburg said to me, 'You've already been to Masada, and you'll have other opportunities to go there. Now come and help me collect some local plants.' I didn't turn the old man down. I went with him. While we were collecting grasses, he straightened up and, pointing his finger, said, 'This little country has twice as many plants as Germany. In Germany we can identify thirty thousand plants, and in this country we can identify sixty thousand, though we still haven't explored it all and there are undoubtedly more varieties to be discovered.' Warburg also told me that the palm tree originated here. Warburg never mentioned this in his books. He was always careful not to write anything until it was thoroughly researched and well documented. Since he didn't get around to validating this hypothesis, he never wrote about it. But he believed that the Jericho Valley was the birthplace of the palm tree, and I may be the only one to have heard this from him."

The universe cast off its shape and assumed it again, at first rapidly, then with restraint; with restraint, then rapidly. In between, it was permeated with brown, yellow, blue, and something more, which the eye couldn't grasp. Its margins were filled with silence that sounded like something audible and looked like something visible. If the eye managed to grasp a bit of that something, it was lost instantly in the endless multitude of colors, shifting in the twinkling of an eye, yet leaving their wondrous trace in the memory of those who saw them. Henrietta sat in a hush, marveling at everything she heard and everything she saw. It was clear to her that whatever she saw, she heard, and whatever she heard, she saw. Manfred was still talking. He told legends about the Dead Sea and the palms of Jericho that added substance to what she saw. Henrietta listened, stroking her husband's hand; Tamara listened and marveled; the other passengers listened and welcomed this family and this scholar, who imparted facts in a manner that was both informative and pleasurable. Before they knew it, they were in Jerusalem.

Tamara leaped off the bus, followed by Manfred, who helped Henrietta down. Henrietta was astonished to see her husband jump so easily, like a youngster. He was astonished too, feeling taller and lighter than usual, the weight of his pack having firmed up his bones, straightened his spine, and stretched his body to its full height. He thought to himself: If I didn't have to take my wife and daughter home, I would go into town and stop at Shira's to show her how lithe I am. Shira would be amazed. Even though she pretends not to notice that sort of thing, her eyes are sharp, and she notes every change. He glanced at his wife, who was standing with him, waiting for the bus to Baka. Their eyes met, and he saw a serene smile on her lips. He was stirred by this smile and smiled back, knowing that he had to go with his wife, thinking in his heart: Too bad Shira can't see me now, lithe, erect, tall. Never in all the time she's known me has she seen me like this.

Waiting for the bus, they were overcome with the fatigue that often

follows a trip. In Manfred's case, it was accompanied by fatigue of
another sort, the fatigue that takes over when you are in one place but
your thoughts have drifted elsewhere. Where had they drifted, and
why did they taunt him? He was tired and in no position to follow
them. Even if he were to go to Shira's, she probably wouldn't be in,
as she often worked at night. While he searched for a reason not to go
to Shira's, the bus appeared. Tamara leaped onto the bus and gave her
mother a hand. Tamara helped her from above, Manfred from below.
He boarded and sat beside her.

The bus began to move, unlike Manfred's thoughts. Fused and confused, they nestled like a cloud within a cloud, like layer within layer
of desert, with Manfred in their midst. He wasn't really there with his
wife. He was far away; and far, far away was Shira's house. She was
at home. She was wearing a sleeveless shirt and shorts; her arms and
knees were bare. She said, "Manfred, dear," and a sweet quiver spread
through his body. He sat across from her, counting her freckles.

Tamara asked, "Why are you staring at me, Father?" Manfred said,
"Am I staring at you?" Tamara said, "You've been gaping at me for
an hour now." Manfred said, "Why would I stare at you?" Tamara said,
"That's just what I was asking." Henrietta said, "Let him be, Tamara.
His mind is on his books." Tamara said, "Why don't you write novels,
Manfred?" "Novels?" Tamara said, "If you wrote novels, I would read
them, and I'd get to know you." Her father said, "And why don't you
write novels?" Tamara said, "I leave that to the waitresses who write
poems and fairy tales. This is such a long trip. It takes less time to get
from Jericho to Jerusalem than from the bus station to Baka. Comrade,"
she said, addressing the driver, "I see you enjoy my company." The
driver asked in surprise, "How is that?" Tamara said, "You're taking
so long. Would you give me a cigarette? My father doesn't give me
cigarettes. He thinks it's unbecoming for his daughter to smoke in
public." Henrietta said, "Are you mad? Do you intend to smoke in the
bus? Besides, didn't the doctor forbid you to smoke?" Tamara said,
"Hush, Henrietta, hush. Don't mention the doctor. That could ruin the
match." Henrietta laughed and said, "What does one do with such a
bizarre creature?" Tamara said, "Look, everyone, the bus is beginning
to move! One, two, three, four / Who is it that walks on four? / Four,
five, six, seven / A natural law set up in heaven. / A boy and a girl walk
on four / When they walk as one with however-many-more."

Herbst tried to sort out his thoughts. He remembered forgotten
things, and, remembering them, they became central to his thoughts.
He suddenly recalled a pleasant fragrance and saw sheets of paper
before his eyes. Not his notebooks, which gave off the smell of ink and

tobacco, but the paper that waitress had given him, the one who wrote poems and fairy tales. He remembered the day Sarah was born and remembered all of that day's events. He reflected: I doubt if anything that happened that day was as pleasurable to me as being in the restaurant and talking to that girl. Still, Herbst was annoyed at his wife for having invited her. He was annoyed for two reasons. First, because sometimes, when there was a guest, his wife wasn't free to pay attention to him, and, when such a girl visits strangers, she is sure to require special attention. And second, when Henrietta is busy, she expects him to deal with guests, although he is involved with his work and his mind isn't free for company. He hasn't even found time to call Lisbet Neu, although her uncle has done him several favors. And when he was about to call her, he didn't, because of Shira.

On another subject: Has Lisbet Neu left her job with that old bachelor? But why do I call him old, when he is no older than I am and, no doubt, looks younger, since he isn't married. I will now put the world out of my mind and devote myself to my book. But will I be permitted to devote myself to it? As soon as people sense you are busy, they come and interrupt you. Since I published my chapter on the four rulings of Leo the Heretic, editors of all the quarterlies have been asking for articles. Even the National Library has sent me a book to review.

Herbst took out his notebook to see when the review was due and realized he hadn't been given much time. Tomorrow he would probably be tired from the trip, and after that is Shabbat, when guests usually come. When do religious people have time to write their books? On Shabbat, they waste the day walking to a synagogue. "Personally, I don't like religious people," Shira said when we were walking on the new road to Beit Yisrael. "Fred," Henrietta was saying, "get your things. This is our stop."

— 4 —

When Herbst was in bed that night, he took out the book the National Library had asked him to review. After getting an overview of the book he read the jacket and noted: This book is right up my alley. It's about Theodora, the empress described by Procopius as the whore who ruled Byzantium.

Herbst moved the lamp closer to his bed, adjusted the wick, and began reading. He found nothing new, but still he was interested. Because there was no new material, the task was not demanding. But something about it irritated him. He didn't know what, which was all the more irritating. He mused: The author is certainly an expert and knows how to present his views convincingly. But . . . But . . . I'll sleep on it, and tomorrow I'll read more and find out.

The "but" that he couldn't identify kept him from sleeping. Herbst was not short on imagination; he was not one to get stuck on details, to see the whole. Nor was he one of those who drown the truth in some hypothesis, who appear to be reviving forgotten times, whose words have the aura of poetry, but, since they are not poets, their books are neither poetry nor truth. In addition to these negative virtues, Herbst knew how to clarify the material he dealt with and how to make a concrete picture for himself, certainly in the field of Byzantine history, to which he had devoted considerable thought.

Herbst lay in bed picturing Theodora in action. This woman, whose early years were spent in a circus, was empress for twenty-one years, assigning tasks to her lieutenants as a director assigns roles to actors. She seated and deposed popes, patriarchs, viziers, and generals; arranged divorces and marriages; had total command of her subjects. She committed scores of murders. Her victims were almost all male. One would suppose that, having been degraded by men in her youth, she was determined to avenge herself when she achieved high position. The most violent ruler of her time, she intended to exercise her power over these men, as they had done when she was the inferior. In any case, late in life she behaved charitably, freeing young girls from the circus masters who owned them and maintaining homes for them.

After reviewing her behavior, he compared it with the behavior of her husband, Emperor Justinian. Justinian enacted laws of chastity, which she overruled. He forbade women to bathe with strange men, to go to circuses at night without an escort, or to spend the night away from home. Theodora, on the other hand, supported adulterous women, and her rulings favored them over their faithful husbands. As someone has rightly said, women should be grateful to Theodora. She secured many rights for them and should be regarded as an early champion of emancipation. If women were historians, they would recognize her as the first patron of women's rights.

His thoughts about Theodora put other thoughts out of his mind. On the face of it, the author conveyed the essence of the subject, even analyzed it adequately. But, because of that undefined deficiency, Herbst decided to review the book at length, to the extent that space would allow. He didn't know yet what he would write, but he considered it his duty as a scholar to write about this book. Not because of its significance, but because of similar books that take a historic period, a scholar, a poet, an emperor, or a pope as their subject. One who is not an expert finds in them a mix of history and poetry, but in truth they are neither history nor poetry. As for this particular book, although it provided an adequate picture of the period, it was no different from all the others.

Upon concluding that the author was among those who approach history as if it were polite conversation, Herbst recognized the flaw he couldn't at first identify. He now realized that the book wasn't worth reviewing, since it wasn't a scholarly work. If one were to review it, it would certainly be adequate to write two or three lines indicating that, since it was not a scholarly work, it was not relevant to us.

He reached for his watch, which was on the table beside the bed. As he groped for it, it occurred to him that he could put a nail in the wall and hang the watch on it, so he wouldn't have to take his hand out from under the blanket to look at it. He was surprised that something so simple had not occurred to him before. He was so involved in the fact that this simple thought had never occurred to him that he forgot to look at the watch and found himself back where he started—with the book he planned to dismiss in two or three lines. For what reason? This was something Herbst preferred to hide from himself. Yet he was already beginning to scheme, and this is roughly what he was thinking: Now that they're going to promote me, I'll prove that they're not wrong.

He considered each professor and which of them was likely to oppose him. First of all, the one who hates me. Why does he hate me? Because I don't like him. But the real issue is, Why does he have the power to make trouble? Not because he is wise, for wise men are reluctant to take charge, knowing that there are people who are still wiser and that it is they who should rule the world. Meanwhile, fools and villains leap into the breach, take charge of the world, and conduct it willfully and foolishly. This is how it happens that wise men allow idiots and criminals to destroy the world. Since the wise men are wise and growing ever wiser, what they regarded yesterday as ultimate wisdom they realize, a day later, is not wise after all. They seldom maintain a position or remain committed to anything, because wisdom keeps leading them a step further. Not so with fools. Whatever they fix their eyes on, they stick with, never letting go; should they let go, they'd have nothing. Their entire life is a strategy, a way to keep the world in their hands. When Herbst arrived at this insight, he laughed and said to himself: Now that I've achieved such wisdom, I'll act as those fools do and take charge of my world. If I'm unacceptable to someone, I'll call on him and be friendly. I don't expect him to fall in love with me; I don't want him to fall in love with me. What do I expect of him? I expect him to keep his mouth shut, rather than indulge in hostile chatter about me.

5

Although he didn't sleep very much that night, he woke up healthy and refreshed. The trip of the previous day and his decision about his job soothed his soul and gave him strength. He put on his robe. In his youth, it had been his favorite garment, and he used to wear it from the moment he woke up until he left home. He had done his favorite work in it, the writing that became the great book for which he was known in the world. Now that the robe is tattered, he wears it only to go from his bed to the bathroom. He glanced at the desk and saw the book he was assigned to review. He opened it and looked it over. Again, he was drawn to read it and yet irritated, not by the things that had irritated him the day before, but by other things. To support his position, the author leans on a certain scholar, without acknowledging that he had changed his mind and wrote, "I was mistaken, I changed my mind." More disturbing is the fact that the author quoted from a secondary source without verifying it. Even more disturbing is the fact that he contradicts himself. In one chapter, he went along with Ranke, who disputes Procopius and contends that what Procopius wrote about Theodora is sheer nonsense and vicious fabrication; however, in another chapter, the author described Theodora's actions when she was empress as a consequence of her wanton youth. So the author admits that in her youth she behaved wildly and improperly. In another context, he wrote that religion was remote from her heart, that all her actions were directed toward the welfare of the state, while, in yet another context, he wrote that, being Syrian, she was attracted to the priests, for in Syria everyone adhered to one of the many religious sects. How does the author explain her interest in the Syrian priest Maras? True, she was Syrian and priests were highly respected in Syria; but this was not her reason. It was because she had noticed how vulgar this priest was, in all his ways, and wanted to make him into some sort of priestly court jester. In summary, although the author appears to be an expert in Byzantine history, he has no clear theory and no overview. He included in his book every trivial detail that crossed his path and gave it prominence. Coming upon some further detail, even if it contradicts a previous one, he would add it to the book and highlight it, like a ferret that forages everywhere, making no distinctions. Still and all, Herbst saw a need to review the book—not to display his erudition to the trustees of the university, but because it was written in a vigorous style, engaging the reader and deluding him into thinking of it as a scholarly work, when in fact it was a compilation of details that the author had skillfully molded into a single essay.

Herbst was suddenly enraged. Some years back, he had put together a Byzantine anthology for a foreign publisher. Five or six months later, he happened on an essay by a renowned scholar. He read it and saw that its entire substance was taken from that anthology, except for the conjunctive clauses: "Hence, one can arrive at a conclusion that provides definitive support for this hypothesis . . . It becomes clear that . . . Though at first it appears otherwise, one could argue . . ." This entire essay, which had nothing original in it but its scholarly jargon, was widely acclaimed, although the anthology itself was barely noticed. He recalled a similar incident involving a scholar who wrote an introduction to a book by a friend that was being published posthumously, about codification of the liturgy in the proto-Slavic church. All the material on Byzantium presented in this introduction was lifted from Herbst's anthology, except for the conjunctive jargon. Neither of these authors bothered to mention the anthology from which they copied their material, typographical errors and all.

He could hear Henrietta's footsteps, light and jaunty, as she prepared breakfast, then the sound of coffee being ground. That good, dry smell, pervasive and stimulating, began to filter through and cling to the veins of his throat. Body and soul craved the brew—its appealing taste, aroma, and sight—so invigorating that it erodes the boundary between ability and will. Herbst put down the book and went to wash up and shave, so he would be ready to drink the coffee while it was hot and fresh. On the way, he stopped to say good morning to Henrietta and added, "Don't bother about me, Henriett, I'll have coffee alone today, and I'll have breakfast later, after I'm into my work."

A little later, Henrietta brought the coffee to his room. She was pleased to see him with the open book before him and said, "Drink a little at a time. I won't give you more than one cup, because I made your coffee strong today. You didn't shave." "No," Manfred answered.

He lowered his eyes, looked at the book, and took a sip, thinking: I'm drinking now and enjoying it, but suddenly all the coffee will be gone, and there I'll be, my mouth open, looking for another sip and not finding it. Henrietta left quietly. At the door, she turned toward her husband and said, "You could say thank you." Manfred looked up from his book, cup in hand, and said, "Thanks, Henrietta. Thanks. Also, thank you for breakfast. Whether I eat it or not, I thank you for it. The coffee's good."

Henrietta left, and Manfred went back to work. He picked up a pencil and reviewed yesterday's notes. He lit a cigarette, then looked in the cup to be sure there wasn't another drop. Though not a single drop was left, the cup still smelled of coffee. Herbst took two or three puffs of his cigarette, like a winemaker drawing liquid through a tube, and went back to the book. He stared at the pencil marks, took some books from the shelf, and began reading, checking up on the author. As it happened, they happened to lead him to conclusions that were different from the author's. In some cases, this occurred because the author had a superficial understanding of the text; in others, because he had copied fragments of the data rather than the whole, either out of sloppiness or for some other reason, such as political motives of the sort that prevailed in Germany after its defeat. Herbst, who detested scholarship that was being used as a means to a political end, was appalled by this diligent author who had used old texts so cleverly. But he decided to ignore these motives and consider the book in purely scholarly terms.

The house was quiet. Not a voice was heard, not Sarah's, not Sarini's, not anyone's. Sensing that Manfred was preparing to do important work that required concentration, Henrietta took charge of the silence. After a while she came back and asked Manfred when he would like some food. Manfred was startled and said, "Food, what a monstrous thought! But a cup of coffee would be nice. I beg you, Henrietta, be so kind as to forgo your principles and make me coffee. Just one more cup, and I promise that, as soon as I'm done with this book and with the article I'm writing, not a drop of coffee will cross my lips until you invite me to drink it." Henrietta said, "Coffee again. You think I'm running a café here, that I'm sitting and waiting for customers like you. You'd do better to eat something, instead of drinking coffee. Tell me, how many cigarettes have you smoked today? One, two, three. All before breakfast. Not another drop of coffee for you today." As she spoke, she made an about-face; then she left the room and came back carrying a cup of coffee that had been ready and waiting. Manfred leaped up to take it from her, leaned over, and kissed her hand, saying,

"Many thanks, Henriett, for the coffee and many thanks for the timing. Now, Henriett, give me your hand and let's say farewell until the third cup. Then I won't drink any more until the government drives the dragons out of the Salt Sea, so they won't swallow up the herrings. Incidentally, tell me, Henriett, why is it that we don't see salt herrings anymore? Did you tell them I've become a vegetarian? As you can see, Henriett, this cup will guarantee a good job—if not good, then halfway good, for sure. In any case, this book and this author are getting more than they deserve. If you bring me breakfast now, I'll eat it." Henrietta said, "Tomorrow you'll get herring for breakfast. May I ask what you're writing?" Manfred said, "Why not? I already told you that the National Library was so kind as to send me a new book to review. So I am being so kind as to review it. Now you understand why I wanted coffee. As for the herring, I didn't mention it with any ulterior motive. Still and all, if you mean to get a herring, I won't keep you from getting a nice fat one. I myself certainly don't need herring. I mentioned it only by way of association. Since we mentioned the Salt Sea, I mentioned salt herring. What did we drink at that inn near the Salt Sea? Was it tea or coffee? Even if you made me read one of Bachlam's books as a penalty, I wouldn't be able to remember."

Seven or eight days later, Herbst finished his article. It had worked out well, not only in quality but in quantity. He had intended to write three or four pages but ended up with eight and a half, to which he added more than two and a quarter pages when editing—all this apart from the notes or the notes on the notes. As it turned out, in several days he had produced a real pamphlet. It was true that Avgad and Lemner turn out long articles regularly, not to mention Bachlam, whose papers cover the face of the earth. But any discerning reader would discern the difference between Herbst's writing and theirs. Herbst examined his article, word by word, phrase by phrase. He cut it where it was longwinded, and where it was muddled he added clarification. He replaced one word with another, substituting the explicit for the vague. Here and there, he made slight corrections, adding, deleting, tightening, elaborating. He replaced idioms that struck him as Teutonic with Hebrew equivalents, and those that seemed florid he replaced with simpler ones. He then took the pages, held them in his hand, and read aloud, tapping on the table like a musician checking his tone. He seemed satisfied. Then, suddenly, he was sad to have written in Hebrew, a language with no terminology, and, even though he had found appropriate words for all the ideas he wanted to communicate, he wondered to what extent he would be understood. Had he been writing in German, there would be no need to waste time on style, and he would have written the entire article in two or three days, without any question about making himself understood. Just as suddenly, he was overcome with joy no article had inspired before, joy derived from the conquest of language. While he was rejoicing, a wave of sorrow took over, for his words were not likely to be read by anyone with a flair for language. They would be read by Bachlams and Lemners, who have no sense of style.

Henrietta brought him a raspberry drink. Manfred pretended not to see her, not to notice what she was bringing, not to smell the raspberry, not to feel what he always felt when he smelled a food or a drink he was fond of before coming to this country. When she was on her way out, he looked up, waved his papers at her, and called out, "Look, look, *voilà!* The article is ready, finished, done." Henrietta regarded him without an ounce of disdain, sharing his joy. Actually, she valued these articles not for what they were but for his sake. They seemed to make him tranquil, to put him at peace with the world. In the past, in the first year of their marriage, before Zahara was born, when Henrietta saw Fred poring over his books day and night, writing, underlining, typing, editing, she would try to understand the secret of the subjects to which he was devoted and for which he was willing to forgo so many pleasures. Such interests were not his alone; he shared them with other scholars. She read some of this material, but it meant nothing to her, so she dismissed it. Having dismissed it, she turned again for satisfaction to books that could be read without much effort, those that sustain the soul in times of anxiety. When she was young, she loved the poems of Rilke; later, she found herself in the poems of George. Now, too, she often finds in them a source of strength, although their landscape is so different from that of this land and although their subjects have become foreign to her soul.

All of a sudden, Manfred put his hand on her shoulder, lowered his eyes, and said to her, his words measured, his voice a singsong, "Listen and you shall know. Bend an ear to my words. My heart, so full of wisdom, brims with counsel like a mountain stream. Let us fly together on wisdom's wings to the dwelling place of Bachlam the Great, for, if he finds me worthy, you will become a professoress and I a professor. Now, Mother, I will explicate my poem for you. I want to call on Professor Bachlam. Not that I expect to endear myself to him, but, if I seem friendly, he may keep his mouth shut rather than denigrate me when my promotion is considered." Henrietta stared at him and swallowed the words she was about to say. Manfred took her hand and said, "I know, Henriett, that you disapprove. Were you to ask me, I would say that I disapprove too. But it's better to act out of character this once and thereby avoid anger, irritation, gossip, and slander." Henrietta said, "Anger and irritation I can understand, gossip and slander I can't understand." Manfred took her hand and said, "You know I don't enjoy making light of others or maligning them, nor do I understand the pleasure people take in making fun of friends in their absence. But, when it comes to Bachlam, even I join in. After visiting him, I'll have good reason to refrain from such talk. Understand, Mother?" Henrietta said, "If you understand, that's enough." Manfred said, "Does that mean you approve?" Henrietta said, "Whether or not I approve, I'm not holding you back. If you want to call on Bachlam, I'm not about to say, 'Don't go.'" Manfred said, "Not so, Mother." Henrietta said, "What do you mean?" Manfred said, "It's not a proper call unless the husband and wife both come." Henrietta said, "If it's essential that I come along, I'll come along, but don't ask me to put on the charm and stuff my mouth with polite chatter." Manfred said, "Calm down, Mother. Who expects you to put on the charm and chatter politely? I'll be content if you come with me and we sit there together for an hour." Henrietta shrieked and said, "God in heaven, are you out of your mind, Manfred?" Manfred said, "Then half an hour will do. You'll see, Mother, it won't be so awful." Henrietta said, "Awful or not, I've already told you I'm willing to go." Manfred said, "I thank you, Mother. Now what was I going to ask of you?" Henrietta said, "Don't ask anything more of me." Manfred said, "First listen. I may be asking exactly what you would ask." Henrietta said, "So?" Manfred said, "So, if other guests come and detain us there, they can go to hell. We have to be practical, especially now, when I have to produce something to secure my professorship. Why are you silent, Mother? Am I wrong?" Henrietta said, "You're right, Fred. You're right. If only we had always behaved this way." Manfred said, "But you're to blame for that. You're always inviting young women to our house." "Which young women do you have in mind?" "For example, the one we met in the hotel at the Dead Sea. The one who treated us to tea and cakes." Henrietta sighed and said, "Poor thing. If only she would come visit, I could repay her." Manfred said, "Poor thing is right. But there are so many young women in this country; we don't have time for them all. We invite one today, another tomorrow. Between the two of them, time slips away and my work remains undone. Forgive me, Mother. Forgive me for talking like this. It's not me talking, it's the burden of work." Henrietta said, "Do you mean to tell me, my dear, that, after she took so much trouble on our account and showed so much affection, there's any question about inviting her? Think how much money she saved us. Six glasses of tea—that comes to twelve grush—and the cakes she served us would cost more than twelve grush." Manfred said, "Then you invited her as a practical matter?" Henrietta stared at him and said, "Please tell me what you mean by the word *practical*?" Manfred said, "In any case, you can't relate to people in terms of what you get from them." Henrietta said, "Was that my only reason for inviting her? I invited her because I was touched by her problems." Manfred said, "There are young women in this country whose situation is worse than hers." Henrietta said, "Since I'm not acquainted with them, I don't have to worry about them." Manfred said, "It's good that you're not acquainted with life's adversities. I, for example, know a particular young girl, of good family, an aristocrat, the one who was brought here by her uncle, Professor Neu. Surely you remember her? You even said——" Henrietta interrupted, "You're dreaming, Fred. I don't know any such girl, and I can't imagine Neu bringing a girl to our house." Manfred said, "What if I told you she was the girl we talked about for Taglicht? Remember?" Henrietta said, "If I tell you we had no such conversation, will you let me be?" Manfred said, "We didn't talk about her?"

Henrietta stood like a victim, as if she had been abused, as if words she had never said were being attributed to her, as if these words were vile and despicable. She looked gloomy, and one of her blonde curls, which had begun to turn gray, slipped down to her forehead, trailing across her handsome eyebrows. She barely managed to keep from speaking sharply to her husband. She didn't know what was bothering her, but it seemed that every word Manfred uttered was designed to provoke her. Her peace of mind was disrupted by this anger, as were her thoughts of work, of all the things she had to do. Suddenly her face became youthful, and she took on the indignant look of a young woman whose words are being distorted. Manfred's love was aroused by her face and by her rage, but she remained remote because of what he had said, his fragmented conversation, and his plaintive tone, which was particularly grotesque in this light, on this morning, in this land, on this day when a *hamsin*-like sun ruled the world and she had to stand in the heat of the kitchen preparing food for Shabbat. At that moment Manfred was thinking to himself: Who would imagine that this woman has borne me three daughters, that this woman and I were intimate, physically and spiritually? He studied her clothes and her face, and said, "Mother, why are you so angry? Did I say something to make you angry? If so, was it my intention to make you angry?" Henrietta said, "You didn't make me angry. I'm not angry." Manfred said, "Then let's change the subject. What does Madame Herbst intend to wear when we visit Professor Bachlam?" Henrietta said, "Leave that to me. You can be sure my clothes won't disgrace you." Manfred said, "Mother, did anyone say any such thing? Still, I'm annoyed with you for not taking care of yourself. I don't expect you to paint your face like Mrs. Lemner. But there's nothing wrong with lending nature a hand. There are women who grow old and don't merely neglect themselves but go so far as to emphasize their wrinkles." Henrietta laughed and said, "As for age, I'm old. As for wrinkles, even if I camouflage them, they show." Manfred said, "Mother, if I tell you I wasn't referring to you, will you believe me?" Henrietta said, "Why not? Have I ever questioned anything you told me?" Manfred said, "That's true. I've never said anything you saw fit to doubt. I used to think you accepted whatever I said because you didn't care whether I said one thing or another. Now I know that the faith you have in me has to do with what I say. Let's get back to our subject. Not to Bachlam, but to women who have wrinkles and ignore them. Do you remember that nurse, the nurse who brought you flowers the day our Sarah was born? If I'm not mistaken, her name is Shura." Henrietta said, "It's not Shura, it's Shira. I'm surprised she's never come to visit. When I was in the hospital, she took so much trouble with me. She was especially affectionate and promised to visit. What were you going to say about her?" Manfred asked in alarm, "What was I going to say about whom?" Henrietta said, "Fred, you make me laugh. If I say I don't know anything about a young girl brought here by Professor Neu, you insist I know her and I've seen her. If I say you were about to tell me something about the nurse Shira, you look bewildered." Manfred said, "Actually, I was going to tell you about her. I saw that nurse walking down the street, wearing old clothes, her hair half-white, looking altogether like an old hag. Couldn't she dye her hair? There are dyes that restore the original color." Henrietta said, "She's a natural woman who doesn't want to dye her hair. You didn't avoid her, my darling? You asked how she was? She did so much for me, showed such kindness, I wish she would come over, so I could reciprocate." Manfred said, "If not for me, you would open your house to all the women in the world. Let's talk about something else. What sort of lunch do you have simmering in your pot?" Henrietta laughed and said, "You want to know everything. Relax, Fred. It's a meal worthy of Shabbat." Fred said, "If I hadn't written my review today, I would have forgotten all about Shabbat. Mother, we ought to make special plans for Shabbat. It's not right that every day is the same for us." Henrietta said, "How could we make it special?" Manfred said, "I haven't studied the question, but we should honor the day. I had an old uncle who was born in Rawicz. All week he smoked cigarettes; in honor of Shabbat, he smoked a cigar." Henrietta asked her husband, "Are you allowed to smoke cigars on Shabbat?" Manfred laughed and said, "For that matter, are you allowed to smoke cigarettes on Shabbat? My uncle wasn't observant, but he enjoyed tradition. Before making his fortune as a manufacturer, he taught religion in the local school. He was unique. In the end, though he detested rabbis, he left half his wealth to a rabbinical seminary. I'm glad I remembered him. Now I have something to talk about with Professor Bachlam." Henrietta said, "You're an optimist, my friend, if you think Bachlam will give you a chance to talk. Before you can say anything, Bachlam will drown you in a flood of words." Manfred said, "Then I won't have to make any effort. I just mean to pay my respects.

— 6 —

I will omit the Herbsts' visit with Bachlam, which went well. When they left Bachlam's house, Herbst said to his wife, "I don't expect him to praise me lavishly, but I hope he won't be too critical." Now let's get back to Herbst's other affairs.

M. Herbst's article was accepted and published. In style and content, it worked out well. When Dr. Manfred Herbst arrived in the Land of Israel, he couldn't say anything in proper Hebrew, and, were it not for two or three students who corrected him continually, those who came to hear his lectures would be beside themselves with laughter. Gradually he acquired the language, so that it enhanced his lectures and he was able to write in it. Those who see style as more than mere word combinations are moved to exclaim: "This German, who probably arrived with only the rudiments of biblical grammar, writes more elegant prose than many of those learned old-timers who are considered the creators of modern Hebrew style." How can this be? Some said that a stylist in one language is a stylist in any language he touches. Others said that, having learned Hebrew as an adult, Herbst read only good books and didn't fill his belly with vulgar prose that doesn't stick to the ribs.

Until that article appeared, he had produced nothing in Hebrew, so he treated it like a book. He ordered offprints, had them bound, and distributed them to colleagues, including some Jewish scholars abroad. As long as he was busy inscribing these offprints and mailing them out, time was passing but he didn't notice. When he was finished, he didn't know what to do.

He did, actually, know what to do. But, because he was discouraged, that was how it seemed. It goes without saying that he has notes to sort out and, even more important, to classify. If he was going to put his book in order, it would be good to have the notes arranged by subject. Right now, a great deal of effort is being wasted. He often copies material that has already been copied once, because the notes are in a mess and it is hard to confirm whether or not a particular item has been copied. Similarly, he often finds something that is worth copying and doesn't copy it, assuming it has already been copied; later, when he goes through his papers, he discovers this is not so, and, if he still wants to copy it, he has a hard time tracing either the source or the subject.

He would occasionally go back to his box of notes, taking out a note, putting another in, comparing texts, adding marginal notes, et cetera— including them, not because of their content, but because of pedants and polemicists who, should he omit a reference, would argue that, had the author seen what So-and-so wrote in such-and-such a book, he would not have arrived at such a misguided conclusion. Hence those footnotes and citations that add nothing but are inserted to silence critics, a gratuitous display of erudition.

While dealing with these papers, Herbst sometimes formulated fragmentary ideas he didn't hesitate to write down, in some cases briefly, in others at length. He was sometimes caught up in his writing, as in the days when he wrote his first book, when ideas flowed, along with the ability to express them and the documentation to support his views. When this occurred, he mourned the early days, which were gone, never to return again. Herbst forgot that then, too, there were arid times. Now it seemed that those days had been altogether good.

Herbst was distressed about the work that remained undone; about Shira, who avoided him; about himself—about the fact that he needed to get rid of Shira in order to be free to work. It can't be, Herbst would say. It can't be that I'll spend my days and years thinking about women. Many times Herbst cried inwardly: What does she want from me? Actually, it was not that she wanted anything of him; it was he who wanted her. What do I want from you? I want to see you, that's all. Better still, not to see you. If you were to go away, or if I were to go somewhere, I would be rid of you. I would be free. Isn't it enough that

I've wasted two years because of you? And that verse "Flesh such as
yours / Will not soon be forgotten" played itself in his mind.

The Herbst household was in good order. Herbst had his concerns; his
wife had hers. Herbst concerned himself with his books, his lectures,
his students, and his major work on burial customs of the poor in
Byzantium, while Henrietta concerned herself with the needs of the
household—cooking, baking, sewing, ironing, shopping, health care,
family matters locally and abroad. In addition, she tended the garden
and tended her little girl, Sarah, who was no longer a baby in a crib
but was not yet ready for nursery school, which is just as well, for there
is no nursery school in Baka. The closest one is in Talpiot, and how
could anyone find time to take her there and pick her up? Herbst's
salary is barely adequate to pay for household help. The Herbsts really
ought to have moved to a Jewish neighborhood. In fact, they should
have done so right after the riots of '29 and all the more so now, when
Arab bands are wreaking havoc, and Arabs are like wolves to Jews. But,
being so fond of their home and garden, the Herbsts are reluctant to
move. Anyone who has toiled over a house and garden will not abandon them easily. And you know what an investment Henrietta has
made in her house and garden. She rented a heap of rubble and transformed it into a fine home. Henrietta ignores danger and lives as she
did when she first came to Jerusalem, when the high commissioner,
who was Jewish, used to go to the Hurva Synagogue on a special
Shabbat, read from the Torah, and sit between the two chief rabbis on
a throne adorned with the verse "Suffer not a stranger to sit upon His
throne." After the service, he would attend a reception in his honor,
where the country's leaders sang his praises over a full glass of wine.
And the German consul, who sent his children to a Jewish nursery,
used to ask Dr. Ruppin to intercede on his behalf when he needed a
favor from the high commissioner. The German consul's brother-in-
law, who was a frequent guest in Jewish homes, used to praise all the
Carmel wines. At night, after Shabbat, Hasidim would dance down
from Mea Shearim to the Old City and from the Old City back to Mea
Shearim, and young men and women would stroll all night, wherever
they wished. If an Arab met a Jew, he would say hello. If they were
acquainted, he would say more—and in Hebrew, so that those who
presumed to foresee the future predicted that in another generation the
Arabs would become assimilated. How? It remained for the future to
fulfill their heart's desire.

And so the Herbst household is in good order. Nothing has changed
except for the help. Sarini is gone, and Firadeus has taken her place.

Firadeus is alert and agile, dark and attractive. Her eyes are like two sweet raisins, and she never says a sharp word. She is the embodiment of humility, enhanced by modesty and reticence.

Henrietta is pleased with Firadeus's work, Manfred is pleased with her manner, and Sarah prefers her to all her dolls. Firadeus is only sixteen, and she supports six people: herself, her mother, her mother's mother, her father's blind father, and Manawa, the madwoman they found on the road from Persia to Jerusalem, as well as her little brother, Ziyon. He was born the day her father was killed by an Arab rogue when he was on his way to dump Talpiot's garbage. Ziyon the father, who was Talpiot's garbage man, is still remembered fondly by the local housewives; if he found something that had fallen into the garbage by mistake, he would return it. He was mentioned by the chairman at the first meeting of the Talpiot Committee, and all the members stood in silence to honor his memory. How can six souls subsist on Firadeus's meager wages? While most of her friends sit around telling fortunes, fussing with their hair or their jewelry, Firadeus sits with her mother, wrapping pamphlets given to her by a gentleman with a stiff collar who lives near her employer and pays her half a grush for each piece. If he gives her a hundred pamphlets and she doesn't return them all, he's not particular. He pays for the whole lot, realizing that neighbors come by, see writing in the holy tongue, take it to read, and don't return it, and she, being so young, doesn't dare to speak up to her elders and say, "Don't take it." As was already stated, Firadeus is quick, conscientious, and altogether dependable. If she is told to do something a certain way, that is how she does it. Sometimes even before there is time to say anything, it's done. Firadeus has another fine quality: she sees everything. I'll give only one example. The Herbsts were in the habit of having their servants eat with them. The first time Firadeus ate with them, Tamara kept tapping her nose to call her parents' attention to the girl's repulsive table manners. In a very few days, Firadeus learned to handle a knife and fork more skillfully, perhaps, than Tamara. Herbst and his wife are not ethnographers; they're not engaged in studying the different communities. But, when they first arrived in the country, they used to go to the Bukharan streets on Shabbat and holidays to watch the people in their colorful garments. Similarly, they used to take tourists to see the Yemenites in their synagogues. Having had their fill, they no longer concern themselves with all the tribes of Israel to be found in Jerusalem and are no longer able to distinguish the ethnic groups from one another. I would not be mistaken were I to say that Herbst is more attuned to the various Germanic peoples in Jerusalem than to the tribes of Israel. Still, when he hears these peoples being maligned, he responds, "You can say what you like about them, all but the Persians." There is one problem with Firadeus: sometimes she shows up and sometimes she doesn't, because her employers live among Arabs, in a neighborhood ruled by hoodlums, where every stone is waiting to be flung at a Jewish head. When Firadeus comes, she takes on all the housework, and her mistress sits writing letters to relatives in Germany. If she doesn't come, all the work falls on Henrietta, since Tamara is inept when it comes to housework.

At this time, Tamara had an opportunity to visit Greece. How? A group of university students was going on a scholarly expedition. When Tamara heard about it, she wanted to travel too, to breathe the air of other places, never having been out of the Land of Israel except once, when she toured the cities of Lebanon, which she considered part of her own country. Tamara wasn't a student and couldn't qualify as a scholar. Her knowledge of Greek culture could be inscribed on the tip of a lipstick without making a dent. But she was lucky. One of the women backed out, and there was room for Tamara. The cost was minimal, since both governments offered large discounts for students. Also, Mother Henrietta managed to skimp on household expenses to make it possible for Tamara to go.

Tamara "spoiled" her parents with picture postcards. Whenever she found a post office, she sent a card. To spoil them further, she adorned her cards with rhymes about her companions, about the food, the drink, the person who dipped his cheese in wine, and so on. Henrietta reads them and remarks, astonished, "Tamara is no poet, but look, Fred, the rhymes seem to roll right off her tongue." Manfred laughs. "Your good taste has vanished, Henriett. You read Stefan George, and you're enthralled; you read some jingles, and you're equally enthralled." Henrietta says, "Still, it's a miracle to have such control of a language that you can make rhymes." Manfred says, "Rhymes without meter are lower than the lowest prose. Tamara reminds me of Professor Lemner. When he utters a Greek or Latin proverb, he drowns it in a sneeze so his mistakes won't be noticed."

One day a letter came from Tamara with an amusing story. In Athens, a wealthy young man wanted to marry her and had approached the professor in charge of the group to ask for her hand, because Athenian Jews follow patriarchal practices and wouldn't dare ask a girl for her hand without her guardian's permission. Henrietta laughed, as if it were a joke. Manfred didn't laugh. Manfred almost fainted. Until that moment, Manfred had never noticed that Tamara was old enough to marry. Manfred didn't think his daughter Tamara was different from her peers; but, like most parents, he forgot what it's like to be young.

Herbst was pleased that his daughter was superior in one respect: she wasn't involved with those who want both sides of the Jordan as a Jewish state. The subject of Tamara has come up again, and again I am ambivalent about telling her story. Since it is too long to write with one drop of ink, I will leave it for now and get back to where I was.

When he was done with the offprints, Herbst felt listless. He barely made it back to his desk. As usual on such days, he did a lot of sitting and a lot of smoking. The tobacco smell neutralized the book smell, and he himself was neutralized by the clouds of smoke. When Henrietta came into the room, she had to clear a trail with her hands. When she went to open a window to let in air, she found it was open, but a pillar of cigarette smoke trapped at the window prevented the air from flowing in or out.

The air suited his thoughts, which were first and foremost about Shira. He himself—which is to say, his work, from which he still considered himself inseparable—came second. Third was Henrietta. His thoughts about Henrietta were roughly these: In any case, Henrietta's lot is better than that of her relatives in Germany. She doesn't live in fear—of police, of informers, of her husband being suddenly taken away and returned as ashes in a sealed box. She even has a garden with vegetables and flowers, as well as a chicken coop, all of which Henrietta had dreamed of in Germany when they were preparing to leave. She used to say, "I'll go to Palestine, find some land there, and plant a garden, like the pioneers." Someone else occupied Herbst's thoughts: his eldest daughter, Zahara. But she wasn't as persistent a presence as Shira, his work, or his wife, though she was perhaps closer to his heart than the others. His thoughts about Zahara were entwined with thoughts about Tamara that remained somewhat amorphous.

The cigarette smoke was occasionally invaded by the fragrance of the garden, the rooster's cry, a chirping bird, Henrietta's footsteps, little Sarah, or a student or colleague. Herbst deals with each one of his callers in terms of his nature and business, then sees him out and returns to the box of notecards, saying, "Here's another note, and yet another." The notes extended in several directions without coming together. The author of these notes is drawn in several directions too, but he doesn't pull himself together either.

Herbst was like the poet who lost his baggage on a trip and was asked if his shadow was lost too, a question that inspired him to write a wondrous tale about a lost shadow. So it was with Herbst. Having lost the desire to deal with his notes, he became interested in something that, for him, was like a wondrous tale. That poet was privileged to write *Peter Schlemihl,* whereas Herbst wasn't privileged to fulfill his

wishes. I will nonetheless relate his wish. I will also relate the chain of
events that led him to fix his attention on a subject other than his
academic work.

In the realm of thought, this is how Herbst functions. He takes on
a subject, considers it from various angles, moves on to another subject,
and finally goes back to the beginning. Now that he had lost the desire
to deal with his papers, he pondered his book, which was not being
written. He thought about the delays and obstacles, about Zahara, who
was living in the country, and about Henrietta. In the end, his mind
was on himself again. He pictured himself leaving the city, leaving his
home, going to a place where he was unknown, with no one to distract
him from the work he was about to undertake. For he meant to do
something new. He meant to write a play about Antonia, a woman of
the court, and Yohanan, a nobleman in the capital. Several days earlier,
he had intended to engage in research, as usual, but it had suddenly
occurred to him that this was beyond what the researcher could handle,
that the material itself yearned to fall into hands other than a researcher's.

Despite their weight and value, the data peered at him with eyes that
were crafty, shrewd, and clever; resistant, hesitant, fearful. If they had
had words, they would have said roughly this: What do you gain by
making an article out of us? Another article and yet another. You've
already produced enough articles. He watched, listened, understood.
Suddenly his heart felt pinched with painful sweetness, the kind a poet
feels when he comes upon something that asks to be put in a poem. Dr.
Manfred Herbst was resolved to write a play about the woman of the
court and Yohanan the nobleman. Henceforth, nothing was as dear to
Dr. Herbst as this play. If not for Shira, the project would have dominated his heart, and he would have written the play.

Thus far, his work had been nourished by what others provided, data
from documents and the like. Now he would be nourished by his own
spirit and creative imagination. Needless to say, he would no longer
have to refer to books or copy notes to store in a box. He would no
longer need to amass references and would have no use for scholarly
apparatus. He barely managed to repress his sense of superiority, for
he already viewed his academic friends as exploiters who eat fruit
planted by others.

Herbst envisioned himself sitting and writing the play. Scene after
scene unfolds, and the leading characters—Antonia, a woman of the
court, and Yohanan, a nobleman—are engaged in conversation, which
he overhears and records on paper.

It took a while for Herbst to be persuaded to write the play. I'm not a playwright, he thought. That's not my profession, he told himself. At the same time, he was aching to try his hand at it. Aware that most people, unless they are poets, fail in this sort of endeavor—that, when they try to tell a love story, they become sentimental—Herbst was discouraged. But he was determined to write the play. And what would become of his notes? They would help him make the play authentic. So far, all he had was the story as conveyed by the writers of the time, but he was counting on precedent. Anyone who devotes himself totally to a task will not come away empty-handed.

Meanwhile, he investigated a pile of documents and discovered things no one else had noticed that were relevant to the story of Antonia, the woman of the court, and the nobleman Yohanan. He was thrilled with these discoveries and tested his imagination to see what it would add. But imagination doesn't always respond, not to everyone and not on demand. Never before had the material refused to comply. Whenever he put his mind to it, a research paper would take shape, seeming to order itself, the pieces falling into place so that there was a beginning, a middle, and an end—all in language suited to the subject, without academic jargon, to which even renowned scholars are not immune.

Herbst went to the window and stared at the trees. They were blooming, as usual, as if of themselves. Actually, one should not forget that Henrietta had a hand in this, and, in fact, so did he; they both tended the trees, hoed, and watered regularly. Neither he nor Henrietta had worked the land in their youth, but the soil was there, so they made a garden. Though no parable is intended, this reflected Herbst's feelings toward the play. But another feeling, about old age, insinuated itself. Was it old age that drained his energies and disheartened him? So this was why he hadn't hurried back to Shira after that first night, and, because he hadn't hurried back, Shira withholds herself from him now.

Turning away from the window and from the trees, he began pacing back and forth. Finally, he stood still, leaned over to press a cigarette into the ashtray, and either took another one or put the one he had just discarded back in his mouth. Then he took out the atlas in order to research the locale of his play. Atlas in hand, he cried out in amazement, "Tamara is in Greece. What does she know about Greece? I doubt she knows as much as the lowest-level student in a German high school. What do they teach here anyway? Who was it who described Apollo arrayed in *tefillin?* As an ideal, it's defective; as a joke, it's equally defective."

Now, Herbst thought, I'll try one of the cigarettes Julian Weltfremdt recommended. He leaned over and pressed the remnants of a cigarette into the ashtray, took out a long brown one, and smoked it slowly to assess its flavor. Now, Herbst said to himself, now I'll look at the map and trace Tamara's route. He got up, opened the door, and called out, "Henriett, Henriett, do you want to see where your daughter is?"

Henrietta came, parting the clouds of smoke with her hand, went to open the window, and found it open. She laughed in annoyance and said, "Unless your cigarettes induce amnesia, I don't know why I forget the windows are all open." Herbst laughed and said, "They don't induce amnesia, but they do have a trace of mandragora." Henrietta said, "You were going to show me where Tamara is now. Is there another card from her? I didn't see the mailman today." Manfred said, "The mailman wasn't here, and there are no new cards. We can nonetheless look at the map and see her route." Henrietta said, "What a good idea." Manfred said, "But I doubt she is enjoying the trip." Henrietta said, "Why not?" Manfred said, "Because she wasn't prepared. She knows less than nothing about Greece. She hasn't read Homer and doesn't know Plato. She knows nothing at all about that civilization. Tell me, Henriett, how did Tamara qualify for a teaching certificate?" Henrietta said, "She's as qualified as her friends." Manfred said, "I'm not asking only about her; I'm asking about her friends too, and even her teachers. How are they qualified to be teachers?" Henrietta said, "You don't mean to say they became teachers by pulling strings?" Manfred said, "I wouldn't say that, but I judge teachers by their pupils." "What do you learn?" Manfred laughed and said, "I learn, my dear, that they have all learned nothing." "Nothing?" Manfred said, "Anyway, they didn't learn what they should have learned. How many poems did you know by heart when you were Tamara's age? If we were to be exiled somewhere, with no books, I would be content with the poems you remember from your youth. But our Tamara—except for the insipid jingles she sings—probably doesn't know one entire poem." Henrietta said, "It's not her fault." "If it's not her fault, whose is it?" Henrietta said, "It may be Hebrew poetry that's at fault for not lending itself to song." Manfred said, "You have an excuse for everything, only the excuse is more radical than the problem. Now let's spread the map and see what places Tamara has graced with the light of her eyes. First let me get a cigarette." Henrietta said, "And I was going to ask you not to smoke for a while." Manfred said, "You're asking the impossible, but is there anything in the world I'm unwilling to give up for you? You're asking me not to smoke for a while. That's fine. But first let me have

two or three puffs. This is a new brand. Weltfremdt recommended it."
Henrietta said, "Does Weltfremdt smoke?" Manfred said, "If you mean
that secret adviser, Professor Ernst Weltfremdt, he doesn't smoke. No,
he doesn't. But if you mean Dr. Julian Weltfremdt, I can tell you
beyond doubt, beyond any doubt, that the gentleman certainly smokes.
Yes, indeed, that gentleman certainly does smoke." Henrietta laughed
and said, "If I hadn't seen your lips moving, I would be sure Professor
Weltfremdt himself was talking." Manfred said, "See, my dear, what
close friendship achieves. Sometimes the mere mention of a fine gentleman such as Professor Weltfremdt causes us—indeed, it causes us—to
adopt his rhetoric, his very own rhetoric." Henrietta said, "You admit
that you meant to imitate his speech." Manfred said, "Intentionally or
not, either way I succeeded. Isn't that so, Henriett?" Henrietta said,
"Besserman couldn't do any better. Now let's sit down and trace
Tamara's route." After outlining Tamara's entire route with his finger,
Manfred said, "Now I'll give you the Baedeker, and you can read about
all those places."

Herbst had a collection of Baedekers he was proud of. His pride may
have been due to the careless comment of a Scandinavian, one of
Strindberg's last surviving friends, who remarked about Herbst's collection that not even Strindberg had a better one. He searched but
didn't find the volume, and he remembered it had been borrowed by
Sacharson. It was more than a year since Sacharson had borrowed it,
and he hadn't bothered to bring it back. "What a pig," Herbst said, "to
borrow a book and not return it. When I'm done with him, he'll forget
his conversion certificate. But first I have to scold myself. Fool that I
am, I should have learned from experience. I once lent someone the
Baedeker of Palestine, and it was returned to me without the map of
Jerusalem." Henrietta said, "It's possible he took the map out for convenience and forgot to put it back." Manfred said, "If you want to give
people the benefit of the doubt, fine. But not when it comes to borrowing books. I'll have to get Sacharson to return my Baedeker. Now,
Henriett, am I released from the ban?" "What ban?" "The ban on
smoking." Henrietta said, "If you must smoke, then smoke. But not the
black ones, please." Manfred laughed and said, "Why is that? Because
they have a pinch of mandragora, or because they have no mandragora?" Henrietta said, "What's so funny about mandragora?" Manfred
said, "Have you forgotten the erotic properties of mandragora?" Henrietta said, "To think that the father of a married daughter and of
another whose hand is being sought in marriage is making such jokes!
But who can blame you—you are young, truly young. If we were

Yemenites, I myself would find you another wife." Manfred said,
"You? You would find me another wife?" Henrietta said, "Why not?"
Manfred said, "I don't think a European woman could do that." "Do
what?" "Yield her position to another woman." Henrietta said,
"You've forgotten the wife of the teacher from Beit Hakerem." Manfred said, "To whom are you referring?" Henrietta said, "I think what
I said was clear." Manfred said, "One thing is clear, there is a neighborhood in Jerusalem known as Beit Hakerem. Many teachers live in Beit
Hakerem, some of whom are clearly married, and it is also clear that,
though what you said is crystal clear, the heart of the matter isn't clear
at all." Henrietta said, "I know you remember the story, but you want
to hear it from me." Manfred's eyes twinkled with repressed laughter
as he said, "If so, all the more reason why you are required to tell it."
"Required? I don't like requirements." Manfred caught her by the chin
and said, "Nu, nu, tell me." Henrietta said, "Don't you remember? We
were walking in Beit Hakerem, and you were thirsty. We went into
a house for water and found a young woman with a baby in her arms."
Manfred said, "A sign within a sign. A young woman with a baby in
her arms." Henrietta said, "It seems to me that you know a woman who
isn't so young with a baby in her arms. If you want me to speak, don't
interrupt." Manfred said, "And then?" Henrietta said, "Why should I
repeat things you know as well as I do?" Manfred said, "What do you
care? So then the woman said, 'I can't go with my husband because the
children are small.'" Henrietta said, "You remember every word, yet
you let me wear out my tongue. Do you want to bore us both?"
Manfred said, "If I ask you, what's it to you if you do as I ask? Do you
have some special reason not to tell?" Henrietta said, "What reason
could there be?" Manfred said, "Then tell me." Henrietta said, "So the
woman continued, 'On a teacher's salary, I can't afford to hire help.
What's the solution? My husband could have two wives. When he is
out with one, the other one could look after the child, and then they
would switch.'" Manfred said, "De jure but not de facto." Henrietta
said, "What do you mean, 'de jure but not de facto'?" Manfred said,
"Those are common terms, meaning 'easier said than done.' What
woman could see her husband in someone else's arms and be silent? In
any case, I wouldn't subject my wife to such a test." Henrietta said, "Do
you ever have such thoughts?" Manfred said, "Me? What are you
saying? Me, God forbid." Henrietta said, "You stuck another cigarette
in your mouth. You still have one, and you're reaching for more.
Another woman, in my place, would see that as symbolic." Manfred

pressed his palms against each other, folded them over his heart, closed
his eyes, and crooned a song:

> I am tender, my heart purē,
>   No trace of sin in it;
> Only you forevermore,
>   My sweet Henriett;
> Only you forevermore,
>   My sweet Henriett.

— 7 —

The play didn't develop. Not for lack of imagination alone did it fail
to develop, nor because the material was insufficiently dramatic, but
something seemingly trivial interfered with the creation of the tragedy.
The insipid jingles with which Tamara filled her postcards had an
adverse effect on Herbst. On the one hand, he considered them meager
and empty; on the other, they led him to look at verses written by poets
who weren't real poets but, inasmuch as they had a command of the
language and could rhyme, were regarded as poets. Because he gave
these works too much attention, it occurred to him that he could set
the story of Antonia and Yohanan in romance or ballad form. Dr.
Herbst was mistaken to think that, having written a scholarly paper in
Hebrew, he would be able to turn out romances and ballads. What
happened in the end was that seven times he dipped his pen in ink
without producing a single verse. After several attempts, he gave up on
Hebrew and turned his pen to the left, intending to write his romances
and ballads in German. An odd thing happened. This scholar—born
and educated in Germany, author of a six-hundred-page tome and
many essays in German, who spoke German to his wife and most of
his friends, who thought in German—when he was about to pour his
lyrical musings into German verse, found neither the words nor the
form. Herbst was caught between two tongues. When he tried writing
in Hebrew, it seemed German would be more responsive; when he
tried German, it seemed Hebrew would be more responsive. In fact,
neither language responded. The Hebrew wouldn't come; the German
fled. Herbst went to the shelf where things he no longer used were
stored, took out his old pipe and cleaned it well, dissected several

cigarettes, filled the pipe with tobacco, and sat on his chair smoking away, smoking and thinking: I'll go back to the beginning and write the tragedy in simple prose, neither rhymed nor metered. He was confident, since the plot, the time, and the place were clear to him, that nothing would prevent him from writing the tragedy. He took out a new notebook and wrote the names of the characters. Then he drew a map of the house and the courtyard, including something he hadn't thought of originally, which added interest: a drawing of the leper colony in which Antonia's slave lived out his final years. His drawing of the place was so successful that he feared his dreams would be haunted by what he had pictured when awake. Oddly enough, although he thought a great deal about the leper colony and the faithful slave who spent his final days there, at night Herbst saw neither the slave nor the leper colony.

Now I'll revert to an orderly account, describing how one thing flowed from another and how everything interlocked, going back to the night after Herbst first wrote the names of the characters associated with the exploits of Antonia, woman of the court, and the nobleman Yohanan. If I omit something that happened to Herbst, I omit it because it's unimportant, though when it happened it seemed essential. When a man has a toothache, the entire world seems worthless. He goes to a doctor, who fixes the tooth; then he forgets all about it, and everything is normal again.

He had another sleepless night. He saw a thousand things, but not a single drop of sleep. Some of these things appeared because he summoned them, because he said, "Come, come," whereas others appeared on their own. Their pace was at first steady and regular, then intense and chaotic. The story of Antonia, woman of the court, and the nobleman Yohanan was so intense that his eyes began to hurt, and he had to close them because of the pain. It was, on the face of it, good that he closed his eyes, but this didn't last, because he had to move to more modest quarters where he could work without being interrupted, having taken it upon himself to write the tragedy of Antonia and Yohanan at the same time that he was assigned by the university to lead a group of young scholars who were touring Greece because Tamara was eager to study the mechanics of poetic meter. It was good that Herbst went with Tamara to Greece. Otherwise, she would have seen him walking with Shira, which was not advisable, because Henrietta was in collusion with the wife of a teacher from Beit Hakerem. They agreed to prohibit their husbands from bringing other women to their studios, declaring, "If they want to draw—let them draw skulls."

Unrelated to the skull or to poetic meter, the map of Jerusalem appeared, the one that was torn from the Baedeker. Unrelated to the map of Jerusalem, the brown cigarettes, distinguished by neither taste nor aroma, appeared. The fact that their long stems filled the ashtray was their sole distinction. Unrelated to the brown cigarettes, Avraham-and-a-half appeared. Not in person, but in the form of something sweet and good that stretches without limits and endlessly. In the midst of all this, he heard a voice calling, "Adam, Adam." He pondered a while and concluded: This probably doesn't refer to Adam Ahlenschlager, whose books I have never even touched. Then to whom does it refer? To Adam Miesckewicz, perhaps, whose poetry was translated into German by two converts, neither of whom was named Sacharson. In the end, everything was covered by a small leather strip, stretching to cover Wechsler and his colleagues, extending over Jerusalem and its inhabitants, and covering Herbst's eyes, which pained him so much that he closed them, asking the strip of leather, "What is this?" He answered, "It's that same leather strip, the *ptygyl* fragment."

— 8 —

Having touched on questions of poetry and language, I won't refrain from relating and clarifying what Dr. Herbst knew about Hebrew literature, what he saw in it, and how he happened to study the language and learn it well enough to write an essay and try his hand at writing a play in Hebrew. Even without the metered verse he had in mind originally, a prose play would be amazing.

As you already know, Manfred Herbst was born and educated in Germany, in German schools, in German scholarship and poetics, like his contemporaries, Jews and non-Jews. I will add some information about Manfred Herbst's progenitors.

Moritz Herbst, Manfred's father, was from a small town in Poznan. Like many other Jews who couldn't make a living there, he went off to Berlin to seek his fortune. He brought no capital to do business with, only the sort of sterling talents that can be converted into silver by their owner: good sense, goodwill, enterprise, and diligence. As a favor to an old man from his town, who, in his youth, had studied Mishnah with Moritz's father, Moritz was given a job in an office-supply store. This store, one of the first to limit its trade to office supplies, specialized in all sorts of business equipment. Furthermore, anyone who was about to open an office turned to Rosenthal and Co. for advice. When Moritz Herbst began working there, he had only the word of his father's childhood friend to recommend him. Before long, his actions spoke for him, his talents displayed themselves, and their outcome became more and more apparent. His employer took note and began to linger over the young man from Poznan, to observe how he arranged merchandise, how he dealt with customers, and the like. The employer sometimes expressed himself with an approving nod; he sometimes allowed him to accompany him home, so he could hear his opinion about various customers—who should be allowed to buy on credit and who should be turned down. At first, the employer suspected that he had hired the boy from Poznan only as a favor to that old man and that he would not last long; he soon began to recognize his worth and to befriend him. After a while, he invited him home for afternoon coffee on the weekend. After a further while, he invited him for lunch. From then on, he often invited him to eat in his home. Little by little, Moritz Herbst relinquished the manners he had brought from his village, especially those he realized were inappropriate in Berlin, and made an effort to please the wife of his employer, as well as his handsome and charming daughter, whose manners impressed the young man from Poznan as ultimate perfection. Though this young man seemed somewhat ridiculous to her, she found that there was something different about him. Not knowing how to describe this quality, she called it loyalty. Unless we project this word into the future, it remains abstract, for so far she had had no opportunity to test his loyalty. By and by, the young man from Poznan became a regular guest in this Berlin household, almost a member of the family, welcomed by all. The lady of the house sometimes made him mediate between her and her husband, and her daughter made him mediate between herself and her parents. The employer, seeing that this young man was dependable, turned over some of his own responsibilities to him and, in every case, was pleased with how they were carried out. Three years passed in this fashion. In this period he received three raises, as well as several bonuses. Moritz Herbst advanced from the lowest position to chief clerk, and, when a buyer left to establish his own business, Herbst was promoted and became the buyer. In all those years, Moritz Herbst gave his employer no cause for complaint or envy, although he introduced many innovations and expanded the business more and more. He never made a move without consulting his employer first, phrasing everything as a request, as if he were saying, "I have a favor to ask, sir," which allowed the employer to believe that everything emanated from him. From the time Moritz Herbst began working in this office-supply store, it never occurred to the owner that he might leave to work elsewhere, nor did Herbst consider leaving. So they grew accustomed to one another, as if they belonged to each other.

As I noted, this store was one of the first to specialize in office supplies. In time, there were many competitors, and Herbst was urged to abandon his patron and work for them. Each tried to attract him with double the salary paid by Rosenthal and Co. But Moritz Herbst remained loyal and continued to work for the allotted salary, never asking for a raise and never considering leaving to work elsewhere at a higher salary. Until something happened that demonstrated that anything can change, even a faithful servant. His employer sent him to transact some business in his name. He discovered, inadvertently, that the transaction was risky and that it would be a mistake to proceed on the basis of credit. He therefore didn't conclude the transaction. On the other hand, another much larger transaction came his way, in which the bulk of the merchandise would be paid for in cash. Not only did he prevent his employer from losing a fortune, but he found him another deal, which was profitable far beyond what was anticipated. When the employer became aware of these events, he immediately doubled Herbst's salary. He expected him to be extremely grateful, to say, "Many thanks to you, kind sir, for your great generosity." Not only did he not thank him, but he said, "I'm sorry, sir, but unless I can become a partner, I will resign to go into business on my own." The employer answered, "You can't be a partner, since it is the custom in our family to include only relatives in the business. And, as you know, we are not related in any way." Herbst said, "That need not present a problem. With your consent, I can become related to you and your family through your daughter." The man was stunned into silence. Then he asked, "What will my daughter say about this?" Herbst answered, "I already have her word. Now we are asking for your consent." Not long afterward, Moritz Herbst married the daughter of his employer, becoming a partner in a business that had been selling equipment to offices, banks, and stores for several generations. It had always been known as Rosenthal's but would henceforth be known as Rosenthal and Co.

From the moment he became involved in the business, Herbst made an effort to adapt his manners to those of his employer, whom he regarded as a model Berliner, a title which since childhood signified real distinction. After marrying the daughter, he became more and more relaxed about the manners he had acquired in Berlin and reverted, though not consciously, to his earlier ways. After his father-in-law's death, he took charge of the entire business. He became less careful about his language, sprinkling his conversation with Yiddish and Polish words from his childhood. He often reminisced about his town, describing it in detail: the teachers there who had studied in the great academies of Poznan and Lysa, and were so intimidating that the rabbis with doctorates didn't dare to challenge them in matters of ritual slaughter or anything else pertaining to religion, although whatever the former allowed, the others forbade, and vice versa. Even his father, Manish, may he rest in peace, for whom Manfred was named, knew the basic texts and studied Mishnah every day in a group that included the town's leading citizens, led by Rabbi Eliyahu Gutmacher. Moritz still had his father's books though he himself had never studied very much, because his father had died when he was young. His mother had married a man whose son by his first wife was already enrolled in a teachers' seminary and depended on his father for support, so there was no money to pay the stepson's tuition. Though he didn't study much Torah, Moritz Herbst was blessed by a man immersed in Torah and even received a coin from him.

This is what happened with the coin. It was the custom in Moritz's town, and probably in many others like it, that, as long as no worm was seen in the cherries, they could be eaten without inspection. But, as soon as the first worm was seen, an announcement would be made in the rabbi's name that the cherries had to be inspected. To facilitate this, the children were alerted to report to the rabbi when they saw the first worm. One year, he was the first to spot a worm in the cherries. He ran and informed the rabbi. The rabbi gave him a coin and blessed him, expressing the hope that he would grow up to follow the straight path, observing the Torah and commandments. Some of this blessing was fulfilled, but not all of it. He never veered from the straight path, but he was lax about the Torah and commandments. On the face of it, he followed the rules of *kashrut;* his house was equipped with separate dishes for dairy and meat, as well as for Passover, but his wife occasionally borrowed a Passover dish for ordinary use without bothering to scour it properly before putting it back. Similarly, if some ritual question arose in the household, she didn't take the trouble to consult an expert. Nevertheless, they considered themselves proper Jews until the Great War broke out, adding to the hardships of observant Jews and undermining those who were lax. At first these Jews were careful not to defile themselves with forbidden foods. But, as the war continued, food was in short supply. When they were lucky enough to find something to eat, they were no longer exacting about the rules of *kashrut.* If they found a food that needed to be certified, they didn't ask whether it was certified, who the certifying rabbis were, or the source of their authority. In Herbst's home, too, *kashrut* standards were relaxed, because Moritz Herbst came down with one of those illnesses that became rampant in the wake of the war and was no longer able to oversee the household, while his wife from the very beginning wasn't strict about these rules.

Moritz Herbst died from that illness. At this point, Manfred was a soldier in the war, knee-deep in blood, and none of the affairs of the world seemed meaningful to him, certainly not business. From the beginning, he was not groomed for business; his father had kept him at a distance from it, coaxing him to study instead. His mother, Amelia, though she was a merchant's daughter, was not skilled in business either. Neither her father nor her husband had included her in it. As she couldn't handle the business left to her by her husband, not only did she fail to derive profit from the store, the equipment, the accounts, and all the rest, but they were a burden to her. Neither mother nor son knew what to do with this inheritance. After consulting relatives, they sold the business for several thousand marks. Like most of the population, they were unaware that the value of the mark was declining steadily, so that a thousand marks were worth a hundred and a hundred marks were worth one. In the end, all that money was worthless.

As I mentioned, when his father died, Manfred was at the front. When he returned, he resumed his studies. A son whose father dies without leaving him any resources ought to learn a trade that can be a means of support. If he is eager for learning, he ought to pursue the sort of knowledge that can be a means of support after a few years' study. But Manfred was drawn to a profession involving a great deal of effort and minimal return. While he was a student, he didn't have to worry. Tuition had been provided for him. Even before he entered the university, an allowance had been set aside to cover his expenses. How? This is how it came about.

When Manfred's father, Moritz, was a boy, his father died. His mother then married a man from Rawicz. The husband had a son by his first wife who was studying at the teachers' seminary in Cologne. The husband joined his mother in her town. Moritz lived with his mother, while the son of his mother's husband lived in Cologne, so they never saw each other. When Moritz grew up, he couldn't find anything to do in his own town and went to seek his fortune elsewhere. He came to Berlin, where he had the good fortune to find a livelihood and a wife. He took over the first store that hired him, and the daughter of his employer became his wife.

Now that you have heard the story of Moritz Herbst, I'll tell you his stepbrother's story. His good fortune was not in abeyance either. He completed his studies and began teaching religion in a small town.

His salary did not satisfy his material needs; teaching did not satisfy his spirit. He suffered, regretting both these facts, but he seemed resigned to his fate, like most teachers, who were in no way inferior to him. In the town where he taught religion, there was an agent for writing equipment and school supplies, whom he sometimes helped with his accounts, letter writing, and the like. Whatever he did was done with no thought of reward. In time, the salesman became paralyzed. His wife invited the teacher to help her with the business. He became the agent's agent. The woman realized he was more adept than she was and left most of the business in his hands. Once he got a taste of commerce, he lost interest in the school.

He gave up his pupils and his fellow teachers, who had lorded it over him because the subjects they taught were needed by the world, whereas he taught religion, and who can say whether it exists to gratify God or to serve man? As soon as he went into business, earning in one month twice what he used to earn as a teacher in half a year, he became ambitious and was not satisfied with being a middleman. He wanted to own a factory. He heard of one that was about to come on the market: a factory that had been producing slates for schools and was operating at a loss, because in most countries students were being given notebooks rather than slates, in order to assess the progress of their handwriting. He quickly bought the factory, confident that he could recover what the original owners had lost. And he was not mistaken. In a few years he had repaid what he had borrowed to buy the factory and made enough profit to convert from the production of writing slates to that of roofs, like those produced by the big slate factories in Thuringia. All those years, the two stepbrothers were blessed by fortune and engaged in the acquisition of wealth; one, as we already mentioned, through office equipment and the like; the other, as we already mentioned, through religion, writing equipment, and slate roofs. Both were determined not to waste a minute on anything unrelated to the acquisition of wealth. They never asked about each other, and, if their paths hadn't crossed, they would have gone through life without knowing one another.

How did they become acquainted? The manufacturer came to Berlin for a board meeting of the Academy for Jewish Studies. Strolling through the streets of Berlin, he passed the showroom of Rosenthal and Co., and went in to see what was new in the way of office equipment. He was browsing through the store, cane in hand, and smoking a thick cigar, since it was Saturday and it was his custom to honor the Shabbat with a cigar, making do with cigarettes on weekdays. The owner stared at him and said, "Didn't you have a father in Myloslow?" He took the cigar out of his mouth, flicked the ashes, and said, "That's right. My father's second marriage was to a woman from Myloslow, whom he followed to her town." The owner said, "And is your name Ringer?" He said, "Yes, my name is Ringer." He said, "Then we are somewhat related." "How?" "My mother, may she rest in peace, was your father's wife." He said, "How did you recognize me, considering that you never saw me?" He said, "I looked at you and thought to myself: I know this man, and I don't know where I know him from. My stepfather's image came to mind. I thought to myself: If I were to dress him in elegant clothes, replace his beard with a mustache, and stick a cigarette in his mouth, a fashionable cane in his hand, and a gold chain on his belly, I wouldn't be able to distinguish between the two of you. Logic led me to conclude that, since you are not my stepfather, you must be my stepbrother. I immediately asked what I asked, and then you answered as you answered. Now, in the name of brotherhood, we ought to have a drink, though I'm hoping for more than that. I have a wife and son. Won't you do me the honor, on behalf of my wife and son, of coming home with me and having dinner with us?" He agreed, and they went off together.

During dinner, Moritz talked about his favorite subjects: the elderly teachers in his town who used to irritate the rabbis with doctorates by sending the slaughterers to them with defective knives, in order to test how well versed they were in the rules of ritual slaughter, and other similar ruses to make a mockery of them. He also told the story of the cherry, the worm, the rabbi, and the coin. He told other things, most of which I have already written in my book. In the course of conversation, he referred to a biblical verse and stumbled over it, like an ignoramus. He laughed and said, "It's because of you that I'm so ignorant." "How?" He explained that, because his stepfather had to pay tuition for his own son, he couldn't afford to have his wife's son study Torah. As a result, both he and the Torah were deprived; he, alas, remained totally ignorant. Mr. Ringer listened and laughed. He had drunk a great deal of wine, and he said, "An injustice that can be corrected should be corrected. I would like to make up, through your son, for what my father did to you. Allow me to pay his tuition while he studies for his degree." Moritz Herbst laughed and said, "How can a little brother turn his big brother down? If that's what you want, fine. Whatever you say." He said, "Let's shake hands on it." He said, "If that's what you want, I give you my hand." Herbst considered the agreement a joke. Ringer considered it an actual commitment. He didn't leave the house before writing a check. He continued to pay Manfred's tuition until his death and then left him enough stocks to pay his future tuition. These funds made it possible for Manfred Herbst to study wherever his heart desired.

When Germany collapsed, most of its industry and commerce was disrupted. The value of Mr. Ringer's securities declined, and there was a chance Manfred Herbst would have to interrupt his studies, since everything his father had left him was lost. He was rescued by a relative. He had an old aunt in Leipzig, the sister of his mother's father, who was married to a noted singer, adored by all the music lovers in Leipzig. When he realized he was losing his voice, he turned away from music and established an advertising agency, which was patronized by all his fans. So it thrived and prospered, and after his death—even during the war and in the years that followed—his widow was able to support herself and to help the son of her brother's daughter, who was the only one of her relatives to survive the war.

— 9 —

I will now go back to Manfred's beginnings, when there was still peace in the world, when Moritz Herbst was alive and Manfred was a student. In addition to his secular studies, Manfred took classes in religion and Hebrew. If the teacher was a scholar, he would call on a student to read something while he sat at his desk proofreading an article on Jewish studies. When the student paused, he would look up, call on someone else, and go back to his proofreading, giving no further thought to his teaching. If the instructor was not a scholar, he would pass the time with words that imparted neither Torah, wisdom, Talmud, nor Hebrew. In any case, Manfred learned neither the elements of religion nor anything related to Hebrew from these teachers. He didn't feel he was missing anything; he pored over the literature of Germany and all the other nations without being aware that, although he was taking in foreign wisdom, his own people's wisdom remained foreign to him.

As I said, there was peace in the world, but woe unto a world that is governed by hooligans. There was harsh news, from a land not so distant, about Jews being massacred. As a boy, he had heard about pogroms, about Herzl, about Zionism. Even before this, he had had a deep understanding of the issues and already tended toward Zionism. The Jewish community in Germany was still serene, diverted by the notion that there was no evil in Germany, that all the Zionist activity there concerned Jews in other countries whose governments oppressed them and instigated pogroms, that it was the duty of German Jews to assist their persecuted brethren in seeking a land that would offer them a haven. And where would these driven, worn-out people find such a haven? In Palestine, under the wing of consuls who would protect their subjects more effectively there than in their native lands. No one realized yet that Germany would be the major source of trouble for Jews, that they would seek refuge and not find it except in the Land of Israel. Since Zionism in no way interfered with the boy's studies, his father didn't interfere with his Zionist activities. He, too, would occasionally glance at Zionist pamphlets and nod affirmatively, saying, "What I see here makes sense, but, if the situation were really as the Zionists see it, our leaders would all be Zionists. Since they are actually hostile to Zionism, it's best not to get involved." Manfred's mother was of another mind. Amelia Herbst loved life, and she loved enterprises that rewarded the people who undertook them. Zionism had neither of these attributes, so she should have rejected it. But, since her son, Manfred, was interested in Zionism, it could not be dismissed outright.

Zionism added little to Herbst's knowledge, beyond the words that are familiar to every Zionist: *shekel, hovev ziyon, yishuv,* Ahad Ha'am, the names of all the settlements in the Land of Israel. From Zionist literature, he learned that those weary, tormented Jews, considered uncultured in Germany, had two libraries in two languages—one in the language they spoke and one in the language of the holy books.

From the time Herbst heard about this, a tune began to sing out from his heart, playing itself in those two tongues. It sounded sometimes like the dirge of an exile lamenting his devastated domain, sometimes like a noble cry. Victims from every era appeared, pouring out their souls in epic poems and stories. Countless events, from the binding of Isaac to the Damascus blood libel and the most recent pogroms, all spoke to him in verse. God's spirit hovered over these poems, stories, and liturgical works, some of which he read in German translation, along with visions of the End of Days, glimpsed only by poets who suffered Israel's pain. When he first read Yiddish literature in German translation, he didn't eat, drink, or go to class. He curled up in a corner and sat reading these stories and poems. His eyes swallowed the letters; he fingered the text, hoping there was more there than was being revealed to him. When he had read an entire book, he studied the title page on the chance that there had been an error, that this volume was actually not from the body of literature he was after. He didn't find what he was after, and whatever he found was not what he was after. Whether it was merely fine or very fine, he knew its counterparts in other languages and was not impressed. This happened again and again. Whether the book was merely fine or very fine, he had seen the genre elsewhere. He tried his luck with Hebrew, to see if he could find there what he hadn't found in Yiddish. No complete works were available in German, only fragments. It is easy to translate from Yiddish into German, because the languages are akin, but it is hard to translate from Hebrew into German, because they are so alien to each other. I can see, Herbst used to tell himself, that Hebrew poetry refuses to appear in borrowed finery.

In those years, the Hebrew high school in Jaffa graduated its first class. Many of the graduates went to Germany for advanced studies. Foreign students commonly support themselves in a foreign country by teaching their native language, which is what those Jaffaites did. Because of the good name of the Land of Israel and of the first Hebrew high school, many people were eager to study living Hebrew with them. As a result, Hebrew teachers from other countries were rejected, although they were endowed with Torah and good manners.

Manfred Herbst was among the first to study with these graduates. He began his studies in a group, but, realizing he wasn't accomplishing very much, he hired a private teacher. He didn't learn from his teachers, nor did he learn from their books. He didn't learn from his teachers because their nationalist sentiments exceeded their learning. As for their books, they used anthologies filled with fragmentary texts in translation. Still, Herbst remained grateful, recognizing that, if not for them, all Hebrew books would have remained foreign to him.

Herbst's relation to Hebrew might have led nowhere, as is often the case, were it not for something he heard from a Christian student, a professor's daughter, whom I think I mentioned at the beginning of this story in a conversation between Herbst and his wife. Among the medical students, there was a short, shriveled Jew, shabbily dressed, altogether sloppy, as if asking to be scorned. In the clinic one day, in front of the entire class, the professor presented him with a copy of his book, *Fundamentals of Pathology,* and inscribed it "In honor of a marvelous human being, a true lover of learning." The gift from this professor, one of the greatest doctors of his generation, made a great impression. His dictum was well known: If I could, I would publish only three copies of my book; I would keep one for myself, and I don't know to whom I would give the other two. In the end, he gave his book to that man and wrote those complimentary words in it. They learned what he had done to deserve the honor. Before enrolling in the university, he had been a rabbi in Lithuania. He gave up the rabbinate and came to Berlin, literally on foot, to study medicine. No one in Berlin knew anything about him. One day, a patient from some town in Lithuania was brought to the professor, and by chance this student dropped in. The patient saw him and cried out, "Rabbi, you are here?" The rabbi whispered, "Hush." The patient ignored him and told the professor the entire story.

Herbst heard about that rabbi and thought: I'll go and study with him. He found him and presented his request. The rabbi said, "When a Jew wants to learn, someone has to teach him." But he was baffled when he heard what the student wanted to learn. How could anyone need to be taught to read such flimsy books? After much coaxing, he admitted to Herbst that he was familiar with only three such texts: Mapu's *Ahavat Ziyon,* the poems of Y. L. Gordon, and Bialik's *Hamatmid.* He considered *Ahavat Ziyon* a florid book that did neither harm nor good; Y. L. Gordon's poems were heresy, and he wouldn't consider teaching them; he was willing to read the Bialik poem, although his diligent scholar was not the one our sages described. It would, of course, have been best to study the books of Israel's true sages, whose wisdom generates wisdom.

Herbst did not have the opportunity to learn very much from him. The strain of study, malnutrition, and whatever else is involved in the pursuit of knowledge depleted the rabbi's strength. He was taken to the hospital and from there to eternal rest. But Herbst acquired a great gift from him: the ability to open any Hebrew book and learn from any text. Once he achieved this, he lost interest in the poetry of his own time. "What's the point," he used to say. "It doesn't move me."

It would be worth knowing why he wasn't moved by our modern poetry. He did, after all, love poetry, and he was acquainted with the poetry of several nations in languages new and old. When he was weary with work and worry, he would soothe his soul with a poem, being truly fond of poetry. He said nothing explicit about our poetry. Still, if one can infer one thing from another, I am almost certain that a comment he once made explains why he said, "It doesn't move me." But first, a story.

The Friends of the University were honoring a Hebrew poet on the occasion of his birthday, and Herbst was among the guests. As is customary at such events, everyone who spoke lavished praise on the poet and his work. Finally, the poet himself took the floor. He spoke, not in praise of himself, but in praise of Hebrew poetry and those who created it.

It is in the nature of such celebrations that, when they are over, no one is really satisfied, so one goes out for coffee and conversation. Herbst was not a conversationalist. Those who are silent in company are always pressed to talk. Herbst was asked for his response to the speeches made in the poet's honor. He answered, "Literature is not my field, so whatever an ignoramus like me says will neither add nor detract." Because they pressed him, he said, "Modern poetry may be good, it may even be very good, but it can't be compared to medieval poetry. And medieval poetry can't be compared to even the most minor poetry of the Bible." Someone laughed and said, "If you mean the Bible as emended by professors, even newspaper articles are preferable, so long as they weren't written by those professors."

Herbst was silent. He considered what he had said and was surprised that it had been so easy for him to speak from his heart. He was also surprised at his colleagues for not taking him seriously. He turned to them and said, "I should have remained silent, but, having begun, I will finish. If you want to hear, I'm ready to speak. For a people to have been granted such a book is quite enough, and it's reckless to turn away from what is granted once in thousands of years in favor of what's granted every day."

These were some of Herbst's attempts to master the Hebrew language. Now I will go back to where I was and recount what happened after that sleepless night.

— 10 —

I took a break between Herbst's dream and Herbst's actions, interjecting some personal history. Now I'll go back and relate events in sequence, as they evolved, recounting one thing after another, incident after incident, as it occurred, as it unfolded, as it fell into place.

By morning, Herbst had recovered from the nightmares that accompanied that mad slumber. A small parcel arrived from the post office, along with other written and printed matter. The parcel was so small that he could have ignored it. But something made him take note of it immediately. After examining what else the mailman had brought, he turned to investigate the parcel.

He took a pencil and slipped it under the string, hoping to loosen it without letting it snap, so he would be able to pass it on to Henrietta in one piece. Good, strong string was no longer available, and what could be bought was rough and ineffectual, like most of the defective merchandise that came in with the war.

He slipped off the string and then the wrappings, treating the paper with the same care. He removed the paper slowly and carefully, so it wouldn't tear in his hand. Good, strong paper was no longer available in stores, and what could be bought was as ugly as all the other defective merchandise that came in with the war. When the package was unwrapped, he found a book inside, one of those book that, as soon as you see it, you feel you have always been waiting for. The book was by Alfred Neu, a distillation of all his articles and papers.

After glancing through the book, Herbst sat down at his desk, as he did when he was about to work. He sometimes sat down to work wishing that he would be interrupted, for even a zealous and diligent worker has to stop. Ideas don't always fly into his pen, and he has to take a break and be idle. No one likes to take this on himself, to admit that he himself is responsible for the fact that he is idle. If he is interrupted, he has someone to blame for his idleness, and he can believe that, if he hadn't been interrupted, he would be working diligently.

Now he was afraid he might be interrupted. He read two or three pages, then sat up in astonishment. He was, after all, well versed in Neu's theories. He knew them by heart, so that, even were he to be wakened from sleep, he could have outlined them without faltering. Still, he found new material in the book. That is the secret of a good book: whenever you read it, you find things you hadn't noticed before. As for this book, there really was new material in it. Some of Neu's conclusions, which had seemed a bit flimsy, were reinforced here. Herbst, who already accepted Neu's theory and was deeply involved with it, made no distinction between what was previously implied and what was now stated with certainty. In either case, he approached the book as a new reader.

I have mentioned Neu on many occasions without mentioning what he does. I have made fleeting references, as if he were a figure that flits from void to void. If he has assumed any substance at all, it derives from Manfred Herbst, who owed his position to him and was introduced to Lisbet Neu because of him. Now I will tell a little something about him, as well as his books. I'll begin with his forefathers, as I did with Herbst, having learned from experience that, if you want to ascertain a man's character, it's worthwhile to consider the preceding generations, to know the quarry whence he was hewed. Also, it is good to begin with childhood, before one has learned to camouflage his actions, a time when everything is still exposed. I will deal only with his early years, before he became famous, because whatever transpired afterward can be found in the monographs written about him.

Alfred Neu was the son of financiers whose business was linked with commerce and industry in several German cities. In the memoirs of the elders, printed only for the family and never made public, there is a detailed account of how the business developed and acquired such a reputation that it became connected with leading banks in almost every country. It was not their wealth that made them famous, for they were not rich, but their loyalty and integrity, for they were scrupulous and rejected any questionable enterprise, any hint of speculation. Whoever preferred loyalty and integrity to avarice did business with them. Until the enemy took over, annihilating them and their business.

In the beginning, it was assumed that Alfred Neu would also go into the family business. It was the custom in the Neu family that, when a son completes his secondary education, he learns banking. This was the rule: he begins at the lowest level. If he is worthy, he is promoted. When he becomes more proficient and more worthy, he is made an assistant branch manager. When he becomes still more proficient and worthy, he is made a branch manager. If there is no vacancy, he waits until there is a spot for him, or another branch is opened with him at its head. So it was with each member of the Neu family, Alfred Neu included. When he finished his secondary studies, he was sent to work in a branch of the bank located in some small town. He spent a year there. He did well, and everyone predicted that he would become a competent financier. No one realized that, what his fathers had done eagerly and willingly, he was doing only out of a sense of duty. He was not yet aware of what his heart was demanding of him, but, unconsciously, he was pursuing its mission. The Neu family, being observant, was careful not to violate the Shabbat, and, since all work stopped on the Christian Sabbath too, he had two free days every week. He used to spend Shabbat studying Torah, philosophy, and science. He spent Sundays hiking, rowing, catching grasshoppers, collecting plant specimens, or fishing, according to the season and the weather. Because it was a small town with a tight economy, in which everyone was worn out by work and the pressure of taxes, because it was becoming more and more difficult to engage in matchmaking because most young men were going off to the big cities, no one was free to invite young Neu for an evening meal, a cup of coffee, or simple conversation, even though he was a bachelor and they were encumbered with daughters. In any case, it seemed clear that a young man from such a wealthy family was not meant for the daughter of some local businessman. So

Neu's time was his own to spend as he wished. He reserved the free days for trips and the like, the nights for books. He read all sorts of things that year. I would be surprised if there was a subject he didn't explore, ranging from the origins of the world and its development to the history of man and all living creatures. Whatever he saw, heard, or read, he summarized in his notebook. The order and precision to which he was accustomed in the bank characterized all his endeavors. On the face of it, what Neu wrote was a diary, the sort a young person writes out of idleness, when there is no one to talk to. But the intelligence for which he later became renowned was already apparent in those note-books. What did he include in them, and what did he exclude? Conver-sations, epigrams, fables, the chatter of children, jokes, riddles, hyperboles, incantations, slips of the tongue, legal verdicts—whatever struck him as special—along with fundamental theories and assump-tions. His basic assumptions about sight, sound, and smell were already apparent in those notebooks, as were his opinions on the influence of smell on human behavior. Before Neu achieved what he achieved, he followed many blind alleys.

Scholars who know what they are after early in life are fortunate. From the start, they prepare themselves for that task, wasting no time on other things. Perhaps still more fortunate are those who don't know what direction they will take and give their attention to whatever comes their way. When the time comes to display their wisdom, they are experts in many areas, like a landowner who knows the lay of his land. Why do I compare Neu to a landowner? While he was in that small town, he made the acquaintance of landowners who had dealings with the bank and, unlike the townspeople, invited him to their homes. He used to go with them and hear what a particular field was worth, whether or not such a plant species was productive, whether rearing livestock or producing cheese was more lucrative, what things needed to be improved, and whether the landowners were doing well with the new machinery some of them had adopted. He also heard about the workers from other countries who came to help with the harvest, whose wages seemed low but were high in the end, because of the thefts and fires that followed on their heels. He sat listening and thinking: I'm here only to learn about business and finance. Providence had other thoughts: He's here to prepare for what he was destined to do from the beginning, to pave the way for discoveries he is destined to make. He spent even more of his time with the farmers. Until he tramped through the countryside, he was as unaware of the fields as any city person. When he began going to the country, he observed the farmers, their practices, and their conversations with their cattle and their fowl; how they tended their bees and worked their land. In this period he began to want to settle in the country, either as a farmer or a landowner, working at work time, resting at rest time, reading books and learning from the wisdom of generations, offering counsel and insight to his neighbors. He did not know then that many people would benefit from his wisdom, though not the country people he was so fond of at the beginning, when he was first moved by the spirit of enlightenment. Neu pictured his future in the country in various attractive forms. But none of his visions was fulfilled, for anyone who wants to work in agriculture must work for a farmer first. All the farmers were gentile, because only Gentiles could own land, so kosher food would be un-available. Even if he were to find kosher food somehow, his parents would never allow their son to become a farmer.

After two years in a small town, it was time for advancement. He was about to be promoted to a high position in a large city. Not only was he himself unhappy, but he made his father and mother sad by asking something no one in the Neu family had ever asked. He wanted to enroll in the university. When his grandfather heard this, he said, "I thought he was talented, and now I hear he wants to enroll in the university!" Upon being told that he was truly talented, the old man said, "Then why does he need the university? Let him leave academic learning to mediocre people. Those with real talent deal in commerce or banking." To appease his father, Neu chose medicine, a field that offers financial security.

I will pause to say something about the Neu family. All the members of the house of Neu loved the Torah, promoted learning, cherished the rabbinate, patronized Jewish and secular studies, and subsidized needy students. One such student lived in their home, so they could study with him in their spare time. They provided him with room and board, and treated him with more respect than they treated rich men. But they never produced a rabbi or a scholar; nor did their daughters marry rabbis or scholars. The first member of the family to turn to philosophy or science was Alfred Neu, who enrolled in the university to study medicine. But he didn't become a doctor.

Medical school is a full-time occupation. Nevertheless, this eager scholar managed to pursue other subjects. He became an expert in some of them, so inventive that he was considered a leader in the field. Before achieving what he achieved, Alfred Neu traversed a long and devious road. The details are known and preserved in monographs and ency-clopedias, so there is no reason for me to dwell on them. I might as well get back to Herbst's story. If, in the course of it, it becomes necessary to return to Neu, I will do so. But not at any length.

After reading Neu's book, Herbst placed his hand on it, as if it were a rare find which he was determined to hold on to. He sat and wondered: How does one arrive at such verbal clarity and simplicity, at the ability to express such mysteries so that they appear obvious, when the fact is that, until Neu revealed them, they were opaque and scholars were unaware of them?

Herbst enumerated some of Neu's sources—fragments of myth, snatches of melody, jumbled proverbs, isolated phrases, magical incantations, legal pronouncements. Such material, unnoticed by other researchers, provided Neu with access to hidden worlds, which he delivered from the abyss of neglect. What was the state of this material before Neu began to deal with it? It was a battered, disjointed mess. Every generation tampered with it, abridging and emending according to its needs, so that its original form was no longer apparent. And what generations did to serve their needs, some researchers did to serve their theories. Neu arrived on the scene and cleaned up everything. Now everyone knows and recognizes this material; everyone is familiar with it. But, until Neu made it accessible, it remained unknown.

Herbst was moved to tears by the modesty of true scholars who work a lifetime to uncover deeply hidden material that becomes general knowledge, so general that those who discovered and revealed it are forgotten. Taking no notice of this, they work on tirelessly, unstintingly, incessantly, with no thought of reward. Herbst went back to the page he had stopped at, bent its corner, and reread the preceding pages. He was astonished. He had read the book and knew what was in it; still, he found things there that he hadn't noticed earlier. Again Herbst asked himself: How does one arrive at this? How can such great and sublime ideas be expressed in such simple, graceful language? Herbst listed some of the ideas that were basic to Neu's theory. The actual life and thought of early man, whose existence we were barely aware of, were outlined in the book. Future generations will surely come up with new and more precise facts, but it is clear that they will follow the path laid out in Neu's books. They will have insights about things Neu never dreamed of, they will challenge some of Neu's assumptions, but his basic theories will remain intact. Like a mountain, his research will not totter. Neu didn't rely on anyone else's work, having arrived at his discoveries on his own. Nevertheless, he gave others credit, beyond what they deserved. Only someone with great scope could have written with such vigor and so lucidly. Not many scholars were able to express their teaching in such terms, concentrating on the essentials without overemphasizing them and playing down the trivial without minimizing whatever quality it had.

Another notable aspect of Neu's book: it exemplified the ideal old man who has acquired wisdom without proclaiming himself a paragon and declaring, "See how great I am." Once again Herbst's eyes filled with tears, because of Neu, because of his wisdom, because of his discoveries, and because of what others could discover as a result of his discoveries. How did Neu merit this? Through his own talent and the relentless pursuit of essential truth, not to mention the influence of the quarry whence he was hewed. This scholar, descended from merchants and bankers, knows how to calculate the past, like a trustworthy treasurer who can account for every cent he takes in and pays out. He has no patience with faulty estimates, invalid hunches, hollow verbiage, or certainties that shift in response to convenience. The entire book is considered, accurate, balanced. Like a large coin that can be exchanged for several smaller ones, his conclusions can be expressed in lower terms, and, like small coins with which small things are acquired, Neu's remarks help scholars to acquire basic knowledge. The nations of the world characterize Jews as merchants whose entire existence depends on coins. What Israel's enemies consider corrupt, we regard as virtue. Since Jews deal in currency, they become experts, buying and selling with the finest coinage. I will depart from the role of narrator and inject a word of my own. How is it that all of Professor Neu's research is accurate and true? It's because he is descended from proper God-fearing Jews, as meticulous in minor observances as in more stringent ones, knowing their Creator tolerates no deceit. Having learned to be meticulous with His commandments, they learned to be meticulous, whatever they do. Professor Neu follows his ancestors' ways, and their merit sustains him.

As thoughts sometimes do, Herbst's thoughts wandered, touching on Neu's visit to this country. The days were especially beautiful, typical of the weeks between Purim and Pesah in the Land of Israel. The earth put forth grass. All the mountains, hills, valleys, and hollows were filled with soft vegetation and the scents of green freshness. Even the aged rocks had buds in their crevices. The sky arched high and blue over everything, with good smells emanating from the earth and the heavens, from above and below. Look down, and a fine smell wafts upward; look up, and a fine scent drifts down from the sky. Between the earth and the sky, new birds dart from tree to tree, from branch to branch, testing their voices in a new song. Not to mention the dove from the Song of Songs by King Solomon, peace be with him, as in the verse: "The voice of the turtle dove was heard in our land."

Like the two-legged creatures above, a host of four-legged creatures—land animals, intimate with the earth—respond with mounting exhilaration. Their voices are renewed when they see the bountiful nourishment provided by the One who provides for all His creatures. They are no longer dependent on their human masters. As they roam about, sniffing the ground, the food seems to reach their mouth with hardly any effort, for the land is generous to all creatures and favors them in every way. This is really how it is. Even thorns and thistles, created because of a snake, are adorned with buds and flowers, and are soft and pleasant in the days between Purim and Pesah. This is not surprising, for Israel was redeemed in the month of Nisan, and, every year at that time, it's as if Israel's redemption were being considered again and again, and as if, knowing this, all creatures were on their best behavior, so that, should Israel be deemed worthy, they too would be redeemed. Already goats and sheep—ewes and kids—dot the landscape with their wool. Though we resent them for destroying gardens and flowers we have labored over, we cherish them in this season and enjoy watching them frolic. Even more so the cows, who are led out of the barns to graze. The meadow gives off the smell of milk, and a small boy leads the cows. If I'm not mistaken, he is the son of a Hasid from Galicia who abandoned his father and mother, his *rebbe,* and his entire community to go to the Land of Israel, acquired a small plot of land in one of Jerusalem's neighborhoods, and bought one cow, then another and still another, all of whom give milk. At first, when there was peace in the land, Henrietta Herbst used to get milk from those cows, praising its quality and exclaiming over its cream content. Now that the roads are dangerous and Jews no longer show themselves in Arab neighborhoods, Henrietta gets her milk from some other source and no longer exclaims over the cream. At first, when that Hasid abandoned his rich family, his *rebbe,* and the entire community, his parents were in mourning, the rabbi spoke of him harshly, and everyone mocked him. Now that Hitler is in power, claiming their wealth and then their lives, they all want to come to the Land of Israel. What deters them? The law deters them. Not only in the lands of exile is that law wielded against them, but in the Land of Israel as well. That land, created for Israel's sake, is governed by strangers who will not allow Jews in.

Back to Neu when he was in the Land of Israel.

The city is full of tourists. They come from every country. They walk from place to place, astonished by Jerusalem's splendor, the good Lord having filled it, from earth to high heaven, with astounding

beauty. Despite the ugly houses, Jerusalem is lovely. At regular intervals the Lord cuts a hole in the sky, as it were, extracts some clouds—
blue, purple, and all the other fine colors mentioned in the Bible—and
decorates His city with them. Just as heaven and earth, cattle, animals,
birds, trees, and rocks are a delight, so are human beings, especially our
people Israel, when they see the Lord's works and wonders—how He
arranges time, shifts seasons, dispels chill, and provides warmth. Just as
He dispelled the chill of winter, its winds and storms, bringing light
and joy in their place, so will He soon dispel our exile and bring on
true redemption.

I have been somewhat distracted by love of Jerusalem and the prospect of redemption. Now I'll get back to Neu when he was a guest in
this country. What a sight that old man was, at his age, skipping up
mountains and leaping over hills to see the sun rise or the moon set.
He made a point of going to different synagogues for morning and
evening prayers, to get to know the customs of every community;
wherever he prayed, it was clear that their God and his were one. I
don't know Neu's views about race. In any case, seeing this wise man
from the west among brothers from the east, north, and south, one
would have to acknowledge that all of Israel is descended from a single
father. Once, Herbst accompanied Neu to the Western Wall. On the
way, Herbst told Neu that the stones meant nothing to him. When they
reached the wall and he watched Neu studying those stones, Herbst's
eyes filled with tears. To this day, when he remembers that scene, he
comes close to tears. Herbst, as you know, is not observant and remains
remote from most things that arouse the hearts of the devout. But
Herbst admires his teacher, and, whatever Neu does, he accepts. Often,
when he watched him pray, he felt like joining in; had he known the
prayers, he would have prayed too.

Neu's visit was wonderful. Herbst was with Neu all the time, in
Jerusalem and everywhere else. Finally, when it was time for Neu to
leave, he came to Herbst's house to say goodbye and didn't find him
in. Herbst missed the opportunity to welcome his teacher to his home
before his departure. When he came, he came with his young relative,
Lisbet Neu. Lisbet had accompanied him to help him find the place.
Neu may have brought her along with some other intention. Perhaps
he hoped to give her entry to his pupil's home, in order to expand her
horizons beyond those of the new immigrants, Orthodox Jews from
Germany, whose world is circumscribed, who don't see past their own
four cubits. Some days later, Herbst called on Ernst Weltfremdt, who
had just become a professor, and found two ladies there, one young, one

old. One of them was Lisbet Neu; the other was her mother. Now he himself is in line for a promotion, and unless there is significant opposition, he may well be appointed professor, as he had been appointed lecturer when the university trustees asked Neu to recommend faculty and Neu directed them to Herbst. Just now, Herbst was concerned with Neu's book rather than the professorship. It occurred to him that Neu might have sent the book to his relatives, who would rejoice over it—not because of its quality, which he doubted they would recognize, but because it was a gift from an uncle. How delighted they would be to have the book analyzed for them. Herbst had not as yet translated this thought into action, and he hadn't as yet designated himself for the job. But he thought: How happy those two ladies would be if someone were to come and say, "I'll explain the book to you, if you like."

It was Shabbat, a day when no business is transacted in the Land of Israel. Since the university and the National Library were both closed, Herbst spent Shabbat writing letters or scholarly articles. But he didn't get deeply involved in the articles, as he was determined to complete his book on burial customs of the poor in Byzantium, a project he had been working on for a long time and was eager to be done with, not only for the book itself but because it was such a bother to him. Now, since his review was published and his name was being mentioned again, all of the country's journals seemed to be after him for articles. As you know, Herbst's energies were depleted. Reading his teacher's book revived him, so much so that he was confident that, if only he would pick up a pen, the letters would fly onto the paper.

Herbst took a cigarette, stuck it in his mouth, lit it, stood up, and leaned on the arm of the chair, looking out the window as he blew a wreath of smoke rings. He suddenly heard a bird and became upset, remembering that he had been in the garden with his baby daughter the day before; they had heard a chirping sound, and the little girl had looked up and said, "There's no bird in the sky." Too bad; too bad he didn't tell Henrietta. Henrietta is so pleased when she hears something clever from Sarah, especially when he reports it to her. He put the cigarette in the ashtray and took another. He meant to pick up a pen, but, since the cigarette had found its way into his hand, he stuck it in his mouth, lit it, sat down, and fixed his mind on writing. He produced an article that later became known by its full title: "To What Extent Did the Emperor Justinian Believe in Those Ministers Who Maintained that He Would Rise to Heaven Like Elijah in His Time?"

Herbst found some relevant notes, clipped them together, took one of the thousands of bulletins showered on us by national institutions, and wrote an outline on the blank part of the paper, beginning with quotations from Justinian's ministers—evidence that often, when they sat together dealing with affairs of state, these ministers were worried that he would suddenly be swept up to heaven in a storm. Since the facts are known, I won't repeat them, but I should note that Herbst tried to establish whether Justinian actually believed in his own holiness and considered himself in a class with Elijah, or whether he was persuaded to believe in his power by ministers who repeatedly said, "When we were in his presence, we were afraid he would be swept up to heaven in a storm."

So much for Justinian's holiness and Herbst's calculations. It is time to get back to Herbst and to my subject, which is Neu's book. Herbst's idea—to explain Neu's book to those two ladies, Neu's relatives, contrived to assign him the role of messenger. Since it is my way to relate outcomes at the beginning, let me say that Herbst didn't get to do it. Why do I tell you this? So no heart will grieve over a good deed that should have been accomplished but never was.

— **11** —

After lunch, when Henrietta lay down for a rest. Manfred put on his good clothes, tucked Neu's little book in his pocket, and went to call on Lisbet Neu. Herbst had never been at Lisbet Neu's, nor had he ever wished to go there. Now that he had her uncle's book, his mind was set on going to her.

Like someone who is about to do something he is not in the habit of doing, he pictured some of what he would see at Lisbet's. Her mother would be sitting in Shabbat clothes, a Shabbat kerchief on her head, her hands on her heart, in the manner of Orthodox women when they are at rest. On the table nearby, he would find a prayerbook, the five books of Moses with Hirsch's commentary, and her uncle's book. She has already read the weekly portion, as well as the commentary, and translated its lofty language into simple terms. Some of her interpretations were the ones she learned as a child; others were her own; still others, imparted by teachers, were outdated and had to be revised. Having done what she was trained to do on Shabbat, what more does her heart desire? It is now her desire to know the contents of her uncle's book. She realizes she won't ever know its contents, for she wasn't allowed to study academic subjects, although she did study some difficult material that not everyone would grasp, such as Hirsch's commentary and ritual law. On many occasions here in Jerusalem, Herbst had spent time with young women—high school students and university students alike—who couldn't deal with that material, not even with its vocabulary. As she sits there, lost in thought, she hears footsteps, followed by a knock on the door. She says, "Come in." He comes in and sees Neu's book on the table. He opens it and begins reading; explicating, interpreting, and analyzing the text; pointing out original insights and discoveries. For Neu has brought many things to light, some of which were totally unknown until he revealed them and others that were illuminated by his insight. The old woman is astonished. She knew her uncle was a great scholar with an international reputation, but this knowledge was not grounded in understanding, and knowledge without understanding is not gratifying. Now that this gentleman, Herbst the teacher, has come and said what he said, her heart expands and her eyes light up, not out of pride and conceit, but in praise and gratitude to the Lord, may He be blessed, for bestowing wisdom on her uncle. Herbst sits with her, reviewing the history of this widow, once rich and aristocratic, which he learned from her daughter Lisbet. Her hand used to be extended to the poor, and countless emissaries from Jerusalem would come to her home and enjoy her hospitality, besides her gifts and charity. Then, suddenly, the world was shaken by a curse; the entire country and its inhabitants became adversaries, so that she and her daughters, like countless other Jews, had to leave their home, their land, their silver and gold—all the property acquired by her family in the course of four or five generations. She wandered through many lands and finally came up to Jerusalem. Lisbet never mentioned whether the emissaries from Jerusalem—those who used to sit at their table and enjoy their bounty—have chosen not to recognize them, or whether it is they themselves who keep their distance, preferring not to put anyone to the test and risk being humiliated. They struggle to live on the meager resources they managed to take with them, supplemented by Lisbet's salary. Suddenly, someone comes to her; he comes of his own accord and reads to her from this book, written by her uncle, a Jewish scholar with an international reputation, even now when Israel's enemies, dominated by this curse, are denouncing Jews everywhere.

These were some of Manfred Herbst's thoughts, reveries, fantasies

when his will contrived to make him the messenger who would explain
her uncle's book to Lisbet Neu's mother. Herbst had seen Lisbet when
he went to congratulate Weltfremdt on his promotion, but since that
day he had never thought of her, and it had never occurred to him to
visit her. Suddenly, he found that his mind was completely occupied
with her. He thought: I'll go to her, sit awhile, and read a bit. Then
I'll tell Henrietta where I was and what I did, and, even if I say outright
that I called on that widow because of Neu, her uncle, Henrietta won't
be surprised. Herbst was not always in the habit of saying "I'll tell
Henrietta"; now he enjoyed saying it: "I'll tell Henrietta."

Herbst went out, closed the door behind him, and checked the fence,
the bushes, the vegetables, and the flowers, which were drooping because of the heat. He felt sorry for them and resolved to come back and
water them before dark. He meant to go back in and tell Henrietta he
would water the garden later. Meanwhile, he forgot what was in his
mind and didn't go back. It's just as well he forgot. Had he gone in,
he would have wakened her, and she needed her sleep, because she had
been up all night with the baby, who had a stomachache from eating
bad grapes and had cried all night. He turned back to the garden and
glanced at the flowers, deciding which to take to Lisbet's mother. He
was distracted and didn't take any. It's just as well he forgot. Had he
brought Lisbet's mother flowers, she would not have accepted them,
because he had picked them on Shabbat. He felt his pocket to be sure
he had the book. He opened it and marked the passages he would read
to Lisbet Neu and her mother. One could not assume the ladies would
understand, but, if he explained, they would surely understand. Again,
he pictured Lisbet Neu's mother, sitting in her chair, hands folded over
her heart, gazing at Lisbet, and saying to her, wordlessly: Listen, my
child; listen, Lisbet. The scene conveyed a message: all the world's
goodness has not been totally consumed, and even in these troubled
times there are ways to help others as well as yourself. Imagine yourself
sitting with two respectable ladies, reading to them, and diverting your
mind from that woman who was created to torment you.

The little neighborhood of Orhot Hayim was unusually quiet. As
in most of Jerusalem's neighborhoods, no work was done there on
Shabbat. There was no one in sight. Some people were at home reading; others were in bed. Six days have been provided for work and
labor; one, for rest and pleasure. Anyone with sense rests on that day
and turns away from mundane concerns. Those with even more sense
pursue wisdom as well as rest. How? By reading the five books, the
commentaries of Rashi, the Ramban, Ibn Ezra. For the Torah is not to

be taken literally and must be studied to be understood. If you find the key to its riddles, you are in on the secret of creation and the wisdom of the world. No day is so suited to such pursuits as the seventh, Shabbat, when the world rests. An object at rest is easier to observe, and observers are quiet, as a rule. Only their eyes are astir, exploring the five books of Moses and the commentaries. God's ways are wondrous. There are realms whose essence is feeling rather than thought. The Holy and Blessed One has granted our sages the wisdom to present these essentials again and again, until you feel you've already heard them. And you have in fact heard them. Where did you hear them? It was at Mount Sinai that we heard them, each and every one of us. For whatever our sages have discovered was already conveyed to Moses at Mount Sinai, and, what is more, the soul of every Jew was there listening. Because of the golden calf, forgetfulness was introduced into the world. Most things were forgotten, and it is the task of true commentators to restore what was lost. Man struggles six days, unable to provide essentials. When Shabbat comes, the intelligent soul pursues its true needs, those that relate to the living God. True sages appear and interpret the Torah and commandments, which they then impart to us effortlessly.

The above ideas are not Dr. Herbst's, but those of the people in that neighborhood, whose grandparents came from the lands of exile to serve God, preserve His teachings, and fulfill His commandments in His chosen city. Dr. Herbst is an intellectual, whose thoughts center on his academic field. Now that he decided to write that article, he walked along thinking about the emperor Justinian and wondering if he really considered himself worthy of being swept up to heaven in a storm. His mind wandered from Justinian to his faithful servant General Belisarius, whom Justinian had blinded out of envy. His mind wandered from Justinian and Belisarius to Antonia, a woman of the court, and Yohanan, who were to be the heroes of the tragedy he planned to write. He didn't dwell on this, because, whenever he thought about his tragedy, he was in the habit of smoking, and it would be disrespectful to smoke out of doors in Jerusalem on Shabbat, especially in an Orthodox neighborhood. Herbst refrained from smoking out of respect, not fear. This was before zealots in Jerusalem started attacking people for violating the Shabbat in public. They still remembered the special committee that supplied water, food, clothes, and medicine to a hungry Jerusalem in the wake of war, and they closed one eye to public violations of Shabbat, realizing that the offenders might be from the very committee whose help they might need tomorrow, for most of the communities they had depended on for support were now dependent on others and could not be counted on.

Even before the war, Jerusalem's vigilantes had learned to close an eye when necessary. The following story is still being told. During the language war, when classes in all the Ezra schools were conducted in German and the Zionists demanded that they switch to Hebrew, an Ezra leader came from Berlin to investigate. All of Jerusalem expected a large contribution from him. Jerusalem's leading citizens went to call on him at his gentile hotel on one of the intermediate days of Passover. He was in the dining room, dipping his biscuit in coffee. It was one of those thin biscuits that German bakers make from flour, egg, and butter. They remarked to him in mock-scholarly terms, "So you agree with those sages who regard watched matzah and soaked matzah as ritually independent of one another."

Herbst abstained from smoking, but his mind did not. It led him to contemplate those brown cigarettes praised by Julian Weltfremdt. Since he didn't think they were superior in taste or smell, he began to wonder why anyone preferred them. He was once out somewhere, and, noticing that everyone was smoking those cigarettes, it began to seem as if there were a secret society whose members recognized each other by this sign. Dr. Krautmeir was there too, with one of those long cigarettes stuck between her thin lips. Was there some special connection between her and Julian? Or was it the influence of Mimi, Julian's wife? Was she also a patron of that skillful peddler, promoting his wares?

It's not likely that there is anything between Julian and Krautmeir. Julian has no interest in women, and Krautmeir is such a cold person, totally devoted to her work, to the young sluts who beat a path to her door, eager to be relieved of their burden of shame. Julian has no interest in women, and Krautmeir, as was already noted, is cold. I wouldn't be surprised if the cigarette in her mouth has a cold flame.

So much for Krautmeir; let's consider why Julian is not attracted to other women. Is it because his wife is so lovely, charming, and gifted, with a fine voice and pleasant ways? Or is it precisely because his wife is lovely, charming, et cetera, that he isn't attracted to others? This is not a paradox. If he has so little regard for this woman who is lovely and charming, he will certainly have no regard for others whose charm and beauty are no match for hers. So the facts explain each other, but what do we know about the workings of the heart and mind? Would it ever occur to you that a man such as Herbst is attracted to the woman ———? We will suppress her name and refrain from saying "Shira," for, if we say who she is, it will be totally baffling that a man with an intelligent, kind, industrious wife would pursue such a woman. And what is even more surprising: in his heart, he doesn't fault himself for his actions. Shira herself, on the other hand, protects and safeguards him, by keeping him at a distance.

When Shira comes to mind, she doesn't soon leave. Now that she was in his mind, she slipped away because of something trivial, because of two bits of wood he remembered leaving in the stove that morning when he took a warm bath. They were being wasted. While he was regretting the wasted firewood, he remembered his little daughter, whose digestion was upset by those grapes. These two causes—the wood and the grapes—were suddenly linked, and he recalled that he had deliberately left the wood burning in the stove, intending to prepare a warm bath for Henrietta. But, since she was so tired, having been up all night with the little one whose stomach was upset by grapes, she chose to do without the bath. The wood was burning, the smoke was trailing upward with no one to enjoy it. Meanwhile he, who would have enjoyed a cigarette, was deprived of this pleasure because those who live in this neighborhood regard Shabbat as the primary day of the week and view its rituals as a source of special sanctity, the core of life's holiness, believing life should be sanctified, rather than wasted.

Like most Jerusalem neighborhoods on a summer afternoon after lunch, this little neighborhood was quiet. The shutters on its small houses were closed, and no creature stirred in the street, except for a dog or cat silently picking at the garbage. Were it not for the fact that dogs and cats are considered ritually unclean, I would suggest that they imposed this silence on themselves, for, when Jews observe the Shabbat, even animals and birds don't disrupt them. Only the sun showed its force. Its intense heat was boundless. The air was filled with the scent of watermelons left to cool on windowsills, so they would be ready to eat when the afternoon rest was over. Herbst kept taking off his sunglasses and wiping them. He stood between the little houses, which were surrounded by bramble. It was the seventh year, so the gardens in the area had been left fallow and were taken over by bramble. The dry bramble would bake in the sun and split open, sending out a sharp, invigorating smell that was quite pleasant. Between the bramble and the houses, a dog and cat stood amicably picking at the same heap of garbage.

Herbst was approaching Lisbet Neu's house. He consulted his watch and saw it wasn't quite three o'clock. Three in the afternoon was not the time to visit, certainly not for the first time, and certainly not in the case of a well-bred young woman who lives with her mother. So all he could do was wait. He turned toward the valley, sat down in the shade

of a rock, and lit a cigarette. Though there were no shade trees, bushes
and rocks warded off the sun and sent up a fine, dust-free scent. When
he finished the cigarette, he looked at his watch and saw he would have
to be patient.

He took out Neu's book and read snatches of it. He put it back in
his pocket, took out a small notebook, and wrote: "Aristotle's *Poetics*,
Sophocles' *Antigone*, Lessing, Herder, *Wilhelm Meister*, Goethe's *Pro-
files*, Schiller's *Horen*, Schlegel's *Descriptions of Character*, Jean Paul,
Hume." Herbst meant to help himself remember some of the books he
ought to read for the tragedy he was going to write. Actually, he had
read all those books and remembered what was in them. He even knew
some of them by heart, but, because he was so exacting, he decided to
reread them. I will now leap ahead: Herbst followed through on this
list, reading all those books, as well as many others, but the drama he
intended to write was never written. Still, nothing was wasted. In
taking stock of the characters he had invented and ordering their lives,
he considered the events of his own life—how they fit together, as well
as their implications. After writing what he wrote, he walked among
the parched bushes and the sun-struck bramble splitting open with a
sound like that of nuts being cracked, reflecting on the characters he
had created.

Meanwhile, the sun began to warm him, shrubs and rock giving back
to the sun what they took so easily. Herbst closed his eyes, hoping to
doze. Mosquitoes came and stung him. He lit another cigarette to keep
the mosquitoes away. The cigarette in his mouth dozed off, and so did
he. The mosquitoes, however, instead of dozing, came back and stung
him again. He got up, yielded his spot to them, began pacing back and
forth, and, as he paced, looked around and began to make archeological
speculations. Leaping from rock to rock, he was no longer in the valley
but had come to a bald spot between the bushes, adorned with thorns
and thistles. It glistened in the sun with countless paths and trails
nearby that vanished among the bushes and rocks. There were other
paths, one of which wound as far as the eye could see, more than likely
extending into town, perhaps even all the way to where Shira lived. He
felt the point of a scalpel cutting into his heart. It was not a scalpel; it
was the anguish of pain. He closed his eyes tight because of the pain
and, with closed eyes, followed his feet. He moved on, his legs striking
each other. Had he looked at his watch, he would have seen that he
could now call on the Neu ladies. But rather than look at his watch,
he looked at the path, retreating and bringing him closer to where he
was going. When he realized he was close to Shira's house, he indulged
in the prayer we are familiar with: Let me find a locked door, let me

find that Shira's out. The gods, who mock each other and don't give human beings a chance to mock them, did what they did. While he was praying that Shira would be out, the gods took charge, brought Shira home, and brought Herbst to Shira's door.

—— 12 ——

Herbst was at Shira's house again. He had been at Shira's many times in the evening, but never by day. Now he was there in the daytime. On which day? On Shabbat, a day when neighbors are free to note nonessentials and their curious eyes scrutinize the very air. Herbst stood at the door, wondering how many times to ring. When their love was new, they had agreed on two long rings and one short one to announce his arrival. Now he hesitated; if she knew who it was, she might pretend not to be in. He decided to be devious and gave an ordinary ring. She didn't answer. He waited and rang again. She didn't answer. He left, came back, and gave two long rings and a short one. He soon heard her footsteps and could tell she was coming. After a while she opened the door. Before he had a chance to look at her, she was gone.

He went inside and found her in bed, wrapped and swaddled to her neck in a blanket that rose and fell over her stomach, which pushed the blanket aside and reared out from under it. A gurgling sound bubbled forth from underneath the blanket, the sound of an inverted water bottle. There was, in fact, a hot-water bottle resting on her stomach and bubbling loudly. He took a chair and sat beside her bed, as if he had come to see how she was, as if his only interest were in knowing what she was doing. She welcomed him as she hadn't done in a long while. Her face was flushed, her cheekbones ashen, and her nose partly red, partly white. The hot-water bottle on her belly continued to rumble. The light was dim, because the curtains were drawn over the window. The entire room had become more like a dingy hallway in which a stranger wouldn't be able to find the door. When he had collected himself, Herbst asked Shira, "Are you sick?" Rather than sympathy, there was a note of irritation in his voice, because she had chosen to be sick at the very time he had taken the trouble to visit. Shira answered, "I was on the night shift at the hospital, and I put myself to bed to make up the sleep I missed." Herbst said, "I'm sorry I woke you." Shira said, "You didn't wake me. Someone rang earlier and woke me, but I couldn't open the door because I was sleeping naked, without a nightgown." Herbst said, "When you came to open the door for me, you put on your nightgown." Shira said, "How do you know that?" Herbst said, "From what you said, I know you were wearing a nightgown. Also, I can see you are wearing it now." Shira laughed and said, "You see everything, my dear Sherlock. Close the window, please, and lower the blinds. The sunlight is in my eyes. Many thanks, darling. Just that blind, the one across from the bed. Thanks, darling. You're not smoking? Would you hand me my bag; it's on the table. Thanks, darling. Now, darling, the little mirror, please. Thanks, darling. Now sit down, darling. You can sit down. I won't bother you anymore. You're probably tired. I assume you had to walk here, since it's Shabbat. Shabbat . . . the God of the Jews knows how to torture His followers even more than the Gentiles torture them. No, that's not the bag I meant. I meant the blue one. Would you please look and see if it fell on the floor? No? Then I left it somewhere, and I don't know where. I'll look for it later. Don't bother. See, when you're used to doing everything yourself and you ask someone else to do something for you, it's useless. No, no. Actually, that is the bag I wanted. My mistake. That's it. I'm surprised at myself. I should have recognized it immediately. I probably didn't recognize it because of the light."

Shira opened the bag, took out a small puff, dipped it in powder, and smoothed it over her nose. She sprinkled some powder on her forehead and said, "So you finished your article and even got it published." Herbst asked in alarm, "Who told you about my article?" Shira said, "I have no contact with angels, and I don't believe in devils, so you can assume it was a person that told me. Not just any person, but someone from Mount Scopus." Herbst stared at her fiercely and said, "I demand that you tell me who." Shira laughed and said, "You certainly are curious, sir. Very curious. If I'm not mistaken, two days after we met I told you I don't like curious people, and you, sir, are not being considerate of me with this display of curiosity. But I will make an exception and tell you." "Who was it?" Herbst needed to repeat the question, though he was afraid he might hear a name that would mean his downfall. Though Herbst knew of no such person, his terror was undiminished. Something akin to laughter leaped out of Shira's eyes, glided over her face, and was intercepted by her ashen freckles before returning to its point of origin. She looked at him out of the corners of her eyes, in which two swirls of laughter shimmered, one filled with malice, the other with affection. She looked at him, laughing, and said,

"You want to know who told me?" Herbst wanted to say, "Yes, I demand that you tell me," but he didn't say anything. Shira said, "Who was it? It was the very person who is here with me now, in this house, at this moment." Even though he grasped that she was referring to him, his fear didn't relent. It took him a minute to recover, feign laughter, move his chair, and say, "Yes, it's true, I told you myself, and I forgot. Now let's put the article behind us and talk about something else." Shira said, "You think I'm too stupid for scholarly chitchat." Herbst got up, took her hand, and held it, stroking it fondly with his other hand, as if to placate her. Shira made no move to withdraw her hand, but she said, "Dr. Herbst is a very learned man; still, there is no reason to stroke my hand." Herbst let go and put his hands in his pockets. Shira said, "I didn't mean to offend you." Herbst said, "I don't consider myself offended." Shira said, "That's good." Herbst said, "Good, good." He leaned to his left and looked at his watch. Shira said, "Sit down and have a cigarette. I'll get dressed, and we can go for a walk."

Shira wrapped herself in a robe and got out of bed. Herbst pretended not to be watching as he strained to follow every one of her gestures. He passed his tongue over his lips, speculating: Now she's putting on her girdle; she's taking off her robe now and putting on some other garment; she's slipping her feet into her stockings. His eyelids covered his eyes, but her every move was revealed to him. His fantasies transformed themselves into vision and showed him everything she did. They showed him every single garment, and his mind was fixed on every one of her limbs. Had he uttered their names, he would have been startled. But his mouth was silent. He didn't have the strength to say anything. Only his lips quivered. Then, all of a sudden, his entire body began to quiver, and he was overcome with sadness.

He was overcome with sadness—because of this woman, because of her clothes, because of her body, because of how she moved, because she paid no attention to him, because she ordered him not to look at her, because she didn't acknowledge his existence. Would she continue to treat him as she had been treating him recently? His mood vacillated between inertia and turbulence. They finally merged, taking the form of devastating despair.

By degrees, his sadness dissipated and vanished. He had already forgotten its source, remembering only that he had been warned not to look up and gaze at what was forbidden. He complied, without cheating, and did not so much as glance at the sight his mind had conjured up.

He suddenly heard the sound of flowing water, like an open spigot with water spilling out. Herbst looked up in alarm and saw a dripping bottle balanced on the edge of the bed. It was the bottle Shira had been using to warm herself. The lid was loose, and it was dripping. Herbst's face turned pale, and he wanted to yell, "Shira!" But he didn't yell; he didn't call her at all. He sat watching, as if he had been appointed guard.

Shira came. Without being called. Neither dressed nor naked. She picked up the bottle, then brought a rag and a bucket. She soaked up the water and wrung the rag into the bucket. Herbert sat watching her, taking in her every move with his eyes. When she had finished, she straightened up. Herbst asked, "May I help you?" Shira said, "It's not necessary." Herbst said, "I didn't mean with the water." Shira said, "What did you mean?" He laughed slyly and said, "I was offering to help you get dressed." Shira said, "I'm not in the habit of having help for such things." Herbst said, "If the answer is no, then it's no." Shira said, "Do you help your wife get dressed too?" He lowered his eyes and was silent.

When she was all dressed, she reappeared. "I see," Shira said, "that you didn't smoke. Let's share a peace pipe, my friend. We won't be able to smoke when we're outside. It's Shabbat for them." She took out a cigarette, stuck it in his mouth, took another one and put it in her own mouth, lit her cigarette, and went over to him, lighting his cigarette with hers. He inhaled, then took the cigarette from his lips and held it between his fingers. "You're burning your fingers," Shira said. "I'm burning my fingers?" Herbst asked. Shira said, "Finish your cigarette, so we can go out." Herbst said, "I'll finish it, so we can go out." Shira said, "You're in another world today." Herbst said, "If you want to go for a walk, let's go for a walk." Shira said, "Didn't we agree to go for a walk?" "We agreed." Shira said, "Then let's go." He answered, "Let's go." She stood there, looking around her room, at her bed, waiting for him to leave.

Outside, they found the road blocked by black-coated figures strolling along expansively, occupying the width of the street, some with their *shtreimels* centered on their forehead, others with their *shtreimels* angled to the left, still others with their *shtreimels* in hand. The figures became entangled with one another and increasingly voluble. "They are Hasidim," Shira said. "From Poland. Listen to them, listen to those accents. *Yach, mach, itchi maya.* They make the city ugly with their getups and their gestures." Herbst said, "In Jerusalem, everyone makes the city ugly. What about that plump morsel waddling by in shorts? Do her fleshy thighs add to the city's splendor? Her two companions— the ones with their hands on their hips—are they any more attractive than she is?" "If they're not attractive on Shabbat," Shira answered, "they're attractive on weekdays. They fix roads, build houses, do what they can to improve the world, undertake any task, eat bread they have earned. But these Hasidim don't do anything to improve the world. They don't work, they're idle. They don't lift a finger to accomplish anything, but at night they breed, producing more of their kind: idlers, nuisances, grumblers, greedy parasites—contentious, in conflict among themselves, with their wives, sons, daughters, the entire world. The more I know them, the more I hate them. They think we were born for the sole purpose of serving them. If they didn't need us and our charitable institutions, they would drown us in spit. The name of God is on their lips, but their hearts are filled with vice. I won't say none of them is decent, but how many? Fewer than you'd guess. With respect to women, they're all the same. Women exist only to satisfy their appetites. One such specimen came to the hospital, a fellow with a goatee, an enlarged Adam's apple, and elaborately curled earlocks. He came to see his wife, to see how she was doing. The poor woman welcomed him, despite her severe pain. He began to press her to come home. She had barely any life left in her, having been worked to the bone. He took no notice of her suffering and pressed her to come home. I saw her anguish and wanted to drag him by his ugly beard and throw him out. But I overcame my rage and asked, 'Do you love your wife so much that you can't do without her for a few days? Wait until she's better, and she'll come back to you.' He laughed derisively and said, 'Am I the one who needs her? The house and the children need her. Since she went to the hospital, her children have been wild. They don't go to school; they play on the street like the children of the godless, may their name be erased. It's not good for a man to be without a wife. It would be all right if there were someone to cover for her when she's stuck in bed.' If Dr. Herbst can't see the difference between these Hasidim and the people who work for a living, I can't teach him." Herbst said, "I don't know about you, but when I read about the lives of holy men, I'm ashamed. I sometimes wish I could drop everything and live with them." Shira said, "How can you compare these bizarre creatures to holy men, who isolate themselves from the world and don't demand anything from anyone? Whatever they demand, they demand of themselves. They want to improve their souls, whereas the Hasidim don't demand anything of themselves. They demand that we satisfy their needs. We have to work, we have to labor, we have to slave, we have to undertake every difficulty, we have to give up sleep—all so those idlers can indulge their appetites. Oh, how I despise them!" Herbst said, "But you enjoy all those lovely stories about righteous men and Hasidim." Shira said, "In my childhood, I avoided them, and I don't understand how a civilized person can see a trace of beauty in that ugly, vapid life. Please, Dr. Herbst, should I be amused because a certain idler didn't bother to take off his socks year after year? Or, for that matter, because another one, who liked to sit around serving God, as they say, never noticed that his wife and children were wasting away? As you know, Dr. Herbst, I don't believe in God. I'm not boasting about it, nor do I regret it. But, when they say proudly that all their actions are for the sake of God, I wonder. I don't doubt that much of our arrogance, conceit, and anarchy derive from that source."

Herbst repeated each of her words and said, "Please, Shira, explain yourself. Tell me what you mean by arrogance, conceit, and anarchy. To me, the Hasidim look humble. They walk at the side of the road with lowered eyes, making do with minimal food, drink, housing, and clothes. As for anarchy, people who are devoted to rules, regulations, customs, even special dress and gestures prescribed in books—can that be termed anarchy? It's hard for me to accept what you say, Shira." Shira glared at him, her eyes flashing with rage, and she spoke fiercely, "If you are so innocent, if you shut your eyes, nothing I say will help you. But let me tell you this: lazy idlers who avoid work to such an extent that they lose the power to engage in anything other than nonsense, retelling tales of righteous men who, with words alone, compel their God to alter the order of the universe on their behalf because of some trivial momentary need, or with a twist of their lip force God to defer His will to theirs—can there be arrogance and conceit to exceed this? Human beings whose arrogance, conceit, and self-love are of such magnitude defy all order and produce anarchy."

Herbst looked at her with admiration and said, "I won't debate the merit of your words, but I am sorry, Shira, that you didn't go into literary scholarship." Shira said, "You don't have to debate with me. I don't mean to win you over to my view, and I'm satisfied to have become what I've become and to leave literature to the scholars. I don't think I would enjoy being a prophet and saying this or that is what the poet had in mind. Anyway, I'm astonished that in such a short time you've changed your mind, and now you think I'm capable of judging literature." Herbst said, "I changed my mind? When did I say otherwise?" Shira said, "Should I remind you of that night and that magazine?" Herbst said, "You *are* vengeful, Shira. You don't forget a single casual remark of mine if it displeases you. In any case, now you see that I don't question the excellence of your taste. I'm merely sorry that you didn't study literature. Now, tell me, Shira, how do you explain the fact that great thinkers, poets, and philosophers consider the Hasidim remarkable and their way of life sublime?" Shira said, "Maybe they are great thinkers, poets, or philosophers, as you say. I'm not equipped to judge. But I can tell you this: if it were in my power to change the world, like the righteous men in the stories those thinkers, poets, and philosophers find so enthralling, I would transform the poets and philosophers into Hasidim, so their bodies could have a taste of what they celebrate. Now, dear doctor, let's not argue about things neither you nor I are interested in. I said 'neither you nor I'; I, as you already know, and you, if you search your heart, will realize that you don't want to be like them, even for a minute. You may sometimes wish to cast your lot with the holy men who have withdrawn from the world, but to be some sort of *yach-mach* or *itchi-maya*—it's clear to me that's not what you want. Their stench alone would drive you away."

Once again, Herbst looked at her as he had never looked at her before and said, "I never met a woman like you, and I never heard such talk from a woman. Your talk would dazzle me even if it came from a man." Shira said, "Because it is your opinion that women were created only to give men pleasure, you don't consider the possibility that women's minds are nevertheless far from empty. Dr. Herbst, I have no wish to offend you, and certainly not to offend Mrs. Herbst, but, when I see how you behave with me and how you behaved with Temima Kutchinsky, I wonder if you and your wife ever have a conversation about anything other than household matters and bodily needs." Herbst said, "So that's how well you know me." Shira said, "Before you were married, you undoubtedly talked a lot about all sorts of German ideals. Humanism, you call it. But afterward, that was no longer necessary, so you flung the household and the children in her lap while you, the great pasha, amble through the palaces of wisdom where there is no place for featherbrains like us." Herbst said, "You sound just like a book." Shira said, "I'm only saying what I see." Herbst said, "And what you say about me is what you see?" Shira said, "It's only a fraction of what I see." Herbst said, "Could you tell me more?" Shira said, "The gypsy whose tune I dance to hasn't been born yet. You will have to make do with what I've already said." Herbst said, "In that case, a thousand and one thanks for your generosity in offering me some of what your eyes have shown you." Shira said, "Please don't bore me by showing how smart you are." Herbst said, "So you have a temper too?" Shira said, "I don't have a temper, but, if there's reason to be angry, I'm angry. The road is clear now. Let's go." "Where?" "To the King David Hotel." "What do you want to do there?" "The gardener there may have some flowers. I'm going to visit someone, a sick friend, and I would like to bring her flowers. The florists are all closed for Shabbat, and there are no flowers to be had anywhere else. We go too far, allowing the Orthodox to do as they like with us. If we don't stop them, we won't be allowed to breathe on Shabbat. How I hate them and all the things they keep us from doing! Smoking on Shabbat is forbidden, wearing short sleeves is forbidden, everything is forbidden. People you have nothing to do with take charge of you, proclaiming, 'Don't do this, don't do that.' I doubt that any of them know what is forbidden and what isn't, yet they forbid us to do anything." Herbst said, "Who is the woman you plan to visit?" Shira said, "Come and see." Herbst said, "Tell me anyway." Shira said, "Again, you're consumed with curiosity. There was a young girl in the hospital who went home a few days ago, and I want to see how she is recovering from her surgery." "Was it serious?" "It was minor surgery, on her jaw." "Who is she?" Shira said, "And if I tell you, will you know? Do you know all the young women in Jerusalem? We're already there. Come up with me. I promise you, it won't detract from your dignity. A little while back, you were willing to give up everything for the sacred life. Now that you have the opportunity to do a good deed and pay a sick call, you avoid it, preferring legends of holy men to an act of charity. You would rather be settled in an armchair, smoking and drinking coffee as you read all about them. Isn't that right, sir?" She spoke without a trace of rebuke, her eyes mirroring her words. Once again, something akin to laughter leaped out of her eyes. Not the laughter with which he was familiar. If he had tried to define it, he wouldn't have been able to find the words. She suddenly slanted her nose in the other direction, to avoid the powerful smell that came out of the dim house.

Herbst, who was perhaps even more sensitive to smells than Shira, didn't notice. But the smell transported him to a desert with snakes, scorpions, caves, tombs, and old men buried alive to the waist in graves they dug for themselves, singing and praising their gods. Other old men, tied to wooden posts or to boulders, stood on one leg, reaching one arm upward, their bodies inert, only their lips moving. They never changed clothes or washed; their tattered garments were covered with vermin, worms, and maggots as they, too, sang and praised their gods.

Herbst was transported to still another place, an emperor's palace, where there was a party for a holy man the emperor had heard about, who had been brought to the palace so the emperor could bask in his holiness. The emperor presided over an extravagant feast prepared for the holy man and for all his courtiers. The holy man sat at the head of the table, within sight of the emperor and his courtiers, neither eating nor drinking, delighting in his sores, which swarmed with worms and maggots. Before their very eyes, a new worm stirred, born in the holy man's flesh, unmindful of the emperor, the feast on his table, his courtiers—unaware, perhaps, that it inhabited a holy body and was feeding on holy flesh. Such lowly creatures lack the capacity to recognize greatness. "Where are you?" Shira said to Herbst. "If you're not in outer space, I don't know where you are. As I said earlier, you seem to be in some other world today. Come on, let's go in." Shira took his hand and went up the dark, dilapidated steps with him.

— 13 —

On a battered bed in a dingy room lay the body of an emaciated young girl. Her head barely touched the pillow, it was so light. Her eyes were weary and filled with longing. Herbst followed Shira to the sick bed, then turned back, looking at Shira as if to explain that he hadn't approached the girl's bed on his own but was simply following her. When he looked at Shira, he saw she was holding flowers. How could that be? When did Shira get flowers, and what sort of flowers were in her hand? In any case, they had no scent; if they had, she wouldn't have had to close her nose against the garbage in the yard. As for where she got them, wasn't I with her at the King David Hotel? And, when we got there, didn't she go to the little hut near the hotel and come out with someone who led her to the hotel garden, from which she returned with an armful of flowers? I didn't pay attention to the flowers, because I was preoccupied.

The sick woman dilated her nostrils to take in the scent. She offered Shira a small, frail hand, gazing at the flowers as if they were some lovely object she yearned for but knew she could never have. She said in a clear voice, unimpaired by sickness, "Please, Shira, let me smell your flowers." I see, Herbst thought to himself, that they do have a smell. He breathed in the scent. Shira handed her the flowers and asked, "Where can I find something to put these in?" Hearing Shira's words, Herbst noted to himself: She said "to put these in," but she didn't say their name. These city girls who have never made anything grow! He turned away from his thoughts to concentrate on the sick woman's voice, which was familiar. While he was trying to remember where and when he had heard it, she offered her hand and asked how he was. Herbst said, "You didn't come to visit us, so I came to visit you. How are you, my dear?" She answered, "I'm fine," laughing wanly. Herbst looked at her, thinking: Why does she say I'm fine, when everything about her belies her words? In the midst of this thought, he answered the question himself: What should she have said to me? She continued, "And how is Mrs. Herbst? And your daughter?" Herbst answered, "Fine, fine," laughing inwardly at himself and at the world, in which everything moves in circles, while the world itself moves in its own circle. A man goes into a restaurant, sees a young woman, and strikes up a conversation. He goes to the Dead Sea with his wife and daughter, and sees the same young woman. She says, "I'm fine"; he says, "I'm fine"; but neither one is fine. Shira glanced at her patient, then at Herbst, and asked, "Do you two know each other?" Herbst said, "My wife knows this young lady too. Isn't that so, my dear?"

Shira found an empty jam jar, filled it with water, and put the flowers in it. "Too bad," Shira said. "Too bad that I had to cut the stems. But they're lovely this way too." "They're beautiful," the girl said, leaning toward the flowers. She smoothed her disheveled hair, took the jar of flowers, and put it to her mouth, as if she meant to eat the smell. Then she extended her hand to hold the flowers at a slight distance. Each gesture seemed to have a message: the flowers that once strewed our path are now far away. . . . Even the hand that smoothed her hair suggested a message: although our paths are scattered, like these stray strands, we can put them in order.

Shira arranged the pillow under the patient's head, took her left hand to check the pulse, then asked her, "What have you eaten today? What would you like me to prepare?" The girl said, "Many thanks, Nurse Shira, but I don't need anything. Really, I don't. I have a girlfriend who takes care of me. She went to the pharmacy to get my medicine."

If that's the case, Herbst thought, she'll be back shortly, and another young woman will be added to those I already know. When your mind is on women, they begin to dangle before you like links in a chain, each one leading to another.

Herbst ran his hand through his hair and studied the girl, as though pondering something. Then he said, "I read two of your poems. If I'm not mistaken, one is entitled 'The Goldfinch' and the other 'The Crane.' They're good poems; they're both equally good." She raised her head, turned to Herbst with a questioning look, and whispered, "Really?" "Yes, really," Herbst said. "They're quite good, with no extra words, and every phrase has integrity and grace."

The young woman had put her poems out of mind. Now that they were being praised, she became as excited as she had been while writing them. Not many people had read her poems, only those to whom she had showed them. He had apparently read them on his own. Since she was a shy and lonely person, this seemed especially wonderful.

Shira said to the young woman, "You write poetry? Then you are a poet." She said, "That's half-true. I write poems. As for being a poet, my dear Nurse Shira, that remains doubtful." Herbst said, "That remains doubtful for most people who turn out poems. There are more poem writers than poets. As for you, my dear, there is no doubt that you are a poet. The two poems I read are evidence." Shira said, "If my life depended on it, I wouldn't know how to write a poem." Herbst said, "You don't need to know how. You have other talents, Miss Shira." As he spoke, a faint tremor swept over him and he whispered, "Flesh such as yours will not soon be forgotten." Shira asked, "What were you whispering?" Herbst said, "You're mistaken, my dear. I wasn't whispering. May I smoke in here? Or would it be better not to pollute the air?" Now, Herbst was thinking, I have provided another witness. One more person has seen me with Shira. I should have been careful not to address her so familiarly.

After they left the sick young woman, Shira asked Herbst, "How do you know Anita?" Herbst looked blank and asked, "Who is Anita?" She said, "Anita Brik." Herbst said, "It's strange, but I didn't know her name was Anita Brik. I've seen her twice and talked to her, but it never occurred to me that her name was Anita Brik. Nor did it occur to me to ask her name."

Shira laughed heartily and said, "Didn't you tell Anita that you had read her poems? If you didn't know her name, how did you know those were her poems?" Herbst laughed and said, "You've stumped me, Shira. I'm sorry not to have a proper answer. From now on, Shira, from now on I'll be more careful and precise. I won't cause problems. Are you pleased with me, Shira? Are you pleased with my promise?"

Herbst suddenly stopped, took out a handkerchief, wiped his brow, and said, "You put a bug up my nose." Shira said, "You must have gotten it out by now." Herbst said, "I got it out, and it came back." Shira stared at him and said gently, "What's the matter, what's the matter?" Herbst put the handkerchief back in his pocket and said, "I ask myself, Why is she so hostile?" Shira said, "Even if I were seventy-seven times smarter, I wouldn't know who 'she' is or what sort of hostility you have in mind." Herbst lowered his voice and said, "I ask myself how you got to be so consumed with hostility toward the Hasidim." Shira said, "Hostility? What does it have to do with hostility?" Herbst said, "Then is it love that flows from your tongue?" Shira said, "In any case, in all of Jerusalem there is no one who would say that Shira the nurse neglects any of her patients and denies them the attention they need or that she favors some patients at the expense of others." Herbst said, "You generalize about their behavior; you are

thoroughly contemptuous and disdainful. Have you never heard about
their good deeds? I assume that even you know the story about the
righteous man who used to get out of bed on cold winter nights, dress
up like a farmer, and carry bundles of wood to the homes of needy
women who were in labor." Shira said, "So he was doing social work."
Herbst said, "But, Shira, in his time there were no social-work agen-
cies." Shira said, "In any case, I don't understand why that *rebbe* had
to dress up as a farmer, and so on. Couldn't he find someone who would
deliver the wood to those poor women? It would make whoever he
hired to deliver the wood a little bit richer, and he could add some
radish, onion, and garlic to his own meal and that of his family." Herbst
said, "Are you joking, Shira?" Shira said, "I'm not joking, but the fact
is, I'm not impressed with good works that depend on tricks. I'm not
especially fond of good works and commandments anyway, certainly
not the ones the Orthodox live by. The way they see it, everything is
a mitzvah. Fill your belly with meat, fish, hallah—it's a mitzvah. Eat
kugel, preceded and followed by wine—it's a mitzvah. Slither into your
wife—yet another mitzvah. So much for them and their mitzvahs,
which don't interest me."

With a wave of her hand, Shira dismissed the subject. She had
already replaced her disdainful expression with the relaxed look of a
hard-working woman who has cast off workaday burdens for a while
and is enjoying a leisurely stroll, relishing each step and every sight.
Herbst trailed along beside her, deep in thought, reexamining ideas he
had always accepted without question. Shira, who had brought this on,
was also subjected to his scrutiny. Those who know their friends well
and are attuned to their thinking are fortunate; their conversation is
always pleasant and reassuring. But friends who suddenly express opinions we never expected to hear from them are bewildering to us as well
as to themselves, as if they have been transformed, reborn in a new
guise. I already mentioned that, in those dark days when Herbst stayed
away from Shira, when he was in such an agitated state, he used to think
uncharacteristic thoughts—thoughts to which he was unaccustomed—
including thoughts about the women with whom he had studied at
various universities. I mentioned that some of them had become prominent and that he was alarmed when he ran into them at scholarly
meetings, talked to them again, and realized they were different from
him, that they were actually female. He was upset by their existence
and by the fact that they had reverted to their essential nature. The
opposite was true of Shira. Shira, who had always been woman to him
and nothing more, had all of a sudden assumed a spiritual aspect; she
possessed thoughts and opinions. What sort of opinions? Opinions that

were totally new to him. But he was uneasy, not because they were expressed in vulgar terms, not because, as I observed, those who know their friends well and are attuned to their thinking are fortunate, et cetera, but because he was in public with a strange woman and anyone who saw them together would think the worst. In any case, it was good that Tamara was traveling in Greece. If she were here, he might run into her when he was with Shira. As he walked on, pondering, he turned to Shira and said, "I have something to tell you, Shira." Shira said, "Only one thing?" Herbst said, "For the moment, only one thing." "And later?" Herbst suddenly had a change of heart and, feeling some sort of pang, answered, "It depends on you and your affection." Shira said, "What is it that my lord requests?" Herbst said, "Remember the café that belonged to that fellow who sent his waitress a wedding cake? Let's stop in and refresh ourselves with some coffee." Shira said, "You're such an optimist. In Jerusalem, if a man does something well, he will certainly not survive. That café is no longer his. It has changed hands several times. After losing everything, he asked his relatives in America for a certificate, which they sent. He left, and, for all we know, he is doing there what he didn't succeed in doing here. Also, it's Shabbat, and all the cafés are closed." Herbst said, "What now?" Shira said, "So what now? What should we do? You'll go to your house, and I'll go to mine." Seeing the gloom on Herbst's face, Shira shifted her tone and said, "Believe me, Manfred, I would invite you to my room, but I'm tired. I was up all night, and, when I got home in the afternoon and flopped on my bed, someone rang my bell and woke me up, and after that you came. Besides, I'm not well. I'm not sick, but I'm not well either. Please don't ask questions." Herbst said, "Then do we have to part?" Shira said, "If you insist, I could walk with you for a while." Herbst said, "If you're not feeling well, how can you walk?" Shira said, "Leave that to me." Herbst said, "I see that I'm irritating you." Shira said, "Perhaps." Herbst asked, "To such an extent?" Shira said, "If you really want to know, think about your words before you say them." Herbst lowered his head and was silent.

Shira noticed and said, "I don't mean to upset you, but you twist things just to irritate me and force me to defend myself." Herbst said, "From here on, whenever I want to say something, I'll ask permission first." Shira laughed and said, "It's not necessary to go that far." Herbst asked sadly, "Then what do I have to do to please you?" Shira said, "What do you have to do? Don't do anything. We've been walking so long that Shabbat is just about over. Unless you've changed your mind, let's stop for coffee." Herbst said, "I was hoping to take you to that café I mentioned." Shira said, "We could go to that café." Herbst said,

"What's the point of a café that's been abandoned by its owner?" Shira said, "Then we'll sit there without any point." Herbst looked at his watch and said, "It looks to me as if we'll have to wait God knows how long before they open the cafés. Won't your legs begin to hurt?" Shira said, "If my legs hurt, I'll rest later." Herbst said, "You're right, Shira. You're right. But it would be good to sit somewhere in the meanwhile. Aren't we close to your place? Wouldn't it be a good idea to wait there?" Shira said, "That's possible. If that's what you would like to do, here's the key. You can wait there." "And you?" "Me? I'll wait for you here or in front of the café." Herbst said, "What will you do if I spend the night there, if I stay until tomorrow?" Shira said, "If that's what you want, you can do just that. I doubt that you'll be bored. There are plenty of books, not to mention that magazine. You know the one, Manfred?" Herbst said, "Look, the sun is setting. Let's see which café opens first." Shira said, "Whoever wants to be first will discover that half a dozen others are already open. Who are those two young people waving at you?" Herbst looked around and said, "I didn't see anyone waving. In any case, if there was any waving, it wasn't directed at me." Shira said, "If you didn't see it, how can you say it wasn't directed at you? I suppose we could head for that café now. By the time we get there, it will be open." As she spoke, she stopped walking. Herbst noticed and asked, "Did you want to tell me something?" Shira didn't answer but stood watching the sun set. After a while she said, "When I see the sun setting, I'm afraid I might never see it again. Not that I'm afraid I'll be dead tomorrow, but I'm frightened by the ugly houses being built, shutting out the view. I don't know whose fault it is— whether it's the architects whose sensibilities are bizarre or their clients who want ugly houses." A little later, she added, "Manfred, you were the one who said that every person here defaces the view. I would like to add that the houses are like the people, and all the houses built in recent years are a blight. Not only are they a blight, but they conceal God's works." Herbst said, "Bravo, Shira. Bravo. Finally, you believe in God." Shira said, "Can I invent a special language for myself? I was using the accepted terms." Herbst said, "No need to apologize. On the contrary, your slip of the tongue is evidence that the devil in you is not so formidable." Shira said, "Good, good. Now let me look."

The sun was still setting, and it looked as if this might go on forever. Even before the eye had a chance to take in the scene, as it was now, it altered totally, and once again it seemed as if it always had been and always would be as it was now. A minute later, it altered again and became rounded, like a magic ball colored by the artist in various hues of gold, untouched by any hand, rolling and tossing itself and altering

everything wherever it landed. Not only was the sky altered, but the
hilltops between earth and sky—even the earth itself—took on a new
look. The hilltops and the earth; each did its best. After a while, the sun
made a golden puddle, into which it was then tossed. It continued to
glitter, to cast its red and yellow glow through the film of sky that
covered it. A little later, it disappeared, leaving no trace. The hilltops
and the earth responded similarly. If not for the light of stores, theaters,
and cafés, which were now open, they would have been unable to make
out the earth under their feet.

— 14 —

Herbst was back in the café he had been in with Shira the night Sarah
was born. The original owner had given up the café, and it had passed
through many hands before being taken over by the present owner,
who felt he had been cheated and was looking for a buyer to whom to
sell the place, with all its equipment. Since he intended to get rid of it,
he made no effort to improve it, and it was like every other café in
Jerusalem. It was poorly ventilated; the chairs were uncomfortable; in
some spots the light was inadequate, in others it was blinding; the
waiter was never there when he was needed, and when he did appear
his mind was elsewhere. With the exception of two people who were
setting up a chessboard, an English soldier huddled in a corner with a
Jewish girl, and a customer who was banging on the table and shouting
"Waiter, waiter," the café seemed empty. When curfews became frequent in Jerusalem, people began to hesitate to go out at night, since
they couldn't count on getting home: a curfew could suddenly be
announced, and, before you could get home, the police would appear
and take you to jail. As he entered the café, Herbst was reminded of
his daughter. If Tamara were in Jerusalem, she might be in this café,
and she would see her father with another woman. Luckily, Tamara
was far away, and there wasn't anyone in sight who knew him. After
Shira chose a table, Herbst asked what she would like him to order for
her. They suddenly discovered that, in addition to the people they had
noticed on the way in, there were two others.

Shira whispered to Herbst, "There they are." "What do you mean?"
She whispered to him, "There are those two young men, the ones I saw

waving to you." Herbst shifted his gaze and said to Shira, "They're my students. The short one with the dark shock of hair is sharp, like a hot pepper. It's too bad he has to waste so much time earning money. His friend, the tall, skinny one with small, inquisitive eyes, he's also——" Shira interrupted, "Why not go over and say hello to them?" Herbst said, "What will you do meanwhile?" Shira said, "You won't stay forever. I may even try to sit here and manage without you for a while." Herbst said, "That's right, I won't stay with them forever, certainly not when I could be sitting with you. Still, how can I leave you alone?" Shira said, "Don't worry about me. I promise that I'll try to make good use of the time." Herbst got up and went to join his students. Shira went wherever she went.

Herbst addressed them in his version of student talk: "What sort of discourse are you guys engaged in?" The small, dark-haired one said, "What are we engaged in? A thousand things, and nothing at all." Herbst laughed and said, "I'm terrific at nothing at all; when it comes to a thousand things, I'm not so terrific. We could turn it around and say, 'A thousand things, maybe yes; nothing at all—that's impossible.'" The young man continued, "We were discussing poetry and literature." Herbst said, "You call such lofty subjects nothing at all? I don't dare to think about them." The tall, thin student responded, "Those are weighty subjects, but what we say about them is not very worthwhile. The words roll off our tongues in set speeches requiring very little thought, though someone like me makes the mistake of thinking everything he says originated in his own mind." Herbst said, "Unless you think my ears are flawed, would you be willing to repeat some of your latest insights? I have often thought that, of all the secrets in the world, the most mysterious ones are the secret of language and the secret of poetry. You are probably familiar with what philosophers have said about the origins of language and the craft of poetry. I myself have done some reading in these areas. But when I disregard what I have read and respond with my heart to the marvels of language—to that which enables people to understand each other and allows philosophers to communicate their wisdom—I am awed and astounded to a degree that nothing else in the world can match. The longer I observe language, the more I regard it as the foremost gift granted to man since he appeared on the face of the earth. It gives him the power to express whatever his heart desires. However, if you end up in a place where your language is unknown and the local tongue is foreign to you, what use is speech after all? As you see, my ideas are neither profound nor novel, but my capacity for wonder is constantly renewed. Beyond language and the barriers of language lies poetry. There are so many words, an infinite number of them, that we don't ever use. The person we call a poet appears, combines a series of words, and, instantly, each word becomes a joy and a blessing. But I came to hear new ideas, and, in the end, here I am, mouthing ancient, outdated truisms."

When speaking to his students, Herbst adopted a modest tone. This modesty, at first a defense against pomposity, was now a subtle sort of bribery, for he was aware that his students risked their lives to protect the country and that he had opted not to join them.

As he talked, the old days came back to him, when Zahara was a baby beginning to say words and make sentences. She understood most of what was said to her, and, when she heard a word she didn't understand, she used to look at him, baffled, and ask, "What, Daddy?" He did not derive the same pleasure from Tamara or, needless to say, from Sarah, because from the day of her birth he had been in a state of distraction. Although he wrote down words he heard Sarah say, he wrote them not on a special pad but on scraps of paper that happened to be at hand, which he never put together. As he jotted them down, he already knew he would not look at them again.

His students saw the gloom on his face and were afraid they had offended him by not answering his question. They didn't know his face was gloomy for another reason; because he paid so little attention to Sarah. And he paid so little attention to Sarah because of Shira, whom he knew because of Sarah's birth. Both of these facts—the fact that he paid so little attention to Sarah and the fact that his attention was fixed on Shira—made his face gloomy.

The students looked at one another and said, "You speak first."

The small, dark-haired student was the one who began. "As I was telling my friend here, Hebrew is unlike other languages, and Hebrew poetry is not like any other. Were we to spot a familiar set of words in a poem in some other language, we would disapprove of this borrowed finery. In Hebrew, the more such combinations, the better. Since Hebrew is not a spoken language, its richness is contained in books, and whoever makes literary allusions in his writing imbues the older text with new life that generates and produces in its own image and form. Nonetheless, I can't forget something that happened to me, which, on the face of it, ought to have been resolved by this approach. But that's not how it turned out. I have been reading Hebrew since childhood. One day I happened on Bialik's poem 'O heavens, seek pity for me.' I read it, trembling and marveling at this poet who had the audacity to turn to the heavens and ask them to speak for him, who considered himself deserving enough to trouble the heavens on his own behalf. I reviewed those six words again and again. Each time, my soul was stunned by their splendor. Days later, I opened the Midrash and found those very same words. 'What's this?' I cried in alarm. 'How did those words get into the Midrash?' I stood bent over the book, my eyes clutching at each word, astonished, for the phrase had lost its impact; it no longer moved me. Was it because I knew it from the poem that it had no effect?"

Herbst lowered his head and reached across the table, touched a dish, withdrew his hand, touched it again, withdrew again. He studied his empty hand, muttering, "Anyone with credit can afford to turn to whoever he wants." The tall, thin student laughed and said, "The author of the Midrash certainly didn't lack the means to cover his words. This is probably equally true of our teacher Moses, to whom these words were attributed. He probably didn't have to look for credit elsewhere." To which his friend added, "Surely both Moses and the author of the Midrash said only what their credit would support." The tall, thin student interrupted. "Since we were talking about language earlier, let me say something on that subject. It seems likely to me that those ancient languages that are no longer spoken, the ones we call Semitic, were pronounced without vowels, exactly as they appear in the early inscriptions. SDNM, for example, should be read as it stands, without adding vowels to make SiDoNiM." Herbst, who was uncomfortable with theories and didn't enjoy speculating in a field that was not his, smoked in silence, putting out one cigarette and smoking another, dropping the ashes everywhere except in the ashtray. Once or twice he looked in the direction of Shira's table. Shira wasn't there. Could she have gone off and left him without saying a word? Then she reappeared. He wanted to leave his students and go to her; he also wanted to invite his students to come sit with him and Shira. These two thoughts were accompanied by a third thought: I have provided more witnesses who could testify that they saw me with Shira.

He got up, went over to Shira, and said, "Come, Shira, let's sit with those two young men. They're intelligent people who express their ideas in vigorous language. I know that you'll enjoy their conversation. This day has been dedicated to literature. On the way here, we discussed hasidic tales; at Anita Brik's, we discussed poetry. Now, what are these two fellows discussing? Poetics." Shira said, "Go back to them. I'm too tired to join you." Herbst said, "Then I'll call the waiter. I'll pay, and we can go." Shira said, "I've already paid. Go back and say goodbye to your students, or, if you like, you can sit with them and I'll find my way home alone." Herbst said, "I dragged you out of the house, and I'll return you to it." Shira said, "Whatever you like."

Herbst said, "If it's entirely up to me, I choose to go home with you and stay awhile." Shira said, "I already told you I don't feel well today."

Herbst ignored her words. Since the day he met her, he had considered her totally dependent on him, in every aspect of her being, as if she lived through him alone. And, as long as she pleased him, all was well with her. It was merely her obstinacy speaking now, an obstinacy he wished to break. His soul suddenly began to sway, and he was on the verge of falling. He dragged behind her, feebly, accompanied by the memory of her affection, which took several forms. "What's the matter?" Shira asked. He was overcome with rage. She asks what's the matter; can't she see, can't she tell? He suppressed his anger and asked, "What did you say?" She answered, "I was asking you if anything is the matter." Herbst glared at her in astonishment and said, "Why do you ask?" Shira said, "You seem to be having trouble walking." "Yes," Herbst answered angrily. "My shoelace is loose." "Your shoelace is loose?" "It's loose, and it broke off." "It broke off?" "Not really. Since it was loose, I thought it was broken." "But it didn't break?" "It didn't break, and it isn't loose. Tell me, Shira, has that never happened to you?" Shira said, "Neither that nor anything similar." Herbst repeated her words and said, "Please, Shira, explain that to me." Shira said, "I always tie a knot." Herbst said, "Even when the shoe has a strap? What sort of shoes are you wearing now?" Shira said, "Do you know what I'd like to say to you?" "What?" Herbst cried, excited. Shira said, "No more questions." "Why?" "Because they bore me." Herbst said, "Believe it or not, I see great things in my questions." Shira said, "In that case, enjoy them yourself; in fact, don't bother putting them into words." Herbst said, "It's not just my thoughts that I want to enjoy, I want——" Shira interrupted him and said, "I thought a scholar's chief joy was his thoughts." Herbst said, "And what about the rest of humanity?" Shira said, "As for the rest of humanity, everyone has his own idea of enjoyment." Herbst said, "See, Shira, in this respect I'm like the rest of humanity; I'm not satisfied with fantasy." Shira said, "In that case, you have my blessing. I hope you find what satisfies you." Herbst said, "Actions speak louder than blessings." Shira looked at him with open displeasure. Herbst said, "I'll explain myself." Shira said, "Don't be angry with me, Herbst. My head hurts, and my brain won't tolerate complicated explanations. I'm almost home. The road has never been so long as it is now." Herbst said, "Is my company so oppressive?" Shira said, "Herbst, let me tell you this: not everything in the world depends on you. There are disruptive factors other than your company. Please, spare me further explanations. Every word I say is fraught with pain." Herbst said, "It's that bad?" Shira said, "Please, don't bother to act surprised. Just give me a chance to recover. I'm glad to be so near home."

Herbst was in the midst of a vexing muddle. He had already given up on the gratification implicit in staying with Shira. Now all he wanted was to talk. He had nothing specific to say to her, but it was hard for him to let her go. He wanted to engage her in conversation in order to hold on to her, another hour, another half an hour. He remembered Anita Brik and was about to make her a topic of conversation. Before he had a chance to set his tongue in motion, she was forgotten. He recalled Shira's disdainful remarks about the Hasidim, among them the statement that no one had ever accused her of neglecting them in the hospital, and was going to bring up the subject of sympathies and antipathies—how they don't always govern our actions. Before he said a word, he forgot what was in his mind. Various other matters muddled his thoughts. Before being transformed into words, they were lost in a muddle. He remembered his students: that he had invited her to sit with them and listen to their talk about language and poetry, and she had refused to join them. He said to her, "Do you ever read essays or articles about authors and books?" Shira said, "Why all of a sudden?" Herbst said, "It's not so sudden. I'm asking because you rejected the opportunity to hear a discussion of poetry." Shira said, "I was tired, and I'm still tired." Herbst said, "Yes, Shira, you are tired. Still, you could answer my question." Shira said, "What did you ask?" Herbst said, "When a good book about poetry or poets comes your way, do you read it?" Shira said, "Why read books about books?" Herbst said, "A good essay can sharpen a reader's perception of a poem." Shira said, "If I can read the poems themselves, why bother with the critics' opinions? If I can master something with my own mind, why do I need other people's?" Herbst said, "True, but they might reveal meanings you wouldn't be aware of on your own." Shira shrugged her shoulders and said, "You know something, Manfred? Since my teeth grew in, I've been in the habit of chewing my own food. Dear doctor, I see that metaphor seems crude to you, so I won't speak in metaphor. From the day I learned to read, I read without inviting critics and essayists to chew the words of storytellers or poets beforehand and thrust the results into my mouth." Herbst said, "You don't admit that there are some things essayists and critics can elucidate for us?" Shira said, "My dear Manfred, when I was in nursing school and my fellow students used to sit around discussing the professors, the doctors, and the head nurses, I paid no attention. I haven't changed in this respect, even now that I'm a licensed nurse. Their chatter and opinions had no effect on the doctors' behavior. What they had in common was the fact that they all went right on doing what they did, and, since the nurses were so used to the doctors, they went right on making them the subject of their conversation."

Herbst was at a loss for words. His tongue set itself in motion, uttering nothing. Herbst knew that at some point he would challenge her, but there was no way to eradicate her opinions. Your metaphors are certainly crude, Miss Shira, Herbst thought to himself. "Good night," Shira said, her key in hand. "Good night," Herbst answered. Shira said, "I should have stopped by the pharmacy." Herbst said, "Then let's go back." Shira said, "I can't." "Why?" "Why? Because I'm too tired." Herbst said, "Say the word and I'll go." Shira said, "My dear doctor, I'll forgo the pharmacy and you'll forgo the good deed."

— 15 —

As always when coming from Shira's, he made his way on foot. Although the roads were desolate because of Arab shells, and Herbst was not without imagination, it didn't occur to him that the perils that menaced others menaced him as well.

The bus was still running. In fact, service was more frequent, so those in outlying districts who had to congratulate a friend on some joyous occasion and couldn't call on him on Shabbat because of the distance could go in the evening. But Herbst, as always, was on foot. His mind was brimming with the day's events, and he didn't want to be distracted by the crowd on the bus.

Sacharson attached himself to Herbst. Before he could hide from him, there he was. Enraged, Herbst lowered his eyelids and reflected: Only the devil could calculate the precise moment when just about anyone would be unwelcome and then proceed to inflict this nut on me. But he said, "I'm glad I ran into you, Mr. Sacharson. My daughter Tamara went to Greece, and her mother would like to trace her route. If you're done with the Baedeker and no longer need it, I would like to have it back. Right now, if possible." Hell, he was annoyed with himself. That nut deserves to be scolded for not returning my book, and I pamper him with words as if I'm asking a favor.

Sacharson smiled abjectly, which was how he responded when he saw someone stumble, and scratched his mouth to camouflage the smile, as he always did at such times. While scratching his lip, his fingers found their way into his mouth, and he began to gnaw at his nails. It was a dark night, and one couldn't really distinguish his fingernails from his skin, so it wasn't necessary to camouflage the smile. But, out of habit, he scratched his lip and gnawed at his nails. After spitting out some bits of nail, he coughed to clear his throat and threw out a word, as if adding to what had already been said. It was Sacharson's style to begin in the middle, as if he were adding to a previous statement. After he had talked for a while, Herbst perked up and said, "You mentioned Norway. What does Norway have to do with us?"

Sacharson's smile could be seen again, and then it was gone. He said, "I was recounting some of what happened to me a few years back, when I still bore the yoke of the commandments accepted by our people. I say 'our people'; yes, our people, my dear Mr. Herbst. I still consider myself absolutely Jewish—more so than those who are regarded as proper Jews, more than ever since I associated myself with the new covenant between God and Our Savior, and even more so now that I have the privilege of considering myself faithful to God and His people Israel." Herbst fixed his eyes on an approaching bus, hoping to be able to flee homeward on it and get rid of Sacharson. But it was headed elsewhere, and Sacharson tagged along behind him, walking and talking. Herbst looked back at him and said hastily, "So, Mr. Sacharson, what were you going to say?"

Sacharson draped his cane over his arm and said, "I see, Dr. Herbst, that your ears didn't accommodate you by taking in my words. I'm not offended, and I don't want to appear offended. That's how people are: some talk, others don't hear. It's often better not to hear than to hear what wasn't said. No need to show signs of displeasure. I don't intend to offer clever aphorisms. I'll get right back to the beginning of the story, and you'll hear what you missed before." Herbst said, "Tell me, Mr. Sacharson, do tell me. This time I will pay attention."

Sacharson cleared his throat because of the stiff collar that pinched him, because of the bits of fingernail that were caught in his throat, because of the story he was about to tell. He jerked his thumb at Herbst and said, "It happened during the war between Russia and Japan." Herbst said, "Then it's an old story." Sacharson said, "What I mean to tell is not a war story." Herbst said, "If it's not a war story, then what do you mean to tell? Whatever it is, tell it, Mr. Sacharson. Tell it. So, it occurred during the Russo-Japanese War. I don't think you said what the story is about yet. Or am I mistaken? Anyway, no need to go back to the beginning. So, it happened during the Russo-Japanese War."

Sacharson said, "Yes, during the Russo-Japanese War." Herbst said, "An unnecessary comment, Mr. Sacharson. I remember every word you said. If you like, I can repeat it. Now then . . ."

Sacharson repeated, "So, I was on my way to America. I was escaping, Mr. Herbst. Escaping from Russia, like many of my people who had no wish to risk their lives for the brutal czar. You people from the liberal countries can't imagine the pain of young Jews in Russia. Denied all civil rights, members of a battered and trampled people burdened with harsh rules that were becoming worse with every passing day, all of a sudden we were told: 'Rise up and join hands with your persecutors to fight a nation you don't know, that has done you no wrong.' Anyone who could, escaped this war, as I did. I won't subject you to the entire story. Imagine it for yourself: fellow Jews, brothers in misery, who ought to stand by each other in time of distress—not only did they not stand by me, but they treated me like merchandise, an object to exploit. They stole my last penny, leaving me with nothing. I'm not here to accuse them, nor do I mean to suggest that Jews have no compassion. But compassion is one thing, and avarice is another. Those Jews who are willing to skin a poor man for a price are the same ones who contribute to charitable causes and, of course, to anything holy. In the great synagogue in my town, there is a Torah scroll donated by a renowned philanthropist. Who was he? A man who used to snatch poor orphans and hand them over to Nicholas's soldiers in place of the sons of the rich. And the rich men—those same rich men—were God-fearing, performed all of the rituals and commandments, and contributed to every cause. Some built synagogues and seminaries or funded schools. Others supported assorted charities, especially those with a sacred purpose. Jews are attracted to that sort of thing. Remember the Kishinev pogrom? When it was over, a fund was set up for the victims, who were without food or clothing. A famous rabbi—one of the most famous in your country—was among those who responded. How? By sending them a very large supply of *tefillin.*" Herbst said, "Please, Mr. Sacharson, tell me, how are *tefillin* related to Norway?" Sacharson said, "You're joking, doctor. Wait and you'll see that it's all one subject—*tefillin* and Norway, or Norway without *tefillin.* As you see, Dr. Herbst, Sacharson can joke too when he wants to." Herbst said, "Excuse me, Mr. Sacharson. I wasn't joking. I merely asked a question. Since you began with Norway, I was reminding you about Norway." Sacharson said, "I'm not fussy. Still, let me remind you that I didn't begin with Norway. Before I said anything about Norway, we were discussing something else: the Russo-Japanese War and the escape of poor Sacharson, who is now privileged to join you

on your walk, a short walk as befits a short tale. Now I'm coming to
Norway in my story. After many difficulties, I reached Norway. I
arrived with swollen feet and torn shoes; hardest of all, empty-handed.
The money my mother had given me for expenses was extorted by our
Jewish brothers who were supposed to smuggle me across the border.
Actually, those swindlers didn't get rich on me. My mother was poor.
She plucked feathers for a living. How did she have money to give me?
She skimped on meals, filling the gap with fast days. If I told you how
much she gave me, you would laugh. But all I ask of you is that you
hear my story without making fun of me. I ask one further thing: a bit
of patience. I'm getting back to the heart of the matter. So I arrived in
Norway empty-handed. My paltry sum of money had been stolen at
the border. I was allowed to keep my other possessions: three faded
shirts, an old set of *tefillin,* and a frayed prayerbook inherited from my
father, whose merit must have worked in my favor. You can't imagine
my misfortune. Empty hands, empty stomach, aching legs. Still, I did
not despair. My physical anguish didn't allow me to indulge in a
spiritual response such as despair, but it nonetheless glared forth from
my eyes. Some fellow from Norway noticed and said, 'Come with me.'
He was a merchant who had dealt with Russian Jews and had learned
some Yiddish. I went with him. He took me to a hotel and ordered a
meal for me on his account. Even if you were never in Scandinavia, you
have probably heard that it is the custom in most of the big hotels to
offer a great assortment of food for breakfast, twenty or thirty varieties
at a time, mostly meat and fish. I couldn't eat meat, because it wasn't
kosher; nor could I eat fish, because it could have been cooked with
shellfish. The sardines had been preserved in wine, so I avoided them
too, for fear the wine was unkosher. I took some of those thin crackers
called Norwegian bread and ate until my throat felt scratchy. I was still
hungry. My benefactor, who had invited me to eat, was confident that
a starving man about to faint from hunger would eat whatever he was
offered and didn't notice what I was eating and what I was rejecting.
But the waiter noticed and reported to the kitchen. The cook came and
asked, 'Why aren't you eating any of the good things we're providing
for your pleasure?' I told him they were forbidden by our religion, et
cetera, et cetera. He listened, astonished. Finally, he glared at me,
outraged, and this is what he said: 'Who are you, and what sort of
religion is it that forbids you to enjoy the good food any decent person
enjoys?' At the end, my dear Mr. Herbst, at the end, if you will excuse
me, he spat in my face. Those northern people are very fine, but there
is something in the Jewish religion that enrages even the best Gentile.

And rage, my dear Mr. Herbst, leads to ugly deeds, such as spitting in someone's face."

Once more, Herbst's attention wandered. Sacharson didn't notice and kept on talking. Sacharson said, "You can't imagine the contempt of the hotel workers. I myself took a hard look and began to analyze the rules. It wasn't the crucifixion of Christ that aroused hatred toward Jews. Even if we accept the lie, which we know by now is a lie, and say the Jews betrayed Christ, it was without the people's knowledge that he was betrayed. It was the high priest Caiaphas, a Roman lackey, who betrayed him, and it is an accepted fact that Caiaphas was killed by the Jews for delivering Christ to the Romans. It is the Gemara and our legal codes that arouse hatred, setting Jews apart from other nations through rules governing food and drink and every other human function, training Jews to consider themselves so refined, excellent, superior, and attractive that it would be beneath the dignity of such aristocrats to eat at a table with Gentiles, much less marry them. All this in the name of a religion invented by the rabbis."

Herbst said to Sacharson, "I'll make a confession, if you promise not to report it to the Orthodox authorities. I don't avoid forbidden foods." Sacharson sighed and said, "You're teasing me, Mr. Herbst. You're joking. It's not fair to tease a person when he exposes his wounds." Herbst said, "Forgive me, Mr. Sacharson, I'm no theologian. Religious faith and practice are not my subject." Sacharson smiled bitterly and said, "Of course, of course. Religion and faith are of no interest to the learned Dr. Herbst. The renowned scholar Dr. Herbst, is engaged in study. As we all know, Dr. Herbst is engaged in . . . in . . . Forgive me, Mr. Teacher, but I have never inquired or been informed exactly which department you are in. I don't distinguish between disciplines, and academicians are all the same to me, in that they know everything. Except for one thing: what that highest element in us is after, the wretched soul lent to us by our Creator to endow us with generosity and mercy." Herbst shrugged his shoulders as he calculated how many meters it was from here to his home and how much chatter he would have to endure from the convert before being rid of him. Sacharson kept talking. "A schnorrer, afflicted with boils, begs at every door and gives thanks to God every morning for not having made him a Gentile. The Gentile he deplores is a workingman whose labor supports those Jews who throw occasional coins to beggars. Were it nor for that Gentile, who allows those Jews to support themselves at his expense, the philanthropists who serve Abraham's God would starve to death, and the rabbis would have to do without that daily blessing directed to

God, who has 'not made me a Gentile.' Isn't that so, Mr. Herbst?"
Herbst said to him, "I'm not very knowledgeable when it comes to
prayer." Sacharson added, "A Jewish whore who makes herself available to every British soldier for three or four shillings is certain that God
values her more than a Christian nun who devotes her life to God's
work, good deeds, and curing the sick and caring for orphans."

Herbst scratched his head and said, "Mr. Sacharson, I don't get the
drift of your words. I hear only one thing: you want to justify the fact
that you abandoned the religion of your fathers and took on a more
permissive one that lightens life's burdens." Sacharson's smile was
erased, and he said sadly, "Dr. Herbst, you know where my words are
headed, and you know what I mean. You and your friends, having cast
off all the rituals, are no different from a Gentile or a heretic, yet you
consider yourselves superior to me. If you please, Dr. Herbst, in what
way are you superior? Is it because you are without religion and without faith? Do you think it's possible to exist without God? Let's assume
that an individual can get by for a while without faith. For an entire
lifetime, it is definitely not possible. Even if he could live a lifetime
without faith, no community, no nation could survive. Without religion, anarchy takes over. Anarchy allows evil to prevail, which, in turn,
leads to annihilation." Herbst answered calmly, "Then are you saying
that all Jews lack faith? Anyway, Sacharson, I don't deal with these
issues. I don't mean to offend you when I say that your entire conversation is superfluous to me." Sacharson sighed and said, "My conversation is superfluous to you, but not to me. It is the welfare of my brethren
that I'm after. You are good people, Herbst. You and Mrs. Herbst. And
it goes without saying that you wouldn't exploit anyone. Still, ask
yourselves: how does your Firadeus support her family, whose bread-
winner was killed over the garbage of Talpiot? Yes, he was killed over
the garbage of Talpiot. Do you know what that means? This is what
it means. A band of bourgeois Jews—let us call them devoted Zionists—build themselves a special neighborhood far from the city and
from the stench of other Jews in order to enjoy the fresh air, or, in their
words, to rebuild the country. They live in new houses, in a healthy
environment, eating and drinking, enjoying life, and filling their bellies
with delicacies. The surplus—what they don't manage to deposit in
their intestines—spoils and is put in garbage cans, which they hire a
poor man to dispose of. You have a term for him in modern Hebrew,
in your Hebrew that invents new words and puts the old ones out of
mind, so that those who are proficient in the new language can't understand a line of Scripture. The garbage man goes from house to house,
clearing away the garbage. He is often disheartened by what he sees in

those garbage cans, because what a Talpiot housewife throws out is enough for a poor man and his family to live on contentedly. Patience, Mr. Herbst. I'll get back to Firadeus. You hired her for three lirot a month, and you pay her promptly, like the university, which pays its professors promptly. And, for this sum, she is allowed to expose herself to those dangerous armed marauders. Your conscience is clear because, after all, you are paying her. If Firadeus is killed, you and Mrs. Herbst will call on her grieving family, and I have reason to assume Mrs. Herbst would bring something from her own kitchen and leave some money on her way out. My words are not directed only to you, honored doctor. They are directed to all the just and righteous souls in Jerusalem and elsewhere who see their brethren wasting away and leave them to starve. You know, honored doctor, were it not for us, disciples of Christ, who stand by them, scores of Jews would have been erased from the world." Herbst said, "Once again, I must inform you that you've come to the wrong address. I don't do social work, and this sort of conversation goes in one ear and out the other." Sacharson said, "Let me repeat what I said: I strive to improve the lot of my brothers, though you see me as someone who has sold his soul and his God for financial gain. Isn't that so, Mr. Herbst? I don't deny that among my friends there are some who have no conscience and convert for material gain. I am not one of those. I am definitely not one of them. Whatever I do is directed toward spiritual improvement, and I am especially eager to rescue Jews from oppression by the rabbis. Israel has suffered at the hands of Esau and Ishmael, but Karo's Code of Law, preceded by the Talmud and the writings of Maimonides and, above all, the dictates of the rabbis, have been even more harmful. Those sadists, in the name of the dot on an *i*, because of a trace of impurity in the Passover food, see fit to starve an entire city, forbid contact between man and wife, doom an abandoned young woman to a solitary life, and . . . and . . . I've already forgotten the teachings and the villainy that are heaped on our unfortunate people through the righteousness of the rabbis. The rab——" Before he could complete the syllable, he grabbed Herbst's arm, shouting, "Get down, all the way down!" Herbst dropped to the ground, thinking: Why is he yelling at me, and why did I get down? While he imagined he was asking Sacharson this question, or that he had already asked him but hadn't heard his answer, the air was pierced by an explosive sound. He smelled gunpowder and realized a bullet had been fired. His thoughts were arrested, his hair stood on end, and he felt a chill that seemed to run between his skin and his flesh, as if the skin had been peeled back and a chill had been trapped in the exposed space. His perceptions were clouded by an odd sensation. Odder still, the very sensation that clouded his perceptions made him more alert. "We're safe," Sacharson whispered. He took off his hat and wiped his brow, then his head, looking to see if there was any blood on his hand. Then he whispered to himself, "It was foolish to walk." He took Herbst's hand and repeated, "We're safe, we're safe, but it was foolish of us to walk."

They went on in silence, their hearts pounding, each of them deep in thought. Sacharson was thinking: If that Arab knew I was not one of those Zionist Jews, he wouldn't have aimed at me. Anyway, anyone who was born a Jew shouldn't go out at night. When an Arab bullet leaves its barrel, it doesn't distinguish between the guilty and the innocent.

While Sacharson lamented the bullet's error, Herbst kept on walking and thinking: Every day I hear the list of casualties—to think that I was almost one of them. I was spared today, but what about tomorrow and the day after? I live in a dangerous place, and I'm endangering both myself and my family. If I don't move, I'm risking my life and theirs. What happened here? He reviewed exactly what had happened, replaying the sound of the shot as the bullet left the pistol, and realized that the danger had exceeded the terror, that terror isn't always relative to danger.

They walked on in silence. They were no longer afraid, but their hearts were distraught and heavy. Too bad it's a moonless night, Herbst thought. It's so delightful when there's a moon. Something seems to be changing up there in the sky. It's a fact, something is changing there. The moon is rising. We'll have moonlight. We'll have moonlight, but there's no joy on this road. No joy. Our hearts are uneasy, uneasy, and we keep on walking without making any headway. Shira is already sleeping. She's in her bed, asleep, unaware, knowing nothing of what happened to me. If the bullet had accomplished its mission, I would be dead by now. Tomorrow they would find me in a pool of blood and take me to the morgue at Hadassah or Bikkur Holim Hospital. Henrietta and Tamara would come and see it wasn't my fault that I didn't get home last night. It was because I was hit by a bullet and murdered, and my corpse is here for them to cry over. A crowd has gathered around them, men and women, friends and acquaintances. Those who know how to put on a sad face are doing just that; those who don't know how, clench their lips and put on a look of outrage, at the murderers for victimizing the innocent and upright, at the Mandate government for standing by in silence. The Brit Shalom people find further support for their views: we can no longer depend on British soldiers to defend us but must be quick to come to terms with the Arabs at any price. Among those who surround me are some who didn't know me at all, who never even heard of me, but, now that I've been defined by death, they feel obliged to join the crowd. Shira may have come too. No, Shira wouldn't come. Shira is in her room, reproaching herself—she should have acceded when I begged to go home with her. Now for my funeral. Shira won't be standing there with a cigarette dangling from her mouth, as she was during that young man's funeral when the riots first began. How could it be that I didn't think of Zahara? Am I to conclude that in emergencies we don't necessarily think of what is most precious to us? As for Shira, it is not the soul that remembers her, but the body; the body—ungratified, remembering, like a worm that keeps wriggling after it is cut in two. My corpse. That's how I refer to my body. That's the correct term for such a body. For you, my soul, I would prefer a finer designation. By my calculations, I ought to be home by now. Actually not, I was mistaken. After the shot, we shifted paths. Now we are on the right track again. I should be grateful for Sacharson's silence. One word could crush my head.

Sacharson addressed Herbst. "I'm walking here, but my mind is somewhere else. I know we are in dangerous territory. Even if we are out of danger, it's still necessary to be cautious, and we have to alert our senses to look, listen, smell, in case there is an Arab nearby scheming to kill us. Despite this, all my senses are elsewhere. I am pondering the event that occurred ten days ago here in Jerusalem. Yes, right here in Jerusalem, near Gethsemane. Some of the facts were reported in the Hebrew press, particularly in *Ha'aretz*. I'm referring to the story of the two brothers who were killed together." Sacharson brushed his hands over his eyes, stretched his thumb toward his collar, and pulled on it. Herbst took note of his gesture and concluded: He's preparing to tell a long story, but, when we arrive at my house, I'll leave, even if he's in the middle of his story. Just because he's my neighbor, does he have the right to harass me? Deep down, Herbst sensed it had less to do with the fact that they were neighbors than with what had just happened to them. The thought occurred to him: He said Gethsemane; the name relates to the event. This was followed by a further thought: What is there to lose by listening? Then he began to be worried that Sacharson had decided not to talk. Again, Sacharson reached toward his collar with his thumb. His eyes were enlarged by moonlight, and a great and bitter sadness dripped down from them, covering his face, wrinkles and all.

He resembled an old woman peering into her own open grave with a bitter heart. They continued to walk, walking awhile, then stopping, stopping in silence. Sacharson seemed shorter; his cane seemed taller.

He looked more and more like an old woman. The cane in his hand cast a shadow wrapped in shadow. Because he was staring at this shadow, Herbst forgot about Sacharson and the story he had in mind to tell.

Sacharson stood still and leaned on the cane. After a bit, he raised his head and began walking again, muttering, "We were almost like those two brothers who were killed together. One of them had already found true faith and embarked on eternal life, whereas his brother was not equally privileged." Sacharson's eyes filled with tears, and he reached out to embrace Herbst but withdrew his arms midway, sighing. Herbst heard his mutterings and glanced at him although he had already forgotten the man wanted to tell him something. Sacharson hadn't forgotten, and he began. As usual, he began in the middle. But for the fact that Herbst had read some of the facts in *Ha'aretz*, he wouldn't have been able to follow. The story was roughly this: Two brothers, who were Jews, escaped from Hitler's Germany. They wandered through many lands before arriving in Jerusalem. They fell on hard times and didn't find what they were after. What were they after, and what was it that they hoped to find? I doubt this was clear to them. In any case, what they found was not what they were after, and what they were after they never found. This account is, more or less, what was reported by people who knew them fairly well. One of the brothers was so desperate that he converted and found himself room and board in a monastery in Gethsemane. The other brother found shelter in a Jewish school inside the wall, where he prayed a lot, entreated God, and fasted. Ten days ago, he set out from there to visit his brother, either because he missed him or to try to convince him to return to their fathers' faith.

Now I'll tell the story as Sacharson told it, in his terms. "One of the young men enrolled in a school in the Old City, where he spent the time weeping and fasting, imploring God to have mercy on his brother and return him to his fathers' faith. God, knowing what is best for man's soul, closed His ears to the poor fellow's pleas, ignored his fasts, and fortified the other brother's faith in salvation. When weeks and months passed, and still the brother who had been saved didn't return to his old faith, the unfortunate fellow went to Gethsemane to urge him to return to the religion of his fathers. Or, it may be that he went because he missed his brother. Oh, Mr. Herbst, do you know what it means to miss a brother? So, just ten days ago, he put aside his prayers and studies, and left for Gethsemane. He found his brother. They fell on each other's necks and wept. Then they sat together and talked. What did they talk about? Only God knows. They may have discussed questions of faith, or they may have not mentioned them at all. Anyway, there is no reason to believe that either one of them was converted to his brother's way. Finally, they got up to leave, walking part of the way together. An Arab spotted them and decided to shoot. One of them fell in a pool of blood. The other one bent over him, shouting, 'My brother, my brother!' While he wept over his brother, the Arab fired another shot. They died together, one on top of the other."

Herbst knew the story, and Sacharson had added nothing to it, except for his drone. He told it as if chanting a sacred text. From the moment Sacharson latched onto him, Herbst was irritated. Now his irritation was compounded. At a time when there are so many victims, singling out one to mourn ignores the common plight. As for the brother who converted, his decision probably had very little to do with a quest for God. So why did he do it? To change his circumstances, because he was having a hard time. He was sick of it and began to cast about for alternatives. Whatever it was that he lacked seemed to exist in those other settings. He began to compare his own situation with what they offered. Meanwhile, he found an opening there, went in, and never came out. You want to know if his new faith was a success. Even if he tells you he's happy, if you look at his face, it's obvious that he's dejected. Perhaps because his new faith requires that he believe what he doubted to begin with, and now he is lost in both worlds. Near the train tracks, in Lower Baka, Herbst used to see a sign with the names of two doctors, a husband and wife. He was in general practice, she was a gynecologist, and they had a Jewish name. One day, he noticed that a Christian name had replaced theirs. Several days later, he happened to be at Bamberger and Wahrmann, where he found some books with those two doctors' bookplate, giving the name he had seen on their sign before it was changed. Bamberger told him he had bought the books from an Orthodox doctor who came from Frankfurt, that he and his wife had converted and purged their household of all Jewish books. If they had not been forced to leave their homeland, they would have lived their lives as Jews. They might have become leaders of the community. But, since they were uprooted and unable to thrive in the new environment, their spirits were low, their minds vulnerable, their hearts despondent. When the riots broke out and there were so many casualties, they began to have second thoughts about their Jewishness, which seemed to be a constant source of trouble. Because they were Jews, they had to leave Germany; and, because they were Jews, they were being persecuted in the Land of Israel. They finally said, "We don't need all this trouble," and converted, since being Jewish was merely a matter of religion to them. We have learned from Sacharson's experience that their Arab neighbors won't necessarily make a distinction between them and other Jews.

Sacharson felt sorry for himself as well as Herbst, since they had almost been killed together. He said to Herbst, "Dear sir and brother, come home with me, and let's sit together and reflect on what happened to us, so we can recover from the shock. I said 'recover from the shock,' when I really should have said 'thank, praise, celebrate the One who wrought a great miracle and saved us from death, keeping us alive so we would be grateful to His name.' I am bowed by sin and don't deserve to recognize the full glory of the miracle. My Creator has allowed me merely the privilege of noting it, nothing more. It seems to me, brother, neighbor, that I'm not asking too much of you. Come home with me, and we'll sit for a while. Then you can go home with a tranquil heart and a joyous soul." Herbst remained silent. He didn't answer. Sacharson changed his tone and said, "If you come in, Mr. Teacher, I can return the Baedeker. You were asking for it. I don't need it any longer. That sort of guide, made out of paper and words, is not what I need." Sacharson's face was distorted by pride and disdain. He feels the sting of my words; a guide made out of paper and words— that's what I told him. Paper and words. He knows, that stuffy academic knows just what I mean. As long as he doesn't convert, any Jew, even one who violates all of their strictures, is, nonetheless, a pharisee. Herbst shrugged his shoulders and said, "There's time for that tomorrow." Sacharson sighed and said, "How many years have we been neighbors, yet I haven't had the privilege of seeing Dr. Herbst cross my threshold. Neither he nor Mrs. Herbst, nor the two young ladies. Even now, when our lifeblood came so close to being mixed, even now Mr. Herbst refuses to come into my house. But I have nothing against Mr. Herbst, and I am sincere in wishing you, my dear Mr. Herbst, a good night. Good night, Mr. Herbst. I'll send over the Baedeker tomorrow."

When they had taken leave of each other, Herbst turned back and said to him, "Just one word, Mr. Sacharson. Please don't say anything to my wife about what happened. No need for her to know I was in danger. There is a further reason to forget the matter. Mrs. Herbst has invested her youth in the house we live in and in the garden she has planted. If she hears what happened to me, she won't rest until we move, though she'll never find a place like this one. It would be hard for me to move as well. It's not easy, Mr. Sacharson, to transport more than three thousand volumes. You can understand, Mr. Sacharson, why I'm asking you to conceal the incident from my wife. Actually, it is something that happens in these times, nothing more than an event that never took place. Isn't that so, Mr. Sacharson?" Sacharson nodded in silence. At this point, Sacharson was content to be silent and to allow Herbst to be the one to leave, albeit without an answer. Sacharson didn't report what had happened, and Herbst tried to avoid thinking about it. Whether or not he was successful, he never spoke of it.

— 16 —

Zahara came, and Avraham-and-a-half was with her. We knew Zahara had found a mate, but we didn't know who he was, for events had given us pause to question whether, in the interim, some other *kvutza* member might have claimed Zahara's heart. Now that she had come with Avraham-and-a-half and was pregnant by him, there was no room for doubt, and the impression that Avraham-and-a-half was indeed her mate was confirmed.

Father Manfred sees, but doesn't grasp, that little Zahara is a full-blown woman; not merely a woman, but halfway to motherhood. Having barely become accustomed to the fact that she was growing up, he now has to see her as a woman about to be a mother. What did Zahara do, and why did she do it? Such a charming little one, her father's pet . . . She has shed all her graces and become a woman like the others.

Father Manfred sits talking to his daughter, as always. But in the course of conversation he notes that his voice is different; something is missing, and something else has been introduced. This is true of her voice as well. Where is the lilt that used to be so refreshing? He had a daughter once, who belonged entirely to him, but someone came and took her away.

Father Manfred sits and talks to his daughter, thinking to himself: How did this transformation occur? It had nothing to do with him, that was certain. It took place before he became aware of it. Father Manfred smoothed his temples. He smoothed them again, thinking to himself: First I smoothed my temples unconsciously; I smoothed them again, deliberately. He looked directly at Zahara to see if she was responding to the message. She hadn't even noticed that her father had smoothed his temples twice. Father Manfred was accustomed to having Zahara question everything he did in her presence. He had just now smoothed his temples twice, and she hadn't reacted.

Father Manfred got up and went to take one of the cigarettes he had tucked away in the closet for a rainy day, though there was a full pack on the table. Zahara saw him get up and made the mistake of taking this as a signal for her to leave, so her father could get to work. He noticed and said, "Sit down, my child. Sit down. I didn't see that there were cigarettes right here on the table, so I was going to get some from the closet. You might think I'm hiding them from Tamara, but I don't even hide them from myself. It's a lost cause. I'm already doomed to end my days in smoke. Everyone has faults. Your father isn't short on faults, and smoking is not the worst one. I say this, not in self-reproach, but to be truthful." Just as it began to seem to Father Manfred that he had access to his daughter again, that he could talk to her in their usual mode, he realized that this was not their usual mode. Then what was it? He was testing himself to see how much he could say to her, now that she was transformed. Again he wondered: How did that transformation take place? Actually, that was not the proper form for the question. He should have asked: When did it begin? Between the time it took to strike a match and light a cigarette, Manfred remembered that once, several years back, when Zahara was still a girl, he went into her room as she was taking off a dress and putting another one on, and that she shuddered when she saw him. This was the first such shudder, the response of a newly adolescent girl when a man sees her half-naked, even though he is her father. In any case, it was adolescence that brought on the change, and I took no notice until she appeared with him, that is, with Avraham-and-a-half.

Father Manfred is curious about Avraham-and-a-half and engages him in conversation. Father Manfred has two motives: first, to find out what the young man is like and get to know the qualities through which he prevailed and won his daughter; and, second, to show his daughter that he is fond of her mate. Be that as it may, Herbst's conversation is an empty gesture. He asks questions without hearing that they have already been answered. He makes a statement without hearing that he has already said the same thing several times. The young man realizes this and has no interest in chewing over what's already been chewed. Manfred realizes this and makes a move to placate the young man. How does he placate him? With a cigarette. But he's not a smoker. Manfred searches the recesses of his heart for something endearing and finds nothing. Again, he offers him a cigarette. He takes the cigarette, lights it, but doesn't smoke. Father Manfred notices and says, "I just remembered that you're not a smoker. How I envy you. I wish I weren't a smoker." The young man says, "Does anyone keep you from quitting?" The father smiles graciously and says, "Really, there is nothing easier than giving up smoking. Isn't that what Mark Twain said—'I know from experience, because I've given up smoking dozens of times'?" The young man listens but doesn't laugh. Father Manfred thinks to himself: This young man has no sense of humor. Father Manfred doesn't realize that most of the jokes being told in town have already made the rounds of the kibbutzim and have lost their punch. Father Manfred eyes the young man intently. What does Zahara see in him? How could she leave her father for him? The young man gets up and leaves. Father Manfred remains alone, whispering to himself, "I hope he didn't notice what a failure I was."

Avraham-and-a-half didn't notice Manfred's failure, nor did he notice his efforts. People like Herbst are of no interest to Avraham-and-a-half. Having never paid attention to avuncular types, here in the Land of Israel he was certainly not burdened by the yoke of excessive manners imposed by the leisure classes. It was merely Avraham's good nature that kept him from walking away in midconversation. After each conversation with Avraham, Herbst felt as if a weight had been lifted from his heart. Herbst had made many attempts to ascertain just what it was that oppressed him when he was with Zahara's young man, but without success. He did not want to admit to himself that he couldn't talk to a young person about anything but academic subjects.

Mother Henrietta was different from Father Manfred. Even before she knew Avraham, Henrietta approved of him, and the first time Zahara brought him home, she became quite fond of him. Now that Zahara had chosen him, Henrietta considered him to be the most splendid young man in the world. Whatever Avraham-and-a-half did was just right.

Henrietta moves through her house marveling over this young man, whose manners and conversation are so appealing, whose timing is so perfect, who can answer any question. Subjects that were far from her heart, in which she had no interest, suddenly engage her. When Avraham brings them up, they become important, and she wants to hear more. She declares, "I always wanted to know more about that, but I couldn't find anyone to explain it to me until Avraham appeared and made it all clear." Manfred hears this, and an angry sneer distorts his lips. He had tried many times to explain just those things to Henrietta, who had put him off, saying, "Let me be. I don't have to know such things." Along comes this whippersnapper whose learning is minimal, and she sits at his feet, a humble student, devouring his every word with no thought of fatigue, displaying her ignorance shamelessly. Manfred tries to say something to her, but she interrupts to sing the praises of Zahara's Prince Charming, who embodies all the finest qualities one could look for in a young man. If it's a question of tact, there is no one so tactful as Avraham; as for kindness, there is no one kinder. Henrietta has never even imagined a young man finer than this one.

Manfred jokes with her and says, "You pride yourself on being a good judge of character. In that case, how did you happen to choose me?" Henrietta says, "In those days, when we first met, you were all right." "And now? Am I not all right?" Henrietta answers, "Now, my dear, I am tired, and I'm not in the mood for conversation." Manfred says, "You're not too tired to listen to that maypole of Zahara's." Henrietta says, "Please, Fred, cut out the nonsense. It doesn't suit you at all." "It doesn't suit me because it's nonsense, but if I said something smart, would you prick up your ears and listen?" Henrietta says, "Judging by what you just said, I doubt you could say anything smart." Manfred says, "Then let me try." Henrietta said, "I already told you, I'm tired." Manfred says, "And what was my answer to that? Have you already forgotten?" Henrietta says, "Whether or not I forgot, I don't have the strength to hear any more." Manfred says, "Very well, then. That's how I'll treat you too." Henrietta says, "Go right ahead. Whatever you like, Manfred." Manfred says, "I'd like to see if I can really do as I like." Henrietta said, "Since when don't you do as you like with me? Anyway, I already told you, you have your rights, you can do as you like. Don't you always claim your rights?" Manfred said, "Just when did I ever claim my rights?" Henrietta said, "When, when, when. Every day, all the time, at any hour, you always claim your rights. Anyway, Fred, you know what I'm going to say. It might be best to conclude this silly conversation." Manfred said, "If it's best for you, it's certainly best for me. Now, what was I going to tell you?" Henrietta said, "Maybe you could put it off until tomorrow." Manfred said, "I could put it off forever." Henrietta said, "What were you going to tell me?" Manfred said, "Curiosity has gotten the better of you." Henrietta said, "If you think it's curiosity, let it be curiosity. It doesn't matter at all to me. I've given up on having an ounce of understanding between us. You can't stand to see me happy for a minute." Manfred said, "So you're happy. I didn't know that." "You didn't know?" "I didn't know." "Yes, yes. A father's eyes are too dim to see his daughter's happiness." Manfred said, "It's enough for me that the daughter's mother sees her happiness." Henrietta said, "So let me be happy with her, and don't interrupt with complaints and grievances. If I were as hard as a rock, I'd be worn thin by your complaints. You think I don't see how your every move is one more gesture of protest. I wonder what you would do if . . ." Manfred asked in dismay, "If what?" Henrietta said, "Better to be silent." Manfred laughed bizarrely and said, "Let's be silent, madam. Let's be silent."

If not for the mailman, who brought them a card, the two of them would not have been silent. Henrietta took the card and looked at the picture. Whenever she saw that heroic figure with the outstretched arm, she regretted her inability to remember who he was. Now it wasn't her forgetfulness that she regretted, but the fact that the figure occupied half of Tamara's card. Manfred peered over Henrietta's shoulder and marveled at the fact that even on such a cheap postcard one could see the splendor of the sculpture. Henrietta soon handed the card to Manfred and said, "You read it now." Henrietta had learned to decipher her daughter's handwriting, but she wasn't always sure she got everything right, so she was in the habit of reading it to herself, then giving it to Manfred to read to her. Now she had tried unsuccessfully. She handed the card to Manfred and said, "What is this? Is it Greek?" It wasn't Greek writing, but every word was surrounded by the scrawl of some member of the tour group, and the entire picture was surrounded by greetings and good wishes, such as the message inscribed under Apollo: "We're all having a marvelous trip. We were in Athens, Delphi, and Olympus, and tomorrow we'll travel through Arcadia as far as the eastern shore of the Peloponnesus. With best wishes . . ." Under Apollo's arm was another message: "Greetings to you, Herbst. Olympic greetings. Sorry I can't convey them in person." The message was signed by the professor who was leading the group.

"I see, Fred," Henrietta said, "that, when it comes to your daughters, you have reason to complain. Tamara is so attached to you—she goes on a short trip, and every day there's mail from her. I forgot to tell you. Sacharson returned the Baedeker. Why does that startle you?" "I wasn't startled. You imagined that I was startled." Henrietta said, "If you say you weren't startled, I believe you. It's all right to lend Sacharson a book. Not only did he return it in one piece, but he put it in a beautiful cover. Here's the Baedeker. Find me Arcadia." While Herbst was opening the Baedeker, Henrietta leaned her head on his shoulder and began singing, "I too lived in Arcadia . . ."

Zahara and Avraham didn't stay very long. They spent four days with the Herbsts. Not counting the day they ate only breakfast at Henrietta's table and the half-day they spent at Kiryat Anavim visiting a friend who had been on the training farm in Germany with Avraham, but adding the extra half-day they threw in for the yeast cake she baked them.

There was work to be done in Ahinoam, and it could not be postponed because of the sentiments of the old people, who would have had them stay on day after day. The air of Jerusalem, its cool nights, the friends from all over the country whom one runs into everywhere, the secrets the city reveals to its guests—all these things make it special. But to someone from a *kvutza*, particularly to a founding member, the *kvutza* is even more special. If there is still not a single tree—no shade, only thorns, briar, snakes, and scorpions—all the more reason why one has to hurry back to water the fragile plants, clear away the thorns and briar, and wipe out the nests of vipers.

When Henrietta realized that the children were determined to hurry back to Ahinoam, she tried to work out a compromise, to have Avraham go back to Ahinoam and leave Zahara to spend another two or three days in Jerusalem. But Zahara would not agree to stay even an hour without Avraham. Henrietta set about collecting all the things she had made for Sarah and passed them on to Zahara, specifying with each item, "This is for your baby, not for anyone else's." To which Zahara answered, "I can't accept your conditions. In our *kvutza*, we each get what we need." Henrietta said, "Still, this shawl, which I made myself—don't give it to anyone." Zahara said, "You can trust me." Henrietta surveyed everything, praying to herself: I hope at least some of these things will be used by Zahara's child.

Finally, she took another tack. She stopped praying, fingered the items she was especially fond of, and appropriated them with her eyes, reflecting: It's not possible, it's not possible that Zahara would offer this to the first taker. She couldn't possibly give this up. She looked at Zahara and was amazed that her daughter didn't seem to appreciate the baby clothes. And what baby clothes they were! Henrietta roamed from room to room, from closet to closet, from drawer to drawer, taking out everything, saying to herself: This will be good for Zahara. I'll give this to Zahara, this will be very useful. As for Zahara's statement "I can't keep these things for myself," those were just words. Zahara was joking. It was impossible that a treasure her mother gave up expressly for her could be offered to the world at large.

Henrietta had already forgotten what Zahara had said and was looking over other things that might suit Zahara and her unborn baby. She was suddenly overcome with worry that she had forgotten the essentials. In fact, she was certain she had forgotten the essentials, that everything Zahara and her infant were sure to need had slipped away from her mind, so that, when Zahara got back to Ahinoam, she wouldn't find what she hoped to find, nor would she find what she needed. The pile she had dragged from Jerusalem to Ahinoam would have none of what she needed in it. Nor would those essentials be

available in Ahinoam, for the entire community was made up of youngsters who had no idea what a mother needs. Henrietta refocused her
thoughts, and it was not her mind that roamed through all her rooms,
but her soul that roamed and fluttered like an anxious bird.

Henrietta paused for a bit, trying to remember what she had put in
Zahara's box and what she should have put in it. She did not realize that
her hands were idle and her heart was empty, that her thoughts were
being dispersed and no new ones were replacing them. The alarm she
had felt a few minutes earlier seemed to subside, and she was utterly
relaxed. Hardly conscious of the swift change, she stood beside the full
carton and gazed into it, her eyes remaining fixed on its top. It seemed
to her that something hidden kept emerging, some aspect of a thought
about what she meant to put in the box. Her thoughts came to a sudden
standstill, and all her ideas were suspended. She ignored the fact that
Zahara was going to give birth. She was unaware of Zahara's very
being, as well as of her own. Like mother, like daughter: Zahara's
thoughts were dispersed too, and, between the two of them, the room
was silent, like those frequently silent inner rooms on a hot summer day
in Jerusalem, in houses surrounded by gardens and far from the road.
In the stillness, the space within the room was suffused with the palest
gray light, tinged with pale blue—paling, then darkening; darkening,
then paling, until it took on an undefined hue. I don't know whether
the light was created from the space between shutter slats or from the
objects in rooms. The two of them, mother and daughter, were unaware of each other and unaware of their own being as well. If I had
a tendency to coin phrases, I would call this a state of "annihilated
being."

Sarah came into the room and stood there in dismay. After a moment
or two, she backed up and knocked on the door from the inside, like
someone who knocks before entering, and said, "Come in." She went
over to Zahara, wrapped her little arms around her big sister's knees,
and said, "Sarah loves Zahara." Zahara bent down, placed her lips on
Sarah's, and said, "Zahara loves Sarah very, very, very much." Sarah
said, "No, no, no. Sarah loves very, very, very much." Mother Henrietta bestirred herself and said, "Sarah, Zahara is leaving us." Sarah
looked at Zahara and said, "Zahara is leaving us?" This was not so much
a question as a matter of words that were inconsistent with reality.
Zahara kissed her sister again and said gravely, "I have to go home."
Sarah's eyes scanned the room as she wondered: What did Zahara
mean, 'I have to go home'? Isn't this home? And why did she say 'I have
to'? Mother Henrietta said to Sarah, "Tell her there's no need to
hurry." Sarah said to Zahara, "Mother says——" She stopped in the

middle, turned to her mother, and said, "You tell her." All of a sudden, she turned away from both of them. "What's this?" she asked. "This . . . this here, this?" Zahara said, "I don't know what you mean." The child pointed with her thumb, repeating, "This." Zahara turned to her mother. "Maybe you know what she means? Sarah, show me with your finger." Sarah was annoyed at Zahara. "What I'm pointing with is a finger, isn't it?" Mother Henrietta said, "She means the grasshopper playing on the window. It's a grasshopper, Sarah." Sarah repeated the word with a mixture of agreement and doubt. She said, "A grasshopper. Can I step on it?" Zahara responded with alarm, "Why step on it? Such a fine grasshopper—see how nice his wings are, what long legs he has." Sarah said, "You don't understand anything." Mother Henrietta laughed and said to Zahara, "She doesn't mean to step on it with her feet. She means to catch it." Zahara said, "Then why did she say 'step on it'?" While they talked, Sarah chased the grasshopper with her fingers. Zahara repeated, "Why did she say it that way?" Mother Henrietta said, "This is what happened: the first time Sarah saw a caterpillar in the garden, she was fascinated by it and finally stretched out her leg to trap it, so she could pick it up. Since then, whenever she tries to catch a butterfly, she says 'to step on it." Zahara said, "To think that I suspected she would crush it. Come, sweetheart, let me give you a kiss. Who's that coming? Why, it's Avraham."

Avraham arrived, his lashes casting bars of gold on his wife and her mother and sister. He picked up Sarah, sat her on his shoulders, and began to prance around with her. Zahara shouted, "Careful! You'll bang her head on the ceiling." He bent down and began to crawl on his knees, holding on to Sarah, who was perched on his neck, clapping her hands and chanting the words of a song she had learned from Firadeus. Then she began tapping her feet to the music. Henrietta called, "You're hurting him." The child leaned over his ear and asked, "Does it hurt?" Avraham flung the golden bars from his eyes to the child and said, "It hurts, it hurts as much as eating chocolate. Do you like chocolate? Oh, dear, we forgot to bring you chocolate. Next time we come, we'll bring some chocolate. Take my handkerchief, Sarah, and tie a knot in it to remind me to bring Sarah chocolate. What else should we bring you? We'll bring you a baby girl, and then you'll be an aunt. Aunt Sarah. How would you like to be an aunt? To someone real, not just a doll. What do you think of Zahara? She knows that sort of trick; she knows how to make you an aunt. Now, honey, I'll put you on the grasshopper's back. He'll carry you to Ahinoam. All the young women will see you and wish for a little girl just like you."

After Henrietta finished wrapping everything, she handed the packages to Zahara, who handed them to Avraham, then kissed her mother and her little sister, Sarah, and said goodbye to her father. Henrietta said, "You'll come back to Jerusalem soon, right?" Zahara said, "What do you mean, 'soon'?" Henrietta said, " 'Soon' means when it's time to have the baby. The setup for childbirth is better in Jerusalem than anywhere else in the country." Zahara laughed and said, "What are you saying, Mother? You want me to give birth in the city? Do you expect me to have a city child? I'm a country girl now. I belong to a *kvutza*, and I'll give birth in the hospital in Afula, like everyone else."

Avraham and Zahara left, loaded down with all sorts of paraphernalia. After Henrietta had finished packing a large box, she remembered other things it would be good for Zahara to have. So she filled Avraham's arms, warning him not to lose anything, for it would all be needed by Zahara and the infant she was about to bring forth.

A contented smile spreads over Zahara's face, the smile of a woman who has found her mate and is going off with him to his home. Avraham-and-a-half is taller than anyone. He is twice as tall as Zahara. Unless you've seen those two together, you have no concept of large and small. Now, imagine this small creature, this mere girl, with a baby inside. Isn't that a truly moving sight? It's no wonder that Father Manfred is more and more moved, and has no further complaints about her, that he accepts everything, whatever his daughter has done.

Zahara and her young man left, and the house was as it had been before. Well, not really. As long as Zahara was single, Henrietta felt that she still lived there. Even when Zahara went to the *kvutza*, Henrietta regarded the move as temporary. Now that she had left with her mate, there was a void in the house. All that day, Henrietta couldn't get her bearings. Wherever she turned, there was something missing. The things Zahara took from the house were not what was missing; something that eludes and at the same time occupies every sensibility was missing. Henrietta told herself again and again: Nothing has actually changed. To which her heart's response was: No change? Things have changed. Yes, they've changed.

When she went to bed, she was confronted by all these voids, which were accompanied by concern for her daughter. Zahara might not find anyone to guide her during pregnancy, since all the women in Ahinoam are young, except for the nurse, and, having never been pregnant, they have no concept of caution. They undertake every kind of work, pay no attention to their own needs, and are totally ignorant about pregnancy and childbirth. She was suddenly overcome with joy on account of her daughter, who had found a mate, and on account of this mate, who was so delightful. In the midst of her joy, Henrietta forgot about Avraham and thought again about Zahara, who was about to become a mother. First she scolded herself for having said so little to Zahara about what she should and shouldn't do. Actually, she had talked to her a great deal, but she should have told her more, for Zahara is young and doesn't know anything. Before she had fully explored her thoughts about her daughter, she was reliving the days when she was pregnant with Zahara. The two feelings mixed together—those pertaining to Zahara, who was pregnant now, and those about herself when she was about to give birth to Zahara. Twin joys were born in her heart. With them came sleep, the sort that doesn't seem like sleep but is in fact the sweetest and most exquisite of sleeps.

At the same time, Herbst was lying on the couch in his study, lying there and thinking about Empress Theodora, about the women of her court, about his two friends the Weltfremdts, about Professor Bachlam and Professor Lemner, about Axelrod and his son, and various other things—a blend of thoughts that have no connection with the heart, yet grip it and induce vacant emotions. From there, he arrived at the strip of leather, the amulet Professor Wechsler had identified as a fragment of an ancient garment. From there, to the the elderly nurse who showed Sarah to him the day she was born. In the midst of all these things, something unfolded, sort of a cake on which MAZELTOV was written. Although a lot of time had passed since he had heard the tale of the waitress and the Histadrut official, Herbst realized that the reference was to the cake the café owner had sent them for their wedding.

Avraham-and-a-half belongs to the Histadrut too, but he is taller than all those officials and as innocent as a child. You can't seduce him with words, because he doesn't need anything from you. Nor does he want anything from you, having already gotten whatever he might want from another source. What is more, he doesn't need you, either. When he sat with you and listened while you talked, he was doing you a favor. Where does that firmness come from? Is it from the *kvutza?* We know several young men from the *kvutza* who don't have Avraham's quality. This firmness comes from Zahara, who gives her whole heart to Avraham. Father Manfred was suddenly alarmed. This Zahara, this baby, is a woman like other women. Not just a woman, but halfway to being a mother. And Father Manfred is halfway to being a grandfather. Were we to analyze the subject, we would find . . . I'll turn out the light now and try to sleep before other thoughts come and intrude on my sleep. However, it would be good to devote two or three moments of thought to the tragedy. Aristotle says, in the *Poetics:* One of the conditions for tragedy is . . . And most tragedians make the mistake of thinking that, if the events are tragic, that in itself constitutes tragedy.

When Herbst turned off the light, the thoughts he was afraid of took over. Though more than two years had passed since he first met Shira, he continued to think about her. His thoughts about her were different, a mass of contradictions. Love and hate, regret and longing; above all, wonder at himself for continuing to pursue her and wonder at the powerful attraction she exerted, though she was neither beautiful nor intellectual. What would be of interest to any intellectual, Shira dismisses with a disparaging twist of the mouth. Admittedly, this gesture of hers often led him to reexamine a subject and reflect further on it.

In addition to waking thoughts, there are his nighttime reveries and the succession of dreams they bring on. In one such dream, he met her one night at a concert hall. When did he meet her? Many years after they had parted and stopped seeing each other. But his love for her still filled his heart. That night she appeared to be a distinguished woman whose conversation with him was purely intellectual, and, though that tends to enhance a woman's appeal, there was between them no hint of what transpires between a man and a woman. By his calculation, she was about fifty years old at the time, but she looked perhaps thirty, certainly not more than thirty-five. One further thing, her manner was exceedingly female. This led him to fantasies he did not at first dare to entertain. And these fantasies were so powerful that he became so bold as to stroke her skin. She didn't object. On the contrary, her pleasure was evident on her face. But his joy was mixed, because her autocratic manner was replaced by submission and the desire to please.

Herbst lay in bed, thinking: It was a fatal mistake not to go back to her immediately after that first night. If I had gone back, she wouldn't have slipped through my fingers. Like a penitent who regrets his sinful actions, Herbst regretted his inaction. Again, the same question: How to explain Shira's actions? She is welcoming, but she doesn't allow real contact. Is there someone else in her life? He reviewed a series of men Shira had mentioned to him, as well as men she hadn't mentioned, whom he suspected of having relationships with Shira. That driver, for example, the son of Axelrod, the hospital clerk. Herbst was surprised at himself for not being jealous.

Herbst was not jealous. But he imagined their contact with Shira, or, to be more precise, the amount of contact she allowed them. In Herbst's imagination, this took many forms, arousing his heart to the point of pain.

— 17 —

Zahara left, and Tamara arrived. Before Henrietta had time to read about the places Tamara had visited in Greece, she was back to tell about them. If not for his interest in order, Manfred could have left the Baedeker in Sacharson's hands, especially since another book on Greece now occupied its space on the shelf. Mother and Father listen to Tamara's tales of her travels in Greece. He suppresses his laughter, and she laughs uncontrollably. Tamara herself is silent, like those Greek goddesses in the professor's pictures whose eloquent silence is so amazing. In truth, Tamara has not a trace of the sublime beauty bestowed on Greek goddesses, but, when she wants to, she can make herself look like one of them. If you examine the contours of her face, you find nothing sublime there; on the contrary, there are traces of vulgarity. You wonder: Can this face transform itself into that one? You say to her, "Please, Tamara, just how do you do that?" And there she is, standing before you like one of those goddesses. She looks serene, tranquil, impassive; yet whoever sees her is unsettled. Even British officers are willing to change their ways for Miss Tamara. But she no longer frequents their haunts.

As soon as Tamara was back in Jerusalem, she went back to work. She spends part of the day and part of the night with tubercular girls in the Mekor Hayim neighborhood, teaching them writing and language. It is her fervent wish that the girls learn to speak Hebrew, rather than pollute the air of the Land of Israel with seventy tongues, so she stays with them until midnight and comes home even later. Henrietta doesn't worry about her safety, because Tamara is always accompanied by a troop of young men. Further, Tamara is a strong and valiant young woman, and no one would dare to offend her. When she was a child and a teacher kissed her on the mouth for knowing the Isaiah chapter by heart, she reached out and slapped his face in front of the whole class. They say that, because of her, several elderly teachers who had been in the habit of rewarding female pupils with kisses were forced to give up the practice. So Henrietta doesn't worry about what might happen to her daughter. But Manfred worries about his daughter all the time. Even a brigade of young men can't intercept a bullet fired from a distance. All in all, Herbst isn't pleased by Tamara's presence in Jerusalem. Not only is there no chance that she'll find a paid teaching job in Jerusalem, all the jobs having been taken by old hens who sit on them and never let go, but a new factor adds to his displeasure. Rumors are beginning to circulate about a band of young men who are not content to let Arabs kill Jews at will. Jerusalem, a city populated by Arabs and Jews, is a vulnerable spot, where trouble is likely to begin, and an unemployed young girl is particularly vulnerable. Being unemployed, she is especially likely to join this embittered group that defies the policy of self-restraint. Seeing this cheerful young girl, who regards the entire universe as something to laugh at, anyone would conclude that political concerns are remote from her mind. Nonetheless, there is reason to worry; if not because of her, then because of her friends. On the face of it, they are all charming and uncomplicated—so much so that they appear to be spiritually defective, mentally retarded, cognitively limited. Even those who appreciate their primitive quality are sometimes concerned that it may be excessive, certainly when compared with their peers in Europe, who, at the same age, are thoroughly mature. Even their peers in Eastern Europe, who study in yeshivas or one-room schools, seem to surpass them. Academically, this is what we would expect. But it is true in emotional terms as well. Still, the children of this country sometimes startle us with their words, and we have learned from experience that, in our time, words are the precursors of action. Until yesterday, we sneered at grandiose words. Yesterday, we were alarmed and frightened by the actions that followed on these words. Today, our lives are at risk. Since fathers don't have the power to influence their daughters, Herbst takes his mind off Tamara and concerns himself with others. Man doesn't control his thoughts, saying to some, "Come," to others, "Go." But, in the case of Herbst and Tamara, it's different. Herbst puts his daughter out of mind and turns his thoughts to others. Who are these others? Since people are in the habit of saying "by chance," I will also say "by chance." By chance, he is thinking of Anita Brik.

Since the day Herbst visited Anita Brik, he has noticed that his mind sometimes wanders in realms that were previously alien to him. True, the first time he saw her, in the restaurant, when she gave him paper on which to write to his daughters and inform them of their sister's birth, he gave some thought to the factors that had led such a girl to

leave her home and come to the Land of Israel, where she worked as
a waitress. When he found her in a dingy room, on a sickbed, his soul
was stirred by her plight, by the plight of German Jews, whose glory
was stripped away, who were now displaced and forced to hire themselves out for a crust of bread. When the Jews of Germany were first
beset by trouble, when they began to be oppressed and lose their
footing, all of Israel was alarmed and asked, "Can it be that the world
will stand by in silence?" The world was silent, as it had been silent
in the face of Jewish misfortune in Russia and other countries. What
is more, the world granted the villains recognition, making it possible
for them to thrive. The Jewish community in Germany lamented and
cried out. What did the Jews in other countries do? They went about
their business and said, "A regime such as Hitler's cannot possibly last."
It lasted. Seeing its increasingly disastrous effects, they tried to reassure
themselves, saying, "New conditions will arise that it will be possible
to live with." The new conditions were more difficult than the previous
ones. They were followed by conditions cruel and severe beyond what
could be grasped or imagined. Yet most Jews still sat tight, reassuring
themselves, saying, "When were we ever without trouble, and when
was Israel unable to withstand it?" But whoever could, sought refuge
beyond the range of the disaster, waiting for its force to be spent, which
is to say, they took flight, intending to return. The Jewish dispersion
in Germany dispersed itself to many countries. Some went up to the
Land of Israel, bringing with them remnants of their wealth, and some
of these were lucky, in that their money was not lost by benefactors
who invited them to invest in flimsy ventures. This is a story that
should be told. Many immigrants from Germany were innocent about
the people in the Land of Israel, trusting them much as brothers would
trust one another. But these brothers were worse than enemies, involving them in enterprises that were shady, dubious, or nonexistent. In
some cases, this was done in all innocence by individuals who had faith
in their business acumen and believed that, given some capital, they
could make a profit for themselves as well as for the investors. Others
acted with less conviction, on the chance that they might succeed; and,
if not, what was there to lose, since the money wasn't theirs? Still others
acted deliberately—to get their hands on other people's money. When
the good Lord wants to degrade someone, not only does He strike out
through some cruel and vile Gentile, but He degrades him through his
own people as well. This was demonstrated in the case of the German
refugees and, some years earlier, in that of refugees from Russia, who
escaped the pogroms and came to the Land of Israel. Here, they were
beset by unscrupulous individuals who took their money deceitfully,

advising them to buy land and, when they were about to buy it, persuading the Arab landowners to raise the price, because, in the meanwhile, they had found other buyers who offered more. Though one shouldn't mix misfortunes, I must note, in this context, that the people of Israel, forgetting how these swindlers had behaved, began to regard some of them as builders of the *yishuv*. Although their ill-gotten fortunes, which were left to the next generation, stemmed from an ignoble source, their children saw how much the *yishuv* valued and respected them, and did what they could to have them proclaimed founding fathers.

Dr. Manfred Herbst, as we know, had the good fortune to come to the country a few years earlier. He had the good fortune to arrive with his books and belongings, and to find a respected position that enabled him to support himself and his family, and to continue to devote himself to scholarship in the field he had chosen. Professor Neu had done well to recommend that he be appointed a lecturer, for Herbst was well suited to the job. And if he still hasn't been appointed a professor, this is due to the laziness of the university trustees, who never bother to open their eyes and see who he is. It is also Herbst's fault for not pulling strings.

When refugees began to arrive from Germany, among them several of his acquaintances, Herbst sought them out as best he could, insofar as his schedule allowed, for a proper schedule determines one's capacity to work, and, what is more, a proper schedule determines the quality of everything a man produces. There is a big difference between work undertaken at intervals and work that is uninterrupted. This is evident in the product. The one is flawed by gaps and excesses; the other is correct and thorough. There are famous professors in the great European universities who go to the library between lectures, watching the clock as they browse for a given number of minutes. In the end, they too produce books. Herbst was convinced from the start that such books, which he called "watched books," do not amount to anything. Academic work requires concentration, which brooks neither interruption nor distraction. I will repeat what I said: Herbst, knowing that his work requires concentration and order, doesn't devote much time to immigrants from Germany, though he fulfills his obligations. He does as much as a man such as himself can do. What he does may be minimal; in any case, his acquaintances ask no more of him. People from Germany are not accustomed to being needy. Whatever help is offered they consider extraordinary, and are grateful for what they get. Herbst's wife tends to overdo. Without regard for herself, she would take immigrants into her home and provide them with food and drink. She would often sacrifice her own routines, and, when a guest arrived at mealtime, she would insist that he sit at the table and eat. She puts up countless newcomers in her home and searches for apartments with them, rather than let them fall into the hands of agents who wear out their customers and then charge for the wear and tear. All this was in addition to Henrietta's efforts on behalf of relatives she was trying to deliver from their suffering in Germany. Had it not been for those heartless officials in the immigration office, several members of her family would have been with us here. The country would have benefited from their presence, since most of them were intellectuals, active individuals who did useful work in Germany. In fact, many German Gentiles were whispering among themselves, "Too bad that these good people were relieved of their jobs." When Henrietta sees the sloppiness of officials in this country, her heart begins to cry out: If this or that relative of mine were here, he would teach them not to be idle; he would teach them that clerks were not invented to waste the public's time. The plight of his brethren in Germany did not disrupt Dr. Herbst's routines. I don't mean to suggest that a photostat of some Byzantine document or the discovery of some trivial Byzantine practice was more important to him than the fate of his brethren. Nonetheless, he gave more thought to Byzantium than to Israel. He was certainly pained by the plight of his relatives, acquaintances, and fellow scholars who lost their positions, yet these heartfelt sentiments did not alter his preoccupations. The day he saw Anita Brik lying on a broken bed in a dingy room and reaching out for the flowers Shira brought her, he was suddenly confronted with an embodiment of the calamity. Herbst was not one of those who delude themselves with the thought that they can change anything. He therefore turned from what he couldn't do anything about to something he could affect: his academic pursuits, his book. Between chapters, he filled his notebook with phrases and snatches of dialogue for the tragedy he planned to write. Herbst was planning to write a great tragedy about Antonia, woman of the court, and Yohanan the nobleman, which I mentioned earlier in this book.

Herbst took comfort in the tragedy, especially on sleepless nights when he was unable to read—because of ambivalence, because of emotional discord, because the text seemed to dissolve before he could grasp it—and drugs no longer brought sleep. He lay in bed picturing the lives of Antonia and Yohanan, of everyone else close to them in time and place, pondering, considering, plotting, arranging for them to meet. At times, it was all so sharp and clear that it could be written down and put in a book. Whether or not you believe it, Herbst sometimes saw

the actual image of an image. Whether or not you believe it, he sometimes felt the tiniest trace of what a poet feels when he sees the character
he has fashioned in his mind begin to take on flesh and blood. However,
as joy is tinged with sadness in all of life's pursuits, Herbst's joy was
tinged with sadness too, on his own account and on account of an
imaginary character he had added to the tragedy, though the character
was neither necessary to the tragedy nor validated by history. Who is
it that Herbst invented from his imagination? A slave he called
Basileios, whose soul was bound to his mistress and who suffered his
love in silence. Needless to say, his mistress was unaware of this; nor
did it ever occur to her that a slave would dare to covet her, for such
a sentiment on the part of a slave would be offensive to his mistress. It
was Schiller's mistake, in his play about Mary Stuart, to allow young
Mortimer to fall in love with her. Schiller, who knew only German
duchesses and princesses, was misguided. Had he known a real queen,
he would never have made such an error. In this connection, Herbst
applauded the Scandinavian mythmakers who tell about a Norwegian
queen who had several kings tortured and put to death for daring to
seek her hand in marriage.

Let me return to Basileios clarifying and explaining how he interfered with Herbst's happiness. Herbst didn't know what to do with this
slave who had sprung out of his imagination, much to his delight. He
didn't know what to do with him, yet he didn't want to give him up,
because, of all the characters in the tragedy, he alone was his creation.
And, having created him without knowing what to do with him, he
became a bother—so much so that Herbst was in despair and considered abandoning the tragedy altogether. After some manipulation,
Herbst was able to deal with Basileios in such a way that his absence
would not be a problem; that is, he found a way to account for his
sudden disappearance.

I will reveal what he did and where he hid him. He made him a leper
and hid him in a leper colony. Actually, in terms of the tragedy, this
was a mistake, because Herbst was afraid to immerse himself in that
disease, and explore it, to picture various aspects of leprosy, such as how
do lepers relate to each other or how they function in conjugal terms.
But, unless the mind becomes immersed in a subject, that subject remains vague. This is especially true in the realms of poetry and imagination, which require that the soul expand, and this expansion occurs only
if two souls merge, giving life to a new soul, which the Creator deems
worthy and endows with breath, as much breath as it can hold. Herbst
didn't achieve this, because he didn't immerse his mind in the subject,
for he was sensitive and found it difficult to tolerate infected blood.

Despite the fact that he had been knee-deep in blood and pus when he fought for Germany in the last war, now that he was Jerusalem, in peacetime, he avoided the whiff of a whiff of blood, the trace of a trace of pus—even more so leprosy, whose very name arouses metaphysical terror. So how was he to immerse his mind in a man with leprosy? I won't be so ridiculous as to suggest that Herbst was afraid the leper would appear and display his leprous state. Nevertheless, he resisted thinking about him.

Most of all, Herbst was terrified of moving. Since the night he had heard gunfire at first hand, close to his ear, he recognized, understood, knew that he should move. But moving a household with three thousand books—apart from journals, offprints, and pamphlets—would involve giving up work for weeks, months, a year, even longer. Such an interruption, at a time when he was deeply involved in his work, would be emotional suicide.

I said three thousand books, but it's not necessarily so, because books are sometimes counted by title, sometimes by volume. And sometimes, as a sign of affection, one includes a pamphlet or a booklet. So don't be surprised if, in another context, I cite another figure in accounting for Herbst's books.

His terror of moving led him to think about transporting the books from one apartment to another and arranging them in a new place, for he really must leave this apartment in Baka, where he has lived since he arrived in Jerusalem. Books that stand on shelves for many years are sedentary citizens, who prefer order and permanence to wandering. Even if they are sometimes willing to step out, to visit in another home, they have no desire to leave their place forever. True, years ago they were accustomed to wandering, but they were young then and few in number. Some of Manfred Herbst's books remember being able to make do with two planks hung from four tightly woven wires on the wall opposite his bed. How charming Manfred was in those days. He was extremely appealing, with his chestnut hair, a lively devil who fingered those books constantly, covering them in colorful paper and showing them all manner of affection. He spread silver paper over the planks and fastened the paper with tacks that gleamed like gold. Some of the books are not very old, but their contents are ancient. They like to recall how and when they were acquired by Manfred. It happened at Manfred's bar mitzvah. Some of his friends and relations, knowing there was nothing he cherished so much as books, brought them as gifts. How dear they are to Manfred. Though he has read them many times and actually knows some of them by heart, he still treats them graciously. Other books here are also not very old, but their discourse is like that of an aged relative. Were it not for the fact that they are scholarly books, which don't deal in legend, they would have recounted the number of nights he did without sleep on their behalf, struggling to uncover their secrets, for the deep secrets they contain are disclosed only through great effort. There are still other books, four, five, six generations old, though they have been with Dr. Herbst not longer than half a generation. Although the authors of some of these volumes were mortal enemies, they live together in peace on Herbst's shelf, clinging to each other in filial harmony, content with their situation, with the dim green light shining on them from the windows and garden, and with little Firadeus, who brushes them with a soft towel and sweeps off their dust. They don't complain about the odd smell Dr. Herbst inflicts with a gadget that breathes smoke, to which they are unaccustomed. And now, my good people, lovers of peace, enemies of war, isn't it criminal to uproot such books and crowd them into a tight city apartment? True, Henrietta is capable and conscientious, guided by good taste and intelligence, but her youthful vigor has been spent. Much as she would try to make the new apartment attractive, it wouldn't be like this one. Surely not for the books.

Now let's look at the state of the books in the homes of Herbst's friends who live in town and in the new neighborhoods, beginning with those of Julian Weltfremdt. Julian Weltfremdt arrived in Jerusalem laden with books. He spent half the money he brought with him on import taxes, brokers, and porters; the other half, on shelves and the construction of a book shed, since there wasn't enough space in his apartment. He didn't arrive in proper style; he shipped his possessions, as well as his wife Mimi's piano, in assorted crates. His books had been scattered in the towns and cities of Germany, for he had wandered from place to place, and, wherever he settled, he left some of his belongings and some of his books, until he arrived in the Land of Israel, where everything came together. When he went up to Jerusalem, he brought all his books along and built bookcases for them, as well as simple shelves. The books that were in the house, he placed in bookcases; those in the shed, he placed on simple shelves. He was so busy arranging his books that he didn't concern himself with his livelihood, assuming that whoever had any use for someone such as him would take the trouble to find him. But those who might have had use for him didn't bother to look, settling for those who took the trouble to make themselves available. Mimi shopped on credit, while Julian occupied himself with his books, climbing up and down the ladder, taking out a book, putting it back, cursing and deploring the villainy of inanimate objects, for the books he was looking for eluded his fingers, while the ones he had no interest in jumped into his hand. He kept running between the house and the shed, climbing up the ladder and down again. Once the books were arranged by subject and ordered in terms of his needs, he gave some thought to a job. What he had in mind was to teach at the university, but those jobs were already taken. What was true of the university was true of all the other educational institutions. When he agreed, for the time being, to consider a position in a secondary school, someone else had preceded him. At first, he laughed at the educational administrators for not knowing what sort of teachers the younger generation needed. Then he began cursing them, as well as the teachers who had taken all the jobs—above all, his relative Ernst Weltfremdt, who didn't lift a finger on his behalf, out of snobbishness masked by a cloak of self-righteousness. Be that as it may, I didn't mean to discuss Julian Weltfremdt; I meant to discuss matters that pertain to books.

And so, Julian Weltfremdt's extensive collection of books was in good order. Those that were not in frequent use were put in the shed in his yard; those used more often stood upright in bookcases in his house. Consequently, he spent his days running from the house to the yard, from the yard to the house, sometimes to get a book, sometimes to catch a mouse, sometimes to dispose of a mouse stuck in the trap. It would have been a good idea to keep a cat in the shed. Not only did he fail to get a cat, he chased cats from the premises, because Mimi used to leave the milk and the meat on the table while she was at the piano. The cats would take over, leaving only scraps. He therefore decided to do without a cat and trap the mice instead. Mousetraps are more hazardous than mice. For example, when he found a mouse in the trap and tried to remove it, the spring would snap on his finger. And when he found a live mouse in the trap, he didn't know what to do with it. He couldn't just kill it, because he was squeamish; he couldn't burn it alive, because that would have been too cruel.

In addition to the hazard of mice, there was the hazard of the elements. A sweltering summer that damaged the books was followed by a snowy winter. Snow fell, covering the houses. Their upper halves were in snow accumulated from below, the lower halves in snow falling from above. All the roads were covered with snow. No earth was to be seen, and nowhere could one find solid footing. Business was at a standstill. One could not even find a crust of bread for a child. But this is not what I want to tell. I want to tell the story of the books and the snow. Roofs began to sag under the weight of snow piled on top of them, while snow piling up from below weakened the substructures. The snow was accompanied by a violent storm that uprooted trees and damaged houses. When the snow stopped falling and the storm subsided, people began to venture outside. Julian Weltfremdt went out to his yard and found that his shed was crumbling. Heavy branches had been torn from the trees, and entire trees were wrenched from their places and scattered all over the shed, as well as along the path leading to it. Here and there, the snows were melting, producing a stream of water that gushed into the yard. Melting snow dripped onto the shed from above, so the entire space was water upon water. Julian Weltfremdt didn't hesitate. Blazing a trail through the snow, puddles, and broken branches, he arrived at his shed, only to find himself knee-deep in water. His wife was standing in front of the house, shouting, "Julian, Julian, come back before you get sick, before you catch your death of a cold." He gave no thought to his own welfare or to her warnings. He was determined to save his books. He saved what he saved, and what he didn't save didn't get saved. Meanwhile, Mimi caught a cold, as well as an ear infection, from standing outside without warm clothes. But I don't mean to tell about Mimi now; I mean to tell about books. After the destruction of the shed, Julian Weltfremdt began to console himself with the books in the house. One day he took a book off the uppermost shelf and discovered that it was damp. This was true of a second, third, and fourth book, and so on, down the row. Not only that row, but most of the books on the upper shelves of the bookcases in his house were steeped in water. He took them down and put them out to air. He assured himself, every so often, that they would recover and, just as often, plunged into despair over his books and himself—to think that they could do this to him, after all his efforts on their behalf. In the end, some of them had to be rebound. You know, of course, how bookbinders are: not only do they do an inadequate job, but they leave out pages and expect to be rewarded for their vandalism. And how was he to pay? From the paltry funds sent by his wife's family. This is the tale of some of Julian Weltfremdt's books and their trial by water. What about his good books, those that weren't damaged? They escaped destruction but didn't remain in his hands. Though they withstood the cruelty of the elements, they did not withstand human cruelty. Julian Weltfremdt didn't find a job and was forced to sell some of his books. After selling some of his possessions when his daughter took sick because of the drafty apartment, he had to sell the remainder in order to get food for her and pay her medical bills. His relative Professor Ernst Weltfremdt often boasted that he paid for the grave and burial expenses, but the doctors' fees and medications were paid for by Julian. Things came to such a pass that, even while he was writing his popular pamphlet (*The Seventeen Primary Factors Leading Us to Unequivocally Oppose the Ap-*

pointment of Master Plato of Greece to the Position of Lecturer in Philoso-
phy at Any University, Particularly One in Germany), when he wished
to refer to some of the books he called "professors' books," he had to
quote from memory. Needless to say, he made some errors, which
provided a pretext for the charge that his work was unscholarly.

Having become so involved in Julian Weltfremdt's books, I will be
brief about those of Dr. Taglicht.

As is often the case with bachelors, Taglicht was a subtenant in the
home of a gentleman who rented out one of his four rooms for the price
of the entire apartment. Since he had only one room, he couldn't collect
very many books. He, too, had come to Jerusalem laden with books.
The rare ones were borrowed by collectors, who never returned them,
the ordinary ones were borrowed by ordinary people, who didn't
return them either. Taglicht often commented about this. "Why should
I be upset? It's enough that others are upset about this sort of thing."
Taglicht's library is now limited to what fits on his windowsill.

According to the Gemara, books and bread were bound together
when they descended from heaven. As for Taglicht, he often had to
forgo his loaf to buy a book. Let me report a delightful exchange
Taglicht liked to relate. "When I lived in Berlin, I often used to visit
Shestov's father, a sick old man. Once, the old man saw I was in distress.
He asked me, 'What's the trouble?' I told him, 'Every month my
landlady demands a rent increase.' The old man said, 'That's because
of all the books you collect. She sees you laden with books and thinks
to herself: Such a person is not likely to move, so I might as well raise
the rent. It would be costly to move, so you choose to pay more rather
than leave. But a young man should first build his resources, then send
a representative to acquire the books he needs—or thinks he needs.' "
Taglicht ignored the advice of the philosopher's father. Not only did
he starve himself because of his books, but in the end they were taken
from him.

It's only two or three steps from Taglicht's house to Lemner's. He
has many bookcases filled with books. Books are stacked inside the
bookcases as well as on the top of them. These books are not friendly
to one another or even to themselves; that is to say, one volume of a
set might be on one shelf, another on top of the bookcase, another who
knows where. If a set contains a total of four or five volumes, it is
doubtful that Lemner has them all. Lemner is an elegant and amiable
person, and, since he is more concerned with others than with himself,
he tends to wear soiled and faded clothes at home and to dress more
attractively when he is out. His books' behavior on their shelves is like
his behavior at home. They are soiled and faded. Spiders spin webs on

them; some have become a cemetery for flies and bugs. If he needs a book, either he can't find it, or, being too lazy to brush off the dust and insect remains, he borrows it from the National Library. So why does he keep buying more? To occupy himself with something. Some people choose a social cause or some similar enterprise. Professor Lemner is engaged in the acquisition of books. Anyway, books are related to a professor's occupation. If his wife hadn't restrained him, he would have bought every book he was offered.

I might as well skip Professor Bachlam's books. He was so busy writing his own that he didn't have time to collect other people's books. Nonetheless, he owned a great many volumes. If you wonder about them, look in the books he wrote and you'll see them in his references. Surely his books also included opinions from books he had merely borrowed, but that doesn't change anything.

I have yet to tell about the bookcases in the homes of Professor Wechsler and Professor Ernst Weltfremdt. Having begun with one of the Weltfremdts, I'll conclude with the other. But first I'll describe Professor Wechsler's books. Actually, they are not really books, but folder upon folder filled with newspaper clippings about his discoveries and interviews with journalists. No professor in Jerusalem is as busy as he is, and no one keeps others as busy as he does. All of Jerusalem's thirteen bookbinders are employed by him, making portfolios to contain the clippings that praise him and his work on amulets. Those who don't envy Professor Wechsler regard the praise he receives as praise for the university, and praise for the university is praise for the entire community of Israel.

Now let's have a look at Professor Weltfremdt's books. There is no difference between Ernst Weltfremdt's library and the libraries of most professors who marry rich women with large dowries that provide the means to buy many books in handsome bindings and construct handsome shelves for them. His bookcases have two sections: one for patrologists, the other for Hellenists, since he was first a lecturer in patristics and then in Hellenistics. In addition, on the corner shelves there are quite a few Hebrew books acquired here in Jerusalem.

I will now add a few words about other book collections in Jerusalem. A city of many scholars will have many bibliophiles. There are many scholars in Jerusalem who deprive themselves of a crust of bread in order to buy a book, whose passion for books is so great that they ignore their children and don't bother about their education. In the former category are those who sell a book when their wives demand money for Shabbat provisions; in the latter category there are those who take no notice, even when members of their household are expiring from hunger. In the end, when they die, book dealers and collectors converge to buy from the orphans, who, not having been educated by their father, are unaware of the value of the books and sell them for a paltry sum.

Now, to get back to Herbst's books. They are not arranged on handsome shelves, like Ernst Weltfremdt's books, and are not as numerous as Bachlam's and Lemner's; nor does he have portfolios such as Wechsler's. For the most part, they are plainly bound, resting in bookcases constructed from the crates in which they were shipped from abroad. But the grace that prevails in his library is not to be found in the library of any other scholar in Jerusalem. Henrietta's good taste had left its imprint on the arrangement of the books, and the vaulted ceiling added charm to the room. It is easy to picture how sad Herbst was when he thought it would be necessary to move and house his books in the skimpy rooms one finds in those new neighborhoods.

I now mean to get back to the tragedy, and I will try to prove how worthwhile the tragedy was to Herbst. For years Herbst had been working out of habit, amassing notes and quotations without involving his emotions. Not so with the tragedy. Although his imagination proved inadequate, the tragedy shook the very foundations of his soul. What he had produced so far didn't amount to very much, but he had faith in the future, that something would emerge, turning it into a tragedy. That is to say, the actions would unfold, justifying themselves, not only in terms of their own inevitability, but in terms of the intense power inherent in them from the beginning.

When a bookish person is about to create a book, he looks at other books to see how they were written. Herbst, who was reared on German poetry, went back and reread it. He was familiar with some of the poets from childhood; others, he had read as an adult. Of course, you know the power of good books: one never emerges from them empty-handed. Whenever you open such a book, you find something in it that you hadn't noticed before. Even if you have read it many times, even if you know it by heart, when you go back to it you find a new message. Whether or not it is the one intended by the author, it is embedded in the text.

I'll now turn to another matter. Herbst was aware that Germany was afflicted with a big dose of anti-Semitism, so that, of all the Hebrew words fixed in the tongues of German Jews, the word *rishus*, meaning "viciousness," was most widespread. But he never considered the change in its meaning, for now one says *rishus* to warn Jews not to behave in this or that manner, so as not to provoke Germans to be vicious, that is, to behave badly toward Jews.

Now back to my original subject. When Herbst went back to those books, he realized that even the finest of Germany's lyricists did not eschew such viciousness, that they celebrated and transformed it into a virtue, giving their approval to all manner of cruelty toward Jews. In the course of this, they distorted words, twisted the straight, perverted justice. But truth is so great that it is evident even in a lie. They meant to portray the Jew as a paradigm of evil, and, as a result, all the evil charges with which they disparaged Jews were like the skin of a garlic—of no consequence compared to the evil of the Germans. Furthermore, the very words with which they disparaged Jews were used to praise Germans. It is worth mentioning here that many slanderous and vicious books were given to Herbst by Jews for his bar mitzvah. The Jewish spirit was so totally dominated by Germany that Jews didn't realize how much hatred permeated those books. But what the Jews didn't recognize was recognized by the Germans, who learned what they learned. Even Herbst was now learning what he hadn't learned before, and he began to be aware of Germany's behavior toward Jews, especially toward his family and friends, who were forced to flee and to cast about among the nations, their frenzied souls adrift between borders. They were not allowed to live in one country; they were forbidden to enter another. Between countries, they perished. Once again, I must repeat what we well know. You sit at breakfast, open the newspaper, and read about a scholar who took poison or a poet who hung himself from a tree in the woods. International figures—about whom one boasts, "I was privileged to know So-and-so"—are persecuted by border guards, only to end their lives with a bullet or by jumping from a high place and being crushed. Once in several generations, the good Lord is generous to His creatures, sending into this lowly world a rare soul who glorifies it with his deeds, only to be intercepted by some authority and destroyed. Whenever Herbst sees two or three lines in the newspaper about a scholar who committed suicide or a poet who took his own life, if it was someone he knew and corresponded with, he would take out the letters and read them, then tie them with a string and put them in a special place. There are more and more such bundles. I hope I am wrong, but there seem to be more letters from the dead who have already died than from the living who are still alive.

From the dead to the living. Herbst puts down the letters of the dead. His mind turns to those who still are hovering between the living and

the dead, and from there to those who have found a temporary haven
in the Land of Israel. Having failed to grasp that the doors of Germany
were closed to Jews forever and ever, and that they would never return
to Germany, they reassured themselves, maintaining that the ignomini-
ous regime would be overturned and the exiles would return to hear
the rustle of Germany's forests and the roar of her waters once again,
delighting in the culture they had helped create. For the moment, they
are here temporarily—as foreigners, strangers, guests, sojourners—
until the anticipated day when Germany's cultural elite roots out the
heinous government and the exiled children come home. Many were
already helped by Henrietta, and just as many are being helped by her
now. Even Dr. Krautmeir, who is the busiest doctor in Jerusalem, was
helped by Henrietta. If not for Henrietta, she would have been lost. She
came here empty-handed and unknown; she had never had any contact
with Jews and had associated only with Germans all her life. One day,
soon after she arrived, she left her hotel, pondering to herself: How
long can I tolerate this? Henrietta appeared, and they recognized each
other, having lived on the same street in Charlottenburg and taken the
bus together regularly. Though in all those years they hadn't talked to
one another, when they met again here in the Land of Israel, they
considered each other a friend. Krautmeir said to Henrietta, "We lived
in Charlottenburg for almost a whole generation and never engaged in
the most casual conversation, and now I consider you a childhood
friend." Henrietta invited her over, provided her with room and board
in her home, and found her work with an elderly doctor who needed
an assistant. Krautmeir took an apartment, paid the import tax due on
her furnishings, and began adjusting to life in Jerusalem. After a while
she bought the old man's practice and, since most of the patients were
by now accustomed to her, they continued to come. She acquired some
new patients too: young women in trouble as a result of their involvement with British soldiers, who made contact with the lady doctor,
knowing she would see them through.

As the number of immigrants grew, Henrietta could no longer deal
with all of them, and already there were those who didn't know Mrs.
Herbst at all, as well as those who knew her but didn't have the
opportunity to enjoy her hospitality. Anita Brik, for example. Why do
I mention Anita Brik? Because Manfred believed that, had Henrietta
invited Anita Brik, Anita would have been helpful to her. Henrietta
complained that work was piling up that neither she nor Firadeus had
the time to do. If Anita Brik had been in the house with them, she could
have been helpful to him too, copying texts. Often, he would stop in
the middle and say, "I'll copy it tomorrow"; then, "day after tomor-

row." And sometimes he would think to himself: Is it really necessary for me to sit and copy? Couldn't I just mark the passage and give it to someone else to copy for me, as many renowned and prominent scholars do? Some of them don't even read through a text before instructing a secretary or assistant to seek out certain material, which they locate in books and copy out, presenting the finished product to their employer. It wasn't arrogance that made Herbst think he deserved to have others do his work, but fatigue and weariness.

Remembering Anita Brik, the idea that she might be helpful to him, and that he might help her too, was appealing. Several mounds of books cluttered his desk, and he didn't get to copy what he needed from them, so let her come and copy. Most of all, he needed help with books he sometimes borrowed from Ernst Weltfremdt. Weltfremdt was a fussy person who lent books only to those who promised to return them in three weeks, saying, "If I leave my books with you indefinitely, you'll put off reading them from day to day and from week to week, and, in the end, you won't even glance at them. That won't be the case if I limit the time, forcing you to read, find, and copy what you need." In the past, it was simple for Manfred to say, "Henrietta, invite such-and-such a young woman." Now it is hard for him to mention any woman to Henrietta. He even hesitates to mention Lisbet Neu, Professor Neu's relative, to Henrietta, despite all the favors Neu had done for him. He had been a student of his and become a lecturer through his efforts, and Neu would surely be consulted about his promotion. All this notwithstanding, not only does he not invite Neu's relative to his home, but he avoids mentioning her name. That woman—that Shira—has made him tongue-tied.

— 18 —

Now that I have mentioned Shira, I will get back to Shira, who is the core of the book *Shira,* and whatever doesn't pertain to Shira doesn't pertain to the story. Again, Herbst's thoughts were of Shira; some to her credit, others to her discredit. Herbst was thinking: If only Shira would say, "Go away and let me be." Herbst was assuming that if Shira were to say "Scram," he would take off and leave her. But Shira says no such thing and he, therefore, continues to come. Whenever he comes, she receives him warmly, so that, if we didn't know what we know, we would imagine she was sitting and waiting for him. Herbst, seeing he is welcome, reaches out to caress her. Shira takes his hand and bends his fingers, like a hunter who catches a bird and clips its wings to keep it from flying. Herbst nurses his fingers and wonders: What does she have in mind? Her face is welcoming; her hands are rejecting. He takes a chair and sits down, or he paces around the room. He takes a cigarette and fills the room with smoke, his face registering rage. Shira is surrounded by clouds of smoke, enveloped by them. She too takes a cigarette, smoking and talking from within the clouds of smoke, telling him everything that has happened to her since his last visit. One day, she sprained her leg. Dr. Zahzam came. She describes the examination, how his hand glided over her leg. Herbst has a dim vision of Shira's legs, which he recalls in all their intense loveliness as soon as they are mentioned. Herbst is perplexed: Why is Shira telling me about Zahzam? If she means to arouse my jealousy, I'm not the slightest bit jealous. Is it true that he's not jealous? Yes and no. In Shira's case, he's not jealous; in other cases, he is. He once ran into Lisbet Neu and saw that the hairs above her lip had been removed. He was upset, as if she had taken something away from him. What did she take away? Was he expecting to kiss her lips? His entire relationship with her was quite straightforward. But any knowledgeable person knows—and it is true—that a woman who does such a thing does it because of a man. Which is to say that there is a man who is so close to her that he can say, "Those hairs are unbecoming," or he may have said, "You would look better without them." And, hearing this, she has the hair removed.

Back to Shira. Shira's behavior is consistent. She invites and rejects, rejects and invites. Once, he sat her on his lap. Though she seemed not to mind, she suddenly slipped down and fled. Herbst repeats the same question: If she means to reject me, why is she so inviting? If she means to be inviting, why the rejection? When he pressed her, she said to him, "I don't want to upset your wife; I have nothing against your wife." If that's the reason, then why was she so inviting to begin with? When he examines the situation, he sees that, even when she is inviting, there are limits.

As it happened, the thought occurred to him that Shira might be sick—that she was surely sick and was afraid he would catch her disease, which was why she had mentioned his wife, saying, "I have nothing against her and I don't want to upset her." Because, if she did have something against her, she wouldn't have worried about infecting her with a disease that could be transmitted to her through him. This would explain why she had been at first inviting and then rejecting. As long as she was healthy, she welcomed him; when she realized she was sick, she began to reject him. In that case, he ought to have been grateful for the rejection. Not only was he ungrateful, he resented the fact that she rejected him. But Shira was different from him. Shira was in good control, imposing her will on his. Herbst took leave of Shira, sad and distressed—distressed by the rejection, and sad that he might already have contracted her disease. If he had the disease, then he was sick; if he was sick, he needed to be careful not to kiss his wife and daughters; above all, not to kiss Sarah, because children are more vulnerable to illness than adults.

A man's imagination generates his actions. Herbst pictured his wife and daughters with an illness the doctors could not identify. Only Herbst knows the source of their malady, and he doesn't disclose it to the doctors. They are in the throes of disease, all three of them. He goes from bed to bed in silence. It is a grave disease, all the more so because the doctors don't recognize it, and, until they recognize it, they don't know how to treat it. Picture this: There is one person in the world who could open his mouth and reveal the nature of the illness so the doctors could find a cure, but he is so cruel to his wife and daughters that he ignores their pain and refuses to tell the doctors anything. Who is that person? He is that woman's husband and the father of those girls.

Angry and confused, Herbst went home, afraid he would find his wife and daughters in the throes of some painful disease. A host of afflictions, which Herbst had become aware of during the war, when he mired in blood, came back to haunt him. Recalled through the power of memory and powered by imagination, they took over. Not content with skin and flesh, the blight was everywhere, and as it expanded the body expanded too. But what he witnessed during the war was inflicted by enemies, whereas now his wife and two daughters were afflicted through him. Zahara was also afflicted. You might think she was spared because she lived elsewhere, but she was exposed when she came to Jerusalem.

Herbst despaired of salvation. What he would have liked at that point was to find refuge, to be alone and consider what to do. In truth, there were no helpful thoughts available to him, and he didn't have the power to change anything. But he must concentrate on what has happened to his wife and daughters before he loses his mind and does something crazy.

Herbst sneaked into his house like a thief in the night, compressing himself as he had never done before. He dwarfed his body, stuffed his head between his shoulders, tightened his limbs, shut his eyes, and held his breath. He would have been willing to crawl on all fours, just so no one would hear him come in.

Before he had a chance to emerge from his dwarfed state, Henrietta came toward him, holding out a letter. He stared at his wife and at the object she was handing him, wondering if the facts were already known. He was struck by two simultaneous thoughts. One was: Woe unto you. The other was: Now that the facts are known, there is nothing you can do.

Henrietta said, "A letter from Zahara." Manfred asked in a whisper, "From Zahara?" Henrietta said, "Yes, it's from Zahara." Manfred repeated his wife's words and said, "The letter—it's from Zahara." Henrietta said, "The child writes that she is about to go into the hospital." Manfred heard and thought to himself: Then Zahara is the first victim. If Zahara was stricken, then her husband was probably stricken too. Since no man is likely to stay with one wife an entire lifetime, he would probably take another woman, and Zahara would probably take another man; four people would be afflicted because of him, because he was afflicted by Shira. These thoughts about the disease were intercepted by a dismaying thought: I heard Zahara was going to the hospital, but I wasn't shocked.

Manfred was sad and depressed. He had never been so depressed. He forgot that he had the cure for his wife and daughters in his hands, but he didn't forget that he was responsible for their illness. Henrietta said, "Don't you want to read Zahara's letter? She's about to go to the hospital." Manfred peered at Henrietta and asked in a whisper, "She's going into the hospital? Why all of a sudden?" Henrietta laughed and said, "Why all of a sudden? What a question! It's not sudden. She's about to have the baby." Manfred said, "So that's it. I imagined all sorts of illnesses, but I never imagined she was going to the hospital because she was about to have a baby." At that moment, he felt neither joy nor sadness, but his heart was pounding violently and relentlessly. Henrietta saw his agitation and said, "I'll bring you something soothing to drink." Manfred said, "If you're going to bring me a drink, make it coffee." At that moment, Manfred had no desire for coffee or any other drink in the world, but, to prove to Henrietta that he hadn't changed in any way, he asked for something she wasn't eager to give. She brought him strong coffee, which provoked him. Her conversation provoked him too. Actually, she spoke only of Zahara and said nothing that could irritate a fatherly heart. But he was concerned with something else, and two simultaneous concerns are more than a mind can tolerate. Henrietta, however, was unaware of this and didn't stop talking.

Once again, day follows day. The sun shines; the moon and stars give light. The days are hot. At night, a pleasant coolness sweetens the city, treasured dew is released, grasses impart a fine fragrance, and people strive to enjoy what can be enjoyed. They leave work, come home, eat dinner, and take out chairs or a blanket, which they spread in front of the house to lie on. Before they have a chance to settle down, a curfew is announced, and they go back inside, annoyed at themselves and their entire household, only to be startled by the sound of gunfire, far away or nearby. There are two aspects to the curfew: it locks in and releases. Jews are locked in, forbidden to leave home; triggers are released, spewing rounds of terror and death. If this puzzles you, here's another puzzle: these deadly rounds land wherever the people are.

The days are orderly, as is Dr. Herbst's household. But now, instead of writing often to her relatives in Germany and those who left Germany and were dispersed throughout the world, Henrietta writes to her daughter Zahara. Henrietta's letters are long. Sometimes, after putting the letter in an envelope, she has to weigh it to see if it needs an additional stamp. What does she write, and what doesn't she write? She has never written such letters, nor has she ever written as often. If letter writers are rewarded, Henrietta receives her due, for Zahara loves her mother and answers every single letter. It must nonetheless be noted that the daughter's letters are not as lovely as the mother's. Don't be surprised by this: Henrietta was born when the world was peaceful, and she could concern herself with such things as elegant script, whereas Zahara was born into a world debased by war, and everything in it was debased—handwriting, language, and all the rest. In any case, her heart is steady, and so are her letters; steady and easy to read. Even Henrietta, who never studied Hebrew, reads her daughter's letters herself and considers each one a gift, every word a kiss. These are not words Henrietta would use to praise Zahara's dispatches. Joy and deep delight go beyond language, beyond the words we utter.

Another letter arrived from Zahara. The first part was written in the hospital in Afula, the rest in Ahinoam. It was scrawled on wrinkled paper in gray pencil. The lines ran into each other, and some of the letters were unclear. Out of affection for Zahara, let's take the time to read it. As we read, we'll correct the language, close an eye to the spelling, and omit buts, onlys, alsos, indeeds, becauses, and various hemmings and hawings, as well other superfluous and redundant words.

"Dear Mother, I was mistaken when I wrote to you last night that I was due to deliver. I can tell you now that, when they brought me to the hospital in Afula, it became clear that it was a gross error, so they sent me home as fast as they had brought me. When I got back, rather than let it go at that, everyone agreed that I was going to have twins. When I came back, they made a huge fuss, as if a baby had been born and left in Afula for the time being, until its brother was ready to be born. When everyone was tipsy on wine, they teased our nurse, who had taken me to the hospital, and a bunch of people came to ask her if it wasn't time for her to give birth, too, and whether they should hitch up the automobile and rush to Afula. Oh, Mother, if you had seen their grave, worried faces, you would have laughed. But she didn't allow them to tease her and presented me and Shammai, the driver, to attest that she had said right away, in no uncertain terms, that the trip was not necessary. She said she had taken me to Afula because of Avraham, who had stirred everyone up, in order to show him there was no need to worry. But, Mother, dear, the drive back from Afula was so beautiful. The moon lit up the roofs of our villages in the Emek, and, wherever we went, we saw a welcoming crowd. As our vehicle drew closer, we saw that there were no people, only trees and bushes. Oh, Mother, we saw some small animal on the road too, with red eyes that seemed to be filled with yearning. I don't know what kind of animal it was. Shammai, who is very well read, said what we saw was a rabbit. But Avraham said it was a fox. The nurse joined in the argument, but I don't remember exactly what she said. Actually, it doesn't matter. All I know is how adorable that little creature was, scurrying from left to right, from right to left. If it really was a fox, I am astonished not to have observed a single trace of slyness. The one thing I saw, as I already wrote you, was the longing in its eyes, a megadose of longing. Mother, you don't know what *mega* means. It's a very modern term. Everyone uses it a lot now, in cooking and in poetry. When writing a poem, you throw in that word. It means roughly this: a very, very large amount and a little more than that. You understand me, dearest Mama. Another thing. I kept hearing the sound of a violin. I thought it was my imagination. Then they asked me, 'Do you hear that, Zahara?' I thought I was imagining the question too, so I didn't answer until I heard the nurse, Shammai, and Avraham arguing about the sound, unable to decide what instrument it resembled. Then I knew I was really hearing music, but there was no instrument there. It was simply the night, with its magic. Now, to end this letter, I'll get back to my affairs and tell you what Avraham said: that my entire adventure is described in the Bible. That's what he said. He's in the fields now, so I can't ask him the precise words. Go to the Book of Ruth and you will find a verse more or less like this: 'I was full when I went off and just as full when the Lord brought me back.' Oh, Mother, I've written so much that I'm afraid I'm wearing you out with all this scribbling. So I'm telling you that you certainly don't have to read everything, nor do you have to show it all to Father. Just tell him that Zahara sends a megakiss, also a pat on the forehead. For you too, dear Mother, a kiss or two. No, no, no, Mother—I'm sending you megakisses. For you as well as for Father and Sarah. Your daughter, who loves you very much.

"If Avraham were here, he would send regards to all of you, so I can truly send regards in his name. Also, my regards to Firadeus and Tamara. To all of you, without exception. Zahara.

"See, Mother, when I can, I write a lot to you. So, remember, if you don't hear from me, it's because I'm busy and don't have the time or because I have to get ready to go to the hospital. Stay well. Megakisses to you, to Father, to Sarah, and to all the people I already mentioned in my letter.

"Mother, I am really worried that you won't have time to read all that I've written here. I see that I've written quite a lot. Still, I ask of you, don't let it keep you from writing what's going on at home. Write everything, including news of Jerusalem. I've heard that terrible things are happening there. That the Arabs are doing things it is hard to believe human beings are capable of. But I'm sure our neighbors in Baka wouldn't behave like those savage Arabs. They have absolutely no reason to harm us. We have always been kind to them, and you, dearest Mama, helped many of them so much that they consider you an angel. What you did for Lucy from Lebanon, for example, whose babies were always stillborn and who wanted more than anything to have a child. You found her a trustworthy doctor, and she had a little boy. Is it possible that her boy would harm us? But I have no desire to philosophize or politicize, that is to say, to get into politics. Again, megakisses. Avraham just came in from the field. He says his hands are beyond holding a pen and asks me to send his best to all of you. Which is what I am doing, absolutely, as you see. Again, a kiss. Not one but many, many kisses, as I already wrote. Once again, Z.

"Mother, I almost forgot. Tamara must be back from her trip. What does she say about Greece? She is probably full of stories. Tell her that she is (pardon the expression) something that begins with a *p*, ends with a *g*, and has an *i* in the middle. She knows. She never once wrote me even half a word. Still, I love her, though she doesn't deserve it at all, not one bit. Love and kisses again, Z."

The days are orderly. Herbst maintains his order too. Out of a sense of duty toward the university, he puts aside the woman of the court and the nobleman Yohanan, to devote himself to his students. He confers

with them and provides them with material for their papers. He reaches
into his box of notes, takes out a handful, and offers to share them. He
is generous and ungrudging toward his students, who will write articles
based on references he has discovered, labored over, and collected,
material that was previously overlooked. Some professors require their
students to gather material for them. And there are professors who put
their own name alongside the student's, making themselves the coau-
thor, assuming, in their vanity, that it will be to the student's advantage
if they lend their name to the work. Not so with Herbst. Herbst takes
what is his and offers it to his students without patting himself on the
back and saying, "See how wonderful I am—how decent, how generous—while others are stingy." His students sense this and are drawn
to him. They allow themselves to venture beyond academic matters to
personal concerns, to their deepest secrets. One of his students even
confessed to an emotional tangle centering on a young married woman
with a child, who shares his desk at the university. Herbst, too, allows
himself to discuss nonacademic matters with his students. His conversations with them are like conversations with peers. One of the two
students he ran into that Saturday night when he was with Shira was
sitting with him once, later on, and Herbst was on the verge of saying,
"Remember that woman you saw me with in the café, when you and
your friend were arguing about poetry and linguistics, discussing the
verse 'O heavens, seek pity for me'? I said anyone with the courage to
ask the heavens to plead for him is certainly fortunate. Now, my friend,
though I know I don't deserve it, I too sometimes hear my heart cry
out, 'O heavens, seek pity for me'!"

Gradually, the storm in his heart, which had been stirred up by
Shira—by the thought that she might have transmitted some disease to
him and from him to his wife and daughters—began to subside. You
can't imagine the scale of his terror. He leaped up repeatedly, alarmed
for no reason. When a spoon or fork fell, for example; when the door
was opened. After he began to calm down, Herbst felt as if he had a
wound that was bandaged too tightly. When the bandage was removed,
the pain vanished and he felt normal again. Herbst felt like someone
who went out for a walk but was unable to move his legs. When he
opened his coat and took off his hat, his feet felt light. Herbst had many
metaphors for his soul. I have included two of them, relatively simple
ones, for in that period his imagination was vivid, and his images were
odd and remote. In one realm, there was no change—the realm of
impending disease, which sometimes remained vague to him, formless
or nameless. At other times, each disease assumed its classic form, its
characteristic symptoms. He considered himself the primary source;

the rest of humanity, both a source and an outcome. Before long, all the victims, including himself, were forgotten, along with their diseases, except for his wife, who succumbed to an illness the doctors were unable to diagnose or cure. He, too, forgot the source of her disease and no longer tormented himself with the fact that he could have shed light on its nature and thus its cure. All the fantasies that at first led him to rage, to self-torture, were transformed into pity for this innocent woman assaulted by so many ills. Because he pitied his wife, he tried to please her. There wasn't a single good thing it was in his power to do that he didn't try to do. Which wasn't easy, at this particular time. Because Zahara was about to give birth, Henrietta was unusually nervous. She forgot about serving meals on time; she forgot to do his laundry; and, when the mailman gave her a letter for him, she forgot to pass it on. It happened once that an urgent letter arrived and was left in the kitchen, among the pots. If Manfred hadn't needed a match for his cigarette, the letter would still be there. Luckily, it was a silly letter, an invitation to a testimonial dinner, one of many such events that take place in Jerusalem every day, honoring some guest who is passing through. Tables are set up for cakes, cookies, pastries, and wines and other beverages, and prominent men and women are invited. But not every prominent person is the master of his own time, and many of them have other invitations for that very hour. In such cases, a moderately prominent person—the lecturer Herbst, for example—is invited and introduced to the guest of honor as a professor at the Hebrew University. Being a well-mannered person, he remains silent and doesn't say, "No, I'm not really a professor." Fortunately, it was a silly letter, and, if he had never received it, he would have lost nothing. But the same thing could have happened with an important letter. Nevertheless, he did not scold his wife. On the contrary, he made an effort to reassure her. And this is how he behaved whenever possible.

This effort purified his soul and allayed some of his anguish. But it left its mark on his face, and the strain was quite obvious to the world.

It is the way of the world to see one's own worries reflected in a friend's. A man with a miserable wife blames his friend's sorrow on his friend's wife, a man who is having trouble with his children blames his friend's trouble on his children, and so on. Taglicht was a bachelor and childless. What troubled him at that time were those factions that split off from the Haganah to act on their own, contrary to the policy of restraint adopted by the moderates in the *yishuv*, by the Jewish Agency, by the binationalists, by the best of the English. When Taglicht heard that Tamara Herbst belonged to one of these factions and was involved in terrorist activity, he surmised that her father was worried about her.

It didn't occur to him that Herbst knew very little about Tamara's activities, that, like most parents, he was not well informed about his children's lives. Especially in matters such as these, which are carefully guarded and concealed lest they reach the wrong ears.

Taglicht was nineteen years older than Tamara. She therefore thought of him as a member of her father's generation. Until Tamara went to study in Tel Aviv, he used to address her as if he were an old man talking to a child. That was how he behaved until the day Zahara came from the *kvutza,* bringing Avraham-and-a-half with her, at which point Taglicht began to treat Tamara as an adult. Henrietta took note of this and said, "Dr. Taglicht, why do you make an old lady out of Tamara? Why, you knew her when she was in the cradle." Taglicht answered, "One of these days I'll have to treat her as a grownup, so I might as well begin now." Since Tamara remained silent, he said no more. After this exchange, Tamara tried to justify his new attitude and was careful not to respond to Taglicht in her usual frivolous way. When Taglicht saw Herbst's worried face, he understood that he was distressed because of Tamara, because she belonged to that faction, and because she was involved in terrorist activities. He decided to seek her out in order to talk things over with her, to convince her to reconsider. At first, he had intended to revert to his original manner, to approach her as he used to when she was a child, so she would see she was still young and immature. After further consideration, he realized that she would be more likely to acknowledge the implications of her actions if he approached her seriously.

It was easy for Taglicht to go to Herbst's house but difficult to find Tamara there, for she would fly off as soon as she finished breakfast. Where to, who knows? Still, he found her. He addressed her seriously, without reproach, speaking not as someone with a monopoly on the truth, but as someone whose heart is filled with concern. He talked on and on, until he came to the subject of politics. He began explaining English diplomacy and the strategy of the Colonial Office, which were designed to defeat Zionism and abrogate the Balfour Declaration. Terrorist actions that disrupted the policy of self-restraint were thus welcomed as a step toward the destruction of the *yishuv.* Tamara stood and listened. She gazed at Taglicht as if she did not know to whom his words were directed. She let him talk and assumed a bewildered expression, as though what was being said had nothing to do with her. Then her expression became questioning, as if to say, What are you after? and these two expressions alternated with a coy one: Though I don't understand what you are saying, I'm willing to listen. When he paused to give her a chance to respond, she looked disappointed and said, "I thought you were going to say something nice. That you are in love with me, for example. Instead, you talk politics. Tell me, dear doctor, why haven't you fallen in love with me? I can provide endless evidence that you won't find another girl like me." Taglicht looked at her and said, "I admit, Tamara, that I was denied a clowning tongue. Not that the subject can't be treated lightly, but I was denied the talent bestowed on you in such profusion."

As he was leaving, she called after him, "I was sure you would look back, that our eyes would meet and disturb you. But you went off without looking back. I didn't turn to watch you go either. If you like, we could stop at that café on the corner. I hear they have all kinds of ice cream. If you don't eat ice cream, because you believe the old doctors who say it chills the stomach, then you can have a warm drink. I'm surprised at you, Dr. Taglicht, for listening to every old wives' tale. Those old doctors have weak stomachs, so of course they catch cold from ice cream. That's no reason to deprive yourself. You renounce enough things for religious reasons." Taglicht said, "You think it's my idea to renounce them? The Torah requires this of me and of all Jews." Tamara smiled, as she tended to do whenever she felt she had the upper hand, and said, "The Torah doesn't require anything of me." Taglicht said, "Why do you exclude yourself from the general public?" Tamara said, "I assume you know as well as I do that the rules you invoke are no longer generally accepted. They are upheld by stubborn individuals who refuse to relinquish the authority enjoyed by their ancestors in medieval times. Like the clerics, they want to exercise power over everyone. I admit that some of them are tolerant; even though they cling to superannuated notions, they don't hold us in contempt, and they even mix with us." Taglicht said, "Me, for example?" He was obviously pleased with his question. Tamara said, "Actually, I had in mind a young man you don't know." Tamara was about to mention his name but had second thoughts, as he was suspected of a terrorist act in which she had also been involved. Taglicht said, "Didn't you want to tell me something about . . . about the fellow who—how did you put it?—'clings to superannuated notions' and is an acquaintance of yours?" Tamara realized from his question that he knew who she was referring to. She laughed inwardly at the phrasing of the question, at her attempt to conceal, which was, in fact, revealing. She affected innocence, pretending to be unaware of the gravity of the issue. Tamara said, "Last Hanukkah I was invited to a latke party. There was a man there who wouldn't eat, because the pancakes were fried in the fat of a goose that hadn't been slaughtered by one of those fellows. You know whom I mean—a fellow with a chin braid and a braid over each jaw, which the

Orthodox call earlocks and a beard. There was a doctor there, a native of the Caucasus, descended from mountain Jews who had always been armed like free men and never known the yoke of the Diaspora. The doctor asked that man, 'Why aren't you eating latkes? Aren't they good?' He wasn't ashamed to say, 'Because they were fried in the fat of an improperly slaughtered goose.' The doctor said, 'The entire Diaspora is the outcome of those dietary laws. If Jews didn't designate someone special, a *shokhet*, to slaughter animals, they would have to do it for themselves. They wouldn't be intimidated by a drop of blood. They would defend themselves, and Gentiles wouldn't dare to attack them. But Jews are so afraid to spill blood that they deliver themselves to be slaughtered. They would rather let their blood be spilled than spill the blood of their enemies. Why? Because they're not in the habit of slaughtering anything, not even a pigeon.' "

Taglicht asked Tamara, "And what do you think?" Tamara said, "I'm my parents' daughter. They don't observe the dietary laws." Taglicht said, "I'm not asking about the dietary laws. I'm asking if it isn't good that we have rules about slaughter and appoint a *shokhet* to do the job—someone God-fearing and virtuous, who knows that it is only because the Torah lets us eat meat that he is allowed to tamper with life; all Jews are aware of this, and not everyone may slaughter. What do you think about that, Tamara?" Tamara said, "I was never confronted with that question before, so I haven't explored it." Taglicht said, "You want ice cream, and I detain you with words. Let's go into that café." Tamara said, "We don't have to go to that particular one. If you like, we could stand outside for a while or walk a bit. Wherever we go, we'll find other cafés." Taglicht said, "If you want to walk, I'm certainly agreeable." Tamara said, "On condition that we end up at some café." Taglicht said, "Agreed. Meanwhile, let me tell you something." "Is it something that happened to you?" Taglicht said, "I could tell you that sort of thing. My life is no secret. The events are known. I could give you an earful, enough to bore you. But now I'll tell you about someone else. If the subject isn't of interest, the person it relates to may be." "Who is it?" "Hemdat." "The one who writes . . . What is it he writes?" Once again Tamara feigned innocence. She took a mirror from her purse, looked into it, arranged her hair, looked up at Taglicht, and said, "Hemdat. I see." Taglicht said, "Hemdat told this to me. He lived in Jaffa, in the Neve Zedek neighborhood, in a house owned by a Sephardic Jew. A German gentleman lived there too, who was one of the managers of the Wagner factory. He may have even been a partner to the owner, who was a descendant of the Templars. He himself may have been a Templar. I don't recall the details. Hemdat thought this German was an extraordinary person. Before the war, all Germans were considered extraordinary—not to mention the Templars, who were, as a rule, ethical, upright, and God-fearing. Hemdat's manners were such that he kept his distance, rather than risk intruding on these neighbors, and he maintained somewhat inflated illusions about their character, qualities, and intellect, because they were compatriots of Goethe and Schopenhauer. One day, they had visitors from Stuttgart, among them a large blonde girl, a beauty of the sort that had never been seen before in Jaffa. Picture to yourself, Tamara, the meaning of a beautiful girl from Germany in those years, in this country. Now our land is full of lovely, charming Hebrew girls. Hush, Tamara, hush. I include you among the charmers. If you insist, I include you among the beauties too. Are you satisfied? Here's the café." Tamara said, "First tell me, then we'll go in." Taglicht said, "Hemdat, like many poets when they see a lovely girl and are attracted to her, composed garlands of verse to her. Whether on paper or only in his head, he never divulged to me. His manners were such that he kept his distance, rather than risk intruding on her, and as a result he attributed every virtue to her. Besides, in that period he used to read German books, whatever could be found in Jaffa. And all the fine characteristics ascribed to their women by German poets, Hemdat attributed to this girl from Stuttgart. One day, Hemdat was standing in his attic room looking out the window. He saw the girl in the garden, holding a chicken. Her hair was slightly disheveled, her blonde curls mingled with the white chicken feathers, and her blue eyes matched the pure blue sky. In fact, Hemdat recounted, at that moment he thought he detected an evil spark in her eyes, the sort you see when someone is about to do evil but is too ruthless to be aware of the nature of the act. However, a young man, confronted with his idol, sees beauty even in such eyes. He suddenly heard the shriek of an animal, a heartrending sound. He looked up and saw the girl beating the bird on its head. Hemdat didn't immediately grasp what had happened. When he did, he turned away from the blonde with the dead bird in her hand, and, if you'll excuse me, he threw up. Yes, he threw up. On the face of it, the girl was not to blame. It is the way of the world to eat the meat of animals killed in this fashion, and a Gentile woman who needs meat kills, cooks, eats, and serves her family, and no one gives it a second thought. Now for the rest of Hemdat's story, as he himself related it to me. Not about the belle of Stuttgart, but about that fellow with the earlocks and beard.

"After that incident, Hemdat fled from his room and roamed the streets, the avenues, the shore, the beach, the vineyards—any place that wasn't fenced off, with the exception of the German neighborhood, which he chose to stay far away from. After several hours, when it was already night and he was plagued by hunger, he returned to Neve Zedek. He passed the synagogue and, hearing the drone of voices, he went in and found people engaged in Torah study. One of them, with earlocks and a beard like all the others, was leading the lesson. This person was the *shokhet*. Hemdat gazed at him, searching for a sign of ruthlessness, of savagery. He found none. On the contrary, he saw a thread of kindness stretched across the man's face. He asked about him and learned that he was a man of sterling character and high moral qualities, that he was especially generous in offering hospitality and charity for the poor." Tamara said, "Here comes Father." Taglicht followed her eyes and said, "I don't see him." Tamara said, "But I do. Here he comes." Taglicht said, "Now I see him."

Herbst appeared. His face was clear, with no trace of sorrow, proba-bly because he was pleased to find his daughter with Taglicht. Herbst said, "I don't want to interrupt. Continue your conversation and your walk." Tamara said, "Come and join us. We're heading for a café. Come on, Manfred. Come." Herbst said, "How can I come if you call me Manfred? What will people say? He has a grown daughter and sits in cafés with young women. Isn't that so, Dr. Taglicht?" "Of course, of course," Taglicht answered, without having heard what Herbst said. After a few steps, Taglicht stopped and said, "Excuse me, but I can't go with you. Weltfremdt is waiting for me." "Ernst or Julian?" Tamara said, "Father, it's as if you're asking 'odds or evens?' "

Neither one of the Weltfremdts was waiting for Taglicht, but he wanted to give the father and daughter a chance to be alone together. Tamara said, "Have you changed your mind?" Taglicht said, "What can I do? They're waiting for me." Herbst said to his daughter, "We'll let him go now if he promises to come to us for supper." Tamara said, "Eggs in a glass, tea in a glass, and a lump of sugar." Taglicht said, "I'll try to come." Tamara said, "You see, Manf—I mean, Father—how much influence I have. He didn't say, 'God willing.' " Herbst smiled. Taglicht smiled and took leave of them.

It was odd for Herbst to be going to a café with his daughter. He had never sat in a café in Jerusalem with either Zahara or Tamara. After ordering what he ordered, he began searching his mind for something with which to entertain his daughter. He found nothing. He wanted to tell her one of those anecdotes about university personalities. But he felt that the time and place required something special, not the sort of subjects they discussed at home. It occurred to him that he could ask her to do the talking. But he felt that he should entertain her. Again, he searched his mind and found nothing suitable to say to his daughter. While he was searching and failing to find anything, a newsboy came through, shouting at the top of his lungs that eight Jews had been killed on Mount Carmel. There was chaos in the café. The newspapers were snatched up, without much attention to proper change, and were all gone in a minute. Herbst barely managed to get a copy.

Herbst and his daughter sat in the café. He had a cup of coffee, she had a dish of ice cream. She was leaning over him, and they were both reading the names of the victims and the brutal details of the murders. After reading the entire account, Herbst scanned the other items in the paper, one about an attempt to smuggle arms from Syria and one about an interview with a Jew imprisoned in Acre who had been sentenced to hang.

This is how Herbst and his daughter spent the time on the one occasion in their lives when they were together in a café. Herbst suddenly said, "Time to go. Mother might worry about us. You didn't finish your ice cream. It's all melted. I'll order another. You don't want it? Then let's go."

On the way, Tamara said to her father, "We didn't even mention Alfreda Weltfremdt, who just got engaged." "Engaged? To whom is she engaged?" "You didn't see the notice? She's engaged to someone whose name I forget." Herbst said, "Mrs. Ernst Weltfremdt must be very happy." Tamara said, "Why single her out?" Herbst said, "Because now she has something to write a poem or a play about. But we, who will be invited to hear her verses, are not to be envied.

Taglicht was always careful not to lie, because one lie leads to another, ad infinitum. There is no end to the pile of lies, and, even if there was no choice about the initial one, you end up with an appetite for lying. Now that he had told Herbst and Tamara that he had promised Julian Weltfremdt to stop in, he wished to sweeten the lie with a dose of truth.

Julian Weltfremdt was not used to having guests. Since the death of his little girl and the loss of his library, he no longer invited people to his home. If a guest did stop by, it was a red-letter day for Mimi. Apart from her piano and the pretense that she was a protector of the needy, she had nothing to be happy about.

That day, she had bought artichokes for supper. When she saw Taglicht in her house, she was elated and invited him to eat with them. Julian, who knew Taglicht would refuse, remained silent. He could see in her eyes how eager she was to share the pleasures of her table with a guest. He said to Taglicht, "I know you pharisees don't give an inch on ritual, even when it's a matter of pleasing someone. But, if I promise to make sure Mimi doesn't feed you anything unkosher, will you perhaps indulge her and eat with us? What can a kosher Jew eat in the home of an infidel such as me? Mimi, what did your grandmother use to feed that merchant from Galicia, the one your grandfather used to deal with? Pickled fish and whiskey. We don't have any pickled fish and whiskey, but we have sardines and some superb cognac. But I don't know if it's kosher—it was a gift from an Englishman I rescued from an Arab shepherd who was about to thrust a knife in his back."

Taglicht knew it would be right for him to accommodate these two solitary people and eat with them. Since the day their daughter died, they had lived together like two mutes. But he had promised Herbst and Tamara that he would come there for supper, so he couldn't do the decent thing; he did what was required to keep his promise. Mimi gazed at him, her lovely eyes veiled by a film of grief. Julian, like most men who cause their wives sorrow without knowing it, noticed this and was annoyed at Taglicht, a gentle man who had suddenly become harsh. Taglicht stammered a bit and took leave of them.

When he left, Julian followed him out and said, "Wait, and I'll show you a shortcut." Taglicht said to him, "When did you last see Herbst? I wanted to talk to you about him. I don't know anything specific. I know only what I see on his face. He looks tormented. If you see him, pay attention."

— 19 —

When Taglicht left the Weltfremdts', he was haunted by the bleakness that prevailed there, even though it was overshadowed by the happy face of the lady of the house when a guest arrived at her long-forsaken door. Taglicht, true to character, tried to ignore what he had seen, to avoid thinking about his friends, but he didn't succeed. He found himself reflecting on these two solitary people, who had suffered a double blow. After their furnishings and books were lost, their daughter died. When the child was alive, she had sweetened their plight and linked their souls. When she died, the link was severed and their souls became separate. They live together now, like the piano she brought with her from her father's house and the crumbling box of books, the remains of his collection. Julian has no use for the tunes, and Mimi has no use for the books. What connects Julian and Mimi? Fear of change, habit, compassion, and sadness. Mimi's sadness adds to her charm; Julian's sadness makes him angry. They are alike in one respect: they are both kind. But they are different in that he communicates through reproaches, whereas she uses her lovely voice. Taglicht was feeling more and more troubled, until his thoughts shifted back to the Mount Carmel victims. They had been in his mind from the time he left Herbst until he entered the Weltfremdt house. There was no end to the murder, no limit to the massacre. Jews were killed in other countries; Jews were killed in this country too. Before a boy could distinguish between death and murder, he heard about Jews being killed. Taglicht himself remembered that one day he went to school and saw the city weeping. He learned that a Jew, a milkman, had been murdered. After a while, the culprit was found, and he told how he had killed the milkman. They were both early risers. The milkman used to get up early to cart milk from the country to the city, while he used to get up early to cut firewood and bring it to the city. That day the Gentile said to the milkman, "Jew, give me your head, so I can test out my axe." The Jew laughed. The Gentile swung his axe and chopped off the milkman's head. Everyone was still in shock about the milkman when another incident occurred. A Jewish midwife was called to some village by a local gentlewoman and didn't return. The area was searched, but she wasn't found. After a while, the gentlewoman got married. She hired workers to renovate her palace. One day they went to do something in the cellar. They noticed a barrel filled with honey, opened the barrel, and found the body of a woman, the missing midwife. While everyone was still in shock about the midwife, another incident occurred, involving a family of nine, all of whom were murdered. In each of these cases, Jews had been murdered secretly, and everyone—Jew and Gentile alike—was upset by the bloodshed. Suddenly, the events of Kishinev occurred: Jews were killed openly. From then on, it seemed to be acceptable to spill Jewish blood, and pogroms became common.

The massacre continues, and there is no end to the horrors that have transpired in the world, with Jews the principal victims. A Jew seeking refuge from trouble is pursued by trouble wherever he goes. Even here, there is no respite. What can one do to avoid being murdered? Some of what has to be done is being done by the Haganah, teaching us to defend ourselves, to protect our property, to prevent our enemies from destroying us. Taglicht doesn't want revenge; he wants to contain the trouble. He enlisted in the Haganah as soon as he arrived in the Land of Israel. He goes where he is sent, without concern for his own safety,

never avoiding danger. But the Haganah's approach has to be scrutinized, because it protects and defends but never attacks, and, as long
as you don't attack, the enemy has the upper hand. If he kills, he kills;
and if he fails to kill, what has he lost? He is merely driven off, unharmed. This subverts the Haganah. If we were to show the enemy that
we can be like them, they wouldn't be so eager for our blood, and we
could prevent the murder of countless Jews. Until it becomes clear to
the Arabs that Jewish blood does not come cheap, we have to act on
the talmudic principle: "When someone comes to kill you, beat him to
the draw."

Taglicht did not arrive at this conclusion through his conversation
with Tamara. On several occasions, when he was standing guard alone
at night in Mekor Hayim, Beit Yisrael, or some other Jewish neighborhood, he had thought to himself: It's good that we're guarding the
neighborhood; it would be even better if we were to make the first
move.

These thoughts were difficult for him to accept, for they were contrary to the opinions with which he had grown up and which governed
most of his actions. Not only calculated actions, based on consciousness
and understanding, but the simple actions one engages in unconsciously. If he was ambivalent about some issue, when it was time to
act, he followed the logic he had grown up with rather than the dictates
of his heart, gleaned through his own experience. One night, while he
was guarding Mekor Hayim, he had sensed that the enemy was approaching. He had not responded on the basis of "when someone
comes to kill you, beat him to the draw." He had fired into the air,
allowing the enemy to escape. An enemy that escapes returns again.
The trouble is averted for a time, but it isn't eradicated. Raising his eyes,
Taglicht looked around, like someone in conflict who seeks advice from
others. The street was empty. There was no one in sight. Whether or
not a curfew was in force, Jerusalem was shut in. Jerusalem was accustomed to the fact that its citizens stayed in at night unless there was an
emergency. Only Taglicht was out on the street—because he had to go
to Herbst because he had promised to have supper with him because
he had left so abruptly because he had said he had to go to Julian
Weltfremdt's when he didn't really have to go and it was just an excuse.
And later, when he got to Julian's, he left quickly, because he had
promised Herbst he would come there.

This muddle compounded his weariness. His soul was already worn
down by the news of the Mount Carmel attack. In his heart, the eight
victims killed together did not constitute the number reported in the
headlines and announced by the newsboys. To him, every one of them

stood alone, distinct and alive, until he was struck by the murderers'
gunfire and fell dead in a pool of his own blood and the blood of unborn
generations.

A bell was ringing at the top of a tower. Taglicht heard it and
hurried to the bus stop. He wanted to ride to Herbst's house, since it
was almost suppertime. When he got to the bus stop, it was empty. No
people, no buses. He looked in all directions, hoping to find a taxi. He
saw a small car. It was hard to tell whether it belonged to a Jew, an
Englishman, or an Arab. Then, all of a sudden, he heard drums and
dancing. He looked up and saw that one of the two Rabinowitz hotels
was brightly lit, that the porches and the entire building were crowded
with men and women. He realized there was a wedding in town.

Taglicht was a frequent caller at the Herbst home. Julian Weltfremdt was not. That night, Weltfremdt called on the Herbsts. This
was a novelty, since he didn't visit very much, on account of the
comedies and tragedies: the comedies couples perform for guests and
the tragedies a guest sees for himself.

At this point, it seems appropriate to tell about Julian Weltfremdt, as
I have done about most of his friends. Though I already told about his
books, I didn't tell very much. Still, I'll skip the major part of his life
story and relate a most trivial detail, one that was on the lips of everyone
in Jerusalem. It's about those long brown cigarettes that took over the
mouths of Jerusalem's intelligentsia. If I were to go to Tel Aviv or
Haifa, I wouldn't be surprised to find them there, poking out of countless mouths.

Previously, Julian didn't smoke or even touch a cigarette, because he
needed his fingers for his books—to straighten their edges, to collect
hairs he might find between the pages, to brush away specks of tobacco.
As you surely know, it is not only the elders of Israel who keep every
hair that falls out of their beard in a book, but the nations of the world
behave similarly. Not with hair from their beard, as Jews do because
of its holiness, but with the hair of the woman they love, which they
keep in a favorite book. This also applies to the tobacco that drops into
a book while they read.

Previously, Julian Weltfremdt didn't smoke, nor did it occur to him
to smoke. As the number of immigrants from Germany increased, each
seeking a means of support, one such immigrant began peddling cigarettes. He called on Julian Weltfremdt with his wares. Julian Weltfremdt said to him, "I smoke only those long brown ones." Julian
assumed they were unavailable in the Land of Israel. The following
day, the peddler brought what he had asked for. Julian Weltfremdt said

to the peddler, "I see you are conscientious and dependable. Every morning, at 6:30, I would like you to bring me two packs. If you are a minute late or a minute early, you won't find me in." From then on, the peddler came at 6:30 and brought him cigarettes. Weltfremdt would take his two packs, put them in his pockets, and, when the time came, go to teach his students the wisdom he was hired to teach. Then he went to dinner, after which he stopped in a café, where he sat until he had finished the cigarettes in one pocket. He would then go to another café and sit there until he had finished the last cigarette in the other pocket. This is a tale of cigarettes and of Julian Weltfremdt, who was not originally a smoker. But, once he became one, many smokers were influenced by what was on his lips. If I hadn't become so involved in this trivial tale, I would comment on the dynamics of influence. It does seem odd that we set up conferences, arrange meetings, speak, mumble, orate, preach, lecture, publish newspapers, and write articles, pamphlets, and books—and all of these enterprises don't affect even the shadow of a cloud. Yet someone appears, does what he does, quite casually, and attracts a host of followers.

Now, to get back to Herbst.

Herbst stayed at home much of the time. On days when he had no classes, he worked at his desk, with his box of notes at his side. Sometimes out of interest; other times out of habit. Herbst discovered nothing new, but his slips of paper proliferated just the same. These papers seemed to procreate and produce more of their kind. Their offspring were similarly productive. By degrees, he disengaged his mind from Shira, as though she had no reality. He hadn't come across her since that night when he had become alarmed by the idea that she was sick, because he tended to stay home and didn't roam in those places where one might run into her. Nor did he go to her. In that period, Herbst was free of terror, no longer preoccupied by dread of the maladies that can overcome a person. He was working again, not with the great enthusiasm of former days, but as a scholar with work to do.

Something else was new. The colleagues Herbst had thought would undermine his promotion made no effort to harm him, while those he had assumed would be his champions did not lift a finger on his behalf. In a second hearing, things could change and the situation could turn around. It isn't only world history that changes, hostile nations becoming allies and vice versa. This is true of individuals as well. Those we count on to be loyal supporters don't put in a good word for us, and those we consider thoroughly hostile make no attempt to undermine us. This statement may sound severe, but its truth remains undiminished. Since wars have become more frequent, murders more violent, and bloodshed more common, man's value has declined, the power of principles has dwindled, hate has lost its sting, love has forfeited its honeyed flavor, and all things are determined by the impulse of the moment.

Henrietta, a sensible, composed woman, heard that Manfred's promotion was being discussed again, but she was not especially excited, just as her stewpot wouldn't care whether it belonged to the wife of a lecturer or that of a professor. Herbst himself wasn't very excited either. Over the years, he had come to accept that age-old wisdom: when a man becomes a professor, it doesn't add to his happiness.

After his article ("Must We Accept As Truth . . .") was published, Herbst went back to the heart of his book. The vacuum created in his note box because of the article began to fill up. But not his heart. He considered abandoning the central thesis on which his book was to be based and using the vast amount of material for separate articles. When a man is young, he reaches out in all directions, collecting endless data, filling boxes, crates, drawers, pads, notebooks. When he is older, he surveys the array of material and sees that he won't live long enough to make anything of it. Herbst began sorting his papers and saying, "These notes are appropriate for this article, the others for another article." One article, properly written and complete, is more significant than a mass of material over which you have no control. It is a fact that many scholars build their reputations on heavy books, dense with quotations, but a perceptive reader realizes that his conclusions were obvious from the beginning.

Herbst and Weltfremdt were once sitting and discussing the major work of a renowned scholar whose broad knowledge was astonishing. Taglicht, who was also there, didn't say a word. Herbst said to Taglicht, "Dr. Taglicht, either you haven't read the book or you don't realize how great it is." Taglicht said, "I read it, and it reminds me of something." "Of what? What does it remind you of? But let's not get off the subject." Taglicht said, "As a matter of fact, this story makes the subject even more immediate." "All right." "So, it's about a preacher interpreting a text. After twisting several verses, making a muddle of them, and confounding the words of our living God, he wished to validate his ideas and prove them reasonable. How? With a parable. He turned to his audience. 'Gentlemen and scholars, I'll tell you a parable. Once there was a great and awesome king, like Alexander of Macedon. This king attacked his enemies. He mobilized all his forces and defeated them. Now, gentlemen and scholars, another parable to support my ideas. Once there was another great and awesome king, like Napoleon, who attacked his enemies. He mobilized his forces and won the war. Now, gentlemen and scholars, one further parable to support these ideas. There was once a great king, also awesome, like Nicholas, czar of Russia, who was attacked by his enemies. What did this Nicholas do? He mobilized his forces, sent them to war, and defeated his enemies.' "

Herbst and Weltfremdt were totally bewildered. Where was the parable and where was the message? Weltfremdt suddenly leaped up, embraced Taglicht, and said, "My dear friend, come, let me embrace you. I would give a thousand and one of my years to anyone willing to tell those scholars that their books are constructed exactly like that preacher's lesson. He cites one proof after another, though the second one adds nothing to the first. Dear Taglicht, you are such a treasure. Whatever the subject, you have a comment that eclipses it. I would trade all the folklorists for one of your parables. You should write it all down in a book. *That* would be a good book, and I could find good things in it." Taglicht said, "In Galicia, where I come from, they would probably say, 'An ordinary pharmacist is a fool.' " Weltfremdt said, "I assume you brought up pharmacists to make a point. So, where you come from, in Galicia, they would say that an ordinary pharmacist is a fool. Why?" Taglicht said, "A man who spends all those years in school and is content to be a pharmacist rather than study medicine is foolish, right? This applies to folklorists, who have so much material and are content to present it as folklore rather than make it into a story." Weltfremdt said, "Then why don't you write stories?" Taglicht said, "I'm like those philosophy professors who aren't capable of being philosophers."

Having mentioned Taglicht, let me mention Lisbet Neu, to whom Herbst planned to introduce Taglicht. Despite the fact that a number of years have passed since Herbst met Lisbet Neu, she is still at the peak of her charm, as she was when he first saw her. How old is she now? Probably about twenty-seven. She is older than Zahara, but Zahara is already a married woman and almost a mother, whereas Lisbet Neu is alone with her widowed mother, in a world circumscribed by her home and office, with nothing more in it. Living a religious life, fulfilling the commandments, dealing with financial concerns, she is deprived of life's pleasures. If Lisbet Neu were to join a *kvutza,* would she behave like the other young women there? She may already be taking liberties and she may be different than she was to begin with. What do we know about other people's lives? Her body conveys innocence. Still, one wonders about her. She had the hair above her lip removed. A girl doesn't do that sort of thing on her own. Someone else must be influencing her. Who could it be? Herbst suddenly felt a sharp pang, a pang that comes of jealousy. Herbst was sitting with friends, discussing ethnography and similar subjects, imagining: Lisbet, if I ever have the privilege of kissing your mouth, I'll say to you, "Whenever I saw those silken threads that shaded your lips, my own lip began to quiver with the wish to kiss you." The slightest male quality can drive us wild in a woman. Shira, for example, seems part male; yet, when you are intimate with her, you know there is no one quite as female.

My novel is becoming more and more complex. A woman, another woman, yet another woman. Like that preacher's parable. As for the man whose actions I am recounting, he is lost in thought that doesn't lead to action. I am eager to know what we will gain from this man and what more there is to tell. Having taken it upon myself to tell the story, I will shoulder the burden and continue.

—— 20 ——

A young woman arrived from the *kvutza*, bringing good news. The news came as a surprise. For Henrietta there could be no better news. Zahara had given birth to a boy. A boy was born to Zahara. Henrietta knew her daughter was about to give birth. Still, when the news came, it came as a surprise.

Henrietta moves through the house, but her mind is with Zahara. From the moment Henrietta received word that Zahara's son was born, she has been walking from room to room. At times, her heart is light; at others, it is heavy. In either case, the walls of her house are constricting. They keep her from flying off to Zahara. In spite of this, she is totally with Zahara. In a thousand ways that begin in the imagination and then become real, she is with Zahara, even though one of them is in Afula and the other in Jerusalem; one is in a valley, the other in a glen. Let it be known that this is how it is. She sees Zahara in bed, her face radiant with light from her firstborn. Zahara's son lies at her side, wrapped in the tiny garments she gave Zahara for him. Henrietta picks him up and hands him to Zahara, so she can feed him. It would be good for Zahara to drink malt beer every day, for it stimulates the milk. But, with so many new mothers there, who has time to think about Zahara's needs? If her own mother were there, Zahara would lack nothing.

All of which suggests that she isn't there. In truth, she is still in

Jerusalem. Why? Because it's a three-and-a-half-hour trip from Jerusalem to Afula. If you have a car for the trip. If you have no car, then
it's truly a problem. There are people with servants who call and order
a car, and, when it comes, they let it wait as long as they like. Henrietta
and Manfred, even now, when they are so eager to see their daughter,
have to go to the telephone office and look up "Car Services" in the
directory. If the directory is intact, it's simple. Otherwise, they have to
run to another office. There they find what they are looking for and
ask about car service to Afula—when it leaves, whether there is room
for two. By the time they get an answer, the car has left. They ask about
the next one. A clerk answers, "Hey, take it easy." They decide to try
the bus. But the bus station isn't listed in the directory. Why? Because
two competing companies have suddenly merged into one and adopted
a new name. They go into town to look for the bus and don't find it.
Even if they do find it, they don't find the driver. They find the driver,
but he doesn't know when he'll be leaving. Why? Because the road is
closed. Why? Because of Arabs who are demonstrating against Jewish
immigration. Until the speeches are over, the roads will be closed. They
go to the office of the car service, because sometimes what can't be dealt
with on the telephone can be dealt with in person. The clerk in charge
yawns in their faces and doesn't dignify them with a straight answer,
because he doesn't need any more passengers, all the cars having already left. As for tomorrow, he lacks the imagination to think that far
ahead, and, besides, it's too much trouble.

Herbst, who had undertaken the search alone this time, was on the
verge of despair when a passerby noticed him. He said, "Dr. Herbst,
what are you doing here in town? I see you are about to take a trip.
Are you, perhaps, leaving us forever? Just between us, I would run
away too. If not because of the Arabs, then because of the English. If
not because of both of them, then because of our leaders. Our orientation, Dr. Herbst, our orientation is truly—how shall I say?—defective.
And it would be a waste of breath to say more." Rather than waste his
breath, he turned to other, more worthwhile, subjects. What did he say,
what did he not say? Whom did Herbst's daughter marry, and are both
parents equally pleased? Often, the father is pleased and the mother
isn't, or the other way around. Sometimes both parents are pleased, but
not the daughter. He stopped in midconversation. Why? Because a fly
fell into his mouth because the city was full of flies because the streets
were full of garbage, and, when garbage cans were placed on the streets,
their lids were stolen. Before Herbst could escape, the man swallowed
the fly and resumed his monologue, in the course of which he suggested

taking the bus. But first, they had to find the bus stop, as the Mandate police favor the Arabs and are hostile toward us and our buses, so they move the bus stops on a whim.

While Herbst was engaged in his struggles, Henrietta was busy packing. As she put their things in the suitcases, her mind drifted back to Zahara. Again, the two of them are together. One is in bed; one is near the bed. Why not on a chair? Because the chair is occupied. A young man has come to be with his wife, and he sits on the chair, paying no attention to Henrietta but hearing everything she says to Zahara. This prevents Henrietta from telling Zahara some of the things she would tell her if no one else were there.

While Herbst was struggling to turn up a strip of space for himself and his wife, a new car drove by, with a man and woman inside. He was middle-aged; she was young. He was a Zionist official; she was his secretary. They were touring the Emek settlements, because he was going off to the lands of our dispersion to report on the accomplishments of our young men and women in the Emek. But first he was going to the Emek, taking his secretary along. He was traveling in a special car, so he could get back for a round of farewells tomorrow afternoon in Jerusalem and tomorrow evening in Tel Aviv. Or was it the reverse—Jerusalem in the evening and Tel Aviv in the afternoon? His secretary, of course, deserved the credit for writing things down and reminding him of everything in due time.

Back to the Herbsts. I'll leave Herbst outside, struggling to arrange transportation, and turn to his wife, who is busy packing. Henrietta used to go off for several days without much preparation, without luggage. Now, a day trip requires great preparation.

While Henrietta considers every dress—whether to take it or not—her daughter Sarah clutches at her mother's skirt and doesn't let go. The mother studies this child of her old age—how she has grown, how much she needs her mother. She picks her up, as if to test her weight, as if that will determine whether she can leave her behind and go to Zahara. She can't be left with Tamara, who is busy teaching the girls in Mekor Hayim writing and language. If Tamara takes time off, that will be the end of it. Even though she isn't paid, she has many competitors, teachers in training who need experience. Henrietta can't leave the child with Firadeus, because her mother doesn't allow her to sleep away from home.

Henrietta was at a loss as to where to leave the child. She thought of Dr. Krautmeir, who had dealings with young women of every class and ethnic group, and had always found her helpers. But, because of

what had transpired between her and Krautmeir, there was now a
barrier between them. What happened was this. They met at a tea
honoring a prominent woman who had been a social worker for many
years. When Dr. Krautmeir arrived, her eyes were red. Since it was
obvious that she had been crying, she smiled sadly and explained, "I've
come from a condolence call to a mother whose daughter died, a girl
of about fourteen. She died—actually, she was murdered. It was a
double murder. I just hope the daughter's death won't lead to the
mother's death." How did the girl die? In the summer, the mother and
daughter exchanged their Jerusalem apartment for one in Tel Aviv and
spent their vacation there. The girl was thrilled, after being closed in
by the stones of Jerusalem for so long. She suddenly saw, stretched out
before her, an endless expanse of soft sand, a sea full of water. She spent
her days on the beach, running in the sand, bathing in the sea, enjoying
the company of girlfriends, reading. Each afternoon and evening, she
used to come home to eat with her mother. One evening, she didn't
come home. The police were informed. They searched for her all night.
In the morning, they found her lying on the beach, without a breath
of life. She was taken to Hadassah Hospital and revived. The girl
couldn't remember what had happened, other than that she had met a
man, who spoke to her, said various things, and, in the course of the
encounter, lit himself a cigarette and gave her one too. Beyond this, she
remembered nothing. About three months later, she had an abortion,
from which she never recovered. Shortly afterward, she died. It's not
clear if some medical quack was at fault, nor was the seducer and rapist
tracked down, because the family preferred to protect its good name
and hush up the affair. The story of this rape was followed by many
others in which the family chose not to pursue the rapist, in order to
protect its good name. These tales of rape were followed by tales of
promiscuous young women, who make themselves available to anyone,
and, when they become pregnant, find someone to go to for an abortion. Some of them continue on this course; others are permanently
damaged, never regaining their health. One of the guests said, "If these
girls knew that, when they get pregnant, no doctor will perform an
abortion, they would behave less casually." Dr. Krautmeir said, "In
some cases, it is a medical responsibility to relieve a woman of her
fetus." Another woman said, "If it's a matter of health, of course it's
a doctor's responsibility to act." Dr. Krautmeir said, "Not only in the
interest of health, but whenever an unmarried woman is involved.
Otherwise, she'll put herself in the hands of some quack and risk her

life. Until society changes its attitude toward a single mother, she is lost. It is the duty of every doctor, especially a female doctor, to relieve these women of their fetuses, not only because of health considerations, but because not every woman can bear the shame. And it is society that should be ashamed of its shameful attitude."

Dr. Krautmeir was not usually talkative, especially in matters that call for silence. But she was overcome with the zeal of a professional woman who has renounced family life, speaking openly and from the depths of her heart. Dr. Krautmeir said, "Instead of abstractions, it would be worthwhile to have some examples. If you like, I will tell you a bit about my practice. One evening, two strange women came to see me, their eyes darting about nervously, looking into every corner of the room, as though they were being chased by their shadow. One of them looked not quite like a lay person and not quite like a nun. It was hard to judge the other one, who was swaddled from head to toe. I could tell from her shoes that she was young. The young woman's companion began to mutter words that didn't connect, and each series of words was punctuated by curses and imprecations. After the initial torrent, I said to her, 'I can't figure out what you're saying.' She continued to chatter without making sense. I said to her, 'I beg you both, please go. I have no time for fantasies. If you can tell me what really happened, well and good. Otherwise, please leave.' She continued to spout nonsense. I got up, went to the door, and said, 'The door is open. Please go, and take along your swaddled madonna.' She grabbed my knees and said, 'Don't be angry, doctor. This girl comes to the convent sometimes.' I said, 'All right, I understand.' Then I said, 'Take off your dress, my child, and I'll examine you.' Her companion said, 'I told you she comes to the convent, but I didn't mean to say she's one of the nuns. She's from the village, just a village girl whom the nuns feel sorry for. They sometimes pay her to help with the menial work.' I said, 'Very well. Let me see what's what with her.' The girl wept as she undressed. I examined her and said, 'At such-and-such a time, you will enrich the world with a new life.' She began to sob, and the older woman shouted, 'That's impossible!' I said to her, 'Why is it impossible? Everything is all right.' She made some response, swallowing her words. I listened in silence. Finally she said, 'She can't just wait and have the baby. She is a nun. She lives in the convent, and, unless she has an abortion, she will take her own life.' Having confessed this much, she proceeded to tell the whole story. It was not very romantic. One of the gardeners— not one of the young ones—used to hang around the convent garden, and they got to know each other. And so on. Now, I ask you, ladies,

what should a doctor do in such a case? Should the mother be abandoned for the sake of a fetus, or should the girl be rescued from certain
death?" One of the women responded, "To tell you the truth, Dr.
Krautmeir, my interests are somewhat limited, and they don't extend
to Christian girls." Dr. Krautmeir said, "Since your altruism is reserved
for Jewish girls, I'll tell you another story, not about one Jewish girl
but about two or three of them. And if that isn't enough for you ladies,
let me assure you that these girls came to me in a single week—not a
special week, but a perfectly typical one." Henrietta Herbst stood up
and said, "You are worse than Hitler. He destroys the Jews in his
domain, and you destroy Jews who are even beyond his domain." Since
this exchange, the two women had avoided each other and were not
on speaking terms. How did Henrietta Herbst, who was usually so
reserved, come to say such things? Once, when Firadeus took sick, she
sent one of her neighbors, an attractive young girl, to fill in for her. Mrs.
Herbst was pleased with her, but she wondered about the sad look on
her face, unusual for a girl of her age. At lunch, she asked why she was
so sad. She told her that her husband played cards, drank too much, and
sometimes spent his whole week's salary in one night on arrack and
cards—all because they were in such distress over the fact that they
were childless. Why were they childless? Because, before they were
married, she became pregnant by him and was afraid that, if her brothers found out, they would kill her. She heard there was an Ashkenazic
woman, a doctor from Germany, where all Germans come from, who
could arrange things so no one would know what the girl didn't want
to have known. She found out where the woman was and went to her.
The woman doctor asked, "What do you want?" Being too shy to
answer, she was silent. The doctor looked at her and said, "In that case,
this is what you have to pay." She gave her all the money she had. The
doctor counted the money and said, "Is that all?" She said, "I have
more." She said, "How much?" She told her. She said, "And where is
the money?" She told her about a Sephardic woman, the wife of a
government official, who owed her two months' salary and refused to
pay; this woman was so mean that she took back all the gifts she had
given her previously. The doctor said what she said. Then she did what
she did and said, "From now on, you don't have to worry." Now that
she was properly married, she wanted to have a child but couldn't
become pregnant. She was miserable, and her husband shared her
misery. When he recovered from his drunkenness, he would cry and
bemoan his fate. Sometimes, because this was so hard for her to bear,
she would run and bring him arrack, so he could drown his sorrow.

When he was sober, he was likely to go and kill that woman doctor, then take his own life.

So much for Dr. Krautmeir. Now I might as well get back to our friend from the *kvutza*. While Henrietta was tormented because she was determined to get to Zahara, although she had no one to leave Sarah with, help appeared from an unanticipated source. The very person who brought news of her grandchild's birth offered to look after Sarah for however much time Zahara's mother and father wished to spend with Zahara. She had come to Jerusalem to spend some time in a rest home in Motza, and, if she stayed there three or four days less, it would be no great loss to the Jewish people.

Zahara's friend stayed to take care of Zahara's sister so Zahara's parents could visit Zahara and welcome Zahara's child. Henrietta hadn't been out of Jerusalem since the day she went to the Dead Sea with Manfred and Tamara. Now that she was leaving town, she was surprised at how easy it was to go and how easy it was to leave Sarah. She remembered what Manfred had said the day they came back from the Dead Sea: "We should go on a trip such as this once a month." How many months ago was that? Not only had she not left Jerusalem in all that time, but even in Jerusalem itself she hadn't been out for a walk, either alone or with Manfred. Now they were going off together for a number of days to see Zahara and her child. Henrietta was comfortable and relaxed, and so was Manfred. He, too, was surprised to be able to detach himself from all his commitments. Herbst was not one of those scholars who believe the world won't survive without their writings, but he believed he wouldn't survive without his work. It was suddenly demonstrated to him that he could leave his work in the middle. When they received word that Zahara had given birth, he was in the process of copying notes out of a book. He abandoned this task in the very middle, yet his mind didn't wander back to it. When he did think about it again, he couldn't remember where he had stopped. No sooner did he remember than he forgot again, although, when he sat copying, it seemed to him that he was making a great discovery. He put all that out of mind and watched the mountains, hills, and valleys unfurling and changing shape as they unfurled. A single color was smeared across the sky, mixing a variety of hues and altering them continually. Everything is subject to change—earth, sky, people. Henrietta glanced at her husband, wondering about him. He looked so boyish; his face glowed happily, just as it used to when he and she were young. Manfred was vigorous and happy in those days. He carried a heavy stick in his hand, and he sported a Rembrandt-like hat and a small mustache that was something of a joke. His manner was light and easy. She was not unattractive either. Her limbs were light; her entire body was lithe and lovely. Her blonde hair attracted considerable attention. When she walked into the municipal train station, with her briefcase tucked under her arm, more than one young man watched to see which car she went into and followed her. But she had eyes only for Fred, whom she still called Manfred. They were seeing a lot of each other when the war broke out and Manfred had to go to fight. She was convinced that this would be the end for her, because there were already rumors that not everyone who went to war came back alive. Her parents were also convinced that it was time for her to give up Manfred, for, when the sword of war hangs over a man's head, his attachment to any young woman will surely wither. Manfred was of another mind. Two days before he left for the war, he married her. It was a hasty wedding, because he had to leave. As soon as they got up from their wedding bed, he went off to fight. But his steadfast love earned him the goodwill of guardian angels, and he returned from the front safe and sound. Whenever he had leave, he spent the entire time with her. Have a look at Dr. Herbst: here in the Land of Israel, he has not enrolled in the Haganah, but, there in Germany, he performed heroic deeds for which he earned extra time at home. It was still the custom, there in Germany, to reward such deeds, even in the case of Jews. He has already forgotten most of the feats that earned him extra time with his wife, but Henrietta never forgot. He came home in uniform, a dashing hero. Other soldiers saluted him, and when he saluted a superior, the response was respectful, as though they were equals. Until the revolution, when he discarded his arms and came home a free man. They were sure the trouble was over. Eternal joy was on the horizon. But in fact the end of the war ushered in a series of revolutions, making life even more difficult. Before one ended, a more violent one began. Because of these upheavals, life was disrupted. There was no electricity, no fuel for heat or cooking, no milk and bread deliveries. The baker didn't respond to those who needed him. Food was scarce, and shopkeepers either closed their doors or opened them and said, "Come in and see the empty shelves." There wasn't even water in the faucets. Worst of all, the world was ravaged by many serious epidemics, all of which spread to Germany. Many young women died; Henrietta lost quite a number of relatives and close friends. They say that more people died from disease than from combat. When man is cruel to his kind, nature is cruel to mankind. Henrietta was not affected. Except by the shortages. There was no money shortage. On the contrary, they had millions, even billions. But the millions and billions didn't buy food. At about this time, Zahara was born. No one who saw her then could believe that little worm would grow limbs and put on flesh. But she grew, exceeding her parents' expectations. Now that child has borne a child.

Henrietta glanced at her husband, suppressing laughter. It certainly was funny that that child had borne a child and they were on their way to see the child she had borne. Manfred felt he should say something. His mind shifted from birth to birth, from the birth of his daughter's son to the birth of his own youngest child, the child of his old age; to that day when he found the nurse Shira, who attended Henrietta. And events transpired that couldn't be explained logically or in any other way, for, though he had never known any woman other than Henrietta, he was drawn to her. Henrietta looked at her husband again and was puzzled. From the moment she received news of the birth of Zahara's son, she had never stopped thinking of Zahara. Now, all of a sudden, she was thinking about Manfred. She shifted her mind back to Zahara, but her thoughts drifted to Manfred. He appeared again, bent over Zahara's crib, his shoulders so broad that the baby was hidden and only he was visible. Now that they were on the way to see Zahara and her baby, Manfred was doing exactly what he had done then, when she was a baby.

The car leaped down mountains, making its way through the valley. The mountains that had raised themselves along the way were no longer in sight. They were replaced by broad plains, brown and picturesque, dotted with gleaming red roofs. Over the rooftops, the sun was etched in the sky. Clouds of blue, silver, and a nameless whiteness unmatched on the earth below made shapes in the sky. A rare warmth, tempered by breezes, delicately scented, and embroidered in finely tinted color, encircled the earth. Sound, like a song, rose from the brush and bramble; from the wings of insects; from the branches of a solitary tree, a remnant of onetime abundance; from the bell of the ram leading the flock. Then, suddenly, everything was silent, but for the sound of a car with three passengers: a man, a woman, another man. The man was the Zionist leader who was touring the Emek. The woman was his secretary. Their companion lived in the Emek and was telling them what to report to our brothers-in-exile. The car raced ahead, because of the two events the Zionist leader was scheduled to attend before leaving the country. It vanished in a trail of exhaust, allowing the Herbsts to enjoy the sky above, the earth below, the sun, wind, scent, view, sounds, the tiny houses sprouting up from the midst of these Emek settlements. Their driver, who was from one of the houses in one of those settlements, turned toward the passengers, calling out the name of every cluster of gleaming roofs. He called out the name of the *kvutza* he had belonged to before becoming a driver and, with a lilt approaching song, told them when that *kvutza* was founded and by whom, what it had endured, and how many rounds of settlers had passed through. A *kvutza* is short on years but long on history. It isn't years that make history, but what one does with them. The driver had a long history too, having spent time in every *kvutza* in the Emek, either as a member or a long-term guest, and he had earned the right to consider himself a founding father.

The driver succeeded in doing what the road failed to do: distracting Herbst, so that all thoughts of Shira slipped away. When the driver fell silent, the sounds of the Emek—its vegetation and wildlife—took over. Herbst's mind was flooded with memories of events that preceded Shira. How wonderful those days were. If he was occasionally disturbed by fantasies about women, they were short-lived, because it was clear to him that he had no interest in any other woman. Manfred took Henrietta's hand, pressed it fondly, and said nothing. Henrietta sat, her hand in his, choosing not to intrude on him with conversation. Manfred remained rapt in thought. His thoughts were a muddle, but all of them were about Henrietta: how they got to know one another, how they confided their feelings to each other, how they happened to marry, how they were before coming to this country, and how they are now, here in the Land of Israel.

— 21 —

It was an hour before dark when they arrived at the gate. Those who worked in the fields were not back yet. There was no one in sight, not a voice to be heard. The entire village was still, the stillness broken only by a murmur from the water tower. Bright greenish light glowed, and a warm blue, contained in the light and held together by air, floated through the atmosphere. The scent of thistle infused with sunshine radiated from the bushes at the gate. Here I would find the leisure to write my book, Herbst thought, and, at the same time, he was happy that here he would not be burdened by his book or required to do any work. He turned to his wife and said, "So, Henrietta, here we are at Zahara's." "Yes," Henrietta said, "here we are at Zahara's." Though the entire trip was because of Zahara, Henrietta was surprised to have arrived at Zahara's home. She felt she ought to do something—sit up straight, for example; something, the nature of which was unclear to her. She made herself small and stammered, "Yes, here we are at Zahara's."

The gate was closed. In front of the gate, on a crooked pole, a warning was posted: BECAUSE OF HOOF-AND-MOUTH DISEASE, NO GUESTS WILL BE ADMITTED AND ALL STRANGERS ARE ABSOLUTELY FORBIDDEN TO ENTER. This was the announcement posted by all the communal settlements before a holiday, to discourage an onslaught of guests. Though the holiday was over and there were no others anytime soon, the announcement was still posted. Herbst, who was a disciplined person, accepted the decree regretfully and resigned himself to the fact that, despite the long trip, he wouldn't see his daughter. Henrietta was also law-abiding, but it was clear to her that no power in the world was going to prevent her from seeing her daughter, especially now that she had given birth. The driver sounded his horn, a long-drawn-out blast, to get someone to open the gate. The Herbsts stared at him, bewildered. Didn't he see the warning; couldn't he read? They had noticed a book resting on the driver's seat. It was a detective story; still, he must know how to read. The driver blew his horn again. The Herbsts stared at him again, not perplexed, but openly pleased and approving.

A tall, thin young man, with a splendid shock of blond hair poking out from under a battered hat, made his way to the gate and opened it lazily, asking the bus driver in a whisper, "Which hotel garden are these two turnips from?" The driver laughed to himself and didn't answer.

Feigning graciousness, the young man asked, "How can I help you?" The driver answered, "You could, for example, tell Zahara's son to run to his grandpa and grandma." The young man studied the guests and said, "Perhaps you are Zahara's parents?" Henrietta said, "Why 'perhaps'?" The driver added, "If you don't believe them, I can testify that I found them in the Herbst castle." The young man lowered his head, brushed away the lock of hair that dangled over his eyes, and said, "Come to the dining room. You can have some tea while I go and tell Zahara." Henrietta was puzzled. Why to the dining room rather than to Zahara's? Before she had a chance to say anything, she and Manfred were in the dining room. Before they had a chance to catch their breath, a drink was set before them.

Still in their travel clothes, the Herbsts sat at a long table on which
there were a tray with a kettle, two glasses, bread, and jam. A plump
and jolly girl stood by, with smiling eyes and black curls dancing
around her rosy cheeks. She looked at both of the Herbsts and said, in
a tone at once coquettish and absolute, "This jam is good in tea, as well
as on bread. We make it ourselves. The fruit is grown here in Ahinoam.
Please, try some. I've already poured your tea."

The Herbsts sat, tea in hand, their eyes on the door. Henrietta's glass
was already half-empty, and Zahara still hadn't come. Other people
came. But not Zahara, not Avraham-and-a-half, her husband, not the
person who went to call Zahara. Some other young man came in,
accompanied by a young woman. He was the driver who had brought
the Herbsts to Ahinoam, and she was one of the *kvutza* members.
Zahara, however, didn't come. Henrietta looked around, nervous and
irritated. She looked at Manfred, who was sitting there indifferently.
Fred was odd; from the moment he set out on this trip, nothing seemed
to matter to him except the pleasure of travel. The whole point of the
trip was Zahara, yet, now that they had arrived, it didn't matter to him
whether Zahara appeared or not. Henrietta put down her tepid tea. The
driver discarded what was left, took the kettle, and poured her fresh tea.
Henrietta thought: I should offer the driver some tea. She also thought:
I'm not even a tea drinker. It's Fred who drinks tea. He quotes Goethe,
who said he preferred a delicate drink such as tea to poisonous coffee;
still, when it's time for a drink, he asks for coffee. Henrietta was
engrossed in her thoughts when Zahara came. She came running. She
came suddenly. Henrietta didn't see her coming, yet there she was.
Avraham-and-a-half was with her—Avraham-and-a-half, who was
Zahara's husband and the father of Zahara's son. In a flash, mother and
daughter were embracing one another, entwined in each other's arms,
the daughter's arms wrapped around her mother, the mother's arms
wrapped around her daughter. As they embraced, they kissed and
kissed again, holding on to each other and kissing all over again. They
clung and were so tightly entangled that it was hard to tell them apart.
If this was not a manifestation of the wish to merge, to be one body
again, I don't know what it was. Zahara suddenly let go of her mother
and flung herself on her father's neck, hugging him and giving him a
protracted kiss. After a time, she kissed him again and said, "Father,
you're here." Manfred was enveloped in his daughter's arms, unsure
whether he had kissed her or not. After a moment's reflection, he kissed
her on the forehead. Then he offered his hand to Avraham-and-a-half.
Taking his son-in-law's hand, he felt weary, a weariness that irked him.

He heard Zahara's voice. She seemed to be saying something. He looked up at her, noting that her face glowed and her mouth was bright with happiness. She was saying, "Now, my dears, now come and I'll show you my son."

They went down the dining-room steps, which were lined with two rows of well-trimmed myrtles, and past an old cistern on which Shomron, the watchman's partner, was stretched out. Shomron eyed the two creatures who trailed behind Zahara. They looked weird, their clothes were weird, their speech was weird; everything about them was weird. He was debating whether or not to bark at them. He jumped toward Zahara and looked into her eyes for a clue. Zahara didn't notice. He began scratching with his right hind leg, as he always did when he couldn't figure out what to do. He shook his ears and considered: Does Zahara want me to bark at these two-legged creatures who have latched onto her, so she can scold me, thus demonstrating that she is protecting them from me? But no, I won't raise my voice, and I won't abandon my good manners. That may be how Zahara is, but that's not how I am. He flexed his ears, relaxed his leg, and continued to watch the odd pair that tagged along at Zahara's heels, their mouths in constant motion, producing incessant noise. He understood that she was ignoring him because of them. He stood up on all fours, rounded his tail, and opened his mouth wide but made no sound, observing to himself: They deserve to be bitten rather than barked at. He settled down again at the other end of the cistern, keeping an eye on Zahara's retinue.

Zahara pointed out two matching structures, more attractive than the others and somewhat separate from them, surrounded by an expanse of green grass spread with diapers and other such items. Zahara said to her father and mother, "See that house there, to the left, with the red roof? Father, if you insist on looking down, you can't see it." Father Manfred said, "What is that over there, in that box that looks like a hut? Rabbits? There really are rabbits? I haven't seen a rabbit since I came to this country. The red roof you were talking about—what is it? Didn't you mention a red roof?" Zahara laughed gaily and said, "That red roof is the roof of the house chosen by all four village babies—among them your grandchild, who happens to be my son—as their home. Now, Father, you know what I'm showing you. Mother already understands." Henrietta nodded and walked briskly toward the porch, where there were four cribs covered with netting.

Zahara ran to one of the cribs, took out a tiny creature, held him in her arms, and lifted him up so her parents could see him, saying, "This is my son." She took him out quickly, picked him up quickly, lifted him quickly, showed him to her parents quickly, said he was her son quickly—all before her parents could make a mistake and look at some other baby. Henrietta handed her purse to her husband. Manfred looked at her questioningly. Why had she handed him the purse, and what was he supposed to do with it? Henrietta took her daughter's child and stared at him as hard as she could. Then she leaned over him, lifting him close to her eyes, and bent her head over him until his eyes met hers. Anyone who saw his stare would say it was no random stare, that it was deliberate, that Dan knew who she was. Henrietta said nothing. She watched him without a word. As she watched, something occurred in her heart that she had never been aware of before and could not identify. Days later, she understood that a new love had possessed her at that moment. Grandma Henrietta stood gazing at her daughter's son, with no thought of relinquishing him, ever. Zahara stood across from her, gazing at her son cradled in her mother's arms. After a bit, she cooed to him, "Dandani, this is your grandma. And here, on the sidelines, is your grandpa. How about you, Grandpa, aren't you interested in your grandson?" "Me?" Manfred retorted in alarm, "I'm afraid to hold him. He might cry." Zahara laughed and said, "If he cries, let him cry. He's used to it. Take him, Father. You'll see how delightful he is." Manfred stretched out his arms and said, "Come, come to Grandpa." Zahara laughed. "He's clever, but he doesn't know grandfather language, and he doesn't know how to walk either. Put down the purse, Father. I'll hand Dan to you." Zahara took her son from her mother's arms and handed him to her father. Grandfather Manfred was trembling. He finally said, "I'm afraid he'll fall. You take him, Mother." Zahara said, "Which mother do you mean, my mother or his mother? Come, Dani. If you want Grandpa Manfred to pay attention to you, you'll have to enroll in the university."

The dog suddenly leaped out of his spot and, with a yelp of excitement and pleasure, began to run. As he ran, he turned his head to announce that the workers were coming back from the fields. The paths were soon humming with voices.

The woman in charge came out of the children's house and stationed herself on the grass, holding an infant in each arm. Children stood behind and in front of her, waiting for their parents, who were returning from the fields. Some stamped their feet impatiently; others did tricks to show Mommy and Daddy what they could do. Before they knew it, these children were scooped up. One was on his father's shoulders and another on his father's head, having appropriated his father's hat for himself. One was buried in his mother's arms. A little girl was stroking her mother's cheeks and saying, "Love your mommy?" All sorts of pet names and personal dialects were heard.

The workers were all back from the fields. The unmarried men and women ran to the showers, and those with families rushed off to see their children, stopping briefly at the office to ask for mail. Not all the children in Ahinoam were from that settlement. The *kvutza* was still young and hadn't produced many children yet, but, since its climate was so pleasant, several children from less comfortable settlements were spending the summer there.

The entire village was bustling. In one corner, a father was carrying around a child. In another, a mother nursed a baby. Nearby, a young man pranced around with a little girl whose father had been killed on guard duty. Next to them, someone was standing on his head, clapping his feet together. Slim girls with cropped hair, dressed in men's clothing, their shoulders like those of young boys, gurgled at their infants. Alongside each such girl was a suntanned boy with a peeling nose. The setting sun cast its final light, as it did each day, releasing specially created colors in a band that extended around the village from the westernmost reaches of the world. Birds were heard returning to their nests with a final chirp before hiding themselves among the branches for the night. The rabbits scurried around in their box and were suddenly still. A gentle breeze blew. All this lasted less than a minute. Then the bell was heard, announcing dinner.

From all the houses, huts, and tents, they assembled, filing into the dining room. Some had come to eat; others waited. The dining room was small, and there were two shifts, one entering, one leaving. Zahara was occupied with her son, so she didn't come to supper. Avraham-and-a-half was busy helping Zahara, so he didn't come to supper. But her father and mother were seated under the clock, between the windows and across from the door, in a spot reserved for important guests, from which they could see everyone in the *kvutza*.

The Herbsts were in the midst of a circle of young men and women. Some were cutting vegetables; some were spreading margarine on their bread. Some drank tea; others gulped water. Some were calm; others noisy, either behaving as they had learned to at home or demonstrating their liberation from bourgeois table manners. They all ate their fill. Then someone looked up from his bowl and, seeing the Herbsts, leaped up and went to sit with them. Others followed, welcomed them, poured their tea, peeled their cucumbers, sliced their radishes, made them salad and sprinkled it with oil and salt, and handed them dishes, the salt-shaker, the cruet of oil, urging them cordially to enjoy everything. As

Herbst picked up his tea and was about to drink, a pretty young woman came running with sugar she had obtained especially for the guests. Someone asked, "Has Zahara been informed that she has guests?" Someone else answered, "By the time a speedy fellow like you makes a move to go tell Zahara, it will be time to tell Zahara's grandchild that his grandpa and grandma are here."

The entire *kvutza* responded warmly to Zahara's parents. Some knew the Herbsts, because they had been in their house, enjoyed Mrs. Herbst's cooking and Dr. Herbst's conversation, fingered the books on his shelves, and been stimulated by his ideas. Others didn't know them but had heard about them. Everyone welcomed them, as young people tend to do when company is congenial. There were some guests they were required to welcome: tourists who were ridiculous and whose questions were just as ridiculous; official guests from the national bodies that determined the budget; cultural windbags who assumed they were indispensable. But the Herbsts were welcomed because of Zahara and because of who they were. They were "like us," and, even if our problems weren't theirs, when we discussed them, we didn't run into a stone wall. Furthermore, although Herbst was a scholar, he wrote academic papers in ordinary language.

The two Heinzes—Heinz the Berliner and Heinz from Darmstadt— took charge of the Herbsts. They sat with them and told them what had been happening in the *kvutza* and what was about to happen. They sat talking until a few members of the Culture Committee came to invite Dr. Herbst to give a lecture. "A lecture?" Herbst asked in dismay. "As I was leaving, I stored all my wisdom in a desk drawer. It didn't occur to me that anyone here would be interested in my merchandise." He scrutinized the young people, their amiable charm and lively innocence, and it seemed odd to him to stand up and lecture on his usual topics, which, though important in themselves, were of no consequence here. They pressed him, suggesting all sorts of subjects. He listened and responded, answering with repeated qualifiers that contained not a trace of scorn, only wonder that anyone was still interested in such things.

While the Culture Committee was negotiating with Dr. Herbst, a group of young women were engaged in conversation with Mrs. Herbst on such subjects as cooking, baking, sewing, and weaving. Mrs. Herbst thought in wonderment: When they come to Jerusalem, they pursue everything except domestic activities; here, their interests are exclusively domestic. She had some questions too: Why aren't the thorns at the gate being destroyed, when do the thistles wither here? In her experience, they wither in July, yet here they are still in bloom.

Mrs. Herbst also asked why the olives were preserved in soda, which spoils their taste. She still remembered eating marvelous olives when she first came to the country. The two Heinzes left with the Culture Committee, to give Herbst a chance to prepare his lecture. Herbst watched the Heinzes go, thinking: They're both more attractive than that beanpole Zahara chose. He turned to Henrietta and asked, "Where is Avraham?"

— 22 —

When dinner was over, the bell at the top of the water tower rang once again. It was a long time since the bell had sounded so gay, so inviting, so full of promise, saying, "Come everyone, come. You won't be sorry. You can trust me not to mislead you. Remember, when that windbag was sent to talk to you, I hinted that you wouldn't miss anything if you stayed away. He accused you of hating culture, not realizing it was because you are cultured that you stayed away. Now I'm telling you to come. You can count on me. It will be worthwhile."

After the children were put to bed, their parents arrived in the dining room. They had been preceded by the unmarried settlers, who were preceded by those who knew the lecturer. Before long, the room was full. People who weren't particularly attracted to lectures came too; there was nothing else for them to do, since everyone else was going to the lecture.

The supper dishes were cleared, the floor was swept, the doors and windows were opened, and the fan was turned on to disperse the smells. Only the odor of cigarettes clung to the walls and the window screens. The tables were arranged as if for a holiday: a short table connected two long ones, adorned with a large green bowl full of wildflowers. Everyone found a seat. Those who tended to stay until the very end sat near the lecturer; those who tended to leave midway through sat near the door. The chairs in the middle were empty. After a while, they were occupied by the people who had been hugging the door.

Herbst was still wavering about his subject. He was in the habit of lecturing to students who come because of the subject, who have made a choice; when he lectures to them, he knows what they expect. The intellectual level of this group of youngsters is not clear. Some of them know things most people don't, yet they don't know what a beginning student knows. Some of them read a great deal; others never open a book. To whom should he direct his words? In the past, when he gave public lectures, he knew what would be appealing. Now that he hasn't given one in years, it is hard to decide. He considered several subjects and settled on "The Art of Byzantium." Lectures on art are always popular. But he had second thoughts. Without illustrations and a slide projector, such a talk would be boring. He considered lecturing on the Crusaders in Byzantium and thought better of that, because he would first have to review what happened along the way, and it would take an hour to arrive at the gates of Byzantium. He considered lecturing on the Crusaders in general, but there was another problem. It is generally assumed that the Crusades had a positive outcome, opening up the mysterious Orient to Europeans, but he is not of this opinion. If he intends to challenge the accepted view, he would have to elaborate, and this is neither the time nor the place. He considered lecturing on contacts between Russia and Byzantium, and the Byzantine influence on Russia. Since these youngsters are sympathetic to Russia, the subject would appeal to them. But he hesitated, lest this lead to political debate. He hates the political debate that ensues from scholarly discourse.

One of the young women brought him a pitcher of water and a glass. She struck him as a model of Byzantine beauty. It occurred to him that he could lecture on images of Byzantine women. However, he would be embarrassed to discuss their behavior in mixed company. He rejected this and thought of lecturing on the poet Romanos. But the poets who influenced him ought to be mentioned, and he didn't know a single related poem by heart, nor could he expect to find a text here. As he reviewed all these possibilities, they converged, reminding him of Constantinople and bringing to mind the truism "All good things must come to an end." He decided to begin there, roughly in this vein: Constantinople was greater than any city known in Europe, so much so that it became the standard for everything great and enduring. As he began outlining his talk, he pictured a dead body seated on a throne, wrapped in a magnificent cloak, wearing the headdress of the Greek patriarch on its head and flanked by robed priests holding lighted candles and intoning mournful chants and dirges. He remembered that he once went into town to buy an oil lamp, so it would be possible to sit in the garden at night when it was too windy for a candle, which would please Henrietta. He remembered meeting up with the funeral of the Greek patriarch and being unable to buy the lamp, because the stores were closed. Since then, another patriarch had been appointed, who was subsequently removed and replaced by yet another, but he still hadn't bought the lamp. Herbst managed to think many thoughts in a short time and to sort them out before contemplating the patriarch's funeral itself. Now that he was ready to contemplate the funeral, he began to consider lecturing on the prohibition against keeping corpses overnight, which was a rule in the holy cities of Greece. This subject prevailed.

Herbst stood at the head of the table in the dining room. On the table were a pitcher of water, a thick round glass, and a bowl of flowers. On his left sat Zahara, her face beaming with love for the entire world—the world being the *kvutza* and all its members, plus her mother and father. But all this amounts to nothing compared to Dani, who embodies all love. Henrietta sat to the right of Herbst. She hasn't heard her husband lecture in years. Now she is here, at his side, while he speaks. Though she knows him so well and is thoroughly familiar with his voice, she looks up to see if that is truly Fred, for his voice has a new ring, a ring of confidence. His voice has something in it of Neu's tone and of that of all the teachers he is fond of—yet it is his alone, unlike anyone else.'s True, she hasn't heard every voice in the world; still, it is clear to her that his tone is unique and no one in the world can match it. Avraham-and-a-half stood at a distance from the lecturer. He was the tallest person in the room, soaring over everyone, surveying the heads of his friends and trying to determine, by their hair, who they were and how they were at that particular moment. The driver who had brought the Herbsts to Ahinoam stood next to Avraham-and-a-half, surprised at himself for not having noticed right away that his passenger was an interesting man. Before he started speaking, he had seemed like all the others. As soon as he began, he proved he wasn't one of them. Herbst was an experienced lecturer. When he spoke, his words drew you in. Herbst was confronted with a mass of uninhibited listeners, careless of their manners—in some cases deliberately so, to show their indifference to good manners. After a while, habit notwithstanding, they began to listen, each according to his ability and even beyond. After a vigorous workday, they were tired, and some of them had come to listen a bit and doze a bit. In the end, what they were hearing ruled out sleep.

Herbst's mode of thought begins with an overview and includes a range of subjects—skimming the surface, touching yet not touching—until, finally, he ends up where he began. In his lectures, he begins with essentials, never straying far from the heart of his subject, patiently clarifying and elucidating it. He is careful not to startle the listener with new interpretations and refrains from emphasizing any particular word. Just as he wouldn't underline a phrase in one of his books, so, on the same principle, he doesn't emphasize words when lecturing. It is not his way to begin at a barely audible pitch and work up to a crescendo.

On this night, he changed his tack—not in terms of form, but in terms of the lecture itself, introducing material that was somewhat tangential. He began with the prohibition against keeping corpses overnight that prevailed in the holy cities of ancient Greece. In this context, he formulated the very essence of Greek philosophy and the principles of religion. He looked at the arts, theater, the circus, athletic games, and the marketplace, where citizens dealt with issues of state—the entire range of Greek manners and pastimes before Christianity appeared, obliterating everything. Herbst, a disciple of Neu, who viewed economics as a force but not a primary force, mentioned the economic factor without dwelling on it. Finally, he came to the decline of Greece and of all civilization until the rise of Christianity, which delivered the fatal blow. Having mentioned the holy cities of Greece, he remarked on the Greek cities in the Land of Israel, too—how they were maintained, how they were destroyed. Finally, he told of the destruction of Gaza and the struggles of Porphyry, the bishop of Gaza, who witnessed its destruction. Here, Herbst offered facts not noted by Marcus the Deacon or by any other chronicler.

— 23 —

The lecture was successful beyond all expectations. I have already described Herbst's prowess; now let me describe the prowess of his listeners. They listened, not merely with their ears, but with their soul, alerting their ears so their soul could hear. Those who had left school to come to the Land of Israel, abandoning their studies in the middle, remembered things they had been too young to appreciate. Now that Herbst was bringing up these subjects, they recognized what they had lost, and what was lost to the world with the destruction of Greece. When had their loss occurred? The day they left their parents' home and the town in which they were born. Throughout Herbst's lecture, some of our friends sat summing up accounts vis-à-vis the Land of Israel, comparing themselves to the last of the Greek philosophers, who watched as Christian invaders destroyed all that was good in the world, stamping out life's joy and beauty. Were it not for the Land of Israel, they would be with their families, tranquil in their homes, serene in their towns, free from fiscal worries, hostile Arabs, and the woes of *hamsin* winds.

Others, who came from the study houses of Galicia, knew hardly anything about Greek cities beyond what appears in the Gemara and in Josephus. Macedonia, for example they related to Alexander of Macedon, conqueror of Judea in 322 B.C.E.; Athens, to the elders of the Athenian school, and to Rabbi Yehoshua ben Hananiah; Corfu, to news items about its citrons on Sukkot. They were astonished by everything Dr. Herbst said, especially about burial customs. Jerusalem was known to be the only place in the ancient world with a prohibition against keeping corpses overnight; now he claimed that idol worshipers lived by the same rule. They were further astonished to hear him refer to worldly scholars as *zaddikim*. Though they themselves had changed since childhood, their faith in these *zaddikim* was intact. And who were the *zaddikim?* They were rabbis whose greatness was on the lips of everyone, the teachers of the *Hasidim.* When these young people moved away from the Torah and began reading secular books, they found support for much of what they had heard. Herbst, as you know, always responded to young people's questions as if they were those of a scholar and made every effort to satisfy them. Now he was quiet, reflecting on statements he had heard from Shira. Once, walking together on a Shabbat afternoon, they encountered a group of Hasidim. Shira was annoyed and imputed all sorts of evils to those pious people, Hasidim and *zaddikim* alike. But his mind didn't dwell on Shira. The road, the village, the lecture dissolved the image of Shira.

Others, because of poverty or the effects of war on their childhood, had never studied and never read. Still, they considered what Dr. Herbst told them and thought: What Dr. Herbst described may have happened in the past, one or two hundred years ago; in more recent times, such things couldn't happen.

One by one, several *kvutza* members slipped away to do chores. Those who were at leisure stayed on with the Herbsts. They brought tea and cake, and presented Herbst with further questions, which they had forgotten but remembered again. A breeze began to blow. Mrs. Herbst said, "Why don't we go outside. You don't mind, do you, Fred?" They got up, went outside, and stretched out on the lawn behind the dining room.

The fresh grass gave off a fragrance enhanced by the myrtle trees alongside the steps, whose scent was diffused by evening dew. They brought straw mats, which they spread on the grass, and blankets. The

Herbsts sat on their mat and covered themselves with blankets. The affection of their hosts was all around them; bright stars were embedded in the darkness above. A light suddenly began to twinkle in the grove at the edge of the village; it split into several lights, and a bark resounded from the cucumber field where Shomron slept. The bark was followed by three cries, then the call of a nightbird.

From the western part of the village, where the light was, came the sound of singing and the smell of burning twigs. Henrietta looked in that direction and turned so she could listen. Someone noticed and explained, "The Palmach people have built a campfire. They like to sit around it and sing." Henrietta nodded and said, "I see, I see." She was thinking: Tamara is already grown and Sarah is still small. Because of age and circumstance they're safe from such adventures.

Herbst was still holding the glass of tea he had taken with him from the dining room and giving profound answers to the questions he was being asked. Finally, there were no further questions, and Herbst was asked to talk about whatever he liked. He sat talking. It was many years since he had lectured before such an audience, since he had been in the company of such youngsters. It was many years since Henrietta had heard Herbst lecture and since she had heard him say the sort of things he was saying here. On this night, these two things came together. Most important, she understood the lecture, which was not the case when Manfred began lecturing at the university. At that time, she still didn't know a word of Hebrew. At many points during his talk, she had felt like stroking his hand. Now that she was sitting next to him, she took his hand and clasped it in hers, not letting go until they got up.

— 24 —

It was nearly midnight when Avraham-and-a-half and Heinz I accompanied the Herbsts to their room. Heinz I is Heinz the Berliner. The numeral I was appended to his name so he wouldn't be confused with Heinz from Darmstadt, who became Heinz II. Avraham-and-a-half walked with Zahara's mother, while Heinz I walked with Herbst. After a bit, they were joined by Heinz II and Marga—the Marga who had given Herbst the idea of lecturing on images of Byzantine women. Marga adds nothing to the story of Herbst and Shira. Her only relevance is that she had brought Herbst water and now gave Mrs. Herbst some sprigs of myrtle. She had planned to bring them in the morning, but Heinz II had said, "What you picked tonight, bring tonight; tomorrow you'll bring more." As she spoke, Marga was chewing a myrtle leaf. Herbst thought she was smoking a cigarette. Marga and Heinz were accompanied by Shomron, who always joined the night watch. Shomron was pleased with himself for having controlled the impulse to bark at Zahara's retinue. He didn't bark at them now either. But he would have liked to bark an inquiry: Why was everyone nodding at those people. Marga and Heinz had no effect on the Herbsts' walking pattern. Henrietta continued to trail behind Avraham-and-a-half, and Heinz I walked with Manfred. Henrietta's conversation was exclusively about Zahara and Dani, about the arrangements in the *kvutza*, which were ideal for babies but less than ideal for nursing mothers. Even had they been ideal for nursing mothers, they were not ideal for Zahara, who, though we wouldn't call her weak, was nevertheless delicate. Abraham-and-a-half devoured every word uttered by Zahara's mother, although he didn't grasp its meaning. The more she talked, the more fond he became of the old lady who was so fond of Zahara, and his mind raced ahead: In a few years, when we're really settled, we'll build a parents' house. We'll invite Henrietta and Herbst to live with the other old people, and every day, in the evening, Dani will visit Grandpa and Grandma. He will come back and tell his friends that Grandpa and Grandma speak Yiddish to each other. How odd it is that Henrietta and Herbst, who take such pains with their speech and whose German is so literate, will be perceived by the local children as Yiddish speakers. Avraham was deep in thought and didn't realize he was taking the Herbsts the long way around when he ought to be leading them directly to their room. It was already late, and they must be tired from their journey. Heinz and Marga weren't paying attention to the route and noticed neither the Herbsts nor the fact that they had left them without saying goodbye.

Heinz I was still engaged in his conversation with Herbst, in the course of which he mentioned Saint Jerome and his Jewish teacher. So Herbst wouldn't make the mistake of thinking he was an expert on the subject, he announced, "Everything I know about the Church Fathers I learned from a single lecture by Yohanan Levi. I once went to Jerusalem and up to Mount Scopus. I wanted to see the university. I soon found myself listening to a lecture on Saint Jerome." "In any case," Herbst said, "you have a good memory if you remember who his teacher was." Heinz was quiet, offering no further comment. After a while, he said, "It's not that my memory is good, but in the course of

that lecture Yohanan Levi mentioned that Saint Jerome had misinter-
preted a particular biblical verse and remarked that, for Jerome, that
teacher was a poor investment. I only remembered Jerome and his
Jewish teacher because of that joke." Herbst said, "Nonetheless, you
deserve praise. Because of a silly joke, you remembered what was
essential." Heinz said, "If you mean to praise me, I have to share the
credit with Avraham, who was at the lecture too." Herbst turned to
Avraham and said, "I hear you go to lectures. I'm sorry to have missed
the privilege of having you in my audience." Avraham said, "I heard
your entire lecture tonight." Herbst said, "And is it unusual to hear an
entire lecture? If you had left in the middle, Dani would accuse you of
offending his grandfather. Yes, yes, I forgot—you don't smoke, so I
can't compensate you for your time with a cigarette. But you, Heinz,
surely you smoke? Not you either? Only the girls smoke here." "The
girls?" "Didn't you notice that the one with Heinz II was chewing on
a butt? But let's get back to our subject. So, you heard the entire lecture.
Tell me this, my dear boy, how many grammatical errors did you
find?" Avraham said, "I didn't find any." "But my accent is bad?"
Avraham said, "An accent tells where you're from. I can tell you're
from Berlin." Henrietta said, "You're not going to argue about accents
at this hour?" Manfred said, "We've already begun." Henrietta said,
"In that case, stop." Manfred said, "We've stopped." Heinz said, "This
is the place. You can sleep as late as you like. You won't be disturbed
by noise. The person who built this house loved to sleep. He picked
a spot on a hill, with no neighbors. If you leave the lights off, even the
sand flies will leave you alone. You don't have to worry about mosquitoes. The windows are well screened, but nothing keeps the sand
flies out." Avraham said, "Since I came to this country, I've been
hearing about sand flies. I think it's all a fairy tale." "A fairy tale?"
Avraham said, "In the old days, people were afraid of giants. Now
they're afraid of sand flies." Henrietta looked at Avraham fondly and
said to her husband, "Fred, isn't it a pleasure to hear such conversation?
Tell me, Avraham, haven't you ever been bitten by a fly?" Avraham
said, "Not by a fly, not by a mosquito, not by a scorpion, not by any
of those mythical creatures we hear so much about. Why should they
sting me? Do I occupy their space? There is room in this country for
me and for them." Heinz said, "Now I understand why you didn't join
us last weekend when we were clearing away the stones in order to get
rid of the scorpions." "Last weekend? I wasn't here last weekend. I
went to Afula to bring Dan and Zahara back." Herbst said to Avraham,
"Didn't you ever suffer from mosquitoes?" Avraham said, "Yes, of
course. One summer they made my vacation so miserable that I gave

up and ran away." "You ran away? Where did you run to?" "To my mother and father in Berlin." "Berlin? Where were you?" "In Karlsruhe. I had an aunt there, a special aunt, who invited me to spend my vacation in Karlsruhe. I was happier than I had ever been about any aunt, because I was told that my Karlsruhe cousins were going to act out the Karl May stories we used to read. When the vacation began, I went to Karlsruhe. I was attacked by mosquitoes and stung until my hands and face were like sieves. It was impossible to stay outside because of the mosquitoes. Not only was I unable to join in the play, but I couldn't even walk in the park with my cousins because of the mosquitoes. Yes, they had window screens there." Heinz said to the Herbsts, "Even though Avraham denies the existence of sand flies, you should be careful. If you can't get undressed without light, be sure you turn it off immediately, before the sand flies notice. The moon is bright, and there's actually no need to turn on the light."

It was nearly midnight when they brought the Herbsts to the house in which they were going to spend the night. It was set on a hill at the edge of the village, away from the other houses, and had two rooms, one an infirmary, the other for the nurse. It had been built by the engineer who planned the *kvutza,* for himself and his new wife, with the idea that they would come for weekends and vacations. He didn't spend much time there, so he sold it to the National Fund. The National Fund gave it to the *kvutza,* and it served as an infirmary, as well as a place for the nurse to live. The house was sold because of something that happened. The engineer and his wife were once on their way to Ahinoam, looking forward to a quiet and pleasant Shabbat. They met up with an Englishman, a government official whose car had broken down on the road. They offered him a ride. He accepted. The engineer invited the Englishman to stop in Ahinoam and have tea with him and his wife. He agreed to join them. Over tea, he told his hosts that he had been living in the country for six years and had never been invited to anyone's home. The engineer said to his wife, "We ought to make up for all those years of loneliness." The woman said, "We'll do our best." The Englishman spent all of Shabbat, as well as the following day, in the engineer's house, and his hosts did their best to make his stay pleasant. He grew fond of them and became a frequent caller, almost a member of the household. One day the woman said to the Englishman, "I'm tired of this deception. Rather than cheat on my husband, I'm going to move in with you, and we can always be together." The woman left her husband's house and went to live with her lover. The engineer began to detest his country house. He sold it to the National Fund, and it was passed on to the *kvutza.* That night, it was unoccupied. The nurse who lived there had gone to Jerusalem in the morning, to see the psychiatrist Dr. Heinz Hermann about a young woman who had been attacked by an Arab shepherd and was in emotional shock. Herbst didn't know that the quarters he and his wife were occupying belonged to the nurse he had met at Shira's. It's good that he didn't know. Had he known, he would have been afraid Zahara would discover that the nurse knew him and that they had met at Shira's. One further detail: when the nurse returned to the village and heard that Dr. Herbst had stayed in her room, she said, "I'm sorry I missed his lecture," but she didn't mention the fact that she knew him.

Zahara hadn't informed anyone that her parents were used to sleeping in separate rooms. The two of them were given one room, the nurse's room. The infirmary couch was brought in, and the two beds were set up side by side. The Herbsts came into the room. The scent of flowers, along with that of fresh linens, conveyed the fact that these were welcome guests. Henrietta put down the myrtle, undressed, took the flowers out of the room, got into bed, said good night to Manfred, lowered her eyelids, and succumbed to sleep.

Manfred found it odd to be sleeping in the same room as Henrietta, which he hadn't done for many years. From the time she became pregnant with Sarah, they hadn't slept in the same room even once. Now, all of a sudden, they were in the same room, and their beds were so close they were within arm's reach of one another. Henrietta paid no attention. As soon as she got into bed, she dozed off, and, now that she was covered by the light blanket Zahara had brought her, she succumbed to the deep sleep decreed by the day's activities.

Fearing the sand flies, Herbst went to bed without light and without a book. Since his return from the war, he would never lie down without a book. Even in bad times, during the unrest that followed the war— when municipal lighting, both gas and electric, was suspended—he had read by a small candle or a carbide lamp. Here, he lit neither a candle nor a lamp. For a time, the moon lit up the window and shone into the room. It vanished, appeared, vanished, and didn't appear again. It may have reappeared after he dozed off. Anyway, he wasn't asleep now. He was very alert, because of the fresh air, because of the lecture, because of his conversations. The lecture was a success. It wasn't new; he had given the same lecture when he was first appointed to the university. But new elements were introduced tonight. As he presented new insights, many eyes shone responsively, unlike that first night, when the evil eye lurked everywhere, awaiting his downfall. Not that he had been usurping anyone or that there were other candidates for his position, a position that was created for him because of Professor Neu. But the primal law holds; for every Abel there is a Cain, if not to commit actual murder, then to invoke the evil eye that destroys one's spirit. Another thing about the lecture in Ahinoam; it was spoken rather than read.

Herbst lay in bed recalling the people who had been in his audience this evening. Herbst was attached to his university students, knew each one of them, with their particular spiritual qualities, and was fond of them, perhaps more than they realized. But how many were they? Five or six a semester. Here in Ahinoam, fifty or sixty young men and women came to his lecture, healthy, vigorous, lively. And that Byzantine girl—if I were going to add pictures to my book, hers would be the first. All of these youngsters, males and females alike, invest their youth, designed for joy and pleasure, in work and drudgery. They sacrifice much-needed sleep to hear a scholarly lecture on a subject remote from their lives. As for me—the lecturer, for whom scholarship is, presumably, the axis of life—I waste my time on . . . Lo and behold, what he failed to do on all other nights, he succeeded in doing on this night. He took charge of his thoughts and did not dwell on Shira.

That night, as was always the case when his mind was stimulated by work, he resolved to devote all his energies to completing his book, fortifying his conclusions, leaving no grounds for the charge that the author was inventive but unconvincing. Convincing, convincing . . . Who invented that ugly word, and what is it doing in a scholarly context? Are we political agitators? Scholarship involves going with the data. Whatever conclusions this forces upon us, we are required to present them without equivocating, even if they are contrary to what we had in mind. I don't specialize in the Hasmonean period, but, if I were to deal with it, I would conclude that much of what Antiochus demanded of the Jews, the Hasmonean kings did willingly. And I wouldn't hesitate to make this fact public, although it detracts from our glory, demonstrating that, given the chance, we behave like any other nation. Similarly, if I were to write a book about national character, I wouldn't hesitate to generalize about Jews, to declare that it isn't a state and political life that Jews are after, but the opportunity to serve God and support themselves. Which is what Mattathias and his sons were after when they were pressed to violate the rules of their religion. When the Hasmonean kings behaved corruptly, many leaders in Jerusalem chose to give up the kingdom and beseeched Pompey to protect them from the rule of the Hasmoneans. I know that such ideas are a challenge to Zionism, and Zionism has, after all, saved my life and brought me here, at a time when so many fine and prominent individuals are in mortal danger. I am repaying a good turn with a bad one. But those

who engage in scholarship value it, and we must stand by its truths. As
for my book, I must get back to work and finish it. Should new material
fall into my hands, it would be wise to ignore it. It is sometimes better
to close one eye than to add material that pretends to add to the
substance but merely doubles the bulk.

Herbst lay in his bed reviewing his manuscript. He undertook this
review to determine what to highlight and what to play down, in the
interest of completing the book and preparing himself for a new project. It was not yet clear to him what it would be, but he had a sense
of it, as though he were already collecting material.

So as not to interfere with his sleep, he began thinking about a simple
aspect of the work: how to set up a new box for his new notes. Even
if he completes his large work, the boxes won't be empty. Those boxes
are amazing; though he takes out endless notes for colleagues, students,
or minor articles of his own, they always fill up again. When your soul
is fixed on a particular idea, you discover it in everything, and, in this
process, new notes are constantly created. That night, he decided to
abandon the tragedy he had intended to write about the Byzantine
woman of the court, the nobleman Yohanan, and Basileios, the faithful
servant, which I have described in preceding chapters. Even, before this
night, Herbst had begun to suspect that he had nothing to contribute;
that, even if he were to make a great effort, he wouldn't accomplish very
much; that whatever he might achieve would be so slight that it would
not approach even the tiniest fraction of what Gerhart Hauptmann
achieved in *Heinrich the Unfortunate*, his dramatization of a superb
story. Herbst was not presumptuous. He had no illusions about himself
as a visionary. Not in his wildest imagination did he compare himself
to such a famous poet. But, having given up the idea of composing a
tragedy, he began analyzing the work of various authors and ended
with Gerhart Hauptmann and his play *Heinrich the Unfortunate*.

Once he decided to give up the tragedy, he felt a surge of relief and
lightness. From now on, his time was his own. He was free to pursue
his interests and devote himself to his current book, as he had done
when writing the first one. Actually, there was a big difference between
the two. One was written in German, a language with thousands of
volumes on the subject, while the other was to be written in Hebrew,
in which there was not a single pamphlet on the subject. His first book
was written in a language with standard, set, accepted terminology,
whereas Hebrew possesses no standard terminology, and scholarly
writers must improvise, translating or creating terms from scratch.
Either way, they struggle and waste time on something a living language simply provides, demanding no effort. Herbst was pleased to be

writing in Hebrew, rather than in one of the languages of the world, though those languages promote an author's name. And he was pleased to be repaying a debt to the language in which he now lectured, at a time when many far more distinguished scholars were being deprived of their posts and were in mortal danger.

From the bed opposite his couch, he could hear Henrietta's breathing. Her breaths were even and regular. Three long ones and one short one, one short one and three long ones, each breath timed to fit in with the others. Even in her sleep, she wasn't undisciplined. A woman who is orderly when awake is orderly when asleep. He turned toward her and told himself: Those old bones need rest. Let her sleep. She's tired, she's tired from the trip. She was so alert on the way. She noticed every mountain, hill, and forest, every snip of cloud, each bird and grasshopper—everything that crossed the road, man as well as beast, not to mention grasses and flowers. Her eyes soaked up the colors of every blossom. If I were to draw an intelligent woman, one whose vitality has not been diminished by the years, I would draw Henrietta as she was when she sat in the dining room with those girls. Henrietta sat among them like a mother with daughters awaiting her in many different places, with such intense anticipation that their places can no longer contain them, so they come together, and, as soon as she arrives, they swarm around her, fixing their eyes on her lips as she tells each one what she wants to know. This is how it was with Henrietta and those girls: until she spoke, they didn't know what they were after. When she spoke, they knew she was saying what they wanted to hear. More than surprises or miracles, the heart needs answers to unformed questions.

— 25 —

The village was asleep; well-earned rest and tranquility enveloped its houses, huts, and tents. An occasional sound was heard—a cow mooing in the barn, chickens clucking in their coop. This was followed by a second sound, sometimes repeating the original one, sometimes sounding surprised at itself. Then the village was silent again, pervaded with quiet peace. The silence was once again broken by the gurgle of irrigation pipes and noises from the water tower, the smell of fading embers emanating from the campfire.

A gust of wind passed through. Tent flaps swelled, and the lights inside quivered. Those who live in the tents are young and hungry for knowledge. On a night such as this, if they are not working, they are sprawled on their beds, reading by candlelight. There are many problems and many hidden secrets; a few of these secrets have been revealed to wise men and are disclosed in their books. There are those who read about cosmic affairs; others read about human affairs. Some read what was written by historians; others read what the poets wrote—the story of Amnon and Tamar, for example. Amnon and Tamar are names picked at random; if you prefer another set of names, they will do as well. Some are reading about soil mechanics; others, about raising livestock and poultry. There is even someone writing, not reading at all. Perhaps future generations will read his words. It is the way of the wind to shift and be everywhere.

I will get back to those people who receive light from others. Right now, let me mention something that is useful to farmers and fruit growers. Both are at war with birds, for they fly in and consume hard-won crops. Those who tend cows and chickens share their grief, for the birds come and eat the animal feed. For this reason, war is declared, even on songbirds. The assault involves not only noisemakers and scarecrows but rifles and other deadly implements. In some poet's story, we find the tale of a man who had gardens and orchards. He invited birds from near and far to his gardens and orchards, made birdhouses for them, and provided them with food. They grew fond of these gardens and orchards, and became permanent guests. His neighbors said, "Don't you realize they're destroying your crops? You give all that up merely for their songs and their beauty." He said, "Not only do their songs fill my heart with joy. My eyes feast on their feathers. Further, they are useful to me, because they peck at the trees and ferret out insects no human hand can reach."

The village is deep in well-deserved sleep. Many perils menace these sleepers, for all around them are armed bands with designs on their lives. Yet most of the villagers are immersed in sweet sleep that attached itself to them as soon as they lay down, before they had a chance to think about it. In fact, the watchmen who guard the village function in a remarkable way. They appear to be idle, to be doing nothing, but their roving eyes are a warning to thieves, bandits, and murderers that they had better not approach the village. Occasionally, they approach and even enter, but only after killing the watchman. This is what happened to one of the watchmen in Ahinoam itself, the one whose picture is in the dining hall along with other heroes, whose only daughter is being raised with the rest of the children. The watchmen patrol the four corners of the village, each one heading in a different direction. Those with families think of wives and children, whose sleep they safeguard. Those who are single think of someone special asleep in her tent. Since sleep puts everything out of mind, has she, perhaps, forgotten him? Just then, a tent flap is lifted, and she emerges, the young woman he feared had forgotten him. They run toward each other and walk on together, talking—not in a whisper, which would be frightening; not in a loud voice, for that would disturb those who are asleep—but singing as they go, without raising their voices. They choose, not nostalgic songs, but some of the lighter trifles, such as "Sing a song, song, song, / Sound a cheer, cheer, cheer."

Herbst lay listening. It seemed to him that what he heard was a German song that sounded like a Russian song but was actually a Hebrew song. His mind shifted to the question of accents, and from there to the character types he had observed in the *kvutza* and to young women who take on men's work. From there, his thoughts turned to the war, when most men went to the front and it seemed possible that the world would be destroyed. What with war casualties, the casualties of time, and work left undone, how was the world to survive? So women were expected to do men's work. Since they were doing men's work, they wore men's clothing. Some of them were grotesque, some attractive. But he didn't dwell on this and began thinking about his book again. He pondered the books of other faculty members, trying to recall whether anyone had written in Hebrew on a general subject or whether all the Hebrew books were about Judaism or the Land of Israel. His mind drifted here and there, from subject to subject, back to the war, to the agents of war, the victims of war, the events of the war. He thought about some of it a great deal; some, he preferred to avoid.

Now, in connection with what happened later that night, I bring up one of the things he dismissed from his mind. During the war, shortly after his marriage, his aunt in Leipzig asked to meet Henrietta. His aunt was too old to travel to Berlin. They agreed by letter that he and Henrietta would come to Leipzig on one of his leaves. One day, Manfred was granted leave. He went to his aunt's house in Leipzig. He washed up, shaved off his beard, changed his clothes, and went to the train station to meet Henrietta, who was expected on the night train. This plan had been devised in an exchange of telegrams. When he got to the train station, he discovered that he had made a mistake and come a day early. He stood there dejected, watching the Berlin train, which had arrived without Henrietta. As he watched the train, he noticed a girl, dressed in trousers, cleaning one of the cars. His heart began to pound, and he left. Walking back to his aunt's house, he saw her again. She was coming from work, dressed in a winter coat of the sort train conductors wear. It hung on her shoulders in a mannish way, and her coarse boots squeaked noisily. He stood watching her. She became aware of him and slowed down, to be more available should he choose to talk to her. He was taken aback and walked on, his heart pounding rapidly and ablaze with excitement. The next night, he went to the train station an hour early. While waiting for Henrietta to arrive, he went to the newsstand and saw a photograph of two severed legs, accompanied by a caption about a boy of fifteen or sixteen whose severed limbs were found on a bench in the Rose Valley. Near this item was a second item with the same picture but another caption, explaining that doctors consulted by the police believed the legs were those of a woman of about twenty, who was murdered, probably by a rapist, and that, since a young woman who cleaned cars in the central station in Leipzig had disappeared, it was assumed that the severed legs were hers. I am omitting Henrietta's reception that night, but I will add that Herbst reproached himself with the thought that, had he talked to the girl, she wouldn't have fallen prey to the rapist who killed her. Now, back to Ahinoam.

The singing voices were no longer heard. They were replaced by the wail of jackals. This sound didn't usually frighten Herbst. He had lived in Jerusalem for so many years that it was familiar to him; it had been common in the beginning, when Baka was sparsely settled. Now he was alarmed and shaken, but he didn't realize the alarm had been stored in him since the night Shira told him about a jackal that devoured a baby. All the things alluded to here are recounted, described, and elucidated in preceding chapters. When Shira told him about the jackal and the baby, he paid no attention, because he was preoccupied with the tale of the engineer and the whip. Now that he heard the jackal, having already dismissed the tale of the whip, the entire story came back to him. When he dismissed the tale of the baby and the jackal, the tale of the severed legs recurred. When he dismissed the tale of the severed legs, the tale of the baby and the jackal recurred. Finally, between the tale of the baby and the jackal and the tale of the severed legs, he was overcome by sleep.

But it was not good sleep, because in his sleep he discovered whose legs they were and who had severed them. Some brute, returning from war, had found her in the field behind her house and murdered her. Herbst ran to the police station to tell them who the murderer was. Before he even reached the station, he was intercepted by policemen, who arrested him as a suspect. He went with them, saying not a word, for they would soon see he was entirely innocent and release him. But he was upset that, in the meantime, there would be an item about him in the newspaper, and his wife and daughters would be mortified. He was not released; he was led to the death cell. He went to the death cell, saying not a word. He was confident they would soon realize he was innocent and send him home. But he was upset that, in the meantime, his wife and daughters would find out and be mortified. He began to worry that his wife and daughters might suspect him of the murder. He wanted to shout, "I'm innocent of that murder and of any other murder!" His voice was locked in his throat, because Shira was coming and he knew that it was she who was the murderer and it was she who was the rapist. He lifted his eyes and turned toward her imploringly, to arouse her sympathy, so she would attest that he wasn't guilty. But Shira gave no sign that she intended to make a move on his behalf. He raised his voice and shouted, "Shira, Shira!"

He woke up screaming and saw his wife standing over him, comforting him, trying to soothe his distraught soul. What he had seen in his dream was forgotten. He remembered nothing. Then he remembered being led to the death cell, with women dancing before him and singing, "Sound a cheer, cheer, cheer." He was startled and wanted to scream. Henrietta stroked his cheek and tried to calm him. Manfred stared at her and cried, "Mother, are you here? Oh, Henriett, I had a terrible dream. Such an awful dream. The sort of dream that can lead to madness." Henrietta smoothed his brow and said, "Calm down, my love. Calm down, Fred." Manfred said, "I can't calm down. I can't! What a dream, what a dream. Tell me, did you happen to hear what I was shouting in the dream?" Henrietta said, "I heard." Manfred shrieked in alarm, "Tell me what I shouted!" Henrietta said, "Calm down, Fred." Manfred said, "I won't calm down! Tell me what I shouted." Henrietta said, "You didn't shout. You were singing." "Singing? What was I singing?" Henrietta said, "That silly song that Tamara always used to sing." "Which one?" " 'Sound a cheer, cheer, cheer.' " Manfred reached for Henrietta and said, "Come and lie down next to me." Henrietta lay down next to him. He embraced her with all his might and cried out, "It was awful! Mother, a dream like the one I dreamed could drive a sane man to madness." Henrietta said, "Tell me the dream." Manfred said, "I can't, I can't. Don't ask me to tell it to you, and don't mention it. Maybe I'll forget it too. Mother, it was a dreadful dream, an awful dream, and you say I was singing in my sleep. What was I singing, Mother?" Henrietta said, "But I just told you, Fred." "Tell me again what I was singing." Henrietta said, " 'Sound a cheer, cheer, cheer.' " "Is that all?" "That's all." "Mother, you are so good. If not for you, I would have been hanged." Henrietta said, "Hush, Fred. Hush." She kissed him on the mouth, and he kissed her, a protracted kiss. Henrietta said, "Wait. I'll go and cover the window. The moon is shining on my face." Manfred said, "Mother, don't move. You are such a delight, Mother. It's good to have you close." Henrietta peered at him and asked, "Is that so?" Manfred said, "Yes, Mother. Believe me. You please me more than any woman in the world." Henrietta said, "To hear you talk, one would think there were others." She kissed him again and said, "My love, lie quietly. Maybe you'll fall asleep." Manfred said, "I don't want to sleep when you're with me." He embraced her with all his might. She embraced him so that they clung to one another and became one flesh.

With this, I have concluded Book Two of the book of Manfred Herbst and the nurse Shira. I will now begin Book Three, starting not with Herbst or Shira, but with Henrietta. After telling about Henrietta, I will come back to Herbst and Shira—to Herbst first, then to Shira, then to the two of them together.

BOOK THREE

— 1 —

Henrietta kept her secret to herself and did not reveal what was in her heart. In delighted surprise and surprised delight, she mused: The baby I'm going to bring forth is younger than my daughter's child; her own child is older than her mother's child. She was embarrassed before her daughters, yet pleased for herself, for her youth had been restored and she was as she had been in the early days, right after her marriage.

How did she arrive at such a pass? After receiving the news that Zahara had given birth to a son, she decided to go to her in Kfar Ahinoam, and Manfred agreed to come along. They locked their house and went off, spending three days and three nights with Zahara's firstborn, with Zahara, with Avraham-and-a-half, and with all their friends and well-wishers in the village. In all their years in Jerusalem, the Herbsts had never had three consecutive days of rest like these. I am speaking, of course, of Henrietta, whose days, except when Tamara and Sarah were born, were filled with work; but Manfred, too, enjoyed the rest. He wasn't trapped by piles of books, pamphlets, transcripts, notebooks, and cards, nor was he occupied with endless papers that seemed to generate spontaneously, producing more and more of their kind, which he would move from here to there although they belonged nowhere.

He did lecture in Kfar Ahinoam, more than once, in fact. Nevertheless, I maintain that he had never enjoyed such restful days as those in Kfar Ahinoam, for there is a big difference between lectures in Kfar Ahinoam and those at the university. His lectures at the university were required. The lecturer was required to lecture, and the listeners were required to listen, whereas in Kfar Ahinoam it was his wish and desire to lecture, and it was because of their own wish and desire that the listeners listened, most of them being tired of the speeches of political hacks and eager for intellectual discourse. Furthermore, from his lectures in Ahinoam he learned that he could recover what had been taken from him.

I'll explain what I mean. Dr. Herbst was not one of those who are willing to pay any price for a drop of so-called honor. He already understood in his youth that one benefits only from what is won through integrity. But when our comrade Berl Katznelson organized a three-day workshop, inviting various lecturers but excluding him, he was dejected, for he had always been in demand. The lectures he presented in Kfar Ahinoam were well attended, not merely by members of the settlement, but by many people from neighboring communities, proving that he could attract a larger crowd than all the lecturers on all three workshop days combined.

Back to Henrietta Herbst. Since the day she arrived in the Land of Israel, she had not had three consecutive days of rest, other than when Tamara and Sarah were born. Her days were spent working hard in the house, gardening, and dealing with guests. Most difficult of all was the pursuit of certificates.

Many of the Herbsts' relatives were left behind in Germany. Upon hearing that Henrietta and Manfred were going to the Land of Israel, they sneered at them for leaving a highly cultured country for an arid wilderness. When they heard Manfred was appointed lecturer at the Hebrew University in Jerusalem, they were astonished to learn that Jerusalem had a university. When they heard lectures were held in Hebrew there, they were astonished that the language still existed. Between yesterday and tomorrow, events occurred in Germany that transformed it into an inferno—the very country about which it was said: Every Jew should bless God daily for the privilege of living there. Now they wandered from land to land. The nations were grudging, and those who escaped the sword were not allowed to earn a living. At great risk, they returned to Germany, and from there they asked friends and acquaintances in America to send them entry permits. Our brethren in America did everything they could, neither resting nor desisting until they brought them to America. But, in the end, they were helpless before the mass of supplicants, among them the Herbsts' relatives, who were left with no options other than Palestine. They wrote to the Herbsts, "Send us certificates." Henrietta raced around to obtain certificates, making no distinction between her own relatives and Manfred's. The same catastrophe engulfed them all, making them equal before it. Nor did she mention that her relatives had all laughed when they heard she was going to Palestine, and, now that they were in trouble, they were asking her to bring them to Palestine.

I will interrupt the flow of my story to praise Henrietta Herbst.

Henrietta had an elderly relative. He was born in the province of Poznan. When Henrietta informed her relatives that the Hebrew University in Jerusalem had offered Manfred a position, the old man said, "I will tell you something from which you will understand what a Hebrew university is.

"When I was a boy, I neglected my studies. My mother was sad, and my father scolded me. What they achieved through their sadness and scolding could be compared to what our teacher Moses achieved through his sadness and scolding.

"One day, my father took me to a poor neighborhood. We went into a crumbling building. I peered inside and saw shabbily dressed boys crowded together on narrow benches, reading in shrill voices from tattered books, their words a jumble of the holy tongue and ordinary jargon. A skinny man stood over them, wielding a cane and a strap, groaning, grunting, and spitting. He leaped up suddenly, pinched one of the boys on the arm, and shouted at him, 'Villain, what are you looking at? Look at the book, not outside.' The boy burst into tears and said, 'I wasn't looking outside.' The teacher said scornfully, 'Then tell me what the book says.' The boy began to read, stammering. The teacher shouted, 'Villain, then tell me what you saw outside. Was it perhaps a golden whip? I know all of you only too well, you scoundrels. When I'm done with you, you won't have eyes to see with or a mouth to utter lies.'

"When we were outside, my father told me, 'In this school, the children of the poor are taught the Torah and commandments. If you neglect your studies, I'll send you there, and what the teachers in the government school failed to achieve, that teacher will achieve with his cane and whip.' "

What is the point of this tale? The Hebrew University in Jerusalem, where our good friend Manfred was appointed lecturer, is the point. I don't suppose the university in Jerusalem is exactly like the school my father threatened me with in my childhood. But most likely it is similar; otherwise, why would the Zionists want to create a Hebrew university in Jerusalem, when they send their children to universities in Germany? What role is there for Hebrew in our time, our forefathers having renounced it? And what do we, the Jews of Germany, need with Jerusalem? Invoking his advanced age, this relative now begs to be brought to Jerusalem.

Henrietta thought to herself: I'll go to those in charge of certificates, and they'll give me as many as I need, for the certificates are in their hands. After all, they are Jews too, and they know what's in store for German Jews. But she was not aware of the difference between those who seek a favor and those who have the power to grant it.

So Henrietta ran around in pursuit of certificates. She took on the job herself, rather than encroach on Manfred's time, for Manfred was busy with the new book he was writing on burial customs of the poor in Byzantium. The book was still unborn, except in his thoughts. She ran to the office she had been told to go to, only to be told, "This isn't the place, and this isn't the office." She asked where she should go. The clerk said, "I'm not an information service, and it's not my job to tell people where to go." Henrietta stared at him, her blue eyes black with despair. The clerk relented and, departing from the letter of the law, told her where the right office was located, giving her several land-marks: the streets in Jerusalem change names from one day to the next, so you won't necessarily find a street just because you know its name. He told her, "Go quickly, or they'll all be gone for lunch, and you'll find yourself facing a locked door."

She managed to run, unimpeded by the ruts in those Jerusalem streets. The good Lord is not overindulgent; He seems content to have covered Jerusalem with a sky that is uniformly blue.

Henrietta arrived at her destination and found the office open, but it was so crowded that she couldn't get in—either because she wasn't the only one with relatives sighing and moaning in exile in Germany, or because the office was overflowing with clerks. She stood—who knows how long?—until the clerks got up and went home for dinner, locking up for the day. Early the next morning, she was back again. She found that others had preceded her. She stood with them—who knows how long?—and left with all the rest, empty-handed. This was how it was, one day, two days, three days, and many days more.

She was once at a university reception for Weizmann, where she happened to be seated next to a prominent Jewish Agency figure, the one in charge of certificates. There was a long series of speakers, and this eminent man was struggling to remain alert. He saw a well-dressed woman, neither old nor ugly, sitting next to him. He began to talk to her. She sat and listened. He said, "My dear lady, do you take me for one of the speakers?" "Why?" "Because you sit so quietly, without interrupting." She found her tongue and told him about her relatives. He said to her, "It's impossible to bring them all in at once, but they could be brought in one by one. In three months, there will be a new round of certificates, and one—maybe two—could be earmarked for your relatives." The anticipated day arrived. He remembered her, was most cordial to her, and inquired about her health, as well as her husband's. As for the certificates, he said that all the certificates that arrived had been for individuals from a designated country, and every certificate had someone's name on it. "But, in three months from now, there will be more certificates, and, what we failed to accomplish with the certificates that are here, we will accomplish with those that are on the way."

The anticipated day arrived. She went to the Jewish Agency and knocked on the proper door. An assistant appeared and said, "He's away." "When will he be back?" He said, "My boss, the chief, is not in the habit of reporting his plans to me." She stood there, not knowing what to do. She peered in and saw the chief at his desk, polishing his fingernails, like a woman. She felt like screaming, "What use are these people, what good are their promises?" But her mouth failed her; it did not utter a sound. Henrietta didn't know that it was wise not to utter a sound. As long as we don't tell our benefactors what they are, there is still hope. The fact is, we depend on them, for those close to our hearts are crying out in distress.

— 2 —

Let us turn from the anguish of certificates to the joy of a son.

A son was born in Ahinoam. His parents didn't bother about getting him a certificate from the Jewish Agency or the Mandate government, yet he has come, he is here, he lets his voice resound, unafraid that Mandate officials will hear and expel him from the country. When Maria Teresa sought to limit the descendants of our father Abraham, peace be unto him, she issued a clever decree allowing only one member of each Jewish family in her kingdom to marry. The Mandate government behaves in a superior fashion, setting out with rifles to confront our brothers and sisters when they arrive at our shores, the old and infirm among them, as well as babies born en route. They stand ready to fire at these survivors, already debilitated by their woes, so they won't come into the country. But they have issued no decrees limiting births.

So we are happy that a child was born unto us. Rejoicing over this child, the grandmother, Henrietta, and the grandfather, Manfred, have come to celebrate with his mother and with Avraham-and-a-half, her mate. Despite the fact that he was conceived and born in Kfar Ahinoam in the Land of Israel, whereas they were born in another country, he allows them to approach him, even to hold him in their arms. If he kicks them, how much charm there is in his legs, how much power in his kicks! A thousand times a day, Grandpa would willingly subject his face to Dani's kicks, not to mention Grandma Henrietta. She has never enjoyed anything as much, even when Zahara was at Dani's stage of life. You assume Dani's kicks are random? Then look and see. They are deliberate and deliberately delivered. Grandma Henrietta has a gold tooth in her mouth. She had it made when she was pregnant with Zahara; when Dani kicks her, he aims at the gold tooth. He is suggesting to Grandma Henrietta that, if not for his mother, she would still be stuck with a rotten tooth. Despite his modesty, there is something about the shape of Grandpa Manfred's nose that conveys pride, so, when Dani kicks Grandpa, he aims for his nose. I am no expert in physiognomy. Dani, may he have long life, makes it clear that he still remembers the passages from the Zohar that are relevant to this subject. It would seem that the angel forgot to slap him on the mouth as he emerged from his mother's womb, so he still remembers everything he learned there.

The Herbsts are in Kfar Ahinoam, eating, drinking, sleeping, walking, kissing the hands and feet of Zahara's baby. Out of love for his daughter's son, Grandfather doesn't smoke in his presence, much less when he holds him in his arms. It's lucky that Grandpa Manfred doesn't wear glasses, as most professors do, the eyes being so close to the nose. And it's lucky that Grandpa can do without his pipe. Dani isn't accustomed to the smell of tobacco, for neither his progenitress nor her constant companion is a smoker, unlike some people we know, who are never without a cigarette—the fathers even when they hold their child, the mothers even during pregnancy and while they are nursing.

The Herbsts spent three days and three nights in Kfar Ahinoam. They stayed in a single room that belonged to the nurse who had gone to Jerusalem with a young woman who was distraught because of the doctor who had refused to do what she had asked him to do for her. The doctor had said, "How many nights do I spend without sleep to keep a patient alive; how many times do I risk my life, exposed to the hazards of the road, the weather, and Arab gunfire—and you ask me to kill the baby in your womb." Since the local doctor wouldn't accommodate her, she went where she went, to someone who did what he did, causing what he caused. And the nurse had to take her to Jerusalem, because that local doctor had gone off to earn his livelihood elsewhere, for no one had the right to demand that he do what he didn't want to do, what no doctor wants to do. But it's doubtful that he will find work, since the country is full of doctors, among them some esteemed and famous men who escaped the Nazi sword but now have no means of support. Female doctors fare better: they can support themselves doing housework.

So the Herbsts spent their nights in the nurse's room in the infirmary building, a second bed having been brought in for them. Because she was preoccupied with her son, Zahara had forgotten to say that her father and mother should be given separate quarters, as at home in Jerusalem. After the birth of Sarah, the child of his old age, Manfred had moved his bed to his study. So the Herbsts slept in one room, in adjoining beds, and this became their custom thereafter, at home in Jerusalem.

— 3 —

When Henrietta saw that she could no longer conceal what was becoming more and more obvious, she decided to tell her husband. Manfred listened, his face taut from end to end, his eyes altering their aspect. After a moment, he laughed, every limb laughing with him. After another moment, he reached for his wife, embraced her, placed his head on her heart, and was silent. She was silent too. The two of them sat in absolute silence, clinging to one another. Then Manfred looked up at her, afraid he had done some harm when he embraced her. Henrietta, reading his mind, laughed to herself. He saw her face aglow with serene joy. Putting together his assorted thoughts, he saw they contradicted each other. He tried to figure out just how, and found only this: Henriett, who produces female babies, will produce a male; although there is no evidence for this, it would be right and appropriate, since her three other pregnancies brought forth only girls. Which was not the case with Zahara. The very first time, she gave birth to a son.

Let us think and consider, what was it like for Zahara when she discovered she was pregnant and what was it like for him when Henrietta told him, in a whisper, that Zahara was pregnant. So many thoughts darted through his mind that he dismissed them all and concentrated on Sarah, child of his old age, who was born suddenly, arriving in the world suddenly, without his knowing she was on the way. Now that this pregnancy was conferred on her mother, Sarah no longer occupied her previous position.

What happened to him the night Sarah was born? It's impossible to say nothing happened, but it is possible to say it was an error. Now that Shira no longer shows herself to him and he makes no effort to see her, he considers himself liberated.

Herbst was glad to be free of those things whose very goodness is bad. If he still had his youthful energy, he would devote it to his book about burial customs of the poor in Byzantium. He would finish that book and write more. Not because a man's wisdom is measured by the number of books he writes; not because of Weltfremdt, who reminded him that such-and-such a number of years had elapsed since his first book was published, the one that led to his appointment by the university, and in the interim he had written only articles. He would write books for his own sake, because of his ideas, which were so prolific that they could fill several volumes and were already inscribed in notebooks, in papers, and in his heart.

Among the books he meant to write, we will mention the tragedy of the court woman, the nobleman, and his slave, as well as the book about the craft of tragedy. Even before he began, he renounced these plans.

He gave up the idea of writing about the craft of tragedy because he looked at the books others had written and saw that they were written only because their authors had read so much, and, having read a lot, they wrote a lot. He didn't write the tragedy in order to avoid being troubled by those dreadful events, for a great calamity befell the woman of the court, the nobleman, and his slave, sweeping others along in its wake, and they all vanished from the world.

During this period, Herbst took things in hand, got back to work, and achieved in a small number of days what he hadn't achieved in many months. There had been books on his desk, piled half a meter high and extending all around. Suddenly, in two or three days, all the books were cleared away, as if a magic wand had been at work.

The magic wand was a long, thick pencil, the kind factories distribute to advertise themselves. When Henrietta bought a portable stove for Zahara, the shopkeeper gave her the pencil to give to Dr. Herbst. As he read, Dr. Herbst marked what was of interest, copying the material into his notes immediately. When his mind was distracted by thoughts of Shira, he became ineffectual, stopped copying, and placed a scrap of paper between the pages as a marker, hoping to get back to work soon and continue copying. He didn't get back to work soon, and he didn't continue copying. His desk remained full of books, which were piled like two pillars designed to support the ceiling. I may be exaggerating; nevertheless, there is some truth to the description. The space between the books and the ceiling was minimal. Suddenly, all at once, the books were gone and the desk was clear. Herbst managed to copy in two or three days what he had failed to copy in many days. The blank scraps placed in books to mark material to be copied, he now wrote on in pencil. He began copying, continuing to work until everything was copied onto his note papers.

These papers were placed in a box about as thick as a medium-sized book. The enormous pile of books that had occupied the desk was replaced by a box, not large, not long. A box with several sections divided by colored pages—reddish, greenish, pink, dark brown, yellowish—in which his notes were arranged by subject. At the top of each page was a heading to indicate the subject. When there were no books left on the desk, the note box was full. Not one more note could have been stuffed in.

He went to Asher the bookbinder on Ben Yehuda Street to order a new box, so many centimeters long and so many centimeters wide, to match the first one, which he had brought from Germany along with his books. He went to Shiryon on Jaffa Road to buy paper for new notes. He took the paper back to Asher the bookbinder and gave it to him to cut, so the notes would be the right size. Asher the bookbinder cut the paper according to Dr. Herbst's specifications, like those of a publisher who indicates the length and width of every manuscript he sends to the printer.

What is more, before placing a note in the box, Dr. Herbst examined it carefully to determine how important it was. He arranged the notes by subject, then he grouped them, tying a string around each group, for the quantity of notes matters less than the range of categories. And what matters even more is that they be in good order.

Some notes are an asset and some are a liability. If they are orderly and well sorted, all is well. If you are looking for material for a book or an article, you reach into the box of notes, and they fall into your hand. But they can be a liability. If the notes aren't orderly and well sorted, they confuse you. The more you use them, the more they divert you from your purpose, pulling you in their direction and causing you to waste time. Even more troublesome are notes that haven't been checked. They seem to have the makings of a book, but, when you are ready to begin, you discover that you have copied the same thing a number of times. Not everyone can remember what he has already copied and what he hasn't.

Having made order of his notes, Herbst tried to do the same with his notebooks and pads. He erased what was superfluous and discarded what was copied in another place. Seeing Herbst at work, double-checking, writing, erasing, reading, discarding, writing more, discarding more, one might think a pedantic impulse had overtaken the man. But this was not the case. He was taking such care because of a sense of reality.

Let me explain. A scholar sits in the midst of a heap of books, reading, writing, documenting, copying, preparing material for a book he is eager to complete. He does not put down a single volume without copying something from it, for a writer does well not to give anyone the opportunity to say he overlooked what someone or other wrote. He devotes most of his years to this process, and he keeps adding more and more notes; by now, there are many full boxes. His greatest satisfaction derives from surveying his notes, which he views as the core of several books. When he dies, all those notes don't have the making of a single pamphlet to perpetuate his memory. Why? Because he has been so busy accumulating notes that he never took the time to see whether he hadn't copied the same thing over and over.

Anyone who saw Dr. Herbst before he left for Kfar Ahinoam, sitting at his desk, surrounded by books, so that all one glimpsed of him was the smoke from his pipe, would regard him as the prototype of the scholar, renouncing himself for the sake of his work. To be truthful, in those days he was using his pipe more than his pen or pencil, puffing away, letting time go up in smoke.

His desk was now empty. There were only two or three books on it, along with the new box waiting to absorb new notes. It sat there chastely, without shouting: See how learned I am, how much wisdom I contain. Herbst's desk was empty now, and Firadeus could brush off the dust.

The day his desk was dusted, the ashtray was emptied too. It was full of ashes from his pipe, as well as from the cigarettes he used to get from the peddler who considered Mimi and Julian Weltfremdt his patrons. They were brown and slender, as long as a small child's pencil on his first day of school. These cigarettes lasted as long as a lit match, and they left behind a charred tip.

Herbst wished to behave in all his affairs, including those related to becoming a professor, as he had behaved with respect to his book. Like all the other lecturers at the university, Herbst was hoping for a promotion. But it was not his way to reach out for something unless it was close at hand. So he didn't lift a finger for the sake of a promotion. He said to himself: I'll finish my book about burial customs of the poor in Byzantium, the scholarly community will take notice, and their views will reach the patrons of the Hebrew University, who will promote me to the rank of professor. Such was the case with my first book, as a result of which I was invited to be a lecturer at the university. When two lecturers were made professors on one day, Herbst began to wonder. Apart from a dissertation that added nothing to the realm of scholarship, the older one had produced only a small pamphlet distinguished by its meagerness, plus three flimsy articles offering very little that could qualify as scholarship. They found their rightful place in those journals whose editors are publicists, not scholars. The other newly appointed professor, an author of many books, was merely the sum of what he himself had written about them. And there was nothing in his books beyond what was in earlier ones; if I don't admit these books to my house, I am sure they won't be missed.

Herbst began to speculate. Perhaps it was his turn to become a professor. Although he hadn't produced another book, his articles were more important than several books.

Herbst was not a man of action, so he did not want to discuss this matter with Henrietta. Whenever Henrietta heard something congenial from him, she would press him to act on it instantly, as if it were up to him, as if he could declare himself a professor. Herbst knew one thing, and he stood by it: he must be careful not to say anything that might suggest he was eager for a promotion. Herbst did not want to be associated with those pathetic grumblers who considered themselves deprived because they weren't professors.

After two or three days, he dismissed the matter. When he did think about it, he was surprised at himself, for he had come close to doing something that was close to pulling strings, which was close to the sort of manipulation that was so alien to him.

— 4 —

I will forgo the saga of the professorship in favor of a chapter on Shira. But first, let me make two or three comments about Herbst's household.

Once again, Herbst surveyed his world and was amazed to find that all was well. This did not result in an emotional muddle, although surprise usually does muddle the emotions. On the contrary, that very surprise was a source of strength, making him feel fortunate, as if to say, "What applies to others doesn't apply to me." Since it's not in my power to explain thought processes, I will begin with a pronouncement of my own: Herbst felt as if all the household winds were at one with him.

All the household winds were at one with him, and he was at one with the household. How far did this go? It was the custom at that time for Arab boys to hide behind a tree, a fence, or a pile of refuse and, when they saw a Jew walking alone, to shoot at him. Once, past midnight, Herbst was coming from Shira's house. He was close to home when he heard a shot, felt the bullet whiz by, and realized it was intended for him. Herbst recognized that, as long as he lived in an Arab neighborhood, he was risking his life and the lives of his family. Since this never recurred, he regarded the event as chance and dismissed it from his mind.

Actually, it wasn't chance. Those who threaten our lives were intimidated by the Haganah, and, in areas patrolled by Haganah forces, there had been no more shooting. Though Herbst suspected that many of his students were Haganah members, he did not know this for a fact. Since there were no further ambushes, he dismissed what had happened to him near his home that night, after midnight, on the way back from Shira's.

So much for Dr. Herbst and his tranquility. We will now tell what happened to him during his tranquil days, as well as what happened to him when the tranquil days were over, and what happened to the people whose lives intersected with his, at home, at the university, and in several other places.

Since the day the Herbsts visited Bachlam, there was no longer a barrier between him and Herbst, and they grew close to one another. When they turned up in the same place, Herbst always asked how he was, and, if it was convenient, he would walk him home and go inside with him. Occasionally, he went to visit him on his own. Herbst, who was not in Bachlam's camp, had always behaved like those of his colleagues who were not in that camp either. Now that he was a friend, he no longer mocked him. In fact, he praised him. Herbst would now say, "Those two people—Bachlam and his wife—are not what you think they are." Having become accustomed to Bachlam's ways, he didn't notice what was ridiculous about him and tried to see his good side. Bachlam stopped hating Herbst, whom he used to include among the traitors, those professors and lecturers who came from Germany, took over the university, and deserved to be hanged. What is more, he began to treat him generously. He gave him a dozen offprints and wrote, on every single one, half a page or more in praise of his young friend, a man with a glowing future. He gave him a copy of one of his recent books, in which he wrote that he, too, was destined to produce fine and useful work. The phrase "he, too" was an allusion to the fond hope that Herbst might one day become like him. Because he was close to Bachlam, Herbst heard his friends defame Bachlam; he also heard Bachlam defame his friends. He would say, "What's it to them if the old man lets off a little steam?" Or, "What's it to the old man if they joke about him? They are both used to this."

Herbst surveyed his world and saw that all was well. It had always seemed to him that there was an open pit at his feet, a raging surf about to sweep over him. Between yesterday and today, the pit was covered; the surf subsided. The books that had been stacked on his desk were back in place; what he had intended to copy was copied. The copied material was organized and sorted, as were his writing pads, as were his notebooks. As soon as he sat down to work on his book, the notes were going to leap into his hands and offer themselves to him. Herbst had enough material to begin writing the book, but his ideas had so many ramifications that he wasn't sure they would lead to the conclusion he had had in mind at the beginning, before he started collecting material.

Let's have a look at the rest of Herbst's affairs.

His little daughter Sarah is growing up, and she is no trouble to her

parents. Her teeth grew in like a mouse's without causing her parents
a single sleepless night. She caught the standard childhood illnesses and
made short shrift of them. She was never really sick and didn't need
doctors. Whenever Henrietta saw that Sarah wasn't well, she called the
doctor, but, by the time he arrived, she would be all better. But what
will we do when it's time for her to start school? Here in Baka, which
is an Arab neighborhood, there is no Jewish kindergarten. During the
'29 riots, all the Jews fled for their lives and didn't return, except for
the Herbst family. We'll have to take the child to Talpiot, but how will
we manage to get her from Baka to Talpiot and from Talpiot to Baka?
We'll have no choice but to move to a Jewish neighborhood. It would
surely be nice to live among Jews, but how is one to give up the
vegetable garden and the flower garden, in which Henrietta has invested so much effort all these years? Manfred says to her, "Don't fret.
We can get vegetables from the market, and there are flower vendors
in the city from whom you'll be able to buy whatever you like."

So much for the vegetable garden and the flower garden; let's turn
our attention to the houses in the city. Two or three generations back,
there was space between the buildings. Each one stood alone. Now
they are crowded together on rocky terrain that produces no trees, no
shrubs, no grass—only noise and clamor. New neighborhoods have
been built, too. They have no trees yet, but saplings have been planted,
which will grow into sturdy trees. Talpiot is the neighborhood closest
to ours, so close to Baka that one bus serves them both. But I can tell
you this: in Talpiot, the houses are small, with tiny rooms. The roads
are in disrepair, and Arabs from nearby villages pass through, noisy and
raucous, littering the street with food and animal dung. Its streets have
no benches to sit on, not even trees in whose shade one could rest. True,
there is a grove, but every tree in the grove is claimed by a British
soldier and his slut, transacting their business while children watch,
laugh, and make obscene comments. Jerusalem's schoolchildren are
brought to this grove to plant trees on Arbor Day. They set forth with
great fanfare, bedecked with branches torn from trees that have just
begun to grow, and carry scores of saplings, which they stick into the
ground as they sing about the land. The next day, no one remembers
the tender saplings, except the Arabs, who uproot them and use them
to build cooking fires. What remains of that tree-planting celebration?
Dozens of articles about the Jewish National Fund and the teachers
who are engaged in reclaiming the land.

From the youngest of the girls, I move on to her big sister Tamara.
Sarah is not yet of kindergarten age; Tamara is about to be rid of school
or is, perhaps, already rid of it. We will now sing the praises of Tamara.

Her tongue has lost its sting. She is no longer insolent to her father. She doesn't call him by his name; she calls him "Father." And she doesn't say to him, "So, Manfred, you've made us a sister," as she did after Sarah was born. Furthermore, she doesn't malign her teachers, deride our great poets, or make silly remarks about Apollo bound up in *tefillin* straps. She has even changed her mind about Jewish history. She says many negative things about the British—that they have taken over the country, that it's time for them to fold their tents and go. Some people are offended by her opinions; others nod in agreement. One can't deny that there is a grain of truth in what she says. Even if we were to overlook the hardships imposed on us by Mandate officials, we must denounce them for shedding the blood of our brothers before our very eyes. Oppressed and tortured, escaping the Nazi sword aboard battered vessels that cast about for days, weeks, months on end, they finally reach the waters of the Land of Israel, only to be confronted by Mandate police brandishing rifles, barring them from the country, though it is open to Poles and to every other nation. The people that concluded an eternal covenant with this land is excluded from it.

So much for adversity; now we'll tell a little bit about Tamara's other affairs. She engages in volunteer work and does not earn enough to keep her shoes in repair. In any case, it's good that she doesn't interfere in the household routines. One might say she pitches in. We wouldn't be aware of this if we hadn't heard about it from her father, who said, "I'm grateful to you, my dear, for taking my letters to the post office."

I'll mention Firadeus too. Though she doesn't count as part of the household, she counts because of the housework. She arrives in the morning and leaves in the afternoon. If, for some reason, she doesn't come—because of the curfew, the perils of the road, or some other life-threatening situation—she doubles her efforts the next day and makes up what she has missed. On her own, she looks for and finds all sorts of tasks that never occurred to the lady of the house, whose grip on the household has relaxed, due to the stress of pregnancy, so that she no longer keeps her customary vigilant eye on things. This being the case, Firadeus does her best to spare Mrs. Herbst. Firadeus is devoted to Mrs. Herbst and to Mr. Herbst, too, because they are fine people. There are other fine people: Mr. Sacharson, for example, who pays her generously for putting wrappers on his pamphlets, even the ones her neighbors take and don't return. When he sees her looking sad, for someone might suspect she took money for them, he laughs and says, "Silly girl, don't worry. No need to get upset." Still, she doubts that he is really a good man, for there is something about his laugh that isn't right; the mockery in his eyes and his distorted face are signs that something isn't right. The Herbsts are different. They are good and lovable. Firadeus once tried to describe what was so special about the Herbsts to her friends, but she failed. Her friends said to her, "Even you don't know." Firadeus knows that she knows, but she doesn't know how to explain it to anyone else.

I have said so much about seemingly trivial matters that are not actually trivial, for they shed light on the people Herbst lived with. If I weren't afraid to be too abstract, I would say that all the household winds were at one with the man of the house.

——— 5 ———

Herbst sits at home. He doesn't go to Shira's, so, obviously, he doesn't stay there late. But he is at his desk late, with his books and his papers. Some of the papers are in the new box that was made for him; others are on the desk in front of him, so he can jot down ideas that will enhance his book. He is about to turn out a new book, a sequel to the first one. A true researcher—even if he turns out many books, each one brimming with new and different ideas—will relate them all to his very first book, the one that took shape in his mind when he first began to respond to intellectual stimulation, before he even knew why he was responding.

So Herbst is at his desk. He compares one text to another, one document to another, and studies photostats without a magnifier all day and into the night. Since he began to smoke less, his eyes have improved. And, since he began to smoke less, Henrietta comes in more often. When she comes, she brings a flower from the garden, fresh fruit from the tree, or any one of his favorite foods. When she comes, he clears a chair for her, and she sits down to talk to her husband. What does she talk about, and what doesn't she talk about? Things she has talked about already, things Manfred himself knows about, such as the baby boy she expects to give birth to. How does she know it will be a boy? Because that's what Manfred told her, and Manfred is dependable. When she was pregnant with Sarah, Manfred did not predict that she would give birth to a boy, and, in fact, she had a girl, not a boy. The night Sarah, their little daughter, was born was the night Herbst got to know Shira. Now that Henrietta is going to give birth to either a boy or a girl, Herbst has put Shira out of mind.

From the time Herbst first knew Shira to the present, he had never realized just how good it was for a man to be faithful to his wife. The poets have wrought splendid poems about love, yet not many of them celebrate a husband's love for his wife.

Nevertheless, Herbst was surprised not to be tormenting himself over Shira. Was his connection with her such a casual matter? Everything is determined by agreement. If we agree that something is important, then it is; if we don't, then it is of no consequence. This applies to his relationship with Shira.

Herbst makes no effort to see Shira, and Shira makes no effort to show herself to him. If Shira had come to visit Henrietta, as she had promised the day Sarah was born, he would not have minded. He would have welcomed her, asked how she was, spoken to her, as he did to most of the women who called on Henrietta.

He acted on his intentions. Not at home, but when he was out. Once, he was standing in front of a shoe store, considering whether to buy new sandals. His sandals were worn. He had brought them in for repair and retrieved them in worse shape than before, so he decided to get new ones. While he was standing in front of the store, Shira emerged, carrying some shoes in a paper bag. She saw him and said, "You disappeared from the horizon." He said to her, "Would you like me to show myself on your horizon?" Whatever he said was said only to be polite, which was the tone of the entire conversation.

When they parted, she said to him, "I have moved to a new place. If you wish, you can write down my new address." She also said to him, "You are going to buy yourself some shoes." And he said, "I'm not going to buy myself any shoes." She said, "But you're standing here and looking in the window." He said, "The window is full of children's shoes." Shira said, "Are you looking for shoes for your son?" He said, "You mean my daughter." She said, "Your daughter's son or the son your wife is about to give birth to." Herbst said, "Nothing is hidden from you, Shira." Shira said, "In any case, you may visit me in my new apartment." He said, "With pleasure, with pleasure. Let me have your package, and I'll carry it." Shira held the package with one finger and said, "It's light. I can carry it." He said, "No is no." She said, "I'm busy arranging furniture, or I would invite you to come this evening. This is your bus stop. If you're not in a hurry, I'll tell you something. You once asked me if I ever dreamed about you, and I told you I don't dream. But, of all things, the night after I told you that, I dreamed I was in my bed, and near my bed, at an angle, under the Böcklin picture,

some sort of creature was walking along jauntily. I looked more closely
and saw a little hat. Do you understand, Manfred? A little hat was
walking around the room. A little hat, walking, on its own. Here comes
your bus. Goodbye now, and *au revoir*. You didn't take down my new
address. Too bad."

Herbst boarded the bus, sat down, and thought: I was in town, and
I didn't buy anything for Henrietta's birthday. If Zahara were here, I
would consult her about what to buy. I could consult Mimi Weltfremdt, or maybe . . . Before he could think of anyone else to consult,
he was at his stop. Herbst got off the bus and went home.

— 6 —

Even though Herbst had put Shira out of mind, he realized that he
should have written down her new address. Not in order to visit her,
but to be polite, especially since she had told him twice, "Write down
my new address." Actually, she had said, "Write it down," only once.
The second time, before she went off, she didn't say, "You can write
it down"; she said, "You didn't take down my new address." She also
said, "Too bad." It's a bad sign when a man treats a woman he was once
intimate with as if she no longer exists for him. But what's left undone
may be for the best. Why fill our notebooks with useless data? Shira's
name and address would take up only a single line, but, when you
opened the book and saw the name, it would arouse all sorts of
thoughts.

Time plays its part, and Shira plays hers. She doesn't show herself
in any of her usual haunts. Herbst is glad that she doesn't show herself
to him, but he is also puzzled.

The days proceed in orderly fashion; the household functions in its
usual way. Henrietta does her work, and Manfred does his. He is busy
with his books and his students, at home and at the university. She is
busy in the house and garden. It should be mentioned that, were it not
for the fact that Firadeus helped her, Henrietta's work would not get
done. Her body is enormously heavy, and her legs seem to be weighted
down with stones. We will therefore sing the praises of Firadeus, who
is a helpmate to Henrietta. You cannot imagine what a skilled worker
Firadeus is. In addition, she has good sense. Henrietta recognized this

even before she became pregnant, when she could manage without help. Now that she can no longer manage on her own, she gives herself credit for having recognized Firadeus's special qualities early on. She often says, "What I observed earlier in my mind, I now observe with my eyes." Henrietta is pleased with Firadeus, and Manfred is equally pleased with her. Actually, Manfred was always pleased with the household help, to the extent that he was aware of its existence, since his main needs were met by Henrietta. When Firadeus arrived, she took on some of the chores that had always been reserved for Henrietta, both in the house and garden, and in Herbst's study. Since Firadeus has begun to do his room, he finds everything in place. Not just the smoking paraphernalia, the pens, and the ink, but slips of paper, blown under the furniture by the wind, are arranged neatly on his desk. Herbst admires Firadeus for not being lazy. Slips of paper he has lost track of, with notes on forgotten books, are set out in front of him, reminding him of material he didn't remember, although he himself had copied it. For this reason, he is always very cordial to Firadeus, and, even if he is involved in reading or writing, he stops to say a kind word. Firadeus listens and makes an effort to satisfy her employers.

Firadeus has many thoughts in her heart. First about her father, who was killed by an Arab while on his way home from work in Talpiot. As he did every day, on that day he walked home after collecting the garbage from the houses of Talpiot, an empty sack on his shoulders and an Ashkenazi-style hat on his head—a hat he had found in a Talpiot garbage can. It was a fine hat, and, being unfamiliar with the Ashkenazi practice of throwing out something perfectly good, he assumed it had landed in the garbage by mistake. He picked up the hat and knocked on the door of the adjacent house. The man of the house appeared and asked, "What do you want?" He pointed to the hat he was holding and told the man, "I found it in the garbage, sir, and I am returning it to you." The man laughed and said, "It's all yours. You can wear it on Shabbat and holidays." Father took another look at the hat and said to that gentleman, "May many blessings come your way." Father used to wear the hat on Shabbat, on holidays, on all joyous occasions. A fine man and full of good cheer, Father was invited to every celebration that took place in our neighborhood. After a while, he began wearing the hat every day, but not when he was dealing with the garbage. After a further while, he began wearing it when he was working. The day he was killed was the third time he wore the hat to work. Firadeus was sitting in the bus, on her way to Talpiot. All of a sudden, a shot was heard. Everyone began shouting. The driver stopped the bus, and a body was carried in. Firadeus had never seen a dead body and had no wish to see one. But her eyes were drawn in its direction. Her heart stood still. She tore at her heart with her fingernails, shrieking—a terrible shriek that still rings in her ears. After that, she didn't shriek at all; she was taken somewhere and given a drink to induce sleep and inhibit tears. To this day, her eyes remain inhibited, and only her heart murmurs: My sweet father, my sweet father. Unlike that moment when she saw that the dead man was her father and shrieked a single shriek: "Father!"

Mother is second only to Father. Like her neighbors, Mother works all day. At night, another mood takes over. She gets up from her mat and paces back and forth, her eyes closed tight, her spirit lamenting, wailing, mourning the father of these tender orphans, a blameless man whose innocent blood was spilled while God in heaven remained silent. He remained silent as an evil nation had the temerity to murder a righteous man in this land ruled by violence.

Third in the thoughts of Firadeus are her brothers and sisters, who have never known any kindness. She alone has found kindness, in the Herbst household.

Many people come to the Herbst home. Almost all of them are doctors, which is how it is with the Ashkenazim. They smoke a lot and talk a lot. The most peculiar one is the raving doctor whose name she has given up trying to pronounce. She calls him Dr. Felfrem. He is tall, broad shouldered, constantly swearing and cursing. As he rants, he holds the tip of his nose between his thumb and index finger, scowling at everything in sight. When he comes into the house, Firadeus feels as if he were placing his heavy arms on her shoulders, pushing her down to the floor, scowling at her. She is still surprised that he has never once done this. Mrs. Herbst says he's not a bad person, that it's just his way to be angry, which one should never say to his face, or he will become all the more angry.

Dr. Taglicht, the skinny man whose name means "daylight" in the language of the Ashkenazim, but whom Tamara calls Talglicht, meaning "tallow candle" in the language of the Ashkenazim, is the reverse of Dr. Felfrem. He is a fine man, and his manner is pleasant. Whenever he comes, he asks how she is; if he hasn't seen her for a while, he asks about her mother, as well as her sisters and brothers. One Shabbat afternoon, walking with a girlfriend, she said hello to him, but he didn't recognize her. When she told him her name, he reached out his hand and said, "Please introduce me to your friend." This was before she knew about "introducing." What did he do? He said to her friend, "Taglicht is my name, Dr. Taglicht." She will never forget how he said

"Taglicht is my name"—how he added "Dr. Taglicht," so her friend knew that the gentleman who said hello to her was a doctor.

Apart from the doctors who come to the Herbst home, many young people come who aren't doctors yet, but who will become doctors. They go to the room with all of Mr. Herbst's books, the room Mr. Herbst works in. Some of the young men wear flamboyant clothes, but her perceptive eye discerns that they are worn. Often, there are no buttons on their coats. Were it not for fear of her mother, she would sign up at the youth center and sit in the corner examining coats and mending them as she had done for one of Herbst's frequent visitors, a young man who forgot his coat. When Firadeus noticed that its buttons were missing, she took it in order to sew on buttons and saw it was torn as well. She sewed on new buttons, found similar material from which she made a patch, and brushed off the dust. Days later, the young man came to ask about his coat. Firadeus assumed he wouldn't recognize the coat—that, if he recognized it, he would wonder about the transformation—but he took the coat and put it on without even noticing that it had new buttons and was no longer torn.

Along with the young men who come to Mr. Herbst is a young woman, also a student on Mount Scopus. Firadeus assumed she was like all the other young women studying at Mount Scopus, until she learned she was married, the mother of a baby. She leaves her little girl in Tel Aviv with her husband's mother and comes to Jerusalem to study with the young men. We all know of women who abandon their children to go off with some scoundrel who steals other men's wives. But never had she heard of a woman leaving her child to pursue academic studies. The one they call Dr. Krautmeir must have behaved in this fashion, which is how she became a doctor. Not merely a doctor, but a medical doctor—a real doctor, who is paid to see patients, whether they are brought to her or she goes to them. Her lips are always clenched. The whites of her eyes are bright. Her hand is large and plump, her face round and smooth. Her every hair stays in place out of fear of this mistress. Some of the women who call on Mrs. Herbst intimidate Firadeus, though she knows they have nothing against her. There are others she is fond of: the wife of the raving doctor, for example, whose name is Mimi, although Mrs. Herbst calls her Mi. Her blue-gray hair is like the soft feathers under a bird's throat; her entire being suggests that she has no real substance. She is extremely thin; her face is transparent, her eyes bewildered. Everyone enjoys looking at her and listening to her voice, except for her husband, Dr. Felfrem. As soon as she opens her mouth, his attention wanders. Whenever Firadeus sees Mimi, she has an urge to smooth her sleeves, to touch her. Once, Firadeus heard her play the piano, and the sounds that came out of the instrument still vibrate in her ears, like the piano keys themselves when Mimi's fingers darted across them. The same fingers do all the housework; she has no household help, because her husband can't afford to pay the price.

It is not only Persians who are poor. Some Germans are poor too, because a villain named Hitler came and took their money. Some of the Germans came to the Land of Israel before Hitler came to power in Germany, and they have everything—oil and margarine and butter—unlike the recent arrivals, who spice their loaves with spit.

Having mentioned Mrs. Herbst, a few of the Herbsts' callers, and a few of Firadeus's thoughts about them, I will mention Zahara and Tamara, two of Manfred and Henrietta's daughters. In fact, I will mention only Tamara, since Zahara lives in some *kvutza* far from Jerusalem, and, on those rare occasions when she visits, Firadeus isn't always at the Herbsts'. As soon as her work is done, Mrs. Herbst dismisses her so she can go home. Mrs. Herbst knows that Firadeus's mother is a hard woman, and sometimes, out of grief, she beats her children for sins they haven't committed. It is better when Firadeus is there, as she knows how to placate her mother. The only one left for me to tell about is Tamara.

You are already acquainted with Tamara. She looks at you without acknowledging your existence. She probably treats Firadeus the same way. It wouldn't be like Tamara to change her style for the household help. But two things she did for Firadeus ought to be noted: she gave her a fragrant lotion for the bruised skin on her hands, and she explained the workings of a particular object hanging on the wall—how the strip of red glass inside changes its position, jumping sometimes upward and sometimes downward, indicating shifts in temperature. Firadeus was thoroughly delighted to learn the function of that object. She doesn't miss an opportunity to astonish her girlfriends by saying, "Do you know how hot it is today? It's this many degrees." More amazing, her mother was once very sick, so they called the doctor. Firadeus found a thermometer, took the patient's temperature, and told the doctor how much fever her mother had. The doctor looked at her benignly and said, "If you're not a doctor, you are surely a nurse." If she were Ashkenazic, she would be in school. But she isn't Ashkenazic, and she can't be in school because she has to work. Since childhood, she has been working to support herself and her family. She has no great ambitions, although she would like to know about the fat letters in the newspaper from which one can tell in an instant just what is happening in the world. If Tamara would teach her, she would learn and know. But Tamara is busy and doesn't have time to teach Firadeus. Many girls have come from the lands of exile without any knowledge of Hebrew, and they have to be taught. Because they are confined in a sanitarium for tuberculosis victims, in Mekor Hayim, Tamara goes there to teach them. These girls roamed from city to city, from country to country, pursued by border patrols because they didn't have visas. Eluding the border patrols, they arrived at a port in the Land of Israel. But the Mandate police didn't allow them to land, because they didn't have certificates, and, once again, they roamed the seas in battered boats, without food or drink, until our young men took charge and arranged for them to land in secret places. Having been at sea so long, they were vulnerable to many diseases. Tamara volunteered to work with them, to teach them to speak and read the language. She goes there every day and stays into the night. It would be good for Tamara to find a paying job, so she could help her mother with household expenses. But this is good too. These are troubled times for our people, and anyone who can, should help. The Herbsts ought to be pleased with Tamara, with the fact that she has given up her earlier mode, turning away from café life and from dancing to devote herself to the advancement of young Jewish girls. What would they do if she joined one of those suspect organizations that endanger their members, like Herut, the Irgun, or the Stern Group. It would be good if Tamara would find a job, earn a salary, and help her mother with household expenses. In any case, it's good that she keeps busy, and her mind is no longer on cafés and on dancing with British soldiers.

There are times, when Herbst is with his books—a cup of coffee at his side, a cigarette in hand, new documents spread out before him on his desk, his notes arranged by subject—when it seems to him that all the world's tangles are in the process of being unraveled. Even if he should have to move to another house and relocate his books, which he estimates at five thousand volumes, he has a strategy. What is it? You take out the books, row by row, tie a string around each row, put them in boxes, mark each box A, B, C, D, et cetera, and mark the bookcases with numbers and the shelves with letters, so, when it comes time to unpack them, there is no confusion. He has already had a word with Moshe the Assyrian, Jerusalem's chief porter, who is intelligent and strong—who transports pianos from one end of Jerusalem to the other—and he nodded his beard at him to signify agreement.

As I noted, it sometimes seems to Herbst that the world has become less and less tangled. To confirm this, he would remind himself of what happened to him with Shira and be glad that his heart was purged of her. In which case, what did he see in her to begin with? Why was he ever attracted to her? It was an accident of fate. Just as a person can make a mistake, fate can also make a mistake. All those events were one extended accident. Some errors can never be purged, but Herbst's error is not one of those. Just as he seeks nothing from Shira, so Shira seeks nothing from him. The fact that she doesn't show herself to him is evidence. To celebrate his soul, now liberated from its delusion, Herbst goes to his wife and embraces her, whispering sweet nothings invented at that moment. He takes pleasure in his wife, and his wife takes pleasure in him. Those who assume that an older man is no longer capable of inventing an amorous phrase for his wife are mistaken. Seeing Manfred and Henrietta together, although he is past forty-three and she is about thirty-nine—perhaps forty-one—one cannot but marvel and acknowledge that the love displayed by this middle-aged couple may even surpass the love of youngsters. Subjecting himself to the ultimate test, Manfred repeats that verse in a whisper: "Flesh such as yours will not soon be forgotten." Whether or not you believe it, the verse is no longer associated with Shira.

Having observed that the world is being restored and that its tangles are in the process of being unraveled, I should get back to Tamara, whose footsteps don't always lead her to Mekor Hayim. I wouldn't be divulging secrets or gossiping if I were to disclose that I once saw her learning how to handle weapons with some comrades and that they were not from the Haganah, but from the Stern Group. Her mother and father don't know about this, but British Intelligence, from whom nothing is hidden, has her name in their files. They still pretend not to know, but, when it suits them, we will feel the impact of their knowledge. For the moment, I'll say no more about Tamara's activities. In fact, I might as well dismiss her entirely, rather than risk getting sidetracked, by her story, when my real purpose is to tell about Herbst and Shira. Similarly, I'll say no more about Zahara, to whom so much has happened that, even if I were to write about her, I couldn't cover everything. I'll say no more about the daughters and get back to the father of these daughters.

Manfred's life is in good order; Henrietta's life is in good order too. His work is bearing fruit; her belly is bearing fruit. His manuscript continues to grow thicker; her body continues to expand. It's a pleasure to see the two of them together. When they are together, his spiritual quality becomes physical compared to hers, and her physical quality becomes spiritual. That is to say, Manfred's entire thick manuscript has physical reality compared to Henrietta's baby. True, her face is drawn and very wrinkled, and her cheeks have several blotches of color, which are not attractive. She is wan, and her bearing is slovenly. But the new light shining from her eyes is the light that wells up in mothers, who are the foundation of the world and make it possible for the world to survive.

At about this time, it was Henrietta's birthday. Manfred went to town and bought some pretty sandals, pretty and just right for Henrietta. True, the doctor had advised her to pay attention to her shoes, to wear only sturdy footwear, and, of course, to avoid high heels, as her arches were weak and she could become flat-footed. But is it possible to heed all medical advice? It was a lovely moment when Henrietta extended her feet so Manfred could help her slip into the new sandals he had bought her. Little Sarah laughed when she saw her mother suddenly turned into a baby, having her shoes put on for her.

I will say a word or two about little Sarah's cleverness. After watching her mother, she asked whether the baby inside her mother was wearing sandals too. What's so clever about this? She was such a clever little girl that she didn't wait for anyone to come and tell her, "The stork is going to bring you a sister, a brother, a doll to play with." She knew on her own that the baby was growing out of her mother's heart, just as flowers grow out of the belly of the earth.

There are many more things to tell, but they might divert us from the story itself. I will therefore disregard them and tell about something that happened to Manfred. That night, after Manfred said goodnight to Henrietta and got into his bed, healthy and intact, his heart filled with good cheer and his soul content, he saw in his dream something he had heard about from Shira. A small object was walking around the room, but it wasn't walking happily, and it made a sound like that of a new shoe. When Manfred looked to see what was walking around the room, he saw that it was a sandal. Startled out of his sleep, he looked up and saw that beggar, the Turk. He was there with Shira. They both entered the sandal and disappeared. Once again he was astonished, as he had been the day he brought Henrietta to the hospital to give birth to Sarah, when he observed the very same phenomenon. How can two people fit into a sandal, which is only one of the body's trappings? Manfred's dismay was exceeded by his sorrow over the fact that Shira had vanished.

In the morning, Manfred was sad. The dream he had dreamed that night disturbed him by day. Morning light was already beginning to shine, erasing all traces of the night, but his dream was not erased. A more painful consequence: while dreaming his dream, he had been lying in bed, his body seemingly relaxed. Now that he was out of bed, he had to drag himself around, his dream trailing behind him, allowing him no respite from either his body or his dream. For an instant, his

dream seemed to be gone; the next instant, it recurred, and he couldn't
get his mind off it. When Henrietta saw he was depressed, she suggested that he go into town. She was wise enough not to ask why he
was sad; she simply suggested that he go into town, where he would
find distraction. On days when he didn't have to go to the university,
he used to spend the morning at home in his study, dressed in old
clothes and slippers, so it was hard for him suddenly to mobilize,
change his clothes, and go into town. Further, it would be a waste of
time, and he didn't even know what he would do in town. He began
to look around his room for things to occupy himself with instead,
which was his usual tactic when he couldn't work any longer. As soon
as he became involved in something, his passion for work was aroused,
and he could get back to his routine. Henrietta, who knew him better
than he knew himself, repeated, "Go into town and don't wear yourself
out needlessly." He listened to her and went into town. Whether or
not you believe it, on the way into town he met that blind beggar, the
Turk, who stared at Herbst with his mocking, blind eyes. On the face
of it, this was an ordinary event, for it is in the nature of beggars to
wander everywhere seeking alms. But Herbst didn't consider it an
ordinary event. Because of it, he was even sadder than before. All of
a sudden, it occurred to Herbst that this, too, was merely a dream. To
test whether he was dreaming or awake, he took out a pack of cigarettes
and approached the blind man, intending to say, "My friend, would
you like a cigarette?"

Before he could reach him, he was jostled and swept along by the
crowd, until he arrived wherever he arrived. Though he had never been
there, he recognized the place. How? From the tragedy he had been
working on before the visit to his daughter in Kfar Ahinoam. He took
out his notebook and made a drawing of the place that was suddenly
so real to him.

He returned the notebook to his pocket and began to think about the
tragedy he had resolved to put aside when he was in Kfar Ahinoam.
Though he had resolved not to pursue it, he was thinking about it again
and considering: It may have been a mistake to add Basileios to the plot,
since there was nothing in any of the notes or studies on Antonia and
Yohanan about a slave or maidservant at all similar to Basileios. On the
one hand, Herbst was pleased to have added an original element, proving that, contrary to what he thought when he first began to write the
tragedy, he wasn't totally devoid of imagination, for he had added a
character to those provided by history. On the other hand, although he
had washed his hands of the play that night in Kfar Ahinoam, whatever

a man touches, even if he washes his hands of it, retains a trace of this touch, a bit of life that continues to flutter, involuntarily.

We will now dwell on Basileios, the faithful servant. This Basileios was formed in Herbst's imagination. Herbst didn't know what he would do with him at first, but he was unwilling to relinquish him, since all the characters in the tragedy were historical and he alone was a product of Herbst's imagination. It is truly no great feat to take something known and make a play out of it. Goethe used to tell poets: Don't invent material. Use familiar stories. The essence does not lie in the plot, but in what a poet does with it. Herbst, however—and there were probably many others with him—did not agree. When Herbst saw Gerhart Hauptmann's drama *Heinrich the Unfortunate*, he wondered why the poet had seen fit to take a lovely story told by an excellent storyteller and turn it into a play, which added nothing to the story. So, since Herbst didn't know what to do with Basileios, in the end he made him into a leper, confined to the leper colony.

As we have already observed, Herbst's contribution was not essential to the tragedy. One could say about this: It's tragic, but it's not tragedy. Still, Herbst took pride in Basileios, the product of his imagination.

7

As I noted, Herbst put Shira out of mind and didn't feel compelled to see her; indeed, when she wanted to give him her new address, he didn't even take his notebook from his pocket to write it down.

As it happens, it happened that what he could have gotten with no effort he could not get later even with considerable effort. But I won't jump ahead; I'll relate things in their proper order.

At about that time, Professor Bachlam became sick and was taken to the hospital. Herbst went to visit him there. As he sat with his sick friend, it occurred to Herbst that he might see Shira. He felt not a trace of joy, only some curiosity about her. When he left Bachlam without seeing Shira, he decided it must be her day off. Some days later, he went back to visit Professor Bachlam and spent a long time with him. He sat there thinking: I'll see her today, I'll surely see her today. I'll see her soon. In just a little while, I'll see her. There's no doubt that I'll see her.

I hear her footsteps now. As time passed and she didn't appear, he began to wonder: This is the hospital she works in, so why doesn't she come? Why doesn't she come to look after the patient?

He had already stayed too long, and he began to imagine: Now Shira will come and suggest that I leave, so the patient can rest. But Shira didn't come, and he didn't leave, because, when Bachlam has someone to talk to, he doesn't let him get away. Herbst sat with Bachlam, annoyed at the hospital for ignoring the patient, for not coming to ask if he needed anything. Since his arrival, no nurse had been in to see to the patient. Once again, his thoughts were of Shira. It made no sense: he had been here twice, and he hadn't seen her. He finally concluded that she must work on a ward, whereas Bachlam was in a private room. He was annoyed at Bachlam for being in a private room rather than with the ward patients. He pictured the various sections of the hospital, the different halls and rooms, with special attention to the general ward where most of the patients were, where the beds were lined up in row upon row. He searched the vast room in his mind's eye, looking for Shira. But he did not find her. He concluded that she was working elsewhere, perhaps in the maternity section, which explained why she never came to Bachlam's room.

Herbst's thoughts were interrupted by noise from outside. But they resumed their flow. He mused: A patient is lying here in need of rest, and he gets no rest, because the hospital isn't strict about resting. The noise stopped suddenly, and another sound was heard, the sound of footsteps in the hall on the other side of the door. Herbst bent his ears toward the sound, saying to himself: If those aren't Shira's footsteps, I don't know whose they are. She's about to come in. Here she comes. I'm about to see her. Shira won't show her delight, but her eyes will reveal some of what is in her heart. She's already knocking on the door. Her hand is on the doorknob. She has opened the door. Here she comes.

As it happened, it wasn't Shira who came in, but an elderly nurse, the one who showed Sarah to him the day she was born. Herbst was encouraged. If this woman is here, Shira is here too. The two of them attended Henrietta when Sarah was born. This old woman, who worked in Obstetrics at the time, works here now, so Shira must be here too. On the other hand, could it be that, because the old woman works here, Shira does not?

The old woman saw and recognized him. With her sugary tongue, she asked after Mrs. Herbst and the darling baby, born with her assistance, with her hands, her very own hands, though that baby deserved to be carried into the world by golden hands bedecked in jewels. As she spoke, she displayed her little hands. Whether or not you believe it, her irritation at Herbst—for not appreciating how darling his daughter was the instant she showed her to him—had vanished, leaving no trace. She asked about the little one again. Herbst behaved appropriately, responding to every question. He even added comments of his own and reported several clever things the child had said. The old woman was thrilled, despite the fact that the child's cleverness was not news to her. The minute the baby was born, it was obvious that she was extremely clever—so much so that one could say without exaggeration that nowhere in the world was there anyone as clever.

Luckily, none of the grumblers was present. If one of them had been there, he would have jested later that Bachlam was so jealous of the baby that he interrupted the old woman and began recounting his own clever remarks. This is what Herbst was thinking, and what unfolded before his eyes was not very different from what was in his mind. He could see that Bachlam was not very pleased by the old woman's conversation, which was how he reacted whenever he heard someone else being praised. Herbst tried to avert his eyes, so as not to see what he saw. But he failed, for Bachlam's eyes glared disapprovingly, the tip of his nose was flushed, and his thin lips trembled. His entire being seemed to proclaim: So they found someone to praise, so they found someone to praise. As if I don't know what they mean, as if I don't see what they mean. They do what they do to avoid praising the one who is truly praiseworthy. Herbst turned toward the old woman and gazed at her, like a person in pain seeking relief. Looking at her, he realized how very old she was, how very small, and he was surprised to have mistaken her footsteps for Shira's. What could he have been thinking? But, because his mind was totally occupied with Shira, every rustle sounded to him like Shira's footsteps.

The old woman was still there, singing Sarah's praises. In addition to being clever, she was the most perfect child in the world. Beauty and wit have been linked together since the world was created, though beauty sometimes supersedes wit and wit sometimes supersedes beauty. In the case of that sweet baby, however, these two qualities were evenly matched, and this was the source of her rare and incomparable charm.

In deference to Bachlam, Herbst wanted to interrupt the old woman, but he couldn't figure out how. All of a sudden, without forethought, without having any idea what his lips were about to utter, he whispered, "I'll reveal something to you, something you will find very interesting. Mrs. Herbst will be coming to you, because she is soon going to have another baby." The old woman clapped her small but vigorous hands. Her face was illuminated with joy, from her forehead

to the roots of her hair, to the white kerchief on her head. As if to
support an argument, she said, "I can tell you this, sir, doctor, you
ought to be very happy. I have no doubt—in fact, it is clear to me—that
the boy who is going to be born will be even more handsome and clever
than his sister, since the world becomes more and more splendid, and
each successive child outdoes its predecessors. This is what I tell all the
mothers, most of whom are not pleased to be pregnant and bear children. 'What are you after?' I say to them. 'Do you want to be like the
dolls in a toy shop, dressed up in fine clothes, entertaining but producing nothing?' My dear sir, you understand what I mean when I say
'producing nothing.' I mean that the dolls they sell in stores don't even
produce dolls like themselves. 'Or,' I say to them, 'you might want to
compare yourself to . . .' Excuse me, professor. What would you like,
sir, professor? If you would like lunch, I will bring lunch right away.
But, before lunch, I would like to arrange the pillow. Only this pillow,
the one on top. Excuse me, please, sir, professor, for daring to trouble
you to raise your head just a bit. Head high! That's a basic principle
in life. Isn't that so, professor? You are wise, you have written many
wise books, and I don't doubt—in fact, it is clear to me—that you have
discovered this for yourself. Head high. Never let it droop. I commend
Professor Bachlam. He obeys the doctors in every respect. I never saw
such a wise patient, one who knows and understands that good health
is based on hearing and following what the doctors say, for their sole
aim is to cure the patient. I usually tell patients this, and it's true: 'If
you listen to the doctor, then you don't need a doctor.' What I mean
to say is that those who listen to the doctor and follow all his instructions will have no further need of a doctor. They'll already be cured.
Goodbye, goodbye, sir, Dr. Herbst. Goodbye to you, doctor. And
please be so kind as to convey my good wishes to the sweet baby. And
say to her, 'My little sweetheart, try and guess who asked after you. The
old nurse who had the privilege of showing you to your father right
after you were born—she's the one who asked after you.' And if I may
add a further request to that request, I would request that you convey
my good wishes to that dear lady Mrs. Herbst. Tell her that a bed awaits
her, a good bed with a rubber mattress, that lying on it is like—what
shall I say?—it's like . . . like floating on an ocean wave on a bright
summer day. I'm already looking forward to having Mrs. Herbst with
us anytime soon. Such a talent for childbirth! I never saw anything like
it. If she would listen to me, I'd tell her that she ought to give birth
every year. No, not once a year, but twice. The babies she produces
have no equals anywhere in the world. If I weren't so busy, with

patients depending on me, I would take the time to draw them, so they could be in the Bezalel Museum. I once said to a famous woman painter, known throughout the world, 'Why struggle to find subjects for your paintings? Wouldn't you be better off having children of your own, so you would have live models?' It seems to me that the professor wished to say something. I think the professor has something to say. Forgive me, sir, professor, for not hearing. Actually, I did hear, for I am totally intent on hearing what you have to say. But sometimes I am like a fish, immersed in the sea, who sticks out his head to catch a drop of rainwater as it falls from the sky, because it is only natural to be drawn to what comes from far away. I wouldn't presume to interpret this to you, my dear professor, since no one is as wise as you, and you yourself know whatever anyone might say or want to say. Now, my dear professor, I will go and bring your lunch, and, in the meanwhile, I will say goodbye to dear Dr. Herbst. Goodbye, dear doctor. Say hello to Mrs. Herbst, and a special hello to the little princess. So, goodbye, dear Dr. Herbst, and once again goodbye. Now I'll go and bring the dear professor his lunch. I'll let you in on a secret: it's not merely lunch but a symphony of treats."

Herbst paid one more visit to Professor Bachlam. Professor Bachlam was feeling better, and he was about to leave the hospital. The room was filled with books, manuscripts, bundles of proofs to be read, and several kinds of flowers, because, of all the professors in Jerusalem, no one was as popular with students as Bachlam. Several of his female students had denied themselves food to buy flowers for their favorite professor.

Bachlam had no other visitors that day. His friends had received word that he was better and would soon be out of the hospital. Since there weren't many visitors, Bachlam was glad to see Herbst, but he complained that all his limbs were defective and declared that there was no one in the entire world as sick as he, that all the known maladies had converged in him. Nonetheless, he wasn't lying in bed idle; he wasn't pampering himself. Sick as he was, he had managed to write more than a dozen pages, apart from reading the proofs of his latest book, which was about to go to press; preparing another manuscript for the printer; and reading dissertations by several of his students, including a comprehensive five-hundred-page work—yes, five hundred pages—on Nahum Sokolow. Not that Sokolow deserved it. But the student's work on Sokolow was first rate. Then, for Herbst's benefit, Bachlam listed the names of all the prominent individuals who had come to visit him, not to mention the ordinary people, for all who dwell

in Zion were concerned about him. Bachlam showed Herbst the flowers he had received, referring to each by name. One of Bachlam's many
accomplishments was the naming of countless varieties of local flowers.
He had found names for some of them in the Mishnah, forgotten names
that he discovered and revived. Other flowers had never had a Hebrew
name, and, if not for the names he assigned them, they would still be
nameless. Then Bachlam began to talk about his illnesses again, how
all the maladies of the world converged in his body, so one might say
there was no one in the world as sick as he was. But he has overcome
all these ills and recovered. When he looks at himself, he can't help
wondering: How could such a feeble body overcome so much sickness?
It must be that his great spiritual power prevails over physical weak-
ness. He must overcome it, because there is so much for him to do. If
he doesn't do it all, who will? Professor Weltfremdt, perhaps? Or
Professor Lemner? Professor Kleiner? Or maybe Professor Wechsler?
They are interested only in themselves, and they don't respond to the
people's needs. If their advice had been heeded, there would be no
Hebrew University. When Professor Wechsler was invited to teach for
the English, wasn't he willing to accept their offer? Is Lemner any
different? Not to mention Weltfremdt. As far as Weltfremdt is concerned, the university could just as well be German. Such traitors.
They would sell Israel's birthright for a mess of pottage. If not for
Bachlam, who stands in the breach, this would still be Palestine, not the
Land of Israel, which is why those Germans hate him. But the people
are not ungrateful. The people, with their healthy instinct, are aware,
sensitive, and grateful. All these flowers, brought by those dear young
women, provide ample evidence. No other nation can boast of souls as
precious as these. Who gave them life and nurtured them? When he
considers these students of his, he knows it's worthwhile for him to
struggle, to struggle and work.

    After Herbst took leave of Bachlam, he stopped in the hall and
looked all around, as though searching for something. Then he turned
to see if anyone had noticed. A nurse appeared. She was young, her
uniform was new, her shiny new kerchief seemed to retain the heat of
the iron. She herself was new: her flesh was new, without wrinkles or
signs of fatigue, and her thick blonde hair exulted in its freshness. She
glanced up at him, her kind eyes aglow with fresh joy, and inquired
pleasantly, "Are you looking for something, sir?" It took a minute for
Herbst to realize she was asking him a question. Her manner was so
correct that he missed the intonation. Herbst bowed ever so slightly and
said, "I'm not looking for anything. I was visiting Professor Bachlam,

and I'm on my way home. But since you ask, it occurs to me to ask if you happen to know where the nurse Shira is." She lowered her head in sad confusion. She didn't know the answer, since this was her first day at that hospital and she hadn't met all the nurses. She looked at him apologetically and said, "If you will wait a minute, I'll go and ask." Herbst bowed again and said, "Many thanks, but there's no need to bother. I can ask myself. Or I may leave the matter to my wife. She'll be here any day now, and she'll see the nurse I was asking about."

Herbst left the hospital without seeing Shira. He had mixed feelings. He didn't know whether he was pleased not to have seen Shira or whether he was displeased not to have seen Shira. Once again, a quality common not only to Herbst but to most people was manifest. When he decided he was pleased not to have seen Shira, an alternate view asserted itself: You could have seen her here. If you had searched, you would have found her. Because you asked that mere child, whose kerchief is still unwrinkled, who hasn't dealt with patients yet, you assume you've done what you could. But, having said you are leaving it to your wife, it would be best to get out of here. Young nurses tend to be curious, and, if you hang around, she'll ask about you, and who knows what that will lead to. Herbst adjusted his tie, imagining it had slipped out of place. Since he didn't have a mirror and couldn't see if the tie was in place, he adjusted it again. Since he wasn't sure he had adjusted it properly, he pulled at the edges of his collar. By now, he was at the foot of the hospital steps, near the gate. At the gate, he saw Axelrod the clerk. He was hurrying. He was wrinkled; his skin looked old beyond its years. Unless his skin was created before he was born, I don't know how to explain this fact. Axelrod raised his glasses all the way to his bald spot and eyed him in alarm. Whether or not you believe it, the glasses eyed him in alarm too. Herbst nodded and greeted him. He greeted him rather submissively. Axelrod looked back over his shoulder, as though a crowd were standing behind him, and said, "Did you want to have a word with me? Be brief and tell me what you want. You can see I'm busy." Herbst said, "I don't want anything." Axelrod said, "It's good you don't want anything. I'm busy, and I don't even have the time to chase a mosquito." Herbst said, "There was a nurse here. If I'm not mistaken, her name was Shura." Axelrod said, "You mean Shira. You are asking about the nurse Shira. Then why did you say 'Shura'? The nurse Shira isn't here. She isn't here, as I said." Herbst said, "Where is she?" Axelrod said, "If I knew, I would tell you." Herbst looked around. He looked at Axelrod and whispered, "Allow me, sir, to ask: Shira works in this hospital, isn't that right, Mr. Axelrod?" Axelrod said, "Who's denying that she used to work in the hospital? On the contrary, everyone agrees that she performed well." Herbst said, "But what?" Axelrod said, "But she quit." "She quit?" "Yes, my dear sir. She quit and went off somewhere. These things happen. I don't get excited over a nurse who quits her job." "She didn't say where she was going?" Axelrod said, "Maybe she did, maybe she didn't. In any case, she didn't say anything to me. Of course, I'm too busy to pay attention to everything people say. Come, I'll see if she left an address."

Herbst trailed after Axelrod, following him to the office. Axelrod took out a notebook and began to leaf through it. He finally took his head out of the book, turned to look over his shoulder, and said, "What did you want to know? Whether she left us her address? She didn't leave us her address." Herbst said, "And what if I need to speak with her?" Axelrod said, "If you have something to tell her, I can write it in this book. But make it brief, just a few words. You can see I'm busy and don't have time for long speeches. I don't see the point of endless words anyway." Axelrod stuck his head back in his book and didn't look up again, making it clear that the conversation was over and he had nothing more to say. Herbst posted himself in front of Axelrod and risked another question. "She left no clue as to her plans?" Axelrod turned his head toward Herbst again, stared at him in alarm, and asked, "Who left no clues?" Herbst answered in a whisper, "The nurse Shira." "The nurse Shira? We already forgot she ever existed, and he is still talking about her. She left absolutely no clues. Who needs clues anyway? I like things to be clear. Clear facts, not clues." Herbst said, "Then there is nothing more to do." Axelrod said, "What do you mean, 'nothing more to do'? There is a lot to do, but we never have a chance to do it." Again, he stuck his head in the book, conveying the impression that, if the whole world were to come and say, "Lift up your head," he would not lift it.

Herbst left the hospital and stood around for a time. He glanced in all four directions, looking this way and that. Then he followed his feet to the bus stop. When he was sitting in the bus, on the way home, the road became two roads, one leading home, the other leading elsewhere. In all the time since Herbst's return from Kfar Ahinoam, it hadn't occurred to him to visit Shira. At that moment, he was convinced that he had to see Shira, in order to find out why she had left the hospital she had worked in for several years and gone elsewhere—also, where had she gone?

He took out his notebook to look for her address. He knew it wasn't there. When Shira had said to him, "Write down my new address," he hadn't written it down. Nevertheless, he looked for her address in his book. The bus stopped suddenly. A large group of Arabs were gathered for a funeral. An Arab dignitary, a rival of the Jerusalem mufti, had been murdered by the mufti's supporters. The victim's entire clan—his mother's whole family and his father's whole family—as well as many of the mufti's enemies, came to escort him to his eternal rest. It's true, Herbst reflected, that Shira has moved. In fact, she told me she has moved. When I was first getting to know her, she told me she was thinking about moving, and now she has succeeded and has made the move. Too bad I didn't write down where she is. He looked in his notebook again and found nothing. He shrugged his shoulders and made a face, for he hadn't behaved properly. If not for his own purposes, then in the name of good manners, he ought to have taken her address when Shira said to him, "You can write down my new address."

The funeral cortege grew longer and longer. Some of the mourners were in cars and buses; others rode donkeys and horses. There were also those who came on foot. "Too bad he was killed," a fellow passenger remarked. "He was a good goy. Last Passover, as soon as the holiday was over, he sent me a loaf of fresh bread." Another passenger retorted, "Let them kill each other rather than us. Still, it's puzzling that the best of them get killed, while the worst villains are spared. Are you by any chance a journalist, my friend?" "Why?" "Because I saw you take out a notebook. You probably want to write about the funeral." "Is that so?" Herbst said, putting the notebook back in his pocket.

"The road is clear, and we can move on. They create a disturbance when they're alive as well as when they die. A constant disturbance. I never saw such a people. Their days are idle. They do nothing. When we come and take action, they sound an alarm, as if we were depriving them of work. Please tell me, folks, what do these Arabs really want? If not for the Jews, they would still be what they were in Terah's generation, in Terah's time. What haven't we done for them? Roads, water, orchards, electricity. Still they complain. You, my friend, are probably from Brit Shalom and find my words uncongenial." Herbst looked at the interrogator and said, "What makes you think I'm from Brit Shalom?" He said, "If you aren't from Brit Shalom, please forgive me for suspecting you." Herbst smiled and said,

"And if I am from Brit Shalom, what then?" "In that case, you shouldn't have come to the Land of Israel." "Be quiet!" the driver shouted. "This is not the place for arguments. Professor Herbst, we are here. This is your stop."

8

It's possible that he would have found Shira's apartment, and it's possible that he wouldn't have found Shira's apartment; it's possible that he would have found her in, and it's possible that he wouldn't have found her in. But he made no attempt to find her. When he felt the urge to see her, he overruled it with this rationale: If, at the hospital, where she worked for so many years, no one knows where she is, who am I to know? On the face of it, Herbst was at peace with the situation. Not merely in terms of himself, but in terms of Shira, too, he was at peace. If she were to come and reproach him for not showing himself to her, he could say, "I asked Axelrod about you, and he didn't know where you were."

Axelrod didn't know where Shira was, and Herbst didn't know where Shira was. They were different, however, in that one had forgotten her and the other had not.

Shira began to show herself to him again. He saw her dimly, in his imagination. The image was different from previous ones, earlier on, when his heart was aflutter and, more recently, when he was bitter, angry, and eager to be rid of her. Now, the image was ambiguous; even as he saw her, he knew she had vanished. He wanted to ask where she had vanished to and why she had left her job at the hospital, but he refrained, lest his voice disrupt the pleasure of his vision. His thoughts drifted, alighting on the climber, the ambitious young man who had pursued her in her youth and whom she had rejected. He speculated that this man had come to Jerusalem and was at the head of every public institution—perhaps he was even a trustee of the hospital—and that Shira had left her job to avoid having him see her in a subordinate role when his position was elevated and prominent.

One day, Herbst saw that climber's name on a poster announcing a rally in Jerusalem, at which he was to be one of the speakers. Herbst took out his notebook and wrote down the date, the hour, the place. At the appointed time, he went to listen.

Whenever Herbst went to one of these gatherings, known as rallies, he was appalled at the number of people who pushed their way into a noisy, crowded space to hear the same message over and over again—a hundred times, a thousand times—a message that was trivial to begin with. Now that he was at the rally and saw the mob that had come to listen, he changed his mind and decided that the public wasn't crazy after all: if the speaker attracted such a large crowd, he must have something to offer. Herbst had said roughly this about several orators, and he had turned out to be mistaken. But, in the case of this climber, it was clear to him that he was not mistaken. I refer to him as the climber, not because he was unique in his ambition, but because I'm not free to use his real name. Since I prefer not to invent names, I refer to him in terms of his character.

Let me return to the subject. That particular day was hot and *hamsin*-like, a day when the good Lord remembered His land unfavorably. The sky was yellow, gray, and dusty; the earth was gritty and hard. In between, the air was yellow and gritty, searing one's eyes, scratching one's skin, drying one's mouth and lips. Throats and palates became irritated, as if they had been sprinkled with salty sand. There was no wind. The sun peered down with ugly eyes. The murky tar on the roads began to melt, sticking to everyone's heels. Loose dust crawled about, rose up, and seeped into one's pores, one's eyes, and one's nostrils. There were no birds in the sky. Jerusalem had suddenly reverted to an earlier era, before the Second Aliyah, when the only birds in the Jerusalem sky were birds of prey, who came in droves, occupied the land, and behaved as if it were their domain. But the streets of Jerusalem were filled with people, men and women, old and young. On that day, Jerusalem was demonstrating against the Mandate government, whose policies added villainy to villainy, heaped decree upon decree, and made Israel's burden hard to bear. Those who had escaped the sword and eluded the raging madmen, who had wandered over the land, who had gone to sea in battered boats without bread, water, or medicine—with nothing—reached our shores only to be turned away by the authorities and forced to wander farther, until their boats were wrecked, leaving them to drown and be devoured by sharks. Even people who ordinarily shunned public events came to join this demonstration. Without words, without noise, without shouts, in total silence the community of Israel made its way through Jerusalem, with faces that bespoke grief, for there was no one present who did not have relatives at the bottom of the sea.

British policemen were stationed on every corner of every intersection, armed from head to toe. They wore helmets, and weapons were
fastened to their uniforms. In addition, military vehicles stood ready
and menacing, reflecting the attitude of those in charge, as such equipment tends to do. Some of the soldiers were on foot, some in vehicles.
If I'm not mistaken, there were even some on horseback. We walked
in silence, not saying a word. We didn't lift our eyes to look up at those
who inhibit life, inflict death, and rule the world—those conquerors,
angels of fury, villains dispatched by others even more villainous. In our
hearts, there was neither hatred nor resentment, but each face was
covered with sadness, a sadness that begins in the heart and takes over
the entire face. Little by little, whispered words began to be heard.
People who were not in the habit of expressing themselves in public
began to whisper to each other. One man told his neighbor, "My wife
said to me, 'This cannot be.' " What that man said was strange. If that's
what his wife said, what of it? Actually, it was meaningful to us that
even his wife, who was not interested in politics, said, "This cannot be."

Herbst was swept along by the procession. When he left home in
order to hear that climber's speech, he didn't know there would be such
a huge crowd. All of a sudden, he was part of the crowd. One minute,
he found himself among ordinary, anonymous people. A minute later,
he found himself next to a friend or acquaintance. On that day, it made
no difference. Everybody was of one mind. Though opinions might be
expressed differently, the substance was the same. Only on rare occasions is there such agreement.

His mind was suddenly diverted from all this, because he saw
Tamara. He realized immediately that he was mistaken, that it wasn't
Tamara, that it was a boy. How could a man mistake a stranger for his
daughter, and a boy at that? Since it seemed to him that he had seen
Tamara, he began to think about her. Where is Tamara? She is undoubtedly here. She certainly wouldn't miss such an event. Tamara,
who is always denouncing the British and deploring their actions in this
country, is surely here. And it's possible Shira is here too. Not really;
Shira wouldn't be here. She doesn't involve herself in public affairs.
The very first time he saw her, the day a young man from one of
Jerusalem's leading families was killed by Arabs and the entire city
turned out to mourn, she stood on the sidelines, a cigarette in her
mouth, as if to declare, "I'm not with you." This would surely be the
case now, when her rejected suitor, whom she would not enjoy seeing
in such an honored public role, was scheduled to address the rally. On
the other hand, since the crowd was large enough for an individual to

be swallowed up in it, Shira might feel free to come, if not to hear his speech, then to see him.

Herbst suddenly found himself at Taglicht's side. Taglicht's face was grim, and his entire person was a mass of sorrow. "You are here too?" Herbst said to Taglicht. Taglicht whispered to him, "I hope it ends well." Herbst heard what he said and was perplexed. What did he mean by "ends well"? What could prevent it from ending well? People were moving quietly and speaking softly; many were even silent. The police were maintaining order. Soldiers were on the alert. So what could go wrong? He meant to ask Taglicht, but they were swept in opposite directions, and Herbst found himself in the midst of a group of youngsters, dressed in special clothes of a sort he had never seen before. He had, perhaps, seen individuals in that sort of dress, but never a crowd of hundreds, like this one, with that climber in the lead, marching like a war hero, like a commander at the head of his regiment. He had a long face with bloated cheeks. His eyes were filled with rage; his lips were clenched. Even before he began to talk, he had everyone's attention.

It took less than a minute for Herbst to size him up. He was of not quite medium height. His shoulders were curved so that his back and neck sometimes pulled away from each other and sometimes leaped toward each other. His head was egg-shaped; his hat wrinkled and erect, likewise his ears, likewise his nose. He had a thick mustache. His chin was sharp, smooth, and prominent. Though his mustache was thick, it didn't cover his mouth. Not only his chin but his entire mouth protruded, likewise his tongue as it whirled around in his mouth. His tongue wasn't visible, but one could picture it from the shape of his mouth. Nothing about him appealed to Herbst—not his appearance, not his manner, not anything about him. Still, he felt no antipathy toward him.

Pushed by the crowd, Herbst was now at some distance from him. That sort of person, Herbst thought, derives power from his words. His words are power, and his power is words. Words dominate him and allow him to dominate others. Herbst was pushed from place to place, as were his thoughts, and he couldn't decide which was superior, words or power. Which takes precedence—does power precede speech, does speech precede power, or do they overlap? At times, one relies on words; at times, on sheer power. In either case, such a person is sure to appeal to this crowd, one that is moved by words. So why did Shira reject him? Shira is a one-of-a-kind creature.

Shira is a one-of-a-kind woman. Yet though he remembered her, he didn't think about her. At that moment, Herbst was impelled not to think about anyone in particular. Being swept along with the crowd, everyone seemed equivalent to him.

He suddenly found himself in an empty lot, one he couldn't identify, though it may have been the one that belongs to the high school. It was too congested to see anything, except for that man, the climber, soaring over everyone, swaying in midair; since this was impossible, the crowd must have been carrying him. How comfortable could it be for such a heavy person to be carried? As he began to orate, his booming voice interrupted Herbst's thoughts. Herbst pricked up his ears, soaking in every word and straining to find the message. There was a message in the words, but not the trace of an idea. The voice became more and more excited, excited and inspired. Every phrase was accompanied by a gesture, a raised or lowered hand. If you would like a visual image for this speech, imagine nails being hammered into a wooden floor. With each stroke of the hammer, as it drives in the nail, the wood cries out.

By now, all the youngsters who stood listening were becoming agitated and restless. Every word the speaker said inflamed their blood, and each and every one of them was prepared to risk life and limb for his people and his land. Could they somehow be sure that their blood would not be shed in vain? This, he didn't say. His thundering voice continued to arouse and enthrall, to arouse and inflame. There was no stemming the passion of these youngsters. There was not one among them unwilling to die for the people and the land. Since they didn't know what to do, they became more and more enraged; their fury mounted, and their hearts seethed with wrath and the desire for vengeance.

The moderates listened and were upset. Others, too, who were hostile to the Mandate government, asked him with their disapproving eyes: What do you want from these youngsters? What are you suggesting that they do? Herbst was suddenly overcome with terror and with the fervent hope that all would end peacefully. What was there to worry about? He saw his daughter Tamara again. And again he saw he was mistaken. It was merely a young man who resembled Tamara. He was reminded of the girl at the train station in Leipzig, of the photographs of severed legs that had appeared in the newspaper, of the fact that one caption had said a boy was murdered while the other caption identified the victim as a girl. As it happened, his thoughts happened to be with Shira—what she was like when he visited her that first night and she was wearing slacks. His limbs sud-

denly felt weary, because of the *hamsin,* because he had been stuck in
the crowd for several hours. He decided to stop in a café for some
coffee, since he knew from experience that coffee has an invigorating
effect in such weather. But the cafés, like all other businesses, were
closed on account of the rally.

Again he was swept along by the crowd. He found himself in a small
space between twin buildings. Wechsler was standing next to him. I
wonder, Herbst mused, I wonder if he will tell me some new scheme
for making portfolios; if not new ones, then old ones, antiques.
Wechsler didn't discuss either of the above. Even he was caught up in
the public anguish.

Little by little, the crowd began to disperse, some going this way,
others that way. Mostly, they were like a shepherdless flock, wandering off and returning, only to wander off once more, in circles. In
any case, Herbst remarked to himself, in any case, the event has
ended peacefully.

Herbst turned homeward in silence. But he didn't feel like going
home. After a hectic day, he, like most people, would have liked to find
something else of interest to do. He didn't find it, but he did find people
with whom to spend an hour or two. Because there were so many to
choose from, he didn't choose any of them, thinking: I'd rather be
alone, I'd rather be alone—doubling the message to reassure himself.
Even as he reassured himself, he doubted that he really preferred to be
alone. He was again joined by a stranger, who announced that a young
man had been arrested for shooting a British officer. Before Herbst had
a chance to digest this news, another bystander reported that a young
girl had shot the Englishman. As he was talking, someone else informed
them that she hadn't shot but had been about to shoot, and that she
hadn't been arrested, since her friends appeared in time to spirit her
away. As he was talking, someone else said, "I tend to agree that she
didn't shoot. I would have heard the shot, and, since I didn't hear it,
obviously she didn't shoot." Herbst stared at him, and he stared at
Herbst, each imagining the other had something to say to him. Herbst
finally took leave of them all, wishing them well, to which they responded, "May we meet again on a happier occasion."

Herbst was suddenly alone. Only a little earlier, the streets had been
mobbed. Now there was no one left outside. Had a curfew been declared? A curfew was likely, and Herbst didn't have permission to be
out. He could be stopped, taken to the police station, and detained until
morning. Nevertheless, he did not hurry home. I'm all alone, I'm all

alone, he reflected as he walked, feeling neither sad nor happy. But anyone who chose to join him would not have been unwelcome, so long as it wasn't one of the people he was accustomed to—his friends, for example; not even Shira, Lisbet Neu, or any other young woman. Herbst, at this point, had in mind a type of person that most likely doesn't exist. If this seems odd to you, it seems odd not because of Herbst but because of my inability to express it adequately.

In the past, when Herbst finished his business in town, he turned toward Shira's. But, for a long time now, ever since he and his wife came back from Kfar Ahinoam, Herbst had not gone that way or even considered going that way. You know that Shira once ran into him somewhere and told him, "I've moved, so take out your notebook and write down my new address." He didn't take out his notebook, and he didn't write in her address, because he knew it was superfluous, that he had no use for her address, that he had banished her from his mind. Now, after the rally, having had a chance to see the climber Shira had told him about, whom he found to be of no interest, it occurred to Herbst that it would be worthwhile to talk to Shira. Two things converged here. In and of themselves, they were unimportant; but together, they assumed importance. Shira was not important to Herbst; neither was that climber important to Herbst. But now that they were allied in his mind, he wished to discuss the man with Shira. For this reason, he turned toward Shira's apartment. The earth was abandoned. All its children were gone, they had been plucked from the face of the earth. There was not a soul in sight, nor any vehicles either—not a bus, not a car, not a bicycle. Only implements of war filled the land, whose bulky parts looked malevolent and reeked of foul-smelling grease. A policeman, armed from head to toe, stood by, holding a rifle or a gun. A car, belonging to an Englishman or an Arab, suddenly loomed into view. It whizzed by, leaping, skimming the ground, leaving its fumes behind.

It was almost twilight when the *hamsin,* which had been so oppressive all day, finally relented. But no one remarked, "Thank God the *hamsin* is over," for the entire city was enclosed in its houses. There was no sound from within. Those who had food were eating; those who had nothing to eat were hardly aware of hunger, because of the woes that burdened their hearts and because of their impotence. A radio was turned on. Perhaps there would be news of salvation and mercy. As was its wont, the radio offered the sort of news it is hard to hear when one's heart is sore. After a minute or two, the radio was turned off. The city and its inhabitants were, once again, silent.

Herbst walked on in solitude. He had already disengaged his feet from the road that led to Shira's house, but he hadn't turned toward home. His soul was devoid of will; his feet had no direction. He wasn't drawn toward Shira's, nor was he drawn toward home.

Suddenly, a human figure emerged from the stillness, and Herbst heard a girlish voice addressing him. Herbst asked the girl, "Firadeus, what are you doing here?" Firadeus said, "I'm coming back from the pharmacy. I have some medicine for my mother." Herbst said, "Yes, that's right, I did hear that your mother was ill. Where do you live? Do you live in this neighborhood? Imagine, here I am. I have suddenly landed in your neighborhood. I don't remember, did I ask about your mother's illness? I may have asked and forgotten. Yes, yes, your mother's illness is also due to the government of Palestine. The government's vile politics. Today it seems to me that all our troubles are due to politics. Because of politics we die, because of politics we're murdered, because of politics we get sick, and because of politics people make speeches and shoot at each other. You may have heard that a young girl shot a British officer. Did it ever occur to you that a girl—a Jewish girl, a daughter of Israel—would be capable of picking up a gun and killing someone? I myself cannot digest the news. Luckily, she didn't hit him, and he wasn't killed. Anyway, he was almost killed. If he has a wife, she would be mourning and lamenting. What are those voices I hear?" Firadeus answered, "That voice is my mother's. She is mourning my father, who was killed by Arabs. Until today, she used to mourn at night. Today, she has been mourning all day. Some say she is this way because of the *hamsin;* others say it's because of the rally." "Yes, that's right," Herbst said. "It's because of the rally. Go inside, Firadeus, and bring your mother her medicine." Firadeus went in, and Herbst stood listening to the woman's lament for her murdered husband.

This man who cleansed the streets of Jerusalem:
His spilled blood flowed like water through them.
This man who cleared the dusty roads of this quarter:
They spilled his blood like dirty water.
You, God, who are great, enlightened, supreme,
See them ravage his body, once sacred and clean.
Enlightened God, who reigns in the skies.
Do you hear orphans and widows when they cry?
Your right hand, our support, you have withdrawn from us,

And we are at the mercy of the villainous.
I loathe my life, for he is gone whom I cherish.
Take my soul too and let me perish,
And perhaps I will again see my longtime mate.
Then will my heart rest and my suffering abate.
Sweet as a mountain goat's were his eyes.
Now covered with earth in the grave he lies.
Sweet as a mountain goat's were his eyes.
Now I see darkness by death, multiplied.
My heart yearns for you, to be dead at your side,
In your grave on the Mount where you now abide.

—— 9 ——

Let's return to Herbst's household and family. As I mentioned, Henrietta is going to give birth, either to a boy, as Manfred believes, or to a girl, as is her habit, for Henrietta is in the habit of giving birth to girls. We will know in due time. For the time being, Henrietta tolerates the indignities of pregnancy rather gracefully. This woman takes great pride in her pregnancy, unlike most women in this country, except for those in the older communities, who welcome children. Firadeus is Henrietta's mainstay. Firadeus knows what her mistress wants. Not merely from the heaviness of her movements, but from her face as well. Every line of her mistress's face communicates her needs. Henrietta smiles and says, "You are a prophet, Firadeus. You know what's hidden in my heart. You guess what I want, and I don't have to bother with words." Firadeus tells her mistress, "I only did as I was told. It seems to me that I was given an instruction, which I fulfilled." Henrietta thinks to herself: I may have whispered something without realizing it. But this was not the case. It was love that whispered to Firadeus, conveying the wishes of her mistress.

Tamara treats her mother with affection too. She doesn't contradict her, avoids arguing, and stays home a lot, so her mother won't be alone and Tamara will be available should she be needed. She herself, rather than remain idle, corrects her students' notebooks. Just between us, they aren't really notebooks; they are the proclamations of youth leaders not yet fluent in Hebrew, written in other languages and translated into Hebrew by Tamara, so they can be posted in public places and circulated among prominent members of the *yishuv* community. To prevent British Intelligence from discovering these proclamations and confiscating them, they are sent out under fictitious names, like those of nonexistent businesses, charitable institutions, and schools. When every name had been used, they resorted to Mekitzei Nirdamim (We Wake Those Who Sleep), after a publisher of classical Hebrew manuscripts that were never in print before, an enterprise that goes back about four generations and was directed by some of our greatest leaders. British Intelligence, from whom nothing is hidden, were unaware that various highly respected Englishmen (Moses Montefiore, for example, as well as the chief rabbi of Great Britain) once led this enterprise. When one of these proclamations fell into the hands of Intelligence agents, who read the text and realized its goal was to wake those who were asleep so that they would rebel against the government of Palestine, they decided to bring the directors of this venerable publishing house to trial. If the actual nature of the enterprise and its history hadn't been uncovered just in time, the eminent persons at the head of the publishing house would have had their peace disturbed. Since this error adds nothing to the story, I'll say no more about the activities of British Intelligence and get back to the Herbst household.

A further miracle befell the Herbst household. The day Jerusalem demonstrated against the Palestine government, Tamara had undertaken a mission. Perhaps you took notice when I related that twice it seemed to Herbst that he saw Tamara, that in the end he realized he was mistaken, that it wasn't Tamara, that in fact it was a boy. And when I related this, I commented: Isn't it odd for a father not to recognize his daughter? Now that it has all ended well and there's no need to worry about saying too much, I can tell the whole story. A handsome officer worked with the Jerusalem police. He was known as the Bloodhound, for anyone who fell into his hands came to a bloody end. There was a plan to take revenge. Tamara, who was especially hostile to him, because whenever he saw her he greeted her warmly—as in the old days, when they used to see each other in cafés and dance together—was determined to retaliate. That day, she dressed as a man, so she wouldn't be recognized, took a pistol, and set out to do away with him. Someone had preceded her, firing at the Englishman but missing his mark. The police also missed the mark.

Before they could seize the culprit, his friends managed to snatch him and hide him away.

Having told about Henrietta, Firadeus, and Tamara, it's time to tell about Sarah. But it's easier to write a long book about adults in this country than to write a short page about a child. Our eyes are still not trained to observe the behavior of the children here, which calls for a new approach. Some people consider them extremely primitive; to others they are like children anywhere else in the world, the product of a particular education. I disagree. They are not primitive, nor is it a matter of education. It is the land and sky that form them. Our children are like the land and the sky above. The land is sometimes parched and brittle; it is sometimes saturated with pleasing dew and bountiful rain. It is sometimes violent, like a raging wind; and sometimes it is sweet and amiable, like a breeze from the north. This applies to the sky and to our children.

So much for comparisons. I'd like to get back to the Herbst household now. But first, a brief tour of Kfar Ahinoam to look in on Zahara and her son, Dani.

Kfar Ahinoam is expanding. Not in farm produce or cattle and poultry—that is to say, in barns and coops—but in the realm of woodwork. A new carpentry shop has been set up. Wood is brought in from Hadera and from abroad, and made into bulletin boards, which bring in more revenue than agricultural products. A friend of the nurse who replaced Temima Kutchinsky when she left Ahinoam is supervising the work. Since I won't be mentioning him again in this book, I won't mention his name or the name of the place Temima Kutchinsky went to. But I will say a few words about the carpentry shop. Some *kvutza* members are dissatisfied, for this was not their purpose in coming here. They came to work the land. Other members argue that, though the land needs agriculture, it needs industry too. Both factions benefit from the carpentry shop. It adds sugar to their tea and meat to their stew. Having given Zahara's environment its due, I will dwell on Zahara.

Zahara is a good mother to her son and a good wife to her husband. She is loved by all her friends. Manfred's mild, gentle nature and Henrietta's talent for action were both transmitted to Zahara, engendering several fine new qualities. She suspends her own needs for the sake of others and exerts herself in matters others are casual about. I was once visiting Kfar Ahinoam on a miserable *hamsin* night. We set up our bedding out of doors, since it was too hot to sleep inside. The walls, floor, and ceiling emitted heat that had been accumulating all day. When I lay down outside, I heard a woman saying to her husband, "The water tank is dripping. We're wasting water. Go and turn off the faucet." He answered her, "Do you think I'm fool enough to get out of bed now that I finally found a comfortable spot?" Zahara got up and went to turn off the faucet, though no one told her to do it and it wasn't her job. She has another fine quality: patience. You know how hard it is to be hospitable in these times, and you know how scrupulously *kvutza* members fulfill this obligation. It often happens that a worker comes back from the field hungry and tired, expecting to sit down and eat, only to enter the dining room and see a guest occupying his place. He has to stand and starve, waiting for the guest to finish eating and reliniquish his spot. But guests are often leisurely; they eat slowly, and, after concluding their meal, they tend to sit around and listen to the conversation of *kvutza* members. So much for mealtimes. As for the intimate questions many guests are in the habit of asking, which even someone as tolerant as Hillel the Sage would be reluctant to answer— even when they are endless and absurd, Zahara responds graciously. Finally, the guest goes off to tell his wife how smart he is, what good questions he asked, how he impressed the young lady with these questions. This is a fine quality, isn't it? As for Avraham-and-a-half, the Avraham-and-a-half we met in Jerusalem, the Avraham-and-a-half we met when the Herbsts visited Kfar Ahinoam after Dani was born—he hasn't changed at all, except that he shaves regularly, so his whiskers won't scratch his baby's cheeks. Something else is new: he is now amused by those who devote themselves to guarding the language. The newspapers allot them a great deal of space. Avraham says their rigors will undo them, that Hebrew is still developing, and when they rule out a usage, why, one should be sure to use it—one should assume that what they rule out is, by definition, acceptable. Enough about these guardians of language, for better or for worse. I prefer to concentrate on Dani. Dani is still indifferent to language. When he starts talking, he will talk proper Hebrew.

What can I add about Dani? You know as well as I do what *kvutza* children are like. He is healthy and vigorous, free of even the slightest blemish. I won't compare him to his aunt Sarah, who reflects Jerusalem's charm. Still, compared to his peers in the *kvutza,* I would say he is as superb as the most superb of them.

Now, a word about Herbst. There is nothing new in Herbst's world. He still hasn't been promoted. Those who have the power to

appoint professors are not as diligent as the candidates would like
them to be. So Herbst is still a lecturer, like all the others. As for
Shira? He spoke to Axelrod at the hospital that day and asked about
Shira, but he hasn't found Shira yet, and he seems to be making no
attempt to find her.

—— **10** ——

One day Herbst was walking down Ben Yehuda Street, going to the
French Library to see if any new novels had come in. Although he had
resumed his academic work, happily and unequivocally, putting out of
mind the tragedy he wanted to write, he nonetheless had a desire to
indulge himself with a new novel. Some of Herbst's friends boast that,
since they became adults, they haven't read a novel, a story, a poem;
some claim they read only detective stories; some make do with the
literary supplement of the newspaper, others with what they find on
their children's bookshelves. There are those with still other odd reading habits—collecting words for crossword puzzles, for example.
Herbst is different. He reads poems, stories, novels, plays—whatever
happens to be in his house, as well as what has to be brought in from
elsewhere, even if this involves effort and expense.

I don't know how you feel about poetry. Most people like poems
with a patriotic theme, an ethical message, a pathos that stirs the soul
and inspires the heart. Herbst loves poetry even when it has none of
those qualities, even poems Bachlam or Ernst Weltfremdt would reject
because they don't make sense. This is equally true of stories, novels,
and plays. Most people like books that enrich the reader, enhance his
character, add to his wisdom, or teach about the way of a man with a
maid. Some readers look for a well-developed plot, shrewd argumenta-
tion, refined speech, clever dialogue, and rich language. Others read to
pass the time or to acquire an understanding of problems that engage
the world. There are idealists searching for a cause, who scorn everything new in favor of what they read in their youth, when novels had
genuine heroes with genuine ideals. As far as Herbst is concerned, the
essence of a book lies in its poetic intensity, its vitality, the imaginative
power and truth it contains. This is how he behaves when he is trying
to assess a book before taking it home: he opens it at random and reads

half a page or so, from which he generalizes about the entire book, on the theory that a true author leaves his mark on every page, in every line.

Herbst walks down Ben Yehuda Street with all the other pedestrians, past stores, business offices, printing houses, cafés, peddlers' stalls, newspaper stands, offices. The street noise becomes more and more intrusive. One sound fuses with another. Each and every sound generates another sound, and these sounds, compounded by one another, make an infinite number of sounds. They fill the ear as well as the eye, which was created for vision and flinches before the noise. When Herbst came to Jerusalem, the entire space this street occupies was empty. Herbst was fond of the spot because of its restful silence; because of the olive, almond, and eucalyptus trees that cheered the eye on a winter day and provided shade in the summer; because of the mossy stones; because of a lizard sunning itself; because of a bird flying through the sky; because of a chicken pecking at the garbage near the hovel of a contented pauper. Now all the plants have been uprooted, all the fruit trees cut down, the stone walls destroyed. The birds and fowl have migrated. Instead, there are houses, built of stone and concrete, raising the noise level, increasing the tumult, adding to the din, producing dust, din, and tumult. The air is filled with the aroma of coffee, cocoa, baked goods, warm butter, grilled cheese, fruit preserves. It is the coffee hour; cafés are bustling with men, women, and children. Not every mother who wants to be out in the world can hire a maid to leave her children with, so she has no choice but to bring the child along, feed him ice cream and all sorts of sweets, soda, ice water— anything to entertain the child, so the mother can have a cigarette and conversation with a friend, male or female. Several years ago, Herbst ran into Lisbet Neu and went to the Café Zichel with her. He had coffee, and she had cocoa without milk. She told him many things that were new to him. Afterward, he walked her home and promised he would call her. By and by, intending to keep his promise, he went to call. He got to the telephone booth and found Shira. When was this? After he left Henrietta when she was about to give birth to Sarah. Many days have passed since, and many things have happened. If we were to try to recount them, we would not be able to. The events consume time, and time consumes memory. Which is to suggest that not everyone must always remember what is best forgotten.

Herbst had already put the past out of mind and was trying to picture what he hoped to find in one of the new books he planned to borrow. This was not too difficult, because he had read some reviews and recognized the names of some authors, and because of the powerful

imagination to which he occasionally had access. Before he could con-
jure up a clear image, he found that he was standing on a rug that was
spread out in front of an antiquities store. Before he could get his
bearings, he was studying the window display. The objects on display
had been thrown together with no connection to each other except
physical proximity. Surely the dealer knew why he had placed a portrait of a monk next to a statue of a nude woman, the idols of some
extinct people next to a *mezuzah* case, a Torah cover near a piece of
needlework found in the tomb of an Egyptian king. We can only note
this arrangement and wonder about it. Whoever is equipped to do so
will invent a rationale suited to his sensibilities and talent. When he
turned away from the window, Herbst heard someone say hello to him.
He looked around, but, since the street was so crowded, he couldn't see
who was greeting him. He did, however, recognize the voice. It was
the voice of Anita Brik, whose two poems he had read.

As it happened, it happened that Anita Brik had reason to retrace her
steps. When she came back, she noticed that Herbst was looking somewhat bewildered. She approached him and said, "You don't recognize
me, Dr. Herbst." He seized both of her hands, clasped them warmly,
and said, "Not recognize you! Is it at all remarkable to recognize a
young lady such as you? Believe me, even among black women or
red-skinned women, I would recognize a woman such as you. How are
you, Anita? It's so noisy here. Let's find a café to go to. The cafés are
hectic too, but, when you have something in your cup, the noise is less
irritating. How are you? What have you been doing? Idle questions. I
ask them only to pass the time until we can sit down together. Have
you written any new poems? Let's sit down and read them. Which do
you prefer, Zichel or Atara? Perhaps you know the utopia of cafés, a
place that surpasses them both? Wasn't it you who said that in Jerusalem new cafés open every day? If you have no preference, we can go
to Zichel." Herbst chose Zichel because, never having heard Tamara
mention the place, he concluded that she was not in the habit of going
there.

They went in, found a table, and sat down. Anita said to Herbst,
"You asked me, Dr. Herbst, whether I have written any new poems.
I haven't written any poems. I stopped writing poems. If you don't
have language, you can't produce poems. I have almost forgotten my
German, and I haven't learned Hebrew yet. If the present is any
indication of the future, I can truthfully say that I won't ever learn
Hebrew, and I never will write in Hebrew either. I never considered
my poems essential, but it's a pleasure to find words—even rhymes—
for what is in your heart. In the course of time, my heart began to be

empty, and I was no longer confronted with this task. Sometimes, when I'm alone, I think it was a mistake to write poems. The most vile reality is more powerful than fantasy, and it doesn't promote delusions of grandeur."

Herbst sat in silence. He looked straight ahead, rather than directly at her. Twice he wanted to light a cigarette, but he didn't light it. Twice people came to look for lost eyeglasses and the like. Anita kept on talking. Her voice was feeble, but her words had vigor.

The waitress appeared. She was small, blonde, and pretty. Her golden hair encircled her head like a golden tiara, and her dainty cheeks had a golden cast about them. Herbst assumed she was a student, of either music or art, who was waiting on tables temporarily. When she appeared, she forgot about her job and stood chatting with Anita. She asked Anita how she was, and Anita congratulated her for having dealt with the Arab so successfully. Herbst was puzzled by their conversation. Anita said, "I see that Dr. Herbst is puzzled, so, with your permission, Trudel, I will tell the story. Just a few days ago Trudel was walking to work, as she does every morning. She encountered an Arab, who wanted to have his way with her. She was carrying a copper kettle that needed to be repaired. She smashed his nose with the kettle, and, while he was occupied with his nose, she fled. Isn't Trudel a hero?"

Trudel laughed and said, "Woe unto this hero. She had to pay for her heroics. In that transaction, I lost the kettle I had borrowed from a neighbor so I could make something warm for my little girl to drink. My Zigi is out of work, as usual, earning nothing. And you, Anita? I hear you're working with children now." Anita said, " 'Children' is an exaggeration. Only one child, the son of Professor Weltfremdt's daughter. Let me introduce you: this gentleman is Dr. Herbst, and this is Trudel, my good friend Trudel. We both worked in that restaurant where you first saw me, Dr. Herbst." Trudel said, "I'm standing here as if I were on my own time, when, in fact, everyone is after me. So many parched throats demanding something to drink, and the boss, who sees me standing idle, is glaring at me. What can I bring for the doctor? And you, Anita, what would you like? If your tastes are unchanged, I know you would like . . ." Herbst said, "Pull over a chair and join us. Bring three cups of coffee, cakes, cookies, tarts, pastries— everything good. And if there is something beyond good, bring that too. Not in one of those little dishes meant for the misers you usually serve, but on a platter. And if it gets too heavy for you, we can call Moshe the porter, the he-man who carries pianos from the center of town to Montefiore as easily as I carry this chair." Trudel laughed and said, "If it were up to me, I would certainly choose to sit with you."

As she spoke, she turned in several directions, calling out, "Right away, right away. I would bring your coffee now, but you asked for café au lait. Yes, madam, I'm bringing ice cream. Yes, yes, vanilla. Also strawberry. Made from fresh strawberries, not preserves. Coffee with cream or without? With cream. Yes, yes, I'm bringing it. Right away."

When Trudel went off to serve the other customers, Anita Brik said to Herbst, "Trudel and I worked in the same hotel, and we had the same dream: to create a children's book. I would write some stories, and she would illustrate them. She has golden hands, and her drawings are real drawings. Those who know say she is an artist." "And what do you say?" "Me? I'm not in that class." "Why not?" "Why not? That's how it is. Most of my friends are proficient in one of the arts. They write poems and stories, they draw; some are involved in music, some sculpt. Our parents were wealthy. They provided us with fine teachers in literature, music, the graphic arts. Since we didn't have to bother about supporting ourselves, we could afford to open our minds and train our hands. How does one distinguish between craft and work, talent and proficiency? I hope you won't dismiss my words as mere fanciful phrases, Dr. Herbst, but what we need is an expert on experts. I'll relate something that happened to me. I was once in Haifa. I went to visit a woman who had been my mother's friend and was from one of the country's older families, having arrived here even before the war. One of her grandchildren was sick. She sent for the doctor, an Italian Christian. I said to her, 'Are there no Jewish doctors in Haifa?' She answered, 'There are as many doctors as patients, but, let me tell you, most of the Jewish doctors studied medicine, not because they were interested in it and not because they wished to devote themselves to curing the sick, but because their parents wanted them to be doctors. And since they were well-to-do and could attend the university, they divided up the professions, assigning medicine to one, law to another, and so on. This was not the case with gentile doctors, who chose a profession because of their interests, not because of their parents' wishes." Herbst made a face and said, "How did you answer that woman, that old-timer who was living in this country even before the war?" Anita said, "It's not my way to moralize or argue. Besides, there was someone sick in the house, and she was occupied with him, so how could I challenge her?" Herbst said, "And what is your opinion?" "About what?" "About that very subject, about that woman and what she said, that woman who believes that most Jewish doctors studied medicine because their parents wanted them to? I can tell you a story too, if you like. I knew a *rav* once—a traditional *rav,* not a modern rabbi—who had such a passionate interest in medicine that he gave up his position and walked to Berlin. He learned both German and enough science to be admitted to the university to study medicine. All those years, while he was a student, he lived meagerly, on a diet of bread and tea, in a space so small that, when he lay down to sleep, he had to leave the door open in order to have room to stretch out. I have him to thank for the fact that I live here, because, even as a confirmed Zionist, I, like most other Zionists, didn't feel compelled to come to this country. Although this *rav* was unique, he was not the only Jew to choose medicine out of personal inclination and interest, just as I was not alone in choosing a profession without consulting my father. To get back to the subject, you wanted to write stories, which your friend would illustrate. Why didn't it work out?"

Anita said, "Trudel didn't have time to draw because she had so much to do, and I didn't have time to write because another dream took over, the dream of all who labor: to sleep without dreams and to be able to withstand another day's work without mental stupor or physical collapse. If you are puzzled, Dr. Herbst, I should repeat what I already said: truth is more powerful than fantasy. Truth is reality, and reality is truth." Herbst said, "In what language did you plan to write the stories?" Anita said, "As you know, sir, I have no language other than German. I don't know French or English well enough to write stories in them. I assumed I would write them in German and have them translated into Hebrew. I would be able to find someone to translate the stories. Trudel, however, wouldn't be able to find anyone to translate her drawings. You are wondering how drawings are translated. The fact is, when I see the picture books that are given to children here, I see that Trudel's drawings are not for them. She has talent and good taste, whereas our children have become accustomed to kitsch." Herbst laughed wholeheartedly, clasped Anita's hands in his own, and said, "Apart from being a poet, you are a perceptive critic." Anita said, "Being a critic is easy. When you're young, you criticize the bad things you encounter; as you get older, you criticize the good ones. All the bad things you see influence your taste." "For better or for worse?" Anita said, "I'm getting older too, and how will I be able to tell good from bad?" Herbst said, "A pity we don't meet more often. I have no chance to hear what you have to say." Anita said, "From that point of view, it's best that you don't see more of me, since one's tastes change with age, and, if you hear something tolerable from me today, you will hear something intolerable tomorrow." Herbst said, "If taste declines with age, I have surely been affected." Anita said, "I would guess that

Dr. Herbst's sensibilities are constant, impervious to change." Herbst said, "You consider me so old that my mind is totally calcified." Anita blushed and said, "Believe me, sir, that's not what I meant. Trudel, it was good of you to bring our coffee. I'm thirsty. What is that, Trudel? That mountain of cakes. Who is it for?" Trudel said, "They're for you, because they're tasty and good." Anita said, "And whatever is tasty is also good for me?" Trudel said, "There are many good things that even a girl such as you can indulge in." Herbst said, "Many blessings, Mademoiselle Trudel, for fathoming my mind and bringing something tasty. Though it wasn't intended for me, I will allow myself to enjoy it." Trudel said, "I intended it for both you and Anita. Eat while it's still warm. Anita, you must come and tell me all about your job. I have to go now and fill the gullets of the other customers. They're beginning to get angry with me."

After Trudel left, Anita told Herbst about her work. She works for Professor Ernst Weltfremdt's daughter. They are good people, who don't expect too much of her. They maintain an efficient household and insist on having everything done on time, according to a schedule. She tries to meet their demands, and they pay her a full salary, regardless. Even when she breaks something, they never deduct it from her pay. Once a week, on Wednesday, she has the afternoon off. If she wishes, she can go out; if she wishes, she can stay in her room. The old woman, the professor's wife, is especially warm and affectionate. When she visits, she always takes the trouble to come all the way up to her room and ask how she is. But even a good turn is not altogether good. The old woman is addicted to writing. She composes poems, plays, and the like, and, since she has no one to read them to, she has made Anita Brik her audience. A week doesn't pass without a new play or fantasy in verse. Because of these plays and fantasies, Anita Brik has no time to get involved in a book. The old woman comes every single Wednesday, before Anita has a chance to leave. She comes directly to her room, takes out her notebooks, and begins reading to her. If not for the fact that the professor's birthday happened to fall on a Wednesday—today, to be precise—so the dear old lady had to stay home and receive well-wishers, Anita would not have been free to go out today either, and she wouldn't be sitting with Dr. Herbst, who is asking her about the poems she no longer writes. Instead, she would be captive to Mrs. Weltfremdt and her poems.

To mitigate the anecdote, which could be construed as a complaint, Anita began to describe the house she was working in—its elegance; the cleverness of the baby she was taking care of; the room she had been given, which was on the roof, a small room with a large terrace over-looking the Judean hills. When she sat alone at night, looking out at those hills, at the moon and the stars, she was in a state of euphoria, lacking nothing. But the better off she was, the worse she felt, remembering her father and mother, trapped in Berlin, bemoaning their miserable fate. Yet she could do nothing for them. She sometimes asked herself: What are we? If we are human, how can we be so heartless? We enjoy every advantage here, without responding to the distress of our brethren in Germany and in other lands where they are oppressed. Anita concluded her tirade against Hitler and his followers, savage animals who behave like savage animals. "But," she continued, "we in the Land of Israel—Jews with Jewish hearts—how can we sit complacently, eating, drinking, sleeping, as if nothing has occurred? I sometimes wake up in the middle of the night with the urge to scream, 'How can we be so complacent? Doesn't anyone hear the cries of our brothers and sisters?' I step outside, search the four corners of the sky, and ask, 'Whence will our help come?' All of a sudden, I hear a voice calling, 'Wake up, hurry, bestir yourselves.' I see light in windows and Jews coming out of their houses, quickly, on the run. I think: They hear the cries, and they are responding. Then I realize they're hurrying to the synagogue, so they can finish praying and be free to pursue their business, like yesterday and the day before."

While Anita was talking, Herbst sat with one finger bent to help him remember the question he wished to ask. When Anita stopped her monologue, he didn't relax his finger, nor did he ask his question, because she seemed sad and because of the people at the adjacent table. When most of the tables were empty, Herbst placed his hand on hers, looked at her somewhat evasively, and said, "What I've been thinking . . . What it occurred to me, by association, that I might ask you . . . You may remember that once, when you were sick, I came to visit you with the nurse Shira. If I'm not mistaken, she brought you flowers that made you very happy." Anita said, "How could I not remember her? I have never met as fine a woman." Herbst said, "What I mean is, I wonder . . . I haven't seen her in several months." Anita said, "As a matter of fact, I'm in the same situation. I've looked for her several times, but I haven't been able to find her. When I asked her neighbors, they couldn't say when they had last seen her." Herbst said, "She probably moved, and you were at her old apartment." Anita said, "No, I'm talking about her new apartment. I even asked about her in the hospital, but she apparently didn't say where she was going. She really doesn't have to account for herself, but I'm sorry she didn't say where she was going. I don't think she's left the country. If she left Jerusalem, she may have gone to Tel Aviv, to Haifa, or to some *kvutza,* and she may return just as suddenly as she left. If you would like, Dr. Herbst, I could tell you where she lives now."

All this time, Herbst sat thinking a variety of thoughts. One thought was: Something could have happened to Shira; she could have become pregnant and gone off to a place where she is unknown. When was he last with her? He did the calculation more than once. She had been putting him off for years. If she was pregnant, he wasn't responsible. He felt gloomy. He sat with Anita, unaware of her and of everyone. But he was aware that something had happened to him.

He smoothed his hair with his hand. Then he looked at the hand and extended it toward Anita. He had the impression that his hair had turned gray, and he thought about asking Anita for a mirror. Seeing that he had extended his hand to her, Anita said, "Dr. Herbst, would you like me to write down Shira's new address?" Herbst looked at her and said, "Shira's address? I might as well write down Shira's address." But his face indicated that the gesture would be wasted, that, even if he knew where she lived, he would not find her.

He took out a notebook and pen, and handed them to Anita. She wrote down the address and drew a map of the street, on which she marked the position of the house. Herbst took back his pen and notebook, and stuck them in his pocket, looking neither at the address nor at Anita. After a while, he stole a sideward glance at her, to see if she had seen that he was keeping Shira's address. After a further while, he took a spoon and began tapping on the glass. Trudel appeared and gave him the check. He stood up, then sat down again. All of a sudden, he roused himself, looked at Anita Brik, and said, "How are you, my dear?" As he spoke, he realized that, in light of their lengthy conversation, the question was superfluous. He smiled, an odd smile, and said, "Actually, you have told me everything, but is all of everything really everything? I talked so much without mentioning that my wife asked about you. You know where we live. We are still in Baka. You can take either the number six or the number seven bus. If you're ready to leave now, I'm ready too. I'm sorry I troubled you to write down the address of Shira the nurse. It was a waste. If I show you my book, you'll find a thousand addresses in it, and I doubt that I've used a single one. I wrote down the nurse Shira's address out of sheer habit. In this country, we do so much writing. I was told about a consul who said he had never been in a country where people write as much as they do in Palestine. It is common that, when a child begins to write, he writes a lot, his hands become skilled, and he learns to write nicely. It's the same with a young nation. What I just said doesn't pertain to writing good poems. So, goodbye, my dear. Oh, I have inundated you with words, as if I were some sort of a Bachlam-and-a-half. I did actually visit Bachlam a few days ago. I suspect his manner is contagious. Goodbye, my dear. Goodbye."

— 11 —

The shock that had overwhelmed him began to dissipate. By the time he took leave of Anita, there was no discernible trace of what had agitated him a short time earlier. Herbst found some consolation in the new address he had written in his notebook; should he want to, he could go to Shira. There was no need to go immediately, but, whenever he wanted to, he could go.

He left Ben Yehuda Street, turned to the left, and walked as far as the Café Europa. Before the shoeshine boys who were stationed there had a chance to grab his feet and begin shining his shoes, he himself placed one foot on the box that was set up for the purpose. While the boy was at work, Herbst took out his little book, noted the new address, and studied the drawing, picturing the precise location of Shira's new apartment, the place where she now resided. It was easy for Herbst to imagine the place, but it was hard for him to imagine what sort of people lived there. Jerusalem is unlike cities in other countries, where rich neighborhoods and poor neighborhoods are distinct, so that where one lives is predetermined. In Jerusalem, people live anywhere, without such distinctions, and the population is not segregated. In fact, one actually finds, in all the older alleys of the new city, dilapidated structures alongside new ones. Here, the rich and the poor—all the social classes—are considered equal. There are areas where we assume no one we know would live; still, when we happen to be there, we are sure to run into two or three familiar faces, the ones we least expected to see. Herbst, who had been trying for years to hide his affair with Shira from his friends, was interested in knowing who her neighbors were, as a precaution. But, as I said, he was after the impossible.

The shoeshine boy pressed the bell on his stand to announce that one shoe was done and he was ready for the next one. Herbst put the notebook back in his pocket and switched feet. The shoeshine boy began again, dipped his finger in polish, smeared it on the shoe, spread it all around, and rubbed it with a rag, until the shoe began to shine. The bell sounded again, announcing that it was shined too, but that the gentleman should put the first foot up again so both of his shoes would have the same amount of shine. Meanwhile, being fond of experiments, Herbst tried to test himself, to see to what extent he was capable of taking his mind off Shira, who was troubling him once again. He began to chat with the shoeshine boy, asking him what he earns in a day. He told Herbst his earnings, as well as his expenses. He earns up to forty grush a day; sometimes more, sometimes less. Before Shabbat and on holidays, he makes more than seventy grush. But expenses are high: six lirot for rent, six grush for six tins of water. And now that his wife has given birth to a new daughter, there are even more expenses. He has to buy seven tins of water, because the nurse at the clinic instructed his wife to bathe the child every day. So they have to buy an extra tin of water in addition to the first six. Herbst made many errors in the course of that conversation. He assumed that the six lirot for rent covered a quarter of the year, whereas actually they covered the entire year. He assumed the boy was a boy, and it turned out that he was married and burdened with sons and daughters. He thought the six or seven tins of water were for a day, not realizing they were for the week. But all of this is beside the point, the point being that Herbst was testing himself to see how capable he was, at that moment, of occupying his mind with remote matters. The bell sounded again, not a signal to shift shoes but a jubilant sound, for the job was done. The gentleman could now display his shoes to the sun, the moon, the stars, to all of Jerusalem, including the rival shoeshine boys. Herbst gazed at his shoes and at the boy's face, which came close to outshining his handiwork. Herbst paid him double his price and moved on. He stopped to take out his notebook and copy Shira's address in his own hand. Then he turned and walked on.

The day grew dusky. A disorderly stream of workers emerged from those offices that close before sunset and mingled with the passersby. They were dressed in all sorts of finery, and their leather shoes glistened. Their skin, however, was not fine. Their manner was not fine. In fact, there was nothing fine about them: for example, the woman with black hair that had suddenly turned brown, the smooth-shaven gentleman who now sported a mustache very much like Hitler's. The details are hardly worth mentioning, but because these people were so invested in them, I have chosen to mention them.

The French Library was still open. If Herbst wanted to, he could go there and get the novels he was after. But he gave this up for

Henrietta's sake, having promised her he would be home before dark. She was making artichokes with butter sauce for dinner, which they usually ate out of doors. And when they ate out of doors, they usually ate before sunset. Actually, Herbst had changed, in that he was no longer enthusiastic about artichokes and butter. It was a bother to deal with them, leaf by leaf, before getting to the heart. Those outdoor meals were also a bother, because Henrietta always forgot to serve at least one dish, which she remembered after he had had his fill, so he ended up overeating and not enjoying it. But, since he hadn't said anything to her, he must get back. He hurried to catch the bus and arrived home before sunset.

When he got home, he changed his clothes, took the watering can, and went out to the garden. He watered and watered. Each bush and every flower thanked him for each and every drop. He thanked them too, for their scent and beauty, for helping him collect his scattered thoughts. Now that he was busy watering, he began to feel more collected.

The sun was setting, and the garden began to grow dark. A flock of birds appeared, on the way back to their nests. They were followed by other birds, who appeared one at a time, their chirps ringing out from the branches themselves. From the branches themselves—how could this be? Because it was dark now, no bird, not even the wing of a bird, could be seen, and the branches themselves seemed to be chirping. A sudden hush enveloped the trees, the branches, the birds in their nests, the garden, and the house. In the hush, only Sarah's voice was heard. She was lying in bed, singing a song without words.

Warmth, lush and lively, rose from the moist earth and from the water that hadn't soaked in yet and continued to bubble up between the clods of dirt. Underground waters became one with the swelling earth; surface waters gazed upward at the waters of the sky above until they were covered by darkness, then continued to peer through the darkness till their eyes were lost in earth and air. The smell of wood and fire blew in from nearby yards where supper was being cooked. Henrietta turned on the lights and set the table in the dining room rather than outside. She served freshly baked bread, fragrant with the aroma of contentment and peace, making this seem like the domain of tranquility and peace. But in Manfred's heart there was no peace, no tranquility. His heart was in turmoil. At any given moment, it seemed to him, he would now be able to find Shira at home. Why didn't he go to her? He moved his lips, to form the name of the alley she had moved to. The alley itself had no name. But the apartment was marked on the drawing in his notebook, along with the name of the landlord, and so on. He put all this together and tried to form an image. Since the image was vague, he rejected it. He summoned up her first apartment instead, his mind's eye feasting on it. He was startled by Henrietta's voice, asking, "Where are you, Fred?" He picked up the watering can and answered, "I'm watering the garden." He lifted it high, so she wouldn't say, "You're a liar." Henrietta said, "You are pampering our garden. You've already given it enough water. Get ready for dinner." Manfred answered, "I'll do just that, Henriett." He put down the empty watering can, went into the bathroom, showered, changed his clothes, and sat down to dinner with Henrietta.

The meal was light and pleasant, as was the conversation. Henrietta was through with the anguish of certificates, of officials who speak but don't act, who promise but don't perform, and her heart was at one with the world again. Henrietta had not succeeded in bringing even one relative to the country, but, when she began to be aware she was pregnant, she had stopped running around for certificates. As soon as she stopped running, her worries diminished. When a letter arrived from abroad, inscribed with grief, misery, woe, she responded with a sigh and returned to her own affairs, as most people did at the time.

As soon as Henrietta stopped running around to arrange for certificates, Manfred felt compelled to do something on behalf of their relatives. Since he did nothing, I have nothing to report, and I'll get back to Henrietta.

Once again, Henrietta's heart was at one with the world and all its creatures, as in the old days, when she first knew Manfred. Except that then she was worry-free, and now she had daughters to worry about, though worry was inappropriate in the case of two daughters such as hers. Zahara lives happily with her husband, and they will continue to be happy as long as it suits her. Being a steady sort, she isn't likely to jeopardize her own well-being or the well-being of others, all the more so now that she has a son, who serves as a new bond between his parents.

And Tamara? She is somewhat more problematic. Unlike most girls, she has a piquant intelligence, a sharp tongue, and an audacious spirit that would endanger anyone else. She was once walking down the hill from Talpiot with one of her friends. They encountered an Arab, who attacked the young man, hoping to snatch his leather briefcase. While the Arab wrestled with him, Tamara picked up a rock and threw it at his head. She did this two or three times, until he fell in a puddle of blood, half-dead. When he managed to pick himself up and crawl back to his village, Tamara followed him to see where he lived and bring him to justice. Those villagers—heroes when it came to attacking aged Jews and solitary women—saw her, yet didn't dare lift a finger. But it's unfortunate that she hasn't found a job yet and still works without pay. In fact, there is a real job awaiting her. She herself says that the superintendent of schools, who observed her at work in Mekor Hayim, has given her a glowing reference and told her she could have a job in one of the settlements in the Sharon. She would have to teach somewhere else first, until the end of the term, substituting for a teacher who went to Scandinavia on a Histadrut mission. The Histadrut, of course, considers only its own needs and feels free to pull out a teacher in midyear. It is they who end up paying. In this case, for instance, a teacher of their political persuasion will be replaced by Tamara, who detests the Histadrut as much as she detests the British.

More about Tamara. She has found herself a boyfriend, a lapsed yeshiva student. Whether or not he is worthy of her, it's too soon to consider him her mate. Many of Tamara's friends are attracted to her, and there is no reason to single out anyone in particular as her mate. Furthermore, an impulsive approach to marriage suits neither Henrietta nor Manfred, though Henrietta, with a mother's intuition, is sure that such a mate would always be faithful to his wife, despite their differences in education, origin, and background. His parents are from one of those renowned Jewish communities, whereas her parents are from Germany. Though they themselves were both born in Jerusalem, it is doubtful that their characters are similar. Actually, Tamara's views are not contingent on her parents', and she does as she pleases. In any case, I have presented her parents' view.

And then there is Sarah. For the time being, she is little and hasn't arrived at the age of worry, but she is ever so clever. She has never been to nursery school and hasn't heard a teacher's voice, but she gains knowledge constantly. From what source? Father Manfred doesn't teach her, because he is occupied with his students, and Tamara doesn't teach her, because of her concerns. Henrietta, who would like to teach her, is hampered by the discomforts of pregnancy. So, from whom does she learn? She learns from everyone she sees and from everything she sees, even from the cat, the dog, and the chickens; most of all, from Firadeus, whose knowledge is very limited. Firadeus can't even read the prayerbook, but she knows things not everyone knows, such as why the moon and stars give light by night while the sun gives light by day: because the night was made for sleep, for which the moon and stars provide sufficient light. This is not the case by day, when workers need abundant light, which is why the sun shines all day, giving abundant light. Similarly, on Yom Kippur night, when a lot of light is needed for prayers, many candles are lit in the synagogue. And why did the sea choose to locate itself in Tel Aviv rather than Jerusalem? Because Jerusalem is high up, and the sea prefers not to undertake the climb. And why are there wild animals in the world? So wicked people, when they see us running away from wild animals because of their wickedness, will realize it's not good to be wicked. Sarah learns many other things from Firadeus. Since she loves Firadeus, she loves her teachings as well.

Now for Henrietta herself. Henrietta is at peace with herself and with her unborn baby. He is at rest in her womb, not troubling her at all. Not that she is absolved from all the troubles of pregnancy, but, since she tolerates these troubles well, it's as if she were untroubled. When she has no household chores to do, she sits watching Sarah play with an insect, the lid of a jam jar, a toothpaste tube, singing to herself and not bothering anyone. At such a time, Henrietta says to herself: I was mistaken to avoid getting pregnant all those years.

— 12 —

Henrietta and Manfred are at dinner. The table is set; the salad provides a riot of color; the bread, made of sprouted wheat, is nutritious and tasty, as are all the other dishes. Henrietta didn't cook artichokes, as she had planned, but she made several other dishes Manfred was fond of, which he would eat and enjoy. They are having dinner in the dining room, not outside, because of Henrietta's fatigue, which prevented her from setting the table in the yard and dragging out whatever might be needed for dinner. Henrietta and Manfred are in the dining room, enjoying the bounty of their table.

The windows to the garden are open. A pleasant scent wafts in from the bushes and flowers Manfred has watered. An oil lamp lights the table without producing soot. Why do I mention the oil lamp? Because there are people in Jerusalem who assume that, without electricity, there is no light. I mention the oil lamp for this reason. Although it is one of the old ones, it gives light that is modest and discreet, light that may even be more pleasant than electric light, so long as it doesn't produce soot. All of a sudden, they hear a bird call. What is this call? It is the call of a bird returning to its nest and finding it changed. Or is it the bird himself who is the source of change, and is he apologizing to his mate for being so late? What do we know? All we can do is speculate, and we have offered two speculations as one.

Henrietta got up and brought two bottles of tomato juice she had chilled—not on ice, though she has an icebox—but by hanging them from a rope attached to a pole placed over the water tank, which is what she is in the habit of doing with watermelons and other foods that are at their best when chilled. Some women are in despair if their ice isn't delivered every day in the summer; some women feel that the world is about to end if their refrigerator breaks down. I therefore applaud Henrietta Herbst, who never loses her equilibrium. Along with the juice, Henrietta brought a pie filled with potatoes, squash, and eggs, and topped with sour cream. The Arabs are scheming to starve us, blocking the roads to prevent their women from bringing us poultry, eggs, fruit, and vegetables. As it turns out, they don't know what to do with their poultry and eggs now, and we, because we are no longer supplied with Arab food, raise our own chickens, who lay eggs that are now on our tables. Arab shepherds send their sheep into the gardens in our towns to demolish the fruit and vegetables, but our rural communities make up for the loss, providing the produce that adorns our tables. I don't mean to celebrate the *kvutzot* and *moshavim*, but merely to commend Henrietta Herbst, whose table is not wanting, whose meals are no less ample since the women from Bethlehem and Kfar Hashiloah stopped bringing in their eggs and produce. The eggs aren't visible, because they are mixed into the potato pie I described, but anyone can see the vegetables and fruits. What is more, they are superior to those from Kfar Hashiloah, which are irrigated with sewage water from all over Jerusalem, whereas our settlements rely on the generosity of the good Lord, who seems personally to provide rain and dew for watering. Even when we don't do His bidding, so that He causes the skies to withhold, His mercy is not depleted, nor is the water in the wells and cisterns depleted. We turn on the sprinklers, and they make the waters rain down. Rabbi Samuel Mohilever, of blessed memory, was asked the following question: A young Jew, a student at the university or perhaps at the Technion, invented a device that produces rain. Is he required to publicize his invention to advance humanity, or does he have the right to hide his secret in the interest of settling the Land of Israel, first buying land and installing Jews there? For, if the nations of the world were to discover that even such arid earth as ours could be reclaimed with the help of this device, they would refuse to sell us a single handful of soil. I don't know how that wise man responded, nor do I know if

the inventor disclosed his invention or how that device was constructed. In any case, as we see with our own eyes, as soon as Jews
began returning to their land, subject as it is to drought and barely
responsive to being worked, God was compassionate and imbued His
sons with the wisdom to devise sprinklers that water the earth and soak
it thoroughly, as needed.

Summer evenings in Jerusalem are delightful; summer dinners are
delightful too. One eats, enjoys, is satisfied. To whom does this apply?
To a man with a wife such as Henrietta, who is attuned to her husband's wishes. If only Manfred were as attuned to his wife's wishes. I
must nonetheless state that he didn't upset his wife, nor did he reveal
his innermost thoughts to her. Which was both good and not good. It
was good for Henrietta not to know; it was not good for Manfred to
withhold his innermost thoughts. They began to press on his heart,
with a force that was intense and unrelenting.

Henrietta sat holding a slice of buttered bread with white cheese on
it. She gazed at Manfred and, adding a dollop of honey as thick as a coin
to her bread, remarked, "Fred, I'm also convinced that our new baby
will be a boy." Manfred answered, "You're telling me something new?
I already know that, but what is your source?" Henrietta said, "This
appetite of mine informs me that there's a male child inside." Manfred
said, "How can you consider such a small slice of bread a sign of
appetite?" Henrietta said, "Small, but brimming over. Have a bite.
Here, from this end." She handed him the bread, and he bit into it, but
not where his wife had suggested. She said to him, "It's sweet and good,
isn't it?" Manfred said, "I meant to ask you before: did you notice the
song Sarah's been singing? At first there were no words. Then I
thought I heard some sort of refrain, the words 'graves, graves.' Isn't
it odd to hear such a song from a child?" Henrietta laughed and said,
"She's been singing 'graves, graves' all day. I suppose you want to
know where she got that song from. She got it from Firadeus. One day
I heard Firadeus singing a song. At first I thought it was a love song.
Doesn't this sound like a love song: 'Sweet as a mountain goat's were
his eyes / Now covered with earth in the grave he lies'?" Manfred said,
"How lovely it is, and how sad." Henrietta said, "It's a woman's dirge
for her slain husband." Manfred said, "A eulogy for a hero." Henrietta
said, "A eulogy for the garbage collector of Talpiot, who was killed by
an Arab on his way from Talpiot to the city, right at the railroad station.
And who composed the song? The victim's wife composed it. This is
what Firadeus told me: every night her mother gets up from her bed,
paces back and forth, and laments our murdered father. She sometimes
repeats the same verses and sometimes recites new ones." Manfred said

to Henrietta, "Do you happen to remember another verse or two?" Henrietta said, "I knew you would ask that, so I asked Firadeus to tell me some other verses. Before she had a chance to say anything further, we were interrupted by a guest. See if you can guess, my dear. Who do you think it was? You can ask ten questions, then you'll be able to figure out for yourself who was here. Now, begin with question one." "A man or a woman?" "A woman." "A woman?" "That's another question." "Where is the question?" Henrietta laughed and said, "That's a question too." "Young or old?" "Ummm. What shall I say? Not young, not old." A middle-aged woman?" "Ummm. Middle-aged." "A woman, right?" Henrietta said, "How can you be so devoid of intelligence—you just gave up one entire question!" "How? I hope the word *how* doesn't count." Henrietta said, "If I were being strict with you, I would count it as a question." "Which question are you thinking of?" "Another question." Herbst let his head droop to the left, extended his hands, and sighed, saying, "I'm not good for anything, Henriett. I give up. I'm a birdbrain." Henrietta laughed and said, "You have no brains, but you do have intuition. Where did you learn that word?" "Which word?" "Another question." "What question?" "All right, now it's my turn. Where did you hear the word *birdbrain*?" "Where did I hear it? I don't mind admitting that I haven't applied myself to the question." Henrietta said, "Then I'll tell you where you first heard it." "Where?" "Wasn't it our Sarini?" "Sarini? Sarini visited you? Why did she come all of a sudden?" Henrietta said, "First, I should inform you that she has a wetnurse in mind for our son." "What son?" Henrietta laughed and said, "You're the one who's so confident, who says, 'I'm certain that you're going to have a boy.'" "Ah . . . Ah . . .," said Manfred. "And who is the wetnurse?" Henrietta said, "Guess. Five or six questions, and you'll be able to guess." Manfred said, "Haven't you learned from experience that I'm no good at this game? If you don't tell me, Henrietta, I'm likely to go to my grave in ignorance. Graves, graves. I want to tell you something. I myself heard Firadeus's mother singing 'Sweet as a mountain goat's were his eyes / Now covered with earth in the grave he lies.'" "You heard and you didn't tell me?" Manfred said, "If I didn't tell you before, I'm telling you now. On the day of the big rally, I met Firadeus on her way back from the pharmacy. I walked her home, thinking that, if she was stopped by the police, I could tell them she had to get medicine for her sick mother. When I approached her house, I heard her mother singing as she paced back and forth in her room. Now, Henriett, tell me who the wetnurse is." Henrietta said, "In any case, you must admit that the whole thing is strange." "What thing?" Henrietta said, "You have so

little regard for me that you forget what we were talking about."
Manfred said, "Either I didn't consider the entire subject worthwhile,
or I wanted to tell you but I forgot. Now, Henriett, you tell me. About
that wetnurse, who is she?" Henrietta looked at him with suspicious
eyes but answered affectionately, "So you won't wear out your mind,
I'll tell you." "So?" "Summon up all your patience, my dearest, and
don't let your curiosity show." Manfred said, "It's not curiosity." Henrietta said, "Then let's forget the whole thing." "What thing?" "That
very thing." Manfred said, "You keep saying the same thing in different
words. If our Avraham were to hear you talking like that, he would say,
'Too bad she didn't become an orator.' Is there any news from Zahara's
household?" Henrietta said, "The vegetables you ate are from their
gardens." Manfred said, "Instead of letters, they send us lettuce. They
have become real farmers; they would rather dig herbs than verbs. And
Tamara? Tamara is idle, as usual. She's not even looking for work."
Henrietta said, "You always complain about Tamara. First of all, she
isn't idle. She still goes to Mekor Hayim every day. But if what you
have in mind is salaried work, what can she do? She's waiting for word
from the Education Department. The officials there treat her the way
her mother was treated when she was clamoring for certificates." Manfred said, "All officials are alike. But I have reason to suspect Tamara
has been telling us tales—outright fictions. From the very beginning,
we should have understood the mysterious saga of Mekor Hayim, the
tubercular girls, and all the rest. But not now. Not now, my dear, when
your eyes are drooping. It's time to lay your head on the pillow, to put
the rest of you in your bed. Listen, Henrietta, I have one request. I
know that if I say I'll do the dishes, you won't let me, so I won't ask
anything that major. All I ask is that you leave them for tomorrow.
When Firadeus comes, she can wash them. That verse is not bad. I
didn't know goats' eyes were sweet. It would be interesting to investigate that image. Is it common among the Persians, or is it original? I'll
look it up tomorrow in the poetry of Rückert." "Rückert? I forgot he
existed." Manfred said, "A few months ago, I came upon a biography
of Moses Lazarus, written by his wife. She reports what he said about
Rückert: that if the world were destroyed by a flood and only Rückert's
poems survived, they would make it possible to reconstruct the world."
"He was that great? And you, Fred, remember everything. Whatever
you read sticks in your mind." Manfred said, "I could have remembered
that statement, or I could have forgotten it. But that very day I heard
it again, not about Rückert and not from Lazarus, but from a Hebrew
writer who was referring to a Hebrew storyteller. I have a student, part
clerk and part critic, who enjoys enlightening me with his remarks.

That day I was applauding Neu for having restored so many forgotten worlds to us. To which my student said, 'If we applaud those who restore forgotten worlds, we should applaud the storytellers.' And he proceeded to quote a Hebrew writer who wrote about a Hebrew story-teller, 'If there should be a flood that restores the world to chaos, with only Mendele the Bookseller's stories surviving, it would be possible to reconstruct Jewish life.' These Hebrews, in their excessive narcissism, don't notice that there are countries outside of Poland, Lithuania, and Russia where Jews have lived and endured, that they too are a vital force." Henrietta laughed and said, "Which is an offense to your German patriotism, Fred." Manfred laughed and said, "No offense to my German patriotism, but an offense to the truth. Even someone like me is sometimes moved to protest against truisms that are grounded in nothing. Now, my dearest, rise up, come along. Let me lead you to the bedroom. I'll settle you in your cradle, and you can close your weary eyes and sleep until Firadeus brings you breakfast."

Henrietta's eyes were closed, her tongue weary. She spoke fitfully. If I were to put the words together and interpret her allusions, this is roughly what they would add up to: When a woman is young, in full bloom, capable of filling the earth with sons and daughters, she isn't always pleased to be producing children. When she ages, when her energies diminish and her sons and daughters leave home, her lot is bitter, ever so bitter. Because she is lonely, she would love to bear a child, but this is something she no longer has the strength to do.

I am omitting the rest of Henrietta's remarks, censuring those women who make no use of what the Creator granted them and giving credit to the Oriental communities: "If they didn't behave like human beings, increasing and multiplying in a natural fashion, the land would soon be empty. But," Henrietta added, "even they have begun to act like Ashkenazim." At this point, Henrietta told about a pretty young Sephardic woman, about twenty-four years old, who had given her husband four handsome sons. After weaning the fourth one, she became pregnant. Her neighbor said, "If you keep up at this rate, you won't have room for all your children." They deliberated and went to a certain woman doctor. The doctor did what she did, and the woman aborted. After a while, she began to yearn for an infant to clasp in her arms. She was consumed with longing, but she was no longer able to become pregnant, and she was not fit to give birth again.

The very same doctor has set up a clinic, and her pace is tireless. The country is full of British soldiers, as well as impoverished young girls. Feeling confined by the narrow walls of their homes, these girls go out for a little while, seeking escape. The soldiers who see them are struck by their beauty and entice them to go to a café or a movie. Some are intrigued and respond, at first to scold the soldiers for their impudence, then because of curiosity, then because there's no harm in talking, then because of habit. In the end, some of the girls are seduced by them, and, when they become pregnant, they go to this doctor to get rid of their unborn babies.

So much for those evils and the troubles they bring on. Now let's get back to the Herbst household. Manfred and Henrietta finished their supper, and it was already Henrietta's bedtime. But, like most women at leisure, she didn't tend to look ahead. Henrietta remained seated, though Manfred stood beside her, taking her hand and attempting to get her out of the chair and lead her to her room. Henrietta, who was comfortable where she was, didn't stir. She was thinking about her daughters. Zahara and Tamara are not here. One lives with Avraham and Dani in the country; the other has gone to see about the teaching position she was promised; Sarah is lying asleep in her little bed. Yet another child is inside his mother, Henrietta, who didn't prevent the Creator from creating a person in her womb. Should the Creator of man alter His ways ever so slightly, He would give her a male child, now that she has produced three females. The world needs daughters too, but it would be nice for this mother of daughters to produce a son.

Henrietta's eyes remained closed, and her hand was in Manfred's. He held his wife's hand and gazed at her. Her eyes were still closed, her face was bloated, and her nose cast its shadow all around. Now I'll say something it would be nicer not to say, but truth goes beyond the niceties. Manfred noted her wrinkled cheeks, flushed and lined with bluish veins, and her body, bloated and slovenly. He also noted how she luxuriated before him, like a bride during the seven-day marriage feast, and he turned his eyes away, commenting to himself: How grotesque. He said nothing, except in his heart, and, like a man who respects his wife, he smoothed her cheek and tried to help her up.

After taking Henrietta to her bed, he sneaked back to the dining room, cleared the dishes, took them to the kitchen, and washed them thoroughly, examining each piece inside and out to be sure it was clean, so as not to give Henrietta reason to reject his work. Then he set the dishes on the slatted shelf to drain, moving about stealthily, so as not to disturb Henrietta and arouse her anger at him for intruding on her territory. Even though she had already allowed him to take on some of the chores, she would, no doubt, scold him. Having finished all the kitchen work, he inverted the dishpans and scanned the room, to be sure he hadn't left anything undone. When he saw everything was in place, he turned out the light. When the light was off, he saw that one burner was still lit. Henrietta had forgotten about it, but it was serving no purpose. He turned it off and went to Henrietta, thinking: If I had left it on, Henrietta would surely complain. But when she does it, it's all right.

Henrietta was lying in bed in her clothes. He began coaxing her to undress. When she was ready to comply, he helped her take off her clothes, just as he used to do when she was pregnant with Zahara.

I have something to say about Shira. That was a good question Shira had asked: "Do you help your wife, too?" Yes, Shira. Dr. Herbst helps his wife take off her clothes, and he does it expertly. His hands don't tremble at all. But Shira is far away. In fact, she has moved. But we won't be looking for you. Not today. It's enough, Shira, that Herbst asked about you in the hospital. He also asked Anita Brik about you. Tomorrow afternoon, we might perhaps go and see where you live. If we find you, good. If we don't find you, it's your fault for not sitting and waiting for us.

After arranging his wife's clothes, he embraced her and kissed her on the mouth. She kissed him too, if not on his mouth, then on his forehead. Manfred's forehead is an integral part of him, you might say his finest part, with all his great thoughts plainly written on it. Henrietta assumes that these thoughts derive from the major essay he is working on. We will allow her this error, rather than divulge one or two of the schemes he is considering. Henrietta asked Manfred to go and see if Sarah was asleep and if she was perspiring. After he had done so, he took leave of his wife, with a kiss, and went to his room to read some papal history and find out just when Damasus became pope. This wasn't actually why he went back to his room. He wanted to be alone for a while. He was worn out by the day's concerns. He hadn't had a moment's rest. In the morning, he had lectured on the earliest known Byzantine coins with Greek inscriptions, as well as on the coins associated with Heraclius, which we assume were minted so they could be used by soldiers during the war against Persia. After the lecture, a guest, who had come to hear a Hebrew lecture at the Hebrew University, arrived and offered a somewhat dated insight. He stated that, even after Constantine became Christian, he continued to be attracted to idolatry, which is evident from the motifs on many artifacts from the Constantine period. Herbst wore himself out conveying to this genius, without being disrespectful, that, with coins, as in various other areas, such motifs are not always conclusive, because they often continue to appear even after they have lost their significance. When he got rid of the guest, he was joined by two of his students, who needed books they couldn't find in the National Library. If I'm not mistaken, they were

looking for the works of G. Finelli and W. Schultze. They went home
with Herbst, and, like all bright students who are full of their own
wisdom, they were eager to impart it to their teacher and enhance his
wisdom. In the end, after they came home with him and he gave them
the books, they found that the wording was ambiguous and Herbst had
to confirm whether or not what they said was right. He was left with
only a small portion of the afternoon break, time for lunch but not for
a rest. Because he was so tired, he was afraid Henrietta would be
talkative, which made him unable to rest. We would imagine that he
did try resting right after lunch, but what use is such an attempt? As
soon as he stretched out on his bed, he heard a sound at the door. He
hurried to open it, so no one would ring the bell and wake Henrietta.
He found a man at the door, a leather briefcase on his arm, his face like
the face of a thousand other solicitors from national institutions. He
began to barrage him with words about a particular individual who had
just reached the age of fifty and in whose honor a grove of trees was
being planted. Dr. Herbst was asked to contribute a tree. After the
solicitor left, Herbst went back to bed, but he found no rest. He got
up and went into town, to the French Library, hoping to find comfort
in a new book. On the way, he met Anita Brik and went with her to
Zichel's, where they had a long chat. After leaving her, he took the bus
home and heard news about some of the unfortunate events that had
occurred that day. When he was finally home, he sat down to eat and
had a long chat with his wife. If his mouth and mind had been with
his wife, all would have been well. But his mouth was in one place, and
his mind was elsewhere. This is why he was exhausted and eager to be
alone.

   He went up to his room, turned on the lamp, and surveyed his books.
He stood there, closed his eyes, and concentrated, straining to remember what he was looking for. He opened his eyes and moved toward
the row of books on the Church Fathers. He took down Tseckler's
book about Saint Jerome, not because he was interested in Tseckler, but
because of an article in manuscript that was appended to the book.
Since the article had no name, I'll relay its subject: how Saint Jerome
contributed to the work of Damasus on religious texts. It is very likely
that the news Herbst heard on the bus, about a young scholar who was
killed by Arabs, was what reminded him of that article, for Herbst had
inherited the book, with all its appendices, from a young researcher
who fell in battle.

   Herbst sat with the book, studying the shape of the letters, scrutinizing them as if to analyze the writer's character. He studied each letter,
searched every line for a sign that the author was destined to die young.

Several years had passed since his friend's death. Others had died, others had been killed, others had committed suicide. But, whenever he thought of him, he felt his death anew. Why was this? Because he was killed at the beginning of the war, when people were not so accustomed to casualties. Now that the book was in his hand, he was overcome with fatigue, which led to a desire for sleep. He glanced at his bed, thinking: I'll stretch out. I'll have a rest. Actually, there's no reason not to spend the night here, as I used to do before I went to Ahinoam with Henrietta to welcome Dani. He put Tseckler's book on the table near his bed and slipped off his shoes to prepare himself for sleep. He was holding one of his shoes, inspecting it for traces of the shoeshine boy's labor, when he realized that Tseckler's book was not the right one for now. He returned it to its spot, scanned the shelf, and took down a book of Saint Jerome's letters to read in bed. He undressed and climbed into bed.

After reading for a while, he came upon the letter in which Jerome tells about a chaste Christian woman who was falsely accused of betraying her husband, of the brutal torture to which she was subjected to force her to confess to a sin she hadn't committed. The great event that occurred after she was tortured was also described. The ghost of a smile spread across Herbst's lips, the smile of a literate person responding to an eloquent passage. He put down the book, placed his hand on it, and pursued his own train of thought: Jerome was a great writer. He succeeded in portraying all sorts of vicious tortures to achieve a desired end. Torture has been a common phenomenon since men first began to seek dominance over others. Still, the agonies described by Jerome were merely figments of his imagination. That broad-minded, saintly Christian concocted all those tortures. Gentiles! What an example of their corruption and brutality. Corruption and brutality that culminated in Hitler.

The light suddenly began to flicker, as an oil lamp does when it is about to go out. He blinked his eyes and was baffled, for he had just filled it with oil the day before. In fact, it was more than half full, but the wick was too short to reach the oil. He was too lazy to get up and add oil for the wick to draw on. He lay there, abandoning himself to all sorts of thoughts.

His mind wandered, settling on the last war. As he tended to do whenever he was reminded of it, he made an effort to forget what he had seen during the war, as well as the fact that he had actually fought in it. To some extent, he succeeded; to some extent, he failed. In any case, he didn't really succeed in getting rid of war thoughts. Kings are at war with kings, nations with nations, religions with religions. A destroys B, B destroys C; they are all, finally, destroyed. If at first there was some logic to this scheme, it soon vanished, leaving only devastation in its wake. Herbst fixed his gaze on the wick that could no longer reach the oil because the fire had consumed it, and yet its light continued to flicker.

I am not one to infer connections, and I don't mean to suggest that the sight of the lamp, et cetera, led him to think about Israel and the nations of the world. But I do allude to it, because it is appropriate. He gazed at the wick that didn't reach the oil, thinking: The nations of the world berate Israel for considering itself a chosen people, and, in truth, it must be admitted that, compared to other nations, we have superior qualities. I don't mean that every single one of us is virtuous and just, but, overall, the people as a whole are truly fine. There are intellectual women, concerned with the Jewish religion, who say, "Before, while we were in Germany, we didn't doubt that the Jews were a chosen people. When we came to the Land of Israel, we saw that Jews are like everyone else, no better and no worse. Now that we have lived here several years, having seen what we have seen, we see that we are inferior to other nations." These women have arrived at this conclusion because, when they lived elsewhere, they saw many Gentiles and knew very few Jews. Here, they see the entire people. Despite this, Herbst reflected, despite this, I believe that we are finer than other nations. What is so fine about the people of Israel? I, in any case, am not especially fine. The pursuit of bodily pleasure and the drive to create books are surely not fine, nor are these Jewish qualities. In this respect, I am no different from my peers. Yet I stand by what I said earlier: If a man sins once and doesn't sin again, I don't claim the sin is erased, but at least it isn't compounded.

When did he make that statement? The day he got to know Shira. All his dealings with Shira have since been suspended. Only her address is written in his notebook. Should he want to, he could erase her address, and he could erase Shira from his heart, as if she no longer exists, as if she never existed, as if she would never return. If they should meet somewhere, and if she should say to him, "Why don't you show yourself to me?" he could say, "You moved to a new place and didn't tell me where you live. When I asked about you at the hospital, they said they didn't know either." Though he was feeling peaceful, on the brink of sleep, he took the trouble to get up and erase Shira's address. He went back to bed, blew out the light, and delivered himself to sleep.

Sleep took over, all at once, wielding its power over each and every limb. You might remember that, when Henrietta was about to give birth to Sarah, Manfred brought her to the hospital, and he was sitting in the waiting room with her when the nurse Shira, whom he called

Nadia, appeared and sat down with the women. At one point, a blind beggar from Istanbul appeared, and the limbs of that Shira–Nadia woman enveloped that beggar, as if to embrace him. The two of them finally began to dwindle and dissolve, until all that was left of them was a sandal. In the end, they were both enclosed in that sandal and vanished, never to emerge again. What had happened to that blind Turkish beggar was now happening to Herbst. His limbs were dwindling, until all that was left of them was sleep. From the depths of sleep, the hint of a human face seemed to surface. At first, it was hard to recognize. Little by little, the face became sharper, and Herbst realized that it belonged to one of the early monks who appear in so many Christian legends. This monk went into a place that resembled the building Shira's new apartment was in, though it didn't resemble the building Anita Brik had drawn. The monk was transformed too, and he began to resemble a certain monk from Gethsemane with whom Herbst had become acquainted at the post office, when he was mailing out offprints of his articles. There is something I should have mentioned earlier; not having done so, I will mention it now. When Herbst, who was mailing out his offprints, was standing at the window in the post office, there happened to be a monk in line behind him with whom he struck up a conversation, at the end of which the monk invited him to visit his monastery. Herbst promised to do so. I didn't mention this event at the time, because it wasn't relevant. Now that it has come up again, though only in a dream, I may as well mention it.

In the morning, Herbst appeared in the dining room with an armful of thick Latin books in pigskin bindings. While he was waiting for Henrietta to bring his coffee, he glanced through the books. "Such diligence," Henrietta remarked, with a show of laughter and concealed admiration. Manfred answered, "Diligence that doesn't do me any good. The very thing I need is missing." Henrietta asked, "And where can it be found? In the National Library?" Manfred said derisively, "The National Library, the National Library. Whatever we don't need is there, and whatever we do need is not there. Even Ernst Weltfremdt has more good books than that warehouse they call the National and University Libraries. But Professor Weltfremdt doesn't have the volume I need either." Henrietta asked in a worried tone, "So what will you do?" Manfred said, "I'll do what one does in such cases. I'll do without."

During breakfast, Manfred said to Henrietta, "I have the urge to go to Gethsemane, to the monastery there." Henrietta said, "To look for that book?" Manfred said, "I doubt that those monks are familiar with the book I'm looking for, but I would like to go, because I once promised to visit a monk who lives there. It's not urgent, and the visit isn't essential, but for those very reasons I think I ought to go. I don't know if you grasp my meaning. Those things that aren't really essential are often particularly appealing. Going there is just such a thing. Several months ago, I became acquainted with a monk, who invited me to visit him. I promised I would come. He didn't expect me to keep my word, nor did I intend to keep it. Suddenly, all of a sudden, I see that I must keep my promise. What do you think about this?" Henrietta said, "I assume you won't be back for lunch." Manfred said, "I see from your response that you approve." Henrietta said, "To be sure you don't get hungry, you ought to have an egg for breakfast—one of the eggs Zahara sent us." Manfred said, "You have a one-track mind, Mother. Give me your lips, you monster, you."

— 13 —

When Herbst got off the bus and found himself on the street, in the midst of a bustling throng, under a sky full of heat and light that blazed, stretched, and expanded with each person, where each structure and each sound took on the whiteness of light, like some substance that dims the eye and deafens the ear—when this happened, his will began to diminish and fade away. He was sorry to have left home on such a hot day, at such an hour. Though he had promised whomever he had promised that he would visit him, though he felt obliged to keep his word and fulfill his promise, he hadn't set a time and wasn't obliged to visit on any particular day. He took off his hat and wiped his brow, as well as the inner band of his hat and his sunglasses, scanning all four directions to find the Gethsemane bus stop. As in the case of all quests that are undertaken without conviction, he only half stirred, and he would have remained in his spot if he hadn't been swept up by people going to the post office and the bank, and by other pedestrians whose swift pace stemmed from the same source as his stationary position: they, too, were unsure of their direction. Time passed, and he didn't remember where the bus stop was, but he realized that he didn't have to make the trip. He decided not to go. Having decided not to go, he was pleased; for, even if he had found the bus, he would have had a long wait. Buses from the outlying districts make the return trip only after their riders have concluded their businesss in town, which they never seem to do until the day is nearly over.

Having ruled out Gethsemane, he didn't know what to do. Unless their work compels them to go into town early in the day, those who live in outlying neighborhoods tend to make the trip only for a specific purpose. This was true of Herbst. If not for the trip to Gethsemane, he wouldn't have come. Now that the trip was off, he had no purpose. He didn't really belong in town. Here he was, with three or four sizzling stones underfoot and a blazing sun overhead. Actually, he could have been standing in the shade of the bus from Talpiot that had arrived in the interim and could have taken him home to his books. But, since he was in town, it seemed a shame to go right back. After all, it isn't every day that he stops working without some sense of guilt. So what should he do? He can't very well visit a friend, because everyone is at work. Anyone who isn't lecturing is either in the library, looking for material for an article, or engaged in writing a book. There are people who sense when a friend is at work, and, in a flash, they are there to interrupt. Herbst was not that sort. He was simply looking for a place to spend an hour.

There are very few places in Jerusalem where one can spend an hour at that time of day. If I list them, there won't be more than two: the Bezalel Museum and the B'nai B'rith Library. In the past, before the National and University Libraries were built on Mount Scopus, the B'nai B'rith building was always buzzing with people. Herbst went there quite frequently, and he used to bring guests from abroad, though he was embarrassed that the collection didn't live up to its reputation. When the university was built on Mount Scopus, all the good books were transferred to its new libraries, and the one in town began to be forgotten. Now that he was looking for a place to spend an hour, he didn't remember it. He forgot about the museum, too. This forgetfulness of his is probably puzzling, so I will explain it. In the early days, when he first came to the country, these two institutions were his favorite haunts. Now that the population had grown larger and the city's limits had expanded, he himself was taking smaller steps, and it was not as easy to come and go. He began to go to those places less and less often, then not at all. Since he no longer frequented them, they began to fade from his memory and were soon forgotten.

Herbst stood on the street near the post office and was astonished to be looking for a place to go and unable to find one. Only a few years back, this would not have happened. Even before he could quite picture a place, he would find himself there, whether it was night or day, sunny or rainy. If someone tells you, "We used to take night walks along the top of Jerusalem's walls, and outside of the city as well," you will think that's a fairy tale. Let me tell you, it's absolutely true. What is more, we used to walk through the Old City to the Western Wall and find Hasidim and other pious men standing there, bemoaning the exile of the Divine Presence. At what hour? At midnight. From there, we used to go to an Arab café, drink coffee, and smoke narghiles, to the accompaniment of their singing or their gramophones. The Arabs welcomed us, and we weren't afraid to go anywhere. Isn't it amazing? Our community was small then, but its horizons were broad. Now that it has expanded, its horizons are narrow, and no Jew is safe from the murderous assault of a knife or a bullet. At any rate, in the area between the post office, Mahane Yehuda, and Beit Hakerem, there is nothing to fear.

Herbst abandoned his spot near the post office and went to look at the window display in one of the stores while debating where to go. The windows were covered, to shield them from the sun. This was true of all the other stores, too. He had no choice but to go to a café. Herbst didn't usually go to cafés. If we saw him there, it was not because of him, but because of Anita Brik, because of Lisbet Neu, because of Shira. Moreover, it seemed odd to him to do today what he had done the day before; he had spent several hours at Zichel's just yesterday. There are, of course, people who spend a great deal of time in cafés. Julian Weltfremdt, for example, who goes to two cafés every day. Herbst met Julian Weltfremdt, who was leaving one café on his way to another.

Herbst asked Julian Weltfremdt, "Are you in a hurry?" He said, "Not at all. I'm running away from the noise. What a nation we are! Each individual makes as much noise as an entire people. Why so much noise? Remember the teachers in our German elementary school? When a Jewish student raised his voice, they used to scold and say reproachfully, 'Not so much noise—this isn't a Jewish school.' If they were exaggerating about the noise there, here it's no exaggeration. What brings you to town? You are ordering a new sign, I suppose?" "A new sign?" "A sign saying Professor Dr. Manfred Herbst. I heard the faculty senate is considering your promotion. Since they are considering it, they'll promote you. Not because you deserve it, but to show the world that they're not idle, that they accomplish something. Good luck and congratulations, Herbstlein. From the depths of my heart, I hope you get a full professorship. Did you see my cousin's book? No? You can see it in any bookstore window. It's as fat as a watermelon.

In another country, such a book would earn professorships for generations to come. Here, he'll have to make do with a title that's good only for himself. Poor fellow."

They went into the café and sat down together. Weltfremdt took his cigarettes from his pocket, placed them in front of him on the table, and sat talking about the things he had talked about yesterday and the day before: how there is never anything new in Jerusalem; that, if you do find something new, it's a second-rate copy of something old. Nonetheless, he had some news. He had found a job. He would soon be teaching in a secondary school, either Blumenkohl or Lilienblum.

"This is the story of the school," Weltfremdt told Herbst. "There was a land speculator, a stupid and ignorant man, who made a fortune. He put up a building that was large and not especially ugly. If it were ugly, I would suggest to the authorities that they turn it into a prison in which they should install the builder, his partners, his partners' partners, and all the high officials who accepted bribes from him openly and secretly. When it was built, he didn't find tenants that suited him, so it remained uninhabited. It upset him not to have any tenants—to have no one to oppress, no one to skin alive—so he decided to set up a school. In this country, schools are a lucrative enterprise. Everyone is after an education and a degree, and those who are too stupid to achieve this for themselves want their offspring to be educated. Where does one acquire an education? In schools. There are new ones everywhere. Anyone who lacks the competence to open a kindergarten opens a secondary school. For the moment, they are content to call the school a gymnasium. Before long, they will all become universities. The Jews are not a people known to be content with the minimum. As long as the university is more highly regarded than the gymnasia, every gymnasium is destined to become a university. And you, Mr. Innocent, aren't you wondering why the headmaster saw fit to have me teach in his gymnasia. It's because of my name. He can boast that Weltfremdt is one of his teachers, and people will assume he means Professor Weltfremdt. So you see, Herbstlein, one can do a good turn without lifting a finger. Whom do I have in mind? I'm thinking of my cousin."

The waitress came and asked, "What would you gentlemen like?" Weltfremdt deliberated and said, "I would like an ashtray." "And what else would the gentleman like?" Weltfremdt said, "Just a minute, I'll see if I forgot matches. I forgot. Yes, I forgot. I truly forgot, so please bring me some matches, too." The waitress laughed and asked Herbst, "Tea or coffee, sir?" Weltfremdt said, "I would like to have some coffee, but make it iced coffee. Take my advice, Herbst, and have some

iced coffee. You'll be eternally grateful to me. Miss, bring two glasses
of iced coffee—but iced, truly iced, not the kind that's called iced and
isn't iced. I found matches. Forgetfulness is an unfortunate trait, but
memory is even more of a misfortune, as it includes remembering and
forgetting in one, for, if you hadn't forgotten, you would have no need
to remember. Do you or do you not understand? I assume you don't.
So let's go back to the beginning. The idiot who set up that gymnasium
had never, in his entire life, seen a school. But he was a skilled merchant
and a good businessman. He understood that the parents' goal was to
acquire good credentials for their children. For this reason, he instructed the staff to ignore the stupidity of the students. This is how
they prepare students for the university. My dear Herbstlein, I'm talking, but you're not listening. What's that in your hand?"

Herbst was holding his notebook, but he wasn't looking inside it. He
was repeating Shira's address to himself, having erased it the night
before. Startled by Weltfremdt's rebuke, Herbst tucked away the notebook, stared at Weltfremdt, then surveyed the café. A few years earlier,
he had been here with Shira. Someone else had owned the place at the
time. He had been here another time with Shira and found yet a
different owner. Cafés change hands often. A proprietor who serves his
customers well, who provides good coffee, ends up selling the business
and leaving the country.

All of a sudden, Herbst took Weltfremdt's hand, looked at him—
either at him or through him—and said, "I have to go." Weltfremdt
collected his things and stood up. Herbst remained seated. Weltfremdt
noted this and laughed. Herbst said, "Why are you laughing? Is it
because I'm sitting down? I really have to go. Yes, I have to go."
Weltfremdt said, "I would assume, dear Herbstlein, that need is determined by desire and desire by need." Herbst smiled, a confused smile,
pretending not to understand, as if he had been about do something but
was interrupted and was now making every effort to recover. Herbst
looked down at the table and called out after Weltfremdt, "You forgot
your matches." "It's an empty box," Weltfremdt explained. Herbst
picked up the matchbox, looked inside, and said, with a confused
chuckle, "That's right, the box is empty. You're going already?" "Yes,"
Weltfremdt answered, "I have to go too." The two friends took leave
of each other and went their separate ways. Weltfremdt went to another café to glance at some newspapers, and Herbst turned toward the
bus stop, meaning to go home.

On the way to the bus, he thought: Henrietta isn't expecting me for
lunch, because I told her I was going to Gethsemane. If I come home

now, I'll disrupt her routines. She probably hasn't prepared lunch, or she has prepared it but plans to serve it for dinner, so she can have time to pursue some of her other interests. I really should stay in town as long as possible. What if I did tell Julian I had to go? Herbst arrived at the corner and stood in the shade of an awning that was shielding a display window from the sun. He looked at his wristwatch and pondered, wondering why he had left the café in full knowledge that, at this hour, there was no better place to be and no better conversation-alist than Julian Weltfremdt. He looked at his watch again. No, the French Library wouldn't be open yet. He suddenly cried out, "Fool! How could you forget . . . ?"

Like a person who remembers something he has to do and regrets every wasted moment, he didn't say just what he had forgotten. But he directed his steps toward a store that sold foreign books, one of many that sprang up when German immigrants arrived, bringing with them many books but not enough money for spacious apartments with room for bookcases, like the ones they were accustomed to in Germany. Thus, they were compelled to sell their books for next to nothing. Herbst's interest at that particular moment was not in those books, but in the collection of a certain orange-grove owner from Petah Tikva, which the proprietor had recently purchased from his heirs. True, for the most part these books were German classics, the best of which he already owned, and the lesser ones were unappealing. But these were elegant editions, bound in leather, and Herbst was considering an exchange. He wanted to trade his ordinary editions for these handsome ones, adding to the deal a number of books he was ready to dispose of anyway.

This is how these collectors operate. A wealthy man, of German origin, settled in Petah Tikva, where he owned fields, vineyards, cit-rus groves, houses—assorted liquid and nonliquid assets. He married a woman from the Hungarian community. They each received a sti-pend. They didn't know what to do with these funds, provided by Jews all over the world to support their counterparts in the Holy Land, for they were self-supporting. They decided to order the works of Germany's great writers, and, since the communities in Germany and Hungary had such ample resources, they were able to include handsome and elegant bindings for the books, beyond anything any-where else in this country. The couple also ordered various novels for their own pleasure. This was their practice until the outbreak of the Great War. After the war, the English language began to enjoy the respect that had once belonged to German, because the English were now in charge. This man and woman died, leaving their collection of German books to their children. As the number of newcomers grew and apartments became expensive, the heirs began to resent the books their parents had collected. They took up an entire room, and space was worth money. So they decided to call in a book dealer, who appraised the books and gave them what he gave them for their collection of German classics and novels. This is the tale of the books Herbst had in mind to pursue.

— 14 —

Herbst remembered the books that were brought from Petah Tikva, and he was glad to have remembered them while he was in town, so that he might see them first, before anyone else. At this time of day, most people were occupied and not free to deal with books. He consulted his watch and turned toward Jaffa Road, which he would follow to Hasollel. He took one shortcut, then another, from Haneviim Street to Harav Kook. He passed the big bakery, as well as the offices of the rabbinate at the beginning of the street, and went as far as the flower garden near the entrance to Doctor Ticho's eye clinic; then he veered toward Jaffa Road. Remembering that, to the left of Harav Kook Street, there was another cut one could take, he turned back, followed it up three or four steps, and came to a narrow lane. A boy with a basket full of baked goods was coming toward him. Herbst saw the boy and was reassured that he was on the right track, for these streets were not to be trusted. They could have been closed off since the last time you were there, making the route longer rather than shorter, as intended. The boy pressed himself to the wall to let Herbst pass, since the road was too narrow for two bodies moving in opposite directions. Herbst nodded in gratitude and surprise that the boy was so polite as to let him pass first. The boy laughed. Herbst asked him, "Why are you laughing?" The boy answered, "Because." Herbst said, " 'Because' is no answer. Tell me, please, why were you laughing?" The boy answered, "I remembered a funny story, so I laughed." He said, "What funny story did you remember?" He said, "Something I learned last night." He said, "You go to night school?" The boy nodded, with the basket still on his head. Herbst said, "What are you studying, and what was the story you remembered? Isn't that basket heavy? I'll take it down, and you can tell me the story." The boy said, "Heavy? If I wanted to, I could dance the hora without letting the basket fall, without losing a single cake or one sesame seed." Herbst said, "Is that so? But don't you want to tell me the funny story? Tell it, and I'll listen." The boy said, "If I want, I can tell it word for word." Herbst said, "Word for word? Does the teacher expect you to know it word for word?" The boy said, "I wanted to learn it." "Word for word? How did you arrive at that?" The boy stared at him and said, "It happened, all by itself." "By itself? How come?" The boy said, "I thought it was such a good story that I read it again and again and again. Meanwhile, the book slipped out of my hand, and the words kept coming out of my mouth, just like in the book. I picked up the book, glanced at it, and saw that every word I said was in the book." Herbst said, "Meanwhile, you probably forgot half of the story." The boy said, "If you like, you can test me." Herbst said, "I'm not a teacher, so I won't test you. I just want to hear whether you really still remember the whole story." The boy said, "But if someone comes, we'll have to get out of the way." Herbst said, "Then we'll get out of the way." The boy said, "I'll move backward. Which way will you move? Forward or backward?" Herbst said, "What would you suggest?" The boy laughed again. Herbst said, "When the time comes, we'll worry. Now for your story. But put down the basket. It must be heavy." The boy shook his head back and forth, studying Herbst's face to see if he noticed that the cakes in the basket hadn't stirred at all. He said to him, "I could stick one arm on the ground and stretch the other toward the sky without disturbing the basket. Want to see?" Herbst said, "If you tell the story first." The boy said, "Good. I'll tell it.

"There was once a river. There was a bridge over the river so one could cross to the other side. It was such a narrow bridge that only one person could cross at a time. One day, two billy goats approached the bridge, one at each end. Each one of them stood his ground—one on this side of the river, the other on the other side of the river. When they finally got to the middle of the bridge, one goat insisted that he had seniority and should be allowed to pass first, that he was greater and more distinguished than his brother, being descended from a herd that originated on Mount Gilead. The other goat, goaded by his lineage, claimed seniority too. He considered himself especially distinguished because of the verse in Exodus 'Those women whose hearts were stirred by wisdom spun goat's hair,' a reference to the very goats he was descended from, whose hair adorned the tabernacle. They stood confronting each other, making no move to back away. They stood there

interminably. One of the goats became enraged and goaded the other
goat, trying to provoke him. 'You haven't made a move yet. Bestir
yourself and get going, before I reduce you to goat dung.' To which
his rival answered, 'How dare you speak so brazenly?' They fought,
seizing each other's heads and locking horns, until they both fell into
the depths of the river."

While Herbst stood listening to the tale of the goats, he heard the
sound of young legs and saw a courtyard, half-obstructed by boxes and
battered crates, half-screened by woven wire that formed a shedlike
structure, which was draped with sacks and branches. Inside the shed
were six or seven girls in exercise clothes. A woman, wearing a summer
dress and a straw hat, seemed to be in charge. With one hand, she issued
orders; with the other, she wiped her sweaty brow. An old man in
hospital clothes surveyed the scene from a window in the wall that
overlooked the shed. Putting these elements together, you realized that
the courtyard was next to the hospital and that next to it was a girl's
school with no facilities for calisthenics, so this spot was used for that
purpose.

Herbst wiped his eyes and his forehead. Then he turned onto Hasollel Street. He came to the offices of the *Palestine Post* at the head of the
street and scanned the newspaper in the display case on the wall,
making an effort to avoid the bad news, such as reports of those distress-
ing events known as "riots" that were occurring at the time. He heard
the noise of the printing press, which was on the ground floor of the
building, duplicating the news. Herbst stood there, his eyes tightly
clenched, listening with his feet. He was straining to remember something, but he didn't know what. He found himself at the window of
Bamberger and Wahrmann, the bookstore, where he saw Samuel Kar-
weiss's book on the history of the Jews in Byzantium and remembered
that it had been recommended to him several days earlier. In fact, this
is what he had been trying to remember. But he didn't linger, because
he was eager to be the first one to get to see those German classics, and
he had wasted too much time on the boy and his story, which wasn't
worth hearing after all, even had he been at leisure, and all the more
so when he was in a hurry. At that moment, the barber was stationed
outside of his shop, waiting for someone to appear for a haircut or a
chat. The barber saw Herbst and said to him, "I see, Dr. Herbst, that
you're in a hurry. You probably don't want to be detained. Still, it
occurs to me to tell you something that pertains to delay. I ask that you
listen, not on my behalf, but on behalf of the man who is credited with
these remarks. I don't know if you were already here when Balfour
came to this country to celebrate the founding of the university. I don't

imagine you were here yet. The English weren't allowing Jews from Germany to come in, because they were too German. This doesn't affect the story itself. As you can imagine, I would have liked to see Balfour; not merely to see him, but to be near him, on the great day of the opening of the Hebrew University in Jerusalem. I wasn't among the guests. Even in my dreams, I didn't see a way to get a ticket. But how could I give up? I said, 'It would be enough for someone like me to stand in proximity to Balfour, who was granted what no king or nobleman since Cyrus was granted. If not in proximity, then in the same territory.' I put on my best clothes and was ready to go. I say 'to go' when I should say 'to run.' If someone had come and said, 'Bernhardt, would you like a mule to ride on?' I would have given him the very shirt off my back right after the celebration. No such person appeared. But my neighbor did appear, a Hasid from Breslau, God-fearing, happy, and innocent. I love all Jews, especially the Hasidim from Breslau, whose manner is so pious, and most of all my neighbor the Hasid, for the very fringes of his coat trail good conduct and righteous ways, not to mention what comes out of his mouth. At any time, on any occasion, for any event, he has a phrase of his *rebbe*'s to offer, or some other pleasantry. Every person has his moment, but not every moment is equivalent for all people. I told him, 'I can't stop now, not even for one breath.' He smiled, a bewildered smile, and said, 'What's the hurry?' I knew that if I told him I was running to see Balfour, he, in his great innocence, would not be able to grasp the importance of the event. I told him I was going on a trip and was in a rush. He smiled broadly, rubbed his hands together, and said, 'You're going on a trip. Then let me tell you something relevant. Our holy *rebbe,* may his merit protect us, used to say that when someone is going on a trip, no one should interfere; he should be allowed to fix his attention on it, lest he forget something.' Now you tell me, Dr. Herbst, wasn't it worth your while to linger for the sake of that pronouncement?"

As it happened, after he took leave of the barber, it happened that he was needlessly delayed once again. How did this come about? I won't refrain from telling all about it, though it compounds the delay.

For about half a generation, most of Jerusalem's porters have had their headquarters on Hasollel Street, because most of the stores and businesses in the city are located on Jaffa Road. Hasollel Street cuts into the center of Jaffa Road, which is why the porters chose Hasollel. When they are needed to transport something, they are accessible.

Here they are, our redeemed brethren from Media and its environs. The younger ones sit at the upper end of the street, the old-timers at

the lower end, a scheme that predates the houses and the road, going
back to a time when the entire street, as well as the section of Jaffa Road
that faces Nahlat Shiva, was a heap of rubble, and it didn't occur to
anyone that houses would be built there and stores would open. The
older men sit cross-legged, with colorful turbans on their heads. Their
beards are black, with a glint of silver that inspires respect. Their
trousers are floppy; their waists are girdled with heavy ropes; and on
their backs is a small pillow. Their faces are like the face of some ancient
king. On any given workday, they are there, many or a few, depending
on the volume of business in town. And they offer their backs—lovingly, willingly, happily, skillfully, in heat, chill, rain, wind—to carry
any burden. No load is too heavy, even if it has to be transported from
one end of Jerusalem to the other. Why did our brethren from Media
elect this particular line of work? Because they derive from the tribe of
Dan, and it was the Danites who carried Micah's idol on their shoulders
and worshiped it, though God's house was in Shiloh. David, king of
Israel, and his son Solomon rooted out the idol, but only temporarily,
for the people continued to transgress and behave corruptly until the
first exile. Now that the era of Israel's redemption has arrived, and
David's son, the Messiah, will not appear until all the exiles are gathered
together in Jerusalem, our people pour in from all over. They have
come too, ready to shoulder any burden, because of the sins of their
fathers, who were weighted down with idolatry until the first exile.
Now that they do their job lovingly and willingly, they are hastening
the final redemption.

Our brethren, who are the porters in Jerusalem, take on any load,
yet they themselves are totally self-effacing when they work. You find
a large oak chest with three heavy doors, the sort of chest one uses for
clothes and linens, ambling from yard to yard, from alley to alley, from
street to street, neighborhood to neighborhood. Its three mirrors are
smiling. All this is unnatural, for the chest is made of wood and glass,
both of which are inanimate. How is it possible for a lifeless and
inanimate object to amble from place to place? If you look very, very
carefully, you see that the chest is balanced on someone's back, that a
man is under the chest, transporting it, that he is bowed by its weight
and effaced because he is so small in proportion to this mammoth object.
This is also true of barrels, lumber, rocks, and other movable goods that
are several times broader and larger than a person. When a porter has
no work, he sits among his ropes. If he is a contemplative sort, he begins
to contemplate, taking delight in his wife, his sons, his daughters, his
home and sleeping mat, the foods and beverages that give strength to
those who eat and life to those who drink. And if, because of sins, the

Angel of Death should take charge and bring on untimely death to someone, he has the good sense to deal with the orphans and raise them, so they don't fall into the clutches of secularists who would steer them away from the laws that express the will of our holy Torah, which was brought down from God by our teacher Moses, peace be unto him, with thunder and lightning, at Mount Sinai. When these thoughts begin to spill over, he shares them with a neighbor. Not everything that is on your mind can be conveyed. We can convey some of our thoughts, and, because the subject is timely, we can discuss the Arabs—how misguided they are to be making trouble, for they, too, are in exile under English rule. As for us, our king, the Messiah, is on the way, and every single one of us will rule one hundred and twenty-seven realms, like old Ahasuerus. As for the Arabs, if one of them is ever king, he will be a minor king, enthroned by us, by our Herbert Samuel, who called in Abdullah and told him, "I'm giving you a thousand pounds a year to rule the Bedouin in the desert. Be clever and crafty, so Weissman, the head of the Zionists, has no pretext to cast you out and overthrow your kingdom." Among these porters, there are those whose minds reach no further than their eyes can see. They reflect on the Ashkenazim, who spend their days running around in an agitated state, trading apartments, trading possessions, casual with money, as if it showers down from heaven, many of them as cruel as the idols Gentiles worship. If a porter asks two or three pennies more than what was agreed, the Ashkenazim roll their eyes in anger, curse, and abuse him as if his offense were on the scale of the golden calf. The porters' leader, Moshe, is unique. He knows how to get along with all the Ashkenazim. With a smile on his lips, a hand on his heart, he can deal with them. Even those who come from the land of Hitler, that depraved son of a she-devil—they also seek out Moshe.

There is a special relationship between Moshe and Herbst. Since their consultation about the books—transporting, organizing, packing them, et cetera—Moshe has remained fond of him, even devoted to him. As soon as he saw Herbst, he approached him and asked if he was now ready to have his books transported. Moshe stationed himself in front of Herbst and stuck his hands back into the ropes on his hip. Herbst realized he was expected to say something to him. Meaning to be polite, he asked him how he was doing. Moshe extricated his right hand, placed it on his heart, and began relating some of the troubles that had befallen him, some of the troubles he had been involved in because of bad luck, some of the troubles he was subjected to as a test, and yet other troubles whose nature was still unclear, for there are troubles that turn out to be for the good. As he listed each and every trouble, Moshe either

turned his face to heaven and then closed his eyes or closed his eyes and
then turned his face to heaven, saying, "May the Lord have mercy."
It was strange to Herbst that this mighty man was so tormented. And
what torments! A chronically ill wife, who, because of her condition,
was constantly bearing children only to bury them, bearing and burying, so that, after the last of her children was buried and she didn't give
birth again, they adopted two orphans, a boy and a girl. The boy was
one of those children whose parents had died en route from Media to
Jerusalem; the girl was the daughter of a relative who was crushed
under a safe he was carrying to a bank. They raised the orphans,
indulged them with fine food and clothes, bought them shoes to fit their
feet, even toys like those the Ashkenazim buy, making no distinction
between the two orphans, though the girl was a relative and the boy
was not. Moshe and his wife were contented, and they didn't ask
themselves, "Where are our own children?" It was decided that, when
the two orphans grew up and were of age, they would marry each
other. The boy suddenly took sick. He recovered, but he was unable
to walk, because he had infantile paralysis. They carried him from
Jerusalem to Tiberias for the holiday of Rabbi Meir the Miracle
Worker, and from Tiberias to Miron on the festival of Lag Ba'omer.
He was brought to the cave there and placed next to the resting place
of Rabbi Shimon Bar Yohai. Three wise men were hired to stay with
him and recite the Zohar. After they recited the entire Zohar, he was
taken back to Jerusalem to be married, so the demons would realize he
was no longer a child and it was time to release him from that illness,
which was, after all, an illness of childhood. Wedding clothes were
ordered for him and for the girl. The girl went outside in her finest
dress and new shoes. A vile and loathsome Yemenite saw her. That
villain cast a spell on her, and, on the Shabbat of Lamentations—three
weeks before the Shabbat of Compassion, when the wedding was to
take place—he carried her off to one of the new settlements, where they
were married. The boy remained crippled. An elderly divorcée appeared—actually, she was not so old—and said, "I'm willing to marry
him." Moshe's wife said, "Go marry the Angel of Death." She had a
grudge against her because, when they were both girls, that witch had
poured bird bile on her, which arrests childbirth. If she hadn't washed
herself with the urine of a woman giving birth for the first time, she
wouldn't have been able to bear children at all. Even so, all her children
had died.

The boy lay in the house, on his mat, with no one to lift him and
carry him outside to warm up in the sun. When they came back from
Miron, Moshe's wife was stricken with yet another disease, compound-

ing her ills, so that now she herself had to be tended. This is roughly what Moshe told Herbst. If Moshe's fellow workers hadn't come to tell him he was needed to move a piano, Moshe would still be talking. A man's troubles give him eloquence, and Herbst, who was anxious about the books, would have stood there listening.

— 15 —

It took Herbst half a minute to get where he was going. By the time he got there, he had forgotten about all the delays and was reminded of Ernst Weltfremdt's book. He peered in the bookstore window and saw the book there, open. Weltfremdt was a lucky man. In these troubled times, when books by Jews were being publicly burned all over Germany, he had found a respected Swiss publisher, who put out a splendid edition of his book. Neither of them will suffer. All over the world, scholars who read German will welcome the book. Even in Germany, scholars will not ignore Weltfremdt's theories. They will take his book into their homes, if not openly, because of government intimidation, then discreetly. Zealots in the Land of Israel shriek that we ought to do unto Germany as it has done to us—that, just as Germany has issued a ban on Jewish books, so should we ban all German books, without recognizing or realizing that whoever deprives himself of intellectual discourse jeopardizes his own soul.

Herbst stood and studied Ernst Weltfremdt's book, thinking: What about my own book? In Germany, they probably burned it. And here, in this country? I never once saw it in a bookstore here, and, if I hadn't contributed it to the National Library and to some of my colleagues, I doubt they would know I wrote a book. Some authors put their books in the parlor, so whoever comes in will see them, and they do the same with offprints. That's not my way. True, I haven't produced many books, but I have published a great many articles, and they could be made into a bound volume and placed on the bookshelf. Why haven't I done this? Why not? Herbstlein, Herbstlein, Herbst said, using Julian Weltfremdt's language, from the depths of my heart, I hope you get a full professorship.

Manfred Herbst was not like Julian Weltfremdt. Julian Weltfremdt disparaged Ernst Weltfremdt's scholarship; Herbst did not. Many of

Ernst Weltfremdt's qualities were distasteful to him. Those we might
call Prussian were particularly ridiculous in this country, yet he admired Weltfremdt's research. In every single study he undertook, he
came up with something new; if not actually new, then at least il-
luminating. Now that a new book of his was out, Herbst wanted to see
what was in it.

What he wanted to see, he didn't see. What he didn't want to see
is what he saw. He wanted to see the book, but he saw the author. He
wore a summer suit of the whitest white silk. His heavy walking
stick—yellowish brown, shiny, and heavily knotted—and his soft gray
hat were lying on a stack of music books. Of all the well-dressed people
in Jerusalem, Ernst Weltfremdt alone knew that hats are in a class of
their own and should not be expected to match the rest of one's outfit.
He was standing next to a skinny, long-legged old man wearing colorful clothes and an altogether festive air. He was the painter who had
attracted attention at the artists' Winter Exhibit with a not very large
oil painting: a portrait of Weltfremdt's granchild, the son of Professor
Weltfremdt's daughter. Now that the painter had run into the professor
in the bookstore, he took the opportunity to convey in words what he
hoped to convey in paint. The painter described to the professor, in
painterly terms, his own image of the professor holding his little grandson on his lap, with the professor's hand on the baby's head. In an even
lovelier scene, the baby is on the lap of his grandfather, the professor;
they are seated at the professor's desk; the professor's book is open; the
baby's little hands are fingering the book, and his angelic eyes are fixed
on it. Professor Weltfremdt listened, studying the scene in his mind's
eye as the painter formed it in his imagination. He didn't interrupt. On
the contrary, he gave him every chance to embellish the picture. Influenced by the expression on the professor's face and by his eloquent
silence, the painter took on something of the professor's expression,
looking back at him with visionary eyes. All of a sudden, he stepped
back, ever so slightly, turned his head to the left, lowered his eyelids
halfway, leaned over, and gazed at the professor with eyes that dismissed what they had previously seen and were enthralled by a new
vision.

While the painter was standing with the professor, an old woman
who had emigrated from Germany was in the store too, in a corner.
She was dressed in faded finery, and her entire presence bespoke onetime splendor. Her mouth was agape, either to express reproach, as she
had learned in her former life, or to ask for pity, as she had learned more
recently, for she was sorely grieved by the fact that a hat and walking
stick had been placed on top of her vocal scores. Her circumstances

were such that she was forced to sell them, and she had come to see if a buyer had been found. They used to be kept in her mansion, in an ebony case with hinges, locks, bolts, and pegs made of pure silver. It had been crafted by a skilled artist commissioned by the bishop of Mainz and was originally designed to contain a sacred bone of the Christian saint known as the Miracle Worker of Gaza. The bishop had sent this case, with the bone in it, to one of the German princes as a gift. The case, as well as the bone, remained in the prince's bedroom and performed many miracles. In time, dissension took its toll, and the ideas of the Reformation prevailed. The bone refused to perform for an unworthy generation. It lay idle and forgotten, until, finally, it vanished. The case was then used for cosmetics and jewelry. Eight generations later, it fell into the hands of a singer famed for her beauty and remarkable voice. In it, she placed a vocal score given to her by Felix Mendelssohn-Bartholdy, who had been her teacher, as well as letters from Schleiermacher, who had converted her to Christianity. This singer's grandson had Zionist friends and was attracted to a Jewish girl, whom he married, abandoning his parents' religion and returning to the religion of his forefathers. His wife gave birth to a daughter, who also became a celebrated singer—the old woman now standing in the corner of the store, noting the ravages of time in the form of a walking stick and a hat deposited on top of a vocal score handwritten by Felix Mendelssohn-Bartholdy.

Professor Weltfremdt was engaged in conversation with the painter and didn't notice that Manfred Herbst had entered the store. But Herbst noticed him and slipped away, so as not to intrude on Weltfremdt and the painter.

Herbst went upstairs to the inner rooms. He inhaled the scent of old books—dust, aging paper, leather, linen—with the added smell of all those generations that had handled the books. He was overcome, like any booklover entering a store full of old books, with an emotion akin to yearning, a yearning that turns into a passion all the books in the world can never satisfy. He closed his eyes, tightening his eyelids so that they pressed down on his cheeks to the point of pain. He groped in his pocket and took out a crushed cigarette that had fallen out of the case. He lit the cigarette, took a puff, and made an effort to collect himself. Little by little, he began to feel more composed, and his anxiety receded. Since he woke up, he hadn't been as comfortable as he was at that moment. In the presence of these ancient volumes that dominate the heart, he assumed a blank expression, so no one would recognize how much he coveted the book whose price he was asking. Herbst flung the cigarette in the ashtray, took out his case, and offered a

cigarette to the clerk who was standing by to serve him. The clerk
noticed that the cigarette was brown and longer than most cigarettes
in the country. He began to discuss the various types of cigarettes he
had smoked, arriving at the subject of wartime smoking. Many times,
when he was at the front and couldn't find a cigarette, he used to wrap
grass in newspaper and smoke it. He moved on from newspaper to
books. Soldiers used to tear out a page, wrap some grass in it, and make
cigarettes. He once saw a soldier tearing up a book to use as toilet paper.
He looked and saw that it was a first edition of Schiller's *The Mission
of Moses.* He scolded him and yelled, "You idiot, how can you be that
scornful of our great poet Schiller!" The soldier said, "I thought it was
one of those Jew books, written by one of their little rabbis." Herbst
suddenly lost his composure. His face turned pale, and his nerves were
on edge. Could it be that, even as he was dealing with those German
classics for the sake of their fine bindings, he was losing out on first
editions of rare books? Hadn't it already happened to him once that
bibliographers denied the existence of a book even though it was mentioned by its author? Why did they deny its existence? Either because
they thought the author was exaggerating or because they were trying
to outsmart everyone—to show that they trusted only what they saw
with their own eyes. Three hundred years later, the book was discovered here in Jerusalem, by a tourist who acquired it, along with considerable fame, for some paltry sum. The ludicrous, perhaps even tragic,
part was that, only an hour before, it had been in Herbst's hand. Why
hadn't he bought it? Because he had never opened it. Why hadn't he
opened it? Because it was bound with another book whose title was
displayed on the cover. He, however, knew very well that the volume
was too thick for its title, and he should have realized that there must
be another book in the same binding. Nine years had passed, but there
was hardly a day when he didn't think about that event. It remained
unresolved in his mind, like a wound that doesn't heal. He took out
another cigarette and reviewed the entire incident: how he himself
brought the tourist to the bookstore, how he led him to the special room
rare books were kept in, how he praised this man to the owner and
arranged to have the clerks show him all their treasures. And, finally,
it happened—a book that he himself had been holding only an hour
earlier fell into another's hands, making Herbst's loss his gain. Herbst
was not a grudging person, nor did he make a pretense of friendship.
It is no exaggeration to say that, among the scholars we know, there
are few as generous as Herbst, as ready to enjoy a colleague's success.
Nevertheless, he remained haunted by the saga of that book.

    Herbst put the German classics out of mind and went into the other room. He began to sort through familiar and unfamiliar books, with his eyes and with his hands. Some were books he had been looking for; some, he began to covet as soon as he saw them. If he had had seven eyes and ten hands at each of his fingertips, he would not have been able to satisfy his desires. It didn't occur to him that each additional book would require further effort and strain, especially on moving day, and it was essential that he move because of the riots, which were becoming more and more severe. It was impossible to remain in Baka, hemmed in by Arabs. Once again, he recalled the night he was ambushed and nearly killed right near his home. The bullet came so close; what a close brush with death. Had he been hit by the bullet, all the books in his house, the ones he had let friends borrow, and the ones he had sent to be rebound would have remained unclaimed by heirs. His wife and daughters—even Avraham, his son-in-law—don't recognize the value of his books. All of the city's book dealers would come—those vultures who prey on corpses, who run to the widow and orphans as soon as a man dies and offer next to nothing for his valuable books.

We ought to picture the anonymous person who borrowed books and never returned them, as well as the bookbinder who kept some of the books he was to have rebound. When we are dead, will the books be returned? Or will the borrower say to himself: That fellow is dead, and no one is demanding the books; why should I be virtuous and return them? Books are a commodity, and not everyone realizes that it is a crime to take a book and not return it to its owner. Herbst suddenly blushed in embarrassment, recalling something that had happened in his childhood. A young doctor, the son of a widow, lived in Herbst's neighborhood. One day, he was told that the young doctor had hanged himself in the woods. Herbst had a book he had borrowed from the doctor, but he didn't return it to the doctor's mother. The book was part of Nietzsche's *Collected Works,* so he was responsible for spoiling the set. To take revenge on those scoundrels who might behave as he had, Herbst decided that he would make a comprehensive list of all the books that had been borrowed, and, in the future, when lending a book, he would add it to the list. For further revenge, he decided to keep the list in a sealed envelope labeled "To be opened twelve months after my death," in order to expose those individuals who, given the chance, would choose to ignore the fact that they possessed someone else's property. What is this all about? Herbst asked himself. Why am I suddenly thinking such awful thoughts? Again, I'm involved in books; again, I'm eager to add books to books I won't have time to read, leaving me less air to breathe.

He stuck another cigarette in his mouth, shook the book dust from his clothes, and turned away to wash his hands and be off. As for the pile of books he had chosen, they could sit there until the clerk decided to put them away. Which was also true of the splendid editions of those German classics. While he was washing his hands and intending to go home, the clerk who had served him was replaced by a former student of Herbst's, who had abandoned academia to earn a living. Most university students in the early days tended to be drawn to one or another of their teachers; he had been drawn to Herbst. He whispered whatever he whispered. Herbst peered at him as if he had heard something he wished to believe, although it was unbelievable. The clerk smiled and said, "Yes, yes, Dr. Herbst. What I told you is absolutely true." Herbst asked, "When did it happen?" The clerk answered, "They're already here. They haven't been sorted yet, or priced. In any case, if you want to have a look, I'll get the key and open the room."

Let me explain what the clerk whispered to Herbst and why it was hard for Herbst to believe it, the meaning of "They're already here," and all the rest. He had told him, "We succeeded in buying a major library that belonged to that scholar who was murdered by his Arab driver. The books are already here, in a special room. They haven't been sorted or priced, and, if Dr. Herbst wants to have a look, I'll unlock the room so he can see what's there." Herbst's heart was unlocked by this news and he trailed behind the clerk as he went to get the key. The clerk came back and opened the door. The room was so full that it was hard for them to find a place to stand. Herbst contemplated the books, pile after pile, bundled and tied together with twine. His heart began to pound. His hands were eager to touch whatever his eyes lit on. His eyes were flaming; his brow was ablaze; his hands were hot. His arms, shoulders—his entire body responded similarly. Which is no surprise. How could anyone, confronted with such a treasure, remain calm?

I'll put aside Herbst's story and tell about the owner of the books.

When the Great War was over, in which England triumphed over Germany, subjecting the Land of Israel to English rule, various people from various lands came to Jerusalem. Among them was Sir Davis Birkenthal, a wealthy man and a scholar with an international reputation, the author of *Strange Gods in the Land,* an exhaustive study of idolatry in the Land of Israel from earliest times and considered a useful source to this day. When he arrived, he bought himself a large house on the road to the Mount of Olives, brought in many books that filled several rooms, surrounded himself with Arab maids and menservants, and, in that entire period, had no contact with any Jews, not even Jewish scholars.

He gave money to several young Arabs and sent them to study abroad at his expense. He was especially generous to his Arab driver, a handsome young man. On the first day of the '29 riots, he took his car and went to see what was going on. He arrived at the Damascus Gate. The Arabs who saw Lord Birkenthal, thinking he was an Englishman, suspended the violence to give him safe conduct. The driver made a sign and whispered to them that he was Jewish. They shot him immediately. He fell out of the car, steeped in blood. The driver took the car and set off in it to have his way with the Jews. After the riots subsided, when Birkenthal was buried, his relatives arrived to deal with the inheritance. They divided everything up, leaving the books until they could agree on a plan for them. They wanted to donate them to Oxford or Cambridge in his name. It was even suggested that they be given as a memorial to the National Library in Jerusalem, since the English libraries were willing to accept only the volumes they didn't already own. Over a period of time, an impasse was reached. Still, many Jewish scholars remembered his books with a sigh. They, too, finally despaired.

All of a sudden—I don't know why—most of the books were sold. To whom were they sold? To a Jerusalem book dealer. And now Herbst had the privilege of being perhaps the first of Jerusalem's scholars to be informed.

Little by little, his limbs began to falter, to be overcome with an odd weariness. He felt another sort of weariness in his shoulders. He turned his head and looked behind him, as if someone had placed a heavy load on his back and he was trying to make it lighter. Feeling sick to his stomach, he snuffed out his cigarette with his fingers, crushed it, discarded it, and tried to open a window to let in some air. The window wouldn't open, and no air came in. Some old books, along with a bunch of pamphlets that were piled on the sill, fell to the floor in a shower of dark yellow dust that gave off a foul smell. The clerk didn't notice what was happening to Herbst. He was busy extricating a particular pile of books from the larger mass. It was tied with twine. like the others; the letters on the spine of each volume announced its title. Any single one would make a collector proud; all of them together were extraordinarily rare. The clerk stood there, casually dropping names of world-famous dealers and the books each one had inquired about. They had touched on only a small part of the collection, which included books it didn't occur to them to ask about, as they had been searching for them for so

long that they had despaired of ever finding them. The clerk talked on
and on. Herbst stood listening, but it is doubtful that a single word
registered. He felt extremely faint. He turned to the door and, on his
way out, jokingly tossed off the Latin equivalent of "everything depends on luck, even a Torah scroll in the Ark." He added, "These
books are unlucky; I don't mean to buy them."

As soon as he left the room, his pain vanished, his shoulders relaxed,
and his stomach no longer bothered him. He felt not a trace of faintness.
He was on the verge of going back to that room, back to those books,
especially the ones every collector was after. The telephone rang, and
the clerk ran to answer it. Herbst stood and waited for him to finish
talking. When Herbst saw that it was likely to be a long conversation,
he wandered into a room he was unfamiliar with, because there were
art books in it, and he wasn't an art collector. Herbst didn't collect
works of art. In his home, he had no drawings, no sketches, no art
folios, because he knew himself well enough to realize that, if he allowed even one piece of art into his house, many more would soon
follow. He was the sort of man who was moved by anything artistic,
and he had to be very careful not to let himself be captivated by
whatever he saw, to leave time for his work, for his research, for the
things he was required to do. This is why he gave up chess in his youth;
this is why he had put his poems aside and resolved not to write any
more of them; this is why he had renounced various pastimes he once
enjoyed. Now that he was waiting for the clerk to finish talking, because he was interested in the books left behind by the murdered
scholar, which had led him to relinquish those German classics, he
wasn't afraid to go into the fine-arts room and pass the time there.

So Herbst went into the room with the art books. He glanced at the
shelves before catching a glimpse of the paintings and drawings that
hung on the walls between the bookcases. Without having so much as
picked up a folio yet, he remembered that, before he came to this
country, he used to say, "I could give up anything to settle in the Land
of Israel, even theater and concerts, but not the sculpture and paintings
I can see in the lands of exile." By now, he had been in the country
quite a number of years, and it hadn't occurred to him that he had given
up things he once thought he could never do without.

He took a folio of drawings off the shelf and leafed through it
aimlessly, not bothering to see who the artist was. Putting down one
folio and opening another, his mind wandered back to Ernst Weltfremdt's book. He found himself thinking about a chapter that had
already appeared in some collection, the chapter about the major forces

that impelled Valens to allow thirty thousand Goths to cross . . . As he examined Ernst Weltfremdt's argument, he began to wonder why he hadn't emphasized the fact that Valens had allowed the Goths to enter Roman territory so that some of their regiments could fight the Persians. While he was considering this idea, he opened a folio containing the work of several artists. He gazed at the drawings and muttered: "They're from Brueghel's school, but, unlike Brueghel, they don't give one pleasure. Now I'll go and see what the clerk is doing."

His eyes were pulled in several directions. He stood trembling and astonished. What is this? A leper. A painting of a leper standing at the city gate, ringing a bell to warn the people to keep their distance. Herbst picked up the picture and stood it up so he could see it better. The eyes were awesome and sad. Their sockets had, for the most part, been consumed by leprosy, yet they were alive and wished to live. Sadder and more awesome was the hand holding the bell, a hand consumed by disease that could not be reversed. Even sadder and more awesome was the bell, warning people to keep their distance. The painter was a great artist to see the bell as the source of pestilence. Why? This cannot be explained, but it is surely correct.

Herbst stood before the picture, examining it first from one angle, then from another, looking into the leper's eyes, at his hands, at the open city gates. Within the city, on one side of the gate, people were milling about, on the way to church, to a tavern, to do business, or just to pass the time. The infected man stood on the other side. In his leprous hand, he held a little bell, and it alone was unblighted, although it was the source of all blight. Who painted this picture? What is the name of the great painter who imbued the inanimate with the breath of life? The men and women of the town fade in and out of view, yet the figure of the afflicted man is extremely clear; he, his hand, his bell. The entire city—the men, the women, the houses, the marketplace, the well—are serene and unconcerned. But the sound of the bell is already disengaged from it, rattling, tinkling, moving out of the afflicted man's hand. A great calamity is imminent. Herbst looked at the picture once again; at the leper, at his hand, but not at the bell, because by now he recognized that the blight was not in the bell. All this time, Herbst had avoided touching the picture, as if it were alive and afflicted. Readers, you know me by now. You know that I don't exaggerate. And if I tell you something, don't say, "What an exaggeration!" At that instant, it was clear to Herbst that he heard a voice from within the bell the leper was holding, cautioning, "Go away, don't touch me." Herbst listened to the cautionary voice and didn't touch the picture. But he looked at it, again and again, with panic in his eyes and desire in his heart. Then he took down another folio, which he placed on top of the picture of the leper, and left. He came back again, exposed the picture, but didn't look at it. Then he took down a folio of Rembrandt drawings. He looked at several reproductions, then took out *The Night Watch* and studied it. What happens to anyone with a discerning eye happened to Herbst. The melancholy that emanates from Rembrandt's work soothed his spirit and brought on tranquility—a tranquility known as harmony, though I call it understanding and certainty.

The clerk appeared and apologized to Herbst for having abandoned him in midconversation. Some consulate or other called about some dictionary or other for some language or other. When the conversation with the consulate was over, the phone had rung again, and someone from the high commissioner's office inquired about the new location of a certain bookbinder, a woman to whom the high commissioner always sent his books.

"The high commissioner is a celebrated collector. He haunts the bookstores, especially this one. His car swallows up an infinite number of volumes. He doesn't admit Jews to Palestine, but he craves their books. I see you have been leafing through the pictures, Dr. Herbst." Herbst pointed to *The Night Watch* and asked the price. He told him. He said, "Wrap it up and add it to my account. I want to send a gift to a doctor I once consulted, who refused to accept a fee. I'll leave it with you for now. Tomorrow or the next day, I'll pick it up."

Herbst lit another cigarette. After putting the case back in his pocket, he took it out again and offered the clerk a cigarette. "They're black," he said. "Since I came to this country, I haven't smoked a black cigarette." The clerk put down *The Night Watch* and lit his cigarette. He studied it, then he said, "Actually, it's not black, it's dark brown." Herbst stood in front of *The Night Watch*, considering: Shira told me she wanted a reproduction of *The Night Watch* but couldn't find one. I'll take it to her tomorrow; she'll be pleased. Henrietta is eating lunch now. Firadeus is eating with her, watching Mrs. Herbst's gestures to learn how to handle herself. Firadeus is a good student. She learns the manners of the Ashkenazim very fast and regards them as the only truly well-mannered people. If I were to go back now, Henrietta would say, "But, Fred, you told me you wouldn't be back for lunch, so I wasn't expecting you and I didn't prepare anything. But, if you give me a minute, I'll fix something for you." Herbst looked at his watch and considered: It's lunchtime, and I really ought to leave. The clerk is probably eager to be rid of me, so he can have his lunch. He looked at his watch again, not that he had forgotten what time it was, but to be sure he was right. It crossed his mind that he ought to go to Gethsemane, not because of the monk, but because he had told Henrietta he was going to Gethsemane. He knew he wouldn't go to Gethsemane, that, if he did set out, he would turn back midway. In that case, Herbst told himself, I won't go, and I won't have to turn back. I'll go to a café, have some coffee, and look at the newspapers. Then I'll go home and get back to my work. Work that follows leisure is twice as pleasant.

He left the old books and went down the steps to the main store below. Like all modern establishments, it was closed for lunch, but the display windows were exposed to view. He stood looking at Weltfremdt's book, thinking: I suppose I'll have to buy it. He had another thought: I have mentioned Gethsemane a hundred times without thinking of those two brothers, the brothers who were killed together near Gethsemane. It wouldn't surprise me to find a study of this phenomenon: certain place-names evoke memories of events that have occurred there, while other places can be mentioned without evoking any such events. With regard to Gethsemane and the murdered brothers, I blame Sacharson, whose name I don't like to invoke. Having mentioned him only in order to resolve a dilemma, he has been mentioned, and I won't pursue the paradox any further. I'll just go into the café, sit down, and have some coffee.

He went into the café and ordered hot, not iced, coffee. He waited for it to cool, then drank it up all at once, took out his cigarette case, and sat smoking and reading the paper he had found on the table. He was watching the office girls who were taking a break. They wore good clothes that they couldn't afford to buy on an office salary. They sat over coffee, tea, or cocoa. Their faces, dimmed by clouds of cigarette smoke, were weary from work and from the weight of the fine clothes on their backs.

One of them approached Herbst and asked for the newspaper that was next to him. He handed her the one he was reading, assuming that was the one she meant, when actually she had meant the one on the table. She returned his paper to him and picked up the other one. As soon as she was gone, Herbst went back to his paper, but he didn't continue to read, because his mind was now on her. He hadn't had occasion to talk to her, but he knew she was married and had children, maybe two, maybe three. She spends eight hours in the office, leaving her husband and children to depend on a housekeeper, who, one imagines, behaves as if she were the lady of the house. What moves this woman to leave her husband and children, to wear herself out eight

hours a day in an office, surrounded by the rattle of typewriters, shrieking telephones, squabbles with office mates? If she is competent, her
friends are annoyed. And the males in an office still find it hard to
accept a woman who surpasses them in skill or earnings. He looked at
her and saw that she was sitting with her cup in front of her, a cigarette
dangling from her mouth, the newspaper slipping out of her hands as
her eyes opened and closed, opened and closed, eager for sleep but
afraid to doze off, lest she be late getting back to the office. Herbst
looked at his watch and was overwhelmed by sympathy for her and for
all the weary workers who would soon have to go back to work. He,
too, went back to what he was occupied with earlier: Weltfremdt's
book, the spread of the Goths into Roman territory, and the famine
they were confronted with almost as soon as they arrived. The famine
was so great that, after the Germans had used up all their resources,
offering their cash, carriages, and armor in return for food, Syrian
merchants brought emaciated dogs to their camp and traded them for
a male or female child.

Herbst suddenly found himself watching a particular young woman,
though there was nothing special about her that would account for his
interest, except for her face, which was quite childlike. This young
woman, Herbst thought, works for a printer; she works in the office
of a printing press. She looks German, but she isn't. Anyway, I'm
clearly right about the work she does. She works in the office of a
printing press, and I can even describe what she does there. Henrietta
would say, "You have such great intuition, Fred." While he was celebrating the fact that he had guessed her line of work from her face, she
was called to the telephone. Now that she was gone, Herbst turned to
the waitress and asked who she was. She told him. Herbst said, "A
lawyer, just as I thought. It's perfectly obvious. What was I about to
say?" The waitress stood waiting for him to say it. Herbst noticed and
said, "Excuse me. I was going to say something to myself, not to you."
Because she was so tired, she wasn't paying attention and didn't find
this odd. When she left, he whispered to himself, without letting the
words reach any ears other than his own, "Another day is gone. What
did I accomplish today? I didn't accomplish anything. I got up in the
morning, picked up half a donkey's load of books, took them in to
breakfast, and told Henrietta I was going to Gethsemane. Henrietta
didn't say, 'Why go to Gethsemane on such a hot day?' When I arrived
in town, I didn't go to Gethsemane, because I had no wish to go to
Gethsemane. When I met Julian Weltfremdt, I went to a café with him
and drank iced coffee. While we sat over the iced coffee, he mentioned

that he had heard I was being considered for a promotion. When he said that the kindergartens in this country will become universities, did he mean to irritate me, because I may be about to be promoted? Another day is gone, one of those days that give us nothing beyond the knowledge that our lifetime is now one day shorter. What significance does this have for a man like me whose days have been decreased by one? How did I use this day? I looked at pictures. True, it's good for a person to look at a fine picture every now and then. How successful that painter was, how vivid the colors on the dead flesh. However, I should say this: I was exaggerating when I said I could hear the voice of the bell in the leper's hand. Tomorrow or the day after, I'll get *The Night Watch* and take it to Shira. If I find her, good. If I don't find her, I'll leave the picture with one of her neighbors. In any case, I can say one thing: It doesn't matter if I find her or not. Wait a minute! Shira was looking for that picture of a doctor, some students, and the patient who is the object of their lesson while all this time I've been thinking of *The Night Watch.*"

He suddenly began to feel the pinch of hunger. He called the waitress and asked for some food that could be considered lunch. "As for bread," he said, "it doesn't matter whether it's black or white." Though he preferred black bread, he had found that, in this country, one often has to make do with wheat bread, wheat being one of the native species. He learned about this from Gandhi, who wrote that every land produces the bread best suited to its inhabitants. He ate, drank, paid his bill, lit another cigarette, and left.

His limbs were light, as they tend to be after a light meal and two cups of coffee. The air outside was not light; burnt gasoline, scorched dust, human sweat, the stench of garbage and titanium produced a mess of smells; the din that filled the air included traffic noise, the clatter of typewriters, the shouts of newspaper boys, the malevolent eyes of policemen, the bold footsteps of young Arabs, the howl of stray dogs, the anguish of human beings wondering what to do next. All this had the potential to unsettle one's mind, but Herbst's mind remained composed. His mind was on many things, even on the waitress who had served him in the café, who must have left work by now, put on good clothes, and looked so different that one would barely recognize her. Finally, he too was unsettled. His capacity to be a simple observer was lost, along with his physical lightness, a lightness he used to enjoy without being quite aware of it, a lightness that was once his characteristic mode. Once, before he knew Shira.

What began to unsettle him again was the tragedy he had wanted

to write but never wrote. When he was with Henrietta in Kfar Ahinoam, after the birth of Dani, his daughter's son, he had decided to
abandon the project, and he had done so. Suddenly, all of a sudden, it
was on his mind again, suggesting that he take it on. Isn't it odd that,
the minute I give up the idea of writing the tragedy, just then I happen
to see a painting of a leper, a painting that could serve as a model for
the faithful slave Basileios?

— 16 —

The day passed, as most days do, partly in eating, drinking, and sleeping; partly in reading books, articles, and dissertations, and adding to
the body of notes. Some notes are definitive; others, tentative, in that
the writer jots them down and stores them in a box until he finds better
ones. There are days when the writing process demands a certain note,
even points it out. On that particular day, most of the new notes were
problematic from the outset. Some, he labored over both before and
while writing them down, only to tear them up and write them over
again, and then continue to vacillate about putting them in the box. We
don't know how he benefited from such a day. Only that his book on
burial customs of the poor in Byzantium gained nothing.

On the other hand, his library was enriched—perhaps his range of
knowledge, too—for he acquired an additional book. How? Professor
Ernst Weltfremdt learned that Herbst wanted his book but didn't buy
it because of the price. What did Professor Weltfremdt do? He sent
Herbst a copy of the book, by special messenger, as a present. We have
heard that it was Professor Weltfremdt's way to honor people with his
offprints, but not with a book that costs enough to pay for a night in
a hotel, even such a place as Bodenheimer's in Haifa. Herbst was
delighted with the book, for he wanted to acquire it but couldn't afford
the price. A lecturer at the Hebrew University in Jerusalem earns only
thirty-five lirot a month, from which he has to contribute to the national funds, the cultural funds, charitable institutions, and so on.

Henrietta noticed how pleased Manfred was and said, "I'll tell you
what I think, Fred. I would have preferred for you to buy Weltfremdt's
book, rather than receive it from him as a gift. I don't know what moves
Weltfremdt to send you presents, but I'm sure he has his own interests

at heart. You had better be ready to repay his kindness." Manfred said, "I don't know what you're talking about. You have an odd habit, Henriett. Whenever I'm in a good mood, you can't resist throwing cold water on me. What do you mean, 'his own interests'? If you mean that he'll ask me to write about his book, I certainly wouldn't mind." Henrietta said, "That's just fine. But, tell me, Fred, are you sure Welt-fremdt will be satisfied with whatever you write about his book?" Manfred said, "Satisfied or not, if I find a misguided opinion in the book, I won't overlook it, and if I find reason to disagree with him, I won't hesitate. Let me make this clear to you: I have never gone in for flattery. To this day, I take responsibility for all the reviews I have ever written. As for Ernst Weltfremdt's book, if I don't write about it, who will? His cousin Julian, whose anger turns him into a madman, or one of countless others whose intelligence could be deposited on a fly's wing without weighing it down. Those who acquired a smattering of knowledge managed to forget it, and those who never studied had nothing to forget. There are some reviewers who figure out from the book itself how to take issue with it, though they know nothing about the subject." Henrietta said, "Then it would be good if you were to review Weltfremdt's book. But, tell me, Fred, are you sure Weltfremdt will be pleased with what you write about his book?" Manfred said, "Whether or not he is pleased, I already told you that, if I find a misguided opinion or an unfounded premise, I certainly won't over-look it. In our generation, there is no scholar I admire as much as Professor Neu. Everything I know, the half a million words I have incorporated from teachers and books—all of this is material I can evaluate because of Neu. Nonetheless, when I found an unvalidated premise in his book, I didn't hesitate to comment on it. Remember the letter he sent me at the time? You don't remember? I remember. I remember what he wrote, word for word. 'My dear Herbst,' Neu wrote. 'You were right to point out the weak spot in my book. I know that I am right, but, unfortunately, I can't offer more support for my position. Nor do I expect to be able to do so. I'm too old to return to that subject. I do hope that what I wrote will lead our younger col-leagues to persist and find ways to validate my premise, which is true, though it is beyond my power to prove it.' Anyway, Henriett, you reminded me of something one should beware of. Not for your reason, Henrietta, but for another reason. This country is small, and the Jews in it are crowded together. Especially the academic community, which is like a ghetto within a ghetto. I already see the problems when a review appears in print. The day the review is published, on that very day the critic and the author are likely to run into each other, in the library, at the university, at another professor's home. Now, imagine what the critic feels when he sees the author right in front of him. Or, reversing it, what the author feels when he sees the critic. Just last Saturday, in Beit Hakerem, an artist saw a critic sitting in an outdoor café with his fiancée. The artist went up to him and slapped his face, because he had criticized his work, and it wasn't until the critic beat him with his cane that he calmed down. Academics don't behave that way, but sometimes words can have more of an impact than a strong arm or a cane. Now that scholars and researchers are coming here from all over, I worry about criticism and critics. In the preceding generation, scholars were well off in Jerusalem. They sat comfortably, playing with ideas while they sipped black coffee and smoked narghiles, enjoying each other's insights, with no breach, with no outcry. Now, my dear Henriett, the idyll is over. Now that so many scholars live in such close quarters, criticism is destined to become less honest. Whether the critic likes it or not, the author's face will confront him as he writes, and he will adjust his words accordingly. I have often asked myself what the main factors are that lead someone like me, if not to lie, then to use words that camouflage the truth." Henrietta regarded her husband fondly and said with surprise, "Why, Fred, you aren't not telling the truth. Because you don't contaminate your mouth by slandering friends, as Julian Weltfremdt does, you consider yourself a traitor to the truth. You know, Fred, I was never impressed with that secret adviser Mr. Ernst Weltfremdt, nor was I impressed by the sharp pronouncements of our beloved Dr. Julian Weltfremdt. Having mentioned his name, let me tell you something else. I resent the way he treats Mimi. What does he want from his wife? She is charming and artistic. If she isn't an expert at cleaning pots, she has many other talents to make up for this deficiency." Manfred said, "The same is true of our daughter, Tamara, though no one would say she is charming." Henrietta said, "But she is artistic." Manfred was annoyed and said, "Forgive me, my dear, forgive me if I have another view. You call her artistic because of the insipid rhymes she makes up when she's bored. If I'm not mistaken, you already know my view of her rhymes; also, of the rhymes of many others who are considered poets. In my youth, I was exposed to some dreadful rhymed prose. Even when there was an idea or a narrative, those were hardly poems. Hardly, my dear, hardly. I am referring to the poets of the world, not to the Hebrew poets, for whom any trace of a political, nationalist, ethical, or social idea embodied in rhyme constitutes a poem. A favorite student of mine, his name is Elyakum Zuf—maybe you know him: the one with dark curls and black eyes—used to show me poems of that sort regularly, in an effort to convince me of their lyrical quality. I like that young man very much, my dear. And I would like to make him happy. But to accept such poems as poetry is impossible for me, though I know that what I say causes him pain. What is there for fine young men like him to do? The earth they came to redeem doesn't respond to them, because their strength is meager. What goes on here is hard on them. Not merely the actions of the English and the Arabs, but those of the Jews as well. Men of action fulfill themselves in the Haganah, the Irgun, Lehi. Those who are not men of action find comfort in poetry. In the end, their teachers and mentors come and say, 'That's not a poem.' I'm willing to close an eye to a researcher's errors. A researcher does his work according to his talent and ability, summarizes his research in terms of his conclusions, and has no special biases. He is content to be given space in some journal so he can publish his findings and have them read by others in his field. Poets are different. If one of them succeeds in arranging his words in rhymed form, it's as if he has created new heavens, as if all the creatures of his world are in place under his sun and moon. Forgive me, Henriett. I don't know what suddenly made me so cross. I'm afraid it's my own fault: because I'm angry at myself, I'm angry at everyone who writes poems." Henrietta said, "Because you're angry at yourself? Why at yourself? Do you write poems? Since our wedding day, you haven't turned out a single poem. Even for my birthday, which was about a week after our wedding, you didn't write a poem. That entire day, Fred, until we went to sleep that night, I was expecting you to present me with a poem or a sonnet. What did that scoundrel do? He pursed his lips and discharged his duty with kisses to match the number of years I was carrying on my back." Manfred said, "I don't write poems. But . . ." "But what?" Manfred said, "If I were to tell you what I am doing, you would laugh." Henrietta said, "Am I allowed to ask?" Manfred said, "You are allowed to ask, but it would be better if you didn't." Henrietta said, "Then I won't ask. I can count on you to tell me yourself." Manfred answered, "I hope you won't be sorry you made me tell you. I'm composing a tragedy. A tragedy, Henriett, a tragedy." Henrietta said, "A tragedy?" Manfred said, "Yes, Henriett. A tragedy." Henrietta said, "Your forehead please, my dearest. Let me kiss your forehead. How did you suddenly come to be writing a tragedy? And what is the content of this tragedy?" Manfred passed his hand over his forehead and rested it there, fingers outstretched, first looking at Henrietta, then turning away from her. Then he began, "I don't recall exactly how I came to be writing the tragedy. But I can outline the plot to you. Believe me, Henriett, I forgot the reason. What I haven't forgotten is the content of the tragedy. But allow me first to finish what

I was saying before. It isn't always good to have scholars crowded together. Still, it could add to the spiritual intensity to have them all struggling to outdo each other's scholarship and, when they can't quite outdo the others, struggling so as not to be lost in the crowd. I already see myself, Henriett, my dear, being stingy with my time, to avoid scattering it to the wind." Henrietta said, "I'm surprised to hear you say that. In all of Jerusalem, is there anyone as busy and involved as you? Lectures, seminars, discussions with students. Also, the book you are writing. Judging by the amount of activity and the number of notes you have amassed, it will surely measure up to Weltfremdt's book. Please, Fred, don't look so indignant. Of course I know that books aren't measured by their thickness. In any case . . ." Henrietta laughed and said, "I might as well admit it. The truth is, I said 'in any case' without having anything to add." Herbst laughed and said, "That's what I love about you, Henriett. You're not afraid to admit the truth, even when it's not to your credit. And if you have nothing to add to that 'in any case,' I'll add to it. In any case, it's to your credit that you tell the truth even when it discredits you. And have you forgotten all about my tragedy?" Henrietta said, "I didn't forget. I'm waiting for you to begin telling me about it." Manfred said, "No, you forgot. And, since you forgot, I'm not required to tell you." Henrietta said, "Please, Fred, don't tease me. Tell me what that tragedy is about." Manfred said, "I once went to get a haircut. While I was waiting my turn in the barbershop, I picked up a magazine and saw a cartoon about a playwright who used to instruct his wife to plan menus to match the plots of his plays. One day he told her, 'My dear wife, cook something happy today. I'm finishing an amusing play.' Henriett, I trust you to understand. Bring on the cognac, and I'll have a drop to match the bitterness of my tragedy."

Because of a solicitor from one of Jerusalem's charitable institutions, Herbst couldn't tell his tale, and Henrietta couldn't hear it. I will therefore take the matter into my own hands and relate the plot of the tragedy Herbst hoped to compose, though I won't break it down into acts and scenes. I'll include the entire plot. I'll tell the story. I'll choose tender language suited to such a tale.

There was once a sweet and fetching girl. She was motherless, and her father was a high-ranking officer in the emperor's army. Because he was busy fighting the emperor's enemies and the like, he couldn't keep an eye on his daughter. The wife of ———, a childhood friend, took her under her wing, invited her to live in her home, and hired teachers and tutors to endow her with knowledge, wisdom, religion, music. In all these endeavors, she was successful. And her success was matched by charm, which increased from day to day.

The wife of ———— had a stepbrother, the son of a woman her father had married after her own mother's death. His name was Yohanan, and he was a nobleman, who served in the emperor's court. When this Yohanan came to visit his sister and saw the girl his sister was raising, he fell deeply in love with her. His sister didn't interfere, for she loved her brother Yohanan and was eager to make him happy. Yohanan loved the girl, and she responded with love. They didn't see each other as often as they wished, because he lived in the capital, far away. But fortune smiled on him, as she often does on those she favors. The emperor's wife was impressed with the girl. She invited her to live in her home and join the other young girls who were members of her court.

When the girl left to serve the empress in the capital city, her mother–guardian sent along a slave she had bought, whose name was Basileios.

Basileios was a God-fearing man who served his mistress faithfully. He knew that God works wisely on behalf of His sons, on behalf of their souls, to be redeemed through the suffering of Christ. He was tied by bonds of gratitude to his mistress and her entire family, who had bought him to be a slave in their household but didn't castrate him, allowing him to remain as he was, as God had created him. Yet that which is a blessing to all men can be a stumbling block to a man in bondage. He had cast an eye on his mistress. Being so close to her, seeing her beauty and charm every minute of every day, he was consumed with desire for her, and his love for her became more intense from day to day.

When the girl arrived at the court of the empress, she hoped to see her true love. And he expected to see her. How despondent they were, how baffled and sad, for, whenever they were about to meet, a sudden obstacle prevented them from seeing each other.

The obstacles were numerous and varied. As the obstacles multiplied, so did their love. They didn't know or understand how it was and why it was that they weren't seeing each other.

All the obstacles and accidents were contrived by Basileios. Basileios devised these schemes to keep the other servants from learning about the relationship between his young mistress and Yohanan the nobleman. Not because he considered himself a rival, for no slave could compete with noblemen and respected citizens. But Basileios knew full well that the emperor had noticed the girl and coveted her, that he was waiting for the day when the empress would be in labor, occupied with the pains of childbirth, oblivious to everything else around her. Then the emperor would have the girl brought to him. If the emperor were to learn of the relationship between her and the nobleman Yohanan, he would have Yohanan sent to the battlefield, never to return. The girl would not see her true love ever again. This was the source of the obstacles that littered the lovers' path. No one other than Basileios, the girl's faithful servant, knew any of this or guessed that anything was amiss.

But every strategy has its limits. Basileios took sick. He was stricken with leprosy, for which there is no cure, and quarantined. He couldn't come into the city, nor was he allowed into the royal court. He wished to warn the girl, his mistress, that it would be very risky to meet with Yohanan the nobleman. The emperor would seek to avenge his lust, not merely through Yohanan the nobleman, but, should he discover that the girl had given her heart to someone else, even as he, the emperor, lusted after her, his powerful hand would strike out at her as well. So Basileios, the faithful servant, sat in solitude, thinking only of his mistress and how to save her from the misfortune in store for her should the emperor discover her connection with the nobleman Yohanan.

Basileios devised many schemes to enable him to sneak into the city and into the emperor's court, so he could see either his mistress or the nobleman Yohanan and warn them that, should their love be discovered, the emperor would have them killed because of his own love for the girl.

One day, Basileios heard about a holy man who lived in the desert, in a home he had made for himself in a broom plant. He was a great and holy man, whose name was celebrated throughout the land. Long before he settled in the desert, making himself a nest in a hollow broom plant, he had served the emperor. He had been a leading general and one of the emperor's favorites. But then he began to disdain the ways of the world and to reject temporal life, in order to secure a place for his soul in a world that is totally good—the afterworld. He traded this world and all its goods for the afterworld, for the infinite bliss it offered to those who fear God and choose to trade this fleeting existence for a timeless one. He left the emperor's court, the city and all its diversions, and all those who loved him—friends and intimates—for the desert wastes. There, he sustained his body with wild grasses and swamp water, so he would be able to sustain his soul with eternal pleasure, for the sake of the Redeemer who saves the souls of those Christians who are true to Him.

Basileios devised many plans in an effort to contact this man of God, to tell him about the emperor's designs on the girl, so that the man of God could rescue her and the nobleman Yohanan, who loved the girl but didn't know what was in store for him because of his love. Basileios had many fine plans. But what use are such plans when a man isn't free and is forbidden to leave his quarters? Basilieos, the faithful servant, was not like all the other lepers, who were permitted to come as far as the city limits to collect bread thrown to them by individuals with compassion for those stricken by God. This was not the case with Basilieos, the girl's servant. For this gracious girl, wishing to be kind to her servant Basileios, had bought a house for him to live in and arranged for him to be taken care of and provided for. Those who were in charge of him assumed the girl wouldn't want him to leave the house and guarded him so vigilantly that what was meant to serve his interests became a hindrance. Now, it happened, just by chance, that the Arians in the state became more and more powerful, and the Christians were afraid they would win the emperor's support and take over. The bishops and other leading clerics decided to approach him (the man of God) and to urge him to have a word with the king. He (the holy man) had seen no other human being in twenty years. He had received no one in all this time. Whenever he heard footsteps approaching his shelter, he quickly hid himself away, so he wouldn't be found. Now that the bishops had decided to turn to the holy man, they didn't know how to approach him, for he had isolated himself from human society and allowed no one an audience. When Basileios found out about this from the servants who looked after him, he decided to undertake to convey the bishops' request to the holy man. He was certain that, when he saw his affliction, the holy man would pity him and allow him to approach.

— 17 —

What had happened to Anita Brik happened to Manfred Herbst. When he arrived at Shira's, he found the door locked. The door was locked, and there was no sound from inside. Where is she? She isn't at the hospital. Then where is she? His question recurred like a gnawing refrain. He didn't realize that he had asked the same question many times. He had certainly knocked on the door, but he probably hadn't knocked hard enough, which explains why she didn't open it. Perhaps she was asleep and didn't hear, and, if he were to knock again, she would hear and get out of bed to open the door, as she had done that Shabbat when they went to visit Anita Brik. Until that day, Herbst wasn't aware that Anita Brik knew Shira. That day, he discovered that she knew Shira, and today that information was very useful, for it was she who had told him where Shira lived, at a time when no one knew Shira's whereabouts. But what use is it to us to know where Shira lives if we don't find her in. Still, though we didn't succeed today, we will surely succeed tomorrow. Was it excessive optimism or fear of the truth, was it the suspicion that even tomorrow we wouldn't really know where Shira is, that led Herbst to say what he said? In either case, we must take our mind off Shira, so we will be free to attend to our real concerns, our work and our book, which we have so frivolously postponed. Now that something has come up, reminding us of our work, let us put Shira out of mind and get back to it.

What was it that led Herbst to turn his thoughts to his work once again? It was Ernst Weltfremdt's book that led Herbst's mind back to his work and his book. There are many books one can read and emerge from with nothing; then there are books whose very name stirs the heart. Not because we find something in them that engages us. There are certainly many books that occupy the mind but leave a vacuum in the heart. This is a secret that remains concealed from us. Since it can't be revealed, let us return to our story, which both conceals and reveals.

Herbst tried to put Shira out of mind, along with her new apartment and locked door, as he muttered to himself, "It's good that I didn't leave a note. The witch will never know I came knocking at her door. She has the capacity to observe a person and know what is in his heart. Since she hasn't seen me, since she hasn't observed me, since she doesn't know I was looking for her, she can't see or know what is in my heart. In fact, if I were to analyze the matter, I was merely curious to know where she is."

Herbst left that alley, which was nameless, like most alleys in Jerusalem in those days. In order to give it an identity, we'll refer to it as Shira's Alley. In those days, most alleys in Jerusalem were known by the name of a man or woman who lived there.

And so, Herbst left Shira's Alley, whispering, "I called her a witch. She is truly a witch, seeing how tormented I am because of her and not lifting a finger to relieve me. She's not a coquette or a sadist. She's not one of those women who torture their lovers, only to cast them aside. I'm no expert when it comes to women, but, judging by the ones I know, whether from history, fiction, or at first hand, I see that Shira is different. I say this not to praise Shira nor to disparage her, but because her character makes her different from the rest of her sex."

Throughout the ages, poets have created many characters and imbued them with spirit and soul. The men and women who were created from the verbal breath of poetry have produced offspring of their own. Not only in literature, but in life. A man meets a woman who seems familiar to him, although he has never met anyone like her. But he knows her from the work of some poet. That woman found a woman, described in a book, who was so attractive that she decided to fashion herself after her; she found a model and followed it. Where was Shira created? Shira is a totally new creature, created out of her very own essence.

Herbst remembered some of the things he had heard from her about her early life, things she had told him when they were getting to know each other, when she was still open with him. She didn't say that much about herself. What she did say came out in pieces, and she never repeated the facts or provided further details. Nonetheless, he was able to put the pieces together and extract the story of her life, though many chapters were missing. The facts were not pleasant. They didn't add to her glory, but they hung together and were consistent. What emerged from the facts was a coherent image.

Much as we contemplate the facts Shira related about herself, we find nothing pleasant. Only a question: Is it Shira's self-confidence that allows her to relate such unflattering facts, or is it out of disdain for us that she reveals what any other woman would conceal? Is what she has told us largely invented, things she wishes were true? In that case, we can learn about her feelings from these inventions, the sort of life she desires. If this is the case, the life you have chosen is ugly, Nurse Shira.

I will continue to do what I have been doing. I will transmit the rest of Herbst's thoughts in words. If they themselves aren't new, then they are new in form, sometimes leaping beyond the realm of thought to sight, becoming elevated and transformed into a vision. But he didn't begin to intone that poem again, "Flesh such as yours, et cetera."

The life force is very powerful. Each and every event generates new ways to interpret human experience. Sometimes to one's regret, sometimes to one's relief. How did Herbst interpret Shira's willingness to present herself in a bad light? It is clever of her, he thought. Shira knows her way of life is not exactly proper, that those who hear about it will disapprove. So she takes the initiative and tells her version of the facts, adjusting them to suit herself. What does Shira gain? When someone hears her life story, it won't make quite such an impact; having already heard it, it will have less of a sting. When it comes to rumor, the old can't compare to the new. One is already stale; the other grips our heart.

— 18 —

The next day, he went back and knocked on the door again. The door was locked, and no one opened it. Did I make a mistake? Is this the wrong house? He stood looking at the house, scrutinizing it intently, then took out his notebook and strained to decode the address under the erasures. The address was gone. He couldn't discern the shape of a single letter. But the building took shape, as Anita had described it: there it was, in all its reality. It stood there, in all its reality, solid and unmovable. So this is the building. This is where she lives. I couldn't be mistaken; there's no way to make a mistake. This is the house, and this is where she lives. He bent down and peered through the keyhole. He went to each window and looked inside. The curtains were drawn. All he could see was the shape of a skull and a strip of neck. It was his own skull and a strip of his own neck that were visible to him. The shape of his skull was inside the house, and he was outside. He went back to the door and banged on it. No response. Not a sound was heard from the house, except for a hollow echo. He turned away from the door and left, with faltering knees and a dejected heart. I'll find her, I'll find her, Herbst assured himself. I'll have no rest, no peace, until I find her. If not today, then tomorrow. He suddenly shifted pronouns and said: I'll find you, I'll find you. But he didn't find her. Not the next day and not the day after.

As it happened, he happened to meet a young man when he was coming back from Shira's, one of the young men one meets on the streets of Jerusalem who are not from the new communities. It wasn't obvious, at first glance, whether the coat he was wrapped in was long or short. He himself was long. His shoulders were broad and his stance self-assured. He was blond, with golden yellow hair. But the black hat on his head, the zeal in his face, the tightness in his eyes gave the misleading impression that his mind and mood tended toward darkness.

Herbst didn't recognize him, although he recognized Herbst. Herbst really should have recognized him; it would have been only right. Since he didn't recognize him, I'll let him remain puzzled until he does.

The young man addressed Herbst. "Dr. Herbst, what are you doing in this neighborhood? You must be lost. You are probably looking for an address and unable to find it. If you would allow me, I would be glad to take you wherever you want to go. I know Jerusalem well. I'm familiar with every byway." Herbst pondered: How do I answer him? If I don't say anything, will he realize that I don't welcome his company? When these people ask a question, they don't notice if you don't answer. But Herbst was polite, and his heart was more generous than his mind. Having decided to be silent, he went on to answer him, "I'm out for a walk. I'm not looking for anything. I see there is nothing new here. This alley looks as it always did, no different. Or am I mistaken?" As he talked, he was thinking: All these alibis won't convince him that I'm simply out for a walk. I'll say something to convince him that I'm here because of my work. He continued, "I have to prepare a lecture that demands concentration, and I expected that here, where I don't know anyone, I would be able to concentrate." The young man laughed abruptly and said, "In the end, professor, in the very place you were so sure you wouldn't be stopped by an acquaintance, some joker intercepts you. I'll be gone, leaving you to enjoy this neutral territory." Herbst was thinking: If only he would go without any further talk. But if I were to let him go now, my conscience would plague me for offending him. I might as well let him keep chattering until he gets tired and moves on. Hard as I try to figure out who he is, I can't remember. I don't even know which set of people he belongs to. But I won't ask, for, like most people in this country, who make things harder when they ought to make them easier, he might say, "Imagine not recognizing me. We were together once, and and we had such-and-such a conversation." If, after all that, I ask him his name, he will surely be offended that I have so little regard for him that I don't remember it. As he continued to search his mind, he remembered seeing him with Tamara. If so, Herbst thought, he must be the yeshiva student Henrietta told me about. In any case, I won't change my manner with him; then he won't realize I didn't recognize him from the start. To extricate the young man from his confusion, for he was still standing there, silent, making no move to go, he added, "There are so many different patterns of concentration. Some people need total inactivity to concentrate; others could be stuck between two millstones, and their concentration would remain unaffected. Wallenstein used to close down half of Prague, lest the echo of an echo of a sound disturb his mental processes. On the other hand, some old man told me about a Reform rabbi in Berlin, who used to preach in their temple. He delivered marvelous sermons that he planned as he walked through the city, choosing to follow the most crowded streets. A Reform rabbi doesn't have much work to do. His congregants don't ask for rulings on milk and meat or ritual baths. Apart from saying a few words at weddings and delivering eulogies for the dead, his main task is the sermon on Shabbat, which they observe on Sunday, the Christian Sabbath. And he did very well with these sermons. He was a great scholar, an expert in Midrash, kabbalah, and philosophy. He had a head full of ideas. One thing was missing: the ability to suspend most of his learning and, at the same time, organize the remainder. Such an enterprise demands enormous concentration. At home, he was unable to marshal his thoughts and organize a sermon, as every corner of his home was filled with books, and he loved to read good books. Some people love science; some love poetry, even if it's their own. So what did he do? Every Shabbat, after lunch, when it was time to plan the Shabbat sermon to be delivered on Sunday, he left home. Where did he go? To Friedrich-strasse, near the train station, the busiest spot in Berlin. This is what he used to do: He used to go to the cigar store, choose the thickest cigar, stick it in his mouth, light it up, and venture into that endless and infinitely bustling throng. He would then choose a verse from the prophets, or a line from Goethe or Angelus Silesius, to which he would give a timely turn, rephrasing it to catch the ear of his listeners. Old-timers, who were there, report that he himself was the size of a dwarf, that his top hat was as tall as half of his body, that his cigar was as long as the other half, that he moved like a squirrel, that, in this manner, he forged himself a path, advancing through the bustle of Berlin. They report that they had never heard sermons as magnificent as his, though Berlin was not short on great preachers. As you see, Mr. Schlesinger," Herbst said with a flourish, having finally managed to identify the young man, "there are all kinds of people with all kinds of ways. Insofar as I am a Berlin Jew, I ought to behave like that Berlin rabbi, my compatriot, but I am more like the Gentile, Wallenstein. And because I don't, alas, have the power to close off half the city, I have come to this quiet spot to organize my lecture."

It was already dark, so it was impossible to see how Schlesinger reacted to all this. However, it was obvious that he was surprised. Schlesinger had given up all things related to religion, yet there was no subject that interested him as deeply. He regarded religion as an impediment to Israel's freedom, and, if not for the immediate urgency of fighting the English and the Arabs, he would have devoted all his energies to the fight against religious coercion. Now that Herbst had brought up the subject of Reform Judaism, he was mystified. What was the point of a synagogue, a preacher, and all those trappings for Jews who had discarded the yoke of religion to the extent of trading the Jewish Shabbat for the Christian Sabbath? While one talked and the other listened and pondered, they continued walking and, before long, arrived at the Baka bus stop.

There was no one in sight. A bus had left only a minute earlier. Who knows how long it would be before another one arrived and was ready to leave? In those days, a time of unrest and confusion, people didn't come and go very much, and there weren't very many buses in service. Herbst, who had put Shira's place out of mind for a while, was thinking about it again. He pictured it as it was when he stood peering through the keyhole. According to Anita Brik's description, that was definitely Shira's place. It was definitely the place Anita Brik had described, but Shira wasn't there. He gazed at his fingertips and would have liked to be thinking about Shira, but he felt a barrier between himself and his thoughts. He glanced at his companion, who was standing beside him, and it seemed to him that a moment earlier he had been thinking, but he couldn't remember exactly what he had been thinking. His mind drifted to Tamara, his daughter, and this is roughly what he thought: My daughter, Tamara, isn't enthusiastic about talking to me, whereas this young man, whose only significance is his link to Tamara, detains me for a chat, unlike Avraham-and-a-half, who never bestows his presence on me. If I didn't know Oriental Jews, I would think his was an Oriental manner, attaching himself to a person, being so persistent. Unless I dispel the mood with well-chosen words, he'll be offended. He expects me to say something, but I remain silent. Herbst began searching for something to say and found nothing. He thought to himself: I'll discuss the yeshiva with him. Since he used to be part of that world, he must know all about it, and he probably enjoys discussing it.

Herbst said to Schlesinger, "I've lived in Jerusalem so many years, and nothing is as close to me as education. Still, when I get the annual announcements of various yeshivas, I never stop to wonder how they are different from each other or what their curricula are like. One announcement is from the Great Yeshiva; another is from the Institute for Advanced Talmudic Studies; yet another is from the Central Yeshiva. They have endless titles, expressing glory, grandeur, eminence. Please, Mr. Schlesinger, tell me how to distinguish between them. Are they organized in classes on different levels—some as secondary schools for Talmud study, others as Talmud universities? I'm totally ignorant about the educational affairs of the older communities. I'm familiar with such terms as *heder, Talmud, Torah, yeshiva,* but I'm not familiar with the curriculum."

Schlesinger's lips were tightly pursed, and his face communicated distaste for Herbst's conversation. Herbst took no notice and continued, "What is the difference between the Grand Yeshiva and the Greater Yeshiva, and how are they different from the Most Revered Yeshiva?" Herbst wanted to ask about other yeshivas, but, being unsure of their names, he didn't want to say anything ridiculous, lest Schlesinger think he was making fun of him. He included them all in a general question: "What is the curriculum of these yeshivas? I've heard it said that the main difference lies in the fundraisers, who know which names contributors respond to, guaranteeing the flow of money into their own pockets. I don't have to tell you, Mr. Schlesinger, that I am not of that opinion." When, after a few minutes, he still hadn't received an answer, he said to Schlesinger, "I have no luck with my questions. An idiot's questions are hard to answer. Would you rather give me your own version of the ways of the yeshivas?" Schlesinger answered, "As it says in the Gemara, 'Never throw stones in a well that once gave you water.' Since I left the yeshiva, I make a point of not discussing it." "Why?" "Why? How can I explain it? Because I have nothing good to tell about it, and it's pointless to tell about its evils. If one were to tell about evils, he should tell about the evil that comes from the source of all evil." "The source of all evil? Are you suggesting that there is a place that all evil comes from?" "Of course." "And what is it?" "What is it? Is that a real question?" Herbst laughed and said, "As you know, my friend, my path was always orderly. I first studied in an elementary school, then in a high school, then at a university. What I mean is that all my knowledge comes from what I was taught; I know only what I was taught. If my life depended on it, I couldn't come up with anything I wasn't taught." Schlesinger stared at Herbst to see if he was teasing or if he was, truly, just a naive German. He finally decided not to divulge his thoughts to him, for, if he knew what he thought about England, he would surely disapprove of his relationship with his daughter. Herbst was German, after all. And, being German, he probably adhered to the program of Brit Shalom, a covenant of peace.

Other passengers were assembling. Most of them were young men, who didn't look familiar to Herbst. He was sure they didn't live in Talpiot or Mekor Hayim; certainly not in Baka, whose inhabitants were Arabs. He noticed that one of them was nodding to him. He looked more closely and realized that he was a student of his. Herbst asked him, "Where's everybody going?" Someone answered, "To a *brit.*" "A *brit*? A circumcision? I never heard of a *brit* at night." "This *brit* will be a covenant of blood, all right." Most of the young men laughed, and the one who was his student whispered something to Herbst. Herbst said, "Now I realize that I shouldn't have asked." "Not at all. It's just that there was no need for such a brash answer. I see, Professor Herbst, that you still live in Baka. That sort of courage is not to be commended. In truth, other neighborhoods are no more secure. It would take two hundred people to protect Mekor Hayim. Neighborhoods are established without much thought, expanding the sphere of danger." As he spoke, he lowered his voice to a whisper. "The air has ears." He raised his voice again and said, "All right, everybody, let the turtle crawl at its own pace. We'll go on foot." Someone else said, "Not on foot, not on foot." "Why not on foot?" "Why? Because the roads are dangerous." "Quiet, quiet. I can already hear the brakes of the bus. Please, everyone, not so much noise." "Is silence any better? Lord only knows what's good and what isn't. When we're finally rid of them, we'll know what's good."

From the moment Herbst got on the bus until he got off, he was alone with his thoughts. They were no different than the ones he had been thinking before he met Schlesinger. Anyway, it was good that he had an opportunity to think his thoughts without being interrupted. The young men were engaged in their own affairs, ignoring him. I won't repeat his dialogue with himself, having already outlined it, but I will relay something that becomes relevant later on. Why advance the sequence now? Because what follows later cannot be interrupted.

From here on, he began to be tormented by lurid fantasies. He saw Shira walking in the mountains, sometimes alone, sometimes with a companion. Arabs assault her, then take her life. He saw her bathing in the sea, swept under by a wave, and drowned. The death throes, on sea and on land, were vivid to him. Her soul, struggling to expire, is unable to withdraw from her body because of its intense vitality. As she agonizes, her escort on these walks abandons her to the waves, to the murderer's assault, in order to save his own life. The murderer finally prevails and thrusts a knife into her heart. Her soul expires and she is dead. It is not clear whether he did what he did to her before she died or whether it was after she was dead that he did what he did. Her companion stands among the rocks, observing the scene. Who is he? The engineer with the whip, who returned because he couldn't forget her, and, when he returned, she was afraid he would hit her with the whip again, so she told him she had to go somewhere. He said, "I'll go with you." She said, "Only if you leave your whip behind." He agreed. They went walking together in the mountains, and a murderer appeared. The engineer, having nothing with which to scare off the

murderer, ran and hid among the rocks, from where he could watch
and see everything the Arab did to Shira. Finally, all that remained of
her was two legs, left by the murderer. Not the legs in the notice at the
train station in Leipzig, but Shira's legs, the legs he first saw that night
when he went home with her and sat with her while she put on the
dark blue slacks. Herbst cried out in a whisper, "Flesh such as yours
will not soon be forgotten." He pictured her room as it was the night
he first visited her, when he sat there looking at everything in the room,
with the dead skull peering down at him from one of the walls. As for
The Night Watch, which he intended to bring her, it was still wrapped
and waiting in the store. When he tried to bring her *The Night Watch*,
he found a locked door. He didn't find Shira. Where is Shira? He had
asked this question at least a thousand times. Each time he asked, the
visions I have already described provided an answer. For example: She
was out walking with someone when a murderer came and stuck a knife
in her heart, for these are not good times; the roads are all dangerous,
and those who walk them risk their lives. Herbst, too, is risking his life
when he walks alone. He ought to go home. Otherwise, he risks being
attacked by murderers.

As he walked home from the bus stop, he stopped at every wall and
at each post to read all the notices. None of the notices pertained to
Shira. Unless one concludes that a total lack of information prevented
the authorities from posting a notice about her, then she still exists. If
she exists, he will see her. Still, the question stands: Where is she? No
one at the hospital knows where she is. Anita Brik doesn't know where
she is, but she knows where she lives, and, when he went there, he
found the door locked. The question recurs: Where is Shira?

— **19** —

When Herbst entered his house, he was like a man depressed by dreadful anguish who wakes up only to realize that what depressed him was
a dream. The house was bright. Gay voices were heard from the dining
room. Along with Tamara's voice, hoarse from smoking, was the sharp
voice, the clear voice, of a girl speaking German, though not as it is
spoken in Germany, and a voice like Taglicht's. In fact, it was Taglicht,
as you are about to discover. But first, I'll tell just how this evolved.

Tamara came back from her trip and brought a new friend, a lovely girl she met on the way. She made her acquaintance on the bus and enjoyed her company so much that she offered to put her up until she could find a room.

Her name is Ursula Katz, and she comes from Vienna. Her eyes are large and kind, assuming a blue cast when they laugh. Her cheeks are fresh and full; she is altogether fresh and vibrant. She has soft, blonde hair, not shorn or bobbed, but arranged in four curly braids. Her lips are somewhat fleshy, but they are permeated by a smile that tempers their sensual quality and makes the flesh seem delicate. She is wearing a soft, brown blouse, embroidered with gold thread, open at the top to bare her graceful neck, which is circled by a thin, black chain. The beads are linked by dots of silver, whose glow rises up to meet the laughter in her eyes that turn all things blue, then plunges downward to be reflected in her fingernails. Her shoulders are covered, not exposed; what is exposed about her is a refreshing warmth that clings to her shoulders. But for the fact that she is skilled in office work—typing, shorthand, and the like—we would connect her with another time, three or four generations back, when a girl's honor derived from her beauty, modesty, and reserve.

Across from her, on the upholstered chair that looks out to the garden, sits Dr. Taglicht. He was there because of Ursula, which involved a bit of magic. This is the story. When they were on the bus coming into town, Tamara asked Ursula, "Do you have any friends or acquaintances in Jerusalem?" Ursula said, "No one I know personally, but my father knows someone here who was at the university with him, or in some similar situation. He told me to look him up when I get to Jerusalem." Tamara said, "I suppose your father told you his name?" Ursula laughed and said, "What you suppose is not far from the truth. Father did tell me the name." Tamara said, "Perhaps you remember his name?" Ursula said, "I remember his name." Tamara said, "If it isn't one of those Russian or Polish names, like those of the Zionist leaders that very few people here can pronounce without great difficulty, perhaps it wouldn't be too much trouble for you to tell me his name." Ursula said, "His name is simple and bright, like the light of day." Tamara said, "Could his name be Taglicht?" Ursula said, "I see, Tamara, that you know even more than I've told you. His name *is* Taglicht, Dr. Taglicht." As they continued this bantering exchange, the bus arrived at the station, and they got off. Tamara saw Dr. Taglicht strolling by and called to him. Dr. Taglicht came over. She said to him, "Here's your chance to be chivalrous. You can help two distinguished ladies get their luggage off the bus." Taglicht said, "At your service, mademoiselle." Tamara said, "And at the service of this lady as well. Meet Ursula Katz." "Ursula Katz . . . Ursula Katz. Are you by any chance related to Dr. Ferdinand Katz, a lawyer and notary?" Tamara said, "If it's not beneath your dignity, doctor, she is the daughter of that gentleman." Taglicht joined them immediately and accompanied them to the Herbst home. The three of them sat talking incessantly. Taglicht had many questions about Ursula's father and how he was faring in these dreadful times. Ursula gave leisurely answers. Having expended all her cleverness on Tamara, she was giving straightforward answers now, responses that fit the questions. She wasn't enraged by Nazi actions; she didn't bemoan her fate. She and her entire family had left their home and had stayed in hiding for months, until she succeeded in escaping from Vienna, getting on a boat, and entering this country. Taglicht had already heard stories like those Ursula had to tell. She told them everything, and if he asked more questions, he would gain no new knowledge. Ursula had a simple view of things. She saw only the surface of events, making no attempt to look inside. And, if I'm not mistaken, she repeated the same ideas in the very same words. Nevertheless, from what she said, one could reconstruct the development of events. So Taglicht already knew what he wanted to know. Isn't it amazing—just a short time before I met Ursula, it didn't occur to me that someone like that existed. Now, all of a sudden, my heart is full. . . . Actually, that's not how it was. The fact is, she and her entire family slipped out of his mind immediately. Even as they were engaged in conversation, she had already slipped out of his mind, because of other things. If I were to put them into words, this is roughly how it would be: Tamara is candid and open, but she also has an opaque and elusive aspect. These traits, all of which include their opposites, should be investigated. Most young women in this country are open and candid, having been born and raised under the bright and open skies of the Land of Israel. Tamara's opaque and elusive quality is self-generated and derives from many sources, not necessarily related to the fact that she belongs to an underground group, be it the Irgun or Lehi.

Having mentioned that Tamara went back to her parents' home, that she belongs to an underground group, and that she brought home a friend, this is the appropriate place to note that the trips Tamara referred to, such as the one to negotiate a teaching job, are fictions she fabricated to hide her activities from her parents; this is true of her classes in Mekor Hayim and of various other activities. As for Ursula, Ursula has no connection with these matters. Tamara befriended Ursula with no practical motive. Tamara befriended Ursula because of

Ursula's beauty, kindness, freshness—because of all the qualities one finds in those who have no dealings with politics.

They sat there talking. Tamara, Ursula, and Taglicht. Tamara said, "Wasn't it good that I invited you, Dr. Taglicht? When Ursula told me her father had told her about you, I called out to you right away. As soon as Ursula and I got off the bus, I called to you. When did you know her father? When you were in Vienna? Yes, Ursula is Viennese, like all the Viennese whose parents came from Galicia. You're Galician too, aren't you? I don't mean to embarrass you, doctor. I'm sure there are some decent people among the Galicians. Please, doctor, don't get the idea that I mean to compliment you. What do you actually do? You're not a lecturer. You don't publish books. So why do they say you're a scholar? Papa Manfred says so too. Isn't that so, Manfred? I call him Manfred. I can't call him Fred, because Mother has a monopoly on that name. I call Mother Mother, because the name Henrietta is too long, and it doesn't fit the environment here in the Land of Israel." Henrietta said, "Please, Tamara, don't talk nonsense." Tamara said, "Do you think, Mother, that Dr. Taglicht is here to glean wisdom from me? If he wanted wisdom, he wouldn't have come. Isn't that true, doctor? Be honest and tell the truth." Henrietta laughed and said, "Dr. Taglicht, did you ever see such a strange creature? I don't know whom she resembles. Not me, not Herbst." Tamara said, "If I resembled others, they would bore me. Tell me, Ursula, whom do you resemble?" Herbst said, "Could we change the subject?" Tamara said, "Yes, of course. Say something, and we'll listen. I read your article, Papa. About a certain empress whose name I forget. I have nothing against scholarship, and I have nothing against history. Still, I have to tell you, dear Manfred, if I were to sit and repeat the sort of things historians write, you would scold me for engaging in gossip and slander. I used to think our history was boring, until I began to be a good daughter, took your advice, and began reading world history, as you suggested. I think that particular enterprise induces all sorts of bad habits. Dr. Taglicht probably disagrees, but that doesn't change anything." Herbst said, "And the romances you pore over?" Tamara said, "Which romances are you referring to? The ones I read or the ones I create?" Herbst said, "You're writing a romance?" Tamara said, "Scholars are strange. In their minds, anything you do takes the form of writing. There are romances, dear Papa, that aren't written, and let me confide to you, in a whisper, that they are the most interesting ones." Herbst said, "Then you are involved in romances there with those teachers?" Tamara laughed and said, "Have you ever seen the likes of these people? They think the

entire globe is occupied by teachers. Papa, my sweet, there are other
types in the world, apart from teachers, lecturers, professors. Dr. Taglicht, are you a teacher too?" Taglicht said, "I am a teacher, a reluctant
one." Tamara looked at him and asked, "What do you mean, 'reluctant'?" Taglicht said, "Like you." Tamara said, "I'm actually happy to
be a teacher, but a teacher's wife—that's an honor I would decline."
Taglicht asked, "Whose wife would you like to be?" Tamara answered,
"Only time will tell. Those who write good romances let Amnon die
a thousand deaths before he marries Tamar." "And Tamar sits tight,
calm, and confident, waiting." "Why shouldn't she be confident? She
knows from the start that Amnon is totally committed to her." "And
if Amnon finds someone else, someone more attractive?" "Ursula, you
answer him." "Me?" Ursula answered in alarm. "In your place, I would
have said, 'If Amnon is such a fool, he doesn't deserve my attention,
not even for a moment.'" "It's that extreme, Tamara? Excuse me, I
meant to say Tamar. Tamar is so rational from the beginning that she
is capable of resolving to renounce Amnon?" "I don't know whether
or not she is rational, but I know that, even if all the others, whose
names I have forgotten, even if all the others, are more attractive than
Tamar, Amnon won't forget Tamar." "That's enough!" Herbst
shouted in a rage. Henrietta looked at him, surprised. Herbst caught her
gaze and brushed his hand over his face, as if to brush away his rage.
Tamara said, "Mother, what did you prepare for these honorable guests
who have honored you with their presence?" Henrietta said, "A good
daughter goes into the kitchen and prepares something for the honorable guests." "And what does the good daughter do if she herself is an
honorable guest?" Henrietta laughed and said, "If only we had such a
daughter." Tamara said, "It's possible that just such a daughter is flut-
tering around inside, eager to emerge." Henrietta said, "Stop babbling.
Come, let's get supper ready." "Who will take charge of Dr. Taglicht?
Who will take charge of Ursula? Isn't it my job to make sure our guests
aren't bored? Come, Ursula, let's help the lady of the house prepare us
a feast. I'm really hungry. Surely you're hungry too, Ursula. Good
conversation is a good thing, but it doesn't satisfy hunger."

Henrietta and Tamara left the room and went to the kitchen with
Ursula to prepare the meal, leaving Herbst and Taglicht alone. Herbst
looked at Taglicht for a while. Then he said, "I read the newspapers,
and every day I read names of men and women who were killed by the
Arabs. Tell me, Taglicht, aren't the newspapers hiding the names of
some of the victims? In a country like this, where we don't have
accurate statistics, don't people disappear, leaving no trace? It's easy to
imagine a person who has no written identification, a person like you

or me, stabbed by an Arab knife, murdered, without its being announced. All the more so in the case of someone who has no relatives
in the country. How can I explain my question? I imagine something
similar has already occurred to you, considering what's been going on
in this country. When will there be an end to the murders you people
call 'riots'? I must get back to my original question. Can we really trust
the newspapers to list every single man and woman who is killed? I said
'woman,' because women are more likely to be killed. Even in normal
times, there were incidents in which women were raped and murdered.
Quiet! I think the women are coming back, and I don't want them to
hear what we're talking about. It's not a pleasant subject for a woman's
ear. I don't like talking about it either. Let's change the subject. What
are you up to these days, Dr. Taglicht? Are you still wasting your time
correcting other people's papers? Everything is, to a great extent,
predetermined. We entrust our professors with the keys to wisdom, so
they can teach and instruct. In the end, they have to ask others to
correct their language, transforming themselves into students. Those
elevated professors are lucky to have you for a teacher, but it is high
time you began to look after yourself. I don't suggest that you get
involved in folklore. I heard what you said to Weltfremdt, and I agree
with you. But I have to say that I don't share your views in every area.
Small matters, when properly pursued, can be a key to larger issues. My
mentor, Neu, has no use at all for folklore. Back to that other subject.
You are involved in the Haganah, as you told me earlier. We certainly
have to defend ourselves, and anyone who can handle a gun must not
turn his back. Still, roles must be assigned, so that some people wield
guns while others wield pens. When I see what we are doing, I am
suspicious of those who don't align themselves with us. In the end,
what choice is there? People like us are doomed to continue to do what
they have always done. Whether they like it or not, habit rules. Here
come the women."

Herbst sat in the dining room with his wife, his daughter, Ursula
Katz, and Dr. Taglicht. He discussed, talked, argued, was silent,
smoked, listened, rubbed the tips of his fingernails—continuing, all the
while, to picture himself roaming from from alley to alley, from lane
to lane, turning toward a certain house, surveying it with his eyes,
approaching the entry, going into the building, coming to a door,
knocking on it with his fingertips, receiving no response. As he sat
there, he gazed at Henrietta again and again, thinking: Henrietta is
pregnant, but what connection is there between her pregnancy and the
locked door? He found no connection. And, because he didn't find it,
he was uneasy. He had another grievance: he wanted to find out where

Shira had disappeared to, and he wasn't being permitted to investigate. When he left Shira's apartment, Schlesinger had latched onto him; when he came home, he found a house full of people. He wasn't free to think about Shira, except on the bus among those Haganah people. Now that Tamara had brought a friend home, she, too, would take up his time. And Henrietta? Her baby was already visible. Now what is the actual connection between Henrietta's pregnant state and . . . Before Herbst could pursue these thoughts to their end, supper was served.

— 20 —

Herbst's fears about Ursula were unfounded. In no way did she infringe on his thoughts about Shira. She was no trouble at all to him, and she even had a positive effect. She came to stay with Tamara, and, as a result, Tamara doesn't go out very often. The two of them stay in, and Henrietta no longer needs him, so he is free to come and go as he pleases. But he doesn't go out very often either. He sits in his room, alone, adding cigarette to cigarette, smoking one, then another. We are used to this. It's in no way new.

Ursula still doesn't know what she'll be doing in this country and how she will support herself. She is running out of money, and there is no way for her father to send more. His property was confiscated, and he is not allowed to work. All he can expect is a dry crust and a hard bed. As for her mother, her mother is safe, beyond the reach of any foe or enemy. She is in the Tyrol with her sister, who is married to a Nazi poet. No one there knows the poet's wife is Jewish, and, of course, no one there knows her sister is Jewish. She both looks and sounds German.

Ursula sits with Tamara, and Tamara doesn't allow her to break her head over money concerns. If she finds a job and can support herself, well and good; if not, she can stay on and help with the housework. To relieve her mother of the household chores, Tamara has taken them all on herself, and she is teaching Firadeus how to do things. Firadeus listens and straightens out whatever mess the two girls create. When Tamara sees how much has been accomplished, she is delighted and declares in her pleasant, rasping voice, "Now you see, honey, how these things are done. This is how to do them. The way I told you, honey, not the way you thought." Firadeus gazes at Tamara, her eyes sweet as a mountain goat's, without a trace of bitterness.

Ursula suddenly found a job. She was to work four hours a day. I don't know exactly how it evolved, how the employer found her, or if it was the other way around. In short, Ursula was employed by an Arab importer. The Arab had been looking for a secretary who could write letters for him in German. Even in these dreadful times, when Arabs view Jews with disfavor, claim the Jews are displacing them, and try to dispose of the Jews through violent attacks and murder, they seek them out, because they can't survive without them.

Ursula found a job with which to support herself, and her employer found her to be a peerless secretary. He had hired her to write letters, but she took on other tasks that contributed to his welfare and pleasure. He was an agent for foreign goods, which he also imported. He bought them from wholesalers, who obtained the goods from the factories. It was she who advised him to get the goods from the producers, i.e., from the factories the wholesalers dealt with. Among the products he imported were some thin tea biscuits, produced in the factory of an uncle of hers, her father's brother. When the Nazis came, they confiscated the factory but allowed him to stay on, albeit in a minor position, because they couldn't find anyone to replace him. Ursula wrote to him in the name of her employer, offering to represent him in Palestine and all the neighboring countries. In Jerusalem and throughout the land, these biscuits were already popular. When a customer asked for biscuits, the shopkeeper would suggest that brand. If not for the Orthodox, who are meticulous about dietary laws, all the biscuit factories in this country would have closed down. Even Orthodox shopkeepers can't afford to ignore these Viennese biscuits, because the English have grown so fond of them.

Tamara invited Ursula out of friendship. When Ursula began to earn money, she began paying for room and board. She pays ten lirot a month for room and board, and she gives Firadeus half a lira for her services, apart from presents, such as a dress or shoes she no longer wears. These presents, which seem small, are significant to Firadeus and her friends. Even things that are not passed on directly—the things Firadeus finds in the trash or in the garbage after Ursula discards them—are noteworthy. Here is one example with many counterparts. Firadeus once found a small case made of soft, bright leather in the trash basket. When she opened it, she found a mirror set in a red frame. Assuming it had been thrown away by mistake, Firadeus put it on the table near Ursula's bed. The next day, she found the mirror in the basket again. Firadeus wondered how such a lovely mirror got into the basket. She went and talked to Henrietta about it. She couldn't talk to Ursula, because Ursula didn't speak Hebrew and she herself didn't speak German. Henrietta asked Ursula. Ursula said, "I have a better one, so I have no use for it." Firadeus ended up with a mirror unlike anything her friends possessed. Even Tamara didn't have such a mirror. Firadeus finds many treasures discarded by Ursula. She feels she must tell the lady of the house about some of these finds, because it doesn't make sense to discard such lovely things. When Ursula values an object, of course, she holds on to it; otherwise, she throws it out.

Meanwhile, events are transpiring in the Herbst household that not everyone in the household is pleased with. It's time for lunch. Everyone is hungry and anxious to eat, but lunch can't be served, because Ursula isn't there. They sit and wait until they can wait no longer, because of hunger and because of the dishes. If they put off eating, Henrietta or Tamara will have to do the dishes, since it's impossible to ask Firadeus to stay and do them. They suddenly hear the sound of a car stopping at the house. A driver comes in and brings a note from Ursula, informing them that she won't be back for lunch: her employer has invited her to eat with him at the King David Hotel. She hopes they will enjoy their meal without her. Ursula returns in the evening, in her employer's car. She comes in and tells them what she ate and drank and everything that gentleman told her. He didn't discuss politics, but his conversation was very pleasant. The Arabs have such elegant ways. They know how to order dinner, and they are equally adept with drinks. When you sit with a gentleman of that sort, watching him lift his glass and drink his fill, you are convinced that the notion that Arabs are forbidden to drink wine was fabricated by Christians or Jews. There is one problem: his brother-in-law, Abdullah, a partner in the business, who is trying to take it over and would like her to come and work for him. This would not be fair at all, since it was Mr. Mustafa who hired her, not Mr. Abdullah.

Meanwhile, everything proceeds in an orderly fashion. Ursula spends a given number of hours in Mustafa Effendi's office, and they spend a given number of hours taking trips in his new car, which is more splendid than any other in the country. He shows her the city, its environs, his vineyards and gardens which produce fruit the likes of which she has never eaten before. She now understands that this is a truly blessed land. Despite all this, Ursula isn't happy, because of Abdullah, Mustafa's brother-in-law, who is trying to turn her against Mustafa and to convince her to come and work for him. She loathes the intrigue between the brothers-in-law and has decided that, unless the situation improves, she will quit. Even before she could quit, Tamara took her to the Histadrut Haleumit, and she became a member. Which was extraordinary, for she was admitted, without excessive questioning, by an official who declared that such a competent worker should be working for us, not for others—certainly not for Arabs. This official was right to say that Ursula ought to be working for one of our institutions. But our institutions are, in fact, overstaffed, employing many useless individuals who aren't fired only because they might disclose information against whoever fires them, forcing those in charge to resign rather than risk public humiliation. Another reason why more officials aren't fired: because the general population detests our institutions, and officials who are fired tend to make trouble. It has already happened that an official was caught cheating and was fired on ethical grounds. He was snatched up by another company, which he now directs, using his position to damage the institution he originally served.

After Ursula was admitted to the Histadrut Haleumit, Tamara took her to a café. They sat drinking cocoa and were joined by one of Tamara's friends, a writer and journalist. Tamara told him that Ursula had been admitted to the organization and reported what the official had said about her: that Ursula should be working in our institutions, but that the jobs were all taken by lazy idlers. The writer said to them, "If I were writing a novel about this community, I would call it *The Cake Eaters.* I would describe all the gatherings attended by officials whose main function is to impress guests and to overeat. No doubt they do something between gatherings, but the real accomplishments are not theirs."

Between the two events, between the time Ursula arrived at the Herbst household and the time Ursula was admitted to the Histadrut Haleumit, Henrietta arrived at full term and was ready to give birth. Because I don't know if I'll get back to Ursula, I've told all about her, insofar as her affairs are linked to the tale of the Herbst household, which is an essential link in the tale of Dr. Herbst and the nurse Shira. Now I'll return to the Herbst household and Henrietta Herbst's delivery.

This delivery was different from the earlier ones, because, in this case, Tamara took her mother to Hadassah Hospital and arranged everything, sparing Manfred the father the excitement that is inevitable for a man when his wife gives birth. Father and daughter had agreed to this. It began in this way: Tamara heard about a woman who had read Tolstoy's *Anna Karenina* and was so affected by the description of Levin's torments the day his wife gave birth that, when it was time to deliver her own child, she hid the event from her husband, went to the hospital alone, gave birth, and informed her husband afterward. When Tamara heard this story, she decided she would do just that when she was married and about to give birth. Meanwhile, she did for her mother what she had decided she would do for herself.

As it happened, just when Henrietta and Tamara left for Hadassah Hospital, at one and the same time it happened that Herbst set out to look for Shira. It would have been better if these events hadn't occurred at one and the same time—because of the moral aspects of this coincidence, because of its sensational aspects, because the affair of Herbst and Shira had begun similarly and its course had not run smoothly. So, just when Henrietta was admitted to the hospital, at that precise hour Manfred was walking down the alley Anita Brik had described to him. He was hesitant and hadn't approached Shira's place yet, but now he was ready to approach. He suddenly realized how bizarre it was, how ugly it was: a man's wife is about to bear his child, and he is groveling at another woman's door. But between consciousness and action, there are many twists and turns. Before long, Herbst was knocking at Shira's door. The door, however, was new, and it didn't respond. Six or seven times he knocked on the door, and no one opened it for him.

— 21 —

Henrietta presented her husband with a healthy and sound baby. It was almost daylight when her son was born. She gave birth to her son with none of the anguish associated with childbirth, though he was large when he emerged from his mother. He weighed eight and a half pounds, unlike his sisters, who were successively smaller than each other and all smaller than he was. The obstetrician, who was afraid Mrs. Herbst might have a difficult birth, instructed the nurses to notify him as soon as she went into labor, as she would need special attention. Before they had time to inform him, the baby was born. The midwife, a young girl of about twenty-two, and two other young nurses were the only ones with her, except for the night nurse, who came to the delivery room after the birth.

Henrietta is the sort of woman who remains composed at all times and doesn't like to indulge herself, even when she gives birth. As soon as she woke up from her sleep, she asked that a special messenger be sent to her home to announce that she had given birth to a son. If the messenger would like to take a taxi, he could take a taxi. If he is content with a bus, let him take a bus. It isn't essential that they know instantly; it will be fine if they get the news even after an hour's delay. As long as the messenger arrives by noon, which is when they generally leave the house.

An hour later, Papa Manfred appeared with Tamara. Or, to reverse it, Tamara appeared with Papa Manfred for Papa Manfred was bizarre. He actually didn't know his left from his right, and, if not for Tamara, he wouldn't have found the door to his wife's room. Manfred was truly bizarre standing before his wife. His eyes were fixed less on his wife than on the door, and, when the door opened, he seemed anxious, pale, disappointed, desperate. They were allowed to spend a limited amount of time with the new mother, and even less time with the son. They probably weren't allowed in to see him at all, but were led to a small opening from the hall to the nursery, where they could stand and peer at the newborn infant, swaddled in a white garment, lying in a woven cradle. It was hard to be sure he was human. In any case, Papa Manfred didn't look at him and didn't notice anything, as if determined to deprive his eyes of whatever they might see. But he was aware of the young nurse's glance as she led him toward the nursery, and, when he became aware of her, he tried to dismiss her from his memory, along with the memory of the day he visited Bachlam when Bachlam was sick, when he asked that young nurse about Shira. To prevent these memories from taunting him, as they often did, he turned his mind to other days and other eras. First, to the time of Emperor Theodosius and his chamberlain Cocolus; then to Arcadius, who succeeded his father, Theodosius. Then back to that chamberlain, Cocolus, on whom they both depended, each for his own reasons. Herbst suddenly began to doubt that the chamberlain's name was really Cocolus, because he didn't remember an *l* in his name, and, if there was no *l*, then it surely wasn't Cocolus. Now how does this relate to Theodosia? But was I actually thinking about Theodosia?

The Mount Scopus bus arrived at its stop, near the workers' kitchen. The entire square was full of students, young men and women who were hurrying to the university, to the library, to meet each other, and so on. All around them, a mass of individuals—men, women, babies— pressed forward toward Hadassah Hospital, on their way to visit sick relatives. Herbst and his daughter barely managed to make their way through the crowd, and they barely managed to wriggle out of the line. "Papa," Tamara said in a tender voice, "let's write a letter to Zahara

now, informing her that all is well and that Mother gave birth to a boy."
"Good," Papa Manfred said, feeling that was not the right word. But,
having already said "Good," he said it again, so she would take it as a
deliberate and sober response. Nevertheless, it surprised him that
Tamara had said, "Let's write a letter to Zahara now." How could you
stop and write a letter on such a noisy street? He couldn't imagine how
it was possible to stand and write a letter on a city street, in a sea of
pedestrians.

Herbst followed his daughter in a hush. They were surrounded on
all sides, in front and in back, by all sorts of people in varied dress, by
stores, vehicles, newspaper vendors, kids distributing flyers, policemen,
Arabs, dogs, flying insects—whatever is typical of such a street on a
summer day before noon. All this was fused into a single raucous mass
that couldn't be taken apart, whose segments had no life of their own,
existing only as a crowd, emitting an incessant murmur. Tamara said
to her father, after they sat down in the café, "I assume that, at a time
like this, a cup of coffee would suit you." "And you?" Papa Manfred
said, with a sense of shared fate. "Yes," said Tamara, "I'll have coffee,
too. Until that dunce brings our coffee, I'll have a cigarette. I left my
cigarettes at home, Papa. If you would like to contribute a cigarette, I
would be happy to accept it. What, you left your cigarettes at home
too? Two people and one blunder."

The waiter brought two black coffees and some milk. He didn't
bring any sugar. In those days, there was a sugar shortage in the Land
of Israel. Cafés and restaurants no longer served sugar with coffee and
tea. "Pigs," said Tamara. "The goyim need sugar for their wars, so we
have to drink coffee without sugar." "Without sugar," Herbst said. It
clearly didn't matter to him whether he had coffee with or without
sugar. "Didn't we want to write to Zahara?" "We did, yes, we did,"
said Tamara. "And what we wanted to do, we will do. I'll get paper
and an envelope. You, Papa, dear, will contribute two or three drops
of ink from your blessed pen, along with your pen itself. I promise not
to violate the sanctity of scholarship. I'll merely inform Zahara that
Mother gave birth to a boy and that they are both well." Herbst handed
her his pen and said, "Here. You can write to Zahara." Tamara said,
"I'll get some paper and an envelope." "Yes, yes," Herbst said. "Bring
paper and an envelope." He suddenly noticed there was something odd
either in his voice or in his words. He wanted to prove to his daughter
that he was entirely composed and began searching for a subject that
would prove he wasn't merely babbling. It occurred to him to tell her
that they could just as soon call Zahara, since there was obviously a
telephone in Ahinoam; that, oddly, if they were to call, Zahara would

have the news in Ahinoam even before Sarah, who was at home in
Jerusalem. While he thought about his two daughters, that the one who
was geographically closer would get the news after the one who was
far away, Tamara went to get paper and an envelope. After she returned, with paper, an envelope, and a plate full of warm cakes filled
with cheese, fruit, and jam, she said to her father, "Why write?
Wouldn't it be better to find a telephone and call her? No letter in the
world could satisfy a daughter's soul as much as hearing the news
directly. They have a telephone here, and at this hour it isn't being used
by couples calling each other. No one will disturb us. There may even
be someone in the office in Ahinoam by now, willing to pick up the
phone out of idleness and curiosity." "Yes, yes," Herbst was about to
say to his daughter. "Yes, yes, let's call her." But he was afraid she might
consider these words odd. He could just as soon say, "Good, good,"
but those words had a similarly odd ring. So he restrained himself and
didn't say anything, counting on his daughter to know what was in his
heart, which would make all words superfluous. Superfluous! He was
suddenly overcome with terror. If Tamara knows what is in his heart,
then she knows . . . Before he could follow the thought to its conclusion,
he was confronted with another wave of terror. Tamara laughed and
said, "So that's it. That's how a man looks when his wife gives him a
son. I want to know: does it make a difference whether she gives birth
to a male or a female?" "That's a silly question. Of course there's a
difference." "Papa, dear, you have probably forgotten what you were
like when I was born. But you probably haven't forgotten what you
were like when Sarah was born." Herbst gazed at her, replaying what
was in his own mind: I wasn't thinking about Theodosia, I'm sure I
wasn't thinking about Theodosia. There was no reason to think about
Theodosia, so why does my mind persist in tormenting me with her?
Until I find another reason, it's because her name begins with T, like
Tamara's. I know that's not the real reason, but, until I find another,
this one will have to do. I already said that, so why repeat myself?

When they left the café, Tamara said to her father, "We've informed
Zahara; what else is there for us to do?" Papa Manfred said, "What else
is there for us to do? Believe it or not, I don't know. I simply don't
know." He suddenly looked at her with affection and said warmly,
"You've been treating me like a child who needs a nursemaid. I stand
around, not knowing what to do, until you tell me. Very simply, I don't
know what to do. You see, Tamara, there's material for a tragedy here.
A sensible man, father of daughters, suddenly loses his mind, and, if not
for his young daughter, he would be desolate. If not for you, Tamara,
I would be like King Lear in his time. You never heard of King Lear?

I would normally be furious about that, but I'll let it go for now. So, Tamara, what should we be doing? What, in your opinion, should we be doing? It seems to me that all we have to do is hop on the bus, go home, and tell Sarah that they brought her mother a baby. I leave it to you to figure out how to construct the story about the baby—whether it was delivered by an angel or a stork. They both have wings. Whom did we leave Sarah with? I think that, when we left home, Firadeus wasn't there. No, she wasn't. She definitely wasn't there, and we left the child with no one to look after her! As you see, Tamara, there are times when a sane person has a lapse and does something he shouldn't do. I'm philosophizing while the poor child is home alone! It's possible that Firadeus didn't come at all." Tamara said, "Don't worry, Papa. Sarah isn't home alone." Father Manfred said, "She isn't home alone? How can you say she isn't home alone? If Firadeus didn't come, then the child is surely there alone. How come I didn't think of it sooner? I'll call a taxi, so we can hurry home." Tamara said, "It's not necessary to hurry, and we don't need a taxi." Father Manfred said, "How can you say it's not necessary? I really have to admit that I don't understand you. A little girl is home alone, and you say, 'It's not necessary.' Please, why isn't it necessary?" Tamara said, "Because she isn't alone." Father Manfred said, "You already told me that." Tamara said, "That's what I said, and that's how it is." Father Manfred said, "Please, Tamara, help me understand. I don't have much imagination. We left the house, and there was no one home but Sarah, yet you insist——" Tamara said, "I asked Ursula not to go to her office, so she could be with Sarah." Manfred said, "You asked Ursula to stay with Sarah, but you didn't tell me?" Tamara said, "I did tell you." Father Manfred said, "You told me just now, but earlier, when I was frantic, you didn't say a word." Tamara said, "Until you were frantic, there was no reason to tell you." Father Manfred said, "If you had told me earlier, I wouldn't have become frantic. What do you think, Tamara? Is there something between her and Taglicht?" Tamara glanced at her father questioningly and said, "Her? Whom do you have in mind?" Father Manfred said, "Between Ursula and Taglicht." Tamara said, "I didn't notice." Father Manfred said, "You didn't notice?" Tamara said, "I don't view the world in terms of what goes on between males and females." Father Manfred smiled and gazed at his daughter with a mix of affection, surprise, and envy, and said, "How do you view the world?" Tamara said, "The world? How do I view it? The entire world concerns me about as much as a single nit in an Arab's kaffiyah. Father Manfred asked his daughter, "What are you concerned with?" "What am I concerned with? Our immediate world." Father Manfred asked his daughter, "What about our immediate world?" Tamara said, "The issues that concern me are liberty, freedom, casting off the foreign yoke." Father Manfred said, "What does freedom mean?" Tamara said, "Freedom from the English and their Zionist agents, from Weizmann and his agents, from those who head the Jewish Agency and the Labor Party. Some monstrous Englishman, from some dingy cellar in London or from the House of Lords, appoints himself master of our fate, ruling our world according to the decrees of some other monster, possibly just like him. One well-aimed kick and they'll be out of this country." Manfred said, "The Arabs want to throw us into the sea, and you want to throw out the English." Tamara said, "Out of the country, not into the sea. That's the difference between us and those desert savages. We've improved their lives in so many ways—raised them out of their filth, supplied them with food, replaced their rags with real clothes, provided doctors to cure their eyes—yet they want to throw us into the sea. But they relate to the English like servile dogs. I promise you this, Papa, the Arabs won't throw us into the sea. In fact, they ought to praise Allah and thank him for the fact that the Jews won't throw them into the sea." Herbst pursed his lips and said, "Is that so?" Tamara said, "Yes, Papa. Yes. That's how it is, and more so." Father Manfred said, "Jews are merciful; they're not cruel. But I can tell you this, my child: when a Jew becomes cruel, woe unto his people. When the merciful become cruel, they are worse than those who were born cruel. But back to our subject: how do you expect to get both the Arabs and the English out of this country? Tell me, please, how will you do it?" "How?" Tamara said. "If I were clever, I would answer you. Anyway, it won't happen the way I imagine it. But what I have told you is definite, guaranteed. I promise that you will see it for yourself." Father Manfred said, "And can you promise that I'll enjoy it?" Tamara said, "That depends on you. I myself can imagine no greater pleasure than national power, a people that is vigorous and mighty." Manfred said, "That Englishman from a dank cellar in London will be replaced by a Revisionist from Odessa, or from some village in Poland, Lithuania, Galicia, or Mea Shearim, and he will tell me what to do. This is what I think: a powerful Gentile, from a powerful country accustomed to power, so that its lust for power has been modulated, is to be preferred to a young Jew whose evil ambitions remain unbridled. Dear Tamara, don't look so menacing. I won't say another word, if you wish. But if you have the fortitude to hear the opinion of a man who has seen an orderly world, who has seen war, who has seen revolution follow in its wake, who has read books, I am willing to share my opinions with you, based on what I have seen in books and what I understand from life. I assume, Tamara, that you prefer life to books. Let me begin with my childhood. Will it be hard for you if we walk?" Tamara said, "And you, Papa. Will it be hard for you if we walk?" Father Manfred said, "I don't credit myself with having taught you many things, so let me teach you one thing that is worth learning." "What is it?" Father Manfred said, "If someone asks you a question, don't use the same words when questioning him." "Why not?" Father Manfred said, "As an exception to the rule, I will begin my answer using your words. Why not? Because that proves to the person you are arguing with that he has influence, if not on your ideas, then on your style. Now, my child, we can go back to the beginning, if you like. But tell me first, do you mind if we walk?" Tamara laughed and said, "What do you want to know first, whether I'm a good student or whether you're a good teacher?" Father Manfred said, "It's all the same, isn't it? A good student learns from his teacher, and a good teacher turns out a decent student. I'm afraid that, with so many asides, we'll never get to the heart of the matter. If you're ready to hear, I'll get back to the subject."

But Manfred didn't get back to the subject, not because of all the asides, but because they were home.

— 22 —

Sarah already knew that she had acquired a brother, but she wasn't impressed—not by the little brother who was going to be a present from her mother and not by all the pet names bestowed on the newborn baby. None of what Ursula told her in broken Hebrew, none of what Firadeus told her had entered her ears. And if it entered her ears, it didn't enter her heart. If it entered her heart, she showed no joy or excitement. Actually, the news did make an impression, but not the one the Herbst family had in mind. Attached as she was to her mother, she never asked where she was or even mentioned her. When they brought a message from her mother and told her that she had sent kisses, she didn't offer her cheek, as she usually did when anyone asked to kiss her. On the other hand, she began to be affectionate to her father, clasping his knees, giving him presents—an eggshell, a bird's feather, and the like. His heart was stirred to love her anew.

Again, I'll do something similar to what I have done before. I'll find

words for Father Manfred's thoughts about Sarah and her brother.
They were roughly this: Until now, Sarah was the child of our old age,
enjoying years of privilege. Now that she has a brother, Sarah is losing
out. Her privileges will be passed on to her brother and multiplied
because he is male. I don't know if Henrietta will be able to restrain
herself and keep from depriving the little girl out of fondness for the
boy. In any case, as for me, I will do whatever I can to keep Sarah from
feeling deprived by her brother. I have heard that, in such cases, people
buy entertaining toys and say, "Your little brother sent you these
things," as a way to erase the rivalry. I don't think that material objects
buy love. When love is strong, there is no need for devices, such as
presents. Herbst was suddenly in a panic. Though his mind had been
totally occupied with his son and daughter, it began to grapple with an
issue he should not have been considering now.

Again, I will do what I did before. I will find words for the thoughts
he was grappling with, but I won't dwell on them, for I find that the
birth of a son is more important than anything, certainly another
woman. This is roughly what was running through his mind about her,
about that other woman, about Shira. All that time, when we loved each
other, it never occurred to me to woo her with gifts. All the gifts in
the world don't draw hearts any closer. They don't have the power to
change anything. As for *The Night Watch*, I bought it to give her
pleasure. The skull that hangs on her wall is there because she couldn't
find a good Rembrandt reproduction. In any case, she never received
The Night Watch, because her door was locked. Once again, the visions
and scenes I already mentioned were repeated, in which she drowned
or was murdered. But this is no time to elaborate, for he must concern
himself with the son his wife has borne for him.

I am now confronted with two separate matters, and I don't know
which to deal with first: his visit to Henrietta or his conversations with
Tamara, also his friends and acquaintances, and how they responded
to news of his son's birth. I would like to add to this some reflections
on education. It would have been better if these matters had come up
separately, so I could take the time to give each one its due. But it is
in the nature of events to occur in a disorderly fashion, and it would
require considerable effort to isolate them and establish the importance
of each one. I don't presume that I could do this, but I count on them
to find their rightful positions themselves; even if one of them is displaced in the process, it can surface elsewhere, nonchalant and essentially intact. First, I will recount his actions in general; then I will break
them down, recounting each and every detail.

While Henrietta was in the hospital, Herbst never left home except to visit her, regarding himself as the center of a household that couldn't be left without someone in charge. During this period, he put aside his central work and took on tasks he either hadn't considered before or had considered and rejected. Having put aside his central work because of his son's birth, his conscience no longer plagued him with guilt about wasted time, and he worked out of love and joy. Among other things, he was busy with his books, checking for duplications, discards, alternate possibilities; setting some aside to be read soon. Because he did all this voluntarily, and because he had put aside his work consciously, he was not plagued by guilt over wasted time, and he was utterly happy.

Now I will begin with his daily routine. He used to wake up an hour before the girls got out of bed, move to the kitchen, light the kerosene stove, put on the kettle, make himself coffee, turn off the fire, and go out to the garden to rake the soil and dig hollows around the seedlings, tending the plants until he heard Tamara calling him to the table. Breakfast, which was seemingly no different than ever, amused him now, because Tamara assumed her mother's tone, urging him to eat an egg. And her responses to Sarah—when she rejected her cereal and left milk in her glass, only to be grabbed by Tamara and prevented from clasping Manfred's knees with hands, still dirty from breakfast—were so like Henrietta's. Ursula's conversations with Sarah were most entertaining, one of them speaking Hebrew that isn't quite Hebrew and the other answering in German that isn't quite German—spicing it with Arabic, on the theory that since it, too, is a gentile language, Arabic must be like German.

After breakfast, sometimes during breakfast, Ursula rushes off to work. Tamara turns to her work, correcting the notebooks of her Mekor Hayim students, which serve as camouflage for writing proclamations and sending them out. Because of the proclamations, she didn't go to Mekor Hayim. She said, "I'm taking time off to look after my little sister." I don't know what is involved in looking after her. As for dressing, Sarah dresses herself; as for bathing, Firadeus bathes her; as for looking after her, in the sense of protection, the good Lord protects her, and no other protection is needed. This little Jewish girl spends most of her time outside, surrounded by enemies, yet no harm comes to her. All this time, Herbst is busy in his room, taking books out, putting books in, cutting snips of paper to use as markers in the books he means to read. This would seem to be a simple task; actually, it is quite difficult. Having decided on a book he would like to read and placed a snip of paper in it as a sign, when he comes back to it, he no longer recalls why he had decided it was worth reading. He is about to put the book back on the shelf when he finds himself deliberating:

So why do you need it at all? Just to gather dust or to add to your book count. While he is engaged with his books, a voice is heard. Firadeus appears, stands in the doorway, and says softly, "The table is set, and lunch is ready." If Tamara fails to notice, Sarah jumps up, runs to clasp her father's knees, and presents her cheek for him to kiss. Again, I should mention that, in this situation, offering a cheek to be kissed is equivalent to granting a kiss. And what about this? Herbst, who is fussy about cleanliness, doesn't look to see if Sarah's hands are clean. Even if her mouth is sticky from the colorful candies Firadeus brings her, it doesn't prevent him from kissing her on the mouth. She asks, "Is it sweet?" and he answers, "Very sweet." She runs to Firadeus and reports that her mouth is sweet. Then she comes back to her father, not for a hug and a kiss, for her love has been elevated. It is now spiritual love, and she is content to have her father near her. Father asks, "What would you like me to tell your mother? What should I say to your little brother?" She instantly becomes silent and doesn't answer.

When he is finished eating, Herbst goes back to his room, stretches out on the couch, and reads a book. Not one of the books he had set aside to read, but a book that appeals to him at that moment. After reading for a while and dozing for a bit, he gets up, showers, has some coffee, and goes to visit his wife. If she is alone, he sits with her. He asks her questions, and she asks him questions. She asks what he ate, what he drank, how he slept, what Sarah said, what Tamara is doing, how the garden is doing, what Firadeus is doing, how they are treating Ursula in her office, and so on. He asks how she is, how the baby is, what name she wants to give the child—having already agreed not to name him after one of their relatives with long, old-fashioned German names and not to construct one of those modern names that will sound banal in no time. If he finds some woman friend is visiting, he makes a point of being brief, to give them a chance to talk.

One day, he found a woman there who told a story. Since her story is relevant to the event, namely, the birth of a little brother and a circumcision ceremony, I will repeat what she said, adding a word of my own. "I was six years old when my little brother was born. On the day of his *brit*, I said to my teacher, 'Mrs. Foiese,' which was her name, 'please, Mrs. Foiese, may I go home an hour early?' The teacher said, 'Why?' I said, 'I have a new brother.' The teacher asked, 'What do you people do when a baby boy is born?' I told her, 'We have a *brit* and the baby is circumcised.' *'What?'* the teacher asked. I repeated, 'We have him circumcised.' The teacher said, 'What's that? You mean baptized?' I was terrified. I began to shake and tremble. I was overcome with fear. I knew baptism was a Christian term, and I was afraid that,

God forbid, they intended to convert my little brother. The teacher saw
my tears and said, 'All right, all right, you can go home.' Another thing
happened. A girl of about twelve said to me, 'You should be ashamed.
You crucified the Christ child.' I didn't know who the Christ child was,
nor did I know anything about crucifying. But I realized that my friend
was connecting me with some dreadful event, an event I had nothing
to do with. The teacher, trying to make amends, said, 'She wasn't the
one who crucified the Christ child; it was her ancestors who did it.' I
went home crying and said I couldn't stay in a gentile school. My
parents sent me to a Jewish school. These events led me to Judaism, to
Zionism, to the Land of Israel."

I will mention one more woman who came to visit Henrietta: Mrs.
Rika Weltfremdt, the wife of Professor Ernst Weltfremdt. I don't
remember if I have already said what she is like, and I don't imagine
she adds to the saga of Shira and Herbst. Though this is the case, I
won't neglect her. I'll tell a little bit about her, as an act of charity
toward this unfortunate soul, removed from her source of vitality,
ending up here with us, where no one pays attention to her poems, and
even her family ignores them. Through deception and insipid compliments, they avoid reading her poetry.

Rika Weltfremdt is a small, thin woman, graceful and delicate. Her
eyes are kind and lovely, brown and direct, viewing the world with
deep yearning that tempts others to abuse her sensitivity. Because of her
size, she is overshadowed by her husband. His limbs are gross, his
eyebrows heavy. He deals with words as if he were dealing out new
provinces and adding them to the universe. She relates to her husband
as she relates to everyone else, as she used to relate to her father, her
brothers, her sisters. Her father, who owned two shoe factories and was
especially fond of her, gave her a dowry that exceeded her sisters' by
one part and found her a husband who was a doctor and a lecturer, and,
if not for the horrors that befell the world, he would have been a
professor in a German university by now. Because of these horrors, he
was compelled to move to the Land of Israel. But even here he is
recognized. Though scholarship is not valued here unless it contributes
to nationalist interests, Zionist leaders acknowledge that he is a genuine
scholar. Since he has an international reputation, those in the Land of
Israel take credit for him when it suits them. However, as he becomes
more ample, Rikchen becomes even more slight. No one is left to listen
to her poems, except for a young lady who helps out in her daughter's
household. Now, having heard that Mrs. Herbst did a wonderful
thing—that she gave birth to a son—she was inspired to produce a
poem, which she brought to Mrs. Herbst. She was so modest that she

made it seem secondary to the perfume she brought as a gift. It was
good that she brought the poem, to perpetuate the fine and worthy
sentiments of our sisters, and to convey her feelings about the birth of
a Jewish child at a time when the seed of Israel is, God forbid, in danger
of being eliminated from the earth. If the poem isn't really a poem, the
sentiments in it are truly sentiments, and those of us who look for
opinions and sentiments in poetry regard those lines as poetry and
accept their author as a poet. Since I'm not capable of translating her
poem, I will put it aside and get back to Henrietta and to Zahara, who
has come to see her mother.

Zahara came, bringing with her produce from the earth of Ahinoam,
along with a hat and booties that were her own handiwork. Zahara's
delight in her little brother was beyond all measure. It was the delight
we note in a woman who has been waiting for years and finally achieves
what she achieves. The two women, mother and daughter, sit together,
one in the bed, the other on the chair in front of it. One has graying
hair and wrinkles on her face, her upper lip, and the corners of her
mouth; the other has smooth skin, not a wrinkle on her face, an unwrinkled soul. They sit saying things to each other that they have never said
before, accompanying their words with exclamations of joy and affection, emotions so powerful that they infect the nurses in charge of the
new mother and her son. When they bring him to Henrietta so she can
give him her milk, Zahara says, "How lucky you are to have such an
adorable baby. If only I could nurse him, I would snatch him away and
run off to Ahinoam with him. Tell me the truth, Mother, would you
give him to me? I already told Dani that Grandma has a baby uncle for
him. I think he actually understood. All day he was chirping 'baby
grandpa,' and at night, before he fell asleep, he said 'baby uncle.' Oh,
Mother, if you could hear him, you would be so pleased, so pleased. I
can't begin to tell you how pleased you would be. I tell you, Mother,
Dani already loves his uncle. Really, Mother. He really loves him. And
I love him too. But, Mother, I thought I had used up my supply of love.
You brought me a brother, and new love was created. Where does it
come from? I really don't know, but I feel it stirring inside me, setting
my heart in motion, and I love him. I love you and Father and Sarah
and Tamara, all of you. I love you all. When they came and told me
Father was on the phone, when I ran and heard the news, I was so
excited I wept with joy. You know, Mother, that I don't get excited.
But I was so excited that I said to Avraham, 'Avraham, I'm going to
Jerusalem.' Avraham said, 'If you want to go, go.' So I collected myself,
took off, and here I am. Tell me, Mother, isn't it good that I came? Make
me be quiet, Mother. My heart is full because . . . because . . . How shall

I say it? My heart . . . I won't say anything. Here comes Father. Mazel tov, Father. I'll go out for a minute and wash my eyes. When I come back, we can go home together. They won't let me spend the night with you, Mother. Don't worry about my eyes. They're stinging because of the dusty road. I made our driver go as fast as he could. At that speed, all I could see was the dust in my eyes."

Once again, Manfred sat with Henrietta, and they said things we are familiar with, adding some words about Zahara—that, as she gets older, she gets more and more emotional. But her life seems to be in good order. Would that Tamara's course were as smooth. While Henrietta and Manfred were talking, Zahara managed to wash her tear-stained eyes, to go back to look at her little brother, and to find he had features like those of her Dani. Manfred had already concluded his conversation with Henrietta. If he had sat with her a thousand years, he wouldn't have added anything. For this reason, when Zahara knocked and entered, he leaped up to join her. If not for the nurse, who gave a sign indicating that Zahara must leave too, she would have stayed with her mother another hour and yet another hour—a thousand years, at least.

Father and daughter left for home. Because Zahara wanted to see Sarah and because she wanted to get to see her an hour sooner, she prevailed on her father to waste his money on a taxi that happened by, rather than wait for the bus, since there was no way of knowing when it might be in the mood to come. They arrived with the speed of an arrow and were home before they had a chance to exchange a word. They came home and found Sarah alone. Firadeus had washed the dishes, given Sarah a bath, and gone home. Tamara had gone off, for just a few minutes, to the German colony. Unless my hypothesis is incorrect, she went to the post office to send off some of her proclamations. Tamara is clever, and she knows no one would suspect that mail from the German colony comes from Jews seeking freedom.

— 23 —

From the moment Zahara entered the house, all household procedures were set on end. This applied to the food, to the cleaning, and especially to Sarah. She examined her from head to toe, changed her clothes, and combed her hair, arranging it in two braids tied with red elastics that emphasized its shiny golden lights. As soon as Herbst came home with his daughter, he realized he had someone he could depend on, that he was no longer needed to supervise. But, since he had become accustomed to staying in during the past four days, except for the hours spent visiting his wife, he chose to continue in this mode until Henrietta's return from the hospital. Herbst hadn't spent that much time at home in years. Whatever he did found favor in his daughter's eyes. Her voice was never harsh; she never said anything that irritated him. I must admit—smart as Henrietta was, and concerned as she was with her husband's welfare and peace of mind—she sometimes irritated him with her pedantic ways, which were thoroughly irrational. Much as Herbst tried to defend her, he regarded her behavior toward him in those petty matters as obstinate and cruel. As soon as Zahara came and took charge of the household, not a harsh sound was heard. On the contrary, Zahara accepted every foolish act of Manfred's, even when he himself felt he had done something improperly, as if it were meant to be done that way and as if it had been done well. Tamara, who made a pretense, at first, of keeping an eye on household affairs and on Sarah, was only too happy to pass the reins to her sister. In fact, she said to her, "From here on, it's all yours." Manfred roamed through his house and garden, books and bushes, in a state of absolute repose. He knew that he could now go to Shira and spend the whole night there, without having to invent alibis. Still, he chose to stay home. Moving from activities in his room to those in the garden, he played with Sarah, sharing her bread (actually a sand bun), listening to music made by her wind-up doll, rocking either Sarah or the doll on his lap, singing jingles learned from Ursula. Playing with little Sarah, Father Manfred browsed through the nursery rhymes he found among Tamara's books, as well as other assorted literature written for children. As he rummaged through these volumes, he was astonished to have lived in the country for so many years without considering the spiritual nourishment provided to children in the Land of Israel. His two elder daughters were raised here, so he should have taken an interest in this matter. If he happened to hear a children's poem or to pick up a children's book, he would discharge his duty with an outburst of intellectual ire: To think that they feed children such drivel, that they expect them to develop taste with these contrived rhymes! He was moved to ire rather than to serious study or an attempt at reform. Though I don't mean to compare one thing to another, or, for that matter, one man to another, I will make an exception and say that, in this respect, Manfred Herbst was very much like Julian Weltfremdt. But one of these gentlemen denounced the scholars in the Land of Israel, while the other denounced its educators. In fact, had one of them found a job, he might have instituted some educational reforms, whereas the other was content to rail against educators and their inane practices, becoming particularly irate at the poems written for children and at the entire contrived body of literature designed for young readers. He was irritated to the point of despising that entire body of literature and those who produced it.

Manfred Herbst was a man of integrity, who didn't tend to involve himself in a subject unless he was thoroughly familiar with it. Which may be why he had avoided the area of education all those years. With the birth of his son—because of which he happened to be playing with his little daughter—he begin to think about education. Hear this: he didn't pick up a book to investigate the opinions of educators in other times, but he began, on his own, to consider what would be an appropriate education for his son. I'll try to outline his opinions, what he pictured to himself in terms of how he would like to educate his son. (1) Total control of the body: the ability to fall asleep at any time and in any place, as well as a total ability to wake up whenever he likes. (2) To eat whatever he finds, without elaborate preparation, with no fuss. (3) To pronounce all words correctly. (4) To acquire an aesthetic and readable handwriting. (5) To choose a profession that will not make him dependent on others' opinions and, similarly, to avoid any individual or enterprise that leads to dependence on others' opinions. (6) To learn languages and their grammar. (7) To be meticulous in everything, to stand by his word, to keep every promise, to tell the truth even if it hurts. Manfred included many other matters in the fundamentals of education. I have chosen only a small number of them and have made no attempt to present them in any order, beyond the one in which they occurred to him.

I will now try to transmit some of his thoughts about human affairs and education. Again, I will take up each item in the order in which it occurred to him. Humanity suffers from the fact that the earliest education is in the hands of women. From birth, human beings cling to their mother's breast, and, as they nurse, they become dependent on a woman. If this was the Creator's goal, He was very successful. It is in the nature of man to be drawn toward a woman. In *Sefer Haggadah*, our compilation of ancient legends, I found the tale of a man whose wife died, leaving him an infant son. The Holy and Blessed One granted him teats, so he could nurse the child. In this splendid legend, a free-thinking storyteller proceeds to depict an ideal person: someone who doesn't depend on mother's milk. Alas, he did not tell us about this baby's subsequent development and how he related to women.

Herbst's thoughts about education were interrupted, and once again they settled on a subject I assumed he had already put out of mind. What had happened to him some time back happened that night. He lay in bed, seeing himself either with Shira in her new apartment or in the role of the man with the whip, walking with her, far away. Suddenly, an Arab approached her and did what he did. He himself had been hiding in a hollow, his eyes closed, so he wouldn't see. He fell fast asleep, only to be startled by the bite of an animal or an insect. He tried to get up and escape, but the creature's teeth were in his flesh. He was dripping blood and didn't have the energy to defend himself, let alone get up and take flight. If not for Zahara, who knocked on the door and asked if he was up yet, he would have been late to his son's circumcision.

Before I tell about this event, I should say that Herbst had announced in the newspaper that a son was born to him and his wife, giving the day, the hour, and the place of the *brit*, the ceremony that admits a male child to the covenant of our father Abraham. Actually, Herbst had considered putting an announcement in the paper as soon as the baby was born, but he reasoned: When I read in the paper that Mr. and Mrs. So-and-so announce the birth of a son, whether it says "announce" or "are happy to announce," the information is of no interest to me; this is not the case when they announce that there will be a *brit*, at a given time and place, and invite their friends to come. I can see that they mean to ask me to take part in their celebration, so I figure out what the invitation has to do with me and whether or not I should go. Tamara had said, "I don't understand these things, but, if you want to put an announcement in the newspaper, I assume you want to put it in *Ha'aretz*. Here we are, right near the office. We can stop in, if you like." Herbst said, "But I still don't know exactly when the *brit* will be. When I know the day and the hour, I'll arrange it. Why make two announcements?"

Henrietta presented her husband with a healthy and sound son. Many of her acquaintances, who hadn't seen her while she was pregnant, read on the front page of *Ha'aretz*, "Henrietta and Dr. Manfred Herbst are happy to announce the birth of a son," and were surprised that such a smart woman, at such an age, had done such a thing. When they read the rest of the announcement—"Friends are invited to the ceremony admitting their son to the covenant of Abraham"—anyone who was not otherwise occupied decided to come. Some were dressed in holiday finery, others in everyday clothes. Some brought flowers for the new mother; some sent flowers by messenger, either to Hadassah Hospital or to the Herbst home.

The circumcision ceremony, or *brit,* as it is usually called, was like all such ceremonies performed in Jerusalem and in most of our cities. Men and women were gathered in one of the ugliest rooms of Hadassah Hospital, huddled together because the space was so tight. The room was bisected by two tables filled with all sorts of cakes—large ones, small ones, tall ones, short ones—in a variety of shapes, with white, red, and green icing. There were also tarts and cookies and other kinds of baked goods. Alongside the cakes and assorted confections was a row of bottles—wines, cognac, arrack, and other beverages, both sharp and sweet—adorned with seasonal flowers. Men and women who hadn't seen each other for months were now in one place, eager to talk to one another. What often happens happened here: neighbors they saw every day kept interrupting them. But this was not a loss to everyone. You can often learn something new from a person you see every day.

Meanwhile, the *mohel,* who was to perform the circumcision, was preparing the instruments. He was a young man, a yeshiva student, skilled and expert at the job. At first, he used to perform this mitzvah for its own sake, without expecting a reward, in accordance with the age-old custom. In time, he began to consider it a skill, like any other, and charged a fee. He was of less than medium height, blond, with a tendency to plumpness, due to so many ceremonial feasts. His eyes were small, blue, and watery; his voice was slightly hoarse; his earlocks were curly, fluffy around the edges but for the most part pressed flat. He wore a clean white robe and a shiny black yarmulke. He did his job carefully, inspecting and testing the knife, the cotton, the alcohol, turning neither to the left nor to the right. But it was clear that he wished to be noticed. In fact, in his heart, he hoped that those doctors and professors, who made a point of scorning the Orthodox, were watching him and observing his hygienic procedures—unlike those of that old man, a partner in a contracting firm, who comes to perform a circumcision in plaster-stained work clothes, with a rag wrapped around an injured finger. Go and understand the workings of the mind! In Jerusalem, people are especially fond of this old man. A certain pediatrician says that, even with the dirty rag on his finger, he is more careful and more sanitary than all the other people who handle babies. The *mohel* finally turned to the crowd, inspected his fingernails in the light from the window, and inquired, disapprovingly, "Why are we putting off the mitzvah? Why not bring in the baby?"

A young nurse entered, carrying an infant enveloped in fine and delicate wrappings. Only the *mohel* noticed her. He shouted and cried out, "Welcome and many blessings." He shouted and cried out, "Elijah, angel of the covenant . . ." Everyone turned and noticed the sweet nurse with the baby in her arms. They made way for her, and Tamara came and stood in front of the nurse, to protect her little brother from harm. The *mohel* elevated the knife, inspected it again in the light from the window, and told the *sandak,* whose job it was to hold the baby, exactly how to sit, how to position his knees, how and how and how. Like most people who perform a mitzvah for pay, the *mohel* made himself conspicuous, whether or not this was necessary. Since Herbst didn't know he could have bestowed this honor on one of his guests, the *mohel* took it upon himself to recite the blessings over the wine. His voice was hoarse and hard on the ears, but most of the guests were attentive and gaped at this miracle worker, who recites prayers from memory as fluently as a cantor reading from the prayerbook.

After the circumcision, he handed the infant to his mother. All those who had come to the *brit* sat down at the brimming tables, ate, drank, and ate more. Tamara had prepared an enormous amount of food and drink, along with an assortment of things to smoke. After the first glass, the *mohel* wiped his mouth with an oddly rapid gesture, pounded on the table, and began to chant traditional verses in his hoarse voice. He then whispered something to Herbst. Herbst got up, left the room with him, and gave him the sum the nurse had suggested as payment for his services. The *mohel* demanded that he double it, arguing that he ought to be treated like a professor and paid on the same scale.

BOOK FOUR

— 1 —

That same day, in the afternoon, Henrietta came home with her male child. After changing her clothes, she stood beside her son's cradle. She studied the red, wrinkled face; the skull, oversized in proportion to the face; the little eyes, so blue in contrast to his white wrappings, and cooed at him, saying, "Now that we're home, you are all mine. No one else has any right to you. Your father is a prophet. Before you were born, he foresaw that your mother would give birth to a male child, and his prophecy has been fulfilled. You are a male child, a man. A little man for now, but in time you will truly be a man." That word, that concept, with all of its ramifications, amused Henrietta immeasurably and endlessly. Little by little, the amusement gave way to a sweet, delightful joy that soothed her soul. If I call it soul-felt joy, I think the phrase is apt.

Avraham-and-a-half came to congratulate Zahara's mother and to take Zahara back to Ahinoam. Not because of Dani, who has already forgotten his mother and doesn't mention her, who doesn't need his mother, because there is good child care in Ahinoam, which makes mothers expendable. Nor did the economy suffer from Zahara's absence, because Ahinoam's lumber factory was so successful that a member with Zahara's standing could be allowed to spend another day, and still another, away from Ahinoam. But it was Avraham who needed Zahara. He needed her, and he therefore constructed an entire philosophical scheme, roughly as follows: When a man takes a wife, he should avoid anything that suggests to him or to his wife that they can survive without each other.

So Avraham-and-a-half came to his wife in Jerusalem. He brought honey and cheese for the household, a snakeskin for his sister-in-law Sarah, and a lovely baby carriage made in the Ahinoam factory, a carriage made especially for Zahara's little brother. The carriage is made of four panels, two long and two short, that can be taken apart and put together quite simply. Anyone who has seen fathers, mothers, and babies in Jerusalem on a Shabbat afternoon—the father carrying the baby in his arms because it is tired of lying in the carriage, while the struggling mother drags an empty carriage through the bumpy streets, filling the air with its shrill squeaks, collecting dirt from the road, along with dog and cat droppings—anyone who has seen this sight will appreciate a folding carriage made in segments that can be folded like the pages of book, with wheels that can also be separated from each other. It doesn't require much imagination to see how smooth and comfortable Henrietta and Manfred's walks with their little son will be. Apart from all the actual presents, Avraham brought regards from Dani, who instructed him to welcome his little uncle. He didn't give explicit instructions, but, when Avraham went to kiss his son before leaving and told Dani that he was going to see Dani's uncle, Dani had cried out, "Uncle, uncle," referring not only to his uncle, but to his uncle's mother as well. That's really how it was, since he had also talked about "uncle's grandma."

Dr. Manfred Herbst's house was full. In the crib was an infant, named Gabriel but called Gabi, because he was so small. His brother-in-law, Avraham-and-a-half, stood over him, trying to ascertain from the lines of his face just what he had in common with Dani. Henrietta was at his side, in all her fullness. If we didn't know she gave birth nine days ago, we would think, from the fullness of her limbs and the fullness of her body, that she was about to deliver. Zahara was at Henrietta's side, waiting for an opportunity to pick up her little brother. As soon as she saw her brother, her arms began to long for the infant. Father Manfred was wandering around at some distance from them. If I include Tamara, who went to her room, unable to tolerate this fetishism—meaning the worship of a tiny morsel of flesh known as Gabriel—then the entire Herbst family and its affiliate—meaning Zahara's husband, Avraham-and-a-half—is accounted for. Herbst has expanded in every direction. He has generated four souls, augmented by two others: Henrietta at Manfred's side and Avraham-and-a-half at Zahara's side.

I'll take the time to voice my opinion about all the members of the Herbst household, beginning with little Sarah and omitting Gabriel, whose existence is still limited to the space between his crib and his wetnurse's bosom. Magicians, sorcerers, and fortune-tellers claim to be able to predict the future of such an infant. Those who judge by what they see can say about him only that he fills his mouth with milk, screams, cries, sleeps, wakes up, and fills the entire house with his screams. Henrietta and Zahara are impressed even by this; Herbst is impressed only when his son is quiet and doesn't subject the ear to his shrieks.

I'll get back to Sarah, which is where I began, though I won't dwell on her. She is still small, and worries are remote from her mind. All one can say about her is that she is native to the land and true to its ways: her needs are minimal, and her concerns few. If she hurts a finger or upsets her stomach, by the time her mother provides a remedy, she is already cured. The sun that belongs to the Land of Israel loves those who live there and cures all of Sarah's ills. Sarah put on a new dress and tore a hole in it. Her mother scolded her. She looked up at her mother with warm, astonished eyes, and pointed a finger at a patch of skin that poked through the hole, saying, "Mother, this is very much nice." She means to say that the skin showing through the hole is nicer than the fabric the dress is made from. She sometimes says, "Mother, this is very much important." I don't know where she got this abstract phrase from. In any case, when it comes out of Sarah's mouth, it is very concrete, and it unmistakably applies to skin and fabric. There are many other nice and important things to tell about her, but I'll leave them for now and move on to Zahara and Tamara. I will add just one thing: whatever she sees in the sky and on the earth, indoors and out, makes her happy. A chicken crying, starlings flying, a turkey strutting, a young ram butting, a dog's bark, cats' eyes in the dark, a rooster's cry, frogs leaping high, a bleating ewe, a cow's soft moo, the wind's force, a neighing horse, a porcupine's bristles, a donkey eating thistles, a burning match, a firefly to catch, a butterfly just hatched—all these things make her thoroughly happy. As well as Mr. Sacharson, when he engages her in baby talk. Sacharson told us she once said to him, "You're a grandpa, but you talk like a baby." If you trust what he says, it's possible that Sarah did say something of the sort. I will now turn to Zahara.

Zahara's life is in very good order. She has no financial worries, nor does she have to worry about housing. She is a married woman and the mother of a child. If she doesn't decide to follow the example of some of her friends, who leave their husbands for other men, the rest of her life will go well. Not many people are as kindhearted as Avraham. I have mentioned Avraham-and-a-half again and again in terms of spiritual qualities, such as devotion to Hebrew, integrity, and the like. Now I will mention some of his simpler qualities. I won't mention them all, but I'll single out one of them: devotion to the land, a positive quality that includes all others. He is attached to the land and to all that grows on it. You know that there is no higher value, because our entire community depends on agriculture, and, if not for the seductions of our time, it would be apparent to everyone that Israel's salvation derives from the good Lord above and the earth below.

I still have Tamara to deal with. Tamara, as you know, is still single. Many young men are courting her, and there is no end or limit to the number of young men who seek her out, only to be rejected. In another context, I mentioned Schlesinger, who was a lapsed yeshiva student. Insofar as I can judge, he is not the mate she will append to the family. Since I hate to speculate, I won't say anything about her other admirers. I won't even mention names.

The entire Herbst family is gathered together. They are all at home, with no outsiders present. Those who are in the habit of visiting the Herbst household know this isn't the time to visit, that the mother of the house is busy with an infant less than two weeks old. Even Ursula isn't at home. She went off on a trip. No one knows whether the trip will be long or short, but that is not what we're worried about. We're worried about the fact that Ursula is in Lebanon. As you well know, in these times, when the entire country is consumed by hate, it is hard to imagine a Jewish girl traveling through Lebanon—unless there is truth to the rumor that she went with a Lebanese doctor, who was taking her to see his birthplace and his family home. Darling Ursula, though we put ourselves out on her behalf, because of her rare beauty, because of her Zionist father, because she asked us for shelter, has taken up with a foreigner, whose country is an enemy. It turned out that her time with us was a brief episode, and, now that she has left us, we have no further dealings with her. Even if we have no dealings with her, her father's sorrow persists. This long-standing Zionist, who devoted his life to Zionism, who went so far as to risk his life for Zionism while at the university, was privileged to see his daughter move to Israel, where she found a home with a good Zionist family. In the end, she abandoned all that was dear to her father to cling to the son of a nation known to be hostile to us. Now that Ursula was gone, Herbst began to think about Taglicht and Tamara again. Years back, before Zahara married Avraham-and-a-half, he had entertained similar thoughts about Zahara and about Lisbet Neu. Now, whether or not he still had Lisbet Neu in mind, he abandoned his schemes about Tamara and Taglicht. If I transmit his thoughts in my own language, they are roughly these: May the One who plots, plot these affairs as He wishes and sees fit.

After Herbst undertook to write the tragedy of the woman of the court, Yohanan the nobleman, and the faithful slave Basileios, he realized and acknowledged how hard it is to connect event to event, action to action, so that they produce harmony or even pleasant disorder. Though he gave up on the tragedy, there is no end to what he learned from it.

Back to Ursula. I meant to dismiss her without further attention, since her affairs are not relevant to the tale of Shira and Herbst, but, in the end, she requires attention. Ursula Katz was lovely and charming. Her ways were altogether pleasant. Even someone such as Taglicht, who isn't taken in by surfaces, enjoyed talking to her and used to call her Droste, after Droste-Hülshoff, the delightful poet whose hairdo was like hers. Soon after arriving in the country, she found work. When she stopped working for Mustafa and Abdullah, she found a better job, with Jews. She walked out on them too, rather suddenly. When Henrietta asked her why she decided to give up such a good job, working for such fine Jews, she answered, "Jews aren't gentlemen," and would say no more. The day before the baby's *brit,* she came to see Mrs. Herbst in the hospital, to take leave of her before setting off on her trip. Mrs. Herbst didn't ask with whom she was going or other similar questions. The information we have was conveyed to us by an official at the Kupat Holim clinic. This, in brief, is the story of Ursula Katz. I won't mention her again, to avoid entangling her in the story of Herbst and Shira or in that of the Herbst family. From the beginning, I hesitated to link her affairs with those of the Herbst household. I now see that what one hesitates about at the beginning is best put aside, that what isn't put aside at the beginning will be put aside at the end, after creating disorder and confusion.

Gabriel, who is called Gabi because he's so small, fills the house with his presence. This chick, who hasn't gotten off the ground yet, is everywhere. Here, water is being heated for Gabi's bath; over there is Gabi's crib; Firadeus is hanging out Gabi's diapers; and that tall, skinny woman there, who looks half-male, would like to be Gabi's wetnurse. Her chest is flat as a board; her eyes are dry and severe. Yet she insists she produces as much milk as two wetnurses. There is also a round, plump woman, sent by Sarini, who is so eager to nurse Gabi that her milk has become a pressing weight. Sarini herself is unable to nurse Gabi, because her milk has diminished because of her sorrow because of her mad husband, because he is planning a long trip, and, if he takes such a trip in times like these, she will end up an abandoned wife. But her eyes and heart are with Mistress Herberist, which is why she sent such a fine woman to nurse Mistress Herberist's baby, as she herself had done for his sister Sarah and for her own children—the Lord alone knows how many.

A few day's before Gabriel was born, Father Manfred transferred his bedding to his study, and, once again, he spends his days and nights amid his books. But he hasn't achieved very much. He hasn't added a single note to his files. While Henrietta was in the hospital, Herbst took time off from his major work and did other things, all of which he did well. Now that he is at it again, not only does no work get done, but other things remain undone too. His fingers are ineffectual; they accomplish nothing. His books are everywhere—piled on the table, on the chairs—making it difficult to tidy up the room and sweep the dust. He really ought to clear away the books and put them back in place, but he does no such thing. He merely moves them from one spot to another. Henrietta, who generally sees what is and isn't happening, saw that he was in a bad mood, which is what tends to happen when he isn't absorbed in his work. One day, Henrietta said to Manfred, "Fred, you have to get to work. You are idle so much of the time. It's almost winter, and you have to prepare for your classes. You mustn't waste a single hour on me. As you can see, I'm surrounded by helpers and assistants dedicated to my welfare. Even Krautmeir came to see if I need her. Yet you, Fred, have been stationed here as if it is your job to take care of me." Manfred answered, "So, Mother, in your opinion, what should Fred be doing?" Henrietta answered, "In my opinion, you should sit in your room and pore over your work." Manfred said, "From what you say, Mother, it would appear that I don't sit at my desk, in my room. In that case, let me tell you this, Mother. All of last night—more precisely, most of last night—I didn't stir from my desk. What did I achieve? Only boredom. The boredom begins to bore me. You laugh at that charming phrase, Mother. It's not mine. It's Ludwig Richter's." Henrietta said, "I won't suggest ways to escape the boredom that is beginning to bore you, but I will say that you don't belong here, in this room. We have a houseful of women, which is quite enough. Stand up, Fred. Let me have a look. You've put on weight. You ought to weigh yourself." Fred said, "I, also, think I've gotten fatter. A dozen Shylocks could each take a pound of flesh from me, and it wouldn't look as if anything were missing. Everything about me is becoming slovenly. It's because I don't smoke as much." "Because you don't smoke as much?" "Yes, Henriett. Yes. Because I'm not as much of a smoker. In the past, when I felt I was missing something—and when doesn't a person feel he is missing something?—anyway, when I felt I was missing something, I used to stick a cigarette in my mouth and begin smoking. Now, Henriett, now I fill my mouth with chocolate or other sweets that turn into fat. What are you staring at?" Henrietta said, "What am I staring at? If I'm not mistaken, your belt is two holes looser than it used to be." Manfred said, "You're mistaken, Henriett, you're mistaken. I've already made an extra hole in the belt. Unless God is a little less generous with me, my belt won't have room for enough new holes. I'm already afraid I may have to make holes in the air. Most people would suggest that I work in the garden. They don't realize that gardening stimulates the appetite." Henrietta said, "You ought to walk." Manfred said, "Do you mean a stroll around my belly? Believe it or not, I already tried that." Henrietta said, "If not for the Arabs, I would tell you to go into the hills, as we used to do when we first came to Jerusalem. Oh, Fred, remember those days? On Shabbat, we used to spend six or seven hours hiking through the hills and come home jubilant and happy. I remember one Shabbat, before I had a chance to set up the burner and heat the food, you devoured everything I had prepared for dinner, except for a bottle of wine, which you drank down in one gulp. After that, you played drunk and insisted you were so hungry you would eat me. I was so silly at the time: even though I knew you were pretending, I was a little afraid you were really drunk, and, when you opened your mouth to bite me, I was afraid you really would bite me. And then the mouth that threatened to swallow me up began to overflow with kisses. Remember? It was the year I got pregnant with Tamara. Sometimes, when I think about her and her character, I wonder if she is the way she is because of how carefree we were on those walks. Fred, I don't want to submerge myself in memories; past memories interfere with current pleasures. As I said before, if not for the Arabs, I would suggest that you go for a walk in the hills. Still, there are places in Jerusalem where you can walk safely. Why don't you invite Tamara to go along? Tamara would be glad to accompany you, and you would be glad too. When it comes to bringing fathers and daughters together, there is nothing as effective as a walk."

Henrietta was silent, and Manfred was silent too. I don't know what this silence was about. It wasn't that he was tired of listening or that she was tired of talking. In any case, Manfred didn't move away from Henrietta, and Henrietta didn't move away from Manfred. After a while, she continued, "Since you mentioned Ludwig Richter, I was reminded of the walks I used to take with my father. At the time, he had been asked by Ullstein Verlag to do some drawings of the countryside around Berlin. Father, who loved Berlin and its environs more than any other piece of land in the world, didn't linger to negotiate the fee or any other details. As soon as he left the publisher's office, he filled his pack with paint and brushes, and set out to work. Father was wearing a hunting jacket; he had a small pipe in his mouth, like the one he gave you, perhaps the very same one; his eyes were fixed on his favorite landscapes. It was obvious to me at the time that Father was unaware of my existence, that he didn't see me and didn't know I was there, that I was superfluous. Just when I was convinced I was super-fluous, Father took my arm and said, 'Look, Henrietta, look at that drooping tree, that carcass of a tree. That particular tree is the one I mean to paint.' He noticed that I was surprised by his words, by his emphasis on 'that particular tree.' So he began to elaborate: 'I know the arbiters of taste will disapprove, but I will do what I like, and, if they don't like it, they can . . .' At this point, Father used one of those words that fathers don't usually use in a daughter's presence. I myself was delighted with that word, with the sense that Father was treating me as he would treat a friend. You remember Father, of course. At home he was very conventional, but I was told that he was totally transformed when with friends, that he became a different person. What do you want, Sarah? Why are you crying? Who put dirty water in your eyes? Let me wipe them, and tell me why you're crying." Sarah forgot she was crying and said, "That lady says Sarah is Sarini's child, Sarah isn't Mama's child. Gabi is Sarini's child too. Gabi isn't Mama's child. If she wants to, Sarini will put Gabi back inside her, and there won't be any Gabi." Henrietta smoothed Sarah's cheek, kissed her, and said, "Go tell that lady, 'Mama says Sarah is her best, best girl, and Gabi belongs to Mama too.' Go call Firadeus to come here, so I can tell her to tell that lady never to say such things again. Sarah is definitely Mama's own girl. Of course she is her Mama's girl." Sarah began to cry again, crying harder than at first. I don't know what made her cry now. When she began talking to her mother, she had stopped crying. Her mother's words may have made her aware of every possible sadness, which made her feel sorry for herself and brought on another round of tears. Hen-rietta picked her up, caressed her cheek, kissed and comforted her. "Why are you crying?" she asked. Sarah answered tearfully, "That lady, she took Gabi back inside her, into her heart." Henrietta said, "Gabi is tough. Gabi took one leap, and out he came. Ask your father. He'll tell you. Tell her, Father." Father Manfred said, "You believe that other lady, but you don't believe your own mother? If your mother says something to me, I listen and believe it. Isn't that so, Mother?" Hen-rietta laughed and said, "Now you'll see, Sarah, that what Father says is true. Tell Father this: 'Mother says, "Go for a walk, Father," ' and, in a minute, Sarah, you'll see Father going for a walk. Sarah, surely

you've seen Father go for walks? What's going on here? I say, 'Go tell
Father,' and you don't tell him." Manfred asked Sarah, "Tell me, Sarah,
what did Mother say?" Sarah said, "Mother said that Sarah should tell
Father that Father should go for a walk." Henrietta said, "Very good,
Sarah. I see that I can count on you, that I can give you messages and
you'll deliver them. Now, Sarah, ask Father when he plans to take his
walk." Sarah said, "What do you mean, 'when'?"

Before she could explain, there was a knock at the door. Before she
could say, "Come in," a man entered, dressed like an elder of the
Sephardic community, an elder's turban on his head and an elder's staff
in his hand. Manfred looked at him, bewildered. All sorts of odd creatures had appeared in his home, but never one like this. Henrietta
peered suspiciously at the sage. She finally said, "You're Sarini's husband, aren't you?" Sarini's husband said, "I'm not here because of the
woman called Sarini. I'm here because of something more wonderful
than a thousand women."

I will try to explain about this. The night of the day his son was
circumcised (the son born to him of the woman Sarini), a year before
Mr. Herberist's son was born (the one Sarini was supposed to nurse),
it was revealed to him that he had been appointed emissary to the Ten
Tribes and to Bnei Moshe. At first he was reluctant and replied, "Who
am I, et cetera . . . ," but his excuses were not accepted, and he was told
not to be obstinate. He has been entrusted with spells against wild
animals, highwaymen, and desert sands, for there are crazy sands in the
desert that can swallow up an entire caravan, camels, riders, and all. But
he will not be harmed, because of the spell he possesses. He is equipped
with a spell to disarm those birds of prey that aren't listed in the Torah
on account of their wickedness—birds that emit fiery sparks when they
encounter a human being, consuming him and turning him to dust.
These are the very birds that destroyed some of Alexander's armies. But
they can't harm him, because he has a spell that counteracts their power.
When they open their mouths to spew their fire at him, the sparks will
backfire and burn up their innards. They will be destroyed by this spell.
He is protected against the perils of the road, savage animals, highwaymen, desert sands, birds that spit fire. So why has he come to Herbst?
He isn't asking for help in financing the trip, for, in addition to all sorts
of trades by which he can support himself wherever he goes, he has
learned to repair stoves and, in a pinch, can also repair a sewing machine. So what does he want? He wants a letter from the Jewish
Agency, which is why he is here. He wants a letter from Mr. Herberist

to the officials of the Agency, asking them to write a letter on his behalf, addressed to the Ten Tribes and to Bnei Moshe. If, for political reasons, it is necessary to conceal this matter from the English—either some or all of it—they can be assured that no information will be extracted from him, not with tongs of fire, not with tongs of gold. If Jewish Agency officials are afraid that he may get lost, leaving them answerable for the loss of a Jewish soul, he is willing to reveal parts of his route to Herberist Samuel or to one of the Ashkenazi elders—Rabbi Kook, for example. If the Jewish Agency insists on testing him to see whether he is familiar with the route from the Land of Israel to where the Ten Tribes are, he is willing to divulge all the roads, as long as they vow not to divulge the information to anyone else until he returns safely from the Ten Tribes and Bnei Moshe. If they are afraid he may, God forbid, partake of those magical grasses and roots that allow a man to see anything he wants to in his dream, he can swear on our teacher Moses, on the Holy Tablets, on the Ten Commandments that he won't even touch any such roots or grasses. He received travel directions from an old Turk, who served in the Turkish army and was told by a high-ranking officer that it was good to befriend the Ten Tribes: they were fond of the Turks because Turks hated Arabs, and Arabs persecuted Jews.

In this period, while he was being pursued by Sarini's husband, who was pressing him to write a letter to the Jewish Agency, Herbst received a letter from abroad inviting him to contribute to an anniversary volume in honor of Professor Neu, who was going to turn seventy the following year. Even before he was invited to contribute to this book, he himself had been thinking of putting out a slim volume for Neu's birthday, and he had begun working on it. Because of Gabriel's birth, he had put it aside. Now that the invitation had arrived, he had in mind to prepare a chapter from his own book for this volume. To this end, he planned to skim through various books and journals to see what was new in the field. These books and journals could be found in two places: in the National Library at the Hebrew University on Mount Scopus or at Ernst Weltfremdt's. Normally, Herbst would go to Mount Scopus. Now he chose to go to Ernst Weltfremdt, though they had drifted apart, and he hadn't even come to his son's *brit*. But he had sent him a copy of his new book as a gift.

I am skipping over Professor Weltfremdt's conversation, which was undoubtedly of a scholarly nature. The day his major work was published, he changed his ways. He no longer engaged in conversation that wasn't scholarly, and, needless to say, he avoided conversation with anyone who wasn't a scholar. If anyone tried to involve him in university disputes, political affairs, or any similarly ephemeral matters, he would respond floridly, "My dear, dear friend, let us leave such matters to those who have nothing in their world beyond these unreal concerns, while we, my dear, dear friend, deal with our own affairs, thus bringing far more benefit to the world than any statesman or public figure." So much for Professor Weltfremdt's conversation. I am now leaving Weltfremdt's house with Herbst, who is laden with books borrowed for a month. Weltfremdt has instituted a time limit when lending books, which is an advantage to the borrower. Knowing that the books must be returned on a particular day, he will make a point of using them and be less likely to waste time.

After Herbst left Weltfremdt, he saw that he would have to take the bus to Baka, because he had so many books that it would be awkward to walk. Herbst was sorry that, now that he was in Rehavia, a neighborhood one could walk in, he had to go home, because of the books. His thoughts turned on many matters, and it crossed his mind that the entire course of his life would have been different if he didn't live in Baka. Moreover, it was clear that he must move out of Baka. It is dangerous for a Jew to live among Arabs, and he is endangering his wife and daughters, as well as Firadeus and all those who come to his house. Years back, before Rehavia existed, he and all his acquaintances were young, and an hour's walk was nothing to them, so it didn't matter to him where he lived. Now, he and his acquaintances have grown old, the city has expanded in all directions, and the Arabs have restricted the movements of Jews and drawn lines that separate one street from another, so it is difficult for a Jew to live in Baka. Before he arrived at the stop, a bus passed him by. When he got there, the next bus hadn't yet come. Herbst stood at the bus stop, his arms laden with books, his mind brimming with thoughts—among them, the foolish ones that are likely to concern a modern man, such as: My hands are full, and, if a woman I know comes by, I ought to ask how she is, but I won't even be able to lift my hand and tip my hat to her. Oh, well, Herbst observed—perhaps joking, perhaps with an ounce of sincerity—one can carry big books and think small thoughts.

The bus finally came. Since it wasn't full, Herbst could have found a seat if he hadn't been intercepted by Sarini, who was on her way to call on Mistress Herberist. She, Sarini, being a truthful person who isn't in the habit of saying Vashti when she means Esther, was prepared, at that moment, to tell Mr. Herberist the whole truth about why she was on her way to call on Mistress Herberist. This is how it was: That villain, that demon from hell, may his name be blotted out, who is her husband and the father of her children, may those who seek to count them lose their sight—that villain, that devil is possessed by madness and is determined to go to the mountains of darkness. Now that all the roads are imperiled by Ibn Saud's wars, a disaster could, God forbid, befall him, and what would become of her? She would be an abandoned wife, doomed to remain desolate for the rest of her days, and her tender young ones would be orphans by default. So she is going to Mistress Herberist, who is probably a soulmate and intimate of the wife of the Englishman who occupies Herberist Samuel's position, who can reproach that villainous husband of hers and forbid him to leave Jerusalem in a bus or a car, on a horse, donkey, camel, or mule, or on foot—not even with magic spells or the assistance of a guardian angel. Sarini interrupted herself and began shouting in a loud voice, "I stand here, my hands empty, my mouth full, while Mr. Herberist stands there, his hands so full. All because of that villain, may he be erased and defaced for having caused me such sorrow and deprived me of sense, so much so that I see Mr. Herberist, exhausted by the load he is carrying, yet make no move to help him. Give it to me, sir. The entire load. I'll take it all home for you, in my arms and on my head. Nothing—not a single page of these books—will be missing. See, you need two hands for it, but when I put it all in my basket, one hand is enough." He hesitated to entrust Sarini with books that weren't his own, that belonged to Ernst Weltfremdt, who was so fussy about his property. Her baskets aren't clean; they may even be dirty, he reasoned. She uses them to carry things home from the market, such things as meat, fish, oil—sometimes even a slaughtered chicken. What will that pedant say if he finds a speck on his book? Weltfremdt would never forgive him and, needless to say, would no longer grant him access to his bookshelves. While he was still considering, she took the books from him and put them in her basket. Sarini lifted the basket until it was at eye level and said to Herbst, "See, here they are. Like an infant in a cradle. I wish my children had found themselves such a cozy nest. You can go where you like. I'll take the books to your room and put them on your desk, one by one, in the right order, not head to tail." Herbst didn't understand what heads and tails had to do with books, but he assumed it was a metaphor for order. He smiled benignly. She smiled back and said, "I won't go with that madwoman," pointing to the bus, which she regarded as a fierce female. Herbst smiled again, said good-bye to her, and repeated, "Goodbye, Sarini. Goodbye, and thank you for making it possible for me not to go home when I have things to do in town. What should you tell Mrs. Herbst? Tell her not to hold supper for me. Now goodbye, Sarini. Goodbye."

— 2 —

As soon as his arms were emptied of his books, his mind was emptied too. He didn't know where to turn, where to go. As long as the books were with him, he knew he had to go home. Now that he was clear of the books, several paths were cleared for him, none of which was useful. Herbst was still at the bus stop where he had been standing earlier, before he gave the books to Sarini. Buses arrived and departed, but he didn't take any of them. Men and women pushed to the head of the line, and he found himself at the end of it. He let himself be pushed aside to make room for people who had to get on the bus. After standing around for a while, he realized he didn't belong there, that he didn't have to stay in line, that he didn't have to stand and wait, that there was no reason to be concerned about finding a seat on the bus. Relieved of the discomforts of waiting, he felt liberated. He could set his legs in motion and go anywhere. Anywhere. . . . Which was a problem, because he didn't want to go anywhere. He thought vaguely about going to see if Shira was at home, but he took no action. He mused: I won't bother myself with something I can do some other time. If my curiosity about Shira has subsided, I won't deliberately renew it.

The day was already dimming, and the entire earth changed its aspect. The streets suppressed their tumult, some roads turning white, others graying. The air close to the ground became black; closer to the sky, it was pink; and the air in between was nondescript, colorless. The trees on Maimon Boulevard, along with the men and women who strolled by, were engrossed in a secret they themselves were unaware of. Some of these strollers seemed to be saying: You don't realize who we are. Not in so many words, yet whoever saw them wondered who they were. After circling several streets, Herbst turned onto the one named for Rav Saadia Gaon; actually, those who name streets had foolishly omitted the title *Rav,* though they generally bestowed it on

Israel's great men. Herbst looked down over the valley, surveyed the
scene that twinkled up at him, and thought: Here we have a remnant
of Jerusalem's splendor, unblemished by new construction. How wonderful it used to be to go down into the valleys and up into the hills,
but nowadays one would be exposed to Arab gunfire and Arab knives.
He forced himself—yes, actually forced himself—to reject the fantasies
he usually indulged in about Shira's disappearance and the circumstances of her disappearance. He suddenly felt that this required no
effort; that, having recurred so often, these fantasies had lost their
intensity and no longer frightened him. I see, said Herbst, in an utterly
peaceful and expansive mood, I see that when one fantasizes a great deal
about something, it loses its intensity. If so, why hasn't Shira lost her
intensity? Is there anything in the world I have thought about as much
as I've thought about Shira? Right now, her name doesn't arouse any
emotion, but it would be worthwhile to know where she is. Isn't it odd?
You begin to count on a person, on finding that person in the places
you know he frequents. He suddenly vanishes, and you don't find him
anywhere. Someone will probably appear now and divert me. In any
case, I shouldn't have entrusted the books to Sarini. Someone else's
books should be safeguarded. I shouldn't have let them out of my hands.
But what's done is done, so I won't dwell on it. Having decided not
to dwell on the fact that he had entrusted the books to Sarini, he began
to think about Sarini's husband: Even if his trip is a total fantasy, he
gains something by leaving his home, as well as the orderly routines
that make boredom inevitable. The world isn't short on ideas, good
deeds, ideals, and love, be it the love of men and women or the love
of sublime ideals. But, when every day is identical, when everything
is the outcome or sequel of something similar, then, whether we like
it or not, ideas, ideals, and love begin to seem flawed. What can a man
do to renew himself, to give meaning to actions whose meaning is lost,
to disengage himself from routine? It may be that monks and ascetics
choose to cast aside wealth and position, and settle in desert caves, in
order to serve their gods, as our history books and our legends lead us
to believe. But there may be another reason for this choice: a need to
suspend their routines and renew their souls. Even such a simple person
as Sarini's husband, who does nothing but eat, drink, and beget children, may have felt the urge to renew his world when that divine hand
directed him, in a dream, to seek out the Ten Tribes. How Henrietta
laughed when I told her I was beginning to be bored with boredom.
I, for one, don't understand this: I went to Ernst Weltfremdt's to get
books for the article I'm writing for Neu's anniversary volume, yet here
I am, wasting my time on sheer nonsense. What is obvious is that what

I ought to do now is review my article to ascertain if there is anything
new in it, anything that will please Neu. Neu, Neu, Neu, Herbst cried
inwardly, like someone in distress crying out for help. Herbst wasn't
in distress, and he cried out only because his heart was full and he had
to express what was inside. Since he was thinking of Neu, he cried
"Neu." In such a circumstance, a naive person invokes God; a simple
person cries "Mama, Mama." Herbst, who was academically disciplined, invoked the name of the teacher from whom he had learned so
much.

Herbst, like most people, found that, having invoked a particular
name, others followed by association. Rightfully, he should have remembered Lisbet Neu. But he didn't. Either he dismissed her from his
mind, or his article was uppermost at that moment. Who can fathom
a man's mental processes? Since I mentioned Lisbet Neu, I will now
dwell on her situation.

Lisbet Neu is still employed at the same place. She works in the store
or the office eight or nine hours a day and is paid the same salary as
before. Employers are difficult, whether they are shopkeepers or run
offices. They are self-involved and don't consider their employees'
needs, especially if the employee doesn't belong to the Histadrut, in
which case the union has no power over them. Even members of the
new society in this old–new country, most of whom came here to live
a new life—a proper and ethical one—fail to restate that old rule to
themselves, the one we have to behold anew every day: "And your
brother shall live *with* you." If not for the threat of strikes and Histadrut disputes, most of our self-righteous brothers would be willing to
ignore their employees' way of life, expecting them to work until they
expire but being careful to avoid getting stuck with the burial expenses.
So Lisbet Neu works eight or nine hours out of the twenty-four in a
day for a paltry salary, supporting herself meagerly. Lisbet Neu has
already despaired of finding a man, so she works doubly hard. Her
employer is pleased. He is generous with compliments, but he doesn't
raise her salary. Leaving the business in her hands, he sleeps late, stays
at home entertaining guests, and goes abroad in the summer. Lisbet
Neu is dependable, and he depends on her. Nothing seems to have
changed in Lisbet Neu's life, except that she has made friends with
several young women, the daughters of parents who came from Germany, with whom she spends Shabbat evenings reading the weekly
Bible portion along with the commentary of Samson Raphael Hirsch.
Hirsch's language is complex, and not everyone understands it. But
Lisbet, who pored over his books back in Germany, interprets for them,
drawing deep meaning from his well of ideas. Some young women

pore over the magazines that come from abroad, studying the pictures to learn what dress one wears on which day, at which hour, in which company; what creams are suitable for skin and teeth; which cosmetics are used by the most genteel women. Lisbet Neu and her friends find contentment in the Torah and the commentaries. Believe it or not, they are well dressed; their teeth are bright, their scent appealing. When Herbst first knew Lisbet Neu, he responded to a scent of innocence that seemed to pervade her person.

Herbst had forgotten when he last saw Lisbet Neu. Other concerns burdened his memory, and there was no room in it for an Orthodox young woman with whom he was acquainted only because she was related to his mentor and guide, Professor Neu. But Lisbet Neu remembers Herbst and thinks of him. Two years ago, she heard that his daughter was married; a year ago, she heard that his daughter had a son; not long ago, she heard that he had a son. Each item led to emotional turmoil. According to convention, she ought to congratulate him, either orally or in writing. Since she wished him well, she surely ought to congratulate him. But, whenever she sat down to write, her hand began to falter, and she thought: Won't it be a bother to him, as if I wanted to force him to relate to me? Once these thoughts crossed her mind, she decided that the less said, the better. But, after choosing not to write to him, she began to worry that this was rude. She did, after all, know him. They had gone on several walks together; he had invited her out for coffee and talked to her. And still she hadn't found time to write two or three words to him. Her mother had even remarked, "Lisbet, you ought to write a note to Dr. Herbst." Imagine this: Herbst remembered everyone who came to his son's *brit* and exactly who came to congratulate Henrietta when she was in the hospital. He even remembered Dr. Krautmeir, who found it necessary to visit Henrietta at home and ask if she could be helpful, despite the fact that they were not on good terms with each other. Yet it didn't occur to him that Lisbet Neu had not come to congratulate him. That's how people are. One person thinks about another endlessly and interminably, yet there is no room at all for him in that other person's mind.

Herbst strolled through Rehavia without going into anyone's house. Two or three times, he sat down on those benches on Maimon Boulevard, but he didn't stay long, because of the couples who needed no witness for their embraces. Hearing the echo of kisses all around him, he thought: These boys and girls imagine I am here to interfere with their lovemaking, but I don't care about them at all. After a few hours, he decided he ought to go home. Even though Henrietta wasn't holding dinner for him, he should have been home already. So he said to himself: We are going home. He wasn't pleased to be going home, just as he hadn't been pleased to be roaming around idly. He had been granted a certain number of hours and had done nothing with them. He felt a sudden weariness in his limbs. Not physical weariness, but emotional weariness—the kind that comes from idleness, from the fact that he had planned to do something and had allowed the time to pass, doing nothing with it because he didn't know what to do. Despite his fatigue he had a desire to walk home, through Talbieh, through the vegetable patches, the fields, the gardens, past the lepers' colony, around Mekor Hayim to Baka. He loved these roads, especially at night, when there was no one to disturb him and he could walk on and on, thinking while he walked. Here was the scent of a grass he knew by name and scent; here, the sound of a small animal; the stare of a dog who recognized him and didn't bark, or barked to announce that he recognized him. Many other adventures, endless and infinite, occurred on the way. Even the telegraph wires in that area have a hum that is not metallic, and, without overresponding to this sound, it would not be far from the truth to compare it to that of rustling garden fences, to the chatter from rooftop nests. But woe unto him who strays from the populated territory, for, with every step, he endangers his life. For this reason, he turned away from all these pleasures and toward Jaffa Road, to wait for the bus to Baka.

Jaffa Road was quiet and serene, with no visible sign of the times. Perhaps this in itself was a sign of the times: the fact that this raucous street was quiet that night. Streetlamps gave off their dim, muted light. In a burst of romantic excess, the head of the municipality, who regarded himself as the last of the Crusaders, ordered streetlamps for Jerusalem with their glass panels divided into twelve sections, to match the tribes of Israel. Jews build synagogues with a window for each of the twelve gates of prayer, so each tribe's prayers can enter the heavenly gates in comfort, while this chivalrous would-be Crusader designs Jerusalem's streetlamps in a way that restricts our light. Here and there, two or three lights shone from windows in the two hotels across from the bus stop. Most of the windows were dark, however. The rooms were unoccupied. Not many people came to Jerusalem in those days, because the unrest brought on by the Arabs made the roads dangerous. What was true of the hotels was true of the stores. And of the entire street as well.

Herbst had been waiting for about half an hour, and no bus had come. Even more strange was the fact that there was no one else at the bus stop. What's this, another curfew? He hadn't heard a curfew being announced. Were his ears so used to it that it no longer registered? He had seen policemen on the street, and they hadn't stopped him, which suggests that there is no curfew, that the streets just happened to be deserted. He was overwhelmed with another terror: that he would have to stand there—who knows for how long?—because the drivers, expecting no passengers, come at such infrequent intervals. It would be a long wait for the bus, if it came at all. These bus companies exist, not to serve the public, but to milk it. Now that the public is ineffectual and no longer fills their pockets with money, why bother? Herbst looked around for a taxi, even though his finances were tight, more so now that he has an added child who needs a wetnurse. Nevertheless, he decided to take a taxi. Sarini meant to do him a favor when she took his books. In the end, he was losing time and money because of her; he would have to spend fifteen grush on a taxi. Since he didn't find a taxi, he continued to wait, contemplating Sarini's favor, and from this subject his mind shifted to her husband.

So Sarini's husband wants to travel to the Ten Tribes. He has a good life with Sarini. She prepares his food and makes his bed, and he has only to entertain himself with adventures. A man leaves home, not necessarily in pursuit of adventure, in pursuit of an ideal, in pursuit of God. A man might run off because he is too comfortable where he is. No bus is coming, is coming, Herbst said to himself, thinking: I sound like Ernst Weltfremdt, who repeats the ends of phrases over and over. However, I must admit that his book is good. Herbst strained to see if a bus was coming. There was no bus in sight.

A woman appeared, holding two baskets, with a cigarette vendor's box stuffed inside of each one. The woman addressed him in Yiddish. "Why are you standing here, Uncle?" Herbst looked at her in surprise. What sort of question is that? If someone is standing at a bus stop, it's a sign that he wants to go somewhere. He answered her pleasantly, in Yiddish, making an effort to match his manner of speaking to hers, in style as well as language. This is what he said to her: "My dear Auntie, this uncle of yours would like to go to Mekor Hayim. Not actually to Mekor Hayim, but to a place on the way to Mekor Hayim, and he is waiting for the bus to come and pick him up." The woman said, "You might as well be waiting for the downfall of villains. The bus you are waiting for won't come." Herbst said, "Why won't it come?" The woman said, "Because the Englishman doesn't want it to." Herbst said, "The Englishman doesn't want it to? Why not?" The woman said, "Because. Who can fathom the mind of an Englishman? He himself may not know why. All he knows is that he has to issue decrees, so he issues decrees. Maybe you know why it bothered him that the bus stop was here, why he suddenly decreed that it had to be moved? Come with me, neighbor, and I'll show you the new bus stop. It's not far, but you'll never find it without me." Herbst said, "We're probably late." The woman said, "Late? Late for the bus? I'm sorry I don't have the energy to laugh. We'll never be late, we'll never be late. The driver waits for the bus to fill up, and still he doesn't budge. Why? Because, even if the bus is full, another passenger or two might come. Otherwise, it's not worth his while. Now that there are so few passengers, he even waits for a poor woman like me." Herbst asked the woman, "Do you come home this late every night?" She answered, "You think you've found yourself someone who is out late every night? Most nights, dear Uncle, I've said my bedtime prayers by now. You might ask, 'Wherefore is this night different from all other nights?' so I will answer that question. We used to be slaves to Pharaoh in Egypt; now we are slaves to the English. A policeman found me peddling my wares without a permit. Tell me this, neighbor: if I had bought a permit for a lira, would the English queen be able to afford an extra feather for her Shabbat bonnet? But I won't be silent. I already saw Moshkeli Royt. I'm hoping he'll use his influence with the Englishman to have my fine revoked. I know you call him Rabbi Royt, but he is as much a rabbi as I am a rabbi's wife. Rav Samuel, of blessed memory, was a genuine rabbi. He was a *rav* in Jerusalem for seventy years, but did anyone call him Rabbi? He was known as Rav Samuel, a title that applies to any proper Jew. Now, anyone who wants to calls himself a rabbi. In any case, it's Royt's duty to keep them from stealing a poor woman's money, though he thinks he does his duty when he feuds with the Zionists. Oy, oy, dear neighbor of mine, the Zionists are the source of all our troubles. It's because of them that the English are here. Here is the stop, and here is the bus. What did I tell you? It's waiting for us. No need to hurry. You can board slowly. By the time he decides to move, you could have walked home at least twice." Though she was still talking to Herbst, she turned to the driver and said, "Getzel, did you hear me? It's true, isn't it?" Getzel said, "When don't you tell the truth? When the policeman stopped you with two boxes full of cigarettes, and you told him they were for your husband, weren't you telling the truth? What did that goy say? 'Do you have so many husbands that you need so many cigarettes?' In the end, you were punished for your version of the truth." The woman said, "Is it truth they're after? They want lies. If I told him the truth, how would that help? Try telling him I'm a poor woman with a houseful of orphans, whom I—I alone—am responsible to feed, dress, shoe, educate. I slave and struggle, drag myself around with these boxes of cigarettes. Maybe you could get your bus to move on, sweetie, so we don't have to wait until tomorrow. What are you waiting for? The bus is full."

— 3 —

Herbst sat on the bus, compressing himself so as not to impinge on his neighbors' space. The bus was very old, one of the oldest, a survivor from the country's first generation of buses. The seats were arranged with two rows running along the sides of the coach and one across its width. They were tattered and worn, with springs that popped out and poked the passengers. The bus company knew that in bad times people are so pleased to be able to go home that they don't notice what they are riding in. Herbst was pleased, too, that he had found himself an inch of space, and especially pleased that he was going home with no secret to conceal from Henrietta.

Henrietta was awake. She still hadn't accustomed her son to do without a ten-o'clock feeding. She didn't actually feed him; a wetnurse, brought in by Sarini, performed that function. But it was Henrietta who prepared the baby for his feeding, then waited until it was time for him to eat.

Manfred came in quietly, so as not to wake the baby. But he wanted Henrietta to hear that he was back. Not because he had anything to say to her, not because he wanted to ask about her or the baby, but for the following reason: if she asked, "Where were you," he could answer honestly, "I was in a certain place, on a certain bench, on a particular boulevard," and so on. He was in a position to enumerate all the places he had been; they were all legitimate and in no way suspect. This was one purpose. Another purpose: should he have occasion to go to a place he wouldn't choose to tell his wife about, the present information would compensate for what he would conceal from her in the future.

The table was set with a light meal, covered by netting, and a thermos bottle. Before Manfred had a chance to take a bite, Henrietta

began talking. She reported that Sarini had brought the books and left
them in his room. When she said "the books," he detected a note of
complaint about money wasted on luxuries, when she needed every
penny for the household. When she heard that the books were borrowed from Ernst Weltfremdt, she was startled, remembering the
poem Rika Weltfremdt had composed for her and the new baby. She
had forgotten to tell Manfred about it. If Rika had asked him about the
poem, he wouldn't have known anything about it, which would imply
that she had so little regard for it that she hadn't thought to mention
it to her husband. But there was no cause for worry. Herbst had spent
about an hour and a half with Ernst Weltfremdt, but Rika Weltfremdt
didn't show her face. Ernst Weltfremdt makes a point of not having
his wife appear in his room when he has a guest, because, when she
comes in, the guest feels obliged to ask how she is, and this interrupts
his conversation.

Manfred wasn't pleased—not with himself and not with Henrietta's
conversation. Though he had every reason to know that Henrietta
wouldn't burden him with Rika Weltfremdt's verses, he was afraid she
intended to read them to him. Determined to spare himself, he said to
her, "I'm not willing to waste even a minute on them." Henrietta
looked at him, bewildered. She was about to respond, but she kept her
mouth shut and was silent, knowing that, if she began talking, they
would end up quarreling. And, after months of peace, it didn't make
sense to have a fight. She looked at him again, trying to find a reason
for his sullenness. One minute, she wanted to scold him, to say that,
if he was in a bad mood, he needn't take it out on her. A minute later,
she felt sorry that he was in such a state. Manfred himself knew that
he hadn't behaved well and tried to placate her, but he didn't want to
say anything openly conciliatory, for that might call attention to his
foul humor. He changed his manner abruptly and said in a firm voice,
"Your boy is taking the lifeblood out of you." Henrietta understood
that he meant to placate her, but his words were irritating, for he had
said "your boy." Henrietta said, "You talk about 'your boy' as if he
were some street child I took in just to annoy you." Manfred said,
"That's not so, Mother. I said that only . . . How can I explain it? Only
. . . for no reason. Just like that." Henrietta said, "Besides, I have the
impression something is not right." "Not right?" Henrietta said, "Everything is all right with me. I'm talking about you, Manfred. I suspect
that something is not so right with you." Manfred said, "When I look
at myself, I see that I've never been in better shape. I don't have a
mirror, but I'm certain that even my tie is straight and in place. Isn't

it, Mother?" Henrietta laughed and said, "You're wrong about that. Your tie happens to be disheveled and askew. I hope you yourself are in better shape." Manfred said, "If it hadn't been a present from you, I would say I myself am in better shape. Since it was a present from you, I would say I'm a rag by comparison." Henrietta laughed and said, "Don't exaggerate, Fred. Hand me my handkerchief." He gave her the handkerchief. She knotted it and said, "Many thanks, Fred. Unless I forget to look at the knot, I'll buy you a new tie, even before your birthday." "Why all of a sudden?" Henrietta said, "So when you say that, compared to your tie, you look like a rag, there will be some truth to your words." Manfred said, "That's what I like about you, Henriett. It's really possible for a person to talk to you, Henriett." Henrietta looked at him and said, "With whom isn't it possible for you to talk?" "With whom isn't it possible for me to talk? You want me to list everyone, beginning with Adam and Eve?" Henrietta said, "And I assumed you had a particular person in mind. A particular woman, to be precise." "A woman?" Manfred cried in alarm. "Is there a woman in the world I have any wish to waste a single word on?" Henrietta said, "If I weren't your wife, I would be interested in talking to you." "Since I am, alas, your husband, you aren't interested in talking to me? Well, it's already ten o'clock, and I'm keeping you from resting your weary bones. If I weren't afraid of offending you, I would leave right now and go off to my room." Henrietta said angrily, "You can go if you like. I'm not stopping you." Herbst said, "That's not how it is, Mother. Don't be angry. You have an odd way of getting upset, all of a sudden. I had your welfare in mind, your need for rest, and you are offended. You tell me: would I want to hurt you?" "You wouldn't want to hurt me, but you've gotten into the habit of saying things that are irritating and painful." "From here on, I will weigh every word before I utter it. Incidentally, has your boy gained any weight?" "My boy is upholstered with fat; he no longer gets cold, as he did a week ago." "It all comes from milk?" "Fred, you don't know how cute you are with your questions. Where does the fat come from? Your cigarettes, perhaps. Mimi was here again. I assumed she wasn't satisfied with seeing me in the hospital, then again on the day of the *brit*—that she wanted to see more of me. But this time she came on your behalf." "On my behalf? I don't feel . . . How shall I say it? I don't feel there is anything about me that would attract her." "But you would like to attract her?" "Why not?" "You old sinner, is that how it is?" "So she came on my behalf. Why does she want me in particular, when I won't scold or abuse her?

Isn't she content with Julian's scolding and abuse? Some women are peculiar: the more a man scolds them, the more attached they are to him. All he needs is a whip to beat her with." "Phew, Fred, I don't think there is a woman anywhere who would be attracted to a man who beats her." "I don't think so either. I don't think there is a woman anywhere who would tolerate a whip. Now, back to the subject of Mimi. So Mimi was here, and she came on my behalf. What does a woman like that want from me?" "What does she want from you? She wants something that doesn't please me. I told her in no uncertain terms that you are cutting down on smoking." "Now I understand. She's trying to help that fellow again, that cigarette merchant of hers! Don't you think Tamara smokes too much? I think I hear a cough coming from her room." "It doesn't sound like Tamara." "Then who is it?" "The woman who nurses the baby. It's time for you to go now, Fred. She just woke up, and she'll be here in a minute." "Good night, Henriett." "Is that it, Fred? I need a kiss first, then a *l'hayim,* then a goodbye." "May you have many long years, Henriett. I could learn a lot more from a woman like you." Herbst went up to his room, stuck a cigarette in his mouth, and lit it with heightened passion, having refrained from smoking the entire time he was with Henrietta, so as not to pollute the baby's air. As he smoked, he surveyed the two heaps of books on his desk. He laughed derisively, reflecting to himself: When it comes to spiritual matters, women and illiterates make the most trustworthy agents. Sarini arranged the books precisely as they were when she took them from under my arm. This woman doesn't know the alphabet, but her memory is formidable. She remembered what order the books were in and placed them on my desk accordingly. Here they are, in two piles, one large and one small, precisely as they were before she took them from me to put in her basket; the large pile is on the right, the smaller one on the left. At that moment, he had no desire to look at the books he had borrowed. But, out of habit, he opened one, then another, and glanced at them without reading them. Meanwhile, he finished his cigarette, discarded it, took another, and began pacing the room, as though troubled by his thoughts. Actually, he wasn't troubled by any thought, but, as he paced back and forth, it seemed to him that there was something he could have done but didn't do. He lit the cigarette and reviewed what he had done that day, including the fact that he had been near the alley where Shira's new apartment was and hadn't stopped by to see if her door was open. He smiled that derisive smile again, directing it at himself. If so, he observed, I am a hero, one of those heroes who control their own impulses. He crushed the cigarette with his fingers and disposed of it. He set his watch, undressed, and looked at his watch again, because he wasn't sure he had set it. After a while, he went to bed, taking a book, as usual, but turning out the light even before he opened the book, which was not usual. He observed to himself: Tonight, having done nothing but walk a lot, I'll fall asleep without a book and without the preoccupations that disrupt sleep. However, something did disrupt his sleep. It seemed to him that it was the anniversary of his father's death, that he ought to say *Kaddish* for him, but he didn't have a *minyan,* a quorum of ten. Bachlam appeared, and Herbst considered asking him to join the *minyan.* Bachlam began to enumerate his aches, his books, his admirers, his enemies. Herbst didn't have the nerve to interrupt, in order to say *Kaddish* for his father, which upset him very much. When he woke up, he was still disturbed, and he began to scrutinize himself and to have misgivings about his own behavior. He searches for Shira, but, when he is near her apartment, he doesn't go to see if she is in. He then returns to his wife and considers himself innocent, pleased to have earned a night's credit to be applied toward a future act that would have to be concealed from her. Even his transactions with Bachlam were improper, for he had begun to court him in the hope of winning his support for a promotion. These thoughts about the *Kaddish* he should have said for his father reminded him of a verse from a Heine poem on the subject, which reminded him of yet another poem that goes roughly like this: *"Darf man die Welt beluegen / Ich sage nicht nein, / Doch wilst due sie betrugen / So mach est nich fein."*

It was already lunchtime, but he hadn't been called for lunch. He had already smoked a cigarette, meaning to allay his hunger, and still he wasn't called. He thought of going downstairs to remind Henrietta that it was lunchtime; that he was hungry; that, even before it was lunchtime, he had been hungry, very, very hungry, really hungry; and, now that it was in fact lunchtime, it was surely time to eat. That's how Henrietta is: she is so orderly and meticulous about having things done on time, yet, when he is hungry and it's time to eat, it doesn't matter to her that it's lunchtime. Is she so busy with the baby that she lost track of time? He may have to go down to the kitchen and remind her that it's time for him to eat. He knows it won't help; that, until he is called to eat, nothing will help; that he might, on the contrary, confuse Henrietta and delay her further. He doesn't really mind about confusing her, except that confusion might lead to anger, and he doesn't want to make her angry. Anyone who has enjoyed several months of domestic harmony isn't eager to get involved in strife. He reached for the cigarettes again, meaning to take one, but he took two. It was because he was so befuddled that he took two. Seeing what he had done, he meant to put one down and light the other. Because he was so befuddled, he put them both down. Meanwhile, he heard footsteps. Firadeus was on the way to his room, leaping up the steps. Then, remembering that was not the proper way, she slowed down. Herbst thought: They're finally coming to call me. My fingers were better informed than I was. They put down the cigarettes even before I heard anyone coming.

Firadeus appeared. She was small, young, weary; weary from the troubles in her mother's house, weary from the work in her mistress's house, which was compounded the day they brought the baby home. Two shining eyes, a fiery mix of reticence and humility, illuminated her pale, dark face. Rarely do eyes convey a message and its reverse at one and the same time; where there is reticence and humility, how can there be such fire? She entered, accompanied by the good smell of peaches, which she brought on a small tray that had been made in Damascus. Herbst gazed at the peaches and inhaled their fragrances, hoping it would quell his hunger. It didn't occur to him that the fruit was for him, because Henrietta was strict about not eating before meals. If fruit was being brought to his room, he couldn't assume it was to be eaten, for Henrietta was not likely suddenly to change her ways. "What is this?" Herbst asked. "You're bringing fruit? Your mistress knows I love fruit, so she sent me some. But it isn't time for fruit now, is it?" He consulted his wristwatch to see if he had misjudged the time. He looked up at Firadeus and said, "It isn't really time for fruit now. Do you, by chance, know what moved our mistress to send up such a thriving garden? I have never seen such splendid peaches, not this year, not the year before. Do you know, Firadeus, if not for Persia, there would be no peaches in the world. Persia is a country that cultivates peaches. I can tell from these peaches that we won't be eating lunch today. Do you happen to know how lunch has sinned to keep us from eating it today?" Firadeus said, "I was told to say we'll be eating later." "Later? Why not now?" Firadeus said, "A guest has arrived." "A guest? Who is the guest?" Firadeus said, "A nurse from the hospital." Even before Herbst heard what Firadeus was saying, he heard himself whisper, "She has finally come." Even before he heard himself whisper, he felt his heart begin to flutter with yearning. He was quick to relax his

left hand, so he wouldn't place it on his heart and let Firadeus see he
was upset. He looked up at her boldly, eyed her fiercely, to inform and
forewarn her that she was to tell the truth, that he would countenance
no deception. He finally asked, in a voice that was neither bold nor
fierce, "What does the nurse look like?" Firadeus repeated his question,
without understanding what he wanted to know. Herbst stared at the
new apron Firadeus was wearing. He stared at the wildflower pattern
on the apron and asked, "Is she old or young?" Before she could answer
him, he twisted his lips in a mock smile and added, "Is she very old?"
Firadeus answered, "She's not young or old. Just some woman who
works with the sick." Herbst said, "Maybe you can describe her to me.
You did see her; what does she look like?" Firadeus said, "She wears
a nurse's kerchief that covers her head, as well as her hair, and white
clothes. A nurse's uniform, like the ones Ashkenazi nurses wear."
Though Firadeus tried to describe everything about that nurse, she was
very sorry not to be able to describe the nurse's face to her master's
satisfaction. Herbst asked Firadeus, "Was she invited to have lunch
with us?" Firadeus said, "The mistress didn't say anything to me."
"The mistress didn't say anything to you? She didn't say anything to
you about the nurse, such as, 'Add a dish, a spoon, a fork'? When a guest
is invited to a meal, you add a plate, a bowl, a knife, a fork. But what
do I know about these matters? You, Firadeus, can't tell me who the
guest is?" Firadeus turned a bewildered face to her master and stared
at him, bewildered and distraught, distraught and bewildered. She had
told him explicitly that the guest was a nurse from the hospital. Why
did Mr. Herbst persist in questioning her, when he had already heard
the answer. She wanted so much to please him by telling him what he
wanted to know, but what was there for her to do when this was
impossible? An Ashkenazi girl would know how to answer, but she
doesn't. Now, when Mr. Herbst wants to know, she can't tell him, and,
even if Mr. Herbst doesn't hold it against her, he probably regrets the
fact that she can't do what would be simple for an Ashkenazi to do. She
was saddened by the fact that there was something she couldn't do for
her master, something that seemed so simple to him. She stood reticent
and humble, her eyes seething with sadness, like her father when he
found a hat in the trash near a house in Talpiot and took the hat to the
owner, who told him what he told him. Herbst suddenly altered his
tone and said; "I shouldn't be keeping you, Firadeus. You are probably
needed downstairs. Did the nurse just happen to come, or was there
something wrong with the baby? Do you know if that nurse was ever
in our house before?" Herbst knew that no nurse had ever been in the

house, and he knew that Firadeus could answer that she had never seen a nurse in his house. He therefore altered his tone again and said, "Now, Firadeus, it's time to eat some of these splendid peaches. I've never seen peaches like these. If I were to examine them with a magnifying glass, I wouldn't find any freckles on them. Tell me this: does that nurse have freckles on her face? You don't know what freckles are? The singular is *freckle;* in the plural, we say *freckles.* I see that I'm detaining you, and they are probably missing you by now."

When Firadeus left, Herbst sat alone, pondering: Henrietta has a guest, a nurse from the hospital. Anyone who has no illusions would know the guest is not Shira. She is just some nurse who attended Henrietta in the hospital, who no doubt promised to visit and came today, keeping her promise, which Shira didn't do. Shira might have also done so, if nothing had transpired between us. Once again, he reviewed the incident in the telephone booth, when he spoke with her there, as well as his visit to her house and her room, which took a turn he wouldn't have thought possible, as well as what transpired the following day, when Henrietta herself put them in each other's hands. Herbst sat reviewing everything that had transpired with Shira. There wasn't anything that he didn't remember, nor was there anything he forgot. He didn't omit anything that transpired with Shira, and he especially didn't omit those things that did not occur between them. He was even more keenly aware of what did not occur between them than of what did, as if what did not occur was the essence. And, that being what he lacked, he would be keenly aware of this lack forever. Now Shira has exceeded everything. She doesn't show herself; she simply doesn't show herself. She has absented herself from the places she used to frequent. She has vanished, vanished so that she can no longer be found. It would be worthwhile to know where she is. He said it would be worthwhile, and his heart began to flutter with yearning, so that he knew he would have no rest until he finds her. He reached for the tray, to take another peach, not realizing he had finished them all, that there was no fruit left. But the fruit he had eaten did not satisfy him. As a matter of fact, it stimulated his appetite. He deliberated awhile and told himself: If I go downstairs, I'll surely find her. He knew clearly that the guest wasn't Shira; that, since she wasn't Shira, he had no interest in her; that all nurses were the same to him, and he had no need to go and see which one was sitting with Henrietta. Nonetheless, he got up to go downstairs.

When he opened his door, the downstairs door opened and the nurse came out. She was taking leave of Henrietta. Herbst already knew she wasn't Shira, but he wanted to see and be convinced that she wasn't Shira. He alerted his ears to listen to the nurse's voice as she said goodbye to Henrietta. Hearing it, he immediately knew her voice wasn't Shira's voice. But he held his breath so he could hear. Was she Shira or was she not Shira? After a while, Firadeus came back again. She came to tell him, "The mistress says lunch soon will be ready."

— 4 —

So as not to delay Sarah and Firadeus, one of whom had to nap after lunch, while the other had to go home and prepare a meal for her mother and brothers and sisters, Henrietta instructed Firadeus to serve herself and Sarah, to sit down and eat, rather than wait for the nurse to leave. Which is why he found Henrietta alone when he came down to lunch. Manfred glanced at Sarah's empty chair and said, "Where is the little one? Did she misbehave? Is she not being allowed to eat with the grownups because of something she did?" Henrietta said, "Sarah's napping." Manfred repeated, "She's napping?" Henrietta said, "She has already eaten. It didn't make sense to have her wait for us to sit down and eat." Manfred rolled his eyelids comically and said, in a tone that made it clear he was anxious to know who had been visiting Henrietta, "So you had important company?" Henrietta said, "How do you know it was important company?" Manfred extended the palm of his hand and said, "There are several clues." He flexed one finger and said: "Because, one, you postponed lunch on account of the visit; two, the guest must be very special if our meal was deemed unworthy of him." Henrietta gazed at him questioningly, "And three?" Manfred said, "Anyone who takes the liberty of calling on Mrs. Herbst is an important person. Who was here—who is he, that you starve your heart's chosen mate because of him?" Henrietta said, "Not because of him; because of her. If I starved you, I did at least send you peaches. If not for that guest, you would never get to see such splendid fruit outside of a display case." Manfred said, "So how did you get the peaches? Did you smash the display case to get them for me?" Henrietta said, "At least you enjoyed them?" Herbst said, "I didn't enjoy them, I didn't enjoy them at all. How could I take pleasure in food, knowing someone was with you, tormenting you with conversation?" Henrietta said, "As it happens, Fred, the guest's conversation didn't torment me at all. As a matter of fact, the entire conversation was a revelation of sorts." Manfred stretched his neck from right to left, peered at her, and said, in a tone that conveyed curiosity, "Is that so? Is that so? It would be nice to hear about that conversation, which was so pleasant that you found it to be 'a revelation of sorts.' I ought to admit that I myself don't know what 'a revelation of sorts' is. In any case, I imagine the guest told you great and important things. If it doesn't involve divulging secrets, maybe you could tell me what that gentleman told you." Henrietta said, "You sound exactly like your daughter." Manfred said, "I sound like Zahara?" Henrietta said, "Is Zahara your only daughter? It seems to me that, apart from Zahara, you have two other daughters." She extended her hand, as Manfred had done earlier, and flexed a finger, saying, "One, Tamara." She flexed another finger and said, "Two, Sarah." Manfred said, "In what way do I sound like Tamara?" Henrietta said, "Why do you pick Tamara? I'm thinking of Sarah." "Sarah? Do I stammer like a child?" Henrietta said, "One, Sarah doesn't stammer; two, it's not a stammer I'm referring to. I'm referring to grammar." "Grammar? You've been studying grammar? Hurray, Henrietta. Hurray. You know my views: one cannot know a language without knowing its grammar. Which is to say that any language that isn't native cannot be acquired without studying its grammar. Who is teaching you? Taglicht? He knows Hebrew, but he surely doesn't know grammar. Let me tell you a paradox of sorts. Grammar is our province—the province of Germans. Among East European Jews, there are those who know grammar. But their knowledge is intuitive; it comes from the heart. They can't externalize it and teach it to others. So, what is all this grammar talk about?" Henrietta said, "Are you thinking of Sarah's grammar? When Sarah wants to say, 'Sarah loves Daddy,' she says, 'Sarah loves his Daddy.' " "What? She still doesn't distinguish between masculine and feminine?" "As a matter of fact, she does distinguish. When she refers to Zahara, she says, 'Sarah loves her Zahara'; when she refers to Zahara's husband, she says, 'Sarah loves his Avraham.' This also applies to hate. Referring to a male, she uses the masculine form of the pronoun for herself; referring to a female, she uses the feminine form." "And for her brother?" "She doesn't mention her brother at all. It's as though he didn't exist." "She ignores him?" "She doesn't ignore him, but she would like us to ignore him." Manfred said, "It's hard on a woman who is used to be being the center of the universe to have her place usurped." Henrietta said, "A woman! You consider Sarah a woman and assume my visitor was a man. My dear

Fred, what is happening to you?" Manfred said, "So it was a woman
who was here. Someone I know?" Henrietta said, "I don't keep a
catalogue of all the women you know." Manfred said, "Bravo, Henriett, bravo. If I were to adopt Sarah's language, I would say, 'Manfred
loves her Henriett.' How gracious you are, Henriett, to assume I know
women other than my own Henriett. That woman couldn't have found
a better time to visit? She had to come at a time when company is
unwelcome?" Henrietta said, "She truly couldn't find another time.
Nurses who work in hospitals are busy. She had a bit of free time and
wanted to see how I am doing. Needless to say, she especially wanted
to see the baby. She was the one who brought us the peaches. An
effendi, whose wife bore him a live child in Hadassah Hospital, brought
her fruit from his garden, and she brought some to us." "What do you
mean, 'a live child'?" Henrietta said, "A live child and not a dead one.
Year after year, she bore dead babies. Thanks to Hadassah and thanks
to our doctors, his wife finally bore him a living child. Fred, we're
developing to the point where very soon we won't be able to talk to
each other. You don't seem to understand what I say anymore, and you
question every word. I wanted to tell you some of what the nurse told
me, Fred, but I see I won't even get to begin." "Why?" "Why? There
you go again. I can't say a word without being asked a thousand
questions." "A thousand questions? That's an exaggeration." "Nine
hundred and ninety-nine may be more precise. My dear Fred, go and
have a rest." "And the story the nurse told you will keep until I get
up?" "I'll have to decide whether to tell it to you." Manfred said, "I see
you're cross with me. Incidentally, I meant to ask: considering the
animosity between the two of you, how did Dr. Krautmeir explain her
visit?" Henrietta was stunned and surveyed her husband in wonderment tinged with suspicion. Manfred felt uneasy, without knowing
why. Henrietta remained silent. Manfred remained silent too. Henrietta broke the silence and said, "Then you didn't hear any of what
the nurse told me? No, no, no. Upstairs, it's impossible to hear what
goes on down below." Manfred said, "Of course, it's always been my
habit to stand up there and listen to what goes on down here." Henrietta said, "That's not what I meant. Anyway, it's interesting that you
mention Krautmeir. The story I wanted to tell you happens to be about
her—a spicy story inspired by Balzac's familiar tales. Too bad, Fred.
Too bad. Even before I began, you stole the sting." Manfred said, "Tell
me." Henrietta said, "How does one begin? I doubt that I can tell it
right. In any case, I learned from this story that Dr. Krautmeir, who
devotes herself to limiting our population, sometimes demonstrates—
personally—how babies are made. Oh, Fred, I've given it away. What

I'm about to say to you is: let's save the story for another time. Because the elements are so good, the story itself suffers." Manfred said, "Curiosity is not a virtue, but neither is it a virtue to stir up curiosity." Henrietta said, "Will you be able to sit and listen without a cigarette in your mouth?" Manfred said, "In your honor, in honor of that lady, Dr. Krautmeir, in honor of all the genteel ladies who don't smoke, I'm willing to forgo a cigarette for a while. Tell me, Henriett, are there many storytellers who have been so royally compensated? Now then, either you begin or I smoke, two cigarettes at a time." Henrietta said, "I really don't know how to begin, but I'll try.

"A young woman from Mea Shearim lived with her husband for a number of years without bearing him any children. They were both very sad, for a man of the ultra-Orthodox community takes a wife to beget children. They heard about a woman doctor from Germany, here in Jerusalem, and that many women beat a path to her door. They weren't aware that those women go to Krautmeir in order not to give birth. One day, they both went to her, the woman and the man. She was about twenty, and so was he. Their longing for a child exceeded their years. Krautmeir undertook to treat the woman. She began coming to Krautmeir, accompanied by her husband. She was a shy and lovely girl. He was handsome, appealing, and as shy as his wife. They were dressed in the old Mea Shearim style, which makes those lovely, demure people all the more attractive. In short, Krautmeir treated the woman, while her husband sat in the adjacent room, looking at the pictures in the magazines one finds in doctors' waiting rooms. Several months passed, perhaps a year. One day, the young man plucked up the courage to go to Krautmeir alone and ask if there was a prospect of children from his wife. Krautmeir's answer is not known. One can assume she addressed him in her usual manner—in simple words, without much empathy—and explained the secrets of sex. The man was interested in what she said. He began to call on her more and more frequently, especially on Shabbat afternoons, when she didn't normally see patients. Krautmeir was interested in this naive young man from the old community, in his long earlocks, in everything about him. Only one thing is unclear, the nurse told me. What language did they speak? He didn't know German; she knew barely any Yiddish. Being one of those fanatics who regard spoken Hebrew as heresy, would he allow himself to speak Hebrew to her? It would still be a problem, because Krautmeir's Hebrew is too limited to allow for much conversation. So much for Krautmeir, for the young man and the young woman. Let's turn our attention to a small fish bone.

"An old man was eating his Shabbat dinner when a fish bone got stuck in his throat. There was a great commotion in his house, and they began shouting, 'Get a doctor!' They remembered that some woman doctor lived nearby and ran to her house. When people from that community go to a doctor, they are usually joined by a large entourage. By the time they arrived at Krautmeir's house, a crowd had collected. To avoid desecrating the Shabbat, and because they were in such a panic, they didn't ring the bell. They merely pushed on the door. Luckily for them, the door opened instantly. Luckily for them—but not for that young man. The crowd was so panicked that someone knocked over a bottle of medicine and stained the young man's *shtreimel,* which was resting on the table near Krautmeir's bed. Not only did it soil his *shtreimel,* but it stained his caftan as well, his elegant Shabbat caftan. He himself was not spared; he was assaulted by many pairs of eyes that wondered just why he was in the doctor's bed, and why she was there in the bed with him. She was probably teaching him what a man does to beget children. Now tell me, Fred, did you expect to hear such a story from me? If you're not astonished, I certainly am."

Manfred said, "Now I know what nurses talk about when they come to visit a respected lady such as Henrietta Herbst." Henrietta said, "Now you know about the ingratitude of respected gentlemen such as Dr. Herbst." "How is that?" "He sits and listens attentively, eager not to miss a single word. Then he expresses disapproval. You got what you deserved, Manfred." Manfred said, "Mother, shouldn't you lie down? I really think you ought to lie down after lunch." Henrietta said, "Don't mind me. If you want to go to your room, go ahead." Manfred said, "I'm going up to my room, but not to lie down." Henrietta said, "Do whatever you like." Manfred said, "I would like to go into town. Believe it or not, I have no specific reason to go. But I'd like to, with nothing specific in mind." Henrietta said, "That's the best reason. A man shouldn't always have specific things to do. As a matter of fact, why not go into town and amuse yourself? You'll come home in a better mood." Manfred said, "I'll try."

As soon as he entered his room, he saw the woven tray with the peach pits on it. Because the household routines had been disrupted by the nurse who chose to visit at lunchtime, Firadeus had forgotten to clear away the tray. Herbst didn't mind. As a matter of fact, he was pleased that the peach pits were still there, so he could crack them open and eat the insides. But a peach pit is tough. It takes a hammer to crack it, and there was no hammer in his room. The hammer was downstairs with all the other tools. He didn't want to go downstairs, preferring not to get involved in conversation with Henrietta, who would hear him and come, or else call to him. He looked around for a hard object or a rock to use to split open the pit. Not finding it, he went over to the window with the pit in his hand. He aimed it at a bush whose roses had wilted. As it happened, he hit the target. He smiled to himself, musing: Too bad I had no scheme for this game. For example: if the pit hits the bush, it's a sign that I'll find Shira today. Again he thought: Too bad. Then he reconsidered, noting to himself: There are five more pits here; what I didn't do with the first one, I can now do with these. He picked up a pit, aimed at the bush, and hit it. He smiled and thought: What do I gain from this activity, if I don't see a sign in it? He picked up another pit and thought: My hand is trained to hit that particular bush; now I'll set myself a different target. He surveyed the garden and noticed a starling, its beak stuck in the ground. Herbst thought: I'll test my power on him. Before he had a chance to pick up the pit, the starling took off with a screech and flew away. Herbst laughed heartily and mused: That starling knew what I was up to and didn't want to oblige me with his body. He looked at the plate and counted the remaining pits. There were three left. He took another pit and was going to throw it. Before he could decide on a target, he saw Sarah ambling through the garden. He called to her. As soon as he called to her, he regretted it. He didn't want to get involved with her, because, if he meant to go into town and find Shira, this was the time to go. It was possible that, at such an hour, when people don't usually visit each other, he might find her at home. It occurred to him to wonder why she would be hiding in her house, having just said that, at this particular hour, when people don't usually visit each other, he might find her in. He looked at his watch and saw that it was four o'clock. It would be good to have some coffee, but that would delay him. He left his room, thinking that it would be good to have coffee first, but that he would get some in town.

— 5 —

Though he guessed that this would be an opportune time to find Shira at home, he nevertheless went on foot rather than take the bus, for he had noticed that he was getting fat from too much food and too few walks. Jerusalem had been reduced to about half its size because of Arab snipers, and there were fewer and fewer areas a Jew could walk in without risking his life. Even in Baka, a Jew's life was not secure, but, as nothing had ever happened to him in daylight, he didn't worry about walking the streets by day.

At about five o'clock, he reached Rehavia. He had encountered no delays along the way. It's not every day that one spends three-quarters of an hour walking in Jerusalem without being delayed.

Herbst was pleased and displeased. He didn't know why he was pleased and displeased. Since he was in the habit of looking for reasons for his behavior and emotions, he pondered awhile and realized he was pleased because he had arrived in town without being delayed and displeased because he foresaw further disappointment. He assumed he would find Shira's door locked once again. But this was not the source of these two contrasting emotions, which were actually one and its reverse. He was displeased because he was sure there was nothing more between him and Shira, so why seek her out? He was pleased with the walk itself and the exercise it provided.

Everything turned out as expected. Shira's door was locked, and he couldn't tell from the windows whether she had been home since he was last there. After looking at the door and the windows again, he began to believe she might have been home in the interim. As for the fact that he saw no perceptible change, did he have photographs to compare the two visits? He was depending on his own eyes, and eyes that have suffered disappointment are biased and untrustworthy. Herbst walked the alley from beginning to end, backtracked, and walked it from beginning to end again. He repeated this course three or four times. Whenever he came close to her house, he hoped he would and wouldn't find her door open. He circled so many times that he began to feel dizzy. He decided to leave. As people tend to do when they want something, although they know it's hopeless, Herbst went back to the house. Once again, he left despondent. Like most people who modify their actions, this way and that, this way and that, to no avail, Herbst became extremely despondent.

Several days earlier, when Herbst had gone there, he had been aware of a person whose eyes seemed to be tracking his every footstep. Though he sensed this, he pretended not to notice, as if they were both pedestrians, passing through the alley with no particular interest in each other. Which was not true of that other person, who sensed that the gentleman had come because of the new tenant, who wasn't living in the apartment he had rented to her; who had, in fact, already put it back in his hands; who had left several days after she moved in and hadn't returned. She left and hadn't returned. The landlord was absolutely confident that the gentleman would return, so he put off talking to him. Whether he was too lazy to initiate a conversation or whether it was wisdom, the landlord assumed that, coming back again and not finding the lady, the gentleman would be interested in chatting about her.

Herbst left the alley despondent and perplexed. He was also annoyed to be wasting time. Having concluded his business with Shira, what did he care if her door was locked? Why did he go back again and again? Did he have such a great need to satisfy his curiosity? And if what was involved was not curiosity, then what was it? For it was clear to him that he had no further business with Shira. Whether or not he knew precisely when his business with Shira had been concluded, he knows that it was concluded and that it makes no sense to revive such things out of curiosity, for there is no telling where that might lead. At the very least, it might lead to wasted time and despondency.

Herbst left the alley without having decided where to go or which way to turn. He didn't feel like taking up his books; he wasn't eager for conversation; it wasn't a good time to call on people about his prospects for a promotion. When your mind is hollow and your heart is troubled, your mouth is not likely to spout words that will impress a listener. Herbst asked himself: Am I so troubled because of Shira? I'm troubled by her because I haven't been able to find her. If I were to find her, how would it be? At least one thing is clear: I wouldn't be happy. I would be relieved of the curiosity that sometimes torments me, but I certainly wouldn't be happy.

To get rid of those thoughts, which were not happy ones, he shifted his mind to the tragedy he meant to write but never wrote. The tragedy unfolded before him, vivid and clear, scene by scene. It seemed to him that, if he were to sit down and write, he would write one scene after another. He might write the entire tragedy. But he had some doubts. Was it a tragedy, or merely a story with tragic events? Herbst, who was a reader, student, and theatergoer, who had analyzed modern trage-dies—those that were updated to make them contemporary, as well as those that dealt with the issues of their time—knew and recognized the distinction between tragic events and tragedy. Modern poets are adept at defining tragedy. Some are even more adept than the early poets were. But those early poets were believers, so the creation of tragedy was entrusted to them. He nonetheless began to reconsider the content, along with the overall scheme, and, again, it seemed to him that, if he sat down to write, he would keep writing and finish. Even if he lacked the excitement that inspires poets to write, he did not lack diligence. He had trained himself to work step by step, note by note, whereas the poetic process demands a different work style, because, when a poet's

inspiration is arrested, it cannot be retrieved. This does not apply to
those faithful workers who forge ahead relentlessly, whether or not
they feel inspired. Fragmentary scenes were already written and re-
corded in his notebooks, along with an outline of locales, such as the
home of Basileios, the faithful servant. It would surely be worthwhile
for him to begin; what followed, as well as the conclusion, would take
shape on their own. Once again, Herbst imagined himself leaving the
university; leaving his colleagues and students; going to some remote
place, where he would rent a wooden hut or find an abandoned stone
house and live alone, solitary, for weeks and months, days and nights.
There, he would write the tragedy of the woman of the court, the
nobleman Yohanan, and their faithful servant Basileios, emerging from
his seclusion only when he finished the tragedy. Out of a concern for
modesty, truth, and avoiding deception, he observed to himself: I call
it a tragedy, not because I believe I'm writing tragedy, but out of
terminological habit. So he observed, imagining this was the reason,
when actually there was another reason that will seem absurd if I write
it. At that moment, Herbst was intimidated by the word *tragedy,* afraid
it would provoke the gods. By degrees, his enthusiasm waned. At first,
he told himself: No need to give everything up; I could take time off
and go to live in Ahinoam for a while, where my daughter is. I could
surely find an empty room there, eat in the dining hall, and be free from
all the concerns of my household. Then he said to himself: I have no
particular reason to live in the country. I could compose the tragedy
in my own home, in my study, at my desk. After which, he said to
himself: Nonsense, this man is destined to write essays. One of these
days, he may even finish his great work on burial customs of the poor
in Byzantium. He scrutinized his soul, examined his heart, and reflected: You are not the sort of person who can change his way of life.
You'll be doing well if you succeed in improving it to some extent.

Improving his life? If he were to try to take stock of his way of life,
he would find that he had never once thought it needed improvement.
He thought about creating books, about writing criticism, about acquir-
ing books, about becoming a professor, about social connections, about
Henrietta. He also thought about Shira. So as not to confound the
woman who confounded his heart with respect to his wife, who had
only his welfare at heart, he stopped speculating about different ways
of life. Although he hadn't thought of personal reform until now, he
had thought of educational reform for his son. As I already related, the
night his son was admitted to the covenant of Abraham, he sketched
out some rules and specifications for the boy's education. Once again,
he outlined a general scheme for his son's education, and, once again,

he pondered the fact that women are in charge of man's education. Even one's earliest nourishment comes from woman. One thought led to another. He remembered the tale of the man whose wife died, leaving him an infant to rear; since he couldn't afford to hire a wetnurse, his two nipples provided milk, so he could suckle his son. Again Herbst's response was: What a shame, what a shame that the legend doesn't tell us the outcome—whether that baby fared any better than the rest of humanity, reared on mother's milk.

He suddenly remembered the time he went into his daughter Zahara's room and she covered her bosom in shame. This may have been the first time the girl herself was conscious of being a woman. What about Tamara? When was she first conscious of being a woman? How would it be with Sarah? Sarah is still a baby. Her mother still bathes her in his presence; she is naked and unashamed. As a matter of fact, she often calls to him, "Father, see Sarah, he's washing." She means, "See Sarah, she's washing." And Firadeus: in all the time he's known her, it never occurred to him that she was a woman. He regards her as a vessel filled with sorrow and anguish, waiting to serve him, reticent, submissive, compliant. Still, when she was upset by the nurse who came to visit Henrietta, she neglected to clear away the dish, which is what caused him to throw the pits. He threw two at the wilted rosebush and one at a starling that took flight, without seeing any sign about Shira in this game. When he finally went to Shira, he didn't find her. But he found someone else, whose eyes tracked his every footstep. Were their circumstances similar? Was he also on intimate terms with Shira? Only the devil knows her ways. That woman is capable of actions and relationships that would be bizarre for any other woman, but not for Shira. Even if there was nothing between that man and Shira, it was good that he didn't speak with him. They would surely have hidden the truth from each other, so what was there to gain from such a conversation?

Herbst was not fanatical about the truth, but he avoided lies, and he had never lied until the night he visited Shira for the first time. What was there for him to do after that night? He had no choice but to superimpose one lie on another, to camouflage his lies with lies, because, in his mind, he was bound to that woman, compelled to seek her out again and again. Marriage is a respected and fine institution which humanity has, no doubt, arrived at as a result of many difficult experiments, but not all marriages promote truth. In the interest of peace and tranquility, one sometimes finds it necessary to heap lie upon lie. What happened to that pious young man who was found in bed with Dr. Krautmeir? What was Henrietta referring to when she called it a Balzacian tale? She was referring to those young people who came to their elders before the wedding ceremony to learn the secrets of sex and were taught on their own bodies. Try to picture that frosty, deliberate woman, without an erotic line on her face, without a tremor of desire, about whose intimate life nothing is known. Picture her in the arms of a young Hasid, half her age, a poor fellow who pays for his love by soiling his black hat, his elegant caftan, and his good name. It's very odd. As Henrietta heard it from the nurse, the fellow's wife is a freshly blooming rose. As for Krautmeir, we all know about her. She isn't ugly, but she certainly isn't attractive. She's quite tall. Her body isn't gross, but it certainly isn't delicate. Her conversation is always deliberate. She probably has some spiritual needs; she might read a nonprofessional text on occasion. What we know about her is very limited. What can we know about a woman we aren't close to? And, even if we were close, we wouldn't know very much. If we were to put together all our information about Shira, it would not be very enlightening. Rika Welt-fremdt's life seems accessible to us, but what we see may be the surface. It is possible that even that woman, whose way of life is simple and obvious, is concealing a monumental secret, the secret of someone who craves poetry and pursues it, only to turn out insipid verse. Though he would have liked to laugh at her verse, he felt melancholy and was depressed by the suspicion that he was remembering her and her verse only because he had once dared to regard himself as the author of a tragedy.

— 6 —

Once again, life's routines are orderly, without any exceptional events. Gabi keeps growing. Gabi, like his sister Sarah, isn't very much trouble to his mother, not to mention his father. It's good that he doesn't trouble his father, because he is busy preparing lectures for the winter semester, and it wouldn't do to confound his mind with irrelevant concerns. Sarah had one advantage: Sarini, who was already mentioned, was her only wetnurse, whereas Gabi has already had to adjust to four sets of nipples, and no one knows how many changes are ahead before he is weaned, because of diminished milk, because of childbirth, because of Arab terror. If Herbst doesn't move, I don't know what's in store for him and his family. The Arabs are insolent. They are a menace to any Jew who shows his face in Baka. By day, they are menacing; by night, they shoot. Sacharson is already planning to move out of Baka, so as not to cause an Arab to kill a Christian when he really means to kill a Jew. The *shokhet* who used to come from Mekor Hayim every week to slaughter chickens no longer appears at the Herbsts' home. Unless Henrietta follows the example of other ladies, who wring the chicken's neck themselves, she will have to deal with the Arab butcher. She doesn't want to get meat from the Arabs, because, as her father used to say, if we give up the slaughterer and the butcher, what aspects of Judaism will we be left with? It's enough that she gets other food from the Arabs. If she orders from a Jewish storekeeper, he won't deliver to her home, because he is afraid. She begins to see herself as someone whose support comes from Jews, without a penny of it reverting to them. How is this? They live in an Arab house. They buy bread from a German bakery; meat from an Arab butcher; fruit, vegetables, and eggs from Arab women; staples from the English. Their books and newspapers are foreign, and, when they want a rest, they go to Father Miller's pension. Whatever Jews earn through their efforts, they hand over to Gentiles, retaining no benefit for themselves. Tamara is not pleased to be living in Baka either. At least once, she didn't come home at night. Not because she was out of Jerusalem, but because she was afraid. If this is how it is for Tamara, who is usually accompanied by two dozen young men, what is an ordinary person to do?

Back to Gabi. He keeps growing. And, when you pick him up, you feel his weight. So far, his magnitude derives from weight, not might or valor. For this reason, he needs to be protected from Sarah's doll and from Sarah. One tries to get her hands on him; the other attacks him with a slipper. Luckily, the doll's slipper is made of silk. Envy is characteristic of all living things, including this child of old age, who was indulged by everyone until a new creature appeared and appropriated some of the attention. A few days earlier, she had cried because some woman said Sarini would put Gabi back in her belly, and today she incited her doll to throw a slipper at him.

Henrietta was occupied with the son of her old age. He occupied her twenty-four hours a day. This is not an exaggeration nor is it hyperbole, for even in her dreams she was occupied with him. Henrietta had so many dreams, and they were so strange. They had no end, no limits, no boundary. A dreaming soul can flit from Jerusalem to Berlin, then reverse its direction, so that the Land of Israel and Germany blend with each other, along with their populations, mountains, rivers, local produce. Sometimes a vegetable that couldn't exist in Germany is offered to her in a Berlin hotel, served up in a Shabbat hat soiled by Dr. Krautmeir's medicines. On what occasion was that vegetable served to her? At her son Gabi's bar mitzvah. You are aware that Henrietta and her family have no commitment to faith and religion. I doubt that she ever saw a pair of *tefillin*, except in drawings and pictures. Henrietta knows that, when a boy reaches the age of thirteen, his father hires a teacher, who is half from the old community and half from who knows where, to teach the boy a chapter from the prophets, sung with monotonous vocal trills no ear would tolerate if it were not for the sweetness of the boy's voice. On Shabbat, the boy comes to the synagogue with his father and his relatives, wearing a strip of silk around his neck, a tallit. He is called to the Torah to read the chapter he learned from his teacher. Then friends of the family come, bringing presents—a book, a picture, a penknife, a camera, and whatever other objects a boy covets. The guests all eat cake and drink an assortment of beverages. Knowing all this, it is strange to us that Henrietta saw her son with *tefillin* on his head. Though I try to avoid the bizarre, I will recount the plot of the dream.

One night, Henrietta cried out in her sleep, because she saw her son's head dripping blood. She wanted to dress the wound but couldn't get a bandage, because the chest was locked. She went to him just as she was, empty-handed, and saw that one of his curls was parted; that there, in the center of the curl, was a small box with curlicues. A four-headed bird was carved on the box, and she knew that she was at her son's bar mitzvah and that those were *tefillin* on his head. This is why I said Henrietta was occupied with her son, not only by day, but by night as well. When his sisters were small, Henrietta used to find time for everything. She managed the household, tended the garden, took in guests from abroad, entertained, wrote letters, negotiated certificates, challenged the accounts of fundraisers from charitable institutions, legitimate and otherwise. By now, Henrietta's hands had begun to falter, and she devoted her remaining energies to the son of her old age. Though she wasn't able to nurse the baby, she was wholly occupied with him; it was as if he never stirred from between her breasts. Difficult as it is to jest about this, just to sweeten the bitterness, I'll lighten the mood with a little humor. The Nazis, knowing that Henrietta Herbst wasn't free to write to her relatives, destroyed some of them and imprisoned others, so they wouldn't bother her with their letters.

Because of Ernst Weltfremdt's new book, Herbst decided to replan his lectures for the winter semester. He had originally intended to lecture on Arcadius II. After reading Weltfremdt's book, he was moved to lecture about the rise of the Goths. By way of thanks, Herbst prefaced his lectures with a comprehensive survey of what was known and what was unknown about the subject before Professor Weltfremdt appeared on the scene with his new book. Some scholars, when they find new material in a colleague's book, respond with silence or drown it out so that the listener can't hear it; there are other scholars who make the new material the cornerstone of their own thinking. Manfred Herbst was unique in this respect. When his friends offered valuable insights, he presented them to his students; when they were misguided, he didn't mention them. He argued that, unless their errors begin to be accepted, there is no reason to point them out, even in the interests of challenging them. He had another virtue. He didn't boast to his friends and report to them, "I mentioned you in my lecture." I recount all this not to elevate Herbst or to discredit others by praising him. But, recalling one of his finer qualities, I am calling attention to it. This quality is praiseworthy. Still, if I should recall a quality that is to his discredit, I won't conceal it either.

— 7 —

The nurse came again. She came to see how the baby was doing and, incidentally, to see Mrs. Herbst. She had been fond of Mrs. Herbst from the outset. Now that they were better acquainted, she had come back for a brief visit, intending to see how she was doing and be on her way. She had an urgent need to know how Mrs. Herbst was doing, because Mrs. Herbst was so exceptional in her charm, good sense, intellect, virtue, manners, and other qualities too numerous to list while standing on one foot. The popular notion that it is a nurse's duty to love everyone and to sacrifice herself on the altar of love is misguided, as it overlooks the fact that nurses are also flesh and blood, that the same good and bad qualities that exist in other people exist in nurses as well. A nurse who is loyal to the truth, who doesn't embellish her outward image, will not deny the natural feelings with which nature has endowed her. But she can assert about herself that, whether or not she has any affection for a particular patient, when she is in charge, she does everything in her power to promote that patient's welfare, health, and recovery. She even forgoes sleep and gives up her private life on his behalf. There are patients she detests when they are in good health, "who are as hateful as mice in the cream." Still, when they come to the hospital and are entrusted to her care, her hostility is suspended. She tends them, tries to please them as though they were loved ones, and stands ready to give her life for them at any moment. When they leave the hospital, even before they have a chance to say, "Goodbye, Nurse Ludmilla," she reverts to hostility, detesting them again, "like mice in the cream."

So, if she calls on Mrs. Herbst, she calls on her because she is fond of her; in fact, she loves her. Love is a simple word that doesn't encompass even a fraction of the feelings that stir her heart. She has loved her for ten years now, or more. Mrs. Herbst knows nothing about this. But this love is engraved in her heart, her skin, her flesh, her bones. On the surface, the reason is simple and uncomplicated. True love doesn't require complicated reasoning. Sometimes a drop of eau de cologne is sufficient to create a sea of love. This is not as odd as it sounds, and not so much odd as bizarre. It is an example taken from life, the sort of life that is typical of the Land of Israel. Ten years ago—to be precise, more than ten years ago—two ladies were traveling in a train from Haifa to Jerusalem. In those days, it was common to take long trips in a train rather than a car. Though lighter vehicles go faster, it is more pleasant to travel in a train than in a car. In a train, the passenger is in control, free to get up and walk around or to remain seated; in a car, you are required to stay in your seat, as if you were strapped in. If you have an open mind, you wonder why a free and intelligent person would surrender his freedom and pay a price for it. In short, the train moved ahead. The two ladies were in the same car, but, like modern ladies, they kept to themselves. As long as they don't know each other, modern ladies remain subdued, though their hearts are full and their tongues all but leap out of their mouths because they are so eager to talk. All of a sudden, something happened. One of these two ladies, Ludmilla the nurse, was traveling with a young girl, who, having suffered what she suffered, was being taken from Haifa to Jerusalem for a psychological consultation with Heinz Hermann. Her mind had been affected by what she had to undergo to rid herself of nature's gift to womankind. In short, the lady traveler was in her seat; Ludmilla the nurse was in hers. She had closed her eyes, hoping for sleep. Nature denied her the sleep she craved. She thought to herself: Nature is cruel. Would it matter if I were granted a drop of sleep, when my brain is empty and boredom is gnawing at my heart? She was still young and unaware that there is nothing as kind as nature, nothing as sensible as nature, that we ought to depend on nature in every realm, for nature alone knows what is good and what isn't. All of a sudden, there was a great noise, and the

train came to a sudden halt. What happened? That young girl had
opened the door and was about to jump. If she hadn't been restrained,
she would have been crushed. Ludmilla the nurse was in shock and
about to faint. She was about to faint, and then she fainted. There was
no one to look after her, because everyone was busy with the girl who
had tried to commit suicide. If not for the lady who was sitting near
her on the train, who rubbed her forehead and the veins of her wrist
with eau de cologne, Ludmilla the nurse would have continued to feel
more and more faint. What had happened was no small thing: a patient
who needs special care is entrusted to you, and you try to nap. And who
was the lady? Mrs. Herbst was the lady. Mrs. Herbst forgot the event.
She so completely forgot it that she was convinced she had never been
on the train from Haifa to Jerusalem and had never used eau de cologne.

But Ludmilla the nurse is trustworthy. Nature has endowed her
with a powerful memory. She even remembers the shape of the smile
that graced Mrs. Herbst's face when she asked the nurse how she was
feeling. Were we to speak truly, Ludmilla the nurse calls on Mrs.
Herbst more for the past than the present, because she has an intense
need occasionally to see herself as she was ten years ago. When she sees
Mrs. Herbst, she imagines herself on the train, with Mrs. Herbst rub-
bing eau de cologne on her forehead. All of this is so vivid that she
actually smells the eau de cologne. Despite the fact that Mrs. Herbst no
longer uses eau de cologne, she experiences its wonderful fragrance—
the fragrance reminding her of the event; the event reminding her of
the fragrance. When she comes, she offers advice and guidance for the
baby and his mother, for the two of them together. Even though the
baby is already separated from his mother's womb and doesn't nurse
at her breast, he is attached to his mother, and his mother is attached
to him. The bond is powerful: physical and concrete, not merely spiritual. Anyone who has mastered the secrets of creation, who knows
what birth is, knows about the nature of the bond between a mother
and the fruit of her womb. There are women, even doctors, who regard
the embryo inside its mother as something you can get rid of, as long
as none of its limbs has emerged into the world. They believe that a girl
who has strayed from the proper path can deal with the consequences
by getting rid of the embryo, that she can be restored to her former
state, which I will describe as youth, rather than use an abstract term
like maidenhood. If she meets up with a naive man, she leads him to
the bridal canopy without any misgivings or regrets. For that type of
shrewd woman, we have something akin to a folktale or ballad to tell,
without ruling out the possibility that the events described in it actually

transpired. Those shrewd women who dismiss the procedure as simply physical, cosmetic, or the like would do well to listen. I am coming to the heart of the story, which I will tell approximately as Ludmilla the nurse told it. Approximately—not word for word—because at first it didn't occur to me that it would be worth conveying. I suddenly remembered the story and realized that Ludmilla the nurse had imparted something very significant. I struggled to recall the details, but without success. I asked myself: Why wear myself out over a story someone has told? We hear so much, and, if we were to try to report it all, we would never succeed. I renounced the story, but the story didn't renounce me. It kept coming back to mind, sometimes on its own, sometimes suggested by other events. So much so that I began to wonder whether the events were meant to remind me of the story or whether the story was meant to help me understand the events. In either case, I couldn't escape it, though I continued to try. It was stronger than I was. If not for the fact that I don't believe in magic, I would say I was under its spell. Every day, every single day, something transpired that reminded me of the story. Seeing that this was how it was, I reviewed it again and again, until the story was gone.

— 8 —

Whenever Ludmilla the nurse appears, Henrietta is happy to see her. Manfred isn't happy to see her, and he is frank with Henrietta about the fact that he isn't pleased by the visits of that mouse in the cream. Ludmilla the nurse isn't a mouse, and Herbst's home isn't cream, but, since Herbst resents her, he gives her a demeaning name. His resentment, which is what leads him to demean her, stems from the fact that, when he sees how often she visits Henrietta, he remembers that Shira never visited Henrietta, not even once. When he remembers Shira, what he remembers torments him. Also, though it is evident from her face that Ludmilla the nurse doesn't dissemble, she causes him to dissemble. He says demeaning things about her in her absence, but he is gracious when she appears. Why does he do this? Because he needs to be on good terms with her. There is no way of knowing what such a woman is capable of. She might even know something of what was between him and Shira. It is common for nurses to keep track of each other's lives, so it is best to be on good terms with her. Otherwise, she could gossip about him and tell Henrietta things it would be better for her not to know. Human beings are surely flawed; they flatter one another for professional advancement and domestic harmony. What else is in store for ignoble mankind? Let us hope that the future, which is an outcome of the present, will be no uglier than the present.

Ludmilla the nurse came again. She came at about noon, as she had done the first time, just as Firadeus was about to spread the cloth and set the table. Ludmilla didn't want to join them for lunch. She turned down their invitation, as she had done the first time. She barely agreed to have a sip of coffee and barely agreed to have a bite of cake, an old cake Mrs. Herbst had baked for Shabbat. Henrietta says these leftovers can't really be called cake, but Ludmilla the nurse says they aren't just leftovers, they are the equivalent of a cake and a half, since each and every crumb has a unique flavor, and no two crumbs are alike; these are not crumbs, but entire cakes. In fact, she uses the term *crumbs* only to avoid contradicting Mrs. Herbst, who calls those large slices crumbs out of excessive modesty, just as she calls the cake old, when, actually, it just came out of the oven. If three or four days have elapsed since the cake came out of the oven, it still retains its warmth—if not the warmth of the oven, then the warmth of a generous heart. Herein lies the greatness of Mrs. Herbst. She offers you the best and most superb delicacy, understating its quality, so you'll feel free to eat as much as you want. But Ludmilla the nurse doesn't want very much. Two or three crumbs satisfy her to such an extent that she is happy not to eat or drink anything else until the next time she comes, if Mrs. Herbst doesn't lock her out. As for the fact that she comes at lunchtime, an hour when people are not in the habit of dropping in, she regrets this more than anyone in the world, because she may be delaying lunch and interfering with household routines. But what is she to do when, suddenly, at midnight—yes, it was midnight and even earlier; of course it was earlier, as she hadn't heard the rooster crow yet—her heart yearned to see Mrs. Herbst and Gabi, sweet Gabi. She assumed this would pass, but the yearning became more and more intense. Then she began to be afraid she would be swept out of the world by these yearnings. Swept out of the world is an exaggeration, but an exaggeration that is close to the truth. Since she had some time off—just a little earlier, she had unexpectedly been told that she could take some time off—she leaped at the chance to come. She came right over without consulting her watch to see if it was a good time for visiting. It's just as well that she didn't consult her watch. If she had, she wouldn't have come, and her heart would have expired with longing. When she arrived, Herbst stepped out of his room and came downstairs. If a man appears in the dining room at mealtime, even his wife doesn't suspect he is there because of his interest in her guest. So Manfred appeared in the dining room, found Ludmilla the nurse sitting with his wife, was taken aback, and made a move to go. But didn't go, because it was only proper for him to welcome the guest first. Then he asked permission to join the ladies, promising not to interfere with their conversation.

The three of them sit together: Dr. Manfred Herbst, a lecturer at the Hebrew University in Jerusalem; Mrs. Henrietta Herbst, his wife; and the registered nurse Ludmilla. Each of them has a history of his own. Herbst and his wife come from the same country, the same city, the same cultural milieu. But Ludmilla the nurse comes from another place, from a city at the border of three countries, and when a rooster announced the dawn in any one of these countries, the people in the other two knew it was morning. This is how it was before the Great War. Now, after the war, it's different. The rooster is no different. The rooster has not changed his nature, but it doesn't matter that he has not changed his nature when he no longer exists. Roosters have been eradicated from the world, and the meat we eat comes from tins. If there is still such a thing as a live rooster, crowing as usual, there is no one to hear him, because human beings have already been eradicated from the world. And if there are still a few people left, most of them are Bolsheviks or Communists. There is no point elaborating on this, for we don't know whom we might offend. Even in the Land of Israel, there is no shortage of Bolsheviks, and it is not in our nature to offend anyone, even someone opposed to our ideals. Before she came to the Land of Israel, she thought the entire country was inhabited by Zionists. Now she sees that the Land of Israel is like other countries. What we find in the lands of dispersion, we find here too: Zionists, Socialists, and so on. Even the Zionists themselves aren't genuine Zionists. There are Labor Zionists and General Zionists. There are probably other types of Zionists from parties she can't name. Her father was unique. He was a genuine Zionist, an outright Zionist. If the concept "simple" hadn't been oversimplified, she would say her father was simply a Zionist. He didn't have the good fortune to emigrate to the Land of Israel, which may be just as well. If he were here, he wouldn't be able to survive. He was a simple Zionist, when what we need here are Zionists who are extremely clever, and even that isn't adequate, because, all of a sudden, a new breed of Zionists surfaces, with new types of cleverness. Does anyone have what it takes to devise new types of cleverness every day? In fact, she admits that she herself has lost interest in Zionism. The day she set foot in the Land of Israel, her heart shed its Zionist sentiments. Spiritual functions are very much like physical functions. A man who is thirsty to the point of madness finds water, and drinks it, and his thirst is gone. Similarly, a man who is starved to the point of madness finds bread and eats it, and his hunger vanishes.

The three of them sit together, engrossed in their conversation. I said "their conversation," though it is actually her conversation. She does all the talking. What does she talk about, and what doesn't she talk about? What does she tell about? What doesn't she tell about? All of Jerusalem rolls off her tongue: Jews, Ishmaelites, Christians alike. She has something to say about them all, a story to tell about everyone. It is the convention to assume that doctors are on the most intimate terms with their fellow human beings, because a sick person is likely to open his heart and reveal what he wouldn't otherwise reveal, not even to himself. But how much time does a doctor spend with a patient? A famous doctor, who has many patients, is short on time, whereas doctors who aren't famous pretend to be busy and in great demand. As it turns out, doctors spend very little time with patients. But a nurse is with the patient all the time, always, even longer. Patients get bored and are eager to extract hidden information from the nurse, such as, Is there a chance they will recover? Is there hope they will live? In this context, they talk to the nurse and tell her things they themselves were not aware of before. They do this to stir her heart, so she will reveal what they want to know, which allows a nurse to hear things not everyone gets to hear. Ludmilla the nurse doesn't say very much about Jews. First of all, because Jewish patients are so preoccupied with their illnesses that, though the illnesses vary, they talk about them in one and the same way. Second, if she were to report what they say, it would sound like gossip and slander. But she tells about Muslims and Christians, because, to the general Jewish society, they are mere names, like those in the tales of *A Thousand and One Nights* and the Brothers Grimm. She admits that she doesn't have the talent of either Scheherazade or the Grimm brothers, but her stories have one advantage. They are true. True, not concocted. True, without a particle of fantasy.

It's impossible to tell all of her stories, but some of them can be told. So I will tell two of them that add up to a little less than two segments of a thousand and one stories. The young wife of Ibn Saud's hangman was both very pretty and very sick. In all of Saudi Arabia, there was no doctor who could cure her. They put her in a bed, which was lifted

onto a camel's back, and carried her from land to land, from country
to country, to each of the seven Arab kingdoms, but they found no cure
for her illness. They took her to Hadassah Hospital in Jerusalem. Back
in Ibn Saud's country, that hangman had a title equivalent to vizier, and
his wife was nobility, true nobility. He had achieved rank because of
his occupation, but her nobility derived from her person. It was the
custom there that, once a year, all the noblewomen in the kingdom
would come to kiss Ibn Saud's hand. She, too, came to kiss his hand.
Hearing she was sick, he commanded that no effort be spared to cure
her, which is why she was finally taken to Hadassah. It was obvious to
Ludmilla the nurse, who was in charge of her, that, apart from being
sick, she was a delicate and well-mannered woman. Having mentioned
hand kissing, she mentioned another incident that revolved around this
custom. Every year, around the time of the Muslim holidays, Master
Salomiac used to bring a gift to the old mufti, who was the father of
Amin Husseini, the current mufti. Master Salomiac was the Russian
emissary, and, as such, he had dealings with Muslim leaders as well as
with the mufti. His relationship with them was one of great affection.
Whenever he came to the mufti, he was offered the seat of honor and
was served coffee, sweets, and a narghile, in accordance with Ishmaelite
custom. While they were discussing politics, Amin Husseini entered
and bowed to the guest. His father scolded him and said, "You insect,
why haven't you kissed the *hawaja*'s hand?" Amin Husseini bowed to
Master Salomiac and kissed his hand. The two of them remember that
exchange to this day. Ludmilla the nurse once went to the Old City to
watch the Nebi Mussa celebrations and found herself standing next to
Master Salomiac. He said to her, "Come, I have something to show you.
See the mufti over there, riding on his white mule, facing the crowd
of celebrants? You're about to see him turn his face away." Master
Salomiac positioned himself in front of the mufti, who immediately
turned his face in the other direction. Master Salomiac moved so that,
once again, he was directly in front of the mufti. Once again, the mufti
turned his face away. This was enacted several times. Master Salomiac
said to Ludmilla the nurse, "It's hard for that villain to look me in the
face from such an elevated position. He still remembers that he once
kissed my hand."

Manfred sits there, his heart pounding with hunger and dread, for
Henrietta the nurse might mention Shira. She doesn't mention Shira.
Is it because she is determined not to talk about Jews, or is it to avoid
upsetting Herbst? Who can fathom a woman's heart? All our speculations about women are inherently contradictory. Ludmilla the nurse
has visited Mrs. Herbst many times. She has consumed a keg of coffee

and a mound of cakes; she has told a thousand and one stories, none of them about Shira. For this reason, I will say no more about Ludmilla the nurse and return to Herbst's essential concerns.

Herbst returned to his own concerns, concerns that have been essential to him since the day he was imbued with an inquiring soul. True, he has made other concerns his concern, but these are not relevant to his essential concern, which is the history of Byzantium. In any case, it is baffling: what does such a man, such a scholar, have in common with Shira? Even if we grant that no scholar can survive on his work alone, in what way are they compatible? Scholarship is totally alien to her. She neither understands it nor wishes to understand it. If he had become involved with Lisbet Neu, I would have said it was because of her uncle. But why does he cling to Shira? Is it because professionals are attracted to the nonprofessional world? I may be mistaken, just as I was mistaken about Ludmilla the nurse, to whom I have devoted so much attention, although she is not connected to the story of Herbst and the nurse Shira. On the other hand, whatever surrounds the core may be essential, just as the whiteness around a letter sustains its shape. Without a context, we wouldn't recognize the text. So much for the irrelevant; now on to essentials.

We are familiar with Dr. Manfred Herbst's work habits, which are probably no different from those of most scholars. He sits at his desk, in his study, bent over his books and his notes, reading, adding notes to his notes, which are filed in a special box. Sometimes, the box fills up before he has a chance to use them. At other times, the hour passes before the box is full. When it's time to write a chapter or an article, he takes out his notes, puts them together, organizes them by subject, ties them in a bundle, then reads them, and writes what he writes. I'm not mentioning the cigarettes and the pipe, because they don't apply to all scholars. He sometimes succeeds in writing a page or two at one sitting; at other times, he barely manages to produce two or three lines. But he adds one line, then another line, until, in time, he can put together half a chapter or even a whole chapter. All this relates to the actual work, to the work process itself.

I will now attempt to clarify just how he handles ideas. A learned man's mind isn't always filled with ideas. Even if his brain is as busy as a beehive, when he looks into it, he might find it empty. Sometimes, inadvertently, suddenly and inadvertently, when he least expects it, a good idea comes to him. When he's alert, he follows through with an action: he writes it in his notebook. When he's less alert, he tosses it around until it floats away. Then, later, when he is ready to write it

down, he finds his hands are empty, unless it was replaced by a similar
idea while he was hesitating. If I'm not mistaken, I have outlined most
of Herbst's habits with respect to his work.

I will now note the fact that Herbst has devised a new approach to
his work. He no longer sits for long periods laboring over books, nor
does he take notes. He does his work outside, on the streets of Jerusalem, in its open spaces. This is roughly his routine: He eats, drinks,
smokes, gets up from the table, says, "Time for a little walk," and goes
out. Some days, he boards the bus and rides into town; other days, he
goes on foot. When he gets to town, he turns toward one of the
relatively uncrowded streets. Not that he avoids those places that hum
with activity, for a person's thoughts reflect the person. At times, he
seeks silence and tranquility; at times, he prefers the human bustle.

Herbst is tall and hardy. His head is somewhat bowed. He has a
cigarette in his mouth, a walking stick in his hand. His mind roves from
Jerusalem to Byzantium. All the emperors of that Rome-of-the-East flit
through his mind. He drives them away sometimes, as an emperor
would drive away irritating ministers. But he sometimes welcomes one
of them and responds, even to the extent of dealing with matters of the
heart. The story of Arcadius and Eudoxia is a case in point. Arcadius
was a young emperor with many fantasies when he married the beautiful Eudoxia. But the beautiful Eudoxia was a cold woman, with no love
in her heart. She cloistered herself in her room or in a secluded chapel,
isolated from people, where she prostrated herself before her God. The
emperor knocked on her door many times, but she didn't open it. The
affairs of Byzantium were in a state of neglect, dire neglect; that great
kingdom was in a state of neglect. The emperor ignored his city, his
people, his entire realm. His mind was totally taken up with Eudoxia,
who rejected him. Why did she reject him? There are many opinions,
but not much truth. Herbst's opinions on this subject are no more valid
than anyone else's. How can we arrive at the truth? How can we
eliminate doubt? How can we eliminate theories that, for the most part,
derive from an impulse to innovate and from a wish to demonstrate that
everything is clear and obvious to us, that we have solved all the
mysteries, though in our hearts we know these theories have no substance? Not only do they themselves lack substance, but they generate
other theories, upon which entire new systems are built. Meanwhile,
there is a mess of documents, hidden away and ensconced in storage
vaults somewhere, unread and untouched. A scholar or researcher appears, unrolls the documents, reads them, studies and analyzes them to
the best of his ability, and, finally, publishes a paper. Those who read
it imagine that they are now holding the truth in their hand. Another

document is suddenly discovered, different from the preceding ones, and what was accepted as definitive truth turns out to be totally invalid. Who can but sympathize with the learned men of the past, who labored, toiled, and lived out their lives under basic misconceptions.

Herbst walks the streets of Jerusalem, responding to greetings, exchanging pleasantries, studying a store window, reviewing his relationship to his own research. One doesn't always know the truth about himself, what he is like at a given moment. But, if he is a person who seeks the truth, he can know, to some extent, what he was once like in specific respects. Manfred Herbst was like a deep well, filled with errors—errors that ensued from one another, engendering still more errors, ad infinitum. He had argued about them with friends, based several theories on them, taught them to his students, built his reputation on them, since they were widely accepted and, presumably, reliable. Suddenly, a photocopy of an unknown document fell into his hands. He read it. He saw and recognized that what was considered definitive truth wasn't true at all. This is not the place to explain why this document was more convincing than the earlier ones. But it is the place to say what Herbst did after he discovered what he discovered and arrived at the truth. Herbst made no effort to protect himself. He wrote, "I made a mistake, which I retract." When he was invited to republish some of his early papers, he declined, because most of them were based on those errors. There are famous scholars who, once they have made a statement, refuse to retract it, despite an abundance of evidence to the contrary. Even when they themselves are aware of their error, they don't admit it. They maintain their position, dismissing the opinion of peers if it suggests they themselves are in error. If they could, they would burn any manuscript that challenges their views. Needless to say, this isn't Herbst's way. In fact, Herbst lives by this axiom: I uphold this view today, because this is what my research suggests. If I see tomorrow that I'm mistaken, I will undo all the structures that are based on this error. Scholarship itself is more important than an individual scholar, and the essence of scholarship is precision. This remains true even if we concede that there are no absolutes in the realm of scholarship, since what was true until today is no longer true in the light of new discoveries, and what we learn from today's discoveries may be a fleeting truth, because further discoveries remain to be discovered, and, when these further discoveries are discovered, earlier truths will be invalidated. But there is one ultimate truth, forever valid: the quest for truth itself, directing our hearts to explore the truth without political or social bias. As long as we have no evidence about the past other than the texts left to us by preceding generations, it is our mandate to examine them thoroughly and meticulously, to be very cautious about offering new theories that can't be supported. In the future, when new data are discovered, more authentic than before, we must discard what is outdated in favor of the new. Herbst repeated this message to his students every semester, in his opening lecture. Needless to say, he repeated it to himself as well. He used to add: Who among us has read travel stories as a child without being stirred by explorers who traveled to remote lands; crossed seas, deserts, uncharted forests; risked life and limb; exposed themselves to harsh environments, deadly disease, savage animals, in order to investigate nature and life in its varied forms— unintimidated by all these perils? We who work in the serenity of our homes, who are guaranteed food, drink, and sleep—will we cling to distorted opinions and be distorted by them ourselves, because of habit, for the sake of our so-called honor? Neu, whose errors are superior to other scholars' certainties, didn't spare himself. On the eve of a gala event celebrating his sixtieth birthday, he published a paper entitled "My Errors," in which he listed every error, every suspicion of an error, that he had ever perpetrated.

— 9 —

In those days, with Jerusalem's area diminished by Arab gunfire, Herbst would meet a growing number of friends on his walks. There is nothing remarkable about this, since most of his walks were in Rehavia and its environs, where many of his friends lived. And those who didn't live there were visiting others who did. Whom did he find there, and whom didn't he find there? Everyone, except for Julian Weltfremdt, who deprived Rehavia of his company because of his cousin and because so many other university scholars lived in Rehavia. There wasn't a day when Herbst came to Rehavia without meeting a friend or acquaintance. If I were to list them all, it would turn into a lexicon of Jerusalem's leaders and learned men. Believe it or not, he even met Gavriel Gamzu. I don't know when this meeting occurred, whether it was before or after Gemula's death. For our purposes, it doesn't matter when it was. What did Gamzu tell him, and what didn't Gamzu tell him? No one has ever talked to Gamzu without hearing something unforgettable from him. As for Gamzu's story, I won't pursue it now, since its subject is remote, but I will tell about someone else whose story is more immediate.

Now then, in this period, when Herbst was working out of doors, when he used to amble back and forth, strolling, pondering, thinking his thoughts, he ran into a friend, a fellow professor at the university who had just recovered from a serious illness. He was an epidemiologist, who used to travel everywhere to study the course of contagious diseases. When the unrest in the world was such that he could no longer travel, he stayed in Jerusalem and worked at home. Now I will reveal in a whisper what was whispered to me. One day, he wanted to study a particularly deadly tropical disease. But, in all of the Land of Israel, he couldn't find anyone suffering from it. He exposed his own body to the disease and tried to cure himself with the drug he had invented. Great German doctors report in their memoirs that, when they were trying to fathom the secret of a disease and its cure, they would expose one of their patients to it. Not this Jerusalem scientist. He tested the disease and the cure personally, on his own body, and in so doing he almost died. Now that he was recovering, he often went out for walks. When Herbst first heard this story, tears rolled down his cheeks. One day, he spotted the doctor in the park at the end of Rashba Street, at the very edge of Rehavia. He and Herbst were not closely connected. One of them worked in the humanities; the other worked in science. But, since they worked in the same institution, they did know each other. When Herbst saw him, he bowed, kissed his hand, and went on his way.

Now I must get back to something I have already given too much time to, namely, the realm of thought. As long as I have no alternative way to get to the essence of the story, I can't give it up. Herbst invested a lot of thought in the scientist who experimented on his own body. Even if we assume that he didn't realize he was endangering his life, he surely knew that he would suffer extreme agony by infecting himself with the disease. He inflicted it on himself in the interest of science and for the sake of those afflicted with the disease. These observations led Herbst to ask himself: Would I do anything comparable? Who, in my field, would willingly risk his life to advance knowledge? Julian Weltfremdt calls our type of scholarship "coffee-and-cake scholarship." What that nihilist means to say is: The person we call a professor sits around with a coffee cup in his hand, his mouth filled with cake, an open book before him. He drinks the coffee, chews the cake, and reads the book, deciding what to copy and put in his note box for the book he is writing. Because of his wrinkled soul, because of his need to deprecate himself and his profession, Herbst forgot about all the true scholars, even Neu, whose entire lives are devoted, truly devoted, to their work. If need be, they would no doubt take risks in order to achieve their end—their sole end being true scholarship. Herbst suddenly remembered something Gamzu had told him, and he began to quake. When he heard the story, he didn't make anything of it, but, remembering it, his entire body began to quake.

I don't know if this story is based on reality or if it stems from the imagination. If it stems from the imagination, it seems to me that it evolved from a real event: some number of years back, a young immigrant from Germany called on Herbst, bringing letters from Herbst's friends, in which they praised this young man and described him as a gifted person with a promising future. Herbst took an interest in him and invited him to come again. He came once, but that was all. If these had been ordinary times, if Herbst hadn't been busy with so many things, he would surely have noted his absence and asked after him. Since these were not ordinary times and Herbst was extremely busy, he forgot the young man. If he did remember him briefly, he soon forgot him for long periods. One day, while Herbst was walking along, thinking about the emperor Arcadius and the empress Eudoxia, he met Taglicht, who was in the company of this young man. Though he had matured in the interim, he was still essentially the same. Herbst asked how he was doing . . .*

This conversation, which was apparently meant to arouse Taglicht, was displeasing to him. I don't know why Taglicht, who spent all of his time with the authors of books, renounced this role himself: whether it was because he preferred to read other people's books that he didn't create one himself, or whether it was laziness—the legacy of rabbinical forebears who had others write books in their name—that discouraged him from setting down his own words in a book. Although he didn't write books, he didn't refrain from editing them. He used to rewrite lectures for various professors. Even famous authors asked him to correct their work. Since he read a lot, studied a lot, and had good judgment, these books may have gained more from his efforts than from those of their authors. He earned a meager livelihood, but, by doing without many luxuries, he could meet all his needs. And, since he didn't have it in mind to marry, he made no attempt to find other work. I said earlier that he came because of Tamara. As a matter of fact, it was by chance that Tamara met him when she was getting off the bus with her

*See p. 561, "Another Version."

friend at the Egged bus station and invited him to come with them, which he did.

We won't dwell on Taglicht and Tamara. Novelists allow Amnon to die a thousand deaths before he marries Tamar, linking one thing to another, and another, and still another. Which takes a lot of time. And, because I am occupied with another matter—with Manfred Herbst and Shira the nurse—I will say no more about Taglicht and Tamara, and get back to Manfred Herbst and Shira the nurse. I will show you Manfred Herbst. I won't show you Shira, whose tracks have not been uncovered, whose whereabouts remain unknown.

FINAL CHAPTER

*This chapter, which originally appeared at the end of Book Three, was
meant to be the final one. However, at a later date, Agnon put it aside
and began writing Book Four.*

Shira came and stood in the tree, looking straight ahead with bewildered eyes. When she saw Manfred, she shrieked, a fierce and bitter
shriek: "What are you doing here?" Manfred answered her and said,
"Shira, I'm here because of you." Shira raised her voice and said, "What
madness! You had better get out while you can." Manfred said, "Let
me tell you something." Shira shouted, "Madman, get out!" Manfred
said, "I beg of you, calm down, and I'll tell you something." Shira said,
"I don't want to hear what a fool has to tell." Manfred whispered,
"Shira." Shira turned away from him and was about to go. Manfred
said, "Stay a minute and listen. Then you can go."

Shira watched him and waited. Manfred said, "Give me your hand,
Shira." Shira said, "You must have lost your mind. Don't you know
what you're risking here?" Manfred nodded and said, "I know, I
know." Shira said, "And you still want to take the risk?" Manfred
sighed and said, "Whether I want to or not, I have no choice." Shira
studied him with her searching gaze and inquired, "How is one to
understand your words?" Manfred said, "It doesn't require much wisdom to understand. What I am saying is simple and obvious. I need to
be with you, Shira. Even if . . ." Shira said, "What do you mean, 'even
if'?" Manfred said, "Even if I end up in your situation." Shira said,
"What will your wife say? What will your daughters say?" Manfred
said, "You ask what my wife will say and what my daughters will say.
I have thought about all that. I have also thought about the son borne
to me by my wife." Shira said, "You have a son? Mazel tov." She

extended her hand to congratulate him, but, before touching him, she withdrew it.

Manfred continued, "Yes, Shira. A child was born to me; I was granted a son. He was admitted to the covenant of Abraham today. Do you remember, Shira, the night my daughter Sarah was born? After three daughters, my wife bore me a son, and the *brit* was today." Shira said, "And you couldn't find a time to visit me other than today?" Manfred said, "Shira, if it had been in my hands, I would have come sooner." Shira said, "The last time I saw you, you didn't seem especially enthralled with me. Remember, the day I bought new shoes?" Manfred nodded and said, "Yes, I remember." Shira leaned against the wall and lifted her leg to display a lovely, graceful shoe, shaped rather like a sandal. Herbst studied the shoe for a while and said, "Yes, a sandal." For a while he was silent. Then he sighed, a deep sigh, and asked, "Shira, how did you get here?" Shira said, "How did I get here? I came willingly. I may have come, not on my own and not willingly, but through the will of a power whose decrees determine our fate. Do you remember, Manfred, that I once told you I had been the companion of a Spanish prince and that I took him to the leper colony in Breslau?" Manfred nodded and said, "Yes, yes, Shira, I know. I have often thought about that. I assume that it's because of him that you are where you are." Shira said, "So you had better get out while you still can, my friend." Manfred said, "My dear Shira, I have decided otherwise." Shira fixed her eyes on him and asked, "Just what did you decide?" Manfred laughed sadly and said, "Can't you see?" Shira said, "I can't see anything, and I don't want to see anything. But I can tell you this—get out! Get out of here, get out immediately!" Manfred said, "If I do go, I'll come right back. Immediately." Shira was mystified and asked, "Why? Why do you say that if you go you'll come back?" Manfred said, "Why? As if I know why. Perhaps this too is the decree of that power whose will determines our actions."

Shira stood gazing at him in silence. Manfred said, "When I was a child, I read a story about an Indian holy man. There was a beautiful woman living in this holy man's town, who was pursued by all the men. I won't prolong the tale, nor will I try to tell you about her beauty and about all the men and their attempts to approach her. But I can tell you this: that monk, that holy man, was the only one in the entire land who had no interest in approaching her, even in looking at her. She sent a message inviting him to visit her, but he didn't come. She sent another message, but he didn't come. In time, she was stricken with leprosy, and all her admirers kept their distance. He, however, went to see her. She said to him, 'My beloved, my holy one, you are too late. I can't be anything to you now.' Do you hear me, Shira?" Shira said, "I hear you. And what was that holy man's response?" Manfred said, "I don't remember his response, but I remember the end of the story." Shira said, "What is the end of the story?" Manfred said, "Wait, Shira. I already recalled the end of the story." Shira said, "Then what is the end of the story?" Manfred said, "In the end, though she had so many admirers, only he stayed with her." Shira said, "And what did he say to her?" Manfred said, "He said this to her: 'In your days of glory, I could already foresee your end." Shira said, "And you saw in me just what that holy man saw?" Manfred said, "I didn't see those things but . . . How can I tell you? I once read a poem, and I found a line in it that sticks to my tongue." "What is it?" " 'Flesh such as yours will not soon be forgotten.' "

While they were standing there, a nurse came and said to Dr. Herbst, "Doctor, it's time to take leave of the lady." Manfred said, "Dear nurse, would you allow me to stay just a few minutes more?" The nurse said, "You can stay another five minutes. Five minutes, and no more." Manfred bowed to the nurse and stood before her in an attitude of mock reverence, saying, "Many thanks to you, kind lady. May the Lord respond to your prayers." He turned back to Shira rather suddenly and said, "He—that is to say, the Indian—stayed on with her." Then he said to her, in an altered voice, "And I intend to do what that Indian did. I'm going to stay with you, Shira." He seized Shira's hand and held on to it. Shira tried to extricate her hand from his. But he held on to it, fervently, until her hand and his were both bathed in sweat. As he held her hand, he leaned his mouth over hers and kissed it. For a long time, her lips clung to his, of their own accord. She suddenly slipped her mouth away from his and brushed his lips with her hand. Then she brushed her own lips. He, in the meanwhile, embraced her lovingly and exclaimed, "Shira, Shira."

ANOTHER VERSION

This fragment seems to fit into the final chapter (at the break on p. 554), though the chronology is problematic.

Herbst asked how he was and what he was doing. The young man smiled with characteristic shyness and thanked Herbst for taking an interest in him and asking about his affairs. But, being too shy to talk about himself, he fell silent. Herbst took no note of this and resumed his conversation with Taglicht. Taglicht interrupted and said to Herbst, "I see that you two are acquainted." Herbst nodded, as if to indicate that there was no need for elaboration, and once more resumed his conversation. Taglicht placed his hand on the young man's shoulder and said to Herbst, "Let's hear what our friend has to say." Herbst gazed at the young man, somewhat surprised, as one might gaze at a person he knows well enough to be certain he has nothing to offer.

At this point, it is worth mentioning that this young man, whose name was Heinrich Reiner, had come to Jerusalem a year earlier to enroll in the university, bringing with him letters to several professors and lecturers, including Dr. Herbst, from colleagues abroad, along with the request that they take him under their wing, et cetera. They may have taken him under their wing; they may have not. In any case, each and every one of these professors invited him to attend his lectures. He may have attended one or two lectures, but he didn't become a university student. Herbst saw him once or twice, after the first time, when he came to his home to deliver regards from a friend. It was not that the young man didn't appeal to Herbst. But Herbst didn't especially welcome him and didn't ask him to come again, because the relationship with that mutual friend was outdated, or per-

haps for other reasons. In the interim, Herbst dismissed the young
man from his mind and took no interest in him. Being somewhat shy,
he didn't presume to call on Herbst again. Now that he was with
Taglicht, they met Herbst, and Taglicht said, "Let's hear what our
friend here has to say." Herbst seemed surprised but willing to listen.
Let me present the substance of his story, some of it in his language
and some in my own.

Heinrich Reiner took on a job with a salary that didn't quite support
him but supplemented the allowance his father had provided. What sort
of job? One could consider it a job or a mission. There is a place in
Jerusalem called a leper colony, inhabited by those whose affliction is
incurable. Reiner took it upon himself to visit them, and he made a
special point of visiting the newcomers, who did not yet accept their
fate and were unwilling to be shut in forever. At this point, Reiner
recounted what we already know from the newspapers: that thirteen
lepers had been found in an old-age home, that most of them had mild
cases of leprosy, but that there was one advanced case among them that
seemed to be the source of the contagion. From which ethnic group and
from which social class did the patients derive? From every group and
every class. Men and women, old and young, Orthodox and free-
thinking, poor and rich. Yes, even the rich. There was a young girl
there from a rich family. How did she contract leprosy? Until yesterday, no one knew. Her mother visited her yesterday. She saw a woman
there who looked familiar, but she didn't know where she had seen her.
She asked her who she was, but the woman couldn't answer, because
half of her tongue and also her lips were so severely infected that she
could no longer speak. But the girl's mother couldn't rest until she
discovered who this woman was. She went to the office to inquire and
was told who she was. She remembered that this woman had worked
in her house fifteen years earlier, when her daughter was born. Reiner
said many other things about those wretchedly afflicted individuals,
who are betwixt the living and the dead, who are not quite alive and
not quite dead. What he related he related so vividly that one could
actually picture it. Now, imagine Manfred Herbst: Manfred Herbst,
who could barely tolerate a leper drawn on canvas, was now standing
with this man who mingles freely with lepers, speaks with them, and
talks about them. True, there are ways to protect oneself from leprosy.
Some people spend their vacations in that place. Professor Dalman, for
example, spends all his vacations in the leper colony, because his wife
is a nurse there. Herbst kept conjuring up images of every deformity,
of each disintegrating limb, and the like. He responded with a revulsion

that superseded any sort of compassion for these living corpses. At home, he found no respite from this sensation. He washed his face and hands many times with soap and eau de cologne, as if they had the power to erase the filth that filled his imagination. The next day, Herbst still could find no respite. He washed his hands several times that day, and, if he touched a book, he washed again. He didn't go out for two days and didn't go to Shira's apartment. He pictured all sorts of ways to contract that affliction. On the third day, when he went out, he met one of the clerks from the home for the aged, who was strolling with Axelrod, the hospital clerk. Herbst was overcome with terror, for the clerk was from the old-age home where those thirteen lepers had been discovered. And Axelrod, who, after all, worked in a hospital, was walking with him. Who knew if the other clerk had the disease, if he would infect Axelrod, if all the patients in the hospital would then be infected, including women in labor and newborns? But Herbst succeeded in controlling himself and resisted making a fool of himself by scolding Axelrod. He walked on, speculating: What do we know about these living corpses, and what don't we know about them? Apart from several myths and inane tales, Herbst knew nothing about lepers. He proceeded to collect all his knowledge about them and to consider it detail by detail. They say that, in days past, yet not so distant, when the Turks ruled the country, lepers used to walk through the city, and the people who lived there would fling them food. Herbst remembered this too: he had once read in the newspaper that some lepers in Rumania, who had been contained in a leper colony, escaped and went to a dentist's office. Several gentlewomen were there at the time. The doctor called the police, who came quickly, aimed their pistols at them, and returned them to the leper colony. Among this profusion of memories, he became aware of the drawing he had seen in the bookstore, with the leper peering at him, studying him, the bell in his hand rattling continually. As it happened, Herbst happened to recall the night he sat with Shira, when she showed him her picture album with an empty space where there had originally been a picture. When Herbst asked about the missing picture, she explained that, when she lived abroad, she had tended a patient who was a Spanish prince, that the prince had befriended her, giving her many gifts, as well as his picture. When, in the end, it turned out that he had leprosy, she was asked to accompany him to the leper colony in Breslau. At this point, she burned all his gifts, removed his picture from the album, and flung it into the fire.

Once again, I will say what I already said. Imagine this: Manfred Herbst enters a bookstore, finds a picture of a leper, hears references to a leper colony, suddenly remembers what he heard from Shira. Could such a chain of events fail to have an impact? Henceforth, Herbst was haunted by these concerns. Although he didn't put them into words, they remained fixed in his mind, so that, when he woke up knowing he hadn't dreamed about lepers, he felt that they had done him a favor.

One Shabbat morning, Herbst went out for a walk. It was one of those delightful Jerusalem mornings, with a lull between rains. Since the day was so delightful, the roads were a delight, his heart was filled with delight, and all his thoughts were delightful too. He wasn't thinking of Shira or of anything else that might confound him. He was seeing every tree, every rock that was there, all basking in the sweet Shabbat morning sunshine. Since he wanted to enjoy these pleasures fully, he turned toward the less frequented spots, where he found himself alone, like in the old days, when he had just come to the country. He kneeled down to collect some of the colored pebbles that were scattered along the road. Now that most areas have been built up, these delightful pebbles have all but disappeared. But, in those days, they were everywhere. If you were clever, you could collect them and make yourself a floor, which probably would not be a source of delight, because mosaic design was already a forgotten art. It's a fact that the territory he was walking in that day was right next to the leper colony. I don't know if Herbst realized this, but, even if he did, he would not have been upset. Because on that particular day he was utterly composed and untroubled.

He returned from his walk refreshed and happy. Henrietta was seated in her chair, all bundled up. Herbst looked at her, at her bloated face, at her belly, and said, "I'm hungry, Mother, hungry as a dozen wolves. I could eat you up, along with the baby that's inside you." Henrietta smiled and said, "I'll set the table right away, and we can have lunch. Please, dear, don't eat anything now, so you're sure to be hungry when you come to the table." Henrietta got up and went to the kitchen. Manfred went to the icebox, which had no ice in it because summer was over, took out the table wine, and poured some into a glass. The cool drink revived him. Meanwhile, little Sarah appeared, with the pipe Henrietta had given him for his birthday dangling from her mouth. That child is so adorable, she makes such delightful noises holding the pipe in her mouth and pretending to smoke it. "Mother, Mother," Manfred shouted. "Come and have a look." Now that she realized she was doing something special, the child continued to perform. Manfred lifted her up, sat down, and placed her on his lap, contemplating the small pleasures a man can enjoy in his own home, reflecting on the cleverness of Sarah, and of Zahara and Tamara when they were small. Now that they were both grown, distant and remote from him, though they caused him no pain, they didn't add to his pleasure. But he expected pleasure from the child Henrietta was about to produce. The fact is, before Sarah was born, it didn't occur to him that she would give him pleasure. But, now that he took pleasure in her, he was also pleased about the baby Henrietta was going to present him with very soon. What should we name the child? If it's a girl, we won't call her Atara. A three-way rhyme, Zahara-Tamara-Sarah, is quite enough.

While they were waiting, Manfred took Henrietta's hand and said, "Now, Mother, it's time you gave us a boy. Do you hear, Mother? I want a boy." Henrietta was quiet. Then she said, "I'll try." Manfred said, "Do you know something, Mother? I have a nice name for a boy." "What is it?" "Shlomo Yehuda." Henrietta said, "The name Shlomo is enough for me. Was your father's name Shlomo Yehuda?" Manfred said, "My father didn't have a Hebrew name." Henrietta said, "Then why is your heart set on Shlomo Yehuda?" Manfred said, "Let me tell you. The very first modern Jewish scholar was named Shlomo Yehuda Rappaport, the Shlomo Yehuda Rappaport who is known as Shiyr." Henrietta said, "Why do you suddenly look so downcast?" "Downcast? I didn't notice. Hand me the mirror," he said, pretending to joke. Manfred was immersed in thought. To keep his wife from noticing, he got up from the chair and said, "It was a mistake to drink wine, especially when I was overheated from my walk." Henrietta said, "Don't worry, Manfred. A healthy man like you can allow himself a glass of wine. In any case, don't have any more today." Manfred said, "Unless you give it to me, I won't have any more." He suddenly looked up at his wife and addressed her with affection, "Just say the word, and I'll abstain until the *brit.*" Henrietta said, "You're certain it will be a boy?" Manfred said, "You must admit, we've had more than enough of this *Weiblichkeit.* You yourself, Mother, and Zahara and Tamara and Sarah, as well as Zahara's daughter Arlozora. I am amazed that no one suspects Arlozoroff was killed by Germans. It's logical that he would have been killed by Germans."

Manfred put his head on the table and smoothed the cloth with his chin. He continued the gesture for a while. Then he lifted his head and stared at Henrietta for a long time. Henrietta felt his eyes on her and returned the stare, waiting for him to speak. Manfred said, "Do you remember the day I brought you to the hospital when Sarah was about to be born?" Henrietta smiled and said, "Now, Father, no woman is likely to forget such a day. Why do you ask if I remember it?" Manfred said, "You may remember the nurse who brought you flowers." Henrietta said, "Her name was Shira, wasn't it?" Manfred said, "If you say her name was Shira, let's assume it was Shira. I want to tell you something now. No one knows where she is." Henrietta said, "What do you mean, 'no one knows where she is'?" Manfred said, "If I say so, you can believe me. She left the hospital three months ago. She didn't say where she was going. She left no trace." Mrs. Herbst shuddered. After a brief pause, she said, "She probably went away and doesn't want anyone to know her whereabouts." Manfred said, "I know what you're thinking. You think she got pregnant and is hiding until after the birth." Henrietta said, "I really didn't think of that, but what you say is logical." Manfred said, "Actually not, Mother. There is reason to suspect she was killed or kidnapped by Bedouins." "And what is the government doing? Is it searching for her?" Manfred said, "The government! What an inspired idea! People are disappearing, and the government doesn't lift a finger to find them." Henrietta said, "Why did you push away the dish? Try some meat. It's very good, Father." Manfred said, "So, in your opinion, she is pregnant, and she'll suddenly reappear on the scene. I am of the opinion that someone like Shira, if she were pregnant, wouldn't be ashamed and wouldn't go into hiding." Henrietta said, "You know, Father, there are women who are daring in theory but timid in practice." Manfred lowered his head, fixed his eyes on Henrietta's feet, and said, "Mother, I must tell you something. I'm not pleased that you wear sandals all the time. True, sandals are comfortable. But, in your condition, there is reason to worry about flat feet, or, to use a more respectful term, fallen arches. When did you buy those sandals?" "When? If I'm not mistaken, I bought them before Tamara was born." Manfred said, "We calculate time by births, don't we, Mother. By now, even Tamara has left home. She is on her own and doesn't need us. In a few years, Sarah won't be dependent on us either. Where is the pipe? Where did it go?" Henrietta said, "Do you want to smoke the pipe?" "I don't want to smoke the pipe, but I don't like it when things disappear." Henrietta said, "We'll find it, we'll find it." Manfred said, "I already told you, the government doesn't lift a finger." Henrietta said, "I thought you were referring to the pipe, but I see you were referring to the nurse Shira." Manfred said, "I wasn't really thinking about her, but, now that you mention her, I remember." Henrietta said, "If we were to think about everything there is to think about, we wouldn't manage at all. Have some pudding. I made it from a recipe in the WIZO cookbook." Manfred said, "You yourself are quite a whizz-o." Henrietta smiled and said, "There are other women who are whizzes too." Manfred said, "I shouldn't have had wine, certainly not a whole glass, and on an empty stomach." Henrietta was amazed. "You had a whole glass?" Manfred nodded. "A whole glass, to the last drop. I was thirsty from my walk." Henrietta said, "You didn't tell me where you walked today." Manfred cried out in surprise, "I didn't tell you? I told you, and you forgot. I definitely told you that I went up to Mount Zion, circled the entire wall, and came down at the Dung Gate. Then I made my way back via the shelters, which is where I met the old printer, the one who printed my article and made the offprints for me. You might have a dress or a blouse you have no use for, Mother. I promised the printer's wife I would find something for one of her acquaintances, a Polish aristocrat who has nothing to wear. I think the wine is wearing off. At any rate, I learned my lesson. A man tries to snatch some pleasure, and it retaliates for hours on end. After dinner, I'll lie down and sober up. Why didn't I loosen my tie before dinner? I've been sitting here feeling this burden on me, as if there were a noose around my neck, as if I were going to be hung from the gallows. Remember the night we spent in Ahinoam, Mother? When Zahara was waiting to give birth?"

Henrietta smiled contentedly and said, "No woman is likely to forget such a night." Manfred said, "I haven't forgotten it either. I didn't tell you the dream I had, nor did you urge me to tell it. If you like, I'll tell it to you now." A tremor passed through his flesh; a similar tremor passed through her flesh as well. Manfred took his wife's hand, caressed it, and said to her, "There aren't many women like you. You don't burden me with questions, for which I am always very grateful." Henrietta said, "Didn't you want to tell me your dream?" Manfred caressed her again and said, "Yes, I did. I will tell it now. That night, I was being led to the gallows." "My God, how awful," Henrietta cried, burying her face in her hands. "Yes, it was awful; it was dreadful," Manfred echoed. "But not for your reason, Mother. For another reason. I knew there was one person who could have saved me. But that person didn't lift a finger on my behalf." Henrietta asked Manfred, "Do you remember who that person was?" Manfred said, "Don't ask, Mother. Don't ask." Henrietta said, "I'm not asking, and I don't want to know." Manfred said, "I don't actually remember who it was. But that night, at that moment, I knew who it was." "That's odd." "Even more odd is the fact that, in my dream, I was upset by the idea that if you— meaning you and our daughters—should hear this news, you would also be upset." Henrietta looked at him in astonishment and said, "Did you doubt that——" Manfred interrupted her and said, "That's not what seemed odd to me. What seemed odd was that I thought I wouldn't be upset if I were to vanish from the face of the earth, though I was aware of the pain it would cause the rest of you. Don't be angry with me, Mother. It's not that you taught me at all times, to be truthful with you, Mother. But your proper life and your upright opinions lead me to tell you the truth, whether I want to or not."

Henrietta took Manfred's hand, placed it on her heart, and said, "Life is so hard for you, Manfred." "Hard for me?" Manfred exclaimed in surprise, as if he had been addressed by a name other than his own. Henrietta said, "What brings on these sad thoughts?" Manfred answered, laughing, "The sad thoughts bring themselves on. It's not a paradox, Mother. That's really how it is. You may think I am sad because I failed to finish my book. Believe me, even if I had finished two arm's-lengths worth of books, nothing would change for me. Do you remember what Goethe said about writing *Werther?* I don't remember the precise words, but I do remember the message. Even if I had a tenured professorship, that wouldn't change anything. My daughters don't need me. You, Mother, don't need me either. I myself have no need of me. So . . ." "So . . . ?" "Now, Mother, don't worry that I'll put a bullet through my heart. People like me don't take their own life. They go on living, even when their strength gives out and they don't have what it takes to live. They live on, to the point of total decay, through all sorts of situations, by any means."

Henrietta gazed at her husband with a cold, analytical eye, with neither animosity nor empathy, and said, "Has something happened to you?" Manfred said, "Nothing happened to me." Henrietta said, "The kind of things you've been saying don't occur to a person all of a sudden." "All of a sudden?" "Henrietta added, "And their cause isn't simple." "Simple?" Herbst already regretted what he had said to his wife and hoped to blur his words. He looked at his wife, searching her face for a sign of affection. Her face looked harsh and was glazed with contempt. She got up, but she didn't clear the empty dishes, nor did she collect the remnants of the meal. Manfred got up, too, and went to his room. He paced back and forth, looked out the window, and resumed his pacing, as though there were no chair or couch in the room. After a while, he lit a cigarette and went to the window. The ashes fell on the rug, but he took no notice. When the cigarette began to burn his fingers, he started, dumped it in an ashtray, and crushed it with a book. Then he went to the bookcase, extended his arms, and, with a sweeping gesture, declared, in the style of Professor Bachlam,

"I am not the author of these books. I don't wish to be an Author of
Many Books. I'm willing to disavow what I've already written, if you
like." He gazed at the two bookcases again and calculated: What will
you be worth to my wife when I'm dead? He pictured his friends
coming to her, feigning virtue to acquire valuable books at bargain
prices. "Damn it!" he shouted, spitting angrily. He began to pace the
room again, scanning the walls, which were lined with photographs of
himself and his friends, each face expressing genius that would be
everlasting and eternal, all of them learned, involved in scholarship and
in the pursuit of wisdom, maintaining contact with scholars throughout
the world. She's first rate, Herbst reflected, contemplating the picture
of his wife that was on his desk. If not for her, I would run away to
the ends of the earth, to far-off isles, leaving you, all of you, to your own
devices, to make a mess of your own—to paraphrase the words of
Augustus, king of Saxony, when he was about to be deposed.

Henrietta opened the door quietly and came in. She said, "So you're
not asleep." She placed her hand on his shoulders and said, "I see you
were working." He glanced at the bundle of notes and offprints, and
said with disdain, "You're deceiving yourself, just as I have deceived
myself. If I were an honest man, I would burn this entire heap of
garbage and scatter it to the winds." "Don't be so harsh. Not everyone
has the privilege of being an outstanding scholar. Who was it you
wanted to name our son after? It was Shlomo, and there was another
name too." "It doesn't matter now." "But it matters to me. Tell me."
"Shlomo Yehuda Rappaport." "I thought it over, and I realize that
Shlomo Yehuda is a fine name." "How could you think it over if you
didn't even remember the second name? We must be honest rather than
deceive ourselves, even in trivial matters. If one allows himself to cheat
in trivial matters, he ends up deceiving himself in important matters as
well." She smoothed his hair and said, "Is that what you think of me,
Manfred? You think I deceive myself?" "You're first rate, but anything
that gets dragged in the mud all the time ends up damaged. It's good
that you've changed your shoes. In my childhood, I never pictured a
respectable woman in house slippers, certainly not in sandals. All these
young women in their odd costumes—in pants, even work pants—are
defacing the Jerusalem landscape. Don't you agree?" He took her hand
in his and studied her face. Then he withdrew his hand and said, "I have
something awful to tell you." Mrs. Herbst was alarmed and said,
"You've had some news about the girls?" "Calm down, Mother. Calm
down. I didn't hear anything about the girls. There's no reason to think

anything bad has happened to them. What I want to tell you is entirely unrelated to our daughters." "You frighten me so," she said. "It doesn't matter. It's best that you know the truth. We were talking about the nurse Shira today. You ought to know that, the very night you were in the hospital, in the throes of labor, I made love to her. Why are you silent, Henrietta?" "And this fills you with the sadness of remorse, though in fact she didn't bear your child." "I expected you to fling your sandal in my face." "But I'm wearing shoes." "You're teasing me. If you knew how much I've suffered and agonized over this." She smoothed his brow and said, "Calm down, Manfred. Calm down. In our generation, men are no longer angels." "But the women are all angels. They're all like you, right?" Manfred screamed, a terrifying scream. "I'm no angel either. If I have restricted myself to this company there are other reasons: because I don't follow my impulses." "If I could reproach you in this respect, it would be easier for me to bear my sorrow. You don't want to hear how it happened." "I can imagine. You were without a woman for several months. Then a woman appeared, and you were seduced." "That's exactly how it was. You don't hate her? But I hate her. My heart seethes with repressed hate for that woman, because . . ." "Because she was your downfall." "Yes. But, to tell the truth, because she doesn't want to be my downfall any longer." "So you continued to pursue her, but she didn't respond. And, as I understand it, you still want her." "How can you say such a thing, when she is dead?" "Dead? Didn't you say she disappeared?" "Whether or not she disappeared, in any case she doesn't exist for me." "But you think about her?" "Is there anyone I don't think about? If I told you all the women I think about, you would be shocked." "Thoughts are permitted." "In your opinion, actions are permitted too." "This doesn't apply to everyone, or to every situation. Let's have some coffee." "Actually, Henrietta, I ought to be pleased that you accepted the news without rage or anger. But, to tell the truth, it would be better if you had thrown me out, if you had called me a villain, slapped my face, spat on me." She took his hand, slapped his fingers, and said, "You're a glutton. That's what we do to gluttons." "You're making a farce out of this." "Would you rather I made it into a tragedy?" she said, somewhat sternly, so that Manfred began to regret having challenged her. She seemed suddenly upset, but then her face was overcome with joy, and she said, "Shlomo Yehuda is announcing himself. See, I also think it's a boy." "I hear someone coming. To hell with the company. I don't want to see anyone." "Manfred, brace yourself. Here's the cologne. Sprinkle a few drops on your forehead, Oh, you spilled it on your papers." "Then it will be easier to set fire to them." "That's how much regard you have for years of work." She, too, grew sad, which she hadn't been in a long time.

Never were guests as welcome to Mrs. Herbst as they were at that moment. She knew it was Herbst's way to be angry when someone came, because of the interruption; that, as soon as he saw the guests, he would enjoy them; that he was looking for an excuse to stop working and would welcome them for relieving him of the choice.

(Describe the various guests as well as their conversations. The young man may be one of them.)*

---

*The sentence in parentheses was added by Agnon in pencil at the end of the chapter. The the guests, and the young man Herbst is expecting, are mentioned in another fragment, not included here. [—Emuna Agnon]

AFTERWORD
by Robert Alter

Shira is S. Y. Agnon's culminating effort to articulate through the comprehensive form of the novel his vision of the role of art in human reality. It engaged him—with long interruptions, during which he devoted himself to shorter fiction—for almost a quarter of a century. On his deathbed, in 1970, he gave his daughter instructions to publish the novel with Book Four still incomplete. Posthumously, the text of *Shira* remains unstable. The first Hebrew edition in 1971 ends with the fragmentary ninth chapter of Book Four, which includes Herbst's musings on the professor of medicine who injects himself with a dangerous disease in order to find a cure (a historical figure at the Hebrew University, Shaul Adler), and breaks off with the narrator's declaration that Shira has disappeared and cannot be found. A subsequent edition in 1974 appended the brief episode Agnon had marked in manuscript as "Last Chapter," in which Herbst joins Shira in the leper hospital; this ending was originally intended to conclude Book Three but was set aside when Agnon went on to write a fourth book. In 1978, another substantial episode, like "Last Chapter" incorporated in the present version, was published: corresponding in fictional time to chapters 8–19 of Book Three, it prepares the way for Herbst's discovery of Shira in the leper hospital and also explores a narrative possibility not raised elsewhere—Herbst's confession of his infidelity to his wife.

Incomplete as it is, and even with some signs of uncertainty in its digressive and repetitive patterns, *Shira* is a remarkable work. The psychosexual realism—most strikingly evident in Herbst's guilt-ridden, violence-prone, sadomasochistic dreams and fantasies—surpasses anything else Agnon did in this vein. What may have prevented him from finishing the book was that beyond any aim of realistic representation of psyche and social milieu, Agnon wanted to imagine in concrete novelistic detail the ultimate relation of art (or "poetry," the meaning of Shira's name) to truth, or, in regard to genre, to pass through the dense medium of realism to allegory, and that was a consummation that eluded him.

It may be helpful to place *Shira* in Agnon's chronological development as a novelist. His earliest Hebrew fiction (there had been a few Yiddish stories before) was published in the half-dozen years after his arrival in Palestine from Galicia in 1907 at the age of nineteen, and consisted entirely of short stories and novellas. Many of these were in the subtly ventriloquistic mode of a traditional Hebrew teller of tales, and it was this identity that figured in most readers' minds as Agnon rapidly made himself a commanding figure in Hebrew prose. Characteristically, his artfully archaizing novella set in premodern Galicia, *And the Crooked Shall Be Straight* (1912), was widely perceived in these years as his emblematic achievement. In 1913 Agnon left Palestine for Germany, ostensibly for a brief stay, but the war and a variety of personal reasons held him there till 1924. It is during the first few years of his German sojourn that he arrives at artistic maturity, rigorously revising his often effusive early stories in a precise, understated, classicizing prose that would remain his hallmark. Shortly after the war, he was working on his first novel, an autobiographical fiction he called *In the Bond of Life.* Though he announced in a letter written in 1920 that it would soon be in print, he must have had difficulties with it because it was still in manuscript in 1924 when it was destroyed in a fire that devastated his apartment in Homburg, and Agnon never attempted to reconstruct the book. His first long integrated work, *The Bridal Canopy* (1931; English trans., 1967), is only marginally a novel, because it reverts to the medieval and Renaissance form of the frame-story—the peregrinations of a protagonist and his companion—into which is introduced a variegated abundance of anecdotes, fables, tall tales, and the like.

Meanwhile, Agnon continued to write realistic short fiction far removed from both the eighteenth-century setting and the formal traditionalism of *The Bridal Canopy,* and this involvement in social and psychological realism culminated in his first proper novel, *A Simple Story* (1935, English trans., 1985), a book more restricted in scope than the novels that would follow but, in the rendering of the evolution of a psychosis and its ironically qualified cure, probably the most flawlessly sustained of all his novels. From this point on, though he continued to experiment with different modes of short fiction, from anecdotal and reminiscent to surrealist and symbolic, his commitment to the capaciousness of the novel form was clear. In 1939, writing with uncharacteristic rapidity, he produced *A Guest for the Night* (English trans., 1968), his personal confrontation, on the eve of the Second World War, with the inward dying of European Judaism. In 1945 he brought out an even more ambitiously original novel, *Just Yesterday* (still untranslated), set in the Palestine he had encountered as a very young man, in which he combines historical realism with intricate symbolism and tragic-grotesque humor (some of the most remarkable chapters, initially composed in the early thirties, follow the canine viewpoint of a Jerusalem mongrel named Balak, who proves to be the most philosophically reflective and the most engaging character in the book).

In each of the three novels Agnon published from 1935 to 1945, he had found ways to go strikingly beyond his previous work in the fashioning of new fictional forms and in the range of themes he was able to sound. It was clearly his intention to go beyond himself once again in *Shira*, and he apparently set to work on the new novel not long after the appearance of *Just Yesterday*. Between 1949 and 1952, he published chapters of *Shira* in a literary yearbook issued by the newspaper *Ha'a-retz*, material corresponding to most of Book One and Book Two of the novel as we have it. The excitement roused in Hebrew literary circles was then frustrated as Agnon confined the continuation of *Shira* to the privacy of his drawer, pursuing other projects in print. In 1966, after he received the Nobel Prize, he allowed two more chapters to appear, and, with failing physical powers, he was working on *Shira* in his last years, still hoping to forge it into what it would in any case, even incomplete, prove to be—his great last testament as a writer.

Shira is at once Agnon's fullest invocation of the nineteenth-century European novel and a deliberate modernist demonstration of the collapse of the thematic concerns and formal strategies of the nineteenth-century novel. Adultery as an attempted escape from the flatness and the stifling routine of bourgeois society is, of course, one of the two or three great recurrent themes of the traditional novel. One could not have chosen a more thoroughly bourgeois realm in the Palestine of the 1930s than the milieu of the Hebrew University with its predominantly German-Jewish professorate, where propriety, conformism, industriousness, self-importance, and social status were the governing values. Agnon, who lived on the margins of the Hebrew University, some of his best friends being members of its faculty, knew this world well and rendered it in his last novel with a shrewd satiric eye. *Shira*, however, turns out to be something quite different from a latter-day Hebrew reprise of *Madame Bovary* and *Anna Karenina* in an academic setting. Herbst, unlike Flaubert's Emma, does not "discover in adultery all the platitudes of married life" but, on the contrary, finds that a fleeting carnal encounter with an unlikely object of desire opens up vertiginous new perspectives, makes bourgeois hearth and home unlivable for him, impels him in ways he is hardly conscious of to do something radically other with his life.

The background of political violence is one of the keys to the difference between *Shira* and the tradition of the European novel that it recalls. The bourgeois academic world from which Manfred Herbst derives is not a fixed datum of social reality, as would be the case in a nineteenth-century novel, but is seen instead as a fragile choreography of complacent social rituals on the brink of a historical abyss. The novel is set in the late thirties, in the midst of the murderous Arab attacks on the Jewish population of Palestine that began in 1936. The ideological tension between Jewish militants, like the underground group to which Herbst's daughter Tamara belongs, and the pacifists of the Brit Shalom organization at the Hebrew University, is frequently invoked. On the European horizon that has the most urgent thematic relevance to all that transpires in the Jerusalem setting of the novel, Herbst's German homeland is preparing the machinery for genocide. In a world moving rapidly from episodic terror to systematic mass murder on the most unprecedented scale, mere private experience—the staple of the classic novel—dwindles to insignificance. Adultery can no longer be even the illusory personal adventure it was in nineteenth-century fiction, and the very premise of the linear plot of the novel of adultery is called into question: Herbst's involvement with Shira cannot go anywhere as a developing chain of fictional events; instead, he circles around and around the idea of Shira, or, what amounts to the same thing, around what Shira's disturbing presence has released within him.

Let me state this in terms of the quest for knowledge that is a central issue in the novel. Herbst and his fellow cultivators of the grove of academe, equipped with their index cards and bibliographies and learned journals, sedulously pursue the most esoteric and distant objects of knowledge—the burial customs of ancient Byzantium, the alphabets of long-lost languages. The purported sphere of these objects of knowledge is history, but do these historical investigations, beyond their utility in advancing the careers of the investigators, tell us anything essential about the historical forces that are about to move the German nation to gun down, gas, and incinerate millions of men, women, and children? The European perpetrators of these horrors are, after all, at least in part products of the same academic culture as Herbst and his colleagues. The most troubling question a Jewish writer after 1945 could raise is variously intimated here, particularly in Herbst's nightmares and hallucinations: Could there be a subterranean connection between forces at work, however repressed, within the civilized Jew and the planners and executors of mass murder who are, after all, men like you and me? At the beginning of the novel, Herbst is unable to write that big second book which will earn him his professorship because he has a writer's block. As the effects of his exposure to Shira sink in, he is unable to write it because it has become pointless, such knowledge as could be realized through it felt to be irrelevant. Instead, Herbst hits on the desperate idea of writing a tragedy, for his experience with the radical ambiguity of eros in his involvement with Shira/Poetry leads him to sense that art, unlike historical inquiry, has the capacity to produce probing, painful self-knowledge, and is able to envisage history not as a sequence of documented events but as a terrible interplay of energies of love and death, health and ghastly sickness. Herbst, with his habits of academic timidity, his hesitant and unfocused character, may not ever be capable of creating such exacting art, but he is ineluctably drawn to the idea of it.

The underlying concern with the nature of art in *Shira* is reflected in its wealth of references—scrupulously avoided elsewhere in Agnon's fiction—to European writers: Goethe, Nietzsche, Balzac, Rilke, Gottfried Keller, Stefan George, not to speak of the Greek tragedians and their German scholarly expositors whom Herbst reviews in his quixotic attempt to write a tragedy (ostensibly, a historical drama set in the Byzantine period but unconsciously a reflection of his own agonizing erotic dilemma with Shira). From one point of view, this is a novel about the impossibility of tragedy in the modern age, and especially after the advent of Hitler—that is to say, the impossibility of a literary form that assigns meaning to suffering, or represents an experience of transcendence through suffering. In consonance with this concern with tragedy, a good deal of weight is given to Nietzsche's notion in *The Birth of Tragedy* of the roots of the genre in an experience of violent primal forces contained by artistic form—Herbst, preeminently a "Socratic" man in Nietzsche's negative characterization of German academic culture, at one point runs across a first edition of *The Birth of Tragedy* in an antiquarian bookshop.

Another manifestation of Agnon's preoccupation here with the way art illuminates reality is the attention devoted to painting, again, a thoroughly uncharacteristic emphasis in his fiction. Three painters figure significantly in the novel: Rembrandt and Böcklin, who recur as motifs in connection with Shira, and the anonymous artist from the school of Breughel responsible for the stupendous canvas of the leper and the townscape (III:16) that constitutes Herbst's great moment of terrifying and alluring revelation. A look at how the three painters interact in the novel may suggest something of what Agnon was trying to say about art, and perhaps also why he found his way to a conclusion of the novel ultimately blocked.

If art, or poetry, is a route to knowledge radically different from the academic enterprise that has been Herbst's world, Agnon sees as its defining characteristic a capacity to fuse antinomies, to break down the logically marked categories—Herbst's boxes full of carefully inscribed research notes—presupposed by scholarly investigation. The Breughelian painting Herbst discovers at the antiquarian's is a multiple transgression of the borderlines of reason, and that, he realizes, is the power of its truthful vision. The leper's eye-sockets are mostly eaten away by the disease, yet they are alive and seek life—a paradox that reenacts the underlying achievement of the painter, "who imbued the inanimate with the breath of life." The medium of the painting is of course silent, but Herbst, contemplating the warning bell held by the leper, experiences a kind of synesthetic hallucination, hears the terrible clanging sound, and feels the waves of the disease radiating out from the leper's hand. The painting from the school of Breughel, as I have proposed elsewhere,* is in its formal and thematic deployment a model for the kind of art embodied in *Shira* itself: in the foreground, the horrific and compelling figure of the diseased person, intimating an impending cataclysm; in the background, half out of focus, the oblivious burghers complacently going about their daily pursuits. Agnon gives us not only the artwork but also an exemplary audience for it in Herbst. The historian of Byzantium is mesmerized by the painting in a paradoxically double way: "he looked at it, again and again with panic in his eyes and desire in his heart." The painting at once scares him and translates him to an unwonted plane of experience, because it both speaks eloquently to a universal truth of human experience and gives him back a potent image, of which he is scarcely conscious, of his own life.

Seeking relief from the terrible intensity of the Breughelian painting, Herbst flips through a stack of Rembrandt reproductions and comes to *The Night Watch,* on which he dwells. Rembrandt would seem to present a kind of art antithetical to that of the anonymous painter from the school of Breughel. The narrator tells us that Herbst now experiences a sense of melancholy accompanied by "inner tranquility" (*menukhat hanefesh,* literally, "soul's rest"), a tranquility usually identi-

---

*"A Novel of the Post-Tragic World," in my book *Defenses of the Imagination* (Philadelphia, 1977).

fied as harmony but which he, the narrator, prefers to associate with the illumination of knowledge. The opposition, however, between Rembrandtian and Breughelian art rapidly dissolves, like most of the key oppositions in the novel. To begin with, *The Night Watch* immediately makes Herbst think of Shira, who had been looking for a reproduction of the painting, and she is doubly associated with disease—the wasting disease that by this point we suspect she has contracted, and her hapless lover's disease of the spirit manifested in his obsessive relationship with her. But a few minutes later in narrated time, Herbst suddenly realizes that his memory has played a trick on him, or, in the psychoanalytic terms never far from Agnon's way of conceiving things from the thirties onward, he has temporarily repressed something. It was not *The Night Watch*, with its beautifully composed sense of confident procession, that Shira wanted, but another Rembrandt painting, *The Anatomy Lesson*. The clinical subject of the latter painting might of course have a certain professional appeal to Shira as a nurse, but what is more important is that its central subject is not living men marching but a cadaver, and thus it is linked with the representation of the living-dead leper in the anonymous canvas.

Death as a subject, in turn, connects Rembrandt with Böcklin, the artist responsible for the painting of the death's-head that Shira keeps in her apartment. Arnold Böcklin, a Swiss painter much in fashion in Central Europe toward the end of the nineteenth century (Stefan George wrote a poem about him), provides one of the teasing keys to *Shira*. Böcklin had a pronounced preference for mythological and allegorical topics, often rendered with a sharp realism of detail, and in pursuing this interest he repeatedly devoted emphatic attention to those figures of classical mythology associated with a riot of sensuality—Pan, satyrs, centaurs, Triton disporting himself with a Nereid. He also produced two versions of an allegorical painting that is particularly pertinent to the central thematic complex of *Shira*: entitled *Poetry and Painting*, it shows two female figures on either side of a fountain (presumably, the Pierian Spring), Poetry on the left, naked to the waist, leaning on the fountain's edge; Painting on the right, enveloped in drapery, dipping one hand into the water while with the other she holds a palette. Interestingly, Böcklin never did a painting of a skull, if one can trust the testimony of the comprehensive illustrated catalogue of his paintings published in Berne in 1977. He was, however, much preoccupied with death, which he characteristically represented in a histrionic mode that has a strong affinity with Symbolist painting. One scene he painted a few times was *The Island of Death*, in which the island looms as a spooky vertical mass against a dark background, with a small boat approaching it in the foreground, rowed by a presumably male figure, his back to us, while a female figure in white stands erect in the boat. One of his last paintings, *The Plague* (1898), exhibits a more brutally direct relevance to *Shira:* a hideous female figure, with large wings and grotesque tail, yet more woman than monster, swoops down over the streets of a town.

The reproduction that hangs on Shira's wall is probably of *Self-Portrait with Death as Fiddler* (1872). It is possible that Agnon simply forgot the self-portrait and concentrated on the skull when he introduced the painting into his novel, but given his frequently calculating coyness as a writer, it seems more likely that he deliberately suppressed the entire foreground of the canvas. In the foreground, Böcklin, wearing an elegant dark smock, stands with palette in one hand and brush in the other, his trim beard delicately modeled by a source of light from the upper left, his lively lucid eyes intent on the canvas he is painting. Behind him, in the upper right quadrant of the painting, virtually leaning on the painter's back, death as a leering skull with bony hand—rendered in the same precise detail as the figure of the artist—scratches away on his fiddle. That missing artist absorbed in his work who stands in front of the figure of death is, in one respect, what *Shira* is all about.

Death is, I think, a specter of many faces in this somber, troubling novel. It has, to begin with, certain specific historical resonances for the period of the late 1930s in which the action is set. In the two decades since 1914, death had given ample evidence of having been instated as the regnant *Zeitgeist* of the century. Herbst recalls wading up to his knees in blood as a soldier in the great senseless slaughter that was the First World War. The novel begins with mention of a young man murdered by Arabs, and in these days of organized terrorist assaults and random violence against the Jews of Palestine that began in 1936, there is a repeated drumbeat of killings in the background of the main action. On the European horizon, German Jews are desperately trying to escape, many of them sensing that Germany is about to turn into a vast death-trap. But beyond Agnon's ultimately political concern with the historical moment as a time of endemic murder, he is also gripped by the timeless allegory of Böcklin's painting: every artist, in every age, as an ineluctable given of his mortal condition, works with death fiddling at his back, and cannot create any art meaningfully anchored in the human condition unless he makes the potency of death part of it, at once breathing life into the inanimate and incorporating death in his living creation. Agnon was nearing sixty when he began work on the novel and an octogenarian when he made his last concerted effort to finish it, and it is easy enough to imagine that he saw himself in Böcklin's attitude as self-portraitist, the grim fiddler just behind him.

Herbst takes due notice of the Böcklin painting in Shira's apartment, and he is several times bothered by an oddly literal question about it: "Did Böcklin paint from a model or from his imagination? Why do I ask? Herbst wondered about himself" (I:29). Why, indeed, should so sophisticated an intellectual trouble himself about whether the painter used a model or not? The question, it should be observed, makes somewhat better sense if one keeps in mind not just the skull but both figures in *Self-Portrait with Death as Fiddler,* for then, since Böcklin demonstrably used himself as the model for the painter, one might begin to speculate about the "source" for the macabre fiddler standing behind the painter, the very hybrid nature of the composition putting to the test any simple mimetic conception of art. A couple of paragraphs later in the same chapter, a clue, or at least a dangling possibility of connection, is provided for Herbst's question. Again he asks himself whether Böcklin worked from a model or from his imagination, but this time he decides firmly on the latter alternative when he recalls that Böcklin "complained that he never had the chance to draw a woman from life because his wife, who was Italian, was jealous and wouldn't allow him to have a model in his studio." There is an instructive overlap, then, between painting eros and painting thanatos from the imagination rather than from a model. The particular link is important enough for Herbst to pick it up again explicitly in a dream somewhat later in the novel (II:7). In the dream he accompanies his daughter Tamara to Greece, where she means to undertake a study of verse meters (the word *shira* is used here for poetry). The father is glad to have gone with his daughter on the trip for "otherwise she would have seen him walking with Shira, which was not advisable, because Henrietta was in collusion with the wife of a teacher from Beit Hakerem. They agreed to prohibit their husbands from bringing other women to their studios, declaring, 'If they want to draw—let them draw skulls.' " One notes that Böcklin's allegorical pair, *Dichtung und Malerei,* Poetry and Painting, follow in quick sequence in the dream.

Agnon gives one further twist to the Böcklin painting by turning it at one point into a kind of reversed portrait of Dorian Gray: as Shira visibly deteriorates, the painting deteriorates with her and so its artificial deathliness becomes progressively more lifelike: "The picture became so darkened that it would frighten you, as though a real skull were staring at you" (II:2). Agnon never entirely renounced the macabre interests of his early neo-Gothicism, and though here the ghastly correspondence between painter and owner is given a perfectly plausible explanation—as Shira neglects herself, she neglects her possessions and no longer bothers to dust the painting—troubling thoughts are stirred about the status in reality of the artwork. Its origins, or at least the origins of the part of the Böcklin painting mentioned in the novel, are not in the representation of a model but in the artist's imagination, and yet the unforeseen intercourse between painting and experience produces a spectral affinity between the two, imbuing the artwork with an air of reality the artist himself had not given it.

Let us try to pull these strands together and consider the kind of conclusion to which Agnon wanted them to lead. Shira, hard-bitten, mannish, unseductive, coldly imperious, neither young nor pretty, seems an unlikely candidate either for the focus of an erotic obsession or for the symbolic representation of Poetry. It seems to me, however, that all these unappetizing traits are precisely what makes her the perfect conduit to carry Herbst from the realm of scholarship to the realm of poetry. Agnon's figure for Poetry is no classical maiden in decorous *déshabillé*. Art as he conceives it is a violation of all the conventional expectations of bourgeois rationality. In Freudian terms, the roots of art are in the premoral realm of polymorphous perversity. It is hard to reconcile anything in the character of Shira with ordinary notions of the good and the beautiful, and once Herbst has learned something about her bizarre sexual history, the initial ambiguity of identity between female and male that he perceives in her is compounded by others in his fantasies: Shira is both the rapist and the raped, the wielder of terrible weapons and the dismembered female victim, the nurturer of mothers and infants and the asocial disrupter of families, nurse and source of contagion. Sexually, she clearly appeals to Herbst because she is everything that his faded-blonde, maternal, sweetly solicitous wife is not, and in the thematic logic of the novel, it is necessary that he be detached from the complacencies of the haven of domesticity in order to be inducted into the soul-trying realm of poetry. The novel stresses the indissoluable bond between poetry and eros, because in Agnon's view what art does is give the revelatory coherence of form to erotic energies (the affinity with both Nietzsche and Freud is not accidental), and, conversely, the many-faced spirit of eros, both god and monster, is the very motor-force of art. It is instructive that Agnon's major fiction before *Shira* repeatedly focuses on some form of gravely impaired male sexuality *(A Simple Story, Just Yesterday,* novellas like *The Hill of Sand* and *Betrothed)*; only in this novel is there emotionally affecting consummation—"Flesh such as yours will not soon be forgotten"—however elusive the object of desire subsequently proves to be.

But the most crucial crossing of opposites associated with Shira is the wedding of health and sickness, love and death. At the beginning, the freckle-like protuberances on Shira's cheeks seem to be merely a token of her mannish unattractiveness; eventually, we realize that they were an early sign of her leprosy, and so the death's-head on her wall becomes an emblem of the fate to which she is consigned, in which Herbst will finally join her. It is reasonable to assume that Agnon, who made a careful study of Freud in the 1930s and probably read him episodically earlier during his sojourn in Germany, followed Freud in positing eros and thanatos as the two universal driving forces of the psyche. A couple of the passages we have glanced at establish an eerie equivalence between the two. If Böcklin, Herbst reasons, was obliged to use only the power of his imagination for the female figures he painted, the same must be true for his painting of the skull. And if Herbst in his dream, constrained like Böcklin by his wife's jealousy, is denied access to female models, he is invited to substitute bony death for woman's flesh as the subject of his art. In the end, no model is required for either, because love and death are so deeply seated in every one of us, constituting the matrix of all our human imaginings.

A small point in Agnon's Hebrew makes the force of his ramified use of painting particularly clear. The standard Hebrew verb "to paint," *tzayer,* is also the verb Agnon uses for "to imagine." A chief reason for Herbst's failure to write his tragedy is that he is too fastidious to imagine, or literally "paint to himself," the concrete suffering of the leper who figures centrally in its plot. "Herbst was afraid to immerse himself in that sickness and explore it, to picture various aspects of leprosy, such as how lepers relate to each other or how they function in conjugal terms" (II:17). The true artist is the person, like Rembrandt of *The Anatomy Lesson,* like the anonymous painter of the school of Breughel, and like Böcklin, who looks on death and disease clear-eyed and unflinching, just as we see the face of Böcklin in his self-portrait serenely scrutinizing his canvas.

If the artist's credo put forth by *Shira* is in one respect distinctly modernist, embracing the idea of art as an unflinching "technique of trouble," in R. B. Blackmur's phrase, it also has an oddly medieval feeling. Herbst is a historian of Byzantium versed in the ascetic practices of the early Christians, and the novel draws explicit parallels between the monastic renunciation of worldly life and the withdrawal to the leper hospital that Herbst will choose as his final fulfillment. In some of his earlier fiction, Agnon had set up a simple alternative between art and eros, depicting protagonists who renounce the gratification of desire in the name of the pursuit of art. Here, on the other hand, desire joins hands with art in the magic circle of imminent death, removed from the shallow egotism and the complacent self-deceptions of everyday social existence. This is chiefly what I had in mind earlier when I proposed that in *Shira* Agnon seeks to move through realism to allegory. And this, I suspect, was precisely the problem that bedeviled him for nearly two decades after the initial élan that produced Books One and Two. How was he to take Herbst, a figure with a certain academic pedigree, a family history, individual work habits and domestic tics, and translate him into the symbolic sphere where poetry, desire, and death were one; and what face could Shira, hitherto also a novelistic character with an individual sensibility and a personal history, show in that ultimate locus of thematic convergences, withdrawn from the worldly realm? There is a structural analogy, though I am not proposing any influence, between the ending of *Shira* and the ending of Stendhal's *Charterhouse of Parma.* Stendhal, too, sought to transport a hero entrammeled in the petty machinations of worldly life to a privileged sphere of lofty withdrawal from the world, and though his novel never actually breaks off like Agnon's, most critics have felt that the conclusion of this masterpiece of European fiction is huddled, leaping too suddenly from all the complications of the court of Parma to the contemplativeness of the monastery at the very end. Herbst's planned route to the monastic leprosarium is persuasively traced byAdiel Amzeh, the protagonist of the remarkable story "Forevermore," which Agnon originally wrote to include in *Shira* and then decided to pubish separately. In the fuller dimensions of the novel, he was unable to find a solid fictional bridge on which Manfred Herbst could cross over from his home and wife and children and academic tasks to that ghastly consecrated realm where a disease-ridden woman whose name means poetry could offer him more than the world ever could. The result was a plot in which after a certain point the central character can only turn and turn again in the circuits of his one obsession, circling back on the apartment where Shira is no longer to be found, revolving in his mind the idea of the tragedy he would write and the memory of the flesh that cannot be forgotten, which are but obverse sides of the same lost coin.

There are certain works of literature that are finally stymied by the bold effort of the writer to pursue a personal vision beyond the limits of precedent and genre. Stendhal's *Charterhouse* is a memorable case in point; another, still closer to *Shira* in its actual incompletion, is Kafka's *The Castle.* Confronted with this order of originality, most readers, I think, will be content with the splendid torso, however much they may regret the absence of the fully sculpted figure. In *Shira* the hero's final way to the place of poetry and truth, where death hones desire, is indicated rather than fictionally imagined. But Herbst's descent into an underworld of eros and art, enacted against the background of Jerusalem life in the gathering shadows of a historical cataclysm of inconceivable proportions, is so brilliantly rendered that *Shira,* even without an ending, deserves a place among the major modern novels.